FIVE SILVER DAUGHTERS

Louis Golding (1895-1958) was born in Manchester and it was the Hightown district of this city which inspired many of his novels, *Five Silver Daughters* and *Magnolia Street* among them. Educated at Manchester Grammar School and Queen's College, Oxford, he wrote over twenty novels, the first of which was the famous *Forward from Babylon*. In addition, he produced a number of collections of short stories and verse and several travel and sporting books. He was a frequent broadcaster and collaborated in original scripts for such films as *Mr Emmanuel* (based on his own book) and *Theirs is the Glory*.

By LOUIS GOLDING

Novels

FORWARD FROM BABYLON · SEACOAST OF BOHEMIA
DAY OF ATONEMENT · GIVE UP YOUR LOVERS
STORE OF LADIES · THE MIRACLE BOY
THE PRINCE OR SOMEBODY · MAGNOLIA STREET
FIVE SILVER DAUGHTERS · THE CAMBERWELL BEAUTY
THE PURSUER · THE DANCE GOES ON
MR EMMANUEL · WHO'S THERE WITHIN?
NO NEWS FROM HELEN · THE GLORY OF ELSIE SILVER
THREE JOLLY GENTLEMEN · HONEY FOR THE GHOST
THE DANGEROUS PLACES · THE LOVING BROTHERS
TO THE QUAYSIDE · MR HURRICANE
THE LITTLE OLD ADMIRAL

Short Stories

THE DOOMINGTON WANDERER · PARIS CALLING
PALE BLUE NIGHTGOWN · MARIO ON THE BEACH

Verse

SORROW OF WAR · SHEPHERD SINGING RAGTIME
PROPHET AND FOOL · THE SONG OF SONGS
POEMS DRUNK AND DROWSY

Travel

SUNWARD, ADVENTURES IN ITALY · SICILIAN NOON
THOSE ANCIENT LANDS · JOURNEY TO PALESTINE
IN THE STEPS OF MOSES THE LAW-GIVER
IN THE STEPS OF MOSES THE CONQUEROR
LOUIS GOLDING GOES TRAVELLING
GOODBYE TO ITHACA

Belles Lettres

ADVENTURES IN LIVING DANGEROUSLY
JAMES JOYCE · A LETTER TO ADOLF HITLER
WE SHALL EAT AND DRINK AGAIN (with André Simon)
THE JEWISH PROBLEM · HITLER THROUGH THE AGES
THE WORLD I KNEW

Sport

LOUIS GOLDING'S BOXING TALES
MY SPORTING DAYS AND NIGHTS
THE BARE-KNUCKLE BREED

FIVE SILVER DAUGHTERS

BY

LOUIS GOLDING

LONDON
VICTOR GOLLANCZ LTD
1987

FOR MY GODSON

RICHARD MAYO MIDDLETON FORDHAM

IN WELCOME

First published in Great Britain 1934
by Victor Gollancz Ltd,
14 Henrietta Street, London WC2E 8QJ

First published in Gollancz Paperbacks 1987

British Library Cataloguing in Publication Data
Golding, Louis
    Five silver daughters.
    I. Title
    823'.912[F]   PR6013.03
    ISBN 0-575-04063-7

Printed in Finland by Werner Söderström Oy

FIVE SILVER DAUGHTERS

CONTENTS

CHAPTER I

THE SILVER KITCHEN

I

IT WAS Saturday night. The anarchists were gathered in the Silver kitchen in Oleander Street. They often turned up on week-nights, too ; but there was something more ceremonious about the proceedings on Saturday nights. That is to say, they all knocked at the front door once-twice, then once-twice again. Within doors things were pretty much the same. They all talked assassination and drank tea-with-lemon.

Vaguely speaking, they were anarchists. All except Polednik, who did not speak vaguely. It did not occur to Mr. Silver that he was not an anarchist ; for why else would all these odd gentlemen be knocking at his door once-twice, then once-twice again, every Saturday night ? But he was a gentle and hospitable creature ; he would have given them house-room if they were a gang of *pogromchiks* who wanted to organise a pogrom in Doomington, and they had nowhere else to go for a quiet talk about details. He would have ushered them into the kitchen, and Mrs. Silver would have made tea-with-lemon for them, too.

None of them was very clear about the doctrines of anarchism, excepting Polednik, who was quite definitely not an anarchist. They had not read Bakunin and Kropotkin, but they would take any amount of trouble to rescue a fly that had fallen into the milk and hold it before the fire till it got dry again. If it got shrivelled up in the process, and curled up its little wings and legs and died, they would look at each other and wonder how it happened. The conversation that was going on during the performance with the fly might be, as likely as not, some vague plan for the assassination of one or other of the European Royal Families.

The conspirators did not drink whisky or vodka or any of the more fiery liquors. They drank tea-with-lemon, sucking it, in the Russian fashion, through a cube of sugar wedged between their teeth. Even the Gentiles amongst them tried to drink that way, though they were not skilful at it, and would much sooner have drunk beer than tea. But seeing that tea it was, and no help for it, they would have preferred to drink it out of pint cups, strong as ink, with any amount of milk and sugar. But they felt it more anarchistic to suck their tea through cubes of sugar ; it was Russian, international even ; it gave the tea a faint flavour of dynamite.

For, of course, there were Gentile anarchists among the *habitués* of Silver's kitchen. The lines of cleavage that were recognised there were between exploiters and exploited, not between Aryan and Semite. If those Jews had been living in the country that had once belonged to them, the conversation would have been all about Jehu and Rehoboam, and the best time and place to have at them with a battle-axe.

It was well known that Silver entertained anarchists in his kitchen. Newcomers to Oleander Street walked past the front door a little fearfully, particularly on Saturday nights, as if they expected one of the anarchists to come bursting out any moment on his way to St. Petersburg. It would be unpleasant if he dropped one of the bombs in his hurry. But older inhabitants took no notice at all. They even said that if Mr. and Mrs. Silver had had no daughters, there wouldn't have been anything like so many anarchists going in and out of the place.

Nobody could have called Mr. Ponski and Mr. Pontrevitch, for instance, really serious anarchists. They were in love with two of the Silver daughters ; they were sometimes not quite certain themselves which two they were. So they never got very serious about it. Or perhaps the truth was that the Silver daughters were so completely oblivious of their existence, that the two young men didn't feel encouraged to get serious about it. They wrote poetry, it is true, but it was not poetry about the Silver daughters. It sometimes got printed in the Yiddish Press. The impulses which drove them to write poetry were not at all the same as those which drove them to be, in a general way, anarchists. It was extremely tender poetry about their mothers, which they read out in high fluting voices to the other conspirators, of whom many could not keep back their tears. There is a whole corpus of Yiddish poetry which celebrates the melancholy condition of being separated from your mother, or, if you are a mother, from your son. It has an anthem, which begins :

> *A brievele der mamen*
> *Sollst du nit versamen*

which, roughly translated, means

> *A letterlet for your mother*
> *Should come before all other.*

That was the sort of poetry that Mr. Ponski and Mr. Pontrevitch wrote. But it was not so succinct as that. It gave them more pleasure to see their poetry in print than it would have done if they had seen Nicholas the Second decapitated before their feet. It also helped to console them for not being loved by the Silver girls. They carried their cuttings about with them in their wallets, and, though they could have recited their poems backward, they always insisted on taking the cuttings out of the wallets and unfolding them as breathlessly as if they were newly found Sappho papyri ; and, indeed, after a few months' hard use that was exactly what they looked like.

You couldn't say of Mr. Emmanuel, either, that he was very much in the way of an anarchist. Mr. Isaac Emmanuel was clerk to the Jewish Board of Guardians, and he lived in Magnolia Street, the next street parallel to Oleander Street on the north side. His back door faced the Silver back door across an entry four feet in width. That was convenient, for a person occupying Mr. Emmanuel's position in society could hardly have been seen paying a public front-door visit to the Silvers. Mr. Emmanuel believed in Love, and so did all the other *habitués*, though none of them believed quite so fervently as he that Love was a solace for all ills, and that everybody should be loved everywhere on all occasions. Mr. Emmanuel was much addicted to addressing public meetings, but he found the Silver kitchen the next best thing to a platform. For it did not in the least matter whether Ponski or Pontrevitch were reading poems about their mothers, or whether Dan Jamieson, the Socialist candidate for Parliament, was rehearsing his election address ; Mr. Emmanuel went striding up and down the kitchen, gesticulating with his pince-nez, talking, talking ; stopping for one moment to gulp down half a tumbler of tea, then once more talking, talking.

The fact was that Mr. Emmanuel did not believe in bombs. He saw no reason why Nicholas the Second and the other crowned heads of Europe should not be loved like any working-man. And in so much as he did not believe in acts of individual terrorism Polednik was no anarchist, either. He was actually a strong anti-anarchist. He was a member of the Russian Social Democratic Labour Party, with whom it was a matter of faith that the enemy was not certain individuals but certain classes in their entirety. They disliked a bourgeois manufacturer of shaving-brushes quite as much as a Romanof, but they held that the spectacular elimination of one or the other did no more than strengthen the hands of reaction. It produced a spasm of nauseating pity even among horny-handed working-folk. It was Polednik's intention some day to eliminate the enemy, not in ones, but in millions. He shared the intention with exiled comrades in London, in Geneva, in Vienna. He shared it with secret comrades in clothing-factories in St. Petersburg, in Ukrainian cellars where intellectuals furtively forgathered to unpack forbidden pamphlets and decipher cryptograms.

So that, strictly speaking, Polednik had no place at all here in Oleander Street, among the Silver anarchists. Yet where else should he betake himself on the damp Doomington evenings ? The sound of his own voice was no enchantment to him, as it was to Mr. Emmanuel ; for which reason he crept away from the clubs and forums where workingmen whistled wordily against each other, like winds on moorlands. He burned with no visible fire like the red-cheeked, red-bearded, red-tied Socialist, Dan Jamieson ; wherefore he stood upon no soap-boxes at street-corners, shaking his fist. His heart was jagged with a blue-green coldness like glacier ice, and the years of his exile had not melted one single needle of his implacable intention. With that intention his eyes, too, were blue-green and cold. There was only one single person living who could, but not invariably, cloud with a faint haze the steely disks of his eyes, This was, in fact, a Silver daughter, the third of them, Susan. Well might the folk of Oleander Street say of the Silver kitchen— no daughters, no anarchists.

Yet Polednik, as we have insisted, was exactly not an anarchist : as Polednik himself once or twice tartly insisted, but had given over insisting long ago. How could you knock sense into the addled pates of the lachrymose poets, Ponski and Pontrevitch ? How could you induce Emmanuel to stop talking for the half-minute necessary to assert that Karl Marx, Communist, and Bakunin, anarchist, had as much kinship with each other as an Atlantic liner and a derelict raft ?

So they went on prating till the tears brimmed over into their tumblers ; and this one wagged his jaw and shook his pince-nez till it seemed that both arm and jaw must fall off ; and this other roared as if the tumbledown Silver sofa were a soap-box ; and Mrs. Silver in a dim dream went about filling the emptied tumblers. So long these things went on, month in, month out, that suddenly the futility of it would rise like bile in Polednik's throat. A pin-point of hard light flared up in the centre of his eyes. His heart thumped, thumped, like a savage thumping on a drum. The praters and roarers no longer had separable faces. They were pale shields of flesh, with a hole in each for a mouth. He ached to have some sort of a gun, a thing he would swivel round upon its base, and launch from it bullet upon bullet into hole upon hole.

None of them noticed the ineffable malevolence of those moments, excepting the girl Susan. She was a lanky creature, devoid of graces. But when these moments came she would hurry over to him with speed and gentleness like a cat, and, with finger-tips normally as rough as sacking, stroke his high damp forehead like a nodding flower. No other softness passed between them at any other time, though they were lovers. The thumping slackened in Polednik's heart, the pin-points of light guttered down in his eyes. He sank down upon his chair. Some minutes later, they would both rise and leave the kitchen, and go along the dark lobby into the sitting-room, even though it was winter. Then they would open their books and read of insurrections and barricades in cities. Or he would bring out from his waistcoat-pocket a phial of secret ink, and inscribe his invisible reports between the harmless visible lines of some matter-of-fact letter destined for the mysterious people he called "contacts," who taught in Russian universities or turned lathes in Russian factories : those people who, whoever they were, year in, year out, wrote letters like these, read letters like these, sometimes were caught writing or reading them ; yet, wherever they were, whether working still undiscovered at their jobs or eating out their hearts in Siberian log-huts, knew that a day would come to them which would be night to their enemies.

Frankly, in the Silver kitchen, they preferred it when Polednik and Susan got up and went into the sitting-room to their books and papers, like a couple of school-children. They all preferred it ; excepting Mr. Emmanuel, who really didn't know who was there and who wasn't, he was so busy striding up and down and talking. So then Mrs. Silver made more tea-with-lemon. The kettle was boiling on the hob most hours of the day and night ; and in the course of years Mrs. Silver had become very expert at boiling water and pouring it on to tea and cutting lemons into slices. It was very nearly her only accomplishment as a housewife, and it was fortunate the anarchists never expected her to serve anything else. By that time practically everybody had had enough intellect and anarchy for one night. So Mr. Silver took out the cards and they played " Pishy-pashy." Mr. Emmanuel left when the cards came out, for he felt that it was not quite fitting for the clerk to the Jewish Board of Guardians to play games of chance. The others felt, too, he was best out of the way when the cards came on, for he talked so much. " Pishy-pashy " they called their game, which has been interpreted as a variant of the words " Peace and Patience." Peacefully and patiently they played for hours and hours. They played for money, too. And the fact is they were, after all, a set of gamblers and anarchists. And one wondered why an evil name did not attach itself to Mr. Silver's house, their head-quarters. But it did not, somehow. For the most part they looked, and were, such kind people. It was impossible to think ill of them.

II

It was the appearance of Alexander Smirnof that makes that Saturday night in the early autumn of nineteen hundred and ten a proper starting-point for this tale of the Silver daughters. Alexander Smirnof was present and Joe Tishler was not. The second fact certainly was, and the first fact may have been, bound up with one and another of Silver's daughters ; which is a further corroboration of the sentiment that prevailed in Oleander Street that the daughters had quite as much to do with the anarchists mobilising at number eleven as their abstract passion for social righteousness.

In the flesh there wasn't much room for the daughters in that kitchen, which was often so crowded that if the fire had not been protected by a metal grid, one or two anarchists must have been roasted alive, particularly on Saturday nights. But even in the absence of all five daughters there was a sense of their presence throughout the whole house, an emanation from their femaleness, a composite ghost made up out of the swish of skirts, the toe of a shoe protruding under a sofa, the sight of a dropped hair-slide, the smell of violet powder, the creak of corsets, the black wink of a hat-pin, a glimpse of white shoulder. It was a ghost of such a quality that it might have lured all the Jacobites in Doomington to make their headquarters in the Silver kitchen, if the anarchists had not got there first.

There often was a daughter or two about, even at the most crowded *séances*. May, the youngest, who was fourteen years old at this time, hardly ever moved from her metal stool on the right-hand side of the fender. Her eyes were wide and grey. Her hair was soft and had a queer grey sheen in it in certain lights. Her eyes were so wide that sometimes she seemed to be hearing all they said and to be marvelling at it all, the wisdom of it or the folly of it. At other times her eyes merely seemed opaque, like curtains drawn to hide the windows of a room in which she lived a secret life, not to be guessed at. But whether at any given moment she seemed to be in the very centre of these people or withdrawn unapproachably beyond their circumference, she would be almost more with her body than with her mind aware of her father, of any need at all that might befall him.

So in a sense it was not just to say that May loved her father, any more than it can be said that the finger-tips love the fretted skin when the brain commands them to minister to it. She would be aware her father wanted his slippers the moment his ankles gave a blind twist, before he himself knew that his shoes were cramping him. It fell to her to make his meals, though she had as much as she could do to keep her end up at her High School, for she was not good at books. He would have eaten little food other than tea-with-lemon if not for her, for that was the only dish that his wife could always bring to a triumphant conclusion. The other girls looked after themselves. They had to, nowadays.

It was four months since May had taken over this duty of feeding her father. Before then, Esther, the eldest daughter, had looked after things. Then she went and married Joe Tishler, the anarchist and cabinet-maker. May did not mind very much that Esther was managing her own house now, and not theirs. It gave the child an opportunity of doing so much more for her father—unobtrusively, as always. Mrs. Silver, too, on the whole, was not displeased that Esther had gone. Mrs. Silver was vaguely aware that meals and cleanings and other household tasks that used to get themselves done in the old days of Esther got themselves done more rarely now.

But Esther was such a *manager*. That was how her mother always thought of her. A manager. She didn't manage quietly and consistently, so that you weren't aware she was managing things. There was a good deal of the sporadic and spectacular about her managing. She would suddenly get up on her hind legs and manage a Friday evening dinner, as if they were a household of rabbis and not a family so lax in Jewish observance that you might as well call them Plymouth Brethren as Jews. She would bring out a linen tablecloth from where it had lain for weeks in a bath-tub and get it washed white as foam. She would get the floors scrubbed till they shone like apples. The brass candlesticks and the trays and the samovar were like a shop-window full of looking-glasses. She got a meal produced that was rather like the Lord Mayor marrying off his eldest daughter, so many dishes were involved, banked round with seasonings so exotic.

She didn't *do* these things herself. She managed them into getting done. She would sometimes get a little help from May, who would polish a brass tray for an hour or so, crooning softly to herself in the heart of the vortex, as if she were sitting quite alone at the edge of a mountain pool, combing her hair. She didn't get much help from the other three girls, least of all from Elsie. So really, in some miraculous way, it all actually got *done* by Mrs. Silver. And seeing that Mrs. Silver in her own right could not boil an egg satisfactorily, miraculous was quite the word. Esther conveyed a demon into her, which gave her all sorts of potencies entirely foreign to her. But she would pay for it for days and days after, so twisted she would be with aches and pains, and her hair falling all over the place, and not able to keep her food down properly, it was sometimes so bad as that.

That was why Mrs. Silver was not very sorry to see Esther go under the canopy to get herself married, however unmotherly the sentiment might be. But, then, she never thought of herself as a mother, though she had five daughters. She sometimes looked at them all in amazement. Where had they come from ? She must have given birth to them one time or another. She found it very puzzling.

Not that she wasn't, in a wide humane sense, a mother. She really had a feeling about trodden-upon working-men and, for that matter, unhappy children, so long as they were not her own children. She spent quite a lot of money each week, chiefly in pennies, on this cause or that. The payments were recorded on hanging cards, divided into a lot of little squares. One of the scullery walls was half covered with these philanthropic records, fly-blown and grease-spattered for the most part, but touching testimonies of her charity, all of them. Some of the causes seemed less relevant to her peace of mind than others. She supported, for instance, a Presbyterian mission to Chinese peasants. She did not quite know how that card had got there, but a gentleman with a frock-coat and a blue chin called, among the other collectors, every Monday, and got his penny, too, whenever there were pennies going.

No wonder that Mrs. Silver sighed happily that Saturday night at the sudden recollection that Esther was safely married, and it was unlikely that she would come swooping down on Oleander Street to do a little managing. She had, as a matter of fact, swooped down a few times since her wedding, just to keep her hand in, but the tornadoes had not lasted so long, and they were getting rarer.

But Joe Tishler, her husband, had not been in once since his marriage, which indicated that he preferred being a husband to being an anarchist. As a lover, too, he had been no bomb-thrower. He had never missed a single Saturday night since he had first met Esther three years ago, and it now seemed pretty sure that Esther rather than Kropotkin was the attraction. At one o'clock in the morning Esther would get up from the sofa, and Joe Tishler immediately got up, too. They went along the lobby, skirting the sitting-room, where Polednik and Susan by that time would be deeply immersed in their pamphlets and secret letters. They went into the parlour, lit the gas, sat down on the pink plush sofa, and held hands for about an hour. It was all quite formal. There in the parlour Esther was still managing the situation. She had managed it from the beginning. She had met Joe Tishler at a social, and determined that this was the man she was going to marry. She then introduced him into the Silver circle, where she could keep an eye on him.

Yes. There in the parlour she was still managing the situation, but not in the dynamic way she got the banquets prepared between periods of semi-starvation. It was all rather correct there. They didn't have much to say to each other ; they just held hands. They wouldn't even have done so much as that if they hadn't been engaged. And after being engaged for three years, a thoroughly proper period, they went and got married. There might be subversive ideas afloat in the Silver circle regarding the structure of society, but Esther Silver and Joe Tishler knew what was proper and what improper.

So did Elsie Silver, the second youngest daughter, who was seventeen. She, too, knew what was proper and what improper. It might even be said that the trouble was that there had been no trouble about it, apart from the trouble Esther had made. Elsie preferred impropriety, and nobody excepting Esther ever lifted a finger in the matter.

Elsie, like Esther, was present in the kitchen that October night when Smirnof turned up. But neither of them was resident in Oleander Street. Esther was married and kept house a few streets away. Elsie was not by any means married. She was a variety artiste, and toured the Gleb Meyer circuit, a number of halls situated chiefly in the North Country.

Between engagements Elsie had a room in the Oxford Road area, a good centre for the Doomington music-halls. It was more convenient living away from home, for various reasons, of which the chief was Esther. Or perhaps it was May. Or they were one and the same reason. She was not frightened of Esther. She turned on her the same sultry *insouciance* with which she faced uncouth audiences in Bacup or Widnes when they were getting restive. But whereas her effrontery as often as not won over the most hard-headed mill-hand, Esther was as impervious to her as she to Esther.

A certain night, about two months before Esther got married, Elsie had not returned home. Next morning she realised very vividly how much more convenient it was not to return home. She knew a number of girls in the profession, one or two not as old as she was, who managed to look after themselves quite nicely. She had the utmost belief in her ability to do the same thing. She was extremely fond of May, but she thought it would be nice to have a room of her own where she could keep herself to herself when she felt like it. She thought May would like it, too, even though she sometimes seemed solitary even in that kitchen of theirs, when the herded anarchists left hardly a square inch of footroom on the floor.

Anyhow, one thing was certain. If she kept away from

home, she would to a large extent free May's ears from the volleying thunder of Esther's eloquence, which rumbled all over the house from scullery to garret. She herself took as little notice of it as of the thud and rumble of the tram beyond the corner. Usually, too, May seemed unperturbed by it ; she did not lift her head from her book till long after the thunder died away. But when she lifted her head, it was only Elsie who noticed that the lips were slightly drawn and the eyeballs slightly dilated.

Elsie had little feeling for the other members of the family. She had rather a contemptuous liking for her father, and she found, to her surprise, that there was a certain magnificence about Esther which she could not help admiring. She had very little interest in her mother and her sisters Sarah and Susan. But for May she cared as she cared for no other living creature, and she had a comforting sense that May was remotely, chastely unaware of it. She liked that. She did not like to be tangled up with people. She accepted the fact of her affection for May, and did not propose to quarrel with it. But she was pleased that May, for her part, did not have to reckon with it. It left May surrounded by her own coolness, as a nereid in the waters of her cave.

Two or three months before Elsie stayed out all night, it was reported that she had been walking along Oxford Road, that a young man had spoken to her, that she had gone into a café with that young man and eaten chocolate éclairs with him. It was only to be expected that Esther should have one of her major calls to management. She realised what a reproach it would be to her family—a respectable Jewish family, after all, however picturesque its politics were—if Elsie were not managed out of the primrose path. She was determined she would force from her an account of what had happened between her and her young man when they had stopped eating chocolate éclairs.

But she got nowhere, despite all her storming. Silver behaved as if Elsie were the daughter of a dealer in Turkish delight in Smyrna rather than a child fathered by himself.

Mrs. Silver made one or two timid and entirely unintelligible noises, and went up to bed with toothache. Esther feared, and several of the anarchists hoped for, the worst. But in a sense what actually happened was worse than that. If Esther had found it out, it is possible that the truth would have dismayed her more than the categorical proclamation that, after finishing the chocolate éclairs, Elsie and the young man had gone off and spent an hour together behind the locked door of the young man's bed-sitting-room.

But she had not done that. She had accepted the chocolate éclairs not so much because she liked them as because she liked men. She ate one after another indifferently ; she hardly said a word to the young man who was paying for, and could ill afford, all those éclairs. He got more and more uncomfortable. He became aware of those hot dark eyes coolly regarding him, how the lids closed upon them till nothing was left but a pair of slits like the small gratings in the doors of prisons or convents, whence eyes, themselves unseen, intently look out. He became damp under the collar. His throat got drier and drier though he emptied down it cup after cup of tea. It was as if in that public place those eyes divested him of coat, trousers, shirt. He sat there naked. He became aware how meagre his chest was and how ugly the birthmark that lay on his hip like a toad. He could have sobbed for joy when she rose and left him. She said not a word. Only her nostrils twitched a little contemptuously.

The neighbours said, " What could you expect ? " They did not approve of Elsie's goings on, nor the way Mr. and Mrs. Silver did nothing about it. But they attributed the goings on to the theatre, and to that they resigned themselves as to a force of nature.

The theatre was too grand a name for it. Elsie could dance rather deftly, rather oddly, and she had a somewhat husky voice which from time to time twanged, or even snapped, like a string. She dressed up as a boy about town with some success, smiting her hip with a cane, pulling her top-hat down over the right eye, nearer to the debonair tradition of Vesta Tilley than to the more hearty mode of her rival, Hetty King. But she was not so affable as either. She was, in fact, a decade or more before her time. Her technique approximated to that of a Beatrice Lillie ; she in some measure anticipated Bankhead and Dietrich. It is not to be wondered at that her elbows stuck outside the pattern of her time. Sometimes she glowered with real malevolence at the hulking louts and blousy women in the pit and gallery. The audiences never knew what to make of her. Sometimes they whistled and cat-called at the very sight of her. Sometimes they brought her back again and again, gaped and goggled at her, as if they would eat her piecemeal, they loved her so much.

Mr. Gleb Meyer—or his manager, at least—found her a puzzling proposition. He might have given her a year or a two-year contract. But he never signed her up for more than a few months' tour. That was why she was sometimes left high-and-dry for a few weeks, or even a few months at a time. That was why the younger anarchists in the Silver kitchen turned up grimly week by week, for you never knew when Elsie might come up out of the nether darkness of Runcorn or Huddersfield, to send the heart tossing uneasily with a glance of those dark eyes and the pout of those vivid lips. But she could not bear to be long away from the smoky public air, the lights, the male faces, silk-smooth and bark-tough, enchanted or hostile. She would go and get a night's engagement at one of the free-and-easies, as the entertain-ments were called, which enterprising publicans put on in the public-houses on the other side of the town. She would sing and dance and slap her thigh, the piano would thud and thump, a girl would go round for coppers with a cap, the ivory handles at the bar would swoop and rise. There would be certain young anarchists from Oleander Street among the beer-swillers, but she was indifferent to their fidelity. Her eyes moved from face to face, watchful, biding their time. It was as if she would recognise what she sought in one white moment of apocalypse, when at length the moment broke on her, how many years or lands distant there was no fore-telling.

To sing in a music-hall was, of course, a little shocking, yet there was something grand about it, too. But it was highly discreditable for a Jewish girl to get up and sing in a public-house, among the spittoons and in a smell of beer. Esther fumed. She had tried to stop it, but failed. The fact was, however, though she never admitted it, that it was all her fault, in a way. It was she who had first spotted the child's talent, how she liked to dress herself as a boy and strut up and down the parlour, singing, swinging her cane. It was she who first induced her to get over her shyness and sing in public ; and, though the public was only the Silver kitchen, it was a little upsetting to Esther to find that Elsie had no shyness to overcome. Before long Elsie was singing in the concerts they held for charity in Unity Hall, a few streets away ; that was before her twelfth birthday. Esther still remembered that she had been as proud as Elsie, perhaps prouder, the first time Elsie's name had appeared on a printed bill—Elsie Silver, Juvenile Male Impersonator. She had stuck the bill up in the parlour window and brought half Oleander Street over to see it. Elsie herself had done nothing so blatant. She merely stood and stared at the bill for long minutes at a stretch, and said not a word. It was impossible to divine the emotion behind those absorbed, coal-black eyes.

Then came her first professional engagement. Esther had nothing to do with that. Elsie showed very speedily that she could take the initiative into her own hands in the matter of her career. Esther and Sarah had taken the two youngsters, Elsie and May, to a performance of *Floradora* at the Queen's Theatre. Susan was not with them, for she thought that was a frivolous way of spending an evening. May was delighted. She clapped her hands and talked a good deal more than was her habit. But Elsie said nothing till the show was over. Then she remarked, not to anyone in particular : " I like that man." That man was probably the juvenile lead, but she was neither asked for nor gave an explanation. Probably she did not know what she hoped to get from him ; but she knew, even then, that she wanted more than an autographed picture post-card.

So Elsie Silver went to the stage door of the Queen's Theatre, and walked straight past the doorkeeper as if she were the daughter of the general manager. She did not meet the light comedy star, for he was on the stage at that moment. But she met the fat gentleman with a cigar who had come to Doomington to arrange the forthcoming pantomime. He enlisted the first member of the chorus there and then, without trial. He assured Miss Silver that the light comedy star would have a leading part in *Cinderella*. She realised in a week or two he had enlisted her under false pretences, but she found she could transfer her interest to the assistant stage-carpenter, who was good-looking. When the fat gentleman invited her to his room, something happened which displeased her, for when he was next seen in public he had quite a nasty scratch down his cheek. She herself did not appear at the next, or any subsequent, performance. Instead she called at an agency, the name and ways of which she had learned from her colleagues in the chorus. She had already started her career as a travelling vaudeville artiste within a month or two of leaving school.

Esther disapproved strongly, but she was less vocal about this disapproval than about others, partly because she was as much to blame as anybody that Elsie was in the profession, partly because Elsie had a way about her which caused eloquence to crumble on the lips like a dried lather. But when Elsie failed to return one night, and came along coolly the next night to announce she had come to collect her things, for she wasn't going to live at home any more, then Esther reached for her armour and her stoutest lance and prepared herself for battle. But, though Elsie was clad in much flimsier material, there was no point at which Esther's lance could force an entrance. Elsie had never been, in the toughest barn of a small-town vaudeville theatre, so bewitching, so insolent, so unassailable. The young anarchists present went watery at the knees with love of her.

Esther remembered wildly that she was going to be married in a month or two. Joe's family was troubled enough that Joe was going to marry into a family of anarchists. What would they say when they learned of daughters of seventeen who stayed out all night, who proposed to go and live on their own off Oxford Road ?

Esther's voice soared and swooped like a swing. Then suddenly, when it had attained a crest higher than it had yet achieved, its moorings broke. It dithered a moment high in air, then crashed in ruin. It lay in splinters around her. Her face—and no one had ever seen it so before, nor was anyone but her father ever to see it so again—was steamy with tears.

" Mother ! Mother ! " she gasped hoarsely. " Do something ! Say something ! "

Mrs. Silver tried desperately to do something, say something. But her voice was as impotent as Esther's. Her hands shut and opened miserably. She formed a syllable or two in her throat, and they stuck there. They stuck there as the thing she had done long, long ago in the deep grass by the Dnieper had stuck in her throat all those years. Though, God knows, she had loved Sam, her husband, then, as she loved him now, and would love him always. But Sam had not yet become her husband, that time long ago. So how can you go about being a pillar of chastity, and glaring on daughters that stay out overnight, if you too, long, long ago in the deep grass by the Dnieper . . . The words were stifled in her throat. She went into the scullery and started peeling a basinful of potatoes that had already been peeled.

Then, like a person drowning who thrusts an arm out desperately towards an overhanging bough, Esther grabbed at her father, sitting at the head of the table with his head between his hands.

" Father, she mustn't go. You know what people are already saying. It's bad enough when she goes travelling about, but in Doomington, when she has a father and a

mother and a family and a home . . . Say she mustn't go
and live on her own. She must be older first."

Sam Silver did not lift his head.

" Father, don't you hear me ? "

" I hear you, Esther."

" Why don't you speak to her ? "

" Did I ask to be born ? " he asked her strangely.

" But what——"

" I did not. And she did not ask to be born."

" Yes, yes, but——"

" She must look after what she does with herself. No
one's got no right to interfere with what people do."

" You're her *father*," she whispered. There was horror in
her eyes.

He lifted his head. On his eyes there was a sort of glaze.
There was a sing-song note in what he said, as if he uttered
a formula, something he did not himself quite clearly understand.

" Oi, a father, a father ! Less than anybody else, a
father ! "

Esther's head ached so much that she felt the top of her
skull would come clean away if she stayed in the kitchen any
longer. She gathered together the pieces of herself and carried
them off to bed.

" Good night, Esther ! " said Elsie softly, without triumph.
Esther was not the sort of triumph Elsie meditated.

Elsie by no means cut off relations with Oleander Street
when she went off to live on her own. In between engagements, she would come in to see May and who the new
anarchists might be, for they were always men. The knowledge conveyed itself by some odd magic to the younger
anarchists. Elsie was in Oleander Street that night ; Elsie was
sitting on the sofa with her slim legs showing well above the
ankle ; Elsie tracing the line of her lips with a rouge pencil.
Young men who were only anarchists, as far as it could be
discovered, when Elsie was at home, turned up and drank

quarts of tea-with-lemon. On such nights the political debate was more inconsequent than usual. Earlier than usual Polednik rose and carried Susan and Karl Marx away dourly into the sitting-room.

III

Because Alexander Smirnof was there that night a good deal of what follows happened. How or why he presented himself at the Silver house was never decided, though it is possible it had something to do with Sarah Silver, for he married her three years later, one year before the Great War broke out.

It was not that people were expected to present some sort of credentials on their first appearance. Strangers often dropped in quite without ceremony—even a detective once or twice. And that matter of knocking on the door once-twice, once-twice again, was not really obligatory. The *habitués* liked doing it, that was all.

Yet as a rule, when a stranger appeared, somebody knew something about him, or he said something about himself. It was not like that with Smirnof. When the girls talked the Smirnof–Polednik incident over later, none of them remembered having opened the door to him. He merely happened. And the odd thing was that even after that supernally strange minute achieved itself and Polednik staggered out of the kitchen with Susan at his heels—the odd thing was that Smirnof resumed the nebulous remoteness out of which Polednik had pitchforked him.

There was room for one chair between the sofa and the wall. The chair was hemmed in by the three steps which descended out of the lobby. Silver usually sat on the chair at the head of the table. But he chose that chair not because he felt himself a sort of Arthur of a Table Square, but because he was a good host. He got whatever draughts were going, both from the yard-door on his right hand and the front-door some distance behind him up the lobby.

So whatever of Smirnof was not hidden by the arm of the sofa was hidden behind Silver. A good deal of this story is summed up in the picture of the large Smirnof hidden behind the small Silver. The arm of the sofa did not go far up Smirnof's waistcoat. His vague size overlapped Silver by half a head and both shoulders. Yet, sitting there behind Silver, he was invisible. It looked as if he had chosen the position with something of the intuitive aptness which was to distinguish all his operations, small or colossal. It looked like that because it was quite an awkward chair to get yourself seated in, even if you were smaller than Smirnof. And no one noticed him getting in, no one for a long time noticed him sitting there—not till Polednik came in, rather later than usual. No one might have noticed his going, even, excepting Sarah Silver. She did not forget him, though more than two years elapsed before he came to Oleander Street again.

There, then, behind Silver, sat Alexander Smirnof. And not many feet away, under the window, sat Sarah, Silver's second daughter, and Smirnof's wife to be. She was twenty. She was nursing a baby. Athwart the talk of terror and dynamite, the sound of her crooning was like the feel of a small woodmouse in the hand. She not merely rocked the baby to and fro in her arms. Her whole body rocked with it, a little like the old Jews rocking in the synagogue, so that there was a ritual air about Susan rocking the baby, and her crooning was like the old Jews praying in the twilight under their breath.

She worked in a cardboard-box factory. When she was not in the factory, she was nursing a baby, or two babies, when they were forthcoming. In Oleander Street they usually were. She, like her elder sister, Esther, survived her own babyhood only by a miracle, for Mrs. Silver was as inconsequent a mother as she was a political philosopher or a philanthropist. She forgot for long hours at a stretch that she had recently given birth to a baby ; and that was not because she was not fond of babies. On the contrary, the first funds she supported with a weekly penny were two funds for babies of two different colours. When she remembered she had a baby, it was, if anything, even more fatal. It did not occur to her that a green apple or a solid wedge of baked macaroni pudding were unsuitable foods for the infant stomach. Esther, the manager, was Sarah's senior by only two years, so that Esther had never been quite old enough during Sarah's infancy to make her the victim of one of those tornadoes of management during which on several occasions she nearly annihilated each of her succeeding sisters.

Susan appeared on the scene when Sarah was only a year old. It is incredible that Sarah started her career as a proxy mother at quite so early an age, but it is certain that she was already cuddling babies while her contemporaries were cuddling the unsavoury blobs of rag they called dolls. So Susan, too, survived. So, in their day, did the two later and final daughters, Elsie and May. When May got too old to cuddle and croon over, Sarah went out into Oleander Street and picked babies from the doorsteps or the gutters, as one might pick gooseberries. She picked them as by right. No one disputed it with her. Oleander Street mothers had far less difficulty in going out of an evening than their Longton neighbours. There was always Sarah Silver, at number eleven, to take the babies off their hands.

She was a little untidy, she had large arms, but there was a certain sweet, almost fat, serenity in her face. Her eyes were mild and dark as plums. Her hair was like the warm deep hummocky gloom of an armchair. She was, if any female in Oleander Street was, a mother-woman. It needed none of the profound ratiocinations of later medico-literary minds to ferret out the blinding truth that what Sarah Silver needed was a baby of her own. One or two anarchists were anarchists because they were ready, even passionately anxious, to provide her with any number. She was a woman to rest in, like a great warm bath. After a hard day's work, her voice slid along the back of the neck like gentle fingers on an instrument.

But she remained indifferent to those anarchists. Some of

them stayed on in the Silver kitchen, miserably hoping. Others angrily became Conservatives, and voted for Mr. Joynson-Hicks at the by-election. It seemed that though Sarah loved babies, she was indifferent to men. She was the mother-woman incarnate, but she seemed no use at all as a wife-woman.

Then Alexander Smirnof turned up out of the void—the Crimea, Austria, Barcelona, wherever it was. He made her aware of him, hidden as he was from all other eyes behind the lesser bulk of Silver. To some women, perhaps even to all women, no man is wholly lovable, however arrogantly malely possessive he is, unless he is to some extent, great or small, to her if to no other man or woman, a baby. Certainly no other man or woman would have detected a vestige of the baby in Alexander Smirnof, in his grey adult self-effacing eyes, his intellectual dome of forehead. But Sarah Silver did. So, in course of time, when he came back again and asked her to, she married him. " My baby ! " she crooned over him, over that dim mass of Smirnof. " My baby ! Sleep, sleep, my baby ! " And when not even violins could soothe him to sleep, after the abstract ardours of his day, Sarah could, pillowing his head upon her breasts, smoothing the wrinkles out of his brow, or endeavouring vainly to annul those furrows on both sides of the bridge of his nose into which it seemed to relapse more hopelessly as the fantastic years danced on.

IV

Polednik came in late that night. He looked tired. The tip of his thin nose was paler than usual. But there was an almost friendly sparkle in his eyes. " Good evening, everybody ! " he said, not, of course, expecting a reply. But such amiability in Polednik was so unusual, that " Good evening ! Good evening ! " came back at him from the sofa, the chairs, the overflow assembly in the scullery.

" Well, Emmanuel, and how are you ? " asked Polednik.

Mr. Emmanuel switched round. " Splendid ! " he said. " Everything's going to be splendid ! " He was organising a great meeting at Unity Hall, a meeting at which he intended quite finally to set up the reign of Love in Longton, and more particularly in Magnolia Street, where he lived.

" Everything's going all right except the chairman ! " said Silver. " He can't get no chairman ! "

" I'll be your chairman ! " said Polednik buoyantly.

" Boris ! " said Susan Silver quietly, making room for Polednik to squeeze in beside her on the sofa. " You did good work to-day, did you ? How fine you're looking ! "

" Yes ! " he said. " Fine ! " But already something had happened. It was as if he had already divined the existence of something that made the fine work less savoursome.

" You've got new letters ? " asked Susan.

" No ! " said Polednik. He shook his head like someone who thinks to get rid of a headache that way, at its first setting in. " A magazine ! They've started a new revolutionary magazine in . . ." He stopped. The words dwindled on his lips.

" Don't you worry ! " Mr. Emmanuel was saying volubly. " I need no Poledniks to be my chairman at my meeting. Do you know who I've got ? "

" The Pope of Rome ! " some cynic suggested.

Mr. Emmanuel ignored the suggestion. " The High Master ! " he said grandly. " From Doomington School ! "

" No evil eye befall him ! " murmured Mrs. Silver, attacking a lemon.

" You have a promise definite ? " asked Silver.

" If I should say definite——" temporised Mr. Emmanuel.

" Hush-a-by, baby, on the tree-top ! " sang Sarah Silver over her borrowed baby.

" What's the matter, Boris ? Where did you say they've started a new magazine ? " Susan insisted. " A factory magazine in St. Petersburg ? "

She shook him by the shoulder. " You hear what I'm saying, Boris ? "

Polednik made an effort to collect his wits. " The

magazine? Oh, yes! No, not in St. Petersburg! In Geneva! I got a whole batch to-day! "

" Who from? Who's writing in it? Why don't you answer? "

But something odd had happened to Polednik's eyes. The light had gone out of them. The lids came down, as if those disks could see nothing, He bent his head back upon his neck, and projected his thin nose into the air, like a dog's nose, sniffing.

" What's wrong with Polednik? " someone asked.

" What's wrong? " Susan repeated tartly. " Nothing! "

Then Polednik brought his head down again. He swivelled it towards that corner of the room where Smirnof sat, ensconced in the small space beyond the sofa. He moved his body forward as if the better to smell what might be lurking there between Silver's chair and the arm of the sofa. Even Mr. Emmanuel stopped talking, so odd seemed Polednik's face, like a somnambulist's. His eyes stared straight upon Smirnof, the round indefinite head muffed by its vague hair. It seemed for several seconds that to Polednik's eyes nothing existed in the corner behind the sofa, nothing impinged upon his vision. Then, in one moment, the blue-green eyes were flooded with an awareness of what they beheld. They were like a heap of bone-dry thorns that crackle into flame. He had flung the table aside with a galvanic thrust of both hands, sending the tumblers, the teapot, the sugar-basin flying. He charged between the knees and laps that interposed between him and the sofa-head. Silver and his chair went crashing back upon the steps. The hands of Polednik were fastened round Smirnof's throat.

" You! " he shrieked. " You again! You! "

Mrs. Silver set up a shrill helpless wailing. Her husband picked himself up and caught at Polednik's wrists, seeking to disengage them from the strange man's throat. Mr. Emmanuel tottered like a schoolboy's top nearing the end of its revolutions. One or two of the anarchists cried " Time! "

facetiously, then stopped at the sight of the purple veins that came out criss-cross on Smirnof's cheeks. Susan cried out, " Boris ! Boris ! " sharply, but Polednik was deaf to her. One young man and another strove to put himself between Smirnof and Polednik, but the fingers did not relax their hold, nor the flames in the eyes suspend their whistling.

It was Sarah Silver who put a closure upon the desperate event. " Take it ! " she said to May, her youngest sister, thrusting the borrowed baby into her arms. She strode up to Polednik, dug all her fingers into his hair, and pulled the head sharply back, till it seemed the neck must break on the vertebræ. His hands relaxed out of the folds of Smirnof's pale neck. In that same moment Sarah's hands unstiffened from his hair. He crumpled up with Susan's arms round him, like some pathetic ape in a cage. He took the breath into his lungs in short spasms, like a child whose sobbing has no more voice in it.

" I've never heard . . ." said Susan. " What on earth . . ." She usually finished what she had to say in brief sharp sentences. But something had happened to-night outside the scope of her reason. " Never in all my life . . ."

But Sarah was not talking so to the victim of the outrage. She had him seated beside her on the sofa, his body lying back against the sofa-arm. His lips were quivering slightly. A tiny froth seethed against the corners of his mouth. The veins on his temple stood out. His lips quivered very slightly, like a leaf. " Hush, now, hush ! " she was saying. " Hush, now ! It's all right now ! " It was as if he were some baby picked up from an Oleander Street doorstep whom none but herself could soothe. With deft fingers she was removing his tie and collar.

" A sponge ! " she bade. " With cold water ! " Mrs. Silver wrung her hands helplessly. " There isn't such a thing ! " she moaned. May went into the scullery and held a face-cloth under the tap. " Throw water at him ! " bade Sarah. " There now, hush, hush ! Isn't that better ? " She soothed the side of his temples with the cloth. " A little brandy, with water in it ! " she requested again. May went into the parlour and brought out the decanter that was kept for high holidays.

" There now, mister ! That'll do you good ! " said Sarah. Smirnof's eyes were settling back again out of their dreadful protuberance.

" I'm all right now," he said. " Perfectly all right ! " It was the first time his voice had been heard that evening. " An angel, that's what you are ! "

They smiled into each other's eyes. " Comfortable, yes ? But no ! " she decided. Shamelessly, before all those eyes, she transferred the stranger's weight from the sofa-arm to her own large soft bosom. " That's better, isn't it ? "

Smirnof smiled and nodded. The normal colour of his cheeks, though it was hardly colour at all, came back into them. He fell suddenly into a profound sleep, lulled against the charity of those large breasts.

Immediately a storm of inquiries and protests broke out from among the assembled anarchists.

" Whoever heard from such a thing ? "

" A Kossack, that's what I call him—a Tartar ! "

" Yes, but who is he, anyhow ? Who brought him ? "

" Isn't his name Smirnof ? "

" Who said ? "

" I don't know. Perhaps he said himself."

" I didn't hear him speak, not once ! "

" Not me, either ! "

" You might think he was the Tsar Nicholas ! "

" Or Stolypin, his big Minister ! "

" Such a year should take him ! "

" I was told only last week Stolypin isn't going to last much longer ! "

" But he's not Stolypin," said Silver, a trifle crossly. He didn't mind much what happened in his kitchen, but when it came to homicidal assault things were going a little too far. " On my honest word, Polednik," he said, looking round for him. He did not know how he could refrain from administering a word of rebuke.

" They're in the sitting-room," May informed him. Yes, they were. He saw the line of light start up under the sitting-room door as Susan, presumably, lit the gas.

" Have some more tea ! " said Mrs. Silver, smiling through her tears. " Yes," she proclaimed eagerly, " we'll brew a fresh pot ! " As if that would explain and settle everything.

At that moment Smirnof opened his eyes. " I would much like some more tea ! " he said. But he did not move his head from Sarah's bosom for twenty minutes or more. Once or twice, watchfully, he slewed his eyes round, lest someone again suddenly launch his fingers round his throat like a noose. And each time Sarah pressed him closer to her, like a mother comforting her child against shadows.

" It's all right now ; don't worry now. There, there. You will take another lump of sugar, yes ? "

Mr. Silver was in great trouble. " I should live so ! I don't know what to say, Mr.—er—Mr.——"

" Smirnof," said Mr. Smirnof.

" That it should happen in my house. But, poor fellow, sometimes he gets that way. Not so bad like that. I can't explain it. You met before somewhere ? "

" I have never set eyes on him in my life before ! " said Smirnof slowly.

" Well, I never ! "

" A madness got hold of him ! "

" If it's true that your Susan is going to marry him, all I say is——"

" Be quiet now," Sarah bade. " It is no good exciting him. It didn't happen. Nothing happened at all."

Nothing happened at all. It was, in fact, the only way to deal with the situation. A beefy young anarchist did, in fact, suggest he would follow Polednik into the sitting-room and slug him in the lug. The idea evoked shrill cries of distress from Mrs. Silver.

" Let be ! Let be ! " ordered Mr. Silver. " You hear what

she said ? Nothing has happened ! It was a mistake !" The others applauded. They disliked violent action nearer than the Nevsky Prospekt. "You have got the entertainments for your great meeting at Unity Hall ? Is that not true, Mr. Emmanuel ? I have heard so much from those entertainments ! "

It was true. Mr. Emmanuel had arranged the most distinguished entertainments for his meeting. They were to be provided by both local and national talent. He immediately plunged into a dithyramb regarding each and all of his entertainers. The talk in Silver's kitchen seethed and hissed again like the kettle up against the fire. Mrs. Silver went busily about filling tumblers and slicing lemons.

"I have just had a new poem printed in the *Phonograph*," twittered Pontrevitch the poet. "Shall I read my new poem at the meeting ? "

"I've joost got statistics of noomber of hours worked per *di*-em by children under twelve on milk-vans in t' Doomington area," cried Dan Jamieson, the Socialist candidate. "That's joost t' chance I've been looking for ! "

Mr. Emmanuel smiled down his nose. "It is going to be an entertainment, not politics. We've got the famous Boy Nightingale from Longton, and from Poyser's grocery-shop, Becky, the daughter. She will play on the piano."

Nothing had happened. It was a mistake. Smirnof, in Sarah's arms, seemed as if that had always been his resting-place. He reached for something, towards the place where he had been sitting. She would not let him exert himself.

"What is it ? " she asked.

"My book," he said. "It is music."

Somebody stooped and lifted a large thin volume and put it on the table before him. He turned the pages till he came to the opening passages of the second movement in Beethoven's Fourth Symphony. And then he read steadily, passage to passage. Now and again he lifted one hand as if it were a melody calling. Then he lifted the other hand, as if it were a melody calling back again.

V

Susan Silver closed the sitting-room door with one hand and with the other kept a tight grip on Polednik's arm to prevent him from falling. Then she felt about for a chair, and, finding one, sat him down in it.

" Are you all right ? " she said.

" Yes."

" Just one moment. I'll light the gas."

She lit it. She saw his check-bones stand out against his skin. A slight moisture rimmed his forehead.

" I'll get you something," she said.

" Please not," he insisted.

She did nothing more about it. Those two made no dalliance out of their sicknesses, their own or each other's.

His head fell forward on his breast. She moved the table forward. " Rest your elbows," she said, in a voice empty of emotion. " It will be more comfortable that way." He let his head lie on his elbows for some minutes. She did nothing. She stared into Count Tolstoi's eyes in the cheap oleograph on the wall before her. Once and again, very infrequently, she tapped the table with the middle finger of her left hand.

He raised his head at length, but not his eyes. They remained blue-green, cold, remote.

" Well ? " she asked, after five more minutes had gone by.

" I have seen him before," he said. Still his eyes gave no sense of the proximity of any person at all speaking to him. It was as if he were replying to a voice within his own brain that spoke, or a voice a long way off, out of his boyhood, a voice in the cold plains that advance under cold moons to the Dnieper's edge.

" Where ? " she asked.

His voice was quite toneless as he spoke. " At the edge of the clearing in the pine-wood. I have spoken to you of it."

" Near the Slobodka, away beyond Kiev ? "

" Yes. In the pine-wood where we gathered, the revolutionaries."

" What was he doing there ? "

He seemed not to have heard her question. He seemed to be rehearsing a dire tale he knew well.

" We gathered there to read the forbidden newspapers and proclamations from our leaders. They would distribute appeals from the workers and to the workers. I was not sixteen years old then. The police did not know of that meeting-place. We came down on it by a dozen paths, or by no path at all. We had markings on the trees to guide us."

He was silent for some time. He lifted his eyes to her suddenly. " I have spoken to you of Vladimir Stepanovitch ? "

She made no answer.

He repeated his question. " I have spoken to you of Vladimir Stepanovitch ? "

" Not often. Once or twice."

" I did not wish to speak of him."

" I knew. So I did not ask you."

" I must speak of him now."

" Speak, then."

" He was the son of the doctor from our town, Tanyev. He was studying in the University at Odessa. I have never loved, and shall never love, any human being as I loved him. I shall never love any human being again."

" That is as it should be, Boris."

" You, of course, Susan . . . that is not the same thing."

" It is the same thing. We must love not ourselves, not each other, not any one person. The mass, the toiling millions . . ."

" Yes," he sighed. " But it was not so then. When I was an ugly little Jew boy and we went bathing in the creek, ' Stork ' they called me, ' Aïsst,' because of my thin nose. The Christian boys threw cow-droppings at me, and when the Jew boys saw them do it they threw twice as much. In the long hot days, when my master let me put aside my needle and thread, I would steal down to the river, hoping that none of them would notice me. But they found me out always. They used to hold my face under the water till I was

more than half dead. Vladimir Stepanovitch found them at
it one day. He was on his vacation. He smashed all their
faces in, till their eyes were swollen and blue as beetroots.

"They did not often attack me after that—down by the
river, at least. They expected he'd crash out on them any
moment from among the willows. And besides, I was sly.
I soon found out he had to pass by our house on the way
down to his bathing. I would not go down unless he had
gone before me. Then I went too. He spotted me, dumb
with shyness, fifty metres behind him.

"'Come!' he'd call. 'Come, little brother! Why do you
hang back there?'

"So I came up to him, but my tongue was stuck to the
back of my throat like a spar of metal, I was so shy, and
I worshipped him so. For he was big and handsome and
had a forehead like . . . like a lump of marble. Sometimes,
on a free day, I stood up against the window hour after hour,
waiting for him to go by, and he would not. I could not eat
or drink. My eyes would not shut all night long.

"Sometimes he came. We went down to the river and
bathed, and lay in the sun, drying ourselves on a small
tongue of sand. A whole summer passed by, and he said not
a word of the things which possessed his whole mind. You
had to walk warily in those days. You had to guard your
tongue even in the presence of an ugly small Jew boy who
adored you. Then, in the second summer, slowly he began
to let me look into his heart. He spoke to me of the poor folk,
peasants on the land, workers in the factories, of their bodies
cast aside like offal when the blood had been drained out of
them. He spoke to me of rich folk, factory-owners swilling
their soup out of golden soup-plates, fat priests rolling with
their women on beds of swansdown. He talked to me of the
coming Revolution. He made me . . . he made me what
I am.

"When he finished his studies, he went into practice at
Kiev. I was fifteen then, and I ran away from Tanyev.
I knew I could be of help to him up there. I got work easily

enough at my trade. But it was not only with scissors I worked, sitting cross-legged on the floor. I was small and could slip about easily, without attracting much notice. I ran errands with documents, leaflets, summonses to meetings. I hid them among the folds of cloth I carried from the store or in the pockets of new suits to be delivered to customers. I helped Vladimir set up a secret press in a stable in the Podolskaya, down in the Jew slums by the river. We carried most of the type single-handed. I knew it could not last for ever. I thought, being a boy, that the Revolution might come to-morrow or the day after. If it did not—I knew that the morrow or the day after they would get us. That did not disturb me. I had a fancy in my mind of Vladimir and myself—no one else at all—standing up against a wall, in the open air, with the first wind of dawn blowing on our foreheads. It blew cool on our chests, too. Our shirts were opened. They offered us handkerchiefs to bind our eyes, but we refused. In one and the same moment . . . in one and the same moment . . ."

He stopped. His throat seemed blocked. Words could not force their way through to his lips. She said not a word.

" Ah ! " he cried, and sprang to his feet. " The bullets ! Hot and sweet and friendly ! In one and the same moment they hit his heart and mine. His blood and mine mingled in one pool on the grey asphalt of the yard ! The red flower of the Revolution springing from the rich ooze ! "

He stood there, his hands raised before him, his eyes shining, as if he were still a small boy, and still, the next day or the day after, the Fates might yield him his lovely death, him and his friend. Then the light went out of him. His hands fell limply. " No ! " he muttered. She could hardly hear what he said. " It was not to be like that ! " He sank down into the chair again, and took up his tale listlessly.

" Some months later I saw that man ! " She started forward. She was almost shocked by the casual way in which at length the tale twisted round to confront the man from whom it had set forth on this journey into long ago and far away.

" Or *did* I see him ? " Bitterly he struck the palm of his right hand with his left fist again and again. " *Did* I see him ? "

This time she was shocked indeed. " What ? " she cried. " You don't even know that you saw him ? And yet you——"

" Oh ! " he shouted, he almost screamed, at her. " Don't you see ? Did you see that face ? It is no face at all ! It goes into nothing at the edges, like a shadow ! Of course I saw him ! I saw him twice, I tell you ! The first time was the last meeting but one we held in the Slobodka pine-wood. He was there amongst us, the revolutionaries. Vladimir pointed him out to me. Vladimir had eyes as keen as blades. ' Who brought him ? ' he whispered. ' How did he get here ? Do you know who brought him ? ' I looked, and looked again, and then I saw. A pale face like—like a peeled bulb in a cellar. A body like a mist. It was the man I saw in the kitchen just now. I saw him eight years ago, in the pine-wood. I went forward to find out how he came, did he know the password. He was not there.

" We met again in the wood a fortnight later. How shall I tell you ? I was uneasy. There was a smell about. I sniffed it in the air. I spoke to Vladimir, but he laughed at me. His eyes were keener than mine, but I could smell, with my long thin nose, like a dog. The meeting went on. There was much to discuss. Then I saw him ; floating, he seemed, between the tree-trunks.

" ' There he is ! There ! ' I said.

" ' You are dreaming, boy ! ' said Vladimir.

" But I was not dreaming. The police were all about us in two minutes more. They chained us man to man and took us away. I'll not tell you of the prison. I have spoken of it already. But this I did not tell you—of Vladimir two cells away from me, at the end of the corridor. Of the rope swishing through the air on Vladimir's naked body. I heard and felt the strokes as if it were my own body they were beating. They wanted to get names from him, where the press was, where he had got the type for it, the names of our people in other towns—Moscow, Odessa. They did not bring a word to his lips. Oh, it was dreadful ; it was dreadful, I tell you ! Should I speak ? Perhaps, if I spoke, it would stay their hands. But I knew he relied on me to keep my tongue. They stopped beating him at length. No, he had not spoken. A prison fever got hold of him. He died there, in the dirt and the darkness. They carted him away on a wheelbarrow, like a load of muck. . . .

" It was that man who broke his body with a rope's end, that man who killed him—that man in the pine-wood. That man. To-night I smelled the dirt in the air again. To-night ! Here ! In your house ! I tell you . . . I tell you . . ."

The words petered out on his lips. He suddenly fell sideways, rigidly. She was too late to prevent his head striking the floor. She ran swiftly to the door and called, " May ! Come at once ! " May came. " Run for a doctor ! " she bade.

But he had come to before the doctor appeared. He was intensely ashamed of himself. " Let me go ! " he said. " Let me go ! " Susan tried to hold him back, but he would not have it. " I'll come with you ! " she said. " I say no ! I say no ! " he insisted shrilly.

" Good night, Susan ! " he said. " Tell your father . . . tell him I'm a fool. I'm sorry ! Good night ! "

" Good night ! "

He was summoned to do some work on the German–Russian frontier some days later, and did not return to Doomington for several months.

CHAPTER II

THE LOTTERY

I

Every morning Silver took a penny tram down Blenheim Road from the Oleander Street corner, opposite the clock-station where the conductors clocked in their times of arrival and departure. The tram took him down to Poulter Street in Bridgeways, a region that lined the pitch-black banks of the River Mitchen. It was a region of small damp dwelling-houses, from which he and his family had graduated a number of years ago. But he still worked there, in an establishment for making waterproof garments, which had once been a dwelling-house, too. The elderly Mr. Horowitz still dwelt in it, as a matter of fact, in one room, though he made waterproofs in all the others. His wife was dead. His one daughter had got married in Leeds without glory. He was an elderly man. What did he want more than one room for ?

There was little else you could say about Mr. Horowitz or his establishment than that they were elderly. He had a grey discouraged beard that had stopped short a long time ago at a stage mid-way between being a short natty beard and a long dignified beard. He had elderly red-rimmed eyes. He was very round-shouldered, and all his bones creaked when he sat down to the machine. His house, like all the other houses in his street, had been built some time in the eighties. But it looked as if it went back two or three centuries before the Industrial Revolution ; as if it had had a special little Industrial Revolution all of its own, to make it so piebald and grimy. In later years, and not many later, it was pointed out that that was the sooty source from which the broad auriferous

Silver river derived. The spectator gaped. Or he chattered glibly of Fuggers, Medicis, Carnegies. A little time later still, he made less respectful comparisons.

But Mr. Horowitz had gratified his one ambition by that time, so he took no stock of the gaping of the silent ones or the chattering of the glib ones. Over in Jerusalem, under the lee of the Temple, he stood up against the Wailing Wall and said his prayers. He swayed his body left and right, or shook it forward and backward. He beat his bosom with his fist. He clapped together the palms of his hands. But the tears that rolled from his almost sightless eyes were a matter more of decorum than of grief. He had gratified his one ambition. They would shovel his old bones into a hole in the sacred hillside of Zion.

It had always been his intention to die in Zion. But he found himself side-tracked to England, which was further in space from his Bessarabian ghetto, but easier to get to. In that wealthy land his ambition endured a blossoming. He would work hard, he would make money, and he would not only die in Zion, he would live there, as the Patriarchs had done, sitting in the cool of the evening under the branches of his front-yard tree, with the hens clucking about the well, and friends hastening along the road to drink wine with him and discuss fine points of biblical commentary. He worked hard, day and night, for years ; so hard that he did not realise he had long squeezed out of himself what little youth and energy he had brought with him. He found at length he had saved sixty pounds. The room his daughter had occupied was vacant, for she had married lately. With his sixty pounds he bought some seven or eight second-hand machines, as rickety as himself, and installed them in the room his daughter had vacated. He dismantled and sold the two beds in the front bedroom, for his wife in her grave needed no bed now and a sofa downstairs would suit his purposes. He then got in a joiner to knock up a few " makers' tables." Here his " makers " would sit, dipping their fingers into pots of rubber solution and smearing it into the seams of the garments that the contractor sent round in ready-cut bundles. The young " seamers " would sew together on their machines the edges where mere " smearing " would be inadequate. They would do the easy work, the straight edges, the belts. Mr. Horowitz himself, with a handful of " machiners," would sew the difficult edges, the sleeves, the collars. He was himself a doughty hand at collars. It was said of him he made collars like for King Edward the Seventh.

Mr. Horowitz evacuated a further room, where the work would be examined and passed. His waterproof factory was ready now to begin operations, those operations which were to buy for Horowitz his passage to Palestine, a roof, a tree, a well, a grave, a stone.

But Horowitz was no bright star to hitch a waggon to. He looked decrepit, and so did his little factory. For some weeks it looked as if the sixty pounds he had earned during these back-breaking years were as much lost as if he had pitched them into the Mitchen. And then one day—rather more than a year before the strange evening of the meeting between Smirnof and Polednik—as Mr. Horowitz was shuffling up Blenheim Road, he met Mr. Silver. They were not well acquainted ; they had, indeed, singularly little in common, for Mr. Horowitz was a devout Jew and a capital-ist, whilst Silver was non-religious and a working-man by philosophy, so to speak, as well as by accident. But they had both worked together for a certain Mr. Winberg of Magnolia Street when he had started off a waterproof factory with the same sort of equipment, if not the same ambitions, as Mr. Horowitz sought to do now. Mr. Horowitz had left Mr. Winberg's employ on the mere suggestion that he should continue working into the Sabbath evening during the " rush " times. Silver was still working for Mr. Winberg, and was making respectable money. And it was convenient, too, just slipping of a morning out of one back door and through another back door, and there you were at your work.

But in a very few minutes poor Mr. Horowitz had told so sad a tale that Silver arranged to go down to Bridgeways as soon as he had worked a week's notice for Mr. Winberg. He would have gone down the very next day and sacrificed a few days' wages, but he could not let Mr. Winberg down. Silver never let anybody down, though he took no credit to himself for that, and no one gave him any. It was merely what was expected from him.

" It's a rush on," said Silver. " Perhaps now he could not get another maker in at a moment's notice. In one week I will be with you."

" Thank you ! How shall I thank you ! " cried Mr. Horowitz, seizing Silver's wrists. " You should live long ! " A tear bumped against the bridge of his nose and collapsed into his beard. Then he stopped a moment. He had a sudden vision of blue skies in Zion and the yellow lamps of oranges in orange-groves. The sense of the hot dry holy stones of the Wailing Wall came up like a moth-wing against his mouth. He was agonisingly aware that his fulfilment of them must be thrust back seven long grey days if Silver did not come down with him, at once, to Poulter Street, if the machines did not start humming, if the naphtha fumes did not arise from the pots of solution like incense at the Golden Altar, the Altar of Incense, in the House of the Lord.

He closed one eye slyly. " And if I give you two weeks' wages," whispered Mr. Horowitz, " you will come down this afternoon ? "

He saw at once he had made a mistake. A spot of colour came into Silver's cheeks. He looked away, as if the suggestion had made him not so much angry as miserable.

" No ! No ! I was making a joke ! " exclaimed Mr. Horowitz hurriedly. " In one week you will come ? We will make money ! You should live long ! " he cried again.

" Let be ! " said Silver. " I am happy ! "

So Silver went down into Bridgeways to help Mr. Horowitz make waterproof coats, after having duly worked his week's notice for Mr. Winberg. Before long most of Mr. Horowitz's machines were manned by machiners and his makers' tables by makers. That was due partly to the fact that people liked Silver, even when they were not anarchists, and they naturally drifted in the direction he had taken. It was due also to the fact that the " rush " Silver had spoken of, the " rush " which might have made it difficult for Mr. Winberg to get another workman in at a moment's notice, subsided as capriciously as it arose.

But for some reason the concern did not prosper. Whereas Mr. Winberg of Magnolia Street came down into the very next street and knocked house after house together till the street was all Winberg, Mr. Horowitz only just managed to keep his head above water. And from time to time he only managed that because Silver furtively remitted part of his wages. The concern lacked youth, energy, or, much more, business ability. Not a garment left Silver's hands the parts of which were not well and truly stuck together. Mr. Horowitz was just as punctilious with his sewing together of their edges. But whereas at first he sewed them as if he were making the sails for a boat which should carry him past flat-land and promontory forward to Zion, he now handled them mournfully as if he were making his shroud. His back creaked louder as he stooped over his machine, his chin fell further down upon his chest. No, not under the golden ramparts would they carry his bones at last to a grave in the holy hillside, but to a hole in Wheatley cemetery, where the Doomington rains seeped down into the clay between the roots of sparse alien weeds.

More than two years passed in this way. It was a cheerless place, that small house-factory in Poulter Street close up against the sluggish blackness of the Mitchen river. But it made Silver look forward all the more eagerly to the anarchistic evenings in his Oleander Street kitchen. Once or twice he even induced Mr. Horowitz to come and join the conference. But the experiment did not add to the old man's joy of living. In the first place, he was a capitalist, a sweater, an exploiter of labour. Dan Jamieson, the Socialist candidate, who had not succeeded in roaring his way into Parliament, tried angrily to convert him to Socialism. The presence of the Silver daughters *en masse* did not quicken his aged heart-beats. And Polednik scrutinised him acidly, as if he were an item in a row of statistics. Sometimes he took him to task quite sharply, for the old gentleman was a Zionist. Polednik had quite early on given up the hope of conducting any serious propaganda among these babblers, but he esteemed it an official duty to pounce on any manifestation of the Zionist impulse. Zionism as a political doctrine was anathema to the Poledniks. They considered it sapped the will to class-war of the Jewish proletariat ; behind its romantic mask grinned the teeth of Big Business.

Looking to right and left of him fearfully, old Horowitz crept away from Silver's kitchen. There was no place for him there. There was no place for him anywhere, saving in that place which is in the holy mountains. He shook his head ruefully. The words of the Psalm dripped from his lips as the tears from his eyes :

" The Lord shall count, when He writeth up the people, that this man was born there."

A small boy in Blenheim Road stopped as the old man shuffled by. He did not like the way the old man was chanting to himself ; so he made a ball out of a dirty newspaper in the gutter and threw it at his dinted top-hat. But the old man went on intoning :

" As well the singers as the players on instruments shall be there. All my springs are in Thee."

He would not hear the singers, no, nor the players on instruments, saving if the Lord should work a miracle.

A miracle ? What, a miracle ? Was it not a miracle, neither more nor less, that Silver should win fifty pounds in a Dutch lottery two or three weeks before Christmas ? If God had not quitted the cloudy tops of Sinai for the express purpose of looking into the matter of Horowitz and his grave in Zion, how was it that Silver had won a lottery as far away as

Amsterdam when he was working for Horowitz in Doomington ?

What is more, almost the first person Silver told about the prodigious money was none other than Horowitz himself. Mrs. Silver had gone marketing in Shudehill and the Silver daughters were gone, too, when the postman delivered the news ; excepting May, who was giving her father his breakfast. And it would not occur to May to suggest what way the money should be spent. A little dizzy with his good luck, but conscientiously aware of a waterproof " rush " which included even the Horowitz factory in its scope, Silver took the tram down to Bridgeways at once, to be in good time for the day's work. He tipped the conductor a shilling. The conductor said " Heck ! " staring at the shilling as if it were a card-trick. Silver blushed like a man who has been caught filching a penny from a blind man's tin. Then he looked through the window, as if nothing at all had happened.

" What do you think ? " said Silver to Mr. Horowitz.

" What ? What ? " the old man began suspiciously. " Well, what ? "

" I have won a lottery ! "

" You are crazy," said Mr. Horowitz. " No ? "

" I am a capitalist," said Silver. " I tell you I have won a prize in the Dutch lottery. From fifty pounds."

" What ? " moaned Mr. Horowitz. " You have won a lottery ? From fifty pounds ? What do *you* want with fifty pounds ? " His bloodshot eyes rolled miserably. " How many *tsentels*, how many tenth-parts, did *you* take ? How many lotteries——" He stopped. He knew. He knew in his bones that Silver had taken at most only one-tenth part of a ticket, and in one lottery only. " I took it for a joke," said Silver. " It was so funny that Cohen, who comes round collecting for the coal, he should be an agent for a Holland lottery as well. So I paid him a shilling a week as well for a lottery."

Mr. Horowitz groaned. For years he had taken shares in Dutch, Swiss, Scandinavian lotteries, spending far more money than he or his factory could afford, in the sick hope that Chance might yield him the passage to the Promised Land that Age, Industry, and Prayer had denied him.

Then suddenly, more overpoweringly than his senses had ever registered them, the blinding blue of Zion's noontime smote his eyeballs. He sniffed the aromatic odour of citrons coming up in baskets from Sharon, from the flat places.

Now, now, or never . . .

" What you will do with those fifty pounds? " he cried. " You do not know what you will do with them! " Which was indeed quite true, for Silver had hardly had a moment yet to consider the matter. " I know! I will tell you! You must not say no! I tell you if you say no——" He wrung his hands feverishly. He was like a lover whose girl has held him at arm's length for years. He can bear it no more. If she does not yield something, everything, now, this moment, calamity is upon them both.

Horowitz grasped the lapels of Silver's coat. " You are saying no! I tell you, it is a bargain! " The old man's red-rimmed eyes glared like a bird's.

" But of course! " said Silver, his teeth knocking. He had no idea that the shrivelled old man had somewhere within him a reservoir of such fierce energy. And it did not occur to him that he could possibly withhold from Horowitz, or anyone else, a thing so craved for, whatever it might be.

" I buy it! " announced Silver.

Horowitz did not hear him. Or only his ears heard. His soul could not permit itself to register a victory earned with a few puffings of breath when the long assault from year to year of sweat and blood and tears had failed.

" It is my business I sell you! I paid sixty pounds! I want no more than fifty! No, I will not take one penny more! Perhaps your daughters have money saved in the savings-bank? I do not want one farthing of it, I tell you. You see what a business we make here! Busy like in middle Market Street! I sell it you! I have finished with it! I am an old man! I will buy my passage to the Land of Israel! This very

morning I'll take the ticket at Garden's Travelling Office !
You will come with me to get the ticket ! " He flung back his
arms in a superb gesture, as of someone who confers an ineffable privilege—the prima donna who permits the gallery
girl to enter her dressing-room, the captain of the ocean liner
who permits a schoolboy to stand on the bridge beside him.

" And you will stay in Doomington," he continued. " You
have bought the business." Insensibly his voice slid into sing-
song. He half closed his eyes. The gift of prophecy came down
upon him. " It will grow and it will grow. It will be like the
oak-tree that has been an acorn and that shall be a wood of
oak-trees. People will look at Winberg's and they will laugh.
They will say : ' Pah ! Is that the place where they feed the
pigs ? ' But you—you will have so many windows that the
Town Hall will look the other way. In Liverpool, in Bradford, in the Wales, they will say : ' Silver, what does *he*
think about it ? ' Men from London and from strange Par-
liaments will come to visit you and bring flowers for your
wife. Your daughters, they will marry Counts from all the
old families . . ."

Then his voice petered out. The spirit flapped its wings
and was away. He put his head on one side and held the
palms of his hands before him, the fingers curling in upon
them like talons. " You will buy my business," he wheedled.
" Only fifty pounds I am asking."

" But of course," said Silver, as it were casually. " Have I
not said already ? I buy ! "

" You buy ? You buy ? " Mr. Horowitz clapped his hands
like a slum child on a char-à-banc who sees the sea opening
before him for the first time. He hurled his arms round
Silver's neck and kissed him on both cheeks.

" Come," he said, " to the Cricketer's Arms ! We will
drink it a *mazel tov*, in brandy ! This very second, I tell you ! "

That was how Sam Silver, of Oleander Street, found
himself a pillar of the capitalist order one morning in
December nineteen hundred and eleven, the year of the
accession of His Majesty King George the Fifth.

II

But the capitalist order reckoned without Esther, the eldest of the Silver daughters.

Silver came home quite late that evening from Mr. Horowitz's factory in Poulter Street. It was as if the contractors had become aware that the concern was passing into new hands. A whole hand-barrowful of extra bundles of work came in during the course of that day.

" What did I tell you ? " gloated Mr. Horowitz. " And if I asked you five pounds extra for the business, would it be a sin ? "

But he did not. Having at the Cricketer's Arms fulfilled his obligation before his fellow-man, he now addressed himself to his Lord. He put on his frock-coat and silk-hat and strode off almost jauntily down the road to the Polish Synagogue a few corners away. It was no more than a weekday noontime service, but he stood there facing the Ark, swayed there, lifted his voice, as if this were one of the grand full-dress services of the New Year festivals.

" What has happened ? Has he had a grandson from his daughter in Leeds ? " the old men muttered to each other. He clasped his hands and shut his eyes in ecstasy like a love-sick youth who has at length heard the sweet incredible " Yes."

So Silver came home late that evening. The family knew of his good fortune. Possibly May had told them. Quite possibly she had not. For fifty pounds, even fifty pounds, was the sort of thing May was quite capable of forgetting. But the family knew. Silver had left the letter of notification stuck behind a brass tray on the mantelpiece.

Mrs. Silver had already acted on the good news. It had happened to be the day on which the Burial Benevolent Society called for its weekly contribution of one penny. She had raised her subscription from one penny to threepence on the clear understanding that the Silver family coffins should be equipped with best handles of real brass instead

of imitation brass and the wood was to be a better quality.
" Three times as good ! " she insisted. " We pay three times
as much ! Tell the Society ! "

" Yes," coughed the collector, " I will tell them. Real
brass handles ; it will look like the queen's crown. Perhaps,
if you pay more, they will make it oxidised copper. And
instead of deal, why should it not be oak ? " He coughed
again—a nasty graveyard cough. The Society had chosen
their collector not without careful thought.

" Come in at once from the fog," requested Mrs. Silver.
" I will make you some tea-with-lemon. And May will go
for some glycerine to put inside. Are you wearing a chest-
protector ? My Sam he has an old one. You can have it."

Sarah, too, seemed to have derived profit from her father's
prize, apart from the still problematic extra-special handles
they might screw on to her coffin. She was nursing a baby.
She had bought for the baby a quite extravagant rattle,
laden with more bells than was good for it—a rattle much
above the baby's station in life.

Elsie was in the kitchen that night. She had been kicking her
heels some time now waiting for a renewed engagement with
Mr. Gleb Meyer, and the Oleander Street kitchen was as
good a place as any to pass the time in. She was sporting a
new pair of silk stockings. Susan was studying in the next
room, making notes with a new fountain pen. May sat on
a metal stool with a new poetry-book on her lap. Esther,
the married daughter, was also there. There was a general
air of well-being in the Silver family. But Esther looked
almost radiant with good-will.

" Good evening, good evening ! " said Silver as he entered
the kitchen. There was a certain self-consciousness in his
voice. Was there perhaps a faint tremor of guilt, too ? He
noticed out of the corner of his eye that Esther was there.
For one panic moment he felt like turning tail and scuttling
out of the house.

" Good evening, father ! " said the Silver daughters.

" Good evening ! " he replied weakly. " You too, Esther ? What a pleasure ! "

" Look," said Mrs. Silver. " Look what Esther has made for you ! " She lifted a soup-plate that acted as tureen-lid to another soup-plate. Silver sniffed the air.

" You are right," said Esther. " Sweet-and-sour ! " As a rule, there was no dish which so enchanted Silver as fish cooked in sweet-and-sour sauce.

" Ah ! " said Silver. " You shouldn't ! "

" It's nothing ! " insisted Esther.

" Sit down to it at once ! " requested Mrs. Silver. " The trouble she had getting it, you would think it was for a wedding ! "

May put a chair to the table. She found him a knife and fork.

Silver thought it would be seemly to inquire what fish it might be, for its preparation completely disguised its specific nature from any but the acutest eye. " And this is halibut ? How I like halibut ! "

" Not for sweet-and-sour," declared Esther. " It should be fresh-water fish."

" The fishmonger," narrated her mother, " he had cod, he had haddock, he had all the fish from all the sea. She turned her nose up at it like it might be stale kippers. It's got to be from the river."

" Yes," admitted Esther. " I knew he had some carp behind the shop for himself. ' Don't tell me you haven't got any ! ' I said. ' Bring it out at once ! ' "

" She got it ! " observed Elsie indolently, stroking her silk stockings.

" Then before she got the flavouring ! " her mother pointed out. " What was it you had to get ? She made Mrs. Poyser take down all she had on her shelves ! "

" Oh, peppercorns. And bay-leaves. There should be little onions, of course. Well, who said it could be too much trouble for my father ? "

" And this ? What's this ? " asked Silver, prodding about with his fork. He knew what they were, but he thought he would feel a little more like eating the rich fish if he put it off a little. He wondered why he felt so sick. He had felt in grand shape all day.

" Raisins," said Esther. " It would be nicer with raisins ! "

" May stoned them," Elsie pointed out. She was in a rather aggressive mood to-night.

Esther ignored her. " It's nice with a pinch of lemon like I gave it," Esther went on, like a pigeon cooing on a tree-top. " I made it a special gravy. With ginger-bread. You like it ? "

" Go in and look what the scullery's like ! " said Elsie. " I wonder who's going to wash it all up ! "

" Be quiet, will you ? " Esther rasped out. " Who's asking you, you . . . you . . . ! " She managed to bite back the word that trembled on the tip of her tongue.

Elsie leaned back and winked one large dark eye. " Tart, I think, is the word ? " she suggested.

" Now, please, you girls ! " Mrs. Silver implored.

" Please ! " echoed Sam Silver. He looked round apprehensively towards his youngest daughter. But May sat silent and withdrawn on her metal stool, her poetry-book open on her knees. The ugly word affected her no more than a leaf that might flutter down on to her shoulders and flutter away again.

Esther swallowed hard. Then she switched round from the provocation of Elsie's eye. The sweet smile came on to her face again, that almost too sweet smile.

" Such a good day, no evil eye ! " she murmured. " You like the fish, yes ? " She became aware that her father's fork lay stranded in the plate. " But why don't you eat ? "

" Oh, Sam, whoever heard," begged Mrs. Silver. " After all the trouble she's taken, you say you don't like it ! "

" I didn't ! " said Silver. To prove he had not, he nearly choked himself with a lump as large as his fist.

" Please, please ! " begged May. " If he wants to eat, let

him eat ! " In whatever visionary world her book took her wandering, among satyrs or heroes or nymphs or trolls, her father, too, was a denizen—Sam Silver, the waterproof-smearer.

Silver went on eating in silence for a minute or two. It was all a little uncomfortable, not merely because his stomach was uneasy. He knew what the sweet-and-sour fish was about. He wondered who would first have a word to say about the fifty pounds.

" Nice, nice ! " murmured Sarah to her baby. She abstracted a morsel of fish between finger and thumb from the plate, sucked it a little, then gave it to her baby to suck, too. " Doodums nice now ? "

" Even the baby liked it ! " Silver jested weakly. His inside swung a little. " A housewife in a hundred ! Your husband, Joe, he's a lucky man, Esther ! "

" What ! " cried Esther. " You've heard already ? Who told you ? "

" Heard what ? "

" You've not heard ? Such a lucky day for us all ! "

Sarah's baby shook its rich rattle. Elsie stroked the silk ankles of her stockings.

" It has been so busy at Horowitz's to-day," observed Silver. " Winberg sent in some bundles of work to-day for the first time."

" But you haven't heard about Joe," Esther insisted. " Wish us *mazel tov*, good luck ! His boss has asked Joe to come in with him and be a partner ! "

" I don't think I will eat any more ! " said Silver.

It didn't now seem to worry Esther that her father wasn't enjoying his sweet-and-sour fish as much as she hoped he might.

" Isn't he lucky, eh ? " she marvelled.

" Yes, he's a good feller, Joe's boss ! "

" No," said Esther, " what I mean is—he should offer him a partnership to-day, just when you win the fifty pounds ! "

" But why—but what——" Silver stammered.

Esther laughed easily. " You wouldn't think he would give him a partnership for a birthday present ? He wanted seventy pounds. So Joe calls me round and I goes and sees him at dinner-time. ' Seventy pounds ? ' I says. ' Has my father won seventy pounds ? Where should we get the extra twenty pounds from ? ' I said. So I argued and he argued, but it's all right. It's settled. Fifty pounds, not one penny more ! Have I got money in the savings-bank ? "

The words rang familiarly in Silver's ears. Who had uttered those same words before, that day ?

" You, too, father," Esther added benevolently. " You will come in on it, too. You can be what they call a sleeping partner."

" But I can't," said Silver, " I can't ! "

" What do you mean you can't ? You mustn't worry about it. The business part of it—I will manage that for you, too. For my father and my husband, it's just the same thing. After all, don't you lay out the money ? "

" I can't," said Silver. " You see——"

" I see what ? "

" Perhaps he wants to get me an outfit for my new act," suggested Elsie. " It's about time I got a new tail-coat and top-hat. And I think a smart little malacca cane——"

Esther treated her like a fly buzzing on the pane. " I think you and me and Joe and Joe's boss had all best have a meeting to-morrow night. Or why not to-night ? "

" No ! " said Silver.

" What do you mean ? Why do you keep on saying no ? "

" Because . . . " He gulped. " Because . . . Well I haven't got no fifty pounds."

" You haven't got no fifty pounds ? Are you mad, father ? Is it a lie ? Haven't you won no lottery ? Doesn't this letter say——What do you mean you haven't got no fifty pounds ? "

" I bought a business myself to-day ! That's why ! " He turned to his wife, in a miserable attempt to change the conversation. " Hannah ! Aren't you going to make me no tea with my dinner to-night ? "

" Listen ! " said Esther grimly. " What shark has been after you ? What do you mean you've bought a business ? Without asking your wife and daughters ? But you haven't ! It's a madness ! "

" I have ! "

" Oh, have you ? And will you please tell us what business ? "

" Hi, who won the money ? " Silver tried to bluster. " Did I or did you ? "

" Please tell us what business ! "

" If you want to know—it's old Mr. Horowitz's from Poulter Street, where I work "

" Ha ! Ha ! Ha ! " laughed Esther scornfully. " You've bought a business from that lump of bones ? You mean he *gave* it you with a tin of cocoa ! "

" I've promised him fifty pounds ! "

" You've *promised* him ? Oh, that's all right ! You've *promised* him ! "

" When I get the money I will pay it to him ! "

" You will tell him to-morrow morning you've got other things to do with the money ! "

" I've promised it him ! "

She stopped. She strode up to him. " Look here ! That old swindler hasn't made you sign any paper ? "

" If I broke my promise it would kill him ! He has been trying for years to save up to buy his tickets for Palestine. If now——"

" Did you sign any paper ? "

" No ! "

" Then it's all right. You're tired to-day. Why should you go out ? I'll go and fetch Joe and Joe's boss and we'll fix it up to-night ! "

" I've promised old Horowitz ! "

No one spoke for a moment or two. The air crackled as if there were lightning about. The baby started whimpering. " Hush ! Hush ! " murmured Sarah, and snuggled him against her bosom. May turned a page and went on reading.

" I wish," said Elsie, yawning, " a few men would turn up ! "

" You will not buy that business ! " said Esther

" I will ! I have ! "

Then the storm broke. The air darkened as with a cloud of torn leaves. Twigs cracked like whips. Whole branches went careering through the air.

" So that is the way you treat your own born children ! Your children who have always looked after you and worked themselves to the bone for you ! " The woman roared and ravined. " Who for did Joe and me want to go into partnership for ? For you ! For your wife ! For all the lot of us ! So that we could live like decent people, and have houses with baths, like the Winbergs ! Who said it was your money ? It was our money, the whole family's money ! Then that old swindler comes along and he thinks he can rob us ! But he can't ! He won't ! Where shall May get books to study with ? And poor mother ! Look at her ! She should have a holiday ! When she goes to the market she's shivering blue with cold ! Why shouldn't she have a new coat ? Do you know what managers are ? How do you expect managers to give Elsie a try-out in the big theatres if she has a silk hat like an old-clothes man ? You must have money in the bank these days, or what will you do with all these daughters ? Do you think husbands grow on trees ? Poor Sarah ! All she wants is a little dowry and she'd have a baby of her own. Must she always go about borrowing babies ? It's a business like a dust-heap. So you give him fifty pounds ! I make you fish cooked in sweet-and-sour sauce and you go and take your children's money and throw it down the grid ! It's a shame, a scandal ! God will not let such a thing happen ! It's against God and man ! "

Minute after minute she continued so. There was little sense and no order in the things she brought out. It was her intention to prevail, as she had prevailed before, by the breath-expelling fury of her impact. She stood there on her hind legs and went on roaring.

Silver was a peace-loving man, even though his talk concerned itself so often with bombs and revolvers. He loved peace, but he loved honour more, for he loved it in the hidden roots of his being, bandying no words about it. He had given his word. He had given his word. The words went on drumming in his brain. " I have given my word. I have given my word. I have given my word." The words pounded on and on, turned round and round like the wheels of a train. All meaning went out of them. " I have given my word. I have given my word." He was tired. He was sick. He must have peace. He would give gold watches and diamond rings if only the noise would stop. Who could get on top of the storm, and pull, pull on the reins, till the storm hung dead in its traces and cold calm peace was in the sky, and in the meadows and in the railway-train that bumped, thumped, thundered along the tracks ? There was a magician somewhere who would get astride that horse and whisper two words into his ear, and there would be no more, no more of these hideous trumpetings. What was his name ? Sam Silver was his name. It was easy. All Sam Silver had to say was just this : " All right, Esther, all right. Am I arguing with you ? "

Silver lifted his left hand. His mouth began to dither with words. The train's bumpings slackened. " All right, Esther——" he began.

Then he felt an oblique pressure upon his eyeballs. It thrust them aslant till his vision lit upon the mouth of May, his youngest daughter, sitting upon her metal stool. It was a mouth fresh as a bud and firm as a fist. " No ! " proclaimed the pursed-up lips, in a silence more imperious than all the shoddy thunders that had pommelled the kitchen walls for these twenty endless minutes. " No ! " bade May. " You have given your word. You have given your word. You have given your word."

" No ! " screamed Silver. " No ! Get out ! " The smell of his sweet-and-sour fish suddenly struck odiously into his nostrils. He lifted the plate with both hands and flung it

hurtling into the lobby. " I hate your fish ! " he cried.
" Take it with you ! "

III

" I wish," said Elsie Silver, yawning, " a few men would
turn up ! "

She said it the evening Silver brought back the news he
had acquired Mr. Horowitz's business. She said it some
evenings later, when she next turned up. Mr. Meyer had
still not signed her up again, and she was rather bored. Perhaps she needed a new tail-coat and top-hat and a new song
or two before they gave her a job. Perhaps she needed to be
a little more respectful towards the local managers, and the
audiences, too, perhaps. It was December, not at all the sort
of weather a girl chooses to go strolling up and down Oxford
Road to see what she can find to amuse her. Not a girl who
can help it, that is to say.

And if ever Elsie went strolling up and down Oxford Road,
it was not for amusement. It was not for profit either. Does
the poet seek the perfect word or the mystic the perfect state
to amuse or profit him ? Or the hungry stomach food or the
desirous loins appeasement or the sea the moon ?

Sharp, dark, and hungry were Elsie's eyes. She knew what
she wanted. No, not quite that. She knew what she did not
want. In the draughty wings of the shoddy little music-halls,
on the blank crowded pavements, in her father's kitchen—
very little, nothing she *did* want, had been given shape, tint,
substance.

Sooner or later, she had hoped, perhaps even an anarchist
might appear who might be worth wanting. A Gentile
anarchist, that is to say ; Jewish anarchists did not disturb
her. Why an anarchist less than a monarchist, a count, a
clerk ? But when her father went and bought old Horowitz's
business, she perceived with displeasure that his new status
severely restricted the supply for quite a month or two.

It was strange how very promptly the drought began. After

all, the news hadn't had much time to get about, but certainly quite a lot of the *habitués* had heard about it by that same evening. A few men did, of course, turn up. Yet you could hardly call Ponski and Pontrevitch men ; those little whining poets, with their noses leaking on to their manuscripts. And you couldn't call Dan Jamieson a man either. Call him a barrel, a fog-horn, a brass band, anything you like, but not a *man*. You don't get into bed with a copy of the *Clarion* and a red tie.

Yes, it was odd how quickly it got about that Silver had become a capitalist. That first evening you could count the number of anarchists on one hand. On Saturday night, the big night, there were hardly more.

" What have I bought these flesh-coloured stockings for ? " sighed Elsie. She got quite jumpy, sitting about on the sofa from hour to hour, waiting for the knock of the anarchists, once-twice, then once-twice again. You never knew what new blood a Saturday night brought in. One or two pimpled youths turned up who had not appeared before, or, if they had, had made no impression on anybody. They were aware of the Polar twilight that seemed to be creeping down on Silver's kitchen, and they felt that in the absence of their betters there might be a look-in for them somewhere with one or other of the Silver daughters. But they mattered as much to Elsie as if they were straws that a gust had blown in through the open door. She settled herself up against the crook of the sofa and closed her eyes, and thrust her head back, dreaming. The glow of the firelight caught the pull of her taut neck and the line was lovely, like a motif drawn by the bow of a master-violinist. In the shallow valley between her breasts all feminine allurement seemed to lie lurking ; yet there was a spirit more masculine in those clenched fists and that strict mouth than a whole regiment could assemble of such youths as gazed on her here in the dark kitchen, their palms sweating with desire for her.

They were blue and cold, the eyes she saw, staring in through the gates of her forehead. The hair was gold once, with a muted sheen. Was that a man's mouth or a woman's mouth, more womanish than her own, of which the corners were so wryly twisted ? That long scar that curled from the crest of the nostril round towards the mouth again—on the cheek of what sort of woman does the rapier impress its so male signature ? That wind- and sun-whipped cheek under which the delicate blood too effetely flows—suddenly a flap of flesh hangs loose and the blood flows—ah, the sweet blood ! Let me dabble my mouth in the spurting of the blood ! Oh, cold blue eyes, never grow warm for love of me !

" Elsie ! Elsie ! " a woman's voice was wailing. Hands were clawing at her shoulder. Sarah, May, Susan . . .

" She's fainted ! She's fainted ! "

Mrs. Silver's hands were clacking loose at the wrists as if the bones were broken. " I have *not* fainted ! " protested Elsie. Sarah was almost smothering her with the excessive comfort of her bosom. " Please let me go ! " requested Elsie, with distaste.

" What on earth *was* the matter, Elsie dear ? " asked May.

" Nothing at all, my pet ! I was just thinking ! "

IV

The fact was, Silver had gone over to the enemy. He had become a sweater, an exploiter. The anarchists couldn't believe it. After all, he had been, in a sense, their ring-leader. It is true that a few people turned up in the Oleander Street kitchen even during the nadir of Silver's repute, during the week or two that followed his defection. But these were either creatures of habit, or young men whose visits had next to nothing to do with politics. As for the others, if chance brought them past Silver's doorstep, they shook their heads sadly. They had not thought Silver capable of such duplicity.

Silver was at least as unhappy as they were. In his soul he couldn't detect that he was in any way different from what he had been before. He had been a workman then. He was a boss now. But he wasn't what you could call a born boss. It had just happened, as it just happens you get caught in a shower or slip on a lump of orange-peel.

He was naturally a friendly soul. He liked to have people about him just dropping in, by the dozen if they liked. There were moments when he devoutly wished he had never won that wretched prize in the lottery. Then he would recall old Horowitz wheezing over his machine, the eyes growing more blurred from year to hopeless year. He would recall the moment of his transfiguration, when hope blazed up in his eyes like a sword. He was far off in Palestine now, perhaps this moment making his way to the Wailing Wall, his step more lissome than it had been in Bridgeways not long ago, dragging along from the factory to the synagogue, the synagogue to the factory. Perhaps even now, in his grave on the hillside, he lay at peace, the holy earth pressing down on his eyelids.

" Well, dead or alive," sighed Silver, " Horowitz is happy, anyhow ! "

But he himself was not happy. In the old days he could hardly move off his doorstep without hearing a kind word or seeing a hand waved at him. Now he fancied that people deliberately turned their backs on him when he went by. If he saw a knot of people talking together, he was sure it was his old friends whispering about him, pointing the thumb of scorn over their shoulders. He crept from place to place like a criminal who thinks that every window goggles with eyes.

It was doing no good to Mrs. Silver, either. She had four unmarried daughters, and a married daughter with a baby and another coming. That might have been enough to keep the hands of most mothers full. But children were not in Mrs. Silver's line. The glory of being a capitalist's wife did not make up for those grand Saturday nights. She laid in great stores of lemon and serried pound-bags of sugar. But it did not entice the anarchists back again. The kettles boiled away dispiritedly on the hearth.

Polednik smiled dourly down his thin nose. " The emperors and kings may breathe freely again. They can dismiss their personal bodyguards now. The Prime Ministers, too, need no longer quake behind their tail-coats and white waistcoats."

" Stolypin ? " asked Susan quickly.

" Poor Peter Arkadievitch Stolypin ! " he mocked. " If he had delayed the Royal visit to the theatre in Kiev but a few more months, until Sam Silver of Oleander Street had disbanded the anarchists, he might have escaped the anarchist's bullet ! "

" There is another Stolypin where that one came from ! " Susan pointed out.

Polednik's eyes darkened. " The fools ! " he cried. " The fools ! Will they never learn that for every victim they bring down in high places they lock up a thousand workmen in prisons or hurl them beyond the Urals into Siberia ? Look ! I've had news to-day from Helsingfors ! ' At this moment the Kossacks are chasing our men along the streets of St. Petersburg, lashing out at them with their *nagaikas* ! Over in Tzarskoe-Selo, Nicholas and Orloff, Alexandra and the fat sow Vyrubova, are laughing till the tears run down their faces ! '

" They will laugh," said Polednik sombrely, " on the other side of their faces before they are many years older ! "

No. Poldednik did not desert Silver during this period. *He* was no anarchist. He did not believe that back-alley capitalists were any more noxious to his cause than those muddleheaded kitchen praters. There was more room nowadays in the Silver house to write letters, forward reports, compare notes with Soho, Vienna. " I congratulate you, Nicholas ! " he muttered between thin pale lips.

V

It did not take more than a month or two before the feeling gained ground that Sam Silver was not, after all, a formidable recruit to the ranks of capital. He was a good honest workman, but no boss. He didn't possess the boss mentality.

In fact, the Silver factory remained about as low down in the scale as the Horowitz factory. Perhaps Silver was too honest. Perhaps he was too easy-going with his workmen. Perhaps he was too ashamed of having turned his back on his old friends to be able to put his heart in it. But there it was. Silver as boss couldn't be taken seriously, even though he developed a rather bushy black moustache at this time, rather capitalistic in shape and texture. It was also possible that the moustache mobilised itself of its own accord, because he was too dispirited to do anything about it.

So gradually the anarchists drifted back to the Silver kitchen. It was never quite the same thing as it had been before. The hands of the clock cannot march back on their traces, nor the stream flow uphill again. But a good number of the *habitués* returned. The happy chirrup settled like a canary again on Mrs. Silver's lips. Silver again took up his seat at the head of the table at the confluence of the draughts from the kitchen door and the front street door. No reference was made to Silver's new status. It was treated as guests might treat a smell of cooking coming up from the kitchen when they are being collected in a drawing-room during the few minutes that precede a dinner-party. It was there. It hung faintly about in the air. But it wasn't talked about.

No, it wasn't quite the same gang of anarchists as had gathered about Silver's kitchen a year ago. But the gang itself had never been identical two Saturdays running. Was it that the *Tendenz*, the *Stimmung*, were not quite what they had been ? Would you say that there had been a slight swivelling towards the right ?

For instance, would Harry Stonier have felt quite at home in the Silver kitchen a year ago, or would not the anarchists have cold-shouldered him into the street again? Harry Stonier was a clerk at the Town Hall now. For two years after leaving school he had worked in a wire factory. He was a working-class man like the rest of them.

Yet he wasn't, somehow. Because he was a clerk at the Town Hall? You couldn't have that up against him. He wouldn't have been the first clerk to find his way into the Silver kitchen. And the fact that he worked for the municipality didn't mean that he was an out-and-out supporter of the old régime. No, it wasn't that. His father, moreover, was a brass-moulder. Had been, and still was. Harry Stonier had once told them so when they had asked him.

They had asked him. That was the point. They had gone as far as that. He didn't carry about with him the atmosphere of the working-man, bone and blood of the working-people. Far less did he seem to belong as of right to their company of root-and-branch rebels. In fact it was said of him that when someone, meeting him in a public park, asked him what his politics were, he looked quite alarmed, as if he did not know what the word meant. He had blushed and been silent for some time. Then he said : " Oh, me ? I suppose I'm a Liberal. Is that all right ? "

But the matter was not brought up in the Silver kitchen. They did not rise with dynamite-stick and bomb to excommunicate him. They let him stay. He was very young, after all ; he was only seventeen. May was sixteen. As a rule he did not stay long. May would look into her father's face and would find there some indication, whether he looked at her or not, as to whether she should stay or go. If she went, Harry Stonier went with her.

Sometimes he left, even if May stayed behind for one reason or another. And that was because Elsie had turned up. Harry Stonier and Elsie Silver did not get on well with each other at all. He did nothing about it, but sometimes she was quite rude, even though she knew how much that pained May, for whom she would do anything in the world except stop being rude to Harry Stonier. She thought him a molly-coddle and a mammy's darling, and said so. So he got up and went. He and May would arrange to meet in Baxter's Moor or Layton Park, if it was likely that Elsie would be about. They were young, those two, but they cared for each other a great deal already. He was Gentile and she was Jewish, but nobody said anything about it, not even Esther, though it was impossible to say how long Esther would remain silent. Possibly she had not said anything yet because Elsie was so rude to the young man ; and those two sisters made a point of never backing each other up. Besides, they were two children ; in one or two important ways they were far younger than sixteen and seventeen. So May Silver and Harry Stonier went on reading *Lamia* and *Epipsychidion* to each other, and thrusting their way through the tangled bluebell drifts in the Mitchen copses.

VI

It was an evening in July, nineteen hundred and twelve, six months or so after Silver had acquired the Horowitz factory. Susan Silver stood at the corner of Oleander Street looking anxiously up and down Blenheim Road. Now and again she doubled rapidly down the length of Oleander Street to take up her position at the Aubrey Street corner. This was Susan Silver, not Elsie. It was more in keeping with Elsie's character that she should stand on the *qui vive* at street corners, to see what men might be coming that way.

" Oh, there you are ! " exclaimed Susan at length. " Where did you get to ? "

" Where should I get to ? " asked Polednik. " Are you losing patience, Susan ? I've waited longer than you ! "

" No, I'm not ! You know I'm not ! That's not why I'm here ! "

" Well, then ? "

" I'd rather you didn't come in this evening ! "

" Why on earth not ? We've a lot to get through to-night."

" I'd rather you didn't come in."

" Is anybody ill ? "

" No ! "

" What's the mystery ? "

" I'd have brought out the stuff myself, but I couldn't stand here with all those pamphlets. I didn't quite know when you were coming."

" All right. If you've got some idea in your head, I won't argue. There are other people to argue with. I'll just come in and help you collect the stuff."

" No, Boris, no. May's in, and that young fellow, Stonier. He'll bring it over to the corner here."

" Now look here, Susan. This is idiotic. If I can't even put my nose inside the place—— What's the matter ? " He paused. " Are you getting nervous ? You don't mean to tell me that the police——"

" No, nothing of the sort. Somebody's turned up I don't want you to meet. That's all."

" Oh, oh ! " He raised his head and lowered it two or three times.

" That fellow ? " he asked.

" Yes."

He turned on his heel away from her and strode ten yards down Blenheim Road quickly, then back again. Then once more, down and back again.

" I don't think you need worry," he said to her dryly.

" You promise that there won't be anything like—like last time ? You understand ? It was—unpleasant ! "

" Listen, Susan," he said. " That sort of rat is only dangerous when you don't see it. When it comes out into the open it ceases to exist at all. He doesn't concern us. He's not there, I tell you."

" We'd best be getting in," she said.

Alexander Smirnof was sitting on the sofa, with Sarah Silver at his side. Sam Silver sat at right angles to them, at the head of the table. Flanked by such supporters, what harm could befall him ? And who would wish to harm Alexander Smirnof ? Who could object to eyes that were so grey and tired ? Who could object to a mouth that was so forlorn ? The faint wash of reddish hair behind the broad bulby temples was fainter than before.

Time had not dealt kindly with Smirnof these two years. He had grown a little fatter, but clearly not through good living. His black coat was shiny with age. It was so tight for him that the buttons strained at their threads. He wore a waterproof dicky, clean enough, but too small for the waistcoat to contain it. His ready-made black bow was shiny, too, from too much touching up with a flat-iron.

" You like it ? " asked Sarah solicitously. " You must eat up every drop." A bowl of lentil soup steamed fragrantly before him.

" Thank you," he smiled at her. " I have never eaten soup one quarter so delicious."

" Eat. Don't mind the others."

He inclined his head to Mrs. Silver and then to her. His manners were perfect.

There were a dozen people there that night who were present on that occasion more than two years ago when Boris Polednik had sought to strangle Alexander Smirnof. They were orating, arguing, drinking, to-night as then.

" Good evening, all," said Polednik, as he entered.

" Good evening," they replied. They did not for one moment suspend their orating, arguing, drinking. If anything, they talked louder and drank deeper. Mrs. Silver dropped a glass. But that meant nothing, for she dropped a glass just as easily when the kitchen was empty as a churchyard.

But did they a little furtively follow Polednik's movements ; how he sat down, how he breathed on his tea to make it cooler, how he took a newspaper out of his pocket and pointed out a passage to Susan ? Did it take them five minutes, ten minutes, to satisfy themselves that he could not have been so long in the room without becoming aware of everyone who sat in it, including the fat threadbare creature lifting spoonfuls of lentil soup so delicately to his lips?

" Yes, Susan," they heard Polednik say—heard him with relief, perhaps. " There's a lot to get through to-night. Shall we go into the other room? "

Susan and Polednik rose. Polednik looked straight before him. Smirnof did not raise his eyes from his plate.

" There's some more," said Sarah. " Are you sure you'll have no more? "

" No, no. I thank you." There was a spotlessly white handkerchief in his pocket. He dabbed his lips with it.

" Listen, father ! " said Sarah, plucking at his coat-sleeve. He turned round. " Yes? "

" Father. This gentleman——"

" Yes? " His voice was gentle. No one could look so side-tracked as Smirnof without bringing all it had of gentleness into Silver's voice.

" This gentleman was a book-keeper in Russia," she said.

" Oh, yes? "

" Well, father, wouldn't it make a great difference? Isn't that what you want, a book-keeper? "

" No, no ! " Smirnof objected. " Please ! "

" A book-keeper? " repeated Silver.

" You know you never know how many bundles you get and how many garments you send out ! You never know how much work you pay for this week that the men carry over into next week——"

" A book-keeper ! " mused Silver. It took him all his time to come out on the right side himself, let alone book-keepers. It seemed to him that the Silver concern could just as well run to an office in Albert Square, a dozen typists, and a commissionaire with gold braid, as a book-keeper.

" Father ! " implored Sarah.

The tone of her voice put his mind round on a new tack. Rather uncomfortably, as if he were spying on the fellow, his eye took in the too small dicky, the buttons that were straining away from the jacket. There were pouches under the fellow's eyes. The way he had taken up the last lentil from the plate, even though he had eaten like a perfect gentleman, even though he had refused a second plateful— it showed he was hungry. But it was the handkerchief that decided the matter. It was so spotless, so gallant—suddenly Silver found himself gulping painfully. He looked away for half a minute, then turned his head again.

" Of course I need a book-keeper ! " he said. " How can my business go on without a book-keeper ? Mr.—excuse me, I'm so bad with names."

" Smirnof."

" Of course, Smirnof. Could it be convenient to come in on Monday ? "

" Oh, Mr. Silver—but I wasn't dreaming——"

" I wouldn't hear of anything else."

" Well, I thank you, I thank you. I'm not bad at figures. Perhaps I can make it worth your while."

Silver waved his hand airily. " Not to mention it, please ! " he said.

VII

Alexander Smirnof quite soon made it worth Silver's while. He found the little waterproof factory in a state of complete chaos. He introduced, and slowly, a hardly more than elementary system of business order, for anything at all complicated, or at all hurried, would have panicked Silver and his men into revolt.

Smirnof moved warily, even gracefully, like a rather plump cat. His courtesy was so unfailing that a word of protest burst on the lip like a bubble the moment it was formed.

He set up a brief system of standing orders, and a simple form of filing, simple but effective. Silver looked at Smirnof ; the men looked at Silver ; the gentle voice of Smirnof purred in his throat—then Silver and the men got down to the machines and tables again, and Smirnof down to his ledgers.

Some of those workmen had been students of Kabbalah in their boyhood. But that was not a more mystical or exacting literature than Smirnof's goods-received book and works-order book. The institution became waterproof in a double sense. There was no leakage of the unfinished material coming in or the finished material going out.

There was a system called " dead horse " prevalent among the waterproof manufacturers, or at least among the more vague-minded of the brethren, particularly during busy periods. A workman " finished out " his week's work on a Friday morning. That day he would receive a fresh bundle of work. This bundle would carry him over into the next week, but he would expect to be paid for it that same Friday night. When next week came, the workman would be reluctant to get down to a piece of work he had already been paid for, if he might get down to a new bundle. Or there might be a rush order for a new type of garment. The " dead horse," duly paid for by the boss, would be thrust out of sight. It might even be dumped into the river.

The following Friday created a new stock of " dead horse." The carcasses were carried over and piled up till certain places stank with it. The contractor got very angry about it. Sam Silver scratched his head helplessly.

Smirnof took the abuse in hand. He daily supervised the workmen's wage-books and checked them up against his own archetypal wage-book locked in a drawer. It took time and tact. The men scratched their heads and sighed a little, but accepted it all. They would have given two black eyes to bluster and kicked it downstairs. But all this suavity reduced them to a sort of sweet dither.

Sarah Silver was not given to deep probing into character or situation. Such a man as Alexander Smirnof was—the whole of him, quite irrespective of what he might be resolved into his parts—she had taken to herself, precisely as she took the casual Oleander Street babies to herself. But this baby was less casual. Night after night, month after month, they met in Silver's kitchen, and repaired after some time to the parlour, the room officially consecrated to Silver love-making. These, too, were wordless lovers, even more than Esther Silver had been, and Joe Tishler, the carpenter. But it was clumsy to call Sarah and Smirnof lovers. She kissed his forehead as if he were her child. He fell asleep against her shoulder as if she were his mother. Now and again he took her to the Hallé concert, or he played chess of a night with Silver or Mr. Emmanuel. But he left his hand in hers, as if something queer might happen to him if he should let go.

But once, when they were alone in the parlour, she said something to him that had quite an odd effect upon him. He was lying cushioned upon her. This is what she said.

" Sasha, it's a funny thing ! "

He took no notice. He did not open his eyes.

" Sasha," she repeated, " it's a funny thing ! "

He was not used to insistence on her part. He sighed lazily. " What's a funny thing ? "

" It's a funny thing about me and father."

" What do you mean, Sarah ? There's not been a quarrel ? "

" No, no. I don't mean that. I mean you and me and father."

" What do you mean ? "

" I know I'm not clever, Sasha. You won't be cross ? "

He grunted dimly.

" I sometimes feel that I'm—I'm only just here."

" Thank God for that ! " he whispered.

" And that father . . . I mean if father had been a girl . . . You've always been looking for a girl like father . . . and you've found it now . . . and . . . you've found it now," she repeated lamely.

He was lying cushioned upon her. When she had spoken, he lifted his head and shoulder from her bosom, thrust himself a foot away from her along the sofa, and placed his hands upon her shoulders. Then he stared with his grey remote eyes into her brown eyes for a full minute, for two minutes.

Then he said slowly, in a far forlorn voice : " Don't talk like that ! " A shiver seemed to pass through him. " You make me lonely." He put his hand up to his eyes and covered them. With his eyes still covered, he said : " Do you know what you're talking about ? "

" Sasha, Sasha ! " she cried, a catch in her voice. " I told you I wasn't clever. What have I said ? I have offended you ? "

Then he said with more urgency : " Tell me, did you think I didn't need a job ? "

She was silent ; her mouth quivered.

" Did you think I hadn't gone days and days without food ? "

" Please ! " she implored.

" Didn't you know I hadn't got a shirt, not one, to my back ? "

" I didn't want to offend you ! " she wailed. " I was only just talking ! "

" You'll never talk like that again, Sarah ? "

" I promise ! " she whispered.

He stared once again into the brown pools of her eyes, to reassure himself that there was nothing at all to see that for one moment he had feared to find there.

He sighed, like a child slipping off into nightmare who is wakened again, and finds the thing mere fantasy.

" Kiss me, Sarah ! " he said. She kissed him. He came back along the sofa to her and rested his head against her bosom. She didn't like to see him with his eyes still open, and still a little frightened. She kissed them both, and then closed them ; so he slid away into sleep. Before long he was snoring gently.

Silver had no doubt Smirnof was clever. But he under-rated his cleverness. He was quite incapable of measuring the skill with which his book-keeper insinuated into his hands the apparent initiative for his various innovations. He was induced to feel that, if not for himself, the systems of filing and checking might never have been introduced into the Silver factory, though he always gave Smirnof full credit for looking efficiently after the mere working details. He was not even surprised to make the discovery that he had harboured within himself these secret stores of business method.

Smirnof's adroitness extended further. For he never introduced any innovation which the other relevant parties, whether they were Silver's own workmen, or the contractors who entrusted him with their work, did not believe that Silver himself, with a little technical assistance from Smirnof, had sponsored.

The contractors smiled upon Silver. They had always believed in his good faith. They now admired his acumen. " Why don't you take in your own cutter ? " they asked, as Smirnof had intended they should. Smirnof had a cutting-table built, and installed a " designer-cutter," as he proudly called himself, to officiate at it. The profits forged upward.

Silver smiled on Smirnof.

" What did I tell you ? " whispered Sarah.

" I am glad," said Silver, " I took him on. He looked so miserable."

" It was so kind of you to take me on," said Smirnof. " It's so rare to come across nowadays—an employer with *go* in him, who knows everything that's going on all the time."

" Please not to mention it," bade Silver. " You are a great help to me, too."

" Please ! " urged Smirnof, and shrugged his shoulders to deprecate what little part he might have played in the improvement of the Silver business.

And then, one night before the year ended, Silver came home and asked for Sarah.

" She's not in," said Mrs. Silver. " Why ? "

" I wanted to tell her about Smirnof."

Esther happened to be in the kitchen at the time. " And what should it have to do with Sarah ? " she asked a little dangerously.

" Oh, nothing, nothing particular ! " he said hastily. He had known quite a long time which way things were going between Sarah and Smirnof. Nobody could pull wool over *his* eyes. And besides, what right had he to interfere, if a man and a woman happen to like each other, just because the woman happens to be his daughter ? Was that *her* fault ?

Mrs. Silver was not entirely so philosophical about it. She consoled herself dimly that someone had once said—it might have been Sarah herself—that Smirnof's mother had been Jewish. " Well, half a Jew," she muttered, " is better than no loaf ! " and let Sarah and Smirnof get on with it.

But Esther wasn't going to take things lying down. If there was any talk of her sister marrying a *goy*, even half a *goy*, they'd have to reckon with her first. In fact, Esther was becoming less of an anarchist every year. She probably had never been much of an anarchist, for she had always had ideas about Jews and non-Jews and marriages . . . not at all the sort of ideas that were current in the Silver kitchen.

And now here was this pasty clerk, Harry Stonier, hanging round the place after May. She'd have to put her foot down heavily, and quite soon, too.

" What's Smirnof got to do with Sarah ? " she repeated.

" I only wanted to say," Silver informed them all, " I've made Smirnof my manager to-day."

" Oh ! " said Esther. She was mollified. She knew Smirnof was a good business-man.

" Yes, my manager," he repeated, with a rather magnificent gesture. " I shouldn't be surprised," he went on, " if we don't make a little money, me and him working together. Though what we'll do with it, if we do make some money . . . " He paused. He stood there and scratched his head. Really, what *would* he do with money, supposing he should make some ? He was happy. He had a wife he loved, and five daughters. And a nice house, in a lucky hour

"Hannah!" he called out. "Hannah! If we should make some money, what should we do with it?"

"Do with it?" She looked startled. "Do with it?" She meditated a few moments, resting her chin upon her fist. Then suddenly she had a vision. Her father's house. It stood in a wide quiet street. Grass grew between the cobbles. In front of the gate there was a grassy ditch crossed by a small bridge. There were green shutters lying back against the walls and friendly windows encased by them, overhung by fretted lintels. At the back of the house there was an orchard. The apricot-tree in the orchard. Her father's house; and, before that, her father's father's house.

Mrs. Silver's eyes shone. She clapped her hands like a child. "Let's buy this house!" she cried. "Let's live in our own house again!"

"Not me!" said Silver. "I never lived in my own house! *You*, Hannah, *you*: I will make it you a present! I will buy it in your name!"

"And the day it is my house——" she started with determination. "Yes, I will!" she went on, more feebly.

"You will what?" her daughters asked her.

"I will wear my pearls, my mother's pearls!"

"And why not?" asked Esther, who was no true proletarian, and saw no wrong in a woman being bedizened with pearls, like any countess.

"You shall, mother, you shall!" sang May.

But Silver said no word. He went up to her and kissed her, as he kissed her one night long ago, when he had made a hooting like an owl and she crept to the door and went out to him where he stood by the apricot-tree. A long time ago this was, over in Terkass, in the Ukraine.

CHAPTER III

THE APRICOT-TREE

I

" TELL ME, Sasha," said Sarah Silver, " before you came to work for father——"

Smirnof's eyes narrowed. He reached for a gramophone record and extracted it from its envelope.

" Were you ever in the waterproof line before ? I mean— you're so clever. Everyone says you're so clever."

" I'm not clever," he said suspiciously, as if it were the one thing in the world he would not have people saying about him.

" All right, dear," she said indulgently. " You're not clever. But were you ? In the waterproof line, I mean ? "

" No, Sarah, I was not. I told you what I was. A book-keeper. And after that I tried to go into business once or twice for myself, but I couldn't manage it. I'm not clever. Your father's cleverer than he looks. Anyhow, he's clever enough not to be a rogue, like all those other people in Bridgeways. He's got a good name with everybody, and I know how to keep books. That's all you need—a good name and to know how to keep things straight. The others, most of them, haven't a good name, and their places are like pig-sties. And they don't know how to talk to people without making them cross. That's all there is to it. Why do you bother your head about these things ? "

" Because I'm so happy. Things are going so nicely."

" That's right, dear. That's what I want. You should look forward to the future. What's gone by "—he paused—" is gone by. What's this ? " He was a little short-sighted. He held the record closer to his eyes. " Oh, this is the new one.

I just bought it to-day. The Mazurka in A Flat Major. . . .
I want you to promise me something."

" What, Sasha ? Anything ! "

" Not to ask me, ever, about those days . . . before I came
to work for your father."

" Of course, Sasha, why should I ? If you don't want me
to——"

" It wasn't the first time we met, that night in July,
when you asked your father to make me his book-keeper."

" No, we met that time when Polednik——" Then she
stopped. Hardly aware what her hands were doing, she
stroked his throat where those other hands had fastened
themselves like a thug's cord.

" Yes, that was the first time we met. But I saw you the
day before. You didn't see me——"

" No."

" And then—the very next night . . . no, Sarah, no. Take
your hands away from my throat. Then I went away—for
nearly two years, it was. And I was thinking of you all that
time. Then I came again. No, not again. I came for the
first time, that was the first time we met. Do you understand ? "

" Yes."

" Say it."

" It was the first time we met."

" You'll never ask me again about the years before."

" No."

" Say it."

" I'll never ask you again about the years before."

" Good girl. Reach me those needles, Sarah, please." He
fitted a needle into the sound-box. " And you'll never think
about them ? "

" Oh, what nonsense it all is ! Of course not, of course
not ! What's the matter with your throat to-day ? You sound
a bit hoarse. Come, I'll make you a gargle ! "

" No, don't get up ! " The fragile Chopin cascade came
tinkling from the smoky ceiling and broke in brilliant spray

on the parlour floor. " You see ? " The fingers of his left hand went rippling down an imaginary keyboard.

She did not see. " You'd best have that gargle ! " she said.

II

Smirnof was courteous with the workmen, but he worked them without mercy. When the rush orders came, he kept them at it till the small hours, or got in other people's workmen to help them thrust the drive home.

Silver demurred a little, but not on his own account. He worked as hard as the rest of them. So did Smirnof. The great thing was, Silver said to himself, he had an honest manager. It was true he had taught Smirnof practically everything he knew. After all he was only a book-keeper when he first came into the business, and how far did book-keeping help you in sewing a first-class collar ? He was inclined to make a bit of a fetish of his works-order book, and his this and that. And, even here, Silver had often to help him out when it came to straightforward common sense.

But he was honest. He insisted the men should be honest, and he didn't want to play any monkey-business with the contractors, either. Silver was well aware that many of his small contemporaries didn't play the game. They got a roll of cloth with the order to make so many garments out of it. In one way or another it was possible to hang on to a certain number of yards of the material, after the garments had been cut out. Out of this surplus, the " cabbage " as they called it, they made a few extra garments " on the side." They did not account for these items, and sold them secretly to small shops.

Quite a few of them did it. Old Mr. Horowitz used to do it. It didn't in the least perturb his conscience. But Silver disliked it, and all the host of kindred practices, like the snipping off of half an inch from the chest measurement, a quarter-inch from the sleeves. And Smirnof disliked it, too.

Silver breathed easily. A manager who would not let the

men cheat him, and who would not himself cheat the contractors, would play straight with the boss. Yes, he thought Smirnof was right. Why shouldn't he come in on a commission basis, on top of his salary? More and more he left the mere detail of the business to Smirnof, though, of course, everything important went through his own hands. Smirnof insisted on it.

They used to take the garments round to Winberg's to have the button-holes done. Smirnof went and bought a second-hand button-hole machine and a second-hand bar-tacking machine, so that they should do the work themselves. He negotiated with the landlord, and knocked out the intervening walls between Silver's place and the two top floors of the next house. He went with Silver to interview the Town Hall people, for there was talk of a big contract to be placed. Silver looked a little bewildered, and Smirnof spoke like a First Secretary at an Embassy. They got the contract. The goods, first class in quality, were delivered ahead of time. The order was doubled.

The firm went on from strength to strength. There had been a fire in a hat-factory at the bottom of Poulter Street. In the new building that was put up in the spring of 1913, there was more space than the hat-manufacturer found he could use. Or Smirnof convinced him he could not use it all. He took over some of the spare space. That gave them elbow-room, without having to pay another builder's bill.

More small contracts came their way. Smirnof would sometimes disappear for a day or two at a time, fixing them up. He would disappear so silently and completely that, for a gnawing moment or two, Silver would wonder if he had ever been there at all. But he came back right enough, with his quiver full of contracts. The firm worked night and day to execute them. There was a reserve of close on five hundred pounds by the middle of the year.

" When it is five hundred," said Silver, " I shall buy the house for Hannah, like I promised her."

" Not yet," Smirnof suggested softly. " Not yet. Didn't

you say we must buy another dozen and a half machines ? "

Silver didn't quite remember saying it, but they bought more machines, and more machines. They now began to make rainproofs, in addition to waterproofs, for Smirnof was certain that bigger money lay that way. They began to develop a direct trade with the big shops, in addition to the warehouse trade.

A day came on which Silver brought home to Oleander Street a garment with a name patented by himself ; or Smirnof, it may have been.

" Look, Hannah, look ! " he cried. He held out the coat to her, and showed her the printed name on the tab. "Waterscapa ! Look ! Feel it ! Have you ever seen anything like it ? Isn't it wonderful ! " He snatched the garment out of her hand and rubbed it against his cheek. " A lining like real silk ! "

" But, Sam——"

" Yes ? "

" You haven't forgotten ? "

" The house ? Forgotten ? I will show you if I've forgotten ! Give me my coat ! "

" Won't you wear your new coat ? "

" What ? My Waterscapa ? No ! This is the first one ! Shall I wear it like it was an ordinary coat ? Hang it up ! They can say what they like ! " he said defiantly. " I want them all to see it ! "

" Where are you going ? "

" To buy you a box of chocolates ! " he said.

He bought her her house, her box of chocolates, though Smirnof had the deposit-money they required him to put down for it earmarked in one or two other directions. Smirnof was beginning to get a sense of the cotton market. There were some clearing-lines he had his eye on. He wanted to get some new machinery. He had got on the trail of a large bankrupt stock of garments.

But he did not press the matter. There would be other bankruptcies.

III

Mrs. Silver could not wear her house round her neck, the night it became her house. But she could wear her pearl necklace. She had not worn it since the day her daughter, Esther, got married, in the spring of nineteen hundred and ten. How could she, the wife of an anarchist, go about wearing pearl necklaces? But she wore it more often during the years to come.

The necklace consisted of five strings of pearls. They were not good pearls. They were of a bad colour, and about as regular in shape as the crumbs in a handful of gravel. But they were important to Hannah Silver. In a sense they were important to her before she was born ; and they kept their importance when she possessed whole boxes of necklaces, as fine as any in Lancashire. On really grand occasions, she never neglected to wear them whatever other jewels she might wear.

Her mother had worn them as a fifteen-year-old bride, when she married Feivel Dobkin, the richest and handsomest young Jew in Terkass. It was a grand wedding. The Jews in the Dnieper villages talked about it for many a day, and not the Jews only, for there were many Gentiles present, merchants from Terkass itself, and farmers from the neighbourhood of the Dobkin farm at Prolensk, some twenty versts away.

For Feivel Dobkin's father, Hannah Silver's grandfather, was a big farmer, as well as a big business-man. In Terkass, he dealt in wine. He imported wine from Kishinev, as his father had done before him, and stored it in great casks in the mysterious cellar under his own house.

The cellar figured as often in Hannah Silver's reminiscences of her girlhood as the pearl necklace itself, and the apricot-tree in the orchard. There were deep bays in it, and sudden declivities ; odd rumblings overhead, and whiffs of sharp air to right and left. Her two elder brothers made her go down with them and play hide-and-seek among the barrels, though she suspected they were almost as frightened as she was.

" Ho ! Ho ! " the boys cried, like bandits, as they sought for her high and low, poking with their sticks in the dark places.

" And, do you know, once," Mrs. Silver used to tell them, " there was a whole heap of sacks left in a big hole, away, away, right at the back of the cellar. And I hid under the sacks. And they couldn't find me anywhere. And they got so frightened, you have no idea how frightened they got. ' Ho ! Ho ! ' they shouted, louder and louder. And then Leon suddenly starts crying like a baby. Then I start crying. Oh, we had great times in that cellar ! "

" Ho ! Ho ! " shouted Silver cavernously in the Oleander Street kitchen, in the days when the Silver daughters were still young enough for such horseplay.

" Ho ! Ho ! " they boomed back at him, making trumpets out of their hands.

" Such a big cellar," said Mrs. Silver. " You could hide a whole synagogue in it. It went all the way back under the orchard. There was a trap-door there, just near the apricot-tree."

" Ho ! Ho ! " said Sarah, her daughter, to this day, making semi-gruff noises at her borrowed babies, in Doomington, a long way from Terkass.

But the Dobkins not only had a cellar where they stored wine. They had barns where they stored wheat and rye, and deep pits where they buried it in the winter, under warm turves. For the father of Feivel Dobkin, being a younger son, had gone off to the wars for the first Nicholas, and had served him well for the full term of twenty-five years. And on his return from the campaign against the revolted Hungarians in the middle of the century, a grateful Tsar permitted him,

Jew that he was, to own land and to farm it. This was near Prolensk, some twenty versts from Terkass, where his elder brother was a wine-merchant.

Feivel Dobkin, the soldier's son, and Hannah Silver's father-to-be, was ten years old when he went to Prolensk to be a farmer's boy. But when he inherited the farm, being then a young man of twenty-five, he inherited the house and the wine-business in Terkass too, for the Terkass wine-merchant uncle had died without offspring.

It was all a little confusing to the other Silver daughters, but Susan kept track of it keenly. She was an intelligent student of the whole Russian ferment—that is to say, not only of the forces of revolution, but of those forces which generated them, which irritated or outraged them into activity. She was interested in the component limbs of the vast Russian carcass, if you could speak so organically of the Ukrainians, the White Russians, the Tartars, the many other smaller nationalities. And for that reason—she was quite certain it was for no other reason at all—she was interested in the Jews, too.

It followed logically that, being interested for that academic reason in the Jewish unit among the Russian agglomeration, she should permit herself to be interested in her own family in Russia, so far as she could trace its origins and render its present aspects to her imagination. She did not need to assure herself that the motive of her interest was not that vulgar bourgeois curiosity which compels the enriched draper to accept the services of a genealogist who will establish a pedigree for him. For she would have found an inquiry into her father's origins much more to her purpose, if she could have pursued it, than her inquiry into the history of her mother's family. She could not disguise from herself there was an almost regrettable element of picturesqueness in the history of her mother's family, as bourgeois as it might be. Her father's family history, on the other hand, was so purely proletarian that there was practically nothing of it. He seemed rather to have happened than to have been born of parents. She reconciled herself with ill grace to the lack of data her father's rootlessness involved.

There was a big family album in the cupboard, which Susan, more often than her sisters, rooted out from time to time, and studied intently. It was as important a document as many another that Polednik brought in to add to their dossiers. Here, in an almost completely faded daguerreotype, was the Tsar's man, the soldier, her mother's grandfather. The Tsar had asked from him twenty-five years of his life, and at the end of them allowed him to settle upon a parcel of marshy acres. This was an act of god-like grace ; for the creature was a Jew—a little subhuman, therefore.

There were one or two photographs of the grandfather, Feivel Dobkin, farmer and wine-merchant. He was an important personage, with a fine full beard, and heavy gold chain stretched across his stomach. One photograph of him was taken in the summer-time, out of doors. You saw the famous orchard. Perhaps this was the very apricot-tree, though mother was not quite sure of that. You also saw a corner of the house, with both the inner and the outer windows flung wide open, and the fretted lintels over them. Grandfather wore a skull-cap, and an alpaca coat twisted and bellied a little by the wind.

This photograph was taken a year or two before the departure of his daughter and her young man for Doomington, and went back about a quarter of a century. There was quite a recent photograph of him in the album, and he seemed hardly to have changed at all. There was a nest of whiteness in the full black beard, and the shoulders were not quite upright. That was all. Still that slightly self-satisfied air. Still that heavy gold chain stretched across the stomach.

Here was mother's mother, taken upon her wedding-day, a fifteen-year-old bride. Malkeh was her name. You could make out the historic pearls ; or it did not occur to you that you could not, for mother had pointed them out so often.

No photograph in the album was more dim than this ; not merely had time faded it, it was almost obliterated by Mrs. Silver's tears.

Little Hannah had been the apple of her mother's eye, for, after having given birth to one boy and another boy in the two years that followed her marriage, seven years had passed before Malkeh had given birth to a girl-child. She was so young a mother that she was almost frightened of the two boys. They were too much for her. But Hannah was her doll, her darling, her princess. Malkeh died when her child was only eight years old. Those years of her childhood were a milky dream, a dim ambience of bliss. Susan did not find it strange that a girl treated in her childhood as if she were a feathery flake from a cherub's wing should develop as a woman into so impalpable a housekeeper as her mother was to show herself in Oleander Street.

The two boys, Alex and Leon, who were so much older than Hannah was, were fond of her, but had little use for her, except for an occasional game of " Ho ! Ho ! " in the cellar. Alex was an outdoor lad, who spent most of his time over at the farm. He would have liked to go off to be a soldier like his grandfather, excepting that it wouldn't have been good enough for him to be a private. He had a good seat on a horse. You wouldn't have thought him a Jew boy, at all. He might have been the son of a Kossack hetman, brought up on the steppe. He wanted to be an officer in the cavalry.

Leon was more for the books. He was going to take over the wine-business when he grew old enough. He played the fiddle too, and Alex played the flute. It was lovely of a summer evening when the two boys played under the blossoming trees, and the neighbours came in, and grandfather opened up a bottle of his special wine that came from the Caucasus.

And little Hannah said not a word in the orchard there. She sat on a stool leaning up against her mother's knee. The flute called to the fiddle, and the fiddle sang back again.

Now and again a petal came down upon your hair. Or it might be mother's fingers playing in it, they were so gentle.

On high days and holidays, mother wore the pearl necklace. " Do they look well on me ? " she would say. " You like them with my new satin dress ? Come, baby, come ! How do they look on you ? There, my sweet ! Look, Feivel, look at your daughter ! An angel, not a baby ! That will be the day, little daughter, when you go under the canopy, the loveliest little bride in all Russia ! And you shall wear your pearls, and he shall wear a great diamond in his tie ! And Leon will play the fiddle—no, no, of course not ! We shall have hired musicians. . . ."

Feivel Dobkin didn't remain a widower long after his first wife died. After all, could you expect it ? He was only forty himself. He had two sons and a daughter to look after, and two businesses. He married Shevka, a widow with one daughter. Perhaps he had found the first wife a little too elflike for so serious and important a man of affairs as himself.

The second wife was no elf. She was a handsome woman, with a good head for business, a good appetite, and a good bosom. There was a photograph of her in the album, plated round with some dress of a thick rich material—brocade, perhaps. A couple of stout gold chains hung over the *massif* of her bosom, and were caught up again on the chinward slope of the shelf into a true lovers' knot.

She had been wearing something round her neck when the photograph was taken ; a necklace of pearls, in fact. It was Hannah's mother's necklace—Hannah's necklace. Hannah had scratched the pearls out of the photographs, no one knew when, long long ago, in some dark fit of desolation. The step-mother had a daughter, Gallia by name, three or four years older than Hannah. Here she was, standing beside her seated mother, her hand reaching with difficulty to the further shoulder. Two fair ringlets spiralled down beside each cheek.

In course of time, Shevka gave birth to several more children. Hannah did not hate any of these as she hated Gallia. Of course, these were the children of her own father, and Gallia was a stranger. But it was not only that. It was Gallia's nose, which turned up a little, and her smell, which was like cheap soap, and her silk dresses with sashes ; and she got the first ripe apricots, and she and the step-mother used to share the same fork, with which they poked into the dish of cut-up chicken and lifted all the best bits before anybody else had a chance.

Not that a stranger coming into the Dobkin house would have known without being told that the same man had fathered this lusty brood of infants squalling on the floor, and the pale Hannah in the corner, sitting solitary. And Alex and Leon were not unkind, but they were both so busy. Alex was in charge of the farm now, and, when he was not working, he'd be out in the countryside, riding, cracking his whip. He was a grand young man, with his riding and his flute-playing. He went dancing, even in Gentile houses. Here he was, his astrakhan cap raked jauntily to one side. There was an astrakhan collar to his coat too—a very tight coat, and trim at the waist. The coat was open, to give you a glimpse of riding-breeches a prince might wear. The leggings shone like water. It was a carefully synthetic photograph. If he had only worn his dancing-shoes too, you would have had a résumé of him in all his elegances.

There was no photograph of Leon. He remained a rather shadowy person, with his spectacles and his ledgers. He remembered Hannah's existence more often than Alex, though that was not often. He went out of his way to be kind to her, and bought her sweets, even when she was a big girl of sixteen.

Things were sometimes very gay in the Dobkin house on Saturday nights in the winter. The step-mother thought it good for the business to have young people in—dancing, and drinking a little and getting merry. It was also a good thing for her daughter, Gallia. Shevka looked very handsome.

presiding over the samovar, and making a sort of punch, with spirits and sugar and tea and lemon and spices.

She wore the pearls. She wore the pearls of the dead wife who had died so young. " She wore *my* pearls ! " said Hannah Silver, the tears starting in her eyes, even to-day, so many years later, with the pearls safe upstairs in a padded cardboard box in her tin trunk. She stared and stared at the big red woman wearing the stolen pearls, till her eyes felt as hot as coals.

For, of course, she had stolen them. Had not my mother said they would be mine on my wedding-day ? Mine ? Were they not mine now, now that she was dead ?

Feivel Dobkin said something on the subject once or twice, and so did Alex, when Shevka first appropriated the pearls. But Hannah was only nine or ten at the time, and it was obviously not seemly for a girl of nine or ten to go about roped round with pearls. So the girl looked on dumb with misery and anger, while the woman sat twiddling the necklace, smiling this way and that on the young men who came to dance with Gallia, and lift their glasses to Gallia. Alex and Leon got married in course of time, and had other things to think of than Hannah's pearls. But to Hannah the pearls grew and grew till they were strung about her horizon like the rings of Saturn.

She felt loneliest of all when there was dancing and singing those long winter Saturday nights. Shevka had always treated her as if her fingers were made of putty. She was never allowed to get busy with the *blintsies* and *varennikis* in the kitchen beforehand ; nor to pour out tea or mix punch or carry round the glasses while the party was going on ; nor to do anything at all but sit moping up against the oven, staring at the pearls that dimmed and glimmered in the lamplight.

But sometimes she would remember the beggars that were gathered over against the fence, their faces big and pale like toadstools. They had come out of their infested shanties, hearing from far off the sound of the rich man's music and smelling his baked meats. They came on crutches, on sore feet bound with coverings of rags and bast. They stood against the fence there, and gaped, and mourned.

So, secretly, she filled her apron with cakes and dainties, and crept out to them and bestowed on them what she had. They blessed her, saying she would be rich with children, and with money, in the fulfilment of time. But it was only her pearls she wanted, which her dead mother had worn once. And the beggars fluttered away in the night like limp moths.

Then at length came the night of her supreme bitterness, the night when she hit her head against the tree-trunks and cried out : " That I might die ! That I might die ! "

But it was not to be a night of death for her, this helpless maid crying in the forest. There would be for her a blowing forth of seed on the wind, to take root, to bud and blossom more strangely than any maid, glad or sorry, had ever known in all that country before, or is likely, it may be, to know again.

That night a rich youth was brought to Feivel Dobkin's house to pay official court for the hand of Gallia, his step-daughter. She was decked out in every finery of silk and gold and jewel. And she wore also the pearl necklace of Hannah's dead mother. She had not worn it before. She seemed as if she would never again, never again remove it from her hell-witch's neck.

Hannah tried to speak, but her tongue was dry leather. She looked wildly into her father's eyes, into the eyes of her two brothers. But there was no response, no flicker of aware-ness. Then a voice cried out in her : " You are worse, my father, than that woman and her daughter. You were her husband and took her to your bed, a fifteen-year-old child. She was a child, Oh my brothers, and she was in labour with you, and you—you have forgotten. For this night's for-getting, evil will come to you all ! "

" What's the matter, girl ? " Leon said to her, peering through his spectacles. " You look hot to-night ! "

"Hello, Hannah! What's wrong?" asked the lordly Alex.

But she did not answer. She rushed out of the big room, out through the front door, across the small bridge that crossed the grassy ditch. She rushed out into the street, and ran, and ran, falling into the big holes, but not knowing she fell. She ran and ran, beyond the edge of the town where the tumbledown shanties of the poor Jews were, out into the open country, and came to the forest at length.

She did not know how long she had lain among the tree-roots, crying her heart out. And when she heard a voice comforting her, for a little time she thought it was her mother, so spent her wits were and the voice was so gentle; so gentle, indeed, that when she realised it was a young man, a stranger, she was not frightened of him.

"Come, now, *dyevushka*!" he whispered. "There now! What is it? Who has been hurting you?"

"They have——" she started. "They have—they have stolen my pearls!" Then she broke down again and cried and cried, and turned her face away towards the hard tree-trunk.

"Indeed!" said the stranger fiercely. "I will get them back for you! You see if I don't!" vowed the stranger, shaking his fist into the darkness.

The name of this young man was Shloime Silver; Sam Silver they called him in the city of Doomington some time later. He was a wandering tailor, who had wandered up the country from Odessa to Ekaterinoslav and Kremenchug, and so from village to village up the river till he should get to Kiev and thence to Vilna. He believed he had an uncle in Vilna, and thought of settling there. But he met Hannah in the wood, and went to Doomington instead.

For they became lovers, it may have been that same night in the wood, or it may have been a few nights later. It did not seem right or wrong to Sam Silver. He had held no other girl in his arms before, and that he should take this one was of the same order of propriety to him as that it should rain or that flowers should grow or bees go about among flowers. To Hannah, on the other hand, it seemed wrong. Often, when she came from being with him, she wept till her pillow was soaked ; but it was a sweet weeping, and she smiled as she wept.

Then she felt the child stir within her, and terror awoke at that same moment. She thought of her father, his thick red lip above the beard, and of her step-mother's cruel bosom. She saw Alex coming in with his riding-whip, and heard him crack it with contempt about her ears. Leon blinked at her through his spectacles, and turned away muttering. The children mocked at her—her half-sister and the three half-brothers. But most of all she was afraid of Gallia, who would sit and say nothing, and turn up still further her odious turned-up nose.

So they determined to leave Russia, as many Jews were doing at that time, for the bad times had begun. " We shall go to a town—they call it Doomington. I have friends there, from Odessa." And when the time came nearer, Hannah, with a fearful sinking of the heart, asked him if he had forgotten the thing he had vowed to her.

" I have not forgotten," said Sam Silver. So he worked out a plan for the stealing, the only dishonest act he had done, or, in the knowledge that he did it, was ever to do at all.

It was the evening of the Ninth of Ab, the fast-day on which they commemorate the destruction of the Temple. All the elder Dobkins were at the synagogue, excepting Alex, who was at the farm. Shevka was there, and Leon, and Gallia, and one or two of the children. And Hannah, of course. On Sabbaths and feast-days, Shevka wore the pearls. But that night she did not, for one must not wear fine things when that sad tale is told.

It was fortunate that Alex was not there when Hannah

said she was half dead with headache and must go home to lie down. For Alex was a cavalier, even to his sister, some-times ; and he might have volunteered to see her safely home. The others had no such thought. So Hannah went back, and struck three matches in her bedroom. And Sam, who had climbed the fence, and was waiting beside the apricot-tree, called like a night-owl when he saw the tiny flame spurt three times. Then Hannah, silent as a ghost, opened the window and let him through, and took him to the locked drawer where the pearls were. He was no adept at lock-picking. They both died several deaths of fright during the burglary. But at length he had forced the lock. He had the pearls safe in his pocket.

" Come, my sweet ! " he said.

So each with a small bag ran and ran the five miles to the station at Terkass, till the sweat poured from their faces, and the stones poked through their shoes. They got into the train there, and got out at Slutsk and boarded a caravan drawn by four horses. And they got to Doomington at length, and there they had five daughters.

IV

" It would be interesting to go to Russia some time," said Susan, returning the album to its cupboard one Saturday evening. " It would be interesting, I mean, to pick up the threads."

She had taken the album down an hour or two earlier, and had set herself to study it, with her usual air of scientific detachment. But, one way or another, the photograph of this uncle or that brother had set Mrs. Silver remembering—the pearls, the cellar, the apricot-tree, the pearls. Only the daughters were there, even Silver was out. So she went on talking, and the others listening. They did not notice, or they forgot, that Polednik had come in, and had sat down on the kitchen-step, not wishing to disturb them.

" I often wonder about them all," Susan went on.

For, of course, there had been no communication between Hannah and her Russian family for years after her disappearance. It certainly had been no credit to the Dobkins, the big Jew family of Terkass, that a Dobkin girl had gone off with a pick-lock wastrel of a tailor, who had no doubt seduced her into the bargain. More recently the lordly Alex had written once or twice and sent photographs. So had Leon, and Leon's eldest daughter, Esther ; she was of the same age as Hannah's Esther, so she, too, had sent greetings. The old man had sent one or two post-cards furtively. He had not been able to do more than that. Shevka kept too tight a hold of him. She had never forgiven the theft of her pearls.

" Yes," Susan said, in a voice softer than was usual with her. " I wonder if Alex is still so grand. And do you think Gallia's nose turns up quite as unpleasantly ? What does cousin Esther do with her spare time ? It would be interesting to go and find out for oneself."

" Perhaps you will go and find out sooner than you think," said Polednik from the kitchen-step. The voice was tart and terse, each syllable a cold pebble.

She turned round suddenly. She felt quite unaccountably furious. She had addressed herself to the grand-daughters of Feivel Dobkin, farmer and wine-merchant, the daughters of a wandering tailor who had been a knight to a sore-pressed damsel, and won her amulet for her at great peril.

She had been talking, or what was worse, feeling, like a romantic schoolgirl, a colonel's daughter. He was always spying on her, spotting the namby-pamby sentimentalist she could never quite exorcise. She was furious.

" I wasn't talking to you ! " she thrust at him. " Mind your own business ! "

He said nothing. He made a polite gesture, apologising for his intrusion.

v

So Hannah Silver duly wore her pearls the evening of the day she became a house-owner, like her father, and her father's father before him. She was a little fuddled with pleasure and excitement, but she presided over the tea-with-lemon like a duchess. She had even made *varennikis* that evening, which her mother used to make of old time, purses of dough, stuffed with *kasha* and dripping with chicken-fat. They were a little underdone or overdone, none of them were quite right. But everyone ate them with noises of exaggerated enjoyment, she beamed so happily as she passed them round.

They did not know—she only dimly knew herself—that Shevka and Gallia were part of her enjoyment. She was getting her own back, at long last, on Shevka and Gallia. Perhaps at this very moment, over in Terkass, they had acid on the stomach, or twinges in the knee, they knew in their hearts that Hannah was paying them back.

Here she was, Hannah Dobkin that used to be, sitting in her own house, with a grandson and grand-daughter already, and four other daughters—she could marry them each twice over to-morrow if she wanted to. And friends on all sides who had come into wish her *mazel tov*. With her own hands she had made *varennikis* for them. Yes, Mrs. Emmanuel, thank you, in a lucky hour they sent me two or three chickens round to choose from ; I don't have to go and buy them myself in the market. A penny or twopence in the pound, what difference does that make to me ?

The pearls are round my neck, Shevka. Ho ! Ho ! If you could see me now, Gallia, you'd smile on the other side of your face. Ho ! Ho ! That's it ! Bandits ! You tried to steal my pearls ! Yes, Mrs. Billig, they were my mother's. She wore them under the canopy when she was a fifteen-year-old bride. Have I told you the story how Sam got them back for me ? I must some day !

Ponski, have another *varenniki*. And you too, Pontrevitch. There are plenty more in the scullery.

You couldn't get away from it. There wasn't quite so extremist an atmosphere about the Silver kitchen nowadays. After all, when you have a hostess in a pearl necklace dispensing bounty, and she's a property-owner, you can't say it's what it used to be. The really intransigent spirits dropped off altogether. Polednik, who was the most intransigent of them all, turned up quite irregularly ; he was always going off somewhere for months at a time. Of course Polednik had never been an anarchist. He had always emphatically *not* been an anarchist. Besides, he was officially courting Susan, so his politics were neither here nor there. A bitter futile little man, most of them thought him—a serpent biting himself with his own fangs. He'd die of poison one of these days.

Polednik was courting Susan, as they put it, and Smirnof was courting Sarah. So that, whatever the secret feelings of each for the other were, neither allowed the existence of the other to affect his behaviour. Or what is more accurate, neither showed himself aware of the other's existence. If that seems improbable, it might be remembered that many a husband and wife, sister and sister, have co-existed within narrower boundaries, for many more years, with few or even none to share that incarceration, and have acted without a moment's respite as if the other were imponderable air.

Polednik and Smirnof remained as remote from each other in the small crowded kitchen as if Smirnof were a turnkey in a Kiev prison and Polednik a prisoner of the Tsar at Tobolsk. And Ponski and Pontrevitch went on reading their poems about their absent mothers ; and a shade of pink crept into Dan Jamieson's red tie ; and though it was rumoured that Joe Tishler had once manufactured a bomb, he made it clearer as time went on he wasn't interested in manufacturing anything more dangerous than overmantels nowadays. As for Mr. Emmanuel, he was less embarrassed than he used to be at the thought of being seen quite patently

entering the Silver house by the front door. He admitted that
the cause of Love had not triumphed as signally as he had
hoped it might during the last year or two, what with these
troubles in South America and North Africa, and the full-
dress wars in the Balkans ; but he was pretty easy in his mind
that by the end of next year the sun of perpetual peace would
have dawned over the five continents. Silver wasn't at all sure
that the same sun could dawn all over the five continents
simultaneously. Smirnof suggested gently he had a feeling
that the biggest war in history was going to break out
in a year or two. The prospect didn't seem to disturb
Smirnof, any more than an astronomer is disturbed by the
prospect that on such and such a date a comet is going
to become visible whose existence he has worked out by a
process of mathematical reasoning. Perhaps he even derived
a certain satisfaction from the thought of the coming war,
for some reason not easy to divine ; for his voice was unusually bland as he made his prophecy, and his eyes were
quite amiable. But the young man, Harry Stonier, when
he heard Smirnof talk of war as a thing purely of political
and commercial stresses, a thing totally disrelated from the
flesh and blood and bones of the human units that were
involved in it, went pale with wretchedness, and his eyes
grew hard with anger.

But, of course, the conversation wasn't usually as serious
as that. It couldn't be, with so many Silver daughters about
the place, and a couple of Silver grandchildren. There
was an air of comfort and plenty at number eleven. The
old sofa had long been re-upholstered, there were new chairs,
a beautiful new wallpaper, with not merely a wainscoting
but a dado. There was as much tea-with-lemon as before,
but there was brandy too, even on weekdays.

For the Silver–Smirnof firm was progressing the whole
time. They took over a factory in Rochdale Road which
had been damaged by fire. Smirnof was convinced that
the damage was not so serious as it looked. The windows

were all out, of course, and a good deal of floor space was unsound. But a certain amount was not. He thought quite a lot could be done with a plank here and there. Silver was rather frightened of the rent, and quite terrified of the rates and taxes ; but when Smirnof began to show him profits that would have justified a considerably bigger outlay he felt that once again he had triumphantly vindicated his own sense of initiative, and that Smirnof's diffidence was rather mean-minded. The firm now dealt with the biggest wholesale houses in the trade, and began, moreover, to develop an important foreign department. Smirnof was quite a traveller ; he had travelled quite a lot for a number of years, though he never opened out on the subject ; or, indeed, on any subject. He still had a Russian passport, but he had put in for naturalisation some time ago. One day he might be in Doomington. A few days later, Sarah might receive a post-card from him from The Hague or Christiania. By a carelessness which was quite unusual with him, he once left his passport on his desk among some circulars. Silver gleefully carried it off, and showed it to the guests in his kitchen.

"Look ! " he was saying. "Would you think such a thing ? Constantinople ! *Constantinople !* " he repeated, mar-velling, as one might say Atlantis or Xanadu. "Constan-tinople, eh ? " And he held up the passport for them all to see.

Smirnof came in at that moment. The faint fluff of his red hair grew stiff with anger. His stomach trembled. "Give it back to me ! " he said. "Who asked you to show it round ? "

It was not at all the tone of voice in which a junior partner should speak to a senior partner. Silver wondered whether he ought not to try and feel indignant. The same moment, or a moment later, he found he was intensely ashamed of himself. There was nothing that filled him with so acute a sense of shame, whether he felt himself or another person to be guilty of it, as the tampering with another's privacy.

"I'm sorry!" he said. He intended the words to be sincere but dignified. They were nothing but a sad croak.

"Oh, please, please, that's all right, Mr. Silver. How about a game of chess? Shall I give you a pawn or a bishop? I insist. Let it be a bishop!"

Perhaps he shouldn't have given away quite so much as a bishop—Silver won with ease. He often won, though Smirnof had the air and the style of quite a good player; and sometimes, when he seemed off his guard, so to speak, he would simply obliterate Silver. Silver knew that, taking it by and large, Smirnof was a better player; and that made it all the more gratifying that he beat Smirnof so often.

"After all," he would explain, "I was playing chess, Smirnof, when you was in your cradle. Oh, well!" he sighed happily. It was a good world, after all. Business was going grand. Look at May, sitting there on her stool by the fire, did you ever see a skin like that, like a jug of milk? Hannah had gone upstairs to put her pearls on. Here she was, wearing them, looking as pleased and handsome as Queen Mary. It wasn't a holiday or a Saturday or anything, and there she was with the pearls. Well, why shouldn't she? He would buy her some more pearls some day. Some day they might go and live in a bigger house, too. It had already been suggested once or twice, by Esther and one or two others.

No. The thought of going to live anywhere else suddenly made him feel sad and empty. No. The way Hannah loved the house, it was a pleasure to see, she wouldn't go and live anywhere else.

But she shall have more pearls some day. And the girls will have fine dresses, too. Business is going grand. It was a good thing getting in that second band-knife in the Rochdale Road factory. How many garments had they checked up last week? Five thousand? Was it possible? *Five thousand?*

"Have a cigar, Smirnof!" he commanded. "And you too, and you too!" he insisted, passing the box round.

CHAPTER IV

SARABAND

I

Esther Tishler came round one morning to Oleander Street to see how the new sideboard looked. It had been made special for Mrs. Silver's parlour by Joe Tishler's firm, Pliskin & Co., and it had wonderful new-fashioned legs—not legs at all, but big balls clasped round by claws. But she didn't get so far as the parlour. As she mounted the steps, the front-door opened, and Sarah, her sister, stood there. It was eleven o'clock, and a weekday, and Sarah should have been at work ; but she had her Saturday hat and coat on, and she was carrying the silver mesh bag Smirnof had given her, which she only used for best occasions.

" What you doing at home, Sarah ? Aren't you well ? "

" I'm quite well, thank you, Esther. How are you ? "

" Have you got a cold or anything ? Is there a strike ? Why aren't you at work ? "

" I'm going to see a house. Up in the avenues, it is. Running hot and cold water."

" What you going to see a house for ? Why do you stand smiling ? "

" Wish me *mazel tov*. I'm going to get married."

" *Married ?* Who ? What are you talking about ? You're mad ! When ? "

" Who do you think ? Sasha, of course ! In three weeks."

" I never heard of such a thing ! It isn't true ! "

" Oh, yes, it is ! "

" Who said you should get married ? "

" Well, Sasha did, and I did. So we're going to."

" It's not true, Sarah. You're making a fool of me ! "

" I say it is. Go and see for yourself in the office in Begley Hill Road."

" In the office ? " She looked absolutely bewildered. " What office ? "

" Where you go when you die and get born and get married ! The register office ! "

" The *register* office ? " Her face looked quite stupid with dismay. " You can't go and get married in a *register* office ! " She had for the moment completely lost sight of the fact of the marriage itself, or who the proposed partner in the marriage was. She was merely aware it was in a register office that one of the Silver girls was proposing to get herself married . . . like an elderly widow, like a girl without two pennies to her name, like a cold-scrubbed Gentile nobody, like a girl who's going to have an illegitimate baby if she doesn't hurry up and——

" Listen ! " She took hold of her sister's arm fiercely. " Has he been up to any nonsense ? Have you *got* to—get married quick ? "

Sarah shook off her arm in disgust. She blushed to her ears. Her full lower lip came out uglily. " How dare you say such a thing ! "

So that wasn't the reason. " Why, then ? In a *register* office ? "

" Because we want to," Sarah informed her coldly. She swept off, lifting her skirt from the ground magnificently. Her silver mesh bag rattled bleakly.

Esther put her hand on to her stomach. She felt exactly as if she had gone up on a swing or on a boat, high to the top of the curve, and she had been left up there, forgotten. She had had quite clear ideas about the next Silver wedding. She hadn't been quite sure which of her sisters it was going to be, for she was not enthusiastic about the various candidates. On the whole, she was definitely opposed to them. But whoever the next sister was, and whoever the man might be, the next Silver wedding was not going to be like the last

one, her own. She and Joe and the whole family were going
to make up for that hole-and-corner mockery of a wedding.
In a sense it was going to be a re-wedding for herself and
Joe, whoever else was going to get married, Sarah or Susan
or anybody, They had had to be content with Unity Hall on
the earlier occasion. Now it would be the Convention Rooms,
in Begley Hill Road, where all the really *classical* families got
married. You should just *see* those chandeliers ! And there
would be a glass of champagne for everybody just after the
ceremony under the canopy. As for the bridesmaids, they
would wear pink silk, with little wings, like angels ! Or would
they think that was just a little, perhaps, Christian ?

Her bosom swelled with rage. No bridesmaids, no champagne, no Convention Rooms ! A register office ! Because
she couldn't marry him under a Jewish canopy ! Because he
was a *goy*. Yes, that's what it was ! Her sister was going to
marry a *goy*. What would they all say in Longton ? Joe's
boss was very particular, too. Joe's boss wouldn't like his
foreman to have a wife who had a sister who married a *goy*
in a register office !

" She will, will she ? Ho, she will, eh ? *We'll* see about
that ! " She swivelled her bosom round and marched off to
the corner. She pawed the ground like an impatient war-
horse till the tram came and, lurching a little, bore her off
to Smirnof's office in the Silver factory in Rochdale Road.

11

By the time Esther had waited twenty-five minutes in
Smirnof's office, some of her fury had evaporated. It was
a small office, but it had a carbolic smell of efficiency.
It wasn't easy to go on being furious in it from minute
to minute. Smirnof was out interviewing a contractor, and
there was nothing to do but wait. She refused to see her
father. Her father was relieved that she refused to see him.
She waited. Smirnof arrived fifteen minutes later.

He was in the room before she was aware he had opened the door and closed it behind him, almost as if he had not come in at all.

" Esther," he said, " how nice to see you. It would have been nicer this evening, after office hours. I have a big order to work out ; it must be worked out to the sixteenth of an inch." He said it all so pleasantly, it was difficult to take any offence. He looked at his watch. " How many minutes would you like me to give you ? "

The thing she had come to see him about was, however, a matter not of minutes but of a lifetime. The watch threw her heart up inside her and tossed it over, like an omelette tossed in a frying-pan.

" Put your watch away," she bade him. " I have come to talk about my sister."

He pursed his mouth as if he intended to whistle, but no sound left it. He sat down and drummed with his fingers on his knee.

" Well ? " she asked, a little flustered by his silence.

" Well ? " he repeated. " It was you who came to talk to me," he reminded her gently.

" Sarah told me to-day you two are going to get married. In a register office ! " she added with a snort.

" That is accurate," he said.

" Oh, is it ? I'm not so sure ! Look here, Smirnof——"

" I'm looking ! "

" Well, it's a shame ! To get married in a register office like a girl from an orphanage ! I've never heard such a thing ! In our family we don't get married in register offices. Do you know who we are ? My grandfather's one of the richest men in Russia. He has farms and wine-businesses and we keep horses. And now my father, too, he's becoming a big man ! I heard last week they're going to ask him to stand for Town Councillor as soon as his papers come through. When we have a wedding in our family, it's going to be a wedding, I tell you. With champagne and bridesmaids and not gold rings—platinum. And if you think——"

He saw she was gradually working herself up like a dervish revolving more and more swiftly on one toe.

" Please ! " he bade her. " Please ! "

But she went on for another three minutes, five minutes. Such a shame, in a register office. Uncle Alex—in England they'd have made him a Sir a long time ago. Champagne. Scandal. Scandal. Bridesmaids.

He leaned towards her and touched her large red cheek with the cold tip of his forefinger. She stopped. There was a white place in the redness, where he withdrew his finger. Then the blood flushed back upon it angrily and obliterated it.

" What—what——" she stammered.

" Listen," he said. " You're a clever woman."

" If you think you're going to get round me——"

" No, I mean what I say. You're a clever woman. You said your father's becoming a big man. Is that so ? "

" Yes, well ? "

" I think you know that I've got a certain amount to do with that. You know that your father and I work very well together, don't you ? "

" Yes, oh, yes, I know that."

" You know very well that if I left the business, things wouldn't go so well."

" I know you're clever," she said reluctantly.

" Now listen. It'll do you no good to be up against me, and it'll do me no good if . . . I want you on my side, Esther."

" What do you mean ? What good will that do me ? "

" You know perfectly well what good that will do you, and what good it's done you already. It's only because our firm's been doing so well Pliskin made your husband his manager. When our firm does a little better, Joe will buy Pliskin out. He'll want capital ; or credit, at any rate."

" Listen, Smirnof," she said. Her anger had quite evaporated. She eyed him shrewdly. " What are you after ? "

" What I'm after ? " He looked her straight in the eyes,

with those eyes which were as grey and vague as cloud. " It's quite simple." But he did not go on. He leaned back in his chair and closed his eyes. Then he opened them again. " You see," he said, " I'm so tired."

" Tired ? What do you take me for ? You work very hard for a tired man ! "

" No, it wouldn't be easy to explain." His head fell forward on to his chest, as if he were falling asleep, there, before her eyes. He was speaking so low she could hardly hear him. It was as if she had stumbled upon him, who knew so well how to keep his own counsel, at a moment when he was in intimate communion with his own heart. " I have my chance," he said. " I know I must work hard. Then I'll rest." He opened his eyes again. " What I'm after ? " he repeated. " I told you, it's quite simple. I think "—he was evidently calculating—" I think—I want to make, yes, a clear twenty-five thousand pounds." He was about to continue. Then he stopped. It was as if he saw before him the figures inscribed on phantom gold-sacks, the sum of money he had, so to speak, already accumulated. He pondered them a moment. The mouth sagged a little ; the chin dropped ; there was weakness in both. But the eyes grew hard, alert. They were windows through which one might have looked into that large skull. And one might have seen ? If one had the fore-seeing eyes, one might have seen green-shaded lights burning chalkily down upon account-books in which columns of figures were marched and counter-marched in subtle strategy. One might have seen men bidding and outbidding under an echoing dome, men bent down towards machines that ticked and ticked like an infernal machine awaiting its moment, while yards and yards of tape emerged from their entrails, and encircled their feet and thighs and bound their arms to the waist, till the grip that held them was more inexorable than the grip of the snakes that held Laocoön.

A crafty smile sat about the corners of Smirnof's mouth. A thin circlet of bluish-whiteness showed under the slightly raised eyelids.

He was lost. He was lost. In that moment he sealed the unrepealable doom.

" I think "—his voice was dry and faint—" I think it should be thirty-five thousand clear."

" Yes," he went on, " I shall need that." His voice was still so low that it was almost inaudible. " I'm so tired, you see. I deserve some rest now. I'll take her away to the South somewhere, where the sun's hot and the sea's blue and warm, like it was that time in Yalta. And there'll be fine music, opera and a famous orchestra. We'll go to Naples. No, not Naples. That's too near. Buenos Aires, I think. Or Rio. Yes, it will be Rio. In the evening, in the cafés, when the moonlight comes through the palm-leaves, I've heard say the little cut-throat players in the cheap orchestras play great music. Beethoven, Handel. They'll play the saraband from *Rinaldo*. How does it go now ? ' *Lascia, ch'io pianga* . . .' " He hummed a few notes and beat time to them almost invisibly with one hand. Then he was silent.

They sat in silence for some minutes. Then Esther sighed heavily, as if her breath, too, had been labouring in some state of trance.

" Yes," she muttered, " we'll be working with you, me and my husband. I trust you to do the right thing by us before you go off. I know you will. You're an honest man."

" You can trust me," he assured her softly. Her eyes were wide open now. He stroked the back of her hand with the tips of two fingers. She did not draw her hand away.

" I know I can trust you," she repeated. " You're clever, but you're honest. Yet why . . . yet why . . ." She was finding it difficult to formulate what she meant—or what she felt, rather.

" Yet why ? " he said after her. " I think I know what you want to ask me."

The words came in a sudden rush to her lips. " If you're so

clever, what do you need *him* for? Can't you do it all your-self?"

"I can't do it all myself," he said softly. "I can't do any-thing myself. Did I look as if I could do anything myself—that night I came, and he made me his book-keeper?"

"What do you mean?"

"I've tried. If you knew how hard I've tried. They won't let me, not me by myself. They listen to me for some time, and they say yes, and then they look at me, and it's as if I wasn't there. They forget they said yes; or they say no, quite sharp, and get down to their papers again. But with *him.* . . . I always knew if I could meet a man like *him* . . . some people think he's soft. But he's not soft. The centre of him is something like . . . like steel. No, not like steel. Something that won't rust or wear out. Diamond. . . ."

"I think you're talking nonsense."

"I think not. Together we can get anywhere." He lifted his voice. "Anywhere, I tell you."

Then suddenly, acutely, she remembered her sister. She remembered who the woman was he had threatened to take away to world's end. It was Sarah—her own sister, Sarah. She remembered what she had come for. After all, Sarah was a Jewish woman. It was not enough, it was not the end of everything, that Joe should buy out Pliskin's business; or that her father should become one of the biggest men in the trade. It was not enough. There had been no piety in her family on either side of it for two or three generations, it was true. But they had been Jews, they had gone on marrying Jews, in blind obedience to a law it had been unthinkable to question.

If Sarah should marry a Jew, there would be no talk of register offices. There would be a canopy and a cantor and a glass broken, and crying and kissing and laughing, and Jewish children and circumcisions and all the timeless intimacy of Jewishness. If Sarah should marry a Jew . . .

"Why, oh, why," she burst out, almost weeping with annoyance, "must you marry Sarah?"

" Because I must have rest," he said.

" *Rest !* " she snorted. " *Rest !* But you're not a Jew ! "

" No ! " he answered shortly. " I am not ! " Then he started again, very quietly : " If it's a matter of interest to you, I am half a Jew. My mother was a Jewess ! "

" So it *is* true ! " she cried hopefully. " I heard that already. Well, listen. Perhaps—perhaps——" The thought she had in her head was not too easy to enunciate.

" Yes ? "

" Perhaps it might be possible," she brought out, the words tumbling over each other, " for you to marry in a synagogue ? I mean, you needn't *do* anything. But for the marriage you could say you were a Jew. See ? Then nobody——"

" I think not, Esther ! " he interrupted her coldly. " I think not ! It would not be suitable."

" And why not suitable ? " She was up in arms. " Wasn't Beaconsfield a Jew ? If it was good enough for Beaconsfield——"

" Please be quiet ! " he said. He looked at her with distaste. " It's got nothing to do with that. It wouldn't be suitable because—because my father was a priest, an unfrocked Roman Catholic priest."

" *A priest ! A galluch !* " She savoured the full hideousness of it by rolling on her tongue the Yiddish word. It was like a pellet of wormwood. Her stomach heaved with the stench of it.

She rose suddenly from her chair. " Go and get married," she cried, " anywhere ! In a pigsty, if you like ! "

III

All that day Esther couldn't get a thing done in the house. She dropped cups and plates as if she were doing it for a living on the stage. When Joe came in and bumped against a table, she nearly bit his head off. She was, in fact, throughly put out.

It was very much the sort of mood in which she liked to go down to Oleander Street and put things straight. In fact, that was the mood in which she had started the day, and the mood got sultrier and sultrier, precisely because she couldn't decide whether her interview with Smirnof had left things straighter or crookeder.

And then she remembered her sister, May, and the young man, Harry Stonier. She remembered them with a snort of triumph. She planted her feet wide, placed her arms on her hips, and stood there snorting with triumph for two or three seconds. Then she strode forth to the hallstand and seized her hat and coat.

It was an odd thing that her nostrils should have been twitching for a quarry since about twelve o'clock and should only now have registered the scent of May and Harry. But it was not so odd if you knew May and Harry. They were so unobtrusive a couple. It was easy, of course, to be unaware of them when the kitchen was full of people. But it was also easy when there was practically nobody else there. They would sit in their corner of the kitchen, May on her immemorial metal stool and Harry on a low chair beside her. They talked a little now and then, of course, but they preferred to go out to do their talking. More often they read a book—the same book, quite frequently—Harry with his right arm round May's shoulder and his other hand holding May's hand, as if they were a couple of children.

When they wanted to talk they would go out. *To talk !* Esther quickened her steps towards Oleander Street. *To talk !* That's how they themselves described it. But a woman of the world knows what talking leads to, if it hasn't led there already. They went out into the country, to the woods, the moorlands.

Esther hadn't been to a wood or a moorland for a long time. She was a respectable married woman and had no need to go to woods and moorlands. May was seventeen, nearly eighteen, but in many ways she was a baby yet. If Harry Stonier *wanted* to, what was there to stop him ? He

wasn't very big, maybe, but undoubtedly he was as strong
as a horse. He had fair reddish hair, with a little curl in it.
They are the sort of people you've got to be most careful of.
They know you wouldn't think it of them, so they take
advantage of it.

Ho, they do, do they ? They think they can pull the wool
over our eyes by all this talk about talk in woods and moorlands ? We'll show them, Mr. Stonier ! A little Jewish
doveling ! We'll show them !

Esther was lucky when she arrived in the Silver kitchen.
Harry Stonier was sitting exactly where she would have
placed him, as a boxer sometimes finds his opponent standing
exactly in the position he has hoped for, exposing himself
to just the lead he delights in. He had, in fact, his right
arm round May's shoulder, and in his left hand he held
her left hand. And, what was more, her chin was cuddled
down into the hollow of his right palm. It was a disgraceful
exhibition. Her mouth twisted bitterly. Perhaps there was
still time to save May. But she must go warily. She must
attack the enemy from the flank. She sidled up to the young
pair to look over their shoulders and see if the book they
were reading might add an arrow or two to her quiver. It
did more than that. It loosened an arrow which hit her
between the teeth. The book was a work entitled *The
Imitation of Christ*.

So the young blackguard was not only trying to seduce
her, he was trying to convert her. She spat. Then she
turned upon her father. She let loose, in the usual Esther
manner, invective piled upon invective. Her bosom heaved.
Her foot pawed the ground like a horse's. But so deeply
absorbed were May and Harry that all her shouting no more
deflected them from à Kempis than if she were a rainstorm
beating against the window, trying vainly to get in. Perhaps,
in order to have them understand who were the objects of
all this eloquence, she would have been forced, fifteen or
thirty minutes later, to march up to the young pair, tear
the book from their hands, and stand directly facing them,

rehearsing all she had said. But before the necessity for
that had arisen she reached the limit of Silver's patience.

" Be quiet," he cried at the top of his voice. " Be quiet !
I tell you I'll not hear one word more ! "

The pain in his voice broke short the thread of May's
absorption. She lifted her head. So, too, did Harry. But
not for one moment did it slacken the pace of Esther's
vituperation.

" A Jewish daughter," she repeated, for there was nothing
she said she had not said half a dozen times before. " And
for why does he come round smarming all over her ? He
thinks we don't know ! We know what he's after ! Look at
his hands now ! How do you know where he had his hands
last night, when they were out on Baxter's Moor together ? "

They knew now whom it all concerned, this uproar that
had struck against the walls of their seclusion as remote and
faint as a bluebottle on the further side of a window. Their
eyes were large with horror. The blood went out of Harry's
face. He became green as a man in dire sea-sickness.

But May's face flamed like a peony, May who was wont
to be as pale as a wood-anemone. She flung herself at
Esther's face like a beast with bared claws. She dug them
into her black heaped hair and pulled and pulled and tore.

" You wretch ! You wretch ! You wretch ! " she shrieked ;
and fell to the floor, and wept and wept, and beat the floor
with her fists.

" Go home, Esther ! " implored Mrs. Silver. " Please
please, go home ! "

CHAPTER V

PROGRESS IN THE FACTORY

WHEN THE GREAT WAR broke out, there were many
for whom the emotion crystallised itself into a few words
in a ditty, a few notes in an air. The air was sometimes
palpable enough in its relevance to the event, as when some
remembered a former war and hummed : " Good-bye,
Dolly, I must leave you " ; or loyalty to their native land
rose like a lump in the throat, and they proclaimed :
" *Deutschland, Deutschland, über Alles.*"

But when Alexander Smirnof went about all day long,
on that fateful fourth day in August, humming : " *Lascia,
ch'io pianga,*" the relevance was not so palpable. Esther
Tishler did not happen to come within his orbit that day,
but, if she had, she would not have remembered that she
had once before heard him hum those notes, beating time
to them with one hand. She had not recognised what air
it was, or been sure that he sang at all, his voice was so faint,
and the hand that beat time hardly moved at all.

But on that day, and on this, the same images were in his
mind. He did not see the lean snouts of guns slowly lift,
swing right or left, recoil ; he had no vision of streaming
banners or streaming brains. He saw moonlight coming
through the ragged palm-leaves that leaned down over
cafés in Rio de Janeiro. He heard the cut-throat players in
the cheap orchestra play great music. It all seemed nearer
and further in the same moment than it had ever seemed
before. It seemed nearer because he saw as clearly as few
men did that day what opportunities would come, in a
doubtful trickle first, then in roaring spate, of making money.

Money ? He was too busy and too happy that day to ask
himself if that forty-five thousand pounds he had once

declared to be his goal would still satisfy him. Or had he, in point of fact, said thirty-five thousand pounds ? To anybody but Alexander Smirnof the thought that that man would withdraw some day from the concern owned by the man Sam Silver with any such sum as forty-five thousand pounds would have seemed as preposterous as that he should some day deal with millions of pounds as if they were pieces on a chess-board. But perhaps the thought would not have seemed preposterous if it had occurred to Smirnof. He never had, and never developed, the sort of imagination which automatically converts money into the things it can buy. He never saw his Rio de Janeiro fantasy encompassed by any luxury which might have been beyond the scope of a retired civil servant's pension. He developed no vision of a wife encrusted with diamonds, like a pier-post with barnacles ; no vision of thousand-ton yachts ; no vision of a grand drawing-room in which the coloratura soprano of the season made lovely and expensive music.

It was true that one or two of these things became imposed upon him, partly by the natural pressure which wealth exerts towards the aggrandisement of one's scale of living, partly as a manœuvre indispensable from the manipulation of capital on a large scale. Yet these were external not internal pressures. To him money was itself a music, which became more musical the more nearly it attained those dimensions in which it becomes, so to speak, intangible. It was a music outside the music of voices and instruments, a chess-board where the pieces were involved in a game as subtle and abstract as Lasker's, a sort of scholastic theology.

" *Lascia, ch'io pianga*," he hummed under his breath ; and the air brought the fiddles and guitars of Rio nearer, for he foresaw that the money was going to be made which might buy them. And it thrust them, in that same moment, further, for his heart leaped, like a lover's, at the thought of money breeding, not fiddles and guitars, but more money, more money, bubbling and hissing like the wake of a ship.

Silver's firm, which had now become a limited-liability company, had an advantage over its rivals from the beginning. Only two or three months earlier, Smirnof had transferred it to a large factory in Rochdale Road, half gutted by a fire. He had a salamander instinct for fire, which would lead him half way across a county almost before the fire had broken out. The factory went for a song, for it seemed useless, until a large capital sum had been expended, to put it to rights. Silver was very miserable about it all and went up and down tugging nervously at his moustache. But Smirnof assured him that his initiative would be handsomely rewarded a lot sooner than he thought. And it was.

Smirnof's nostrils smarted with intimations of the greatest of all fires. He saw all the heavens glow with flame when a few boys put a match to a handful of shavings at Sarajevo, and he quietly transferred his makers' tables and machines to the parts of the building in the new factory which had been declared safe by the surveyors. He would disappear for two days, three days, at a time, softly making his preparations. When the war broke out, there was an initial depression in the industry which made everyone but Smirnof look very hang-dog about overhead expenses. But Smirnof scented at once the torrent of orders that was to come pouring in. He landed the first big Government order. It was easy enough to buy machines, all he needed was joiners to put up more and more makers' tables. As the demand increased, he extended the factory into charred insecure regions of the building, which would have provoked considerable unpleasantness on the part of the authorities at a time of less urgency. He was among the first to realise how invaluable women were going to be to the employer of labour. The output and the profits soared.

A scandal here and there was uncovered at this time, but in other firms than Sam Silver's. The stitching was inadequate in garments apparently perfect ; collars and pocket-flaps were cut cunningly below specification ; there was bribing and corrupting of agents. Silver's face was a book no official could or did distrust. His word was a bond that was never violated.

In 1916 the output had become so vast that shifts working night and day could not keep pace with it. An architect and a firm of builders, with heavy backing from the Government, put up a fifty-thousand square feet one-floor factory for the firm on the Longton brick-croft, with space alongside and behind for unlimited development. The firm's liability to the builders was discharged, as it seemed, overnight.

Smirnof neglected no avenue of aggrandisement. He gave his workers a bigger bonus than all his rivals. He bought over from the most powerful of them a young research chemist of great brilliance, at a salary three times greater than he had been receiving, and his patent processes reduced the cost per garment by twenty per cent. The profits per garment became more and more satisfactory, and in a few months they were turning out ten, twenty thousand garments per week, and more.

In 1917, they opened a proofing-plant so that they might do their own proofing. They were still receiving their cotton cloth in a dyed state, but delivery was not prompt enough for their furious energy. They therefore opened a dyeing-plant near the proofing-works. They then bought up weaving-sheds in Yorkshire, and established a subsidiary company for the sale of cloth to the rivals they had outstripped. In 1918 there was a flutter of alarm among the manufacturers lest the big bountiful War should be over before the year was out. But Smirnof was convinced that the end of the War, so far from withering this golden harvest, would for a certain time increase its fantastic fertility. The soldiers would be coming back, and would need new clothing. New States would be formed, and would want to dress themselves up like gentlemen. He extended the parent plant on the Longton brick-croft. He bought more machinery, another weaving-shed in Yorkshire. He almost did not notice the War had come to an end, he was so busy negotiating the purchase of a cotton-mill in Lancashire, and extending the ramifications of his export trade to half a dozen countries.

Sam Silver was a very rich man by now. Alexander Smirnof was very rich, too. And, perhaps, Smirnof, who had worked very hard, was meditating his retirement, now, or in some months, or in a year or two at most, for he had richly deserved it. And, in fact, Sarah Smirnof, his wife, asked him more than once about Rio de Janeiro, almost worried him—a thing she was not used to do. It would be so good for the children, the sun and the sea.

But Alexander Smirnof did not go to Rio de Janeiro.

CHAPTER VI

IVANHOE TOWERS

I

ALEXANDER SMIRNOF married Sarah Silver, without splendour, in the August before the War. Even if they had not got married in a register office, there could not have been much splendour about a marriage organised from Oleander Street. To have set up the marriage canopy in the Cromwellian fastnesses of the Spanish and Portuguese Synagogue, to have celebrated the nuptials in the Convention Rooms on Begley Hill Road, would have gone some way towards appeasing Esther's appetite for magnificence. But not the whole way.

She wanted the family to get out of Oleander Street as the Winbergs had moved out of Magnolia Street—she wanted them to move out of Longton altogether. Her ambitions were high, but she felt that no ambition could be so high that the secret conspiracy between Alexander Smirnof and Esther Tishler could not realise it for her. She thought, with longing, of the grand castellated mansions near Baxter's Moor, the smart villas in Didsbury. The family would go first, and she and Joe would follow ; they might even live in a wing of the same big house, or have a house built special for themselves in the grounds. That was exactly what Uncle Alex had recently done, as she had been informed by her cousin, Leon's Esther, the one who was the same age as herself. Leon's Esther wrote quite friendly letters nowadays, every two or three months, ever since it had become clear that her Aunt Hannah's family was doing quite well, too, over in England. There used to be a couple of two-roomed peasants' hovels up against the lower end of the orchard of the big house in Terkass. But Alex had pulled them down and put up a neat little bungalow in their place. For his wife and daughters disliked being away from the family at large during the winter months when all the windows were puttied up, and the farm was as dead and stuffy as an empty kennel. And he found it useful himself, too, when he went to a party at one of the fine Gentile houses in the town.

Yes, Esther would have liked a bungalow, too. A bungalow for herself and Joe in the grounds, and father and mother established rather feudally in a main house with an iron-studded front gate, and greenhouses—she thought she would like greenhouses. The Silvers would keep house in a style worthy of the Dobkins of Terkass. The anarchists would not follow them there.

There were only two of the sisters actually at home now, Esther and Sarah being married, and Elsie on tour. Susan and May did not back Esther up energetically in her idea of moving the family from Oleander Street, because they did not believe in backing Esther up in anything. But they did nothing to oppose her. Susan would have liked a large work-room all to herself, for her books, pamphlets and documents had accumulated alarmingly. But she did not feel strongly in the matter. She did not feel her roots deeply planted in Doomington, though she would rather have lived in Doomington than in Buxton, say, for Doomington was, at all events, a town of the proletariat. She still worked in the office of a big foundry, though her father had made it clear to her she could stay at home all day long, if she liked, with her studies. But she preferred to keep herself rather than be kept by money made out of the exploitation of her fellow-workers. She preferred, also, to maintain her contact, such as it was, with the workers at the foundry. That gave her more data, she realised, than a whole library of books. She had already made one or two week-end excursions with Polednik to London, to talk things over with the Russian exiles. She intended to go to Paris and Basle some time this year. She hoped she might some day get enough time off to go so far as Cracow, whence Polednik had returned not many months ago, having conferred with certain of the leaders of the Russian Social Democratic Labour Party in exile—Zinoviev, and Ulianof (usually called by his writing-name, Lenin), and certain others. There was a general air of ferment in Russia and along the Russian frontiers. The years of savage reaction that had followed the abortive revolution of 1905 had grown slack through the excess of their tension. The waters were beginning to seep up from the underground chambers. Soon—who knew how soon ?—the great waters would be rolling, furious and free. Susan Silver was content in the sitting-room in Oleander Street to sit under the chuckling of the incandescent lamp with Boris Polednik beside her, deciphering the code-letters they received, exchanging notes with Stockholm, Prague, waiting, waiting for the signal that would be raised high.

May Silver was content, too, in the Oleander Street house, but less for her own than her parents' sake. She would have preferred a larger house to live in, not because it was larger, but because it would of necessity have been nearer to the rough tangled meadows, the river's shelving banks, where she and her friend, Harry Stonier, were so happy in their wandering that they would hardly speak a word to each other for hours. They would wander there, holding hands like children, or sit down in a small copse, under overhanging boughs, their heads together over some book of verse.

But May alone of the daughters knew how the happiness of her parents was bound up with the small house in Oleander Street. What more did they need ? Neither of them had any sense of comfort. They could sit more comfortably on a chair with a hard seat and a broken back than many folk sit in deep-sprung armchairs. Apart from one or two dishes, which required for their preparation no chefs in complex kitchens, flanked by sauces and spices, food meant nothing more to either of them than the thing you put into your stomach when it feels empty.

It was, of course, inevitable that, sooner rather than later, they would have to leave Oleander Street. It was implicit in the situation. So, on those great revolving disks in fairgrounds, though for a certain time the children perched on them can keep their place, it is quite clear that soon they will be hurled off as the revolutions quicken. You could not go in business the way the Winbergs went, and these, and these, without, like them, being forced out of Magnolia Street or Oleander Street, or wherever it might be, into those regions where you keep servants, and have a garage, and a car in it, and a chauffeur in uniform to look after it, and different sorts of gardens for both flowers and vegetables, and conservatories. It was inevitable, a thing which Sam and Hannah Silver themselves recognised. Money was coming in so fast, and the firm's credit was so high, that it became necessary now to keep up appearances. Smirnoi had shown himself no spendthrift, but he, too, had pointed out more than once that the move couldn't be much longer delayed. What sort of business would the contractors think it was if the proprietor couldn't afford to move out of Oleander Street ?

Only May perceived the real wretchedness with which Silver agreed to move. However many of his friends followed him to his rich house, the old grand nights of talk and smoke and anarchy and cards and tea-with-lemon, would be over for ever. And he knew that very few would follow him, and those few would feel themselves to be poor men sitting at the rich man's board.

As for Mrs. Silver, she was more than wretched—she was terrified. The house in Oleander Street had been beyond her power to manage, even when Esther was in charge, with one or two of the other girls ready to give a hand now and again. She was thankful no one ever suggested a servant. A servant in that house, in that street, would have been more than grotesque. The very thought frightened her. Yet, somehow, the house got its stairs and floors scrubbed, its meals prepared, if not by skill, then by love. She loved the small house with a dumb passion. It was her own, her own, she had papers to show it was hers, and no one else's at all. When she thought no one was looking, she would go up to the wall of any room she might be in, and place the palms of both hands on it, feeling the thrill of her ownership tingling upwards along her arms.

She had all she wanted, much more than she had ever dreamed of. She had grandchildren by Esther, she would soon be a grandmother by Sarah, too. She had money to give away to charity in ample measure. She had her mother's pearls, and her own house to wear them in. She turned in the direction where she conceived, beyond the lands and the seas, her step-mother, Shevka, and her step-sister, Gallia, might be going about their businesses at that moment. She had drawn even with them. She wished them no hurt at all, neither that they should have acid on the stomach nor twinges on the knee. Only that they should *admit* she had drawn even with them. She insisted on that.

She did not want a bigger house. But she knew she would have to have one. Her eyes slowly filled with tears.

The War had actually broken out and was nearly a year old by the time it was thrust upon her. Not merely was it far bigger than the house in Oleander Street ; it was far bigger than any house Esther had presented to her imagination, and her ambition had not been humble. It was, in fact, not quite suitable ; but Esther determined that if she wouldn't get on with it nobody would. Silver and Smirnof were night and day busy with their rainproofs and waterproofs. She was aware that, in the press of terrific events, undertakings even vaster than theirs were controlled from nuclei even meaner than Oleander Street. So she clinched the matter, for fear it might be postponed indefinitely if they waited till a more suitable house came into the market.

The house was a castellated fortress of the Ruskino-Gothic period in the Baxter's Moor neighbourhood, though its name, Ivanhoe Towers, referred it to an earlier period in the evolution of Gothic architecture. It looked down on a bend of the River Mitchen. A thin gauze perpetually obscured the view, for, though the house was only two or three miles away from Longton, there was much more rain about, and the river-mists never seemed to shift. Even in the rare lapses of sunshine there would be a sudden overflowing from the devious roof-gutters, where the rain had been disconsolately roaming for some time in the effort to find a decorous issue, and had, in a fit of temper, abandoned the search. There was an acre or two of flower-garden and kitchen-garden and lawn attached to the house, though it was difficult to decide where one ended and another began ; attached was the word, for windows, walls, borders, trees, were hooked on to each other by a tangle of creepers, burrs, brambles, tropical in their complexity.

The whole place was, in fact, in a ramshackle condition, having been untenanted for years. It is possible that Esther did not try too strenuously to find out why the house had had no tenant for so long. Or, if she did actually find out, the fact that the previous tenant had been a " Sir " may have made up for the fact that he had committed suicide. So, in point of fact, he had, some months after his wife had died of a long and somewhat mysterious illness—the sort of illness concerning which you will not prevent people from uttering unpleasant insinuations up hill and down dale. They said the husband had poisoned her ; so, whether he had or had not, it was not strange that the " Sir " did away with himself some time later.

Esther may have been aware of all this ; yet it would not be kind to condemn her out of hand for moving her parents into Ivanhoe Towers. For in a time when death was busy on a scale that the biggest big-scale industry had never approached, it would have been pedantic to let one suicide and one murder—nothing more was alleged—incommode you. Besides, there was clearly room enough in the garden of Ivanhoe Towers to set up that bungalow which was to

be the vis-à-vis, so to speak, of Uncle Alex's bungalow at
the bottom of the orchard in Terkass across the sea.

The house would have felt and looked empty even if all
the regular anarchists who used to visit Oleander Street
had come along with camp-beds and bivouacked in it.
The Silver parents and the five Silver daughters could have
had a suite apiece and never come up against each other
except by appointment. But of the daughters, only Susan
and May were available, and only one of these ever lived
in Ivanhoe Towers. For Susan was in Paris the week the
War broke out. And, instead of returning to Doomington
to resume her post in the office of the foundry, a call was
issued to her to attach herself to a group of workers, it would
be more accurate to call them conspirators, in Geneva.

Polednik was in Cracow at the same time, where, like the
leader of his party, Lenin, he was arrested. He, too, like
Lenin, was released, on the assurance to the Austrian
authorities that he was at least as implacable an enemy of
the Tsar Nicholas as was the Emperor Franz-Josef. He was
requested to present himself at Geneva, where Susan Silver
had arrived some weeks earlier. There they got married,
partly because they were fond of each other. They had
intended to get married for some years now, but had
decided against getting married in Doomington. They knew
that that could not have failed to involve the sort of fuss
that was repugnant to them both. It had not occurred to
them, either, that they should get married in Paris when
they met there. The word Paris had not the sexual connota-
tions for them that it has for most young men and women.
It did not thrust nightgowns, pyjamas, bidets, into the
forefront of their minds. There was matter enough to occupy
them, very remote from such triviality. As for instance :
when the test came, could it be conceived that the Bolsheviks and the Mensheviks might actually work together ?
The infinitesimal whisper that had gone abroad that

this-and-this comrade was an *agent provocateur*, what substance was there to it ?

Polednik and Susan got married, partly because they were fond of each other ; also, because it made for greater clerical efficiency. So Susan did not return to Doomington to occupy that large room—that whole floor of large rooms, if she had wanted them—in which she had sometimes looked forward to getting all her data scientifically assembled. So, of all the five daughters, it was May alone who accompanied the Silver parents into their tatterdemalion wilderness. And, though the old folk did not know it, it was with a heavy heart that May went with them.

II

May and Harry Stonier were walking through a tousled meadow by Merseyside one Sunday evening in June. Esther had announced triumphantly, a night or two earlier, the acquisition of the deceased Sir's house. It was going to take some months before the whole house was really shipshape, for, of course, it wasn't so easy to get builders and decorators nowadays as it had been. But there was a nucleus of habitability, where an old man and his wife, Hargreaves by name, two retainers of the deceased Sir, had kept the flag flying, not very heartily, since the tragic events at Ivanhoe Towers.

The young people had been discussing the War again, though they had vowed, the last time they had gone out into the country, the matter should not again arise between them, to dim the sun and besmoke the air. To May, as to most young men and women of her age, of all ages in fact, the War was dreadful, but it had necessity, and it had glory. But, unlike most women, she remembered, without a moment's remission, that, being a woman, the ultimate pains would never be demanded from her. So that, even in those moments when she was caught up in a blaze of pride for England, or made white-hot with anger because of the enemy's reported wickedness, a certain fundamental delicacy prevented her from so speaking or so acting that a word or a deed for which she was responsible might influence another human creature to a loss of which she herself stood in no danger—a loss of limb or eyes or life, it might be.

Harry Stonier had been crystal-clear in his mind in his attitude to War long before this Great War started. To him the human body was the temple of God. There was no other sacrilege than to defile it or lay hands upon it in any sort of violence. It was not that he shrank from pain as such, as some shrink, with an almost pathological terror. He was himself capable of bearing intense pain without permitting his own awareness of it to be apparent to an onlooker, outside the purely reflex reactions of the brow that grows damp or the eye misted over, when pain is intense enough. He believed in the discipline of the body, as one who would have God's temple speckless and scoured clean as rocks are by storms. The sacrilege to him was the searing of that holy silk which is the skin, the pulping of that holy bread which is the flesh, the smashing of those holy rods which are the bones, the outraging of those mysteries, so precise, so unfathomable, for which skin and flesh are the casing and bones the support.

It seemed to him a far smaller thing that all Russia should pass to the Kaiser or all Germany to the Tsar than that the ribs and lungs of one lad be confounded, the holiness of his body be violated, in the mingled ooze of damp clay and his own blood.

It had not been possible for them to keep their hearts and their tongues away from this matter of War. Again the shadow came between them. They walked along in silence for some time. The shadow came not because either mistrusted or misvalued the other, but because each was in sore doubt. He asked himself in anguish whether it was seemly to allow his piety to stand in the way of lightening the woes of the million others, if only to the microscopic degree that the participation of one infinitesimal unit would lighten them. She asked herself whether his was not a truer heroism than the heroism of all those marchers who went with the blowing bugles and the flying banners ? And if Harry's heroism was in very truth the *truer*, was there not something vicious in the marrow of the heroism of the patriot, despite all its magnificences ?

And then each answered as, according to the laws of his being, each was forced to. " This," she said, " is the War to end all Wars. After this there will be no more tearing up of solemn covenants as if they were scraps of paper. And are there not times in human history when the individual must suspend his rights in both body and brain, and hand them into the keeping of the time's great necessity ? " So she argued, as most people argued then, and many still do to-day.

And he said to himself for his part : " For the sake of the countless generations still to be, there can be no compromise with Error. If no more than one or two or three have Truth at the heart of them, they are still its guardians ; they must guard it though they die in loneliness and obloquy. In their corruption the spark will not be wholly extinguished. A wind will breathe upon the spark ; a great fire will be lit ; the blaze will go up to the middle parts of the sky and all men be dazzled by it."

The young people walked heavily for some time. But, as they moved, the quiet of the June sunlight came down upon their brows, resting there and fluttering, like the white butterflies that declined in and out of the wood's edge, as if they were that quiet rendered into shape.

They came to a bank which sloped upward into an overhanging of hazel branches. The small woodland flowers, speedwell and dogwood, wood sorrel, campion, star of Bethlehem, spilled down like water. They sat down. He looked down upon the flowers by his right hand, straightened their stalks, and with the tip of a finger delicately stroked their petals. He abandoned these, and with the fingers of his left hand sought for hers where they lay pale in the grass. He found them, and imprisoned them for a time, as if he had feared they might not be there by now, might not be anywhere at all for him to find them. Then his mind, it seemed, became easy again. It was as if he were aware now they were not butterflies and would not take wing. They were flowers. They had roots. He straightened them. With the tip of a finger he delicately stroked their petals.

Then he turned round towards her. Her eyes were shut. He moved his mouth towards the centre of her brow and touched it, no more roughly than a swallow slides against the water. " I love you," he said. Her eyes opened. They smiled back into his. Her lips moved, but uttered no audible sound. " I love you, too," they said.

They rose and walked on again. Then she turned to him. " Harry," she said, " it's going to be so much easier and quicker now."

" *What* is, darling ? *What* can be easier now ? "

" When we move into—into——Oh, it's too ridiculous ! I can't talk of it as Ivanhoe Towers. It makes me *blush* ! " Duly, she blushed. Her eyes twinkled. " But you should hear Esther talk of it—with a frightful attempt at being casual. Can you imagine Esther being casual ? It's like a regiment of artillery going down a cobbled street ! "

" What's going to be easier, darling ? "

" To get out. Those coppices and dingles on the Mitchen where you feel you're five hundred miles from Doomington. Do you remember our bluebell place ? And all those lambs with black faces ? Just like the children at playtime in Aubrey Street School—excepting that the lambs weren't behind railings. Do you remember ? "

" Yes."

" It'll be so much easier, your calling for me at—at— I—van—hoe Tow—ers. . . ." She swelled herself out, took a large stride to each syllable, boomed each syllable like a seneschal summoning his lord to banquet in his raftered hall. She was, in fact, being Esther.

" No, May ! "

His voice was very quiet. So quiet that her heart took fright at once. She shrank down into herself.

" What do you mean, Harry ? "

" I won't call for you at Ivanhoe Towers."

" But, why not ? Harry, I don't understand. Have you heard that story of the old man who—who committed suicide there, and they say that his wife—oh, Harry, it can't be that ? "

" No, it's not that."

" Well, then ? "

" You get hardened to the tragedies of old folks these days. It's not that."

She shook her head, her eyes full of trouble. But he did not perceive it, for on his eyes there was a sort of grey sheen, such as you find on stretches of water before they freeze.

" I can't go to Ivanhoe Towers ! " he said. She saw a muscle harden on the left side of his jaw, which she knew, and loved, and feared. " There are two reasons why I can't go. Your father's becoming a rich man. He's becoming a rich man out of a War which is dreadful to me. You know how dreadful." He closed his eyes, and, in the instantaneous horror of the vision which he evoked, all the colour seemed to go out of the skin of his face, and the flesh to go saggy under the cheek-bones.

" But, Harry," she implored him. " It had already begun, his getting rich. It began last year, the year before that. The time when Smirnof——"

" It's out of the War the big money, the hideous money, is coming."

" What can I *do*, what can I *do* ? " she begged. He ignored her still.

" He's going to be a rich man. It's going to be hard not to

become a rich man out of this War. I'm not going to go hanging round a rich man's door, snuffling after his daughter."

" Harry ! " she cried out. " How dare you talk like that ? Oh, how dare you ? "

The pain in her voice bit deep into his heart. He halted there, in the grassy path by the river. " *You*," he said. " *You !* I wasn't talking about *you* at all ! " Her head drooped. She looked down upon the ground, utterly woebegone.

" I love you very much ! " he said.

" You don't ! " Her voice choked with tears, like a child's. He put one arm around her shoulder, and with one hand forced her forehead back until he made her eyes look up into his own.

" Do I love you very much ? " he asked.

" Ye—e—yes ! " she brought out through the catches of her breath.

" It's going to rain," he said. " We'd best be getting back."

III

The enjoying of money—that is to say, money in a really formidable quantity—is an art like any other ; the practitioner of the art must be born with an instinctive *flair* for it, like the man who some day is to paint pictures or compose music. He must, in addition, assiduously practise the technique of the art.

For some years, at least, Sam Silver never had a moment to acquire the art of enjoying money ; or, if he had, he was far too fatigued to apply himself to it. It would be safe to say that, during the four or five years of his residence in Ivanhoe Towers, he got no more than a very incidental pleasure out of the vast sums his firm was earning. In the year 1916, a good deal of the profits went into the building of new plant, and the acquiring of new machinery. The year

after, the profits were at least thirty-five thousand pounds ;
the year after that, sixty thousand ; the year after, not less
than one quarter of a million.

But, at least, until the time when he moved over to a
smaller but much more comfortable house near Altrincham,
the increment in his private fortune impinged upon his
direct awareness far less than the sudden uprush of his wages
from a slack week of twenty shillings to a " rush " week of
four pounds ten. There, in Altrincham, he began to feel his
way towards a state of things in which money began to be
expressible in terms of diverse pleasurable experiences.
There had been one or two people from the beginning
anxious to help him to such realisations. There were more
by then.

To put it bluntly, he had very little fun in Ivanhoe
Towers, and Hannah Silver had even less. He spent much
less time at home, of course, than she did. He worked far
harder nowadays than he used to, when he had been one of
Mr. Winberg's or Mr. Horowitz's hands. He went to the
factory earlier in the morning, and came back later at night.
He came more and more to leave matters of mere organisation to his assistant, Smirnof, though he kept tight hold of
the ultimate threads of policy. So, at least, he was convinced.
But when it came to the actual manufacture of the garments,
there he could depute the matter to nobody. It did not occur
to him to reproach himself for making a fortune out of the
War, despite one or two incoherent harangues that that
strange young man, Harry Stonier, addressed to him. Indeed, he seemed to be making a fortune entirely independ-
ently of whether he wanted to or not. Money was rolling
down on him like snow tumbling down a gully.

He was, however, extremely conscientious about the
quality of the rainproofs, waterproofs, tunics, ground-sheets,
gum-boots—all the various articles of military use the War
Office commissioned from him from stage to stage. He was
well aware of the manifold chicaneries which some of his
brother manufacturers indulged in. But that seemed to him

not merely disagreeable; it was manifestly, as his own account books showed, bad business.

So he ran about the works all day long, pretending he knew all about the big machinery he had installed, and pouncing with real authority on an untidy end of cotton that some girl had not snipped away. At the works he was busy, and, in a way, happy. He was not happy in Ivanhoe Towers. He might have been a little happier if his wife had not looked so haggard and so woebegone. He crept out in the morning before she was awake ; but when he returned at night, she was sitting up against the curtains of the drawing-room— her nose poked through them mournfully—where she kept her watch. A dismal ray of light fell on the moss-muted gravel and the weed-choked lawn. Every night it felt like the once-a-month visit that a man is allowed to make to a relation who has been so unlucky as to get himself shut up in prison.

There was a nucleus of habitability, it was said earlier, in Ivanhoe Towers. This was a huge basement kitchen, and one or two adjoining rooms, which Mr. and Mrs. Hargreaves, one-time retainers of the deceased Sir, occupied. It might all have been a little less unpleasant if not for Mr. and Mrs. Hargreaves. For, apparently, they went with Ivanhoe Towers, and there was about as much hope of uprooting them as of uprooting the colossal boiler in their basement kitchen. It was the sort of boiler you would have associated with a dye-works rather than with a private house. Not that it occurred to Sam and Hannah Silver, not for a long time at least, to uproot the old couple. The Silvers were not the sort of people to turn a pair of ancients out into the cold world from the home they had occupied for so many decades. But when, later, the idea was forced home upon them that it would make things easier with a younger generation of retainers at Ivanhoe Towers if the Hargreaveses were retired somewhere, it was discovered that they were tied up with the lease in the same serpentine fashion as the hot-water-pipes were tied up with the fabric of the house.

The Hargreaveses were old, but they were formidable. Whether or not they had preceded the tenure of the deceased Sir and his lady, it became increasingly evident they intended to outlive the tenure of Sam and Hannah Silver. Esther was deputed to deal with them, for it was felt, almost with heat, that Esther should have covered the Hargreaves situation when the papers were drawn up and signed. What happened when she went down into their basement-kitchen was not reported ; but she did not venture there again. The Hargreaveses, as a rule, did not issue far from their basement-kitchen, but, during the few days that followed the Esther interview, they were up and about the house with a surprising agility, now shuffling along distant passages, now appearing at unexpected windows, all the time shaking their heads, their fists, tittering, he showing his brown teeth, she showing her shrivelled gums. The purport of all that was to show clearly who was to be considered lord of Ivanhoe Towers, this little upstart Jew tailor and his wife, or the late Master and Mistress, for whom, it was to be concluded, they felt they held the house on trust.

Their duties, according to the documents, were to keep clean their own steps and passages, and to look after the boiler-fire. They looked after the boiler-fire energetically but spasmodically. Sometimes they so banked up the boiler-fire that the basement-kitchen was as hot as a stoker's hold ; and they kept on banking it up till you would have thought no mortal creatures short of a pair of salamanders could have endured such an atmosphere. The poor old people looked more like salamanders, it might be said, than humans, their skin was so shrivelled and reticulated, and their eyes so beady. They used fuel in such quantities that often they found of a sudden it was all gone. It was not easy in those days, even for a Sam Silver, to restock his coal-cellars. But old Hargreaves took no notice of that. He would lie in wait for Silver before he set out for the factory, or after he

returned, and abuse him violently. Then he and his wife would
retire to their bed, and stay there for several days, thus
establishing a further similarity between themselves and the
reptilian species, which is capable of retiring into its hole,
and into complete immobility, for long periods at a stretch,
without being incommoded by any thought of nourishment.
The house would then be plunged into arctic frost ; but
there was nothing to be done about it till Mr. and Mrs.
Hargreaves got out of bed and attended to the boiler-fire
again. It should be added that the house was never warm,
even with the boiler going full blast down in the kitchen-
basement. It was not warmth that the boiler distributed
through the house along its network of pipes, so much as
noises. The pipes in the Silvers' bedroom ticked like an
infernal machine ; even, mysteriously enough, when the
fire was out downstairs. Sam Silver had talked of infernal
machines often enough in the old Oleander Street days, but
that did not prevent him from getting up, cold with fright,
time after time, to hear those ticking shifting noises a few
feet behind the back of his skull. He knew that Hannah,
lying beside him, was awake, too, but he was not sure ;
nor was she sure about him. So, side by side, hour after hour,
they lay looking up into the pallid ceiling, listening to that
clicking and ticking, remembering Oleander Street and their
cosy bedroom there, and their cosy kitchen there, which was
their own, their very own, and none to keep them away
from it with warning finger and beady eye, from the fire,
the kettle, the teapot, the tumblers, the sugar, the lemon, the
warm sweet ritual of their Golden Age.

This would be a mournful document if an attempt were
to be made to tell the tale of the housekeepers, maids,
chauffeurs, and the rest that came and went at Ivanhoe
Towers during the Silver phase of its history. It is doubtless
clear by now that Hannah Silver would not have made a
success of running a big house even under much happier

auspices ; for she had never made a success of running a
very small house, at least in the purely domestic sense of
the word. She would have been grateful for a lot more help
from Esther, and that was a significant development, for
the time had been when there was nothing in the world that
terrified her so much as help from Esther. But after the first
few months, Esther had less and less time to devote to
Ivanhoe Towers. It was clear to her she would have to
postpone till after the War the idea of the Tishler bungalow
to be built at the bottom of her parents' garden. Any
building she could negotiate was in connection with the
Pliskin cabinet-making works, which her husband, Joe,
acquired about this time, by arrangement with Alexander
Smirnof ; which she herself acquired, to be accurate. For
Joe, revealing depths of patriotic sentiment astonishing in
one so lately an anarchist, went to be a soldier, leaving
Esther, who had been a dutiful wife and prodigal mother for
several years, to become a business-woman—a rôle in which
she bore herself with great distinction.

May was not much use, either, at Ivanhoe Towers. The
child had never seemed happy since they came to live in this
Bridgeways Gaol of a house. The young man, Harry Stonier,
never came to see her, although apparently there had been
no quarrel. They still saw each other now and again—
outside somewhere. The child never made any secret of it.
Then he went off to Norwich to serve in the Quakers'
Ambulance Corps. It was one of his funny crotchets, without a doubt, this idea of never coming to the house. He was,
after all, just a working-man, like they themselves had all
been ; or he was a clerk, anyhow, and his father was a
working-man. What for did he have all these funny ideas ?
Mrs. Silver hoped that May would now meet some nice young
Jewish gentleman—he might even be a high-up officer—and
that would be nicer for everyone all round.

Then May, too, went off. She went off to serve in a
canteen in Boulogne, France. The house felt quite appal-
lingly empty without her. Mrs. Silver swallowed a lump in

her throat. At all events, it would be easier for May to meet that nice young Jewish gentleman over in France, who might also be a high-up officer.

She turned again to this desolate business of housekeepers, maids, housekeepers, maids. She wondered what she had done to deserve it all. She snivelled secretly into her handkerchief. It was not really strange that there was all this trouble with staff. If the kitchen wasn't as hot as a furnace, it was as cold as a tomb. The situation was further complicated by the clause in the contract about Mrs. Hargreaves keeping the steps and passages clean. The Hargreaveses were nothing if not literal-minded. He did, indeed, look after his boiler-fire, and she did, indeed, look after her steps and passages. She surrounded the kitchen with a *noli me tangere* of soap and water, and sometimes, for hours at a stretch, connection between the kitchen and the upper house was completely cut off. It did not make for permanence on the part of the new-comers. Now and again a stern lady, old or young, showed fight ; but sooner or later, she was ignominiously worsted. Another maid to find, another housekeeper.

Silver acquired a car. It was impossible to acquire a house like Ivanhoe Towers without acquiring a car, too. It was a car of great magnificence, and a chauffeur of great magnificence went with it. Pulliton seemed to be tied up with the car pretty much in the same way as the Hargreaveses were tied up with the house. Silver wasn't quite clear about it, but the manufacturers seemed to be rather diffident of letting anybody have so grand a car without taking on a Pulliton to maintain it in the state which it was born into.

Pulliton was so magnificent that he had to have an underling to keep the polish on the woodwork and the glass and the metal and the coachwork. Some might have thought that Pulliton was magnificent enough to be in the Army. But that was all right. Either he had been, or he was too superb to be. Nobody could have begun to frame the inquiry, even in the secrecy of his own mind, without being overborne at once the moment the majesty of Pulliton's presence rendered itself.

Pulliton was not merely a noble animal ; he was a distinguished mechanic. But not even Pulliton, sitting at the wheel of even that car, was proof against the hoodoo that Sam Silver established as soon as he seated himself in a car. He belonged to a clearly defined species who live in a state of mystical discordance with petrol-driven machinery. The most shameful things go wrong with the most impeccable engines when they seek to establish relations with them. The radiator starts boiling or the brakes seize or the big-end goes. It takes not many minutes for a puncture to happen. And at night the lights fuse.

Things went wrong in Silver's car so frequently that Pulliton was forced, for the sake of his own credit and the credit of the manufacturers, to reduce Silver's use of the car to a minimum. These things did not, as a matter of fact, happen when Silver was not in the car. When some young female member of the staff was looking the worse for wear—and how was it possible not to look the worse for wear in a house built up on a foundation of Hargreaveses ?—Pulliton never spared the use of the car in the effort to restore the colour to the young lady's cheeks. On those occasions the car moved like a bird.

So, quite often, Silver went to his factory on the tramcar, as he used to in the days when he worked for old Mr. Horowitz in the little sweating-den by the river which had so grotesquely budded and blossomed these last few years. Sometimes he got a lift in a car belonging to some associate or other in the trade, who, like himself, had acquired a house and a garden in the Baxter's Moor neighbourhood, but a smaller house and a smaller garden. However, he was not popular in cars. He was not good for them.

There was not much in the way of a social life at Ivanhoe Towers. Silver and his peers were far too busy at their factories to find much time for that sort of thing, though now and again one or two manufacturers, almost as be-wildered by it all as Silver himself, dropped in and smoked an expensive cigar and drank a glass of expensive brandy, and played a hand at whist, or even bridge, if there were enough of them. They would have preferred to play " Pishy-pashy," it was much more a rest for the nerves, but doubtless it seemed too proletarian a game—the sort of game their workmen played in their houses in Longton and Bridgeways.

Gone for ever, it seemed, were those old days, the anarchist days, the tea-with-lemon days. The anarchists were dis-banded. Some turned out to be straightforward, even fervent, patriots when the test came. As Polednik had always pro-phesied, Dan Jamieson, the Socialist orator, and one or two of his Socialist colleagues, became as imperialist as any born lord when the imperialists summoned them to fight for them in their war. They were fighting, or doing some sort of direct military service somewhere, at a great remove from Ivanhoe Towers.

Some of the anarchists were conscientious objectors, as Harry Stonier was, for instance ; though it would never have been quite right to call Stonier an anarchist. Several of the Russians enlisted in the Army ; others, and amongst these were the poets, Ponski and Pontrevitch, violently objected to fighting in a war of which one of the main sponsors was the Tsar, Nicholas the Second. Their position became a little ambiguous when the February Revolution in Russia dislodged the Tsar. It became really difficult when an agree-ment was presented to both Houses of Parliament by com-mand of His Majesty, King George the Fifth, in July 1917. It was described as an " Agreement concluded between His Majesty's Government and the Provisional Government of Russia relative to the reciprocal liability to military service of British subjects resident in Russia and Russian subjects resident in Great Britain." The situation was more than difficult. It was menacing. For, in fact, Ponski and Pontre-vitch had not much more lust to fight for the Cadets, or the Bolsheviks, or whoever might ultimately gain the ascendancy in Russia, than they had had to fight for the Tsar. They had always pronounced themselves to be quite specifically anarchists, and they were very troubled by the reports that zealous efforts were being made to extirpate the anarchists in Petrograd and Moscow.

But there was the agreement in black and white, signed at Petrograd, in duplicate, by George W. Buchanan and Michel Terestchenko. So Ponski and Pontrevitch, and several other Silver anarchists, were deported to Russia, where, in point of fact, they found it convenient for the most part to forget their anarchist doctrines ; and one or two attained high position in the Bolshevik régime, which a few months later overthrew its rivals and assumed the leadership of affairs.

So Ponski and Pontrevitch, as well as the patriots, were prevented from visiting Ivanhoe Towers, if it had occurred to them to do so. Representations had been made to M. Chicherin, who was active in a committee formed to look after the interests of Russian political emigrants. But without avail. So Ponski and Pontrevitch, and the others, set forth for Russia, leaving their wives and children behind them. Most of these soon fell to the charge of Sam Silver. But, these, too, did not visit Ivanhoe Towers to lighten its gloom a little. They were themselves not very light-hearted.

Hannah Silver acquired a car as well as her husband. Pulliton's underling drove it for her when he was not too busy polishing Pulliton's car's woodwork and glass and metal and coachwork. But she did not like to disturb him at that occupation too often, partly because Pulliton didn't like it, partly because she hadn't anywhere much to go to in her car. The only place she much wanted to go to was Longton, the region of the streets of the flowering shrubs. For there, in the streets of the Oleander and the Magnolia and the Acacia, most of her friends lived. But it was out of the question to go visiting in a car in that region. She would have felt it the acme of bad taste. So she and her husband used the tramcar almost as much as common working-people, though, for one reason and another, as the war years went on, their visits became fewer and fewer.

She was acutely embarrassed the first time she returned to Longton after the removal to Ivanhoe Towers. She was so shy about it that she put off the visit for months. Finally, a fit of such acute depression seized her, that, putting on an old dress which Esther somehow had forgotten to get rid of, she crept forth. She got off the car in Blenheim Road opposite the corner of Oleander Street. It was dusk. It was not to one of her Oleander Street friends she went. She could not have borne that. She turned into Magnolia Street, and knocked timidly at Mrs. Emmanuel's door. It was easier to visit the Emmanuels than anybody else, for Mr. Emmanuel, who was in the habit of visiting rich houses to enlist them in support of his various philanthropic schemes, had more than once visited the Silvers at Ivanhoe Towers.

There was another reason. The Emmanuel back door faced the back door of her own house, number eleven Oleander Street. She knocked. The Emmanuels were unaffectedly delighted to see her. They had great tact, too. They made tea-with-lemon for her, as she so often had made for them. There was *lekkach*, cake sprinkled with poppy-seed. The kettle sang cheerfully on the hob. The reflections of the bright flames danced up and down upon Mrs. Emmanuel's brass trays and candlesticks and samovar. Mrs. Silver's heart uncurled like a bud trembling in response to a spring wind.

They made no song about it when she asked might she go upstairs to the back bedroom, and look down on the yard and the kitchen of her house in Oleander Street across the entry ; for she was still its landlord, and she did not know if the new tenants were treating her property with respect. It was night now, and quite clearly she would not be able to make out very much. But they took her upstairs, and left her there, and closed the door behind her. She came down a few minutes later, her eyes shining somewhat suspiciously. She had forgotten, moreover, to put her handkerchief away into her handbag, and her handkerchief seemed quite damp.

But the Emmanuels made no comment.

" You'll come again, soon ? " they both insisted, when Mrs. Silver left at last. " You promise you'll come again soon ? "

" I will," breathed Mrs. Silver.

" And perhaps you'll bring your husband, too ? It will be like old times."

She brought her husband, he was very happy to come, even though he was so busy in his factory. And, indeed, the Emmanuels were right. It was quite like old times. Except that the Silvers were rich now, and they had been poor once ; and that a Great War was in progress, so that most of the young men of Magnolia Street and Oleander Street were missing, and some were dead, like David, the youngest son of the Emmanuels. Otherwise, it was quite like old times.

CHAPTER VII

HARRY STONIER

I

MAY SILVER and Harry Stonier saw less and less of each other as the war months, like monstrous waves, advanced, roaring, and collapsed, advanced again and collapsed. He knew that she was, after all, a child, and that the first wave had swept her off her feet long ago, in those unspeakably mournful early days of August. There she was, with the countless others, weltering in the chaotic waters. Overhead the seagulls squawked and scuffled ; but their beaks were the beaks of vultures, and slow gouts of blood dripped on to the reddening spume below.

How easy it would be to relax the grip he held with bleeding feet upon the sharp shingle ! From time to time the temptation beset him sorely. How pleasant it would be to be swept where the currents of passion willed, to shriek with the others, to go down, perhaps, into cool oblivion, a sportsman, a hero !

Then he remembered again that, as it seemed to him, heroism lay not there. He thrust his feet deeper among the stones. His lips were thin and white like bleached wood.

He could not bring himself to see May in the house of a man whom the War was so grotesquely enriching. And though they met from time to time to walk in the riverbank meadows or to climb the bare slopes of Kinder Scout, it was impossible that things should be as they had been ; and the little aluminium water-cup they took with them, which collapsed when they filled it, and the twenty times underscored *Golden Treasury* he carried in his sagging pocket, only made it the more sorrowful.

May Silver tried to see it all from his point of view ; she tried hard, for they had agreed on most things till now. She sometimes succeeded for a short while. Then she went away from him, or from the thought of him, and the banners and the fifes made her their own again. The suspicion began to grow on him that she despised him. How could she not ? Did he not let anæmic lads go out and do in his stead far more hazardous things than sitting on an office-stool, reflecting upon St. Teresa and Boehme ?

But it was not true that for the shadow of a moment she despised him. As the War drew on, and she perceived that he suffered a misery so formidable that any physical pain would have been at least as easy to bear, she tried more than ever to reassure him. But he would not be reassured. They saw each other less and less, though each loved the other more than he could bear. She went to Boulogne in course of time, to serve in a canteen. He went to Norwich, to serve in the Quakers' Ambulance Corps, which had been set up in a big factory there.

He had misgivings. For a long time he could not convince himself there could be, in logic and in holiness, the signing of any pact with this Satan whose black wings occupied the whole sky. When he at last persuaded himself to enlist for membership, it filled him with dismay to see the simulacrum of military organisation which these objectors against war had set up. They wore the khaki of soldiers, too. It seemed to him vicious they should not wear garments as coarse and humble as they are made, coarser and humbler than tramps receive in workhouses ; some twentieth-century variant of the sackcloth and hair-shirts which would have been, in very truth, the rightful wear for these protestants, and even then far more gracious than the blood-stiffened, lice-crawling garments of soldiers in trenches.

The colonel, or the major, or whoever he might be, who interviewed him in the matter of his religious or philosophical qualifications for enlistment in the corps, was not very certain about him.

" Are you a Quaker, Mr. Stonier ? "

" No, I am not a Quaker. But I have been reading Fox lately and the early Quakers. They, too, would take life on no pretext. But it is along another road I arrive at their conclusions."

" You are not a Roman Catholic, Mr. Stonier ? "

" If to be specially grieved for soldiers, like Teresa of Lisieux——"

" Are you a Roman Catholic ? "

" No, I am not ! "

" Are you a Christian ? "

" There is no Church that would not call me a heretic. I read much of the writings of the quietists, like Bruno and John Tauler and Meister Eckhart."

The colonel passed his hand across his forehead a little wearily. Then he took to tugging his smart moustache.

" You've read Tolstoi, of course," he said firmly, re-membering that, after all, he was a more distinguished figure in the ranks of conscientious objectors than this tow-headed clerk.

" Yes," said Harry Stonier, perhaps a shade contemptu-ously. " And Madame Guyon."

" Oh ! " said the colonel.

" You remember Eckhart ? " the other asked forlornly. " ' If I love anyone even as much as myself, I would as soon that joy or sorrow, death oɪ life, were mine, as his.' "

" I don't see how that makes you a C.O."

" Because all men are Christ. ' Inasmuch as you did it to the least of these, you did it to Me.' I don't choose to pierce His side with a spear again or drive nails into His hands."

" Oh, I see," said the colonel doubtfully. " Very well, then. We'll take you on."

So they took him on, despite his avowal that he would not ape the khaki of poor doomed soldiers. He became an orderly of the Quakers' Ambulance Corps. He was not popular with his colleagues, for his misgivings haunted him during the whole period of his service, and they mistook this for surliness. For a time he was allowed to do no work more responsible than to scrub acres upon acres of red flooring. In this he managed to attain some degree of forgetfulness of the doubts that harried him. The regularity of the movements, the vast area they must cover, numbed him. But in the huge dormitory at night, with the young men around him chuckling over the latest intrigue with the latest nurse, his doubts came back again.

After a month or two he was promoted to the wards. He was deft with the cleaning and bandaging of wounds. The work he was doing was in itself so palpably humane that for a time he managed to absorb himself in the practice of it by day and the study of the technique of it by night. The colonel smiled upon him, realising that, after all, he had done wisely in not hearkening to the scruples which oddly troubled him when the young man came to demand admission to the corps. Harry Stonier might have served devotedly, if not happily, as a hospital orderly in Norwich till the War ended if it had not been for a young soldier from the depôt in Grantham.

The boy was brought into the hospital on the day when he should have left for France if an accident had not occurred to him. A weight fell on his naked foot, and crushed it savagely. Blood-poisoning set in, but Harry nursed the boy so ably that it was necessary to do no more than remove one of the toe-nails. He looked, and perhaps was, a boy of extraordinary innocence ; but under chloroform he directed against the sisters and nurses the most revolting obscenities. When he came round, the soldiers in the rest of the ward did not hesitate to let him know in the fullest detail exactly what he had said. Some laughed good-humouredly ; others leered. The boy was almost frantic with shame. He would not allow any of the women to touch him ; he threatened so dangerous a hysteria if they should that Harry was permitted to tend him exclusively till he was discharged. So he went back to his base camp again, a fit soldier, after a little time to go forth to the French trenches, Harry Stonier's oblation on the altar of War.

The episode jolted Harry uglily. The doubts that had been torpid in him awoke to throbbing life again, like the nerve in a tooth.

Some months later, a certain great attack having been launched, an unusually large train-load of wounded was sent to the Quaker Hospital. Harry Stonier had been moody, even a little unreliable, of late ; it was not improbable that his nerves were giving way. He had been granted a few days' leave, and was about to go north to Derbyshire, to go roaming the bare slopes of Kinder Scout, where he had been so serene once, with May Silver, the girl he loved. On the arrival of the large train-load of wounded his leave was cancelled. He got himself ready for ward-work again. A soldier in a bed near the window was uttering obscenities in his delirium. He was requested to quieten the boy with an injection of morphia. He hastened to the boy's bed, a hideous premonition already tearing at his heartstrings. He bared his face, he looked down upon his body— the body that he had himself made fit for the impious and appalling sacrifice that had been demanded from it. For one moment he stood swaying by the bedside, his eyes staring wildly. The syringe slipped from his hands. He uttered two or three cries, short and sharp, like an animal's. A moment later he lay crumpled beside the bed, like a heap of clothes.

When he recovered from his nervous breakdown, as it was called, there was no question, on the colonel's part or on his own, that he should resume his service in the Ambulance Corps. Some two or three months later he was sentenced to imprisonment in Dartmoor as a conscientious objector, and there he remained till the War ended

II

Elsie Silver had no conscientious objections against the War, and she was ready to go to a lot of trouble to alleviate the lot of the soldiers. She no longer lived in Doomington, having found it convenient to transfer her headquarters to London a year or so after the War started. She was almost a top-liner in the music-hall profession these days, though there was still a certain insolence in her bearing which prevented her from getting quite to the top of the posters. It may have been a lack of that particular sort of ambition. She was not extravagant. She did not need more money than she made without exerting herself excessively ; though, once or twice, when she had found it difficult to get on without it, she had suggested to her father that he might come forward and oblige her. He obliged her without a murmur. He even suggested he would like to oblige her more frequently, if she would permit him.

This period was the heyday of intimate revue at such small West End theatres as the Ambassadors and the Vaudeville. It happened that one of its promoters spent an evening in Chiswick or Cricklewood or one of the more forlorn suburbs, and there, on the stage of the local Empire, he saw Elsie Silver go through her arrogant paces. He immediately recognised the girl's *gauche* talent, if it was not even a streak of genius, and before long she made her début in the world of smart theatres. Her appeal was quite definitely to sophisticated people ; she even took some real trouble to win their approval ; until she realised that these audiences, far more than her previous ones, were the more disposed to go into ecstasies about her the more she treated them like dirt.

She was amused by her success, and even a little flattered by it. She might have established for herself a position comparable with Beatrice Lillie's, whose art in some sort hers resembled. But during the rehearsals for a revue in which she was going to have a quite leading part, she informed herself, not for the first time, she was in love. This time it was a young captain in the Coldstream Guards. She spent a week of his leave with him in a Dorset village—time long enough to realise the guardsman was a bore. When she returned to London, there was serious difficulty at the theatre, for her absence had dislocated the rehearsals violently ; indeed, another young lady had been chosen in her place. The manager believed in her, however. He was ready to reinstate her, if she promised to resist all further temptations to give lonely officers her company in Dorset, or elsewhere. It was not an unreasonable request, but she found it distasteful to have theatre managers dictating to her in so private a matter.

She was not included in the cast, therefore, and for the time being, at least, she gave up her promising career as a revue artiste. At about this time one or two of her music-hall friends were requested to organise a concert-party by one of those associations which endeavoured to lighten the leisure hours of soldiers at base camps. She accepted their invitation to join them, partly because it seemed a creditable thing to do, partly because, if she became interested in some young man out there, he might turn out to be less of a bore than her recent Coldstream captain. She had more than once been kind to one man or another since the War started. She had been at some pains to show the young men they were not kind to her. One had had the impercipience to offer her a cheque. It was a calamitous day for him, which covered him with more horror, when he remembered it, than any day in his life excepting the day when, in the hall of a college not his own—being in fact a guest there—he was suddenly and violently sick.

She had a third reason for accepting the invitation of her friends, namely her sister, May, whom she had not seen for a long time. She thought it possible that May had been requested by their sister, Esther, to make no effort to see her when she passed through London. On the other hand, it was also possible that she had herself been out of town when May

went through *en route* from Doomington. May was working in
a canteen in Boulogne. It was extremely likely they would
meet out there, for her concert-party could hardly fail to
pay Boulogne a visit.

And so, in fact, they did. The sisters were enchanted to
meet again. Their reunion was a most pleasurable spectacle.

Elsie was a very intelligent girl, especially in what is
termed affairs of the heart. She perceived at once that May
was seriously unhappy. She had intended to go to bed early,
for the party had come a long way and the concert had been
strenuous. There would be time enough for sisterly dalliance to-morrow morning. She would pull May out into the
country by the scruff of her neck, however sticky the red-
headed lady in charge of the hut ladies might prove to be.
She wanted to go to bed early, even though the handsomest man in all the world had sat himself down next to the
red-haired lady in the very middle of the front row, and had
sat there, patently, shamelessly adoring her, like a chinless,
goggle-eyed errand-boy in a threepenny gallery in Runcorn.
She had a feeling that perhaps this might be the young man
she had had in mind when she accepted the invitation to
join the concert-party. He looked quite engagingly not
a bore.

The handsomest man in all the world sat and goggled at
her, yet he was far from being goggle-eyed, excepting in
a metaphorical sense. He had the loveliest brown gazelle's
eyes, big as a schoolgirl's, eyes that at once challenged and
appealed. They sent flutters all down her spine, till it was
all she could do to keep on doing her act without wriggling
a bit, as if an insect had wandered down into the small of
her back. He had the loveliest eyebrows. He had a nose
straight and fine and sensitive. He had the loveliest brown
silky hair. She wondered how he managed to keep it so
brown and silky under the exigencies of wartime. She was
accustomed to appraise such matters. She could do it quite

adeptly, even if she was engaged in a cartwheel, as she sometimes was. Moreover, he was not chinless. He had a good
chin, good enough to have fastened a neat little D.S.O.
ribbon on his chest.

But she determined to do nothing about the handsomest
man that night. Perhaps he only looked so handsome, she
thought, because she was so tired. And he would certainly
be hanging about to-morrow, even if the Great War had
ended before then. To-night must be May's night. There
was something in May's face that made her miserable and
apprehensive. She would take May down into the town, and
get to the bottom of it. They went to a café and sat down
at a table against the harbour's edge.

" A cognac ! " ordered Elsie. " And you ? "

" A bock ! " said May.

" I think not ! " said Elsie. " Two cognacs ! "

" I don't like it ! "

" Take it as medicine ! Just sip it ! You need some ! " She
thought a moment. She wasn't going to charge straight at it
like a mad bull. There was a fairly interesting matter to start
the proceedings with.

" May darling ! "

" Yes ? "

" There was a man in the very middle of the front row ! "

" Of course there was ! "

" Who was he ? "

" How on earth should I know ? "

" He was sitting next to the red-haired lady in charge of
your crowd."

" Miss Rogerson."

" She can't possibly not be Miss Rogerson."

" Tell me more."

" He's the handsomest man in all the world. He's got the
D.S.O. He looked as if he hadn't had a meal for a month
and I was a steak-and-kidney pudding."

" Well, my dear, you *did* look very fetching."

" Well, who was he ? "

" There's only one person he could be. I suppose he *is* good-looking. Bobby something, they call him. Oh, yes, Bobby Malswetting. He's going to be a baronet or something."

" Do you know him ? "

" I don't *know* him. These people come and go. But he's been a bit of a nuisance the week or two he's been here. All the women in our hut and the Church Army hut are silly about him. He comes behind the counter and pretends to help them."

" Yes, that's exactly what he looks like."

" They forget the tap's running in the tea-urn."

" He's good in the eye ! "

" Yes, I suppose so."

" If he's about to-morrow, will you let me meet him ? I mean, unostentatiously. He *will* be, you know."

" I'm sure he will. Miss Rogerson will fix it up. I've hardly spoken to him. He's not my sort."

" Who is ? " She jumped at her opportunity like a trout at a fly.

" Oh, I don't know. I haven't any sort."

" Listen ! " Elsie's voice was quite sharp. " What's it all about ? What are you so miserable about ? "

" Honestly, Elsie, nothing at all ! It's quite hard work, you know, in a way ! "

" Oh, I know, I know ! Hard work doesn't make your mouth drop like a horse's ! You're a strong little devil, May, even though you look such a poor thing ! Oh, it's not hard work ! It's a man ! Tell me all about him, my pet ! "

" Please ! "

" Do you know you're not leaving this café till you've got it off your chest ? Do you know that, darling ? Don't be cross ! It's really because I . . . You know it's not because I like to poke my nose into other people's business ! You know that, don't you ? "

" Yes, I suppose so. Do you know, Elsie, you're oddly like father in one or two ways. His sense of a person belonging all to himself, to do exactly what he likes with himself, and no one else to interfere. Have you ever thought of that ? "

" I don't know that I have, darling, and I don't know that I'm going to now. I'm not going to be side-tracked, my pet. You look down-and-out, so I'm going to get to the bottom of it, see ? "

" Yes, Elsie ! "

" Please, darling ! Out with it ! "

" It's—it's Harry Stonier ! You remember ? "

" What ! " Elsie cried. " *Still ?* I thought that was over long ago ! "

" No ! "

" I got the idea you never saw each other ! "

" He never called at home for me. We met outside."

Elsie sneered. Her mood had changed completely. Her eyes did not seem the same eyes. " What was the idea ? "

" All that money that father's making out of the War——"

" He makes me sick ! What's he doing now ? "

" He's in prison, I think ! As a conscientious objector ! "

" The best place for him ! "

" I think we'd best go now, Elsie ! "

" I'm sorry, May, I'm sorry ! I always hated him ! "

" We can't do any good by talking about him ! "

" You love him, do you ? "

" Terribly ! "

" Listen, May ! " She thrust her arms across the table and seized May's elbows. She seemed to be not at all the same girl as had sat down, so sympathetic, so genial, not more than a few minutes ago. Her eyes were hard. A spot of colour burned in her cheeks. Her mouth looked very ugly. " I tell you he's not worth the dirt on your shoe ! He's a nobody, snivelling about with his poems and his high ideas. I hate him ! "

" Elsie ! I never knew—— "

" I hate him ! I want to see you married to somebody worthy of you, May ! Father's getting so rich there's nobody in the country you won't be able to marry."

" You're mad ! Elsie, how can you talk so hatefully ! "

" I'm sorry ! A touch of the old Esther, my pet ! "

" There's nobody I want to marry ! He wouldn't see me any more. It got worse and worse. Then he wouldn't even write to me ! "

" If he comes smarming around again, May, he'll have me to reckon with ! "

" Let me go, Elsie ; let me go ! "

" May, you're crying ! What a swine I've been ! "

" Yes ! "

" Hell ! I wish I'd never come to this damned camp ! "

" So do I ! "

" Please, please, May, don't say that ! I'm so sorry ! I'm frightfully sorry ! What the hell came over me ? Please don't say you'd rather I'd never come ! "

" It's not been much fun, has it ? "

" Oh, my dear, my dear ! What had we best do ? "

" I don't know ! "

" Shall we get two of the men from the party and go and dance ? Oh, to hell with it ! May, will you forgive me ? "

" Elsie, dear ! "

" You're a pal ! "

" Shall we go for a walk ? "

" Yes, May, a grand idea ! Out there, to the rocks ! See, the moon's coming up ! "

" It'll be lovely, Elsie ! "

" Come now, kiss me ! Will you ? "

" There ! "

" Sport ! *Garçon, alors ! L'addition !* "

CHAPTER VIII

RED BANNERS AT NIGHT

I

THE FIVE Silver daughters were the children of the same father and mother ; three of them had been born, and all brought up, in the same small house, yet it would be just to say they were more distinguished from each other than many women separated by all the gulfs of race and country. In physical appearance the oldest and the youngest were most unlike each other. It would have been impossible not to pronounce Esther Jewish, with her hair, her nose, her lips, her bosom. It would not have occurred to you, seeing May away from her family, that she was not English, or, to be more accurate, Anglo-Saxon.

Unlike the majority of the Jewish families out of the *milieu* of the streets of the flowering shrubs, there was little religious consciousness on the part of the Silvers. Mr. and Mrs. Silver, and all the girls in their younger days, attended the synagogue on the New Year Festival and the Day of Atonement. Out of a sort of inertia, because they were surrounded by people who did such things, and because their parents, perhaps just as inertly, had done them too, the Silvers kept up a show of respect for the Sabbath and the Passover. Of Susan and Elsie, however, it must be said that they suspended even that at a shockingly early age. Susan was early an atheist, Elsie was early a pagan.

But this inertness could not be charged against Esther. She had always been the most race-conscious of the daughters ; after she married, she became an increasingly zealous Jewish matron—in the ritual meaning of the word, too. The same must be said regarding Mrs. Silver, after she moved to Ivanhoe Towers. But it is to be suspected she became more zealous in ritual out of sheer *ennui* ; the house and the housekeeping were so colossal that she early realised how completely outside her scope they were. Quite literally she had less to do at Ivanhoe Towers than in Oleander Street. No wonder the poor lady betook herself to salting her chickens and segregating her milk and meat cutlery and blessing her Sabbath candles with a fervour which would have enchanted most of her late neighbours.

May was as completely English as Esther was Jewish. Judaism did not embarrass her. She merely relegated it in time and place to the synagogue, exactly in the way that many Gentile English folk of the Anglican denomination relegate Christianity in time and place to the church. It is a part of being English, like buying a poppy in its season in these post-war days, or leaving your card on the consul if you happen to be abroad. May had no nostalgia after the oaks of Mamre at Hebron, where Abraham, her initial ancestor, took his rest under the shade. She was far more anxious to meditate among the gravestones of Stoke Poges, murmuring the lines of the *Elegy* to herself—a thing she did, in fact, as soon as she first went down into the south country. She was consciously, happily English. English landscape, English poetry, the English character, were the world of her well-being. It is no wonder she so loved Harry Stonier, who so firmly bore the stamp of all three.

There were times when it might be said there was something of the fervour of the convert about May. This could never be said about Elsie. She took her place and did her job among publicans, mill-hands, country yokels, without a tendency to clap her hands delightedly and cry out : " Oh, how English, how *too* English ! "—a tendency which is to be observed just as frequently among Gentile young ladies from artistic suburbs as among Jewish young ladies whose residence in England is but a generation or two old. Elsie had no traffic with Jewish affairs and people as such. But, like many Jews, she became briefly but very violently Jewish the very moment the word "Jew" was used offensively. She would slap a face, or tear up a contract, in an immediate fury. The fury subsided ten seconds later. She became once more a male impersonator on the English music-hall stage.

She was anti-Jewish, however, in a way which one or two Jews ruefully regretted, more particularly during the War period. She would spend no week or two with any officer from any regiment in any village, if that gentleman happened to be a Jew. It might be said of her she was an instance of that centrifugal sexual force which from generation to generation exercises itself among Jews, as Esther so clearly was an instance of the centripetal force. She did, in fact, meet a Jewish D.S.O. in London, of the greatest charm and social rightness, who fell violently in love with her. He was more than ready to marry her, if she would on no other condition spend a week or two in Brighton with him. He was an urban Jew, and wanted it to be Brighton rather than a desolate village somewhere in the backlands. But she refused, on the ground that he was a Jew, she said. She had already met her Gentile D.S.O. too, Bobby Malswetting, the handsomest man in all the world. She seemed to be rather fatal to D.S O.s. But, even if she had not been carrying about with her so vivid a memory of Bobby Malswetting, she would still have turned down her Jewish D.S.O. And when this same remonstrated bitterly—for he was both hurt and angry—" My dear, my dear," she said, " I like you awfully. But you can never be more than a brother to me. And when I say brother I mean *brother*."

" What the hell are you driving at ? " he said, for he was quite furious by now.

" I mean," she said, " I *couldn't* go to Brighton with you. It would be like incest."

The Jewish D.S.O. knocked over his wine-glass in his

disgust, like any young man who was never educated at a public school and university.

" Perhaps it's because I've never had a brother," she was trying to explain to him. " There were five of us at home, all girls, so any Jewish young man is like the brother we never had." She looked at him rather pitifully, as if asking him to be nice and kind to the poor girl who had never had a brother.

But, of course, that was by no means the accurate explanation, or Esther Silver would never have married Joe Tishler, which she did, and had five children by him. And another sister, Sarah, married Alexander Smirnof, who was half a Jew, at any rate, and she had even more than five children by him. And as for that same sister, Sarah, she would have married her man if he had been wholly a Jew, or wholly a Gentile. Her Judaism and her England were the armfuls of her babies, of whom her husband, Sasha, was the most pitiable babe of all.

There remains the case of Susan Silver, who married the full Jew, Boris Polednik. The full Jew—yet of these various matings with which the chronicles of the five Silver daughters are concerned, the marriage between Susan and Boris was the least Jewish. It was least Jewish in the sense that it most deliberately repudiated the category Jewish, declaring that it was discarded, irrelevant. The orbit of interest for them did not embrace the concept Christian, Muslim, Jew, on the one hand, which is the category of faith, nor the concept Slav, Teuton, Jew, on the other hand, which is the category of race. Their orbit of interest was conterminous with the concept aristocracy, bourgeoisie, and proletariat, exploiter and exploited. It was the orbit of interest at that time for some thousands of their intellectual partners ; it would probably be a great exaggeration to say for some hundreds of thousands. At this present time the inheritors of their idea are the one hundred and sixty million inhabitants of the

Union of Socialist Soviet Republics. The attempt has been made, and is being made, to extend the capacious boundaries of the idea ; and has been countered, and is being countered, with the sort of ruthlessness with which in earlier centuries the wars of religion were conducted. It will take more than one generation before it is decided whether the boundaries of the idea are immensely to extend or immensely to dwindle. Perhaps that debate will give History its main argument for centuries to come.

Russia and things Russian filled the circle of Susan's mind from her childhood, as, later, England and things English were the whole content of May's mind. But it was not the æsthetic Russia, so to speak, as with May it was the æsthetic England. She never attempted to render an image in her mind in St. Petersburg, of the long rococo façades of the Winter Palace ; in Moscow, of the Kremlin's rose-red walls and the gilded cupolas they encircled ; in Kiev, of the Lavra Monastery disposed among its woods that hung down over the yellow Dnieper. The Russian towns, large and small, took shape out of a void, for whatsoever incidental references to landscape were involved in the conversations she listened to, and the books she read, made no impact upon her ; excepting only that certain areas were or were not industrialised, to certain horrific regions the political exiles were banished.

The towns of Russia were, in other words, the places where most of the factories were, or might be, and where the workers worked and lived under such vile conditions. She would listen, fascinated and furious, to the accounts given by the anarchists, many of whom were Russians, in her father's kitchen. Her father used sometimes to tell of the conditions under which he worked as a tailor in his early boyhood in Odessa and Kremenchug ; he spoke with melancholy rather than with anger, for although the anarchists gathered in his kitchen, he was himself no dynamic leader of anarchists. He told how his working-day was often, day after day, eighteen hours long, and the only bed he had to rest his bones on, when the day's work was done, was the cutting-table upon which his master went on cutting, cutting, till dawn came. His wage for that labour was rarely as much as three roubles a week. Others told of the Gentile workers in the factories ; how they were prevented from speaking to each other for fear of the spread of subversive propaganda, so that it was only in the latrine they might exchange a furtive word. The average wage was six to seven roubles per week. Their diet was bread and salt herrings. A cucumber was an occasional luxury.

She realised that the workers in English factories lived in no Paradise, and she became in her early teens, as she described it later, a pap-and-water Socialist. She studied the facts of the labour situation in England and elsewhere, but even before the appearance of Polednik she felt that in Russia lay the greatest woe, and out of Russia the proletariat dawn would come. She was about seventeen when she first met Polednik in a very advanced Socialist club in East Doomington. That was some two years before the evening in the Silver kitchen with which these chronicles opened. To Susan and her colleagues the club seemed very advanced. To Polednik it seemed contemptibly pink. It took him no long time to convince Susan to the same effect. The serious young woman and the secret young man established an immediate contact with each other. It was as if they both realised that there were other far more important things they had to do than oscillate in a state of biological skirmish. They liked each other's flesh ; or, at least, they did not dislike it. Far more important, their minds had registered spontaneous sympathy. They became—and no more nonsense—each other's man and woman. He was also useful for her Russian, and she for his English.

He was only twenty-two when he met Susan, but he had already had a various and exciting career as an underground worker for his party. He did not think of it as exciting. The dangers of arrest, exile, of a chance shot at a frontier putting him summarily out of the way, were merely part of the routine of his vocation. Vocation, in the religious sense, is the word that with precision describes the state of being of the hundreds of Poledniks who honeycombed the European cities at that time ; a state of being in which, often in dire poverty, running great risks, they worked indefatigably night and day, year in, year out, for a consummation they only rarely dared to hope they might witness with their own eyes.

He had been kept in prison in Kiev as a small boy for three months, and was then on the point of being exiled to Siberia when, on account of his extreme youth, he was released. He continued with his revolutionary work—the summoning to meetings, the distribution of literature—but it became clear he was being watched very carefully. Word was brought to him one day in the workshop that a handful of known police spies in plain clothes were posted round the house he lived in. He was given a wallet of fifty roubles and smuggled across the Galician frontier. He worked in Vienna for some time, where, much to his embarrassment, his comrades tended to heroise him, for they had been kept well informed of all the doings in Kiev, and they felt that young " Aïsst " had comported himself with as much decorum as could have been expected from a much more practised revolutionary. " Aïsst," or " Stork," was his secret party name ; it was an irony he did not fail to appreciate that the name with which the little boys of his native village had used to jeer at him was the name under which he conducted his share of those subterranean activities which were some day to abolish all injustice. It was one of his party names, to be exact. It was not unusual to have two or more. It was quite usual not to know a comrade by his real name—if he could still be said to have a real name ; for most of them had travelled under so many passports (the names on which were either totally fictitious or the names of people, totally unknown to them, thousands of miles away) that quite often they would have been hard put to it to remember what names they bore in their innocent infancy.

Armed with certain paroles, and bearing a diversity of letters from " contacts " in Russia concealed in a double-bottomed trunk, he was then sent to England—an easy country to negotiate at that time, for foreigners needed no identification papers and could register under any name that pleased their fancy.

In London a certain journal, entitled *Iskra, The Spark*, was being produced by the intellectual leaders of the Russian exiles abroad. It was the creation of one Vladimir Ilyitch Ulianof, usually known by his pen-name, Lenin. A term of exile in Siberia to which he had been sentenced came to an end early in 1900, and he left Russia in the middle of that same year. The paper was started in Munich the following year, and soon attained a position of much influence ; so much so, that the question of its control, as between the Lenin influence and the influence of Plekhanof (who had been, and still was, the acknowledged leader of the Russian Social Democratic exiles abroad), soon presented difficulties. It was out of those same difficulties that the complete schism of the party arose which divided it three years later, at a congress in London, into the two groups, ultimately irreconcilable, called Bolsheviks and Mensheviks.

The production of the paper was transferred in 1902 to London, and it was to that town that Boris Polednik was despatched to deliver letters and to establish personal connection with the leaders, more particularly with Lenin. Polednik was no enthusiast for personalities. It was for principles that his mind burned with a hard unblinking light. Because a personality was picturesque, it did not tickle him, any more than it would have tickled him to find an engine picturesque. The sole test of its value was its efficiency.

But when he spoke to Susan Silver concerning Lenin, as he did sometimes, when there was no more mail to be sent out to Russia and they had despatched all their own letters and pamphlets, he spoke with an almost stammering excitement, like a small boy who had spent an afternoon in the company of a world-famous athlete, or a little piano-playing girl with her hair in plaits in whose presence a supreme virtuoso has sat down at the piano, and has even asked what her favourite piece of music was, and has played it for her.

" He's a great man, I tell you, Susan, a great man," he would say. " You mark my words ; some day, if any man alive is going to crush the monster, *crush* him, and put the downtrodden toiler at the head of society . . ." He broke off. " If they let him ! They'll poison him one of these days ! Or he'll be fished up from the Thames, or Lake Geneva, or somewhere, with his head smashed in ! "

Then the current of his thought changed again. " I think not. They're too stupid. They don't understand their danger. I've seen him with my own eyes. When we go abroad together, we'll both see him. There's no trouble about that, no grandeur, no holiness. He's not big, not much bigger than me. But his shoulders are broad, and his forehead's big and lumpy. There's a queer smile in his eyes, which are a little close together. They slant a little, too. There's something Buddha-like in him. He comes from the Volga, there's Asian blood in his veins. He's the symbol of Europe and Russia meeting in a single force. You think I'm mad, Susan. I'm not. He's a great man, because he's something more than a man ; he's what I say, a force. He's logic walking in a human body. He's pity, too. But pity clean and sharp, like a surgeon's knife. The diseased flesh that the knife gouges out will think the knife cruel. I suppose the founders of religion were like him—Buddha ; and Christ, too, and Mohammed. You see—don't you *see*—those others made people like me feel as I feel about *him*. I'm not the only one. He doesn't bluster when he comes into a room. But when he comes, other people stop talking. They know what they have to say can't matter now. Or sometimes he's in the room before you go in. You mightn't notice him. He's *listening*. But gradually, however dark the room is, you know he's there. The words peter out on your lips. . . ."

Polednik saw a good deal of Lenin and his wife, Krupskaya, in London. Together they set out from Lenin's lodgings in Holford Square and walked down through Bloomsbury and Soho to Marble Arch, where they listened, amazed, to the feverish orators threshing the air, the amiable bystanders cracking their jokes. They marvelled to see the orators become purple with excitement over teleological minutiæ when, within a stone's throw of the palaces, the London poor swarmed and festered in slums. Or sometimes they drove round upon the tops of omnibuses, to try and establish some sort of a London perspective. They would dismount at Primrose Hill, looking down on the vast city, remembering how an earlier Communist had once stood upon a hill, the world and all its principalities spread out before him.

After Lenin left for Geneva in the spring of 1903, Polednik remained in England for a year or two, to see what chances there were of establishing a group, such as had been founded in Berlin, to assist the party in London and the big cities. It was then he paid his first visit to Doomington. Thereafter, for some time, he was busy with the smuggling of illegal literature across the German–Russian frontier. A good deal was carried across as straightforward contraband, but he and his associates developed a considerable degree of ingenuity along lines more subtle. Newspapers and pamphlets of a kind most noxious to the authorities were packed in small bundles, which were, in turn, packed away at the heart of huge bundles of the most syrupy evangelical literature. Travellers sympathetic to their cause had their luggage treated so that they carried in a false bottom quantities of inflammable material under their folded shirts or chemises. A sort of waistcoat was manufactured for the men, and a special bodice for the women, in which they were able to carry several hundred pamphlets, printed on the thinnest paper available. Trousers and skirts were similarly padded. Letters were pasted inside the bindings of books or slipped behind the backing of gentle religious pictures. It was a labour which Polednik carried out with the agility and silence of a rat, with the ruthless zeal of a priest.

It began to be evident that an *agent provocateur* was at work in the heart of his organisation. The bundles he despatched were mysteriously side-tracked ; a number of his agents were mysteriously waylaid and arrested. He himself escaped arrest, and, once or twice, being shot or knifed, only by great skill combined with great luck. He was sent back further to the rear, to a point of vantage from which he might more unsuspectedly track down the *agent provocateur*. He ran his quarry to earth, but too late to prevent him from going over publicly to the Black Hundred organisation which had secretly employed him. Thereafter, Polednik moved on to Basle, to Paris, and then to Doomington again, where he met Susan Silver, and arranged that in course of time he would marry her.

Doomington was found to be a satisfactory headquarters, particularly because letters and literature emanating from a town so removed from the main revolutionary map were more easily handled by " contacts " than material that arrived from the " intellectual " European cities. None the less, he paid several visits to groups on the Continent during this period, and, as was told earlier, he was arrested near Cracow by the Austrian authorities on the outbreak of the War. He was released and permitted to journey to Switzerland, where he was forced to remain for many weary months, until a month or two after the first Revolution broke out in Russia in February 1917. As for his wife, who had been Susan Silver, she joined him quite early, in Zürich, and worked at her revolutionary labours as grimly and tirelessly as he.

II

There was enough to keep the Bolsheviks, and the Poledniks among them, very busy in Switzerland during the period of their semi-imprisonment, for that was what the next two and a half years amounted to. They were horrified by the behaviour of Socialists on both sides, who, as they phrased it, were entrapped into voting for and fighting for a purely imperialist War. The Bolsheviks were now faced by more serious difficulties than had ever confronted them. It was infinitely more difficult, if it was not quite impossible, to move from country to country, and their contacts either ceased or became much more circuitous. They were faced in every direction by both an official and a popular hostility such as they had not met before.

It was not so much that they were opposed to the War, as such. They set themselves to alter the nature of it, to convert it from a war between rival capitalisms to a war between rival classes. With this end in view, they summoned conferences, they put forth literature, they worked day and night as they had never worked before. There was nothing to divert Boris and Susan Polednik from their ferocious pre-occupation. Susan maintained no communication at all with her people in Doomington. She was bitterly ashamed of the money that her father was making. He was a profiteer out of the imperialist War. He was an exploiter of the workers who had once been his comrades. Her shame was not modified by the thought that he was more conscientious than most manufacturers in the delivery of what was contracted with him ; nor by a realisation that her father's workers were receiving sums of money for their services which they would once have considered fabulous. She was unaware of those facts, or she did not find they more than touched the surface of her resentment.

Polednik had too much contempt for Sam Silver to waste hard language on him. He was aware, though he had been much away from Doomington since the association of Silver and Smirnof, that Smirnof was the real profiteer, the real exploiter. The thought of Smirnof produced in him a cold and steely fury. He took his success to heart as if it were a move in a game between Smirnof and himself in which he, Polednik, had been brilliantly and odiously worsted.

He worked harder than he had ever worked before, but he was not happy. It had never been possible to say Polednik was a happy man, but he had seemed to be able to attain some sort of ease in the degree that he worked hard. His face grew even more pinched than it had been, and his nose seemed longer and more pointed than before, a state of things for which his pince-nez, which he had lately taken to wearing, might have been partly responsible. His eyes flickered hard and hopeless behind the lenses. They had no diversions, Susan and he. They kept away from the *émigré* circles, as being hotbeds of malice and fritterers away of time and energy in a fatuous spate of tittle-tattle. They did not go up to the mountains, where Lenin and his wife used to go gathering mushrooms and berries, gentian and edelweiss. Nature spoke no language they understood.

Polednik's sole diversion was to seek out Lenin, who had a room in the house of a shoemaker named Kammerer. The house was dilapidated ; the room was dingy ; it looked out on a dark alley. But to Polednik it was more lofty than the mountain-tops he did not frequent, and more spacious than the lakes which could not tempt him. He did not go often. He was as loquacious as he chose to be with the other exiles. With Lenin he felt tongue-tied, schoolboyish. But a certain serenity came down upon him which would continue for hours.

"I think," he said to Susan one day, somewhat wistfully —or for Polednik you would have called it wistfully—" I think Vladimir would have looked a little like Lenin."

"Vladimir?" she asked. For, indeed, not from year's end to year's end did Polednik mention the name of his friend who had died in the Kiev prison. And they had known a number of Vladimirs from time to time.

Polednik clicked his fingers impatiently. " Stepanovitch ! " he said shortly.

" Of course," she said. " I'm sorry."

Polednik said nothing more for a minute or two. But when he spoke again the tone of wistful reminiscence was in his voice again.

" He had the same sort of brow, you know, the same sort of lumpy temples. His hair, too, was browny-red. Did I tell you ? I sometimes think. . . . It's queer ; it's quite idiotic. He's like Stepanovitch come back to life again. I suppose he'd have been about the same age as Lenin, wouldn't he ? Or you might say he's Vladimir going on and on from the point at which they stopped him. So that they didn't cart him away, after all, on a wheelbarrow from the Kiev prison. We were too much for him."

" Too much for whom ? "

" Our brother-in-law, rot his bones ! "

She knew that when his mind had switched itself back to his unspeakable hatred for Alexander Smirnof, the wise thing for her to do was to sit in her chair, or lie on her bed, immobile as a stone carving, till the pinpoint of hard light died out of his eyes again and the trembling went out of his hands.

" I'm going to see Lenin," he said at length. " Coming ? " She rose and reached for a hat.

She preferred not to go with him when he visited Lenin. She, too, felt tongue-tied, schoolgirlish ; but she felt somewhat flattened by the man, somewhat appalled. She shared with Polednik his respect for the man's steel-true integrity, his superhuman industry. But he frightened her in the way a wood at night, or the sea at night, frightened her. It was not that the man gave himself any airs. On the contrary, he would be sitting in the kitchen with the shoe-maker's wife, drinking his tea from a cup without a handle, in animated conversation with the other lodgers. He would make noises as he sucked up the tea, perhaps to put the others at their ease. If a child were about, he would jog it up and down on his knee, and pull its hair, and call it comic names. There would probably be a bar of chocolate for it in one of his pockets.

But as often as not there would be a strange silence about the child, and there would be the same strange silence about Susan. A coldness lay about her heart. She was glad when Boris gave up his boggling and at length rose to go.

Outside these visits to Lenin, and despite the colossal amount of work he got through, Polednik was unhappy.

" I can't understand," Susan would say. " It's as if you can't wait any longer, you who've been so patient all these years."

" It's damned hard to wait," he snapped. " Who knows how many years this blasted War has put us back ? "

" Some think it's put us a century forward."

" I know. I *don't* know. That's why it's so damned hard, I say. And yet, in Petrograd, if the War hadn't started just when it *did* start . . . I met a comrade only this morning. They rushed him into the army, then the Germans captured him. Now he's managed to escape. He swam across the Bodensee. He was in Petrograd the month before the War. He told me again. I hadn't heard it before at first hand. He was one of a huge crowd of workers that went marching up the Sampsonievsky Embankment one day ; they sang revolutionary songs and carried red flags, and the police stood by and didn't dare say a word. Next day the crowds came out again. He himself was one of a group that went about overturning the trams. Before long there wasn't a tram running anywhere in the city. They began to build barricades round the trams. It's possible he was exaggerating. I can quite see that. He's looking back on what happened through a haze of revolutionary triumph. But there's no doubt at all there was something to exaggerate. It was beginning, I tell you.

It was beginning, there and then. The Revolution was beginning. And these swines came along with their war-lies. Oh, it was very useful for them, their War. Just when everything we've been working for so long——"

"Now, Boris, try and be sensible. You know how much work we've got to get through. You'll only break down if you carry on like this. Come. I think we might get some food. What would you like? An egg? I think it might run to an egg."

"I don't want any food. I can't eat."

Polednik was sitting alone in a café in the Neiderdorfstrasse one afternoon, a book propped up before him on a somewhat dirty cruet-stand. Beside the book was an untouched cup of coffee. His eyes were open but he was not reading. He did not seem to be seeing anything at all. Minutes passed. His chin slipped lower down upon his chest. But his eyes did not close. The coffee had slopped over into the saucer. It did not look appetising. It was cold, too, by now.

Then a man suddenly rushed into the café—a big man in a threadbare blue suit. He was brandishing a newspaper. He called out two or three words at the top of his voice.

"Hi!" he proclaimed. "Hi! There's been a Revolution in Russia!"

Then he rushed out again. He rushed out before Polednik raised his head. Polednik sat there quite still for a full minute. Once and twice and three times certain words formed inside his skull. "Hi! Hi! There's been a Revolution in Russia!"

The words had no meaning. He sat there with his chin on his breast. Then one shape and another shape began to establish themselves through the dark haze which had obscured his eyes. He saw a book propped up before him on a somewhat dirty cruet-stand. Beside the book was an untouched cup of coffee. The coffee had slopped over into the saucer.

Then for a fourth time certain words formed inside his skull : " Hi ! Hi ! There's been a Revolution in Russia ! "

The words cracked like a breaking ice-floe athwart his ear-drums. He sprang up, and the metal chair fell with a crash behind him. He ran out into the street and seemed, in the street there, two or three times to turn round upon himself, like a shot rabbit. Then he stopped dead. He returned to the café, threw back his head and drained the cup of cold coffee, picked up his book, put a coin down on the table, and walked out. He made his way to the nearest corner and bought all the special editions of the newspapers. Then at his usual pace he went home, climbed the stairs, and let himself into his room.

Susan was sitting before a typewriter, at a desk heaped with papers. She did not lift her head.

" Susan, I've some news for you ! "

Her fingers went on tapping away, a little more slowly, at the keys of the typewriter.

" Susan, I've some news for you ! "

" Yes, Boris ? "

" Susan, there's been a Revolution in Russia ! "

" What ? "

" There's been a Revolution in Russia ! "

" It's not true ! Oh, Boris ! Is it really true ? "

" Here are the newspapers. If you read the stop-press reports——"

Her cheeks flushed slowly. " Boris ! It's terrific ! "

" We'd best get ready to go to Russia ! "

He turned towards a shelf where a number of their books were piled together, as if he was going to start packing there and then.

" And, Boris ! Won't it be marvellous ? "

" What ? "

" I'll be able to see the family ! In Terkass ! "

He turned round like someone who has been lashed from behind with a whip. He did not see her eyes go blank with amazement at the thing her own lips had said.

" What ? " he screamed. " What ? Has there been a
Revolution in Russia just . . . just "—he could hardly bring
out the words, he was so frantic with fury—" just so that you
might see your stinking family in Terkass ? "

She was infinitely crestfallen. " I beg your pardon, Boris.
I don't deserve to have lived to see this day."

III

Polednik had tried on one or two occasions to get to Russia
during the two and a half years since the War started. But
on each occasion he had come up against such formidable
difficulties that he had decided to defer his attempt. There
was, after all, a great deal of work to be done in Switzerland.

On the day when the news of the Revolution came
through, his manner would not have seemed odd to a
stranger, apart from those few seconds when he had rushed
out into the street from the café. But Susan knew that,
despite his apparent calmness, he was half demented. He
collected books, made bundles of them, untied them again,
put them back where they had come from. He sat himself
down at a desk and chewed a wooden pen close down to the
metal haft. If he had not been half mad, he would not have
announced in that casual way : " We'd best get ready to go
to Russia ! " As if it might be Berne or Geneva they were to
get ready for.

But if the difficulties in the way of getting to Russia had
hitherto been formidable, for some weeks after the Revolution they seemed insuperable. The Swiss frontiers marched
everywhere with the frontiers of the countries at war. To the
Germans and Austrians the Bolsheviks were still Russians,
and enemies. There was no hope of getting away by France
or Italy, for it was their known determination to summon
the Russian soldiers from the trenches in order to turn them
against the Russian bourgeoisie.

If there had ever been anything rat-like about Polednik,
now, more than ever before, the quality asserted itself. He

shunned people and open places, and, exactly like a rat in a trap, scurried from wall to wall, from wall to wall, of his tiny apartment. His eyes glared. Susan did not dare to speak to him. Sometimes she crept out of the room, closing the door as if he were a very sick man. Sometimes she sat on at her table, pretending to read, but keeping her miserable eyes on him the whole time, as he scurried from wall to wall, from wall to wall.

Then one day a message was delivered to him, an official notification from the local secretary. The exiles were to be allowed to travel home by way of Germany. It had all been arranged by their Swiss colleague, one Fritz Platten. For the brilliant thought had occurred to the Germans that the presence in Russia of these enemies of the imperialist War might advantage them more than the capture of an army corps. It was officially understood that the Social Democrats on their arrival in Russia would agitate for the transfer to Germany and Austria of an equivalent number of German and Austrian prisoners. But there was not much emphasis on that matter. It was further understood that no one was to enter the carriage of the Russians during the journey across Germany, and on neither side would any attempt be made to establish contact. There was to be no inspection of luggage or passports.

Polednik read the note. Then, very carefully, he doubled it, took out his wallet, and placed the note inside it. Then he turned to Susan. There was not the trace of an inflexion of excitement in his voice.

" Susan," he said, " it's been arranged. We're to take the next train for Berne. We get the Berlin connection there. Then Stockholm, I suppose, and Haparanda, probably, on the Swedish–Russian frontier. Then——"

Still with this almost terrifying self-control he went up to a small table where a railway time-table lay. He turned the pages.

" We leave in two hours," he said. " Let's get down to it."

" I can't believe it," she said. " It's like . . ."

Then at last he cracked.

" Like the beginning of the world ! " he cried resonantly.
" Like the beginning of the world ! Oh, Susan ! Susan ! "
He hurled himself at her. She was sitting at the table. He
threw his arms round her neck, bent down and kissed her
impetuously. She blushed like a schoolgirl. He waltzed like
a dapper little draper in a fairground.

" Isn't it grand ! Isn't it grand ! Oh, Susan, Susan ! "

Then he stopped. The brightness went out of his voice.
" Come along ! " he said quite curtly. " We've only got
two hours to do everything and get to the station ! "

About thirty Bolsheviks boarded the train at Berne. These
included Lenin and Krupskaya, his wife ; Fritz Platten,
who had arranged the journey ; Sokolnikof, one day to be
Ambassador at the Court of St. James's, and Boris Polednik,
who was at no distant date to attain responsible office both
in arms and finance in the Russia of the Soviets—a country
which might never have emerged into history if not for the
carriage-load of exiles that left Berne that day. For that
carriage bore Lenin home at last, and Soviet Russia was the
will and mind of that one man made manifest, splendid
and dreadful.

There travelled also Zinoviev, for long one of Lenin's
closest associates, and the wife of Zinoviev ; also Karl
Radek, the most caustic of journalists in or out of Europe ;
also the wife of Boris Polednik, Susan, the third of the five
Silver daughters.

IV

The journey from Berne to Berlin, Stockholm, and
Petrograd, in what has been described with only metaphorical accuracy as a " sealed carriage," took eight days.
Certain of the exiles had been waiting to return to Russia
for a decade or more, with more or less patience, yet to them

the eight days of this journey seemed to drag on for a life-time. They were jumpy and irritable. When the train stopped at a wayside station, and a peasant chanced to look in through a window, in complete ignorance that he looked in upon the standard-bearers of revolutionary history, they snapped the blind down or hid their faces in their coats. They had an accurate apprehension of the things their enemies would say about their acceptance of the offer of transit across Germany. They would say that they were German spies, that their valises were crammed with German money. They were not patriots, but they did not like it.

Others were garrulous as slum children on a holiday. The wagon-restaurant people had been requested to produce enormous meals for them, so that they might spread the news in Russia that milk and honey were flowing in Germany. They guzzled their *Sahnschnitzel*, their creamed veal cutlets, and their heaped platters of vegetables, and their rich *Mehlspeise* (flour-pudding), fried in butter, all bebuttoned with raisins, and their great slabs of cheese from Tilsit. And when they had finished their first helpings, they moved forward their empty plates and coffee-cups a second time and a third. They had not fed so sumptuously these several years past, up against the Porte Saint-Denis in Paris, or down the Wasnergasse in Vienna.

Lenin sat wrapped in his thoughts. He spoke rarely. He was not impatient. He had waited long enough for this hour, and could wait two or three days longer for it. But he would have preferred it if the train had moved a little faster, and it had been possible it should not stop so frequently. Their arrival a day or two sooner might, as a matter of fact, prevent undesirable developments in one or two directions. The leaders over in Leningrad had not got it *straight*. Some of them were beginning to think the battle was won. It was not ; nothing more was won than a preliminary skirmish. What was this nonsense they had been publishing in the newspaper, *Pravda* ?

He was pale. He sat for the most part with his eyes closed,

but it was evident he was not asleep. His brain was working furiously. Now and again he would start up out of his silence and engage Zinoviev or Sokolnikof or one of the others in a swift discussion on some matter of policy or ideology. It was not so much that he wanted to learn what they had to say as to make it crystal-clear in his own mind that he had the scheme of his intentions as perfectly thought out and arranged as the component parts of a machine. Then he shut his eyes again, and his head drooped upon his chest. The tiny veins stood out on the pallor of his broad brow.

A member of the party had his small boy with him, Robert by name. The child was about four years old. Lenin did not, as a rule, attempt to resist children or simple folk. He was much happier with them than with adults, intellectuals. He held that these had a responsibility for their ideas, and his eye darkened if he thought their ideas false or fatuous. But he had little time for Robert on the German journey. Once or twice, with a faint smile, he pulled the child's curly hair. Then he relapsed into his thoughts again.

It was Polednik who wooed the child, and he wooed it much more than the child wooed Polednik. That was no lap to sit on, Robert clearly thought, that thin neck was no neck to throw the arms round. But Polednik insisted. And the child, a polite child, submitted, excepting for one or two occasions when he felt he had had enough Polednik for the day, and kicked out viciously, or suddenly set up a loud howl.

Polednik was no expert in the child mind, or he might not have pressed his attentions. Indeed, Susan could not remember any previous occasion upon which he had taken any notice of a child at all. The fact was, as she saw, he was almost numb with happiness. To be travelling so closely cooped up with Lenin, his master, for so many days, made him as blissful as a man who has been commissioned to carry a casket of saint's bones to his convent-chapel. He was going home, home, to the Revolution. He did not talk ; he did not even listen, excepting on the few occasions when Lenin provoked a brisk passage or two. He was not taken in, of course, by the prodigality of the *cuisine*. He shovelled it down, and winked knowingly at Susan. After the meal was over, he would lean against the back of his seat with a faint grin on his face. His lower lip hung slack a little. Susan was not in the habit of measuring people in the scale of their good looks, least of all her husband. But she could not prevent herself from registering how unattractive he was, sitting there relaxed, with that faint grin on his face.

" But of course," she assured herself, " the poor chap's on holiday. Don't you realise this is literally the first time in his life he's had a holiday, the first time the tension's slackened?"

But she knew the tension was slackened for a time only. She knew that very few days would pass before it was as taut as steel again.

" Look ! " cried Polednik suddenly. " Isn't it pretty ! " He pointed out a great thatched farmhouse with a pool in front of it and a windmill on a knoll a little distance away— it was a perfect piece of German picture-postcard landscape.

"Yes," she agreed, though she was not thrilled. "Isn't it pretty ! " They had between them only a meagre vocabulary of æsthetic approval. There was a fine sunset that evening. Polednik almost cooed over it, like a schoolgirl poet. " Odd ! " she murmured to herself. He had as much use for Nature, as a rule, as for a cold in the head.

The journey was not a happy one for her. She could not speak Russian glibly enough to keep pace with the conversation. She was rather awed, too, to find herself rubbing shoulders all day long with this distinguished crowd of revolutionaries. She felt herself something of an interloper. It would have been a bit better if Boris addressed a sensible word to her from one day's end to another, instead of worrying that silly small boy with goo-goo talk.

" What ? What's that, Boris ? Oh yes, yes ! It *is* a pretty sunset ! "

v

It was night when Lenin and his companions arrived in Petrograd, at the Finland station. His arrival came as a surprise to some of his most important associates, yet in the hour or two before his arrival the rumour of it spread throughout the city, and half the population seemed to be gathered round the station and in the station square and in every available inch of space under the drab vaults. But there were many who did not come. They stayed behind in their aristocratic drawing-rooms or gathered round their comfortable bourgeois stoves. They did not rejoice in the coming of Lenin.

A guard of honour, recruited from the sailors of the Second Baltic Naval Division, was gathered on the platform. Lenin descended from the carriage and made his way up the aisle which the sailors had left for his passage.

" You know how he cares for that sort of thing ! " Kamenev muttered in his beard to a colleague standing beside him.

" But he's finding it rather amusing," the other replied. " He's not used to being met by guards of honour on his arrival at railway stations."

Lenin was very self-possessed. His intimates had met him further up the line at Beloostrov, the frontier station. There for a few minutes he had given way to the excitement which he, even he, cannot but have felt to be home again, and home under such auguries. His friends threw their arms round him and kissed him again and again. He protested. He threw his arms round them and kissed them in return. There was laughing and weeping and back-slapping and eye-wiping. Then they swarmed back to his carriage. The moment he sat down again, the excitement, the joy of his being home, passed out of his eyes. His mind brimmed at once with its natural pre-occupations—what was to be done now, what mistakes must be rectified at once, what mistakes could wait a day or a week. It was exactly as if he had not been out of Russia all these convulsive years, as if he had been sitting in a party office drawing up minutes and agenda. He turned brusquely to Kamenev, and rated him for the " incorrect " line he had taken in the newspaper, *Pravda*. Kamenev looked down between his boots like a censured schoolboy.

Lenin was thoroughly self-possessed again on arriving at the Finland Station. He walked between the enaisled sailors, his eyes twinkling a little with amusement. A young cadet in charge of the naval detachment stepped forward and saluted, as if Lenin were a visiting admiral from the British Navy. The irrelevant young gentleman hoped that the distinguished returner would see his way clear to joining the Provisional Government. To Lenin the Provisional Government was hardly less indecent than the Tsar's *entourage* of priests, governesses, and doctors. Lenin's eyes turned away from the young man as if he were a piece of newspaper blown by the wind out of a gutter, or, rather, as if he were some silly little fan fallen from some lady's mantelpiece. He stared into the eyes of the crowd, as if they were but one pair of eyes.

" Long live the Socialist Revolution ! " he said tersely.

" Long live the Socialist Revolution ! " the crowd roared, as if it had one voice—the group of exiles who had returned with him, the politicians who had come to meet him, the sailors in their formation, the workers from the factories, the soldiers from the barracks, the blank featureless indiscriminate thousands. The huge streamers of blood-red bunting spread across the vault seemed to shudder slightly in the impact of the wind of that cry.

A fleet of armoured cars had come to greet Lenin, thrusting its way with difficulty to the Finland Station through the crowded streets of the Viborg quarter, the quarter where the Revolution had arisen, where it was to be renewed, where it was a singular felicity that Lenin should arrive, to be hailed by it. On issuing from the station, Lenin was not allowed to go further till he had addressed the multitude. He was borne into one of the armoured cars, and standing there, small, level-headed, nothing at all of the demagogic hero, he uttered a few words, concluding with the same slogan : " Long live the Socialist Revolution ! " But it was that very level-headedness which seemed to the vast crowd something steadfast at last, a rock in the waste of rhetorical waters which had churned and churned these last few weeks. " Húrra ! Húrra ! Húrra ! " they thundered back at him.

The cavalcade set forth at a snail's pace, Lenin still standing on the armoured car, his friends, in ordinary cars, following behind him. The searchlights from the Fortress of St. Peter and St. Paul strode hugely across the sky, now and again picking out and isolating in mid-air a red banner that seemed to blossom out of nowhere. In the lower levels the lights of the fleet of armoured cars dipped and ran. The workers and soldiers that lined the street maintained a roar in volume like the sea ; but, unlike the sea, it did not rise and fall—it continued at one pitch. The returned exiles and the party emissaries in the cars behind Lenin shouted with the rest. Only Lenin remained silent, standing on his car, remembering only spasmodically to cry out to the multitude : " Long live the Socialist Revolution ! "

In one of the cars a woman seemed on the verge of collapse, she was so broken with ecstasy. She still tried to shout, though she had hardly more than a shred of throat left. But no one had any eyes for her, Susan Polednik, who had come a long way, from a damp twilit city, to bathe herself in these fierce fires. " Húrra ! " the last tatters of her voice whispered. " Húrra ! Húrra ! "

She felt someone pulling, pulling, at her elbow. She realised she had felt the same pulling for a minute or two ; but there had been no time—and this was no time—to regard it. The cavalcade was stationary. It had been stationary for a minute now. She registered at last who it was that pulled so desperately. It was Boris, her husband.

" Well ? " her mouth made at him. Her eyes were bleared as if she were quite drunk.

He was trying to say something to her. He was pointing out someone in the crowd. Again he tried to say something to her.

" What ? " she howled.

She brought her ear down nearer to his mouth. At last she heard him.

" Look ! Look ! Do you see ? " he was saying.

" See what ? "

" Just by that lamp-post there ! Look, I tell you ! There's Smirnof ! "

" *Smirnof ?* But you're mad ! Where ? "

" There ! "

" You're mad ! There's no Smirnof there ! Boris, do you hear ? You're mad ! "

The cavalcade was moving again. Susan was shouting again, her lank hair lying across her eyes.

" She's right ! " Boris Polednik's lips formed. " I'm mad ! " The sweat dripped in thick rivulets on both sides of his sharp nose.

At length the cavalcade drew up at the small palace the Tsar had built for Kseshinskaya, a ballet dancer, who had been his mistress. It had now become the headquarters of the Bolshevik Party. Lenin addressed the crowd once again that night from the second floor balcony window. Then his wife took him home to their own people, back again on the north side of the river. They were very thirsty. They drank great quantities of tea, with which they washed down hunks of black bread piled with red Ket caviare.

CHAPTER IX

SARAH AND HER BABIES

"Hush, now, Jackie, hushaby, Jackie!" whispered Sarah Smirnof to her baby, as she bent down over his cot. But Jackie did not want to hush; his mouth made a small *moue*, as if he intended to do anything but hush. She bent down again, and placed her mouth on the tiny bud of the child's mouth, so that he might perceive that, on the contrary, this was a warm, sweet, odorous world, a world of mammy's mouth, her breast, the full flowing waters of her comfort.

The bud of the mouth pursed itself to again. She kept the signature of her lips round it for a moment or two, then she removed it with the lightness of a moth. She went out of the bedroom, leaving the door open, so that she might hear if Jackie finally determined that this world was no place fit for babies to live in. She went downstairs to the sitting-room. It was a dining-room, too, furnished with some of Pliskin's best Jacobean oak. It was also a nursery, for there was a pen in the corner of the room, where Hilda, the first-born Smirnof child, stood, smiting the low parapet with a rag-doll. "La! La!" sang Hilda. "La! La! La!" Then she struck the bar again, once-twice, once-twice—a third time. Then once more she sang, "La! La!—La! La! La!" It had been going on for a long time, and there was no reason why it shouldn't continue for a long time.

"You can go back into the kitchen, Mary," said Sarah, as she came in. "I'll look after her now."

She smiled into the little servant-girl's eyes friendlily. Mary smiled back again with candour and pleasure. Sarah was good with servants, evidently. If she was going to have more servants, and still more, she would be able to manage them. They would even manage themselves for her ; she was clearly that sort of house-woman.

"Thank you, mum," said Mary, positively with a curtsey, as if to a mistress in a country-house who has had servants at her beck and call since she can remember. She went off and joined Mrs. Riley, her senior, in the kitchen. What with its cook and its maid, its well-upholstered parlour and its Jacobean sitting-room, it was really rather an impressive establishment ; not, of course, compared with Ivanhoe Towers, where Sarah's parents lived, but compared with number eleven Oleander Street, certainly. The Smirnofs had moved from the neat little house in the avenues to a neat, rather bigger house near Layton Park. It was necessary, for the children's sake, to get into fresher air. But the new house was just as grand as they wanted it to be. It didn't need to be any grander, for Alexander Smirnof was only a director of Sam Silver & Co. Ltd. ; Sam Silver himself was managing director. And that was exactly as it ought to be. He was a downy one, Sam Silver ; honest as they make them, but a downy one. If you weren't clever, you would think that the director, Smirnof, was the brains behind the concern. But it was Sam Silver, really, who stood behind everything, with the strings tied round his fingers, twitching here, twitching there. Smirnof, of course, was very good with figures, specifications, and so on, a good sound henchman.

Sarah sat down in a deep brown-leather armchair to the left of the fire. She lifted her feet on to a Pliskin-Jacobean footstool. She felt better that way. Already the new baby was beginning to feel heavy inside her ; not heavy as a load is heavy, but as warm smells are heavy, or a soft heaped fur round the knees, a gracious drowsy heaviness.

She turned her head round to the small Hilda. "La ! La !" chanted the child without remission. "La ! La ! La !" She had a pink ribbon in her curly blonde hair. Sarah turned her face again to the leaping fire. She folded her hands across her belly, and her head slipped slowly back into the cushion behind her.

She awoke to hear the child cry, " Da-da ! Da-da ! " The rag-doll slipped from Hilda's hand. " Take me, Da-da ! " cried Hilda.

It was Smirnof's invariable custom, if the child were still up when he came in, to lift her up from the pen and carry her solemnly all round the table. To-night he did not seem to be aware of her. He sat down in the armchair on the further side of the fire.

" Sasha," said Sarah. " So early ? " There was a note of reproach in her voice. It was not because he had come early.

" I'm sorry ! " he muttered. He came over to her chair and kissed her. Then he went back to his own chair. He proceeded to untie his boots.

" Let me ! " said Sarah.

" You'd better not ! You lie still and take things easy ! "

" But why are you so early ? Dinner won't be ready for an hour."

" Early ? Why do you say I'm early ? "

" Sasha ! You said you were going to a committee meeting. About getting up that quartette to play in the dinner-hour."

He looked up. He remembered. " You're right ! Oh, well ! It'll have to wait ! "

" What's the matter ? " It happened very rarely with him that he should forget an appointment.

She rose and came over to him. She sat down on the arm of his chair and played a faint tattoo on his forehead with her finger-tips.

" What's the matter ? " he repeated. " Shall I tell you what's the matter ? The *rats* ! "

" What are you talking about, Sasha ? What's wrong ? "

" Have you read a paper to-day ? "

" No, darling, no. You know I'm too busy to read papers."

" There's been a Revolution in Russia ! "

" Oh, has there ? "

" There has ! Rats, stinking sewer rats ! They've come out now, after all these years, nibbling, nibbling, grinding away with their teeth ! "

" But, Sasha, why should you let it worry you ? "

" Why ? " He looked up at her. " I can't tell you why ! "

" It won't make any difference to *us* ! "

" Don't be silly ! " he said shortly.

" All right, Sasha darling. I told you I don't understand politics. I didn't ask to talk about it ! "

" Give me your hand, Sarah ! "

" There ! "

He held it against his cheek for some time. With her other hand she went on playing the faint tattoo on his brow. She knew it always soothed him. She could send him to sleep that way.

" I'll hurry dinner up for you, Sasha ! " she said at length.

" Oh, please, Sarah, no ! No dinner ! I'll only have a glass of milk and some biscuits. And a little cheese perhaps."

He crunched his biscuits without a word. But that was nothing strange. He often said not a word from one meal's end to another. He was thinking. Now and again he would put his hand along the table and she would pat it. She didn't ask more than that from him, when his brow was all wrinkled with thinking this and that.

Then suddenly he rapped out a word or two that seemed to have some bearing on the matter which had put his appointment out of mind.

" You can always put poison down for them ! "

" What ? " she asked, startled.

" Or shoot them ! That's best ! "

" Sasha ! " she said hurriedly. " Shall I put on some records for you ? What shall I put on ? "

" I suppose that little long-nosed rat—he'll be scurrying along there as fast as his legs will carry him."

" Have some grapes, Sasha. They're lovely. English hothouse."

" Didn't you say he's in Switzerland now ? "

" I heard Susan was."

" He'll be wanting to rub his snout in the muck."

" Listen, Sasha. Be quiet. I asked you what record you'd like me to put on."

" A record ? No, I don't feel like music."

" But it always——"

" No, nothing, not to-night. Tell her to take this away.
I want nothing ! "

" Let me unfasten your collar and tie for you, Sasha !
There. Isn't that better ? Come, sit down in your chair.
Have one of those nice fat cigars to-night. It'll soothe your
nerves. Hush, now ; don't move. I'll get you some brandy
—in one of those big, big glasses."

" Thank you, Sarah. I'd like some brandy."

She lit his cigar for him and poured his brandy out. He
gulped it down. He puffed once and twice at his cigar. Then
he fell to thinking again, whatever those thoughts were that
ran round and round under the arched dome of his skull,
vaguely muffed by its wash of reddish hair.

" Your cigar's gone out, Sasha ! Shall I light it again ?
No, you shouldn't light cigars again when they go out, should
you ? I'll get you another ! "

He threw the cigar away and rose from the chair. He
went towards the door that was only a few feet away from
the staircase that led to their bedroom. " Sarah ! " he said.
He was like a little boy asking a school-mistress to be kind
to him.

" Yes, dear, at once ! I'll ask them to clear away."

They went upstairs, and halted at the little room where
Hilda and Jackie lay. " Hush ! " she said. She turned the
door-handle silently, and they stood there looking from cot
to cradle in the dim pallor of the night-light. They went on
to their own room. They undressed and put their night-
things on.

" Come ! " she said.

He lay encompassed by her warmth and softness. She
placed her mouth on his, and drew at it, as if she drew the
bitterness out.

" Feeling better, darling ? " she murmured.

He did not answer. He was asleep.

CHAPTER X

THE SPY

I

SUSAN could not clearly remember where she and Boris had spent the night of their arrival in Petrograd, though there was very little of the night left by the time they left the house of Kseshinskaya. There had been talk and talk, and again more talk, and she had followed it all keenly for an hour or two. Then the day's long journey, the excitement of the arrival, the mental strain of following this tangle of arguments in a language which, in Russia, seemed suddenly a different language from the one she had been learning for years—all these took toll of her. She became sleepier and sleepier. She was seated on an exquisite damask-covered chair, very frail and elegant ; a chair in which a director of Kseshinskaya's ballet might have been well at ease during the half-hour lapse of a polite little tea-party, but no chair for a long-shanked woman, who has been travelling all day on a hard wooden third-class train-bench, to be sitting on hour after hour. She tried to catch Polednik's eye a few times. But he seemed to get fresher and fresher as the night went on. She wondered where in that thin-chested little frame he hid such enormous stores of energy. His cheeks were burning with excitement, his eyes danced in the glare of the ornate chandeliers.

At last she found he was leading her out of the room, still hurling arguments behind him. She followed him, quite numb. The cold air gave her the strength to walk, but not to waken her, though she mumbled a single question anxiously : " Where's our luggage ? "

"That's all right. It's being looked after," he assured her. They moved on and on.

She thought they were at an hotel—the Smolensk Hotel, she dimly remembered later—but there was no room for them there, absolutely none. They moved on again. On and on, across a street, across a bridge, across a street. She said she would lie down against the parapet. She needed only to close her eyes for ten minutes. But he had met somebody. He took no notice of her. He and the stranger talked together for a minute or two. Perhaps he slipped a note, a Swiss note, into the hands of the stranger. The three of them walked on. They stopped outside a big house. There was tugging and tugging at a bell. A house-porter came. They were climbing endless flights of stairs, the two men dragging her by the elbows. They were in a room now. There were three beds in the room, but there seemed many more than three people on the beds, and on the floor. There was a sofa. Someone was lying on it. A hand pulled at the legs. The creature rolled, grunting, down on to the floor.

"There now," said Boris. "Sleep!"

She did not know where he laid himself. She herself slept like a corpse.

He had been up for hours, and had been out again and had returned, by the time Susan woke. He had been busy. He had hunted up certain of his "contacts." He had managed to find them a whole room to themselves, here on the Petersburgskaya, the island part of the city north of the River Neva.

Polednik had not been deceived, even in Switzerland, even the very day the news of the Revolution was declared. He realised how provisional a Revolution this was compared with the basic uprooting of society which Lenin and the Leninists—and they were not many—had been working for. Susan had nothing like his knowledge, either theoretical or practical. It was only in Russia itself, during the months that elapsed between their arrival in the middle of April and the triumph of the Leninist Revolution in October, that she learned how strong and numerous the enemies of their cause were, and what prodigalities of devotion and energy must be still expended.

They both worked exceedingly hard, far harder than they had ever worked in their lives before. She sometimes could not help marvelling at herself that she could get such colossal quantities of work done in the tiny room they had on the Zvyerinskaya, or in the tenth part of an office she occupied, when they made her Secretary of the Leatherworkers' Trade Union, where the Bolsheviks were not strong. She was often cold, sometimes hungry and thirsty, not only because there simply was no time to eat or drink anything, but because there wasn't anything about to eat or drink.

Polednik combined the activities of several men in his one negligible body. It was soon discovered how effective an agitator he was. There was a complete lack of the sweetnesses of rhetoric about him when he got up on his feet to address working-men and soldiers and sailors. He spoke with absolute simplicity and absolute conviction. When it was reported that the workers in a certain factory or the sailors in a certain battleship were wavering, Polednik was sent to address them, and they wavered no longer. It was desirable that he should be elected to the Petrograd Soviet of Workers' and Soldiers' Deputies. He duly became one of the delegates from the great Pelikhov steel-works. There he founded and edited a Bolshevik factory newspaper. His activities were suspended for a while after the episode usually referred to as the " July Days," when the masses made an abortive attempt to over-throw the Provisional Government. The Bolsheviks main-tained that the movement, being premature, was entirely self-engendered, but that, after it had gathered momentum, it was imperative that they should put themselves at the head of it. The Government, buttressed by a regiment that had arrived from the front, declared the Bolsheviks guilty of treason. Lenin and Zinoviev went into hiding ; Trotsky and certain other Bolshevik deputies, among them Polednik, were locked up in the Kresty Prison.

The situation was grim, from the point of view, at least, of the Bolshevik leaders. General Kornilof was marching on the capital. There was little doubt that, if he got there, he would treat the imprisoned leaders with little courtesy.

" A pretty irony ! " murmured Susan Polednik savagely. " So this is what we've come to Russia for, is it ? This is what he's worked for, night and day, year in, year out—how many years is it now ? Back again where he started from, in Kiev, when he was fifteen ! Back again in prison ! "

But the forces which were in motion now went further back than February. They were such that Kornilof could not reach Petrograd ; nor could Krasnof, nor Denikin, nor Kolchak, nor Wrangel, nor any other of the generals who, then or later, put themselves at the head of the Counter-Revolution. Trotsky and his associates were released from prison. Almost immediately after his release, the Military Revolutionary Committee of the Soviet appointed Boris Polednik to be a military delegate, with the special duty of maintaining liaison between the barracks and the Red Guard factory-units on the Petrograd side of the river. For it had become known that he was no mean authority on tactics and strategy, and that he had made a special study of the science of barricades in cities. It was evident everywhere that it was only a matter of days, even of hours, before the arrested Revolution of February must attain its deferred climax ; or, as others had it, before the Revolution of the democracy must be ousted by the Revolution of the proletariat.

But though, during the night of the twenty-fourth and the day of the twenty-fifth, Polednik was more occupied than even he had ever been since his return, it was not such knowledge as he possessed of strategy and tactics and the barricading of streets that he put into practice. Silently, with that extraordinary silence which could be with him so terrifying a characteristic, he and his colleagues moved about the city, occupying key building after key building—stations, post-offices, telegraph offices, banks. Step by step they reported progress to Trotsky, waiting tense and dishevelled in the Smolny Institute, the Soviet headquarters. The building had been till lately a home for widows and female orphans of impeccable breeding ; if any of their ghosts dithered that night along the enormous corridors, they would have been far too puzzled to be indignant, wondering who these uncouth men might be, and what the fantastic messages were that came through all night long.

All night long, not for one moment did Polcdnik and his colleagues lose touch with Smolny or the various fighting units waiting to be called on. But it was not found necessary to call on them, even when the Bolshevik soldiers gathered closer and closer round the Winter Palace, where the Provisional Government was sitting, their pale anxious faces staring out from under the volutes of rococo plaster-work.

The October Revolution was, in fact, achieved with such effortless politeness that Susan Polednik, who had been away for two or three days on trade union business in a town a day's journey from Petrograd, was not in the least aware of it, on the very night of the twenty-fifth, as she took a clopping droshky along the Nevsky Prospekt towards the Winter Palace. The trams were running ; the cinemas were open ; things seemed to be where they had been.

On the island side of the Birzhevoi Bridge she did, in fact, notice a group of workmen squatting round a brazier, and she thought for a moment that one or two of them had arms. If they had, it was not extraordinary. But it was more likely that the apparent arms were picks or levers or some sort of street-implements. She did not give the matter a second thought. She was not aware that that armed picket of workmen, and another, and another, were the reservoir from which Trotsky and Polednik would have drawn all the additional strength the event needed if their victory had not achieved itself with such sweet ease.

She got home and tried to telephone Polednik at the Smolny Institute, but she could not get through to him. He often enough was kept busy all night. She went to bed. She had a good deal of sorting to do next day among her papers. In the late afternoon of that day he came in. He barely had time or strength to convey the news to her. He had not slept for two days and nights, and had eaten, at most, a slice of bread. He fell asleep, on his feet, before her eyes.

She got him on to their bed, and left him ; and, knowing he would not awaken for some time, she went out to learn more. She learned with intense excitement—and Polednik confirmed it later—that Trotsky had been the pivotal genius of the *coup d'état*. She was excited because, to her, Trotsky was an enchantment. She did not feel, as she had always felt with Lenin, that this man was in most ways more, in some ways less, than a man. She felt Trotsky to be gloriously a man, infinitely alive, blazing with vitality. He had enormous virtues, and he had vices to make them tolerable. He was vain. He was erratic. But what devastating brilliances of oratory ! What flesh-singeing irons of sarcasm ! Whenever she learned that he was speaking at the Modern Circus, which he had adopted as his own platform, she would make every effort to get away, even if her work might suffer. He had the graces of civilisation. He had the strength and speed of the jungle.

She tried once or twice to get Polednik to come with her to hear him at the Modern Circus. But he never had a moment to spare. He had other things to do than to go and see Trotsky juggling with words before a rabble of school-girls and Menshevik clerks. He did not like Trotsky. Trotsky enchanted her.

And then Trotsky was a Jew. And not only a Jew, but a farmer's son, born on the land. Trotsky's father had gone out to be a farmer's boy when he was quite small, just as Feivel Dobkin, her mother's father, had gone out to be a farmer's boy at Prolensk, where the family farm was, twenty miles from Terkass.

It was a coincidence, nothing more. Trotsky meant nothing more nor less to her because he was a Jew like herself. He was only Jewish by race, the mere flesh and blood part of him. The thing that made him Trotsky, and her Susan Polednik, was something that transcended race, as it transcended colour or creed. Those were all outworn categories.

Yet the fact that he was a Jew was part of the data, as she phrased it ; you couldn't get away from that. And he was a farmer's son, too. It surely made it easier to understand how he became—Trotsky. Had somebody told her that Trotsky played the flute ? Her uncle Alex used to play the flute quite well. She recalled the photograph of Uncle Alex they had at home, in Doomington, in the family album. She had seen a photograph of Trotsky looking not altogether unlike Uncle Alex, an astrakhan cap raked to one side, and an astrakhan collar to his coat, too—a tight coat, rather trim at the waist.

Not, of course, that you would say Trotsky had ever been a dandy. The idea was laughable. Or that Alex had ever been an intellectual. She recalled Trotsky's broad brow, his huge mane of black hair, the thick short moustache, the small pointed beard. Above all, the eyes, the intensely intelligent eyes flickering through their rimless pince-nez. They were separated by an unusually broad bridge of nose.

Uncle Alex's eyes were set wide apart, too. But they were not, she knew, the eyes of an intellectual. They were rather gay ; they could look sideways at a woman quite fetchingly.

Were Uncle Alex's eyes really like that ? She did not know. That was the picture she had built up for herself with the aid of the photograph in the album. She would like to find out what he was really like, what they were all really like—

the old grandfather ; and the other uncle, Leon, the studious one ; and her grandfather's wife, Shevka, the villainess of the piece. Or wasn't it Shevka's daughter, Gallia, who was really the villainess of the piece ? It was when Gallia wore the famous pearls to lure a lover that the world went black for poor Hannah ; for her mother, that is to say, away across the seas and the centuries, in England, in Doomington.

It was odd. She had a good deal to think about. Yet her thoughts came back again and again to the family in Terkass, to the apricot-tree that still blossomed, or blossomed no more, in the Dobkin orchard. How could she prevent her thoughts wandering now and again, when she worked so regularly till deep in the night, month after month, without respite—excepting for her occasional furtive attendances at the Trotsky shrine ? How had her people come through the War ? Had any of her cousins been revolutionaries all along, like Boris and herself ? Would there be any harm in trying to get into touch with them ? She did not see what there was against it. She asked Boris. She waited her moment carefully, when something had happened to make him look quite genial, some tactical victory or other that the Bolsheviks had scored over their opponents in the Soviet.

" Boris, look here. I've been wondering. Do you think there'd be any harm in my trying to get into touch with my family in Terkass ? Perhaps some of the younger people——"

" Susan ! " His face did not look in the least genial. " I thought I'd made it clear to you what I think about that ! "

" Have you ? Not altogether, Boris. We could do it through the Party, if you like, at Kiev. There could be nothing wrong with that."

" I thought you were a sensible woman. I wish you'd get this nonsense out of your head. Don't you see ? Your grandfather's a rich peasant. So is his son, the farmer. The other one's a merchant, a bourgeois. It's politically foolish to have anything to do with people of that sort. Do you think that just because you're related to them——"

" I was hoping that perhaps the younger people have brought them over into the Revolution."

" I'm taking no chances. Neither are you. Don't you realise who *you* are, too ? Don't you realise that you, with your father, have particular need to be careful ? Don't be an idiot, I tell you ! "

She looked surlily down on to her bony lap. She felt a blush creep along her rather spotty cheeks.

" I suppose you're right," she said.

" Mind you," he went on, " there's always this. If ever you should be down that way, I don't suppose it would be fatal to look in and see what's happened to them."

" All right," she agreed heavily. " If ever I'm down that way."

Yes, it was strange. After that conversation Terkass and those people seemed further than they had ever been before. Boris, too, seemed further. He sometimes seemed—how should she put it ?—as if he had sprung from the loins of no race, with no family in the half-background, no father or mother even. He seemed—she thought it with admiration and fear— like something concocted in a laboratory. And, indeed, it was exactly such men as he that a revolution needed, if it were not also the intention of a revolution to produce such men as he.

II

It had been a comparatively easy matter for the Bolsheviks to seize the government ; it was a different matter to work it. It is likely that few political parties, on being called, or on calling themselves, to power, have ever been faced with difficulties so tremendous. Even in the big towns they could count on the support of only a small minority. They had no army, and, though their agitators were at work in every regiment they had nothing more to reckon upon than a profound war-weariness, a mood not propitious for the exchange of one military loyalty for another. Among the peasants they could reckon on the vague enormous appetite that was spread amongst them for the appropriation of the land, though this was formidably countered not only by the landlords, but by the middle peasants, the yeomanry, if it is not grotesque to attempt to render conditions in Russia through so purely English a concept. And the Kossacks in their various regions, whom the Tsarist system had maintained, as it could not help maintaining them, in a position of arrogant favouritism, could be counted on for a furious resistance. The food conditions of the country were bad, made the worse by the decrepitude of the railway system, which, in its turn, was aggravated by the perpetual crumbling of the front. There was still a direct external enemy. It could hardly be doubted that the general enmity, not only of the powers that had been recently allied to them, but of all the powers of the opposite system, would mobilise itself against an idea that struck at the very roots of their nature. The mobilisation would express itself, the Bolsheviks anticipated, in various forms—boycott, propaganda, military intervention. At the same time as they were destroying an old system of society and building up a new one, they found themselves fighting on a front of eight thousand kilometres, deploying sixteen armies and numerous irregular formations against their enemies.

It would be no exaggeration to say concerning Boris Polednik that those events, in a real sense, were his sole existence. It would have been hard, in the days before his arrival in Russia, to say of a given moment of his day that it was not devoted to the service of his cause. It would have been harder, from the moment he set foot on the Finland Station platform, on that historic night of the arrival of Lenin. He ate, he drank, he slept. But he did those things exclusively for the further functioning of the political machine he was, and the military machine he became for a time. It would have been true, perhaps not quite so chemically true, to say the same thing concerning Susan, his wife. There were rare moments in which she was, so to speak, human. In other words, an element of incalculability manifested itself in her thoughts or her behaviour. The discovery frightened or shocked her. She was grateful if Boris were no witness of that moment's shame.

Yet it was because the Bolshevik Party, before and after its triumph, enlisted spirits so devoted, minds so acute, as the Poledniks, that it managed to face up to its unparalleled tasks, and to complete some of them, and they were spirits and minds often enough housed in quite second-rate bodies, some broken by previous exile or privation, many undermined by contemporary privation and overwork.

The seat of government was transferred from Petrograd to Moscow in the March that followed the second Revolution. Boris Polednik was called to Moscow some weeks later at the instance of the War Council. Susan remained in Petrograd, for there was a good deal of organisation to do in her own and affiliated trade unions. It would not, in any case, have occurred to either of them that she must necessarily go to Moscow because Boris was called there. They were not the sort of married people who feel it is difficult to continue living if they do not share the same bed regularly and dip their spoons in the same soup-plate.

Susan remained in Petrograd. She was happy, in a way, that she was going to be left on her own for a time. She would have the opportunity to prove herself. She was English by origin, a fact that some of the people she had come in contact with had found it difficult to gloss over entirely. Moreover, as Polednik had reminded her, it was not unknown who her father was—an exploiter of labour and a War capitalist. She could not disguise from herself the fact that it was clear her papers had been looked over during one or two of her absences in the country. She had a feeling that the house-porter registered her goings and comings with some attention.

She did not resent it. There was only one thing for her to do—not for her own sake, but for Boris's sake, or, rather, for the sake of the Revolution : that was, to work as hard as any woman in the Party—and she did ; till sometimes her fingers were quite numb on the keys of her typewriter and her eyes seemed to be starting from her head. But she continued. All day, all night, her typewriter pursued its inexorable revolutionary tattoo.

III

In the sixteen armies the Bolsheviks disposed upon their wide-scattered fronts, they absorbed a certain number of " specialists," as they were called—officers who had received their training under a system pledged to different loyalties from those they now undertook to serve. In their subsequent campaigns upon the industrial " fronts," the Bolsheviks were similarly constrained to borrow " specialists " from the rival system to enable them to establish their own. In both cases the process was accompanied by much contemporary and subsequent criticism. The military as well as the industrial "specialists," though often admitted to be loyal, were often accused of sabotage and treachery. The time has not yet arrived to estimate the degree of success the industrial campaigns have achieved. But there can be no disputing the success of the Red Armies ; and, whether the degree in which the " specialists " helped them was considerable or not, the fact remains that they were predominantly amateur.

The supreme commander, Trotsky, was an amateur, who had no contact of any sort with war, excepting for a month or two as a journalist. The years he might have spent, had he not been Trotsky, in the Tsar's armies, he spent in prison, in exile, and abroad. His commanders, his military commissars, were mainly amateurs like himself. The record of that shoemaker who later became a newspaper-essayist, and, between the practice of his two professions, in the period of Civil War, became a brilliant cavalry general, is typical.

Boris Polednik was one of a whole company of tailors who, without benefit of the West Points and Sandhursts, conceived strategy, directed tactics, in a manner which might have drawn gusts of praise from the professors in those academies.

The generals and chief officers of the armies opposed to them, the Krasnofs, the Yudenitches, the Denikins, the Wrangels, were the fine flower of orthodox professionalism ; but their science, buttressed by the capital funds of their political sponsors, seemed about as effective as a medicine-man's mumbo-jumbo against the manœuvres of these shoe-makers and tailors. The chroniclers of their exploits use flamboyant language regarding them ; but the tailors and the shoemakers themselves are more modest. They knew exactly what they were fighting for, they asserted ; their enemies did not. It was an ignorance more fatal to them than armies of opposing tanks or fleets of aeroplanes.

Boris Polednik served on several fronts and in several capacities during the Civil Wars, between the midsummer of 1918 and the spring of 1920. He served with Trotsky on the Volga Front when the Czecho-Slovakian corps, on its way to Vladivostok, turned and struck, was itself struck, and sent on its eastward journey again. Whether it was demanded from him that he should harangue a crumbling regiment till it coalesced again in a molten mass of revolutionary ardour, or to take charge of a torpedo-boat during a night-raid, he performed the duty simply and efficiently, realising it to be the florescence in the light of day from those roots whose subterranean existence he and his comrades had nourished for so many laborious and dangerous years.

Early in the following year he was active among the Red troops who occupied Riga ; a month or two later he was in command of a flying train sent to harry the advance of Denikin's White Army towards Rostof and Tcherkask. Two or three months later he was on the Dnieper, attacking, being hurled back, attacking again. He saw service in regions half a world apart, in Poland and Vladivostok. He was present at defeats and victories. But he saw the victory of his cause prevail. He was thereafter requested to take his place on a swivel-chair in an office, seated before an enormous Empire bureau and a Remington typewriter. This, too, he did, simply and efficiently, in the due time, as he had once carried summonses to illegal meetings among the folds of cloth he carried from the Kiev warehouse, as he had once gone out against a Kossack sortie, single-handed, swinging a rifle he hardly knew how to use, in order to whip up the courage of a gang of peasant boys recently recruited from their black fields.

It is not stated by the bitterest opponents of the Bolshevik régime that there was any official Terror in Russia before the attempt of Dora Kaplan, a Social Revolutionary, to assassinate Lenin in August 1918. But there were a number of Bolsheviks who were convinced from the beginning that, in the nature of the case, a Terror was from the beginning inevitable. They believed it a sentimental delusion that the nature and the balance of forces in society could be fundamentally changed without a measure of organised bloodletting. They believed that a short sharp Terror early on would have dispensed with the necessity for a long rancorous Terror later on.

Boris Polednik was one of these. Mistrust of the opponents of his cause was with him a passion second only to his ardour for the cause and those supporters of it he believed in. Where he had once seen *agents provocateurs* he now saw spies. He could not bring himself to believe that any inheritance from the system that October had overthrown was not rotten, counter-revolutionary. Whenever an initiative was placed in his hands, he would have nothing to do, if it was at all possible, with the military " specialists " who had been inherited from the old Army. When he became an official, he sought as strenuously to have no dealings with the survivors, such as they were, of the old intelligentsia and the old bourgeoisie. Spies, spies, they were all spies during the time of the fighting. They prevented supplies and reinforcements from getting to the front ; they conveyed information to the enemy within and beyond the frontiers. The offence of the spies later was sabotage. They insinuated gravel into the bearings of machinery. They caused derailings and overflowings. The whole country swarmed with spies.

It is possible that Polednik exaggerated the amount of mischief for which spies were responsible, first in the fighting, and, later, in the economic upbuilding of the country. But that is explicable. He, like many of his colleagues, had lived a subterranean existence for so many years that when at length his Party triumphed, it was impossible for him not to believe that the ground was not being undermined in every direction by the burrowing of just such rodents as he had himself been. In moments of strain the whole landscape seemed to billow like water with their sunken heavings.

An episode occurred during the march of the Kossack general, Krasnof, on Petrograd, immediately after the dislodgement from power of Kerensky by the October Revolution, an episode which made him chalk-pale with fury whenever he remembered it. Informed that Krasnof was already at Petrograd, already at the Narvsky Gate, the cadets of the Vladimir Revolutionary Academy revolted against the new power. It fell to Polednik to suppress the revolt. The suggestion was made that it would be safer to keep them locked up and strongly guarded within the walls of the Academy, as the crowd of soldiers, sailors, and workers that had gathered was so ominous. Precisely because the crowd was so ominous, Polednik determined to march the prisoners down the Bolshoy Prospekt into the city. He felt that here was a moment which, if it were rightly used, would teach a salutary lesson to the enemies of the Revolution.

And, indeed, a moment came when it seemed impossible that the mob could be any longer withheld from exacting its dreadful payment from the pale band of youths, who seemed all the paler because they had chosen to wear, as if ceremoniously, their most shining uniform. It was in that moment that a courier on a motor-bicycle handed over orders of the utmost stringency to Polednik. The convoy was to make a detour at once for the Pelvovsky Park ; the bridges were to be strictly guarded ; no harm was to befall the rebels.

The rebels were, in fact, released to a man. The greater part of them made their way to the south. So did any number of younger and elder officers from the armies of the deposed Tsar. They formed the nucleus of the armies of Denikin, of Yudenitch, and of the other White generals, which on more than one occasion seemed as if they could not fail to bring the Bolshevik power to the dust.

" There would have been no Denikin," muttered Boris Polednik, " there would have been no Civil War, if we hadn't been such fools ! If we hadn't let those Vladimir cadets go, if we hadn't accepted Krasnof's word of honour when we captured him that he'd never take up arms against us, if we hadn't been as soft as schoolgirls——"

" You mean ? " asked Susan.

" I mean ? Of course I mean—they should have been shot to a man ! Or thrown to the crowd to do what they liked with them ! Revolution has a right to its victims ! If you don't give it its dozens soon, it'll have its thousands later ! "

" Of course ! " said Susan. " You're quite right ! " She preferred not to see for too long that expression in his eyes— a certain malevolence, a certain lust, that made her scalp go icy. It was no strange thing to her. It was in his eyes sometimes when he told her of the infinite wranglings of the Petrograd Soviet, in the days before the Bolsheviks attained chief power in it. She recalled it in the old days, in the Silver kitchen in Doomington, when the prating anarchists came together. There was such a tension in his clenched fists that the knuckles went pale as ash. A hard light flared up in the centre of his eyes, white and hard like the low jet of an acetylene burner. But it was most desolating when he spoke of those overt enemies that they had allowed to slip through their fingers, or the secret enemies, the spies, the spies. The whole country crawled with them.

He had a tale of a spy to tell her one day early in 1919. He met her in Petrograd a day or two after the affair of the spy. It had happened in a train travelling to Moscow from the east, by way of Vologda, the junction for Petrograd. Polednik and his orderly, a certain Kronstadt sailor, Zhatkin by name, had boarded it at Jaroslavl, some distance south of Vologda. Of the two, only Polednik got off at Moscow, when the train, or a revised version of the train, pulled up at the Alexandrof Station. It was by the merest chance that Polednik, and not Zhatkin, was not left behind on the railway-line, in a gutted carriage, a charred heap of bones among a mound of bones.

Polednik lost the few things he had with him. It might have been thought, too, he had suffered a certain shock. But he was not susceptible to shock—that sort of shock, at least. It did not occur to him to wait on in Moscow, having been ordered to proceed straight to Petrograd. He handed over a woman prisoner to the station authorities and handed in an official report of what had occurred at headquarters. Then he went straight on. He was able to let Susan know only a day or two after it happened, therefore, the tale of the spy who was now one spy the less.

Susan expressed no surprise when Polednik arrived. He had not been to Petrograd for months, and for all she knew would not be in Petrograd for months again. But he and she did not indulge in the small courtesies of sending each other wires or meeting each other at stations, unless the job in hand called for it.

" But you've got some luggage ? " she asked.

" I had a small bag," he told her. " It got burned in the train."

" In the train ? Where ? "

" Oh, about twenty versts outside Moscow, this side of Pushkino."

" How did that happen ? What a nuisance ! Did you lose anything valuable ? "

" I lost some papers which it's going to cost me a lot of trouble to make out again. And I had two of my good English shirts with me, too. I won't be able to make those good in a hurry."

" Hasn't Zhatkin come with you this time ? You don't seem to move a step without your Zhatkin."

" Yes, he was a good fellow, a revolutionary through and through. I'm sorry about Zhatkin."

" What ? " she asked quietly. " Did they find something out about Zhatkin, too ? Is that possible ? "

" No, no ! Don't be stupid ! He was burned in the fire, I mean ! "

" For heaven's sake, Boris, tell me what you're talking about ! You lost your luggage, and Zhatkin, in a fire in a train ? It sounds frightful ! What *are* you talking about ? "

" Just that ! A fire in a train ! "

She was getting quite angry now. He, for his part, was having rather a good time. He was obviously enjoying himself. He didn't usually waste words when he had any information to impart, but there was clearly something in the train business which had given him, and was still giving him, a lot of pleasure.

" Sit down, Boris ! " she said. " For God's sake get up to the point ! "

" For God's sake," he mocked her, " let me ! " She never succeeded in keeping, and even he sometimes failed to keep, bourgeois concepts—like God, for instance—out of conversation. " This is what happened. Zhatkin and I joined the train at Rostof-Yaroslavski. We got into the first carriage. We'd not had anything to eat all day, so Zhatkin got busy and managed to get some food from somewhere. I'll miss him for that. He'd smell out a bottle of something and a bite to eat in the middle of the steppe. After that, I got down to my lists ; I've had the local Soviets busy for some time getting up lists of reliable Party members, the really sound returned soldiers and so on. Zhatkin slept for some time. He hadn't slept the night before. Neither had I. Then he woke up. I forget what station it was. I sent him off up the train, on his usual job."

" His usual job ? "

" Yes. Spies. I'm always on the look-out on trains. The train's a good place for spies. You get them off their guard." He drew in his lips so tightly that he seemed to have no lips at all. " They get so tired, sometimes, with the slow trains and the great distances. Sometimes you get them talking in their sleep."

" What happened ? Did the train catch fire ? Where were you ? "

" Gently, Susan, gently. I was talking about spies. I went on working. Zhatkin went prowling up and down the train. A careful fellow ; I'll miss him."

" Did he find anything ? "

Polednik's expression changed. " He did ! " he rapped out. His pince-nez twinkled evilly. " He did ! The swine won't do any more spying now ! "

" You shot him then and there, I suppose ? "

" Oh, no ! Oh, no ! I didn't waste a bullet on *him*. I didn't need to ! " His small teeth showed for a moment, white and pointed. He rubbed his hands with pleasure. " Let me go on ! It was at a station well on the other side of Pushkino. Zhatkin lumbered into my carriage. He was rather like a big ape, Zhatkin. You remember, his hands seemed to hang down to the ground. I've seen him strangle a White Guard officer just about as quickly as a dog breaks a rat's neck. As I was saying, he came into my carriage and lifted his finger to his mouth. I knew what that meant. I put the papers away into my case and ordered the guard to look after it. I then followed Zhatkin to a carriage some distance down the train. We got in separately, of course, as if we hadn't anything to do with each other. He made a movement with his head. I knew at once who he meant. I thought it best to send Zhatkin back to the first carriage. I didn't want those papers to go astray and I wasn't too sure about the guard I asked to look after them. Besides, it's easier for one person to hang about listening than two.

" So he went off. And I hung about. What sort of a man was he? He was tall. He had fair hair ; you could call it golden, if you like—sickening. Like a pretty man in a play. Excepting that he'd got rather a nasty scar from his nose down to his chin. It may have been a bit of shell. It also looked like a duelling-scar. I shouldn't be at all surprised if it was that. The man was German, pure Prussian, the purest Junker Prussian. It wasn't at all a clean scar, so it may even have been a bit of both. Pure Junker Prussian ! " Polednik repeated. His voice became thin with wrath. " The insolence ! The clumsiness ! Poor fumbling amateur from Potsdam ! But let me go on ! I sat down on the floor. I pretended to be asleep. Oh, I was very patient. Then he and the woman he was sitting next to started talking again, quite low at first, and then a little louder as they warmed to it."

" The woman? What woman? "

" No, I've not really got to the woman yet. She's alive still. I'll find out all about her when I get back to Moscow."

" Was she a spy too? "

" Of course she was. She wept and she squealed and she tore her blouse off, she got so excited. And then came the shout, suddenly, all down the train—' Fire ! Fire ! '

" But I'm going too fast. As I say, the man and the woman started talking again. They'd been talking earlier on, obviously, and then they stopped. Perhaps one of them dozed off. Or they didn't like the look of me. But I foxed them. Soon they were at it hammer and tongs. They talked Russian at first. She talked perfectly. He spoke badly, with a strong accent. I recognised the accent at once. German, of course."

" Was he dressed as a soldier ? "

" No, he was in civilian clothes. So was I, of course, or

he wouldn't have opened his mouth. I prefer civilian clothes on train journeys. I've often found them useful. It was stuff he'd got in Russia—a black alpaca blouse, elastic-sided boots, and the rest. He'd tried to let his beard grow as Russian-looking as possible. His hair and beard were quite rough. He'd come a long way. From Siberia, I imagine. I heard him say that when they got to Ekaterinburg they changed and had to wait two days for the trans-Siberian express. Then he'd spent the next five days in a corridor, till things got easier, at Vologda.

" Before long he got so excited he forgot he was a Russian. That's what I mean about long journeys. Sometimes even the most practised spies get silly from want of sleep and say far more than they ever intended to. And these two weren't *good* spies. Oh, no, far from it. As I say, he got so excited, he forgot he was a Russian. He started talking German. She talked German, too, but not so well as he did. I'm sure *she's* a Russian. I got it out of her—that was later on—that her husband was a major-general in the old Army. I shouldn't be in the least surprised if it was true—not in the least surprised. Then they talked French. Oh, they played quite a game of languages. Then he offered her some sausage. And he said he had a great luxury—some *Zwieback* ; wouldn't she have some ? She squeaked with pleasure. Then she took out a little bottle of scent. Pah ! It was filthy ! You might have thought we were in Peterhof back in the year 1913. Then she sprinkled a few drops of scent on her handkerchief and dabbed his forehead with it. . . .

" I'd had quite enough. I got up. I turned to them. I took out my revolver. ' Who are you ? ' I said.

" He didn't like it, I suppose. His face went quite green under the tan ; but he didn't move a muscle. ' Would you like to see my papers, *tovarish* ? ' he said. ' I think you'll find them quite in order.'

" ' I would ! ' I said. ' Bring them out ! '

" He brought out his passport. I've never seen such a clumsy bit of work. I suppose there are not many greater authorities on forged passports than me in Russia to-day."

" No," said Susan. " I shouldn't think so."

" No, I shouldn't either," he corroborated. If you could ever have accused Polednik of vanity, you could have accused him at that moment. He jerked his head from side to side like a cock.

" He had the forged passport of a Galician prisoner. You know, don't you, that we allow our Galician prisoners to travel up and down the country as they please ? They're supposed to be friendly to us. The stupidity of it ! I've brought the matter up time after time. Perhaps they'll listen to me now ! "

" Wasn't he ? "

" Of course he wasn't ! The way he pointed out his row of faked counterstamps was enough to give him away. *Galician !* Pooh ! You might as well have said Hindoo ! "

" ' Where are you from ? ' I asked him. He was quite pat. ' From Peludska. Not far from Lemberg ! '

" That was a little unlucky. You remember I once spent four months near Lemberg ? It was in a village two or three miles away from Peludska. Yes, there *is* such a place. I asked him one or two questions about it. How many churches were there ? What was the name of the square ? He tried to bluff for a minute or so. Then he smiled. I almost liked him at that moment. He handed over his passport to me. ' I am a German,' he said. ' I am an officer from Mecklenburg. My name is '—he gave me his name. Von something-or-other, a double name, it sounded like. It doesn't matter what he said. Partly because it obviously wasn't his name. Partly because he's dead."

" Dead ? "

" Yes, I'm coming to that."

" Is there any chance it might have been his name ? You'd caught him fair and square ! Why should he lie about it ? Not that it matters, of course ! "

" ' Liar ! ' I said to him. He looked quite nasty. Then he went on to tell me he had escaped from an internment camp in Siberia—a place called Vitomir, I think he said. It may have been true, and what if it was ? Does that make him any less a spy ? He *was* a spy ! You can trust my instinct in these matters ! "

" Yes, I know."

" He then went on to insist he was a complete stranger to the woman he'd been talking to. She was howling at the top of her voice by this time.

" ' That may or may not be true,' I said. ' There's quite a lot I want to find out about you both.' There were two or three Red soldiers away down the carriage. I ordered them to come up and complete the party. Then I turned out the old man and woman who'd been sitting opposite all this time, and settled down to a good long talk.

" A minute or two later the train slowed down and drew up at a station—Pushkino, it was. Zhatkin came up the line and climbed into the carriage. He saw at once how the situation lay. He grinned all over his face.

" And then—and then.... No, I won't be such a fool. It would be idiotic to say that I had a sort of presentiment. I felt—oh, curiously settled, in that compartment. There was no doubt about the man. I wanted to find out about the woman. It occurred to me that she'd be easier to handle if I sent the German off. He'd be giving her a sense of confidence which it would be useful to undermine. Besides, it's advisable to split up your suspects, and face them up to their contradictions later on. I sent him off with Zhatkin and one of the soldiers to my original carriage. I knew the German would be quite safe with Zhatkin. The train started. I got down to my little talk with the lady. Her papers seemed quite all right, but that, of course, didn't prove she wasn't a spy. It was quite enjoyable ; we had such a lot to talk about. But she seemed to get more upset the more I tried to be nice to her. I told you, she got quite hysterical at one moment ; she simply tore her blouse off."

" Yes," said Susan. Her voice had no edge to it.

" And then . . . and then . . . I don't know what came

first. Whether it was the sharp cry, ' Fire ! Fire ! ' that went down the train like a series of explosions. Or was it a quick smack of heat on the face ? Or did the night seem to open a door suddenly, like the door in a furnace ? The brakes shrieked. The train shivered all down its length and stopped. At once everybody lost their heads. They started flinging luggage out of the windows, themselves out of the doors, howling, howling like dogs. I got out somehow. I still held fast to my woman, of course. I reached the first carriage. It was a roaring mass of flame and hands tearing and bodies rolling, stuck to each other already in a gluey mass of burned flesh.

" I'd like to know what it was. A spark landing on that rotten wood was quite enough to set it going. You know what the coal's like these days, *and* the rolling stock. Or do you think it's possible . . . ? Is it possible *he* could have had something to do with it ? "

His mouth twisted like a worm as he asked again ! " Do you think he could ? Could he have managed it ? "

" I don't know," she whispered faintly.

" But he won't—never again ! There he was, I saw him quite clearly. His face—oh, it was a good sight ! Zhatkin was still beside him. Zhatkin couldn't have got out, even if he'd wanted to. The carriage was jammed by a mass of bodies all alight like torches. He didn't want to get out. His orders were to stay by the prisoner. He was a good fellow, Zhatkin. But he saw me across the window. ' *Tovarish* Polednik ! ' he called out very clearly. I can still hear him. It was upsetting. Then he said something more ; I couldn't hear the words. He wanted something. It was the first time he'd ever asked me anything. But I knew just what it was he wanted. I took out my revolver and shot him through the forehead. It occurred to me to put a bullet through the head of the other fellow, too. He looked at me rather as if he wanted me to. And then I thought better of it. He was done for, anyway ; there was no point wasting a good bullet on him. I saw him just crumple up, like a match-box in flames.

" What ? What, Susan, are you shivering about ? Don't be such an idiot ! Pull yourself together ! All right, if you've had enough of it. Hell fire, what's come over you lately ? "

" It is a little grim, isn't it, Boris ? And you yourself—it's after all only by the oddest chance. . . . I think you'd best— just let me know what happened ! "

" All right then. The soldiers took the cue. The soldiers shot those who weren't dead yet, excepting half a dozen or so who weren't fatally injured. But it would have been much more sensible to have put a bullet through their heads too. They're not going to be any use to anybody again. The fire had spread to two other carriages, but they managed to uncouple the rest of the train. A pack of wolves had come up out of the darkness by this time, the devil knows where from. All the luggage had been hurled out into the snow. It was a foot or two thick, did I tell you ? That's what made it all the queerer—the blazing train and the thick snow. The wolves—they were just like wolves—were slinking off with the luggage in every direction. The passengers went flopping after them like madmen into the snow, crying and tearing their hair. The soldiers stopped a few of the thieves, but a lot of the luggage disappeared. There was no question of going on that night, of course. The train had been crowded enough already ; it was quite impossible to get everybody into the remaining carriages. So we cleared the snow round the smouldering wreck and made a night of it. It was impossible to come too near, because it took your skin off : yet, however near you got, your back was frozen dead. It was a bad night. The relief train didn't come till late next morning. I delivered my woman to the Red Guard at the Alexandrof Station, and made out my report, and came straight on here.

" I'm hoarse, Susan. I've talked too much. Is there anything to drink in the place ? "

IV

Boris Polednik had not made a careful note of the name which the German spy had given himself. He knew it already. Among the young rebels of the Vladimir Military Academy in Petrograd he had not sought to distinguish one from the other. He knew their names already. He attempted no more than summarily to establish the names of the *mouzhik*, the one-time lawyer, the priest, who were brought before him during the campaigns, accused of espionage, and then and there put up before a wall and shot. He knew their real name.

Their name was Alexander Smirnof. In a dreadfully real sense, it was no illusion that Boris Polednik saw Alexander Smirnof, that night of Lenin's arrival at Petrograd, among the crowd, standing over against the lamp-post. He saw Alexander Smirnof sure enough. He was the spy, the *agent provocateur* that had been, the eternal enemy, hovering among the tree-trunks at the edge of the clearing. He saw him again and again during the time of the agony of Russia, from Kiev to Vladivostok, from Archangel to Odessa. He saw him, and that pinpoint of hard light flared up in the centre of his eyes, his heart thumped against his ribs with the demon insistence of a tom-tom in murderous jungles.

Two or three months after the episode of the train, he established a less metaphysical contact, so to speak, with Alexander Smirnof ; but what it lost in psychological poignancy it gained in exterior vividness, in singularity of detail. For, clearly, the handsome young captain of Kuban Kossacks, Yefimof, was Yefimof and not Smirnof. And yet the conversation with Yefimof proved, if it had needed proof, that Smirnof in Russia was no bogey engendered in his own mind, but a danger alert and real as a serpent, unseizable as a belt of poisoned vapours on the horizon.

The incident took place in the third week of April 1919. The White general, Denikin, was mobilising his forces at

Taganrog, on the Sea of Azov. A British Military Mission
had been despatched by Mr. Winston Churchill to give him
every assistance, moral, intellectual, and material. It was
the duty of the Mission to receive and distribute British war-
material among Denikin's forces, and to instruct them in the
use of the tanks and aeroplanes which had been generously
lent to them. The Red troops had advanced in February as
far as the Lower Don and the Manitsch, but the flooding of
the rivers had compelled them to suspend their activity. It
was decided at Moscow that an offensive should now, in
April, be launched on the South Front, before the British
support should definitely tilt the balance in Denikin's favour.
The Red offensive held Denikin up for only a brief time. In
June he had occupied Kharkof, in August Odessa and
Kiev ; in October he was at Orel, threatening Moscow
itself.

And when news came to Boris Polednik, whether through
the wireless on his armed propaganda train or where he
crouched in some Ukrainian peasant's hut, the telephone-
headpiece round his ears, the triumph of Denikin was the
triumph of Alexander Smirnof. But it was from Captain
Yefimof, the handsome Kuban Kossack, he learned one
thing more concerning his enemy—that he was, in fact,
Denikin's friend. He learned other things, too, concerning
him.

A body of Red troops was manœuvring on the River
Manitsch. It had been reported to Boris Polednik, who was
the Commissar to a regiment engaged in these operations,
that a White armoured train was advancing north. In those
vast areas it was not unusual for detachments from either
side to penetrate into the enemy's area, without knowledge
of the danger, or, indeed, without harm actually transpiring.
On this occasion, too, it was reported that the White train
was blissfully unaware that it had left safe ground. As the
reports came in, it was manifest that their unawareness was
so blissful that they were treating the expedition rather as a
Kossack pleasure-party than a military operation.

While these gratifying reports were coming in, Polednik and his men were drawing nearer and nearer to the enemy. They made use of the river, which for some distance in this neighbourhood ran at a slight distance from the railway-line beyond a belt of pines. In this way the enemy's retreat was cut off. They made use of one or two cavalry motor units. It was a dexterously and silently executed manœuvre.

But it need not have been quite so silent. For if they had advanced with drums and bugles they would hardly have attracted attention to themselves. The whole train-load of officers and men was quite drunk. A number lay snoring up against the upholstered backs of the carriages ; for this was a White train, and the amenities of civilised travel had not been disregarded. But the greater part of them were assembled in a clearing between the railway-line and the pine-wood. At this point, in fact, the trees obligingly withdrew, to leave a charming circular meadow not unlike the stage of a vast metropolitan theatre.

Most of the officers wore the Circassian national coats, though some wore Kornilof's uniform, a skull and cross-bones sewn upon their sleeves. To Polednik, looking on through the trees not without pleasure, the uniform of the men seemed oddly familiar. He realised it was identical, except for the minor matter of badges, with the uniform of the British private soldier.

The Whites would not have heard Polednik if he had approached with noise, because they were making noise enough on their own account. An officer was playing an accordion with magnificent verve. A group of his fellow-officers was dancing a wild Kossack dance even more magnificently. Others were clapping their hands to the mad rhythm, shouting " Ho ! Ho ! Ho ! Ho ! " as if they would crack their throats. Others could not clap because the harlots that lay snuggled up against their bosoms gave other occupations to their hands. The cheeks of all of them flared like poppies. Their eyes were almost as red as their cheeks. They were having a good time.

At the edge of the clearing, beyond the circle of the clappers and shouters, there was a heap of six or seven bodies, bound together by ropes and stuck together with their own blood. It was discovered later that these were a handful of Jews and Communists. The White train on its northward journey had overtaken a stranded train full of little peasants and shopkeepers at a small station. The Whites were not so drunk as they became next day ; but it occurred to them here was a good opportunity for a Jew-and-Communist hunt. It was a disappointing bag—not more than six or seven. It was easy to make certain which were Jews. This they did, lewdly and delightedly. The Communists were not so fool-proof, but it didn't matter in the least if they made a mistake or two. Their ankles and wrists were tied with lariats ; they were then thrown on to a truck.

The train proceeded, stopping now and again for a little merrymaking beside the track. But when the big party took place, it was felt that it would not be so good a party as it might be if a little killing were not thrown in. The prisoners were jerked out of their truck and their heads smashed in with rifle-butts, amid the uproarious mirth of the revellers. The mirth became more and more up- roarious. Then Boris Polednik requested two of his men to choose Kossacks they did not like and shoot them. This was done, then the Red troops came out into the open.

The train-load of Kossacks was captured to a man. The personnel included a goodly bevy of harlots and an opera- singer ; for Captain Yefimof, who was in charge of the train, liked music as well as fornication. He was, in fact, thoroughly a man of the world, perhaps even more a man of the world than a soldier. He even had a troupe of acrobats with him, for he did not know how he might go into action without a troupe of acrobats. He also had an extensive library of gay French novels.

Boris Polednik had quite an interesting talk with Captain Yefimof an hour or two later, before shooting him. They held the talk in Captain Yefimof's own carriage, unless you called it a boudoir. For his harlots and his opera-singer had the free run of it, and powder-puffs and scent-bottles and pomades lay about all over the place. As a matter of fact, the toilette delicacies were by no means all theirs. Captain Yefimof was a strapping creature, six feet several inches in height, but he used almost as much scent and grease as they. In fact, before he and Polednik settled down to their little talk he begged with infinite politeness if he might put some lotion on his hair. Recent events had disordered it a little. Polednik said he might. Whereupon he rubbed in a grease, then poured on a liquor, then sprayed a spray, upon his black hair till it was smooth and sleek as a seal. He knew that he would almost certainly be shot after the conversation, but he saw no reason why he should be shot with his hair untidy.

" My dear fellow," said Yefimof, settling himself more comfortably against a cushion, " if I were you I'd give it up. The fact is, you haven't got a dog's chance. A cigarette ? Mind if I smoke ? "

" Smoke, please ! I won't have one ! "

" You don't *really* think you have ? " asked Yefimof, crossing his legs. " A dog's chance, I mean ? "

" We're not here to discuss politics. You know what I want from you."

" I think you must know that I'm going to give you no military information that might be of use to you. Oh, I know, my dear fellow, I know, what's going to happen to me if I don't. We've discussed that already. Or if I do. So we'll wipe all that out, shall we ? "

" If it does you good to talk, talk ! "

" Did you ever hear of a Russian who refused an opportunity to talk ? And I rather think it's a pleasure I shan't be able to indulge in much in future. I've just been having a delightful time with the British, down in Taganrog. A dull little place ; do you know it ? Not a woman on the street, not a sail on the sea, absolutely nothing to buy—dreadful ! But it's where the writer, Tchekof, lived ; did you know that ? No, I thought perhaps you didn't. Anyhow, I had a perfectly delightful time at the British Mess. Who says the English can't talk ? And what good linguists they are ! Do you happen to know England ? "

" Yes. I've spent some time in England."

" Of course. You Bolsheviks were travelling about for years, here, there, everywhere, before you came back to Russia. Do you know Paris, too ? *I've* been to Paris. And Berlin, too ? And Vienna ? And Geneva ? Oh, how I envy you ! I've only been to Berlin and Paris. And Nice, of course. I had a delightful time at Nice. Oh, by the way, you don't happen to have anything to drink hanging round ? I know that we're quite cleaned out in here ! "

" I could get you some tea made."

" Oh, no. No, thank you. It's been dreadful lately, this shortage of vodka. The shifts people have had to go to to be able to offer drinks round ! I was invited on board one of our own ships, with the British officers. This was on the Sea of Azov, of course, outside Taganrog. We came off blind drunk ; blind drunk, I tell you. And do you know where they'd got the drink from ? They told us themselves, later. It was a terrific joke. They'd drained the anti-freezing spirit from the big reserve compass. Isn't that funny ? I ask you—er—er—*tovarish*—that's the right way to address you, isn't it ?—isn't that funny ? "

" What are you telling me all this for ? "

" Well, frankly, I don't quite know. Oh, yes, partly to pass the time. And then it all takes me back to where we started from. You remember ? "

" I don't know what you mean."

" I said, my dear fellow, you haven't got a dog's chance. To begin with—forgive my putting it this way—you're only a pack of Jews."

" I don't think that's accurate."

" Oh, yes, I know. You've roped in some others."

" I don't think we need discuss the race-origins of the members of the Communist Party."

" I quite admit it. Nothing could be less profitable. Excuse me." He reached for a nail-file. " Thank you. But the fact is," he resumed, " you've got the world against you."

" Not the world. Not the workers. Only the capitalists."

" But, of course, the capitalists—the French, the English, the Germans, the Americans—the whole world. I think you'll find it's the capitalists who count. It's the capitalists who've got the ships, the tanks, the aeroplanes. What use against tanks and aeroplanes are a horde of workers with chisels and saws ? "

" You'll find out."

" No, not I, I think. Or am I mistaken ? "

" I don't think you're mistaken."

" No ? Very well, then. Look at this man I was sent to see in Taganrog. Denikin himself sent me. He's a natural-ised Englishman now. But he was born a Russian, and a Russian he remains, till the last man of you is put up against a wall and shot. They'll probably have to adopt much quicker ways of getting rid of you than shooting you singly. There are too many of you now. Machine-guns, probably."

" This man," asked Polednik. His voice was hoarse and faint. " This man, what's his name ? "

Yefimof was for the moment wrapped up in his own thoughts. He found them rather attractive. Then his mind returned to the subject of the Russian who had become a naturalised Englishman.

" His uncle, you know, was educated at the same military academy as Denikin. His father was a priest, I understand. A very good White Russian family. You wouldn't think it to look at him ; a big bulby sort of man, he is, with a faint smear of reddish hair above the ears—but very delightful, so hospitable and charming. And a great business-man, I believe. I beg your pardon, what were you saying ? "

" His name is Alexander Smirnof ? "

" Yes. How on earth do you know ? What's the matter with you, my good fellow ? "

Polednik's heart seemed suddenly to become visible, to be outside him, leaving the vault of ribs empty. It had the appearance of a red sphere rolling away from him towards an abyss. It trembled for a moment on the sheer edge. He exerted all he had of will-power. It felt as if his teeth must be dislodged from their sockets, he clenched his jaws so tightly together. His heart now was back behind the ribs again, beating steadily.

" I've had information about the man," said Polednik.

" I see," smiled Yefimof. " Rather discouraging, wasn't it ? Your information, I mean ? And of course big business all over the world feels exactly as he does. And what big business feels, the politicians feel. All those millions of foreign capital invested in Russia—they won't get a smell of it till they've wiped *you* out."

" That's quite true," said Polednik grimly. He had resumed complete control of himself. " So Mr. Smirnof was in good form ? "

" First rate. He's lately pulled off a big deal with one or two of the Governments that had dumps of war-material in Salonica ; including his own, I believe, the British Government. You know, perhaps, do you ? "

" Yes."

" They were making such a fuss of him at the officers' mess. He was quite the big noise at Taganrog. Funny, wasn't it ? "

" Why ? "

" Oh, he was quite frank about it. Some years before the War he tried to set up business there in Taganrog. And in Baku. And in Batum, over on the other side. He just couldn't bring it off. And now—there he is ; or *was*, rather ; heaven knows where he is by now—there he was, the big noise at

Taganrog. There's been a certain amount of friction between the British naval people at Constantinople and the
military mission at Taganrog. It might have been quite
serious if not for this gentleman."

Polednik's eyes glittered behind the pince-nez. The
young man was blathering rather as he had hoped. The
young man himself had an uncomfortable moment in
which he felt that perhaps he was being a little too loquacious.

" Talking a little, aren't I ? " he admitted friendlily.
" And I assure you I'm dead sober."

Polednik said not a word. There was silence for half a
minute. The young man felt it weigh rather heavily.

" You'll understand, of course," he said, " it's rather
fun to feel the tongue wagging when you know it's going
out of business altogether in about half an hour. Half an
hour, would you say ? "

" About that."

The young man seemed to search for some saliva among
his back teeth, then he swallowed it. Then he went on again,
quite cheerfully : " It'll not do us any harm, I think, if you
begin to realise what forces are drawn up against you. I don't
mean merely the obvious forces—soldiers, and sailors, and
aeroplanes. Your spies can find all that out for you. I mean
the secret forces, the big business-men—the Smirnofs, in
fact. All this war-material, he's simply *giving* it away to us,
just *giving* it away. Anything we need. He's a big manufacturer on his own account, too. You see those raincoats my
soldiers are carrying ? I believe he turns those out by the
million. There, that's one of them, my coat on the seat
beside you there."

Polednik recoiled from the garment as if it were a serpent.
Indeed, indeed, the serpent had crawled forth a long way
from his lair in Doomington.

" My dear fellow," laughed Yefimof, " you *are* jumpy. It
won't bite you ! "

" No."

"As I was saying, anything we need. Our medical material, our tinned food—selling it us for a song, my dear fellow. You can imagine how pleased the general is."

"I can. Is there much more you'd like to say?"

"I say, did you really suggest I might have some tea?"

"I did. I'm going to have some made for myself."

"We'll have some together, shall we? Let's drink to *Tovarish* Smirnof!"

"Shut your mouth, will you, or I'll put a bullet through it here and now!"

"I beg your pardon. Very well then. We shall *not* drink to Mr. Smirnof! A match, please! The box is empty!"

CHAPTER XI

UNCLE ALEX

I

THE REVOLUTION was conscious of the scale upon which it was making history, and did not neglect to keep itself carefully documented even in its darkest hour. In the August of this same year, several months after the capture by Boris Polednik of Yefimof's train, Susan Polednik was transferred to a department of Revolutionary Archives. Among its duties was the formation of a collection of those newspapers, posters, proclamations, leaflets, which were promulgated during these internecine years by the various forces, from the largest to the smallest, from regular army corps to towsled bandit packs.

"We've already sent comrades to the Don fighting area and to the Ekaterinburg area," the official told her. "You might go up towards Minsk, which is at this moment threatened by the Whites. Or you might go into the Ukraine. Your husband is operating in that region, I understand. He knows the country well, doesn't he? There's a lot of material to be picked up in the Dnieper villages."

"Yes," said Susan. "Probably there more than anywhere else. You're right"—her voice remained quite matter-of-fact—"I believe my husband is down beyond Kiev somewhere. He knows the country well. He was born there."

She kept her voice and manner so cool because she knew that, if she showed any excitement, they would decide against sending her into the Ukraine area. They believed that work was more efficiently done when it was in no way bound up with personal emotion.

But it was not because her husband was working down

beyond Kiev somewhere that she was so excited by the
suggestion that had been made to her. She had not seen
him for several months, but, if nothing happened to him,
she would see him again sooner or later.

It was not that. It was the mention of the Dnieper villages. It was the thought of Terkass that had flashed behind
her eyes like a swallow.

The official was uttering certain warnings. He let her
know that it was not by any means plain sailing, the way
the rebel Headman Petlura, or the bandit, Makhno, suddenly swooped up out of nowhere. She wasn't listening quite
so intently as she ought. Her mind was repeating to itself
certain words that her husband had once uttered.

" Mind you," Boris Polednik said, " there's always this.
If ever you should be down that way, I don't suppose it
would be fatal to look in and see what's happened to
them."

It was hot in this room in the Petrograd back street. The
windows were open, but there was no wind. The traffic
clattered on the cobbles below.

There would be shade and quietness in the orchard of the
house in Terkass where her mother was born. She would
talk to her people, she would find out what was left of them
after War and Revolution and Civil War had wrought their
will on them. She would talk to them lying in the shade of
the apricot-tree in the evening.

" So you think you can get ready to go at once ? " they
asked her.

" To-night, if there's room on the train," she said.

A sense of humour is not to be expected from a revolution ;
and there was no one in Kiev, least of all Susan Polednik
herself, who saw how grimly humorous the spectacle of herself was, going about industriously, in the slums, in the
suburbs, in the little villages beyond, collecting material for
her department. It was grimly humorous in the way a

spectacle might be of a party of earnest young people dancing folk-dances or discussing meteorology, on the lip of a sullenly active volcano.

Kiev was exactly like that, those lurid August days, with a heavy bronze sky clapped down over the city like the lid of a cooking-pan. For the time being, Kiev was in the hands of the Bolsheviks. It was hoped by their friends, and feared by their enemies, that the Bolsheviks might stay on for some time now, might even establish themselves there permanently. For though Denikin was advancing everywhere, the peasant forces of Petlura, the " Partisans," as they were called, were giving him endless trouble in the Ukraine ; and the bandit, Makhno, driving from village to village at the head of his assassins in his magnificently caparisoned troika, kept cutting off Denikin's raw drafts the whole time with radiant promises of land and gold and deep baths of Jew-blood.

The Bolsheviks had done well in this region lately. They had cleared the railway-line and the river for some distance southward. It was in these actions that Boris Polednik had been engaged. But it seemed impossible to extirpate the guerilla bands, who, now bearing Petlura's banners, now Denikin's, now the banners of the Bolsheviks themselves, suddenly sallied forth from the forests, burnt a village, massacred its Jews, tore up the lines, and disappeared.

It was not to be wondered at, therefore, that heads slept uneasy in Kiev. Indeed few cities can have concentrated into a few years so mournful a tale. In the summer of 1918 the Germans had established themselves there, not without unkindness. An order—duly docketed in its place by Susan Polednik—was promulgated to the effect that any person who concealed arms would be punished by life imprisonment. In the house-to-house searches that followed, it was sometimes found convenient to convert life imprisonment to instant execution. Then Petlura, " Revolutionary and Friend of the People," appeared. There was bloody fighting in the streets, in which the citizens and their property suffered even

more than the combatants. Thereafter, the city was successively occupied by the Bolsheviks, by Petlura again, by the
Bolsheviks, by Petlura bandits—this time for just one day—
by Denikin, by the Bolsheviks.

It was during the intermediate Bolshevik occupation of
Kiev that Susan Polednik arrived there with her typewriter
and card indexes. She made the nucleus of a valuable revolutionary collection ; and, correctly divining that there would
be further changes in Kiev before the hammer and sickle
definitely established themselves, she did not store her
material in the Party offices. The sense of unease that the
inhabitants carried about with them all day, and took to
bed with them at night, conveyed itself to her. The very
flags in the pavement of the Krestchatik seemed to heave
slightly under her feet, as if the foundations of the city were
unsteady. At night, people locked and barred their doors,
for fear of what might happen. They drew the shutters to
against their windows, despite the sweltering heat, for fear of
the bullet that might come out of the void suddenly. In the
Podolskaya, the low-lying Jewish quarter by the river, the
folk lit no light in their rooms at night, so that, if the Terror
should come, it might pass them by in their darkness. On the
Bibikofski Boulevard, the rich folk thrust their jewels into
the down of their mattresses, and hid their silver plate in
sacks of potatoes in the attics.

Susan Polednik was uneasy. She was afraid, too. And it
did not take her long to realise that it was not for herself she
was afraid, though she had heard grisly tales ; not for herself she was uneasy.

What had happened to the people in Terkass ? She knew
that the Bolsheviks were now master of the river at Terkass,
and a good way beyond. But what had happened before ?
What was happening now ? She leaned out of her window,
almost gasping for breath. She still had a cool summer frock
from England in her trunk in Petrograd, why hadn't she
brought it with her ?

Phew ! It was hot in Kiev. There might be a breeze on the

broad river when the sun went down. Between green bluffs and low sandbanks the Dnieper thrust its floods southward. Here and there were woods along the river-banks. How cool their shade would be ! The next day she demanded authorisation from the local authorities to go to the villages a day or two's distance from Kiev down the river, to increase her collection of documents. They put no obstacle in her way. She could go down by river-steamer they told her. It was believed a skeleton service had just been restarted.

Susan was informed the steamer would start at nine o'clock. She arrived an hour or two early, for, though she had official papers from her department in Petrograd, she thought it would be useful to arrive in good time. On reaching the quay-side she realised that some hundreds, if not some thousands, of intending passengers had camped out all night on the dock, and in the adjacent streets, thinking, like her, it would be useful to arrive in good time. The passengers were for the most part peasants and poor Jews, whose fields had been laid waste, whose small shops had been gutted, in one raid or another, by White or Green or Red soldiers, or irregulars wearing the cockades and flying the banners of Red soldiers. The river-steamers had not been running for some time, either because the places they ran to were in the hands of one enemy or another, or because the steamers themselves were in enemy hands—floating islands of evil that slunk up in the night to discharge their cargoes of bandits upon cowering villages and lonely homesteads numb with terror.

It is certain that without her official papers Susan would not have got within shouting distance of the steamer. But she enlisted the help of a posse of Red soldiers, who triumphantly butted a way through the mob for her and landed her quite close to the gangway, or the place where the gangway would be when the steamer was ready to start. She was by no means a helpless woman, but she was grateful when the large-mouthed grinning little sergeant assured her he would give a special eye to her.

She knew the steamer would not start on time ; she could not remember a train, since her arrival in Russia, which had not started two or three hours late. Many had started at least six hours late. But she knew enough of the conditions of rolling stock and transport in Russia to be grateful that the trains got going at all. The steamer was still at its moorings when night came ; and the next night. It did not start till the evening of the day after. It was not for want of trying on the part of the engineers that the steamer did not start. They worked with revolutionary ardour to start the engines, for thirty-six hours. Now and again certain reluctant responses were achieved, but they were short-lived. An expert turned up from the city from time to time ; he disappeared into the engine-room, comparatively clean ; he withdrew to the shore again, grimy and furious.

Many of the passengers had a certain amount of their bedding with them, as much as they had been able to rescue in their flight. Those who were not fugitives had their bedding, too, for it seemed that the Russian folk were incapable of making any sort of journey without their bedding. Here and there a samovar stuck up its teapot-crowned chimney among the mattresses, and all day long, even in the intense heat of mid-day, all night long, there was a perpetual brewing of tea. There was a perpetual spitting out of sunflower-seed-casings, so that the ground looked like the bottom of a parrot's cage. A variety of live-stock was distributed among the passengers. There were goats, and chickens, and dogs. A small girl on a mattress a few feet away had a string tied round her wrist ; the other end of the string was tied round a leg of a cat. A green parrot, that had made what astonishing journeys to reach this place, that had survived what immense adventures, was perched upon the shoulder of an old peasant, who seemed so weak and listless, and seemed to have been so long weak and listless, that he still wore, now in these dog-days, his winter coat of shaggy brown felt. The parrot seemed as weak and listless as he, and as piebald with age. He had not the energy to pull up the light membrane of his eyelid. He stared before him hour after hour, his head drooped sideways, like a dead bird that has been badly stuffed. Once and again, but rarely, some memory of the vivid woods where once he had squawked and squabbled among the high branches stirred in his dim brain, and he uttered a choked cry that hardly went further than his beak. Or a flea would stick its horn into him, and trouble him into a movement of protest ; but, before his beak had reached the place where the flea was biting, his neck drooped again.

The parrot was less lucky than the peasants, for they had the help of each other to attack the insects which they themselves could not reach. Susan was not squeamish by now, after these more than two years in this tragic land, but she could not help congratulating herself that those labours must mean that a smaller insect cargo would be carried down the river. Also she realised that time would have hung even more heavily upon their hands without that pastime.

Susan was too practised a traveller to move anywhere without iron rations of food in reserve—a hunk of black bread, a length of sausage, she knew it was usually horse-meat, hard-boiled eggs, if ever attainable, and caviare. Caviare, ironically enough, was plentiful, for the export had ceased. But, as the hours went on and the steamer still did not start, the food question began to be a matter of some importance, for it was likely that her iron rations would have to last her considerably longer than she had anticipated —should the steamer ever get going at all. Her large-mouthed sergeant was invaluable. He not only procured for her from somewhere a mattress which looked fairly clean, but he busied himself to buy her some food, too, from the peasants. That business was somewhat complicated by the fact that they refused to deal in Duma or Kerensky notes. They wanted Nikolai notes, they proclaimed firmly, and would not budge. The sergeant saw to it they budged in Susan's favour. So she acquired some more bread, a huge green melon, and a leg of chicken. A little old Jew with corkscrew ear-locks had some salt herring, and managed to boil some potatoes. It may have been that he divined this bony-shanked lonely woman to be of his race, or he may have felt that he, too, was lonely. But he asked her would she not join him, which she did ; and she in her turn offered him green melon and a thew from the leg of chicken. He accepted the melon, but would not eat the chicken, for the bird had not been slaughtered in the way prescribed for Jews. She thought it was a strange thing that she should be eating salt herrings and black bread and boiled potatoes, now on her way to Terkass, sitting on a mattress beside an old Jew. For as a small girl she had often eaten those things in her father's kitchen, in Oleander Street, in Doomington ; but the Jews in that room did not wear corkscrew ear-locks.

And then, after thirty-six hours, when steam had been up for an hour or so, and it was considered they had kept going long enough without stopping, the steamer started. They left behind, of course, far more intending passengers than they took with them. They had proceeded not many minutes —they were still under the bluff where the Lavra Monastery disperses its gilded domes among its woods—when the engines stopped again. This time the damage was quickly put right, and the steamer took the middle stream, hooting proudly like a smart liner.

The sergeant had done her one final service before the steamer went off. He saw to it that she had a cabin, or at least a fourth share of a cabin, on the covered deck. It was a minute cabin, and it smelled abominably. Her senses, which were not over-acute in these matters, told her that the cabin itself, and the two men and the woman who shared it with her, were lively with vermin. But that did not miti-gate her unspeakable gratitude for the hard bench she had, all to herself, to stretch out her racked bones.

She took out a few garments from her bag, wrapped them round her shoes to make a pillow, and lay down. She slept quite soundly for two or three hours, partly because she was so utterly exhausted, partly because it took several hours for the air in the cabin to congeal into the almost

tangible foulness it was during the rest of the voyage. The
minute window would not go down more than an inch or
two, and, as ill luck would have it, it was one of the few
windows in the steamer which were still intact. The three
other occupants seemed so amazed that they had a bunk to
themselves, and so terrified that it would be taken from them
if they left it, that it was only the most imperious demands
of nature which impelled them to leave the cabin, and they
returned so precipitately—within the limits of precipitate-
ness permitted by the tangled lumps of intervening bodies—
one might have thought they had left caskets of jewels
behind them in their little wooden suitcases. They did not
even rise to eat or drink. Somehow they managed to open
the trap-doors of their suit-cases, where they lay full length,
and feed hunks of bread and ends of sausage and bottles of
milk or water into their mouths. One of them went up on to
the top deck once a day with a tin mug, and managed to
get himself some tea. All three spoke not one word to Susan
or to each other throughout the voyage. It was as if each
thought that the others were only waiting for an indiscreet
word to hale him off in triumph before some tribunal. The
two men and the woman were more mysterious creatures to
Susan when finally she left the steamer at Terkass than when
she embarked at Kiev. As the nightmare prolonged its
bourneless length, their eyes, their noses, their mouths, their
chins, became more and more indistinct, their faces looked
like the faces of drowned bodies weltering a foot or two
below the surface of a salt friendless sea.

It was no solution of the problem of ventilation to open
the cabin-door. The door opened on to a covered deck,
divided by a railing into an inner well-deck and an
outer ambulatory. But there was no ambulation in either.
The passengers were clogged together like the cells in a wild
bees' nest. A few feet away was the lavatory, which was so
noisome that Susan did not know how she could fail to die
in it if she should be forced to go again. She slept soundly
for two or three hours. Then the insects proceeded to defile

from their barracks. The air proceeded to ram itself into her nostrils like sour pellets. She rose. She shook the clothes which had been wrapped round her shoes, replaced them in her bag, and put her shoes on. Then, at length, forcing her way through the hooked clot of limbs, she climbed to the upper deck. By great good fortune she managed to find a square foot or so near the steamer-rail—she needed little room—and sat down, her knees drawn up to her chin, her hair coming forward, damp and scraggy, over her eyes.

Susan could never decide in her own mind whether the voyage lasted two days or three or four. She was tough and had done some hard going in Russia, but she was of the opinion later that she would have died, or gone quite mad on that voyage, if the steamer had not drawn up at a succession of small stopping places, and enabled her to step ashore, and stretch her limbs, and buy a pumpkin here, a large coarse tomato there. At one place she heard a peasant woman cry aloud, " *Varenniki! Varenniki!* " Across the hypnotic torpor of her mind, the word came oddly, distressingly familiar. Her mind attained clarity for one moment, and the word became so poignant that tears filled her eyes.

" *Varenniki! Varenniki!* " She looked down into the woman's basket. Yes, there they were, the purses of fried dough stuffed with *kasha* ; the *varenniki* her mother made from time to time, in the Oleander Street kitchen, of better material doubtless, but not so well-cooked as these. And, even in that moment of quite contemptible sentimentality, her bluestocking mind registered the fact, for whatever future use it might be, that *varenniki* were not, as she had always thought, a Jewish dish—the Jews had borrowed it from the Ukrainian peasants.

She duly ate two or three *varenniki*, washed them down with milk, then walked along the strand for twenty yards or so, to the first place where there was room for her to take her clothes off. She stripped and bathed. On both sides of her, males and females stripped and bathed, utterly without self-consciousness. She came out of the water, which was brown, and not too clean, but cleaner than the decks were ; and, like the others, she got hold of her garments and looked through them for insects, and killed as many as she could find. Then she lay back on that warm tongue of sand, and stretched out her thin arms and looked up into the sky.

And as she lay there, she heard the cries of small boys a little distance along the shore, small boys from the village, they evidently were. The cries they uttered were happy and cruel cries, as the cries of boys usually are ; but amongst them was the wailing cry of one small boy, whom, clearly, they were ill-treating. She lifted herself upon the palms of her hands, and looked to see what was happening. It was as she thought. The boys were ducking a small boy, and holding his head under the water till they almost drowned him. As bullied small boys usually are, he was an ugly small boy. And she remembered as she lay there, naked, among the naked peasants hunting for bugs in their clothes, that if it had not been for a small ugly boy whom the small boys of his village were maltreating in this same way, in a brown shallow not many miles from this place, she, Susan Polednik, would not have been lying here in the hot Ukrainian sun, the wife of a Russian military Commissar. She looked round, feeling that something was still lacking. She looked round for Vladimir Stepanovitch to smash the faces of these wicked small boys. But, amongst these cowed creatures that lay around her on the sand, there was no Vladimir. Vladimir Stepanovitch had died long ago, carried out from his cell in the Kiev prison, like a load of muck on a wheelbarrow.

Apart from the few halts the steamer made there was no remission of the misery of the journey. There was almost as little room to move as in those mediæval cages in which prisoners could neither stand up nor lie down. But for Susan Polednik it involved a strange experience the like of which she had never known. Susan Polednik had no sense of beauty. But the unprecedented assault which the Terkass voyage made upon her nervous system from so many totally new angles, awakened into a gnawing spasmodic vitality a nerve of æsthetic excitement which normally was as dead as stone. Her tiredness was such that it compelled a remission of all her usual faculties. The sudden tap upon her eye of a bird in flight, a willow reflecting itself in the water, a stockade of sunflowers before a peasant's hut, the moon driving her clouds before her, sent her dithering into ecstasy. On the second or the third evening of the voyage, a sunset fumed and hissed upon the convulsed water, pouring from its cauldron a stream of molten metal yellow as daffodils. She knew she had never seen a sunset before. The tears rolled without stopping down her thin cheeks.

An hour or two's journey beyond Tanyev a great raft of sawn rough logs was floating down the river. The river spread itself out into an enormous silver width at this point. The raft slid without noise, like something that long ago had been compounded out of the world's primal forest and sent down upon a timeless journey to no sea.

There was a clacking and cluttering of voices about her ears. The peasants were wondering how it came that a log-raft should be unmoored and sent down the river, for these reaches were no longer immune from the sudden sortie-ing of the bandits. It occurred to Susan that perhaps a requisition had been made for logs to build a temporary bridge over some tributary where the bandits had wrecked a permanent bridge. She wondered if it was not possible that her own husband, Boris, had sent orders to Tanyev that timber must be sent to him.

Tanyev. . . . She suddenly remembered that that was his native village, where he had first taken suck from the stern paps of the Revolution.

Oh, she was tired, tired ; her bones felt as if they had become rotten wood inside her. She was tired of the Revolution, of Boris, of leaflets, of slogans, of squalor, of black bread green with mould. She swivelled herself completely round from the memory of them. She sluiced her eyes with the silver width of the river. She looked down upon the raft of rough sawn logs. Before her sluiced eyes the sawn trees suddenly put forth branches, and the branches twigs, and the twigs green leaves. The green leaves trailed in the river as the raft slid southward to Terkass.

It was not to be wondered at that the peasants muttered among themselves to see a raft floating down the river as if these were the care-free reaches of Thames or Loire. An hour or two after midnight she became aware of the glare of fire ; at this distance it could not be said whether the fire might be upon the right or the left bank. She heard one or two say it might be a fire that had arisen in the woods out of itself because of the great heat. But she found it was not so when they drew abreast of it. It was a peasant's homestead, some distance from the bank. All wood, it seemed to be, from the way it blazed, not mud and plaster, as many of the peasants' huts were in these parts. A few of the peasants spoke of the fire in hushed whispers. The others looked stolidly on, like folk who have seen worse. Beautiful and lonely the blaze seemed to Susan Polednik, a great lily sprouting before her iron-lidded eyes, hurling fronds of fire into the air, scattering its own roots with a pollen of orange fire.

There was more evidence of bandits on this latter part of the journey—here the black burned hulk of a boat on a sandbank, there a wood of fruit-trees egregiously lopped down, there the shell of a farmhouse and its ruined husbandry. But Susan was almost not alive by now. These things made an impact upon her mind, as objects do upon sensitive paper in photography. They produced no pain in her, no indignation, no apprehension as to what she might meet, now that in an hour, a day, she should at length arrive in Terkass.

There was a hooting, a long doleful hooting. A hooting from the land, like an owl in a tree, responded. There was a swishing of bows turning against the flow of the river. She had come to Terkass, whence her father and mother had gone forth long ago.

II

She stood with her bag in her hand on the sandy foreshore.
She stood there minute after minute, wondering what was
to be done now. She stood there so long that at last the bag
became too heavy for her, though there was little in it. She
put it down beside her. She realised that the passengers who
had disembarked at Terkass had almost all dispersed. These
others, whose feet slugged softly through the ankle-deep
sand, were waiting till the steamer summoned them. It was
to make one more halt, and then turn, up river again to
Kiev.

It was about three o'clock. There was a milky mistiness
in the air, though there was no moon. Before her feet a road
ascended through the low bluff which overhung the landing-
stage ; it was less a road than a strip of sandiness, a little more
firmly beaten down than the foreshore was. On the crest of
the rise she saw the bony contour of an animal, which the
dimness could not make less bony.

She trudged up the rise to the creature, and, as she hoped,
it was a horse, standing with drooped head within the shafts
of a droshky. There was another horse and droshky beyond.
An *izvostchik* sat in the driving seat of each, his head drooped
just as forlornly as the horse's. Susan's approach did not seem
to interest them. They were old men, their animals and
droshkies were old. They seemed to have been in that place
for days, for weeks. It did not seem grotesque to imagine
that they had been there, drowsing miserably in that same
place, years ago, when Sam Silver and Hannah Dobkin had
fled from Terkass. They seemed so wretched, everything
about them so worthless, that it was not hard to believe that
if Makhno's men, or Petlura's men, had been this way, even
they had scorned to take any notice of them.

It had been Susan's intention to present herself at once
to whatever Party headquarters had been set up here in
Terkass. But she felt three o'clock was no time to present
herself, and that she herself was in no state to provide them

with the explanations they would ask for—if she should find anybody awake.

Then, was it not the obvious thing to go straight to her grandfather's house? Where else in all Russia could she go to with more propriety at three o'clock in the morning, than to her grandfather's house?

But dull-witted as she was, almost imbecile with fatigue, a thought crossed her mind. Oh, no; oh, no! There may have been other callers this last year or two that came suddenly out of the darkness and knocked upon their door at three o'clock in the morning. No, it might be a great unkindness to bring them out of their beds at this hour.

Perhaps there was an inn? Oh, surely Terkass was a big enough place to have an inn, if it had opened up again since the bandits had been last expelled? That is to say, if it had closed at all?

" *Tovarish izvostchik!* " she called out. She had been standing beside the first droshky for some minutes, but the driver had not lifted his head from his chest. " *Tovarish izvostchik!* " she called out again. She pulled at his coat. "Are you awake? Do you hear? I want to go into the town!"

The man shook his head a little and grunted, then his head settled on his chest again.

" Oh, to hell with you! " She went round to the other man. " *Tovarish izvostchik!* Take me into the town! Do you hear? Is there a hotel up in the town? "

This one was a little more responsive. " There is a hotel in the town! " he said.

" Then take me there! " she called out sharply. " Take me there! " Her voice broke.

He uttered some words she could not make out at all. He addressed them to his fellow, who uttered a word or two in return. Neither moved a hand from where it was thrust deep down into trouser-pocket.

She determined to ignore the first *izvostchik*. " I'll give you good Nikolai roubles," she told the other, " if you'll take me up to the hotel."

" How many ? "

" What's the tariff ? What do you want ? "

Then both *izvostchiks* galvanised themselves into activity. As if she were not there at all, they began to discuss the matter over her head. But they talked Yiddish now, they had been talking Russian, and a word or two of Ukrainian, till now.

" She's a foreigner," they were saying. " Who is she ? What's she doing here ? Do you think anything can happen to us if we took her up to the hotel ? How should *we* know who she is ? But we'll make her pay, yes ? We'll make her pay a lot. One of us will carry her, and the other will carry her bag. How much shall we say ? How much shall we say ? "

It was not merely Yiddish. It was that sort of Yiddish which was most familiar of all the variants in her ear. How often had she not heard, in her father's kitchen in Oleander Street, two tailor-cutters, during a " rush " season, arrange to hold up their employer to blackmail, in exactly these words, inflected exactly so !

" Indeed ! Such a year should take you ! " her voice rapped out, in Yiddish as salty as theirs. She was amazed at her own prowess ; for, though with many Party associates Yiddish had been the language she and they had found it most useful to converse in, she talked without fluency, as a rule, as one using a language of no spiritual importance to her. She flailed the drivers with her tongue. She told them what bandits they were. More, she told them who she herself was, a Government official, wife of a military Commissar.

" Please ! Please ! " they wept. " Oh, please say no word ! Oh, a black year ! " They beat their bosoms. The tears streamed down their wrinkled faces.

She seated herself behind the driver who had been a little more loquacious than his brother. " Go ! " she said. The driver cracked his whip, the horse awoke with a start ; the driver cracked his whip again, the horse lunged and pulled. The droshky would not move. The first driver came down from his seat, and pushed with his shoulder from behind. " Hoi ! Hoi ! " they both cried. The droshky found firmness under its wheels at last.

A few low buildings were clustered near the top of the rise above the landing-stage. These were soon left behind. They entered at once into a sort of milky emptiness. A dim lump of shape on the left might have been a house, it might have been a lonely tree. Here and there were small woods, their edges blurred in mist. Almost soundlessly the droshky moved, the horse's hoofs making no more than a hushed watery hissing in the deep dust of the road. She thought they must have been moving for an hour, or perhaps less, before they came to the outlying houses of the small town.

The dust of the country road became the cobbles of a main street. The houses were bigger here ; they had two stories. At this corner was a church. At this corner was a shop. It had been a shop once. It was a ruin now. Here were cross-roads, the main cross-roads of the village presumably. Here were big houses, bigger shops.

She was in Terkass now. She was in Terkass now. She was in Terkass now.

She uttered the words to herself, time after time, to see if they had an effect upon her. They had none. Her brain was like soaked wadding. I am in Terkass now. I am in Terkass now. Twice one are two now. Twice one are two now.

The intellectual part of her brain was out of function. Her eyes saw almost nothing at all. Even if they had been less tired, they could not have made much out, so obliterative was the milky atmosphere.

But her nose twitched with the smells in it. She smelled dust, she smelled burning. She had smelled them from the moment she had set foot upon the shore—dust, dust, and burning.

Here, however, in the town, a smell imposed itself upon those other smells. It was a tinny smell, a sweet, dry, tinny smell. She knew what the smell was among the dust and burning. She smelled blood, she smelled blood in Terkass.

It seemed to her that the smell became harsher, sweeter, the deeper they moved into the heart of the village. A cry was in her throat, beating its wings like a caged bird. She knew she must scream soon, scream at the top of her voice, unless they stopped. She knew it would not be the first time such screaming had been heard at such an hour in Terkass.

The driver did not stop. He went on past one street corner and another. " Stop ! " she screamed. " Stop ! " But the cry she uttered was hoarse and without substance.

"Yes," said the *izvostchik*. "You are right. That is the hotel !"

" Wake them for me please ! " she bade. " Certainly, comrade ! " he said. His voice sounded uncertain. He got down from his seat. She wiped her brow with her handkerchief, then restored it to her handbag, wet as a sponge. Then she got out.

" Oh, here, *tovarish* ! " she said. " Let me pay you ! " She fumbled among her notes. " And tell me," she said. " Where is the house of Feivel Dobkin ? " The words were out of her mouth though she had no intention to utter them.

" Thank you ! " he said. She put the notes away and turned to the door.

" Did you hear what I asked ? " she repeated. " Where is the house of Feivel Dobkin ? "

" It will be very difficult," the old man quavered, " to wake them up."

" Yes, I see," she muttered. This was no land where one asked questions, or answered them, if it was possible to avoid answering them.

" There'll be no difficulty about it to-morrow," she assured herself. " When I've had a rest. Good God, when I've had a rest ! "

The *izvostchik* was quite right. It was very difficult to awaken the people in the hotel. Susan added her feeble knocking to the old man's efforts. The knocking came back muffled and terrible from the further side of the wide dim street.

At last a man's head appeared out of a window on the upper floor. It had become clear to him, perhaps, that the knocking would go on till dawn if no one should appear. His hair was towsled, his eyes gleamed pale with fright.

" What is it ? What is it ? At such a time ! " he whispered, his teeth chattering.

" Come quickly down, quickly ! " said the *izvostchik*. " It is the wife of a Commissar ! Open ! Find a bed for her at once ! "

He came down. With trembling fingers he unlocked and unbolted the door. " If the comrade will permit," he begged her, " if she will only just let me look at her papers, so that if they should ask me——"

She thrust her papers at him. " Oh, for God's sake let me lie down ! " she cried.

So that there should be no delay at all, for he saw the state she was in, he took her at once to his own bed, where his wife lay, shivering with fright. Three children were lying in another bed, whimpering.

" It's all right ! " he assured them. " Go to sleep, all of you ! And you, too, comrade ! There, now, there ! Another pillow ? No, Tanya, no ! She does not need another pillow ! "

III

It was not till six o'clock the next evening that Susan woke.

" You slept like a dead woman," said the innkeeper's wife. The innkeeper was elsewhere.

" Please," smiled Susan, " don't say it like that ! " She was feeling quite fresh. " It would not be easy to have a bath ? "

" We have no baths."

" I can wash then ? "

" There is the washing-room at the end of the passage."

Susan washed in a tin basin, into which water came down, drop by drop, from a small cistern above it. Two men in their vests and pants were washing at the same time. A samovar was going briskly in the family living-bedroom where she had spent the night, and a good deal of the day. The woman gave her tea and a good plateful of soft cheese in sour cream, and a fresh egg, and bread with a thin smearing of real butter. After all, they were in the country.

" Thank you," said Susan. " That was fine."

" There is more cheese and sour cream."

" No. I must get on. Oh, you must tell me one thing."

The woman made no comment.

" Do you belong to this town ? "

" And if we do ? "

" I just wanted to know where Feivel Dobkin's house is."

The woman made no observation. Her face was quite expressionless.

" Do you know where Feivel Dobkin's house is ? " Susan asked again.

At that moment the innkeeper came in. " Ask him," the woman said, indicating him with a thumb. She turned her back on them both, to show the matter concerned her no further.

" Oh, comrade, tell me, do you know where Feivel Dobkin's house is ? "

" Yes, of course," he said. He was easier on the tongue.

" Where is it ? "

" It is—you just walk along——" He stopped a moment, and reflected. Then he seemed to make up his mind that, surely, merely to give an address was not to compromise oneself. " You cross the road," he told her, " turning on your left hand. Then you pass one street, then you pass another. You go up that one. It's there on your left-hand side. It's the biggest house in the street. There's a big door in front, which leads you down into the cellar where they used to store the wine."

Her scalp tingled queerly. Here she was in Terkass. They were telling her quite calmly, she was listening quite calmly, how to get to the house of Feivel Dobkin, the house of her mother's father, where there was a cellar for storing wine. And an orchard, of course.

" And, of course, there is an orchard too ? " she said.

He scratched his head. " If you'd be calling it an orchard."

No, of course not. They'd hardly have had time these troubled days to look after their fruit-trees.

" I must go," she said. " I don't know if I'll spend the night here or not. I'll leave my bag. I'll be back again."

" There's no train," he told her, " if you're thinking of leaving to-night."

" No, there's a chance of my spending the night in the house of old Dobkin," she said in a burst of affability. " You see——" She was about to tell him more ; that the woman who was talking to him now, born in England, a long way from that place, was the daughter of the daughter of that old man. A moment later her instinct of caution, which in this country must be permitted never, or rarely, to relax, reasserted itself. " I don't quite know what I'll do," she said.

" I don't think," he said slowly, " you'll spend the night in that place."

" Why ? " she asked quickly. " Why ? "

" There's trouble there ! "

" Ivan ! " the man's wife called out peremptorily.

" Yes, Anna, yes," he said, crestfallen.

" What do you mean—there's trouble there ? " Susan insisted.

" I've got to be getting on with my work," he said. " I've a lot to do this evening."

She went down into the street. It was clearly the main street of the small town. It was very wide, much wider than the streets of many a metropolis. The cross-streets were very wide, too ; they, too, were almost deserted. There were practically no civilians about. Small groups of Red soldiers were walking here and there, or lounging at the corners. They were all fully armed. There was some sort of municipal building on the opposite side of the street. It was now obviously the military headquarters of the troops operating in this area. A Red sentry stood on guard. Soldiers were going in and out.

One or two shops were open, but practically nobody was buying anything, and there was practically nothing to buy. Grass grew between the cobbles. It was clear, it would have been fatuous to try and hide from oneself, that there had been dark days in the village. Further along the street were houses which had been burned down ; only their shells survived. There were bullet marks and hackings on the walls of certain shops and houses. Certain others that stood side by side bore no mark of violence at all. She knew at once what that meant. These were Jewish places, those were not.

" It would be interesting to go to Terkass some time," Susan Silver, as she was then, used to say from time to time, in Doomington, in her father's kitchen. " It would be interesting, I mean, to pick up the threads."

Yes, she was picking up the threads. This was the corner where she was to turn, wasn't it ? The second corner. Up and down the place there were proclamations stuck on walls and trees. Some had been scratched out ; these were clearly the notices of Green and Whites, and whatever other enemy bodies had infested this region before its present occupation. There were some fresh ones, too, doubtless recently issued by the Red authorities. She was too dispirited to pause and read them now, and make notes on them. It was stupid to conceal it from herself. She was anxious—more than that— she was frightened. She would call at the local Soviet, and perhaps at the military headquarters, too, later on, to get what help she could out of them. It was up to them to give her all the help she asked for.

This was the street the innkeeper had indicated. This was the street in which her grandfather lived. She always had had a vivid image in her mind of her mother running out of the house that night, running out into this street, the night when the step-mother had hung the pearls round the step-sister's neck, the night when the sobbing girl had met a wandering tailor in the woods, and been comforted by him.

This was the street. Her mother must have run the other way, away from the main street. She crossed to the further side. A grassy ditch ran all the way along the side of the broad footpath. The houses at this end of the street were small. They stood alone, locked up in themselves. They were not empty. There was a sense of people behind the doors, people who preferred not to look through windows, not to draw any sort of attention to themselves.

There, just beyond there, was a big house, and it had ground of its own, beside and behind it. There was a fence running this way from the house to the corner. Then it turned, at right angles, along a narrow lane. This then was her grandfather's house. There was no other big house in the street, and none other with land attached to it.

She came abreast with the fence ; it was quite easy to look over it. She sighed. As she had feared, there was little left of what might have been a brave orchard once. The grass was thin and bare, bestrewn with tins and hoops and dry chips. There were one or two discouraged little trees, and one bigger tree, quite handsome still, much nearer the house—quite handsome still, though this year's leaves were already scorched and yellowing. Surely, surely, that was the apricot-tree, the famous apricot-tree. Her heart fluttered. Not everything was gone. There still was the apricot-tree, though the fruit was all gone—if any had ripened this year. But the roots of the apricot-tree were still firm in her mother's father's garden, and there would be blossom and fruit again in their season.

She remembered the photograph of her grandfather in the album they had in Doomington. She saw it in her mind's eye with a vividness which quite startled her. He must have been standing just about there, with that full black beard and that heavy gold chain stretched across his stomach—just about there where the rusty bucket was. The photograph took in the corner of the house, with the fretted lintels over the windows. The day it was taken, both the inner and the outer windows were open. They were closed now.

At the back of the orchard was the little bungalow, not quite so grand as she had figured it to herself, as the main house was not so grand. She stood there, trying to piece it all together. And for another reason. She did not dare to go further. She was afraid.

This fence at her side—it was here, where she was standing now, where the beggars used to stand and look towards the lights and music, those nights when there was merrymaking in the big room. Her mother used to steal out with a lapful of dainties to hand over to them.

Further along the front of the house, she saw the small slope where the barrels with wine from Kishinev were rolled down into the cellar. Beyond the apricot-tree she saw the other door of the cellar—the famous cellar, where Alex and Leon and little Hannah would play a game of bandits, poking with sticks among the dark places, shouting " Ho ! Ho ! " to each other terrifyingly.

It seemed suddenly that a blade of cold steel lay flat upon her heart.

She moved several yards along the fence. As she did so, a man moved from behind the apricot-tree, which had concealed him till now, where he had doubtless been seeking coolness in the shade. It was a Red soldier ; he brought his rifle up against his shoulder as he moved towards the gate.

A soldier ? What was a soldier doing here ? There was a taste of dust in Susan's mouth. " Excuse me, comrade," she said, " but this is the house of an old man named Dobkin, isn't it ? "

The soldier looked at her. " It is not for me to answer questions," he said.

" But—but——" she stammered. How could she tell him she had come all this way, the long journey from Doomington, in England, to Terkass in the Ukraine, to see her mother's father, and her mother's brothers, and to learn how they fared now, in this big house with the orchard. . . .

She was mad, the voyage to Terkass had completely unhinged her. The wife of a military Commissar in the Red Army, a responsible Party member, to be dickering and dithering like a crooning nigger going back to Dixie !

She took out her papers. " I order you to look at these ! Then answer me ! "

" It is not for me to look at papers."

" You refuse ? "

" I have orders to stand on guard at this house. No one is to come in or go out. I must answer no questions."

She stuffed her papers savagely back into her bag. Her long jaw fell in her vexation and misery.

Then she remembered. She had a trump card to play. " If you had looked at these papers, you would see I am the wife of Comrade Commissar Polednik, who is serving not far from here."

" Then if the comrade will go to the Red headquarters, in the main street round to the left, she will meet Comrade Commissar Polednik, who is in charge there."

Her heart surged and pounded. She did not know if she were exultant or terribly afraid. " Thank you, comrade ! " she said, and turned on her heels the way she had come.

She had no difficulty at headquarters. " Take me through to Comrade Commissar Polednik ! " she told the soldier on duty. " I am his wife." He gave the message to a soldier lounging in the small flagged hall behind him. " To inform Comrade Commissar Polednik that his wife is here and wishes to see him."

The second soldier went and came back. " This way, comrade," he bade her.

She was taken into a bare-boarded room furnished with two tables, and a chair at each. There was a third chair. There were maps on the walls and on the tables. In a corner stood a heap of red leaflets. Polednik sat at one table, an officer at the other. The officer said no word throughout.

" Boris," she said, " I'm sorry to be disturbing you."

" What have you come for ? " he asked. It was clear there was to be no ceremony. She had never seen him look so efficient and self-possessed, nor heard his voice so hard.

" You remember you said if I should be down this way, it would do no harm if I came to see how my mother's family were ? "

" I remember."

" They've appointed me to the department of Revolutionary Archives. I wrote you a letter."

" It's not reached me."

" No, I didn't expect it would. You've been moving about."

" Yes."

They said I might come to Kiev. I am collecting proclamations, leaflets, and so on for the museums. I'm authorised to ask for the help of the Commissars and the local authorities."

" I'll do what I can."

" I went to my grandfather's house. There was a soldier there. He sent me to you."

" Nobody's to go into or come out of that house."

" I'm not going to go down on my knees to you, Boris. But I want to know what's wrong."

" I'll tell you. It's my duty to let as many people as possible know. That's why I've had those leaflets printed there—in advance. They'll be all over the place by to-morrow evening."

" In advance ? In advance of what, Boris ? "

For a moment or two, no more, he allowed his voice to depart from its dry mechanical tonelessness.

" Susan, it's going to be bad news for you."

" I'm prepared for something—something bad."

" Worse than you think, perhaps." Then his voice became the thing it had been, a noise coming out of a machine. " The Revolution is in grave danger. The danger is nowhere graver than in these parts. We have often found it difficult, sometimes impossible, to keep up our communications in the rear. It is necessary for the people whom we have come to deliver to give us all help and to obey literally every order we issue to them." He recited these things as if he read them from a paper, though he did not. It was as if they formed the substance of a charge he had drawn up before, and would draw up again.

" Nothing is more important than that we must feed our troops. The small peasants have understood the necessity for that from the beginning. That has not been the case with the rich peasants, the *kulaks*. We issued orders that all supplies of corn must be handed over to us at our various depôts, and as much would be given back as could be spared, when it could be spared. The *kulaks* disobeyed this order. It was clear that there were more supplies in the countryside than were being handed over to us. Orders came through that an example must be made of one or two of the richest *kulaks* in each village in the territory of operations. I grieve to say that we received information that, among others, Feivel Dobkin, and his son, Alex, flagrantly disobeyed our order. It has been found necessary to punish them in a way which will make the other rich peasants understand that our orders are to be obeyed."

He paused. He pointed a finger at her. " I want you to understand one thing. The names of Feivel and Alex Dobkin were supplied to me by the local committee. There was nothing for me to do but endorse their recommendation."

"What is to happen to them ? " Susan Polednik whispered.

" I regret. I wish you had not come here."

" Will you please tell me ? "

" They are to be shot at sunrise to-morrow morning."

She stood stiff as a rod. She did not even blink her eyelids, though for one moment it seemed she had gone blind, for a blackness came down over the room, swallowing the tables, the chairs, the maps, the man who had been talking to her, the man who had been silent, everything.

" You won't prevent me from seeing them ? " she asked.

He paused " I fail to see that that can do harm. You will

understand that I, or one of my men, will be with you throughout ? "

" Please," she said, " let it be yourself ! " The rim of her eyelids lay like a hoop of hot metal in her eyeballs.

" We'll go now," he said, and rose.

All her skin tingled hot and peppery like the skin of her eyelids, yet she was quite cold within. Her heart felt like a cold and heavy lump of metal. She suddenly thought : " I would give a great deal for a good cup of tea." It occurred to her that, in a way, it would not be much to ask her grandfather for, the first time in her life she met him. On the other hand it would not be easy to ask him for it, seeing he was to die in a few hours.

As they walked back, he asked her about her new appointment. He asked her who were the comrades she had seen in Kiev, and what the voyage down the river had been like. She replied to him as if they might be going to some Party meeting of no exceptional importance ; but her voice was a little blurred, her tongue moved at its roots with difficulty.

I must be brave, her thoughts went. I must not give way. It is tactful and intelligent of him to talk like this. I understand. This is the logic of the Revolution. He is not to blame. It is not he who is killing them. It is part of what we have worked for all these years, he and I and all of us.

" The front door," he was saying to her, " must have been broken down in a pogrom earlier this year." They had reached the house now. He was pointing out to her something she had not had time to notice earlier, the fact that the main door of the house, just beyond the gate that led into the one-time orchard, was boarded up.

" They don't seem to have had time to put in a new door since the last pogrom. That is our principal job in these parts, to put down pogroms. Pogroms and counter-revolution are one and the same thing. You remember Lenin on the subject ? "

" Yes ! " She supposed she ought to register a certain sense
of being obliged to Lenin and the Revolution for putting
down pogroms. But she could do no more than utter one
toneless " Yes."

" We'll go in this way," he said.

They passed across the small bridge that spanned the
grassy ditch before the gate. The sentry touched the butt
of his rifle, and opened the gate for them. The side door
into the house was this side of the trap-door that led down
into the cellar. She had not noticed it before, because of the
apricot-tree. The door was not locked. Polednik turned the
handle, and they passed into a narrow passage. There were
a number of doors on the left hand, leading into the smaller
rooms, doubtless. There was only one double door and one
single door on the right hand, for here was the big room of
the house, occupying all the space between the passage and
the street wall. There was a soldier sitting on a chair outside
the double doors. He jumped to his feet, looked inquiringly
at Polednik, and, in reply to a nod, flung the door open.

" This way," said Polednik.

They passed into the big room ; it was so big a room that,
although there was a good deal of furniture about, it looked
empty. There was not much light, because some of the
windows had been smashed and blocked up with wood from
boxes, and because some attempt had been made to draw
the curtains. The curtains were of a dark heavy material,
and had been fine once. They were hanging on by less than
half their rings. There were two big cupboards against the
walls, and a grandfather clock in one corner. There was a
table covered with a big plush cloth. There was an upholstered sofa and several upholstered chairs. Some of these
had been slashed, with a knife, or a sword, or whatever it
might have been. Over the backs of the chairs were a sort of
linen antimacassar worked in Ukrainian embroidery.
There were cushions covered with the same material. An

enormous complicated brass chandelier hung over the table. On the walls there were framed tapestries, and one or two enlarged photographs of Dobkin elders and marriage-groups, of which the glass in most cases had been splintered with a direct blow. A good deal of the further end of the room was taken up by a huge tiled oven.

Susan Polednik did not take in these facts as she entered. There was time enough, during the next few hours, for these details to impress themselves on her mind. She looked round for the two men, and found her eye travelling from object to object and still failing to find them. She thought for a moment she had merely been brought into this room to wait whilst the others were summoned. Then she saw them. They were sitting in the narrow recess between the wall and the oven, two old men. The younger of them sat on a form with his back against the wall. He sat there curiously like a schoolboy who is detained after hours, and lifts his head hopefully when he hears a step outside on the gravel, thinking he is to be reprieved earlier than he thought. The other old man, an old man indeed, was sitting on a wooden chair in the angle between the wall and the oven. He was drowsing, if not asleep. His white beard lay splayed upon his chest. It was as if he had gone for comfort to the oven which for many years had comforted him and all his kindred any time they were cold and unhappy. There was no comfort in it now. Or perhaps he and his son had withdrawn themselves into the part of the room where there was most darkness, because they could hardly hope the light of day would now be of much use to them.

When Polednik and Susan entered, the younger old man got on to his feet. The other did not hear them, or he was too tired to rise.

" It is the Commissar, yes? " Uncle Alex said, for this was he, of course. He and the Commissar had clearly met before.

" This is my wife," said Polednik. Uncle Alex bowed, tottering a little as he did so. Uncle Alex had been a great man among the ladies, and had known well how to comport himself in their company.

" Wake him ! " Polednik ordered.

" Father, father ! " Uncle Alex tugged at the old man's coat. " Wake up ! Stand up ! Here is the Comrade Commissar ! "

" He does not need to stand up," said Polednik.

" What ? What's that ? " the old man grumbled. " I *am* awake ! "

" I have something to tell you both," said Polednik.

" Something to tell us ? " Uncle Alex quivered. " Something to tell us ? "

" No ! Get that out of your head at once ! It is about my wife ! "

" Please," Susan begged. " Let me tell him ! " She turned to Uncle Alex. He moved his head in bewilderment from one to the other.

" I don't know what I can say to you," she said. " I've often hoped to see you."

" Who are you ? "

" My mother is Hannah, your sister ! "

" Hannah ? From England ? What are you telling me ? Are you Hannah's daughter ? "

He looked to Polednik as if to seek confirmation of the astounding news.

" That's true," Polednik said tersely.

" Hannah's daughter ? From England ? It can't be true ! "

" Yes. We met in Doomington, my husband and I."

" Doomington ? Yes ! That's where Hannah went ! " he repeated, as if finding it very hard indeed to convince himself. " Then you're my niece ! Oh, my little daughter ! " He threw his arms round her neck and kissed her. Polednik turned away and strode to the window and looked out. The old man was sobbing, sobbing, on her shoulder, with little dry noises, and without tears.

Then he turned round suddenly, and made a step towards the door. " Manya ! " he called out.

Polednik turned brusquely round from the window. " What's that ? "

" Please ! She's my wife ! She's her aunt ! "

" I think we'd best not bring the women in. She can meet them—later. If she stays on in Terkass."

Uncle Alex drooped. " Yes, Comrade Commissar."

" What ? What's all this you're saying ? " protested the old man. " Why don't you tell me ? "

" Father," said Uncle Alex. " This is Hannah's daughter ! " He suddenly realised he did not know her name. " Hannah had a lot of daughters. Four ? Five ? "

" Five," said Susan. " I am Susan, the middle one."

" She is Susan, Hannah's daughter ! Named after Aunt Susan, your sister, peace be upon her ! "

" What are you talking about—Hannah's daughter ! Hannah's in England. She went off a long time ago, with that tailor ! "

" Yes, father, yes. This is one of her daughters. She was born there. She is married to Comrade Commissar."

" Married to Comrade Commissar ! " He looked up from under his red-rimmed eyes. " Have you come to take us away ? " he said.

" I have not."

" There will be more pogroms," said the old man. " If you are married to such a big man, a Commissar, then you should take us away." His old voice mumbled on. He shook his head protestingly. " You should take us away. Hannah's daughter ? What, Alex ? Did you say Hannah's daughter ? "

" Yes."

The old man tittered into his beard. " Oh, how I laughed ! You remember, Alex, the pearls ? I laughed and laughed ! Were you there ? No, you weren't. You were at the farm. We all went to the synagogue that night. It was the Ninth of Ab. And when we came back from the synagogue—they were gone. The pearls were gone, Hannah was gone, the tailor was gone. Hee, hee, hee ! "

It was clear he remembered far more vividly the things

that had happened, how long ago ?—more than thirty years ago—than the things that had happened yesterday, and were to happen next morning at sunrise.

" You should have seen Shevka, with a face like a beet-root !" he went on. " But me—I laughed and laughed ! I'm glad she got those pearls. They were not Shevka's at all. They were Malkeh's. She was my first wife." He turned suddenly towards Susan. " That is to say, your mother's mother. You understand ? "

" Boris ! " Susan turned to her husband.

" Yes ? "

" I want to ask you something. Please walk away a little."

" You understand there is to be no discussion of the decision that has been taken ? You understand that that is the condition on which I've brought you here ? "

" I do. I only want to ask you something."

" Go on."

" Was my grandfather informed of the decision ? "

" It was read out to him and his son in the presence of my tribunal."

" You realise he's so old he didn't understand what was said, and doesn't understand what's happening ? "

" I've told you I will allow no discussion."

" I'm not discussing the matter. I merely want to ask this. If he's too old to understand anything that's going on, can he have understood the order you signed ? "

" What do you mean ? "

" The order about handing in the grain ? "

" He was associated with his son in the farm in Prolensk in the criminal withholding and concealment of supplies. We have all the evidence we need."

" But how can he be punished for a crime——"

" Listen, Susan. If you say one more word on the matter, I'll order you to get out at once. Try and understand. We believe we are punishing the guilty. But there is one thing more important than to punish the guilty—we must make an example. The local committee decided there is no one else in this neighbourhood who better suits our purpose."

"Yes, Boris," she said. She swayed suddenly, and caught hold of a chair to prevent herself falling. "If I might ask you," she begged, "could they let me have some tea?"

"You're not of the stuff that some of our women are made of," he said. "Yes, I'll get some tea. Sit down now."

"Tea?" Uncle Alex said. He had observed something was wrong with his niece, and had come shuffling out of the recess. "Please, Comrade Commissar, she is faint? May I ask that my wife should make her some tea?"

"My man will see to it!"

"Comrade Commissar, I am to be shot to-morrow morning. My sister's child has come out of a far country. She has come to her mother's home. Will you refuse me this, that my wife should make some tea for her? And for you too, Comrade Commissar. Are you not the husband of my niece?"

Boris Polednik strode over to the door. "Comrade!" he called out. The soldier who had been sitting on the chair sprang to his feet. "Go over to the small house at the back there, and ask for the wife of Alexander Dobkin. Tell her that the niece of her husband has come. Say she has permission to make some tea and bring across some glasses."

"And please, Comrade Commissar, perhaps also she has some cake?" suggested Uncle Alex. "But I hardly hope there will be cake in the house."

"If she has some cake, she may bring it!" called out Boris Polednik to the soldier.

"Service, Comrade Commissar!" said the soldier and went off.

"I could have hoped that if such a guest should come to see us——" Uncle Alex was saying, shaking his head woefully. He stopped. The marvel of it struck him again. "*Such* a guest! Hannah's daughter! Little sister Hannah was just like our mother, the very same big brown eyes and the fat small nose!" He stopped, and looked at Susan. "You are not much like her," he said. "Perhaps the eyes a little? Are you at all like her?"

"I believe," she said, "I am not much like either of them."

"It is like that sometimes," he admitted, though it was clear from his tone he would have liked his sister's daughter to resemble his sister more. Then he went back to what he had been saying. "I could have hoped my wife and I would have prepared a different table for such a guest. She has never had to do any cooking for herself, you know," he insisted, with a note of pride, not remembering that with a Bolshevik Commissar and his wife that might be no recommendation. "But she could always turn out her *varennikis* and her *halkehs* with the best hired cook in the *gubernye*. Tell me, Susan," he said, "about my sister Hannah, and your sisters, and your father." He looked up swiftly at Polednik, to see if he had done anything wrong by asking. He had not, it seemed.

Polednik strode over to a window, and looked out between the curtains.

"The eldest girl is Esther, yes? And then comes Sarah, I think. They are both married. Tell me about their husbands. How many children have they, no evil eye befall them?"

She told him what she knew, though she found him as well informed as herself on certain matters, for her own sister, Esther, and Esther, his niece, Leon's Esther, who were of the same age, had been in correspondence with each other till the Revolution broke out. She had herself been out of touch with them all since the outbreak of the War, except for an occasional letter from her parents and a few more from May. May had disapproved violently of her attitude towards the War, but had accepted its sincerity. A fairly regular correspondence had passed between them until Boris and Susan had gone off to Russia.

"Listen, father, listen!" Uncle Alex interrupted her recital now and again. "Hear what she says! Hannah has got a big automobile. She wears the pearls every Friday night to table. Esther has—how many children do you say Esther has?"

His motive was pitifully transparent as he gabbled away

with a broken simulation of excitement. To talk, to talk, to talk—to keep thrust away from the forefront of his mind the shadow, the bullet. The other old man interrupted cantankerously from time to time. He kept on confusing Hannah's daughter Esther with Leon's daughter Esther. Leon's daughter Esther had only one daughter. The others had been sons. They should have been the utterers of *kaddish*, the prayer-for-the-dead, for Leon. Who now would utter *kaddish* for Leon ?

Leon had always been a shadowy person, with his spectacles and his ledgers. It was he who had taken on the wine-business. There was no photograph of Leon in the family-album in Doomington. What was this about *kaddish* for Leon ?

" Is Uncle Leon dead then ? " asked Susan.

Alex had been about to say something to her. His mouth remained open, though no sound issued from it. He looked at her with eyes in which depths of pain sank, fathom beyond fathom, depths deeper than she knew existed. Then sound came out of his mouth at last, a sound like a bird tapping its beak among gravestones.

" Uncle Leon is dead," he said. His lower lip trembled like a child's, his head drooped towards his chest. He was sobbing ; his whole body creaked and broke.

" Uncle, please ! " she begged.

There was a knock at the door.

" Yes ? " Polednik cried.

The soldier presented himself. " The wife of the younger prisoner has brought the tea. She said it was your intention, Comrade Commissar, she should bring it in. I have no such orders."

Alex and Susan lifted their eyes towards Polednik. Neither dared say a word.

" Oh, hell ! " exclaimed Polednik angrily. " We'd best get it over ! We'll have to be leaving soon ! We might as well have them all in ! Or would you like to see them in there, when we get out ? "

" I don't understand ! Who ? "

" The women, of course ! " he said, annoyed at her stupidity. " That small house at the back there is chock-full of women. They have orders to stay there ! "

" There are only women now," said Uncle Alex.

" Uncle, tell me, who's there ? Is grandmother Shevka there ? "

" She is there. And Manya, my wife, and our daughter. They are all there."

She ventured to take the situation into her own hands for a moment, and addressed her uncle directly.

" Shall I see them there when I go out ? Or shall they come here ? "

He was terrified at the thought of her leaving him, though she had turned up not many minutes ago out of nowhere. The longer she stayed, the shorter this night would be, even though it could only be shortened the way that a sea can be reduced by carrying off pailfuls of salt water.

" Oh, please, have them come here. It will be a gathering of the family, yes ? " A wan smile touched his quite white lips. " We often used to have gatherings of the family in this big room."

" Tell the woman to bring in the tea ! " Polednik called out. " Then tell the other women to come here ! No ! Wait a minute ! I'll go myself ! " He turned to Susan. " I'll ask them to come in in a quarter of an hour. You'd best drink your tea. You look as if you need it. Pour mine out, will you ? I like it to cool down a little ! "

"You can come in ! " a voice said. It was the soldier's voice.

" Thank you ! " a voice murmured.

A woman appeared at the door with a tray. The things on it rattled, the whole tray slanted.

" Let me ! " said the soldier. He took the tray from her, came into the room with it, and put it on the table.

" Manya, come in ! " bade Uncle Alex. A small woman, her face seamed like a scorched leaf, came in. She was trembling down to her feet. Her lower lip trembled so violently that she lifted her hand to control it, but her hand was just as unsteady.

"Now, now, Manya!" her husband reproved her. "We've been through worse things, you and I! Is this a way to receive a guest? And such a guest? This is your niece, Susan. The daughter of Hannah. Hannah who stole the pearls! Did you ever hear of such a thing?"

"Auntie Manya! Oh, you poor, poor Auntie Manya!" The little woman had thrown her arms round Susan's shoulders, and was weeping silently and terribly on Susan's bosom.

"The tea will get very cold!" objected Uncle Alex, his voice very tremulous. "See, here is a lemon, too! Do you drink tea-with-lemon like this in England, Susan?"

"We always drank tea-with-lemon in our house," said Susan.

"There's some cake too. I baked it the day—the day——"

"How beautiful it looks!" said Susan hurriedly.

Aunt Manya took the teapot in hand. Her hand trembled so that at once the tray was swimming.

"Allow me!" said Alex. Yes, Susan remembered, he was always the gallant one. "And for your husband too, it should get cold."

The gallant one. She looked at him. With an eye inside her head she saw the photograph of him in the family-album in Doomington. The astrakhan cap raked jauntily to one side. An astrakhan collar to his coat, too; a tight coat, trim at the waist. Riding-breeches. Leggings that shone like water.

He was a fine one, with his riding, and his flute-playing, and his dancing about in Gentile houses.

He had married a Jewish girl, however—Manya, the daughter of the richest miller in Davno. Gentile girls were all right to go dancing about with.

Here she was, the daughter of the richest miller in Davno. Evidently the state of the tray troubled her. Her hands fluttered with distress. The plush cloth on the table was crooked. Furtively she twitched it straight.

She had clearly been a punctilious housekeeper, Aunt Manya, daughter and wife of rich men.

"Father," said Uncle Alex, "here is a glass of tea for you!"

"Is there cake?" asked Feivel Dobkin.

"Yes, look!"

The old man's hands trembled with pleasure. "No! I won't come to the table! I can hold it!"

Susan looked across the rim of her glass at her uncle as she sipped her tea. The suit he wore had been a good one, but he seemed to have shrunk inside it. The trousers lay like a bag over his knees and round his ankles. The body seemed to have shrunk, and the face to have puffed out. The cheeks were pouches, and there were pouches under the eyes. He would have looked a very old man if his father had not been in the same room.

She contemplated the image of her grandfather she had so long carried about with her. The old man out in the orchard, with a corner of the house showing. The fine full black beard, the heavy gold chain stretched across the stomach. He wore a skull-cap, and an alpaca coat twisted and bellied a little by the wind.

He had no gold chain now, but wore a skull-cap and an alpaca coat, now as then. The black beard was a fierce fall of whiteness, as if it had grown white with terror in an hour or two.

"I must make conversation," said Susan to herself. "I must try to prevent time lagging for them or me. I needed this tea!" she said aloud. "It's good! Oh, Boris! Here's your tea poured out! It's cooled down enough, I should think."

"Thank you. I told them they could come in for a few minutes. It's getting late. We'll have to be going at once. It's quite dark. Is there any oil in this chandelier?" he asked.

"Please don't light it!" Susan insisted.

"As you choose! I told them there was to be no scene!"

"It's good of you to let them come!"

"They're here!" he announced.

A dozen women, or more, or less, came drifting into the room. Some were quite old, some were children. They came drifting in like leaves, making the same sort of unquiet noise as they moved.

" Ah, children, children ! " Uncle Alex greeted them. " To think there should be such a guest to greet you to-day ! Mother ! " he said. " This is Susan, Hannah's daughter."

That was his stepmother, of course, the famous Shevka, who had stolen the pearls, and had them stolen from her. Was this the infamous Gallia behind her, with the turned-up nose, who had worn the pearls that night when her suitor came to woo her, so that Hannah Dobkin went running broken-hearted into the forest, crying as if her heart were broken ? Was this Gallia ? Or had not her husband long ago carried her off to some other Terkass dedicated to blood and doom ?

Susan stooped to kiss a face hardly human in its wrinkled roughness. It was too dark to make out the features of the others—Shevka, Gallia, Leon's Esther, whoever they might be. They came forward awkwardly, formally, as Uncle Alex said who they were. Awkwardly, formally, Susan kissed them all. Most awkwardly she kissed the children ; she had always been uncomfortable with children.

It was like being a fine lady holding a levee, with humbler people passing in turn before her. Her cheeks were hot with embarrassment and misery.

They stood about forlornly in the darkness, the faint mournful noise rising from amongst them, though none seemed to speak.

" Why is there no light ? " suddenly came the querulous voice of Feivel Dobkin.

" Susan, it's time we left ! " called Polednik from the window.

A faint cry of dismay came from among the women. " Please, please let her stay ! " came in a note of sharp anguish from Uncle Alex.

" Do you want to stay ? " asked Polednik.

" Boris, listen ! " She turned to him urgently. She spoke in English. " I want to stay ! I must stay ! Don't you see it's completely out of my hands that I should stay ? Something greater than you or me or anything we know about has brought me here to-day. I tell you——"

" Pah ! Rubbish ! What are you talking about ! There is nothing greater than the Revolution ! "

" All right. Please. I'm not arguing. All I know is that I'm making it easier for my uncle. It doesn't matter about the old man. He has no clear idea of what's going on. I ask you to let me stay—to stay till morning. After all, it's not many hours. I don't expect you, or want you, to wait. You could put one of your men in here. May I stay ? "

He hesitated. He was clearly not pleased.

" I suppose so. I was looking forward to a good night's sleep."

" Then why not——"

" Oh, no. Ridiculous. I'll stay." He turned to Uncle Alex across the room. " My wife tells me she would like to stay with you. I will stay, too. Have you got paper and ink and a pen in this room ? " he demanded.

" Yes, Comrade Commissar."

" And a table-lamp ? Put a table-lamp on a small table."

" It is done, Comrade Commissar. Oh, Susan, my child, my child ! " He went up to her, and kissed her two hands, then he busied himself to get what Polednik had asked for.

" Comrade ! " Polednik called out.

" Present ! " replied the soldier.

" Pull those curtains ! "

" Yes, Comrade Commissar ! "

Polednik tapped about in his pockets. " Damn ! " he muttered.

" Excuse me," said Uncle Alex. He went to a chest of drawers and extracted a packet of cigarettes which had been carefully packed away. " Please smoke these ! " he said. " I will not have time myself to smoke them. Would you like one, Susan ? " He had clearly been a model host in his day.

" Thank you ! " said Polednik.

" Thank you ! " said Susan.

" Excuse me, Comrade Commissar, my mother and my sister, and the other women—they may stay ? "

" Oh, yes ! " said Polednik curtly.

" Thank you, indeed ! Come now, mother, sit down. Here, now. You, Manya, Shevka, all of you, sit down ! There, little one, ups-a-maidel, there's a good girl ! Now we're all comfortable," said Uncle Alex, " quite like the old times, on a holiday evening ! "

There were more lights than this in the old days, were there not ?—and two men for every woman ; and there was dancing and singing, and Uncle Alex played the flute, did he not ?—and Uncle Leon the fiddle ?

Uncle Leon, who had left no son to say the prayer-for-the-dead after him. He was dead ; his sons were dead ; the sons of Uncle Alex ; the husband of Shevka ; her sons . . . where, where were the men of the house of Feivel Dobkin ?

Then once again the voice of the old man came quivering into the room from his place by the cold oven.

" She is Hannah's daughter, I tell you ; Hannah who went to England ! "

It was as if someone had been arguing the matter with him. No one lifted a voice in protest. " There ! " he said triumphantly. Then suddenly he remarked something. " There are five of them ! They're in the photograph ! " He made as if to get up from his chair.

" Oh, yes, of course ! " said Uncle Alex. " How could I forget ! " He turned to Susan. " It was your sister, Esther ; she sent a photograph of all five of you to Leon's Esther. It's a long time ago now. And it's a long time before that that the photograph was taken. Do you remember, Susan ? "

Susan did not remember, but she nodded her head.

Uncle Alex stood doubtfully in the centre of the room. He made a movement towards a cupboard, a chest of drawers. Then he stopped and scratched his head. He turned to one of the women.

" Esther ! " he called out. This was clearly Leon's Esther.

" Hannah's Esther sent it to you. Do you remember where it is ? "

" It's among the other photographs, I think," whispered Leon's Esther.

" Where are they now ? " murmured Alex. " I wonder where they can be. You see "—he turned again to Susan— " ever since the bandits were here, and turned all the drawers and cupboards out on to the floor, it's been almost impossible to lay your hands on anything. It's a pity about those chairs, too," he sighed. " What good did it do them to slash them open like that ? Ah, well, if it had been only the chairs ! Where are the photographs now, Manya ? "

" We put them back in that chest of drawers," whispered Manya.

" But yes," said Alex, " I am getting quite an old man, the way I'm forgetting things ! " He opened a drawer. He fumbled about among some papers and folded cloths. Then he came to the heap of photographs he was seeking. Feverishly he ran through them till he came to the one he had in mind.

" There ! " he exclaimed. " Isn't it beautiful ? All five of you—no evil eye befall you—when you were girls ! "

He took the photograph over to her and put it into her hand. Esther, Sarah, Susan, Elsie, May, the five Silver daughters. The photograph had been taken many years ago ; it was many years ago indeed since any interest could bring the five girls together, even a visit to a photographer. It was a cabinet-sized photograph. The photographer's name was printed in heavy gold lettering : Goldenberg, Deansgate, Doomington. The lettering was very ornate, for Goldenberg was a very " classical " photographer. The gilt stood out oddly rich and clear.

She did not know that Esther had sent this photograph. She had almost completely forgotten its existence. She held it now in her hand, in the big room of her grandfather's house in Terkass, by the River Dnieper.

It was ghostly. It was as if their ghosts, the ghosts of Esther, Sarah, herself, Elsie, May, had added themselves to these. For these women about her were hardly more than ghosts. And she herself was a ghost. And she was not in Terkass at all, a few hours before the execution of her mother's father and her mother's brother, by the orders of her husband, Commissar Polednik. She was in Doomington, scrubbing herself hard to be clean and tidy for the photograph they were all to have taken by Mr. Goldenberg, who was so " classical " a photographer.

"All girls," Uncle Alex said. "Not one male amongst you."

Then the words rushed to her lips. " Where are all the men, Uncle Alex ? "

Her uncle looked at her gravely and compassionately, as if compassion were needed more for her than for him. For he knew already, and she did not yet know.

" I will tell you, little daughter," he said. And as he said this, a dim, an almost inaudible, voice of wailing went up from among the women, like a sound arising out of tragic waters when a wind stirs them.

As the slow wheels of those fatal hours revolved, he told her a tale which seemed to her too sad for the power of her mind to gauge it. Its sadness was such that, from the moment when he opened his lips to speak of it till the moment when the marching men turned in at the gate, she seemed completely removed from the world of reality. Her grasp on reality had, indeed, become steadily fainter since she had first entered the big room and set eyes on the old men. Further, the photograph of herself and her sisters had transported her for a time into a sort of trance state where she could not say if this was Terkass or Doomington, whether she dreamt or was awake, whether she was the small girl of that photograph or a grown woman, a servant of the Revolution.

But the unreality into which her uncle's narrative impressed her was of another order ; it made her feel that whatever pain she had experienced, or her husband, her mother, her father, anyone she had ever known, was a trivial chimera, the smoke-puff of a cigarette, compared with the pain which had been his burden, and was still to be, for three hours, for two hours, for one.

"It was like this, my child," he said. "I will tell you a tale or two, for we have time, no? Oh, this is you, Manya? Yes, sit on this chair beside me here, little wife. Where is your hand? There, my little one, there!

"Where shall the tale begin? Oh, it was all so happy in the old days. Why should I want to live on? It is already like the difference—how shall I say it?—between a bed of flowers and the weeds that grow among the tombstones, in the house-of-eternity. Why should I want to live on? But who wishes to die before his time? And perhaps the morning is about to break now, and the flowers are going to grow again? Ah, there has been much Jewish blood shed to water their roots.

"You should hear the young Bolsheviki in the village talking about the new world that is coming. But I am stupid. To whom am I talking? I forget you are the wife of a Commissar. Yes, Susan, let me say this at once. The Bolsheviki have been very good to us. They have been against the *pogromchiks* all the time, from the beginning. They have said all men are the same, Jew and Christian and Mohammedan, only they must all be *mouzhiks* and working-men. I don't understand it quite. You understand it so much better than I do. But what fault is it of mine that father's father got land at Prolensk when he came back from Hungary?

"Forgive me, Susan. The night is long. What time is it now? But it is not long enough for politics. I would not like to have a headache my last night. No, Manya, my love, no. I have no headache now. I want nothing to eat. Some water only. Perhaps the Comrade Commissar will allow some water, a great deal of water, to be brought in? Thank you, Comrade Commissar. And you, Susan? It is a strange thing to be offering you water, Susan, in this house which once ran with wine like a fountain. But of course the War finished our wine-business. We used to import most of our wine from Rumania, and that stopped at once. And of course it was decreed that no vodka was to be made or sold either. You can understand that a great deal of vodka was still turned out secretly; but of course Leon would have nothing to do with that. That was not the way the business had been built up. It was he himself who had made it bigger than it had ever been before. He was importing fine white wines from the Caucasus—good qualities from Hungary, too. But now—even if a son had been spared to Slatta there, who is Leon's widow, of course the business would be taken from him, would it not, Susan?

"Perhaps that is right. The world goes on and on like a river. It does not stay in the same place, and the sun, too, never comes back where it has been. We must not complain. And it might have been so much worse. If the Bolsheviki take away our land and our goods—you and he will not mind if I speak frankly to-night; I can do harm to no one—if they take away our land and our goods, they saved our lives, at least—those of us who still had lives to save.

"But it was so hard, Susan, sometimes, to know if they were real Bolsheviki, or impostors dressed up to look like Bolsheviki. Oh, we got a fine fright one day, I can tell you. It had all started already, the raiding and the killing and the bandits coming and staying two days and then being driven out by other bandits or by Bolsheviki, and the Bolsheviki being driven out by more bandits . . . oh, Susan, Susan, it was a sad time!

"And one day a party of Red horsemen came into the village, along this street here, and turned round to the square by the church. They had red banners and red bows on their caps, and they had with them an Ataman, the headman of one of the Ukrainian peasant bands. He was in a cart, all tied up. And they sent round for the chief Jews still left in the

village—Leon, of course ; and they made me come. I was
at Prolensk most of the time, but I had had to come in to
Terkass that day. And they asked us had that Ataman done
us any harm.

" Had he done us any harm ? Oh, great God ! It was he
who only a month earlier had come in and issued a proclamation that the Jews had poisoned the wells. It said in the
proclamation that it must be preached in all churches and
taught in all schools that the Jews had poisoned the wells
and they must be wiped out, not one Jew must be left
alive.

" He conducted one of the first and the biggest of the
pogroms in Terkass. For the next day or two you saw the
small Gentile boys learning to shoot, with the bodies of dead
Jews for targets. Their mothers were lying in the arms of the
bandits, dead drunk, in houses swilling with blood. The
animals ran about in the streets with hands and fingers
sticking out of their jaws.

" I must tell you these things, Susan ; it is good for you
to know. For right is right. And it is true that the Bolsheviki
saved us from those things. But, as I have told you, sometimes
it was hard to say who were who. I was speaking of the
Ataman who was bound in the cart. They asked us had he
done any harm to the Jews in Terkass. I was about to tell
them the truth, and Leon guessed it, for he pressed my foot.
He was a quiet one, but he had great good sense. And the
others looked from face to face, with their chins dropping
and their mouths slavering, they were so terrified to utter one
word, lest that word should be the wrong one.

" But Leon said : ' No, he was a great man and a good
man. He wanted the good of all the people.' He went on
singing his praises like that for some time.

" Then at last the Ataman jumped up out of the cart,
for he was not bound at all. Can you imagine how our
hearts leaped up in fright ? And he roared and roared, and
he slapped his thighs, and the tears ran down his face ; and
all the others roared too, you might have thought it was some

famous comic turn in the theatre. For they were not Bolsheviki at all, but masqueraders.

"And there and then they made a price. If we paid them
what they wanted, there would be no pogrom. Need I tell
you that, though we gave them what they asked for that
same day, there was a pogrom that same night? But it was
not so bad as it might have been, for a band—dressed up as
Red sailors, this time—came in on the merry-making, and
there was a great fight between them. They asked for thirty
thousand roubles, and so many poods of bread and sausages,
and so many casks of vodka. You understand, of course,
vodka was made illegally the whole time.

"And then poor little Berel, the parchment-maker's son,
spoke up—you remember he limped on one foot? What am
I talking about, Susan; how should *you* remember? He was
small and he limped, but he was brave. And he said we were
a poor village, and had been robbed so much, it would not
be easy to find thirty thousand roubles at once. So the
Ataman took his bayonet and thrust it straight through
Berel's ribs till it came through the other side. And he was a
big man, the Ataman, and Berel, as I have said, was quite
short. So he lifted him up and turned him round slowly, like
a bird that turns round on a spit before a fire. Berel's father,
Shmul, the parchment-maker, was there."

He paused for some moments. "Yes," he resumed, "it's a
good thing she's dead now, too." No one had uttered any
word or mentioned any name.

"Who's dead?" The question formed itself without
volition in Susan's mind. She did not learn who the woman
was, then or any time, that nameless woman who was the
wraith of a wraith, who had returned for a moment's
spectral existence on the lips of a doomed man.

"You see she was mad, quite mad. Whenever the bandits
used to come, she would wait for them in the market-place.
She had a skull with her. They say it was her son's skull.
She slept with it beside her on her pillow of rags and straw
When the bandits arrived, they gathered round her. They

knew what to expect. She undressed herself before them, and danced and danced, very solemnly and statelily, holding the skull before her like a king's cup. It's a good thing she's dead now," he repeated. " They roared with laughter. They lay in the roadway hiccuping, they found it so gay."

The voice of the old man went on and on, without much modulation of grief or indignation. The women uttered no word, as if the horror had become so completely part of themselves that it did not disturb them now more than the beating of their own hearts.

He was speaking now of one of Petlura's bands. " And, of course, the first thing they did," he said, " was to stick up leaflets everywhere, saying that we must surrender all reserves of corn and oats. We would fail to do so on pain of death. They all did that, Susan, all the bands, one after the other. And once or twice we gave up all we had ; and it was not easy to get more for our own needs, and the needs of our horses at Prolensk. It was not easy, I tell you. So when Petlura's men came the second time, we went and digged pits in the fields and hid a few sacks. For we knew that they would go off soon, like the others, and what would we do when they had gone ?

" Sergei Ivanovitch, of course, was as faithful as a dog. I should have told you, Sergei is our chief agent. He has been with us forty years, fifty years—I can't tell you now. He helped us to dig the pits and carry the sacks. It was his son, Semyon, that betrayed us. He is a hot Bolshevik, and when the Bolsheviki came this time, he came nosing about the farm on pretence of seeing his old father and mother, and went about the fields at night, like a fox, scratching, and so he found out about the sacks ; they were two or three— nothing ; just enough to keep body and soul together.

" You see, Susan, they all said the same thing, all made the same proclamations, and how should we know that the Bolsheviki were so much stronger this time than they had been before ? No, Susan, I am not seeking to excuse myself. It is too late for that. But the old man. Yes, he's sound asleep. It's a lucky thing he spends much of his time now night and day sleeping. I could have wished that he might just have dozed off like that into his last sleep one of these days, instead of . . . instead of this thing.

" You see, he had nothing at all to do with the burial of the sacks. He knew nothing about it. Does he look as if he could lift a sack on to his shoulders ? It was like this. I had sent for him to be brought over to us at Prolensk. In some ways Prolensk was safer, for though we were more exposed over there, there was not so much to attract the bands. They come where the Jews are. Over there, they would not even know that it was a Jew farming those fields. So he came. Then only a few days later. . . . But you know, my child, you see before your eyes what happened a few days later.

" If only one of the boys had been spared, Susan. Not one, not one. They are all gone. It is late. There is not much time left. I must tell you this thing, too. It was the men of Grigoriev that did it. The Bolsheviki had been very good to us. If not for them there would be not one Jew left in all this country. I am about to die, Susan, but I would like to say to him that I know how good and just the Bolsheviki have been. Will you tell him that, Susan ? "

He paused. Susan sought in her throat for the power of speech, but could not find it. He seemed to be waiting for her to convey his word. The silence continued several seconds longer.

Polednik was still sitting at his table, a pen in his hand, and his hand on the writing-paper. He did not lift his head. " I have heard every word that has been said." Again there was a silence, a longer silence now. Then Alex Dobkin resumed his tale.

" It was in the June of this year. News came from beyond Prolensk that a great band of Grigoriev's men was marching upon the Dnieper. So dreadful a band had not been seen yet in these parts. They were burning farms and forests as they approached. We talked it over a whole day and night long, as to whether we should all gather in Prolensk or come

over here, to the big house in Terkass. There was a chance
that they would not come this way ; they might have turned
north quite easily, to Tanyev. But Sergei Ivanovitch thought
it quite certain that when they heard all our family was
gathered together at Prolensk—there would be those who
would not fail to tell them—without doubt they would come
down on Prolensk and not one of us would be left alive, and
not one stone standing on another.

" They skirted the farm at Prolensk. Sergei Ivanovitch put
it about that he had forced us at the point of a pistol to hand
the farm over to him. Two days later a message was brought
in by one of our men that they were marching down on
Terkass ; they were only a few hours away ; they had suddenly changed their line of route.

" I called a meeting at once in the synagogue. Some of us
wanted to build up some sort of Jewish defence force. If we
wanted to do such a thing now, for any purpose at all, it
would be too late. There are no men left to build up any
force at all."

" That would be quite unnecessary," cut in the voice of
Boris Polednik. " We will provide all the defence that is
needed. We expect none will be needed from now on."

A slight sigh went up among the women, a murmur of
oh-that-it-might-be. Uncle Alex continued :

" Perhaps those who were against our getting a force together were right. They said that if we did not fight, at
least the women would be spared ; but if we fought, the
women, too, would be slaughtered. And yet—who knows ?
—if we had fought . . . Ah, well, who shall decide that now ?
You have not seen our wine-cellar, Susan ? " he asked,
almost with a note of proprietary pride, as it were a place
worth commemorating some day with a marble tablet
announcing that here human woe and human vileness
reached their limit, and could no further go. " You have
not seen our wine-cellar ? "

" No," breathed Susan.

" We often used to say it is as big as a synagogue. It

is here under our feet, and goes all the way under beyond the wall there, and comes out by a door near the apricot-tree. News came about three o'clock that the first bandits were approaching Terkass. We got into the cellar all together, all of us, Leon, and father, and the other brothers, and our sons, and the husbands of our daughters, and their sons, and all our women. We pushed empty barrels and earth and some of the broken flooring against the big door in front and the small door into the orchard. We heard them coming in ones and twos. Then in groups. We heard loud laughter and songs and drunken cheers. They were very drunk. They held a meeting some little way down the street there. Quite clearly came the sound of swords sharpened on the stones. Then they began. We were almost the first, for ours was much the biggest house in the street. They had no difficulty at all in breaking in the two doors.

" ' Out ! Out ! ' they cried. ' All of you ! Pig-Jews, out at once ! If you come out at once, we'll not touch the women. Out, I say ! You there ! ' It was Motka, Leon's second son, one of them had got hold of. ' Hide, would you ! ' He smashed his skull in with the butt of his rifle. He was fourteen years old, peace be upon him !

" What else was there to do ? Die there like rats in a hole ? Out they went, all of them, excepting two of us only —my wife, Manya, and myself. You see, it was like this. We had hidden ourselves in the very furthest corner, where the roof came down quite close to the ground. We happened to find some sacks beside us, and lay down there and covered ourselves with them.

" The others went. They told the women to get out into the street, and shoved the men up against the apricot-tree. Thalia would not go. She was the wife of my younger son. She had brought with her—we had not known it—all the jewels of her dowry, and some thousands of roubles beside.

" ' Take these ! ' " she cried. ' In the name of God, take these, and let me have my husband ! ' She threw herself on the ground and kissed their feet. She was getting in the way. They stuck a bayonet into her. She was the only woman they killed. They took her jewels and money, of course. And then——"

Suddenly one of the women, the women who had been silent so long, sprang to her feet and uttered a loud howl. She ran to the window against which the faint dimness of the earliest morning was lapping. She pointed like an avenging priestess at the apricot-tree. " There ! There ! " she cried. " I saw him, my man Leon, his blood pouring from his heart ! Oi ! Oi ! My man, my love, his blood ! "

Then as suddenly she collapsed again. Two of the younger women went up to her, and said, " Hush ! Hush ! " faintly, and led her back where she had been sitting.

" They did not kill the old man, as you see. Perhaps it would have been better if they had. He was too old and wretched for even the bandits to kill ! He was brighter then than now. He has become like this—he can hardly see at all —since that day.

" They finished what they had to do up there. There was not a sound we did not hear, for this happened near the smaller door—and the smaller door was open, not far from where we were. Then we heard one bandit say to another : ' Hadn't we best go down into the cellar again, friend ? What do you think ? There's lots of holes and corners about in that cellar where some of them may still be hiding.'

" So they came down and poked about with their bayonets all over. ' Ho ! Ho ! ' they cried. ' Come out, Jews ! Ho ! Ho ! ' And Manya and I were still lying there in the darkness under the sacks. Then they lit matches. They came quite near us and lit a match. You know," he said, " they were facing this way when they lit that match." He turned towards the oven. Then he turned round at right angles from the oven. " But if they had been turning round this way, they would most certainly have seen us. I felt a movement in Manya's face beside my shoulder. I clapped my hand quick as lightning over her mouth. She was going to scream.

" Then they left. I need not tell you more. I would like a drink, Susan, if you would reach it me. What ? It isn't night any longer ! Can you hear anything ? Can you hear feet ? Yes. It is the feet of men marching. They've stopped at the gate. . . ."

The feet of the marching men stopped. Susan's heart stopped. For one moment the whole mechanism of the universe seemed to have suspended its action. Then Uncle Alex uttered a word or two more. He spoke with the pathos of the schoolboy who hopes that the harsh decree may, after all, be not quite irrevocable. His eyes rested, mournful and inquisitive, on her face.

" Would you ask him," he said, " if there's any way at all——"

Then the whole fabric of her universe broke. She flung herself towards her husband, grovelling on her knees. " Let them go ! " she screamed. " Let them go ! How can you do this dreadful thing ! You won't do it ! You can't ! You're a monster ! All of you are monsters ! I hate you ! I hate your Revolution ! Blood ! Blood ! All blood ! Haven't you had enough blood ? "

She was knocking her forehead on the floor as she spoke, blow upon dull blow.

" You can't do it, I say ! Let them go ! Cowards, butchers ! "

Then she heard a voice pierce athwart her desolation, a voice icy and sharp as splintered glass.

" Get up, woman ! Get up ! If you say one word more— one word more—I'll ask them to take you out with the two others ! "

She lifted her eyes towards the cold blaze of his eyes. In hers were fear and terror, and a dreadful adoration. She heard the gate swing on its hinges, and the feet of men marching forward towards the tree. She heard a cry rise from among the women, long and terrible and mournful, like the cry of an animal under the moon in a desert place, She heard and saw no more,

CHAPTER XII

PENNINE GRANGE

I

IT WAS an afternoon in the spring of 1921. Mrs. Silver was getting ready for a committee-meeting tea-party which was to be held in twenty minutes or so down in the drawing-room. It was a beautiful day. Everything was beautiful all round her. But she sighed. The carpet under her feet was thick and beautiful, and the Pliskin rosewood bedroom furniture was beautiful, and the bathroom which led out of her bedroom was beautiful. And, beyond the little dressing-room which separated her bedroom from Sam's, Sam's bedroom was beautiful, too.

She knew they were high up in the world, really so high up that you couldn't get very much higher up without hitting the underside of the King's throne; but she would have liked Sam and herself to go on having the same bedroom, just as they used to, even in Ivanhoe Towers, though it was two or three times as big as Pennine Grange.

Of course it was different there. Many a night she would never have lasted till the next morning if she had had a bedroom to herself at Ivanhoe Towers. Particularly later on, when Mrs. Hargreaves got to wandering about the house all night. One or two of the maids had sworn they'd seen her with a knife in her mouth, and had given notice. But probably they were looking for a reason to give notice, or had become quite simply hysterical. The Hargreaveses were enough to drive anyone silly.

And then there had been those noises that the hot-water-system made. It was obviously the first hot-water-system that had been put in in any North Country house. Yes, she was happy enough they had left Ivanhoe Towers—excepting for this matter of the separate bedrooms. There weren't any Hargreaveses to be afraid of now. On the contrary, she had a staff of servants at Pennine Grange that was the envy of all the rich women in Altrincham and Didsbury, and she had May to look after them, too. And the hot-water-system, like everything else in the house, ran as smooth as silk.

But it was rather late in life for her and Sam to be separated at nights. They had been through so much together, and, after all, they had had five daughters together, it was a bit lonely and strange at nights. She would never get used to it. You might as well go and live in the Central Hotel altogether.

In the old days, in Oleander Street . . Mrs. Silver adjusted the clasp of her pearls, and sighed.

Of course you couldn't get away from it ; it was Esther's fault. Esther thought it wrong for husbands and wives in their position not to have separate bedrooms. She and her husband, Joe, had had separate bedrooms for a long time. But that might be all right for Esther, Mrs. Silver thought. Esther and Joe weren't so all-in-all to each other as she and Sam. Besides, Esther was a big person at Pliskin's Furniture Company Limited ; so she saw as much as she wanted to see of Joe during the day. It was different for her. *She* saw nothing of Sam all day long, for Sam was just as busy as ever at the works ; even busier, since Smirnof had gone off to London to look after the London end of the business and to start new companies.

And now she saw nothing of Sam during the night, either. It wasn't right. Oh, Esther made no bones about it. When a man and his wife have two separate bedrooms, it means they have two separate suites of bedroom furniture. Esther tried to make out, at first, that it was all really for health's sake. But she didn't stick to that long. It was really for the sake of the Pliskin Furniture Company Limited. When both Sam and herself had pointed out that they were Esther's father and mother, after all, and it wouldn't make much

difference to a firm with such a big turnover as the Pliskins
if her parents went on using one bedroom with one suite of
bedroom furniture, just as they had always done, Esther
said it would set a very bad example. Besides, she said she
would let them have the most wonderful bedroom suites
that anyone had ever put on the market ; in fact, all their
furniture was going to be so wonderful, and Pennine Grange
was such a wonderful place to show it off in, without letting
anyone know that it was being shown off, that people would
want to come from miles round to look at all that wonderful
furniture. And, in fact, they did ; until sometimes you might
think Pennine Grange was just a show-room annexe to
Pliskin's, for which Pliskin's didn't pay any rent. And then
May, gently but firmly, stepped in. It was a good thing she
did, too.

Mrs. Silver looked out through the window on to the lawn
below, and the flower-beds that encompassed the lawn.
Beyond the sitting-out lawn was the tennis-lawn, and beyond
the tennis-lawn and beyond the vegetable-garden the
Derbyshire hills were a purple curtain hung above the
horizon. Beyond the flower-beds, to the right of the lawn,
was a low rose-pink wall that seemed centuries old, but was
only three or four, the age of Pennine Grange itself. At
least, the wall in that assembling of its bricks was only three
or four years old. The bricks before that had been part of
the fabric of a Tudor house which had been pulled down.
The rose-pink bricks in Mrs. Silver's wall were a document
in the social history of the England of that time.

Beyond the brick wall was an orchard flung over with
petals, like a bride and bridegroom's car taking them off on
their honeymoon. There were apple-trees in the orchard,
and pear-trees, plum-trees, and damsons ; there were
medlars and quinces and cherries. There were red currants
and white currants and gooseberries growing among the
fruit-trees. There were fine nut-trees—walnut and hazel.
They had had fan-shaped apricot-trees planted against the
south walls. They would not grow of themselves here, in

Altrincham, as the great apricot-tree had grown in Terkass. The blossom came early, so the gardener had to protect it very carefully with netting. The apricot-tree in Terkass was strong as a horse.

It was a beautiful and expensive orchard they had here, but there was nothing in it so grand as her father's apricot-tree. Pennine Grange was a grand house, and yet, in certain ways, it was not so grand as her father's house in Terkass. It was a happier house than Ivanhoe Towers, but in certain ways it was not so happy a house as number eleven Oleander Street.

She fingered the pearl necklace at her throat. Sam had given her much finer pearl necklaces than that one, but she knew it would be considered showy to come down to a mere committee-meeting tea-party with one or two of the really valuable pearl necklaces on. May wouldn't say anything, but there would be that slightly pained look in her eyes which always got up in them when her mother behaved in what might be called a *nouveau-riche* manner. So Hannah Silver tried hard to behave like a lady who has always been, in that particular sense of the word, a lady. She knew May never felt that the famous pearl necklace counted. It wasn't show to wear that pearl necklace. It was religion, almost.

She fingered the pearl necklace. She looked down on the orchard. She wondered what was happening to them all at Terkass, to her father, and her brothers, Leon and Alex, and her half-brothers, and her step-mother, Shevka, and her step-sister, Gallia, and all of them. She hadn't the least ill feeling in the world against Shevka and Gallia. Far from it. She had more than once suggested to Sam that he ought to make an effort to bring the younger people over. Her father and step-mother were probably too old to travel, and perhaps Alex wouldn't like to leave the farm and Leon the wine-business, but some of the others might like to come, and jobs might be found for them in one or the other of the Silver concerns.

And who knows? Perhaps Alex and Leon wouldn't feel themselves too old to come over either. She was certain business in Russia wasn't what it used to be, what with this Revolution there had been. She had heard them talking about it at dinner-parties, saying that they had taken land and businesses away from the people who had owned them, and were dividing them up amongst the peasants and the work-people. Or, if they hadn't yet, they were going to.

Of course they wouldn't do such a thing with Alex or Leon. They were so good to everybody. But then you never knew how things turned out when they got out of hand. It was a pity that that Revolution had made it difficult, even impossible, to send and to get letters, or something might be done about it. Oh, yes, she remembered. Last year a letter had come from Susan, with Turkish stamps on. " What," May had asked, " what's Susan doing in Turkey? " " A letter from Susan? " Mrs. Silver had asked, entirely unable to believe her ears. " Yes," May had said, " I believe it's possible to get into touch with Russia nowadays, through Turkey." Then she had started reading the letter. Her face had gone quite pale and strange. " What, darling? What's the matter? Is there any bad news? Read it out at once! " But May had said : " You know what Susan is. The first time she writes to me after four years, it's all Karl Marx and Lenin and politics and more Karl Marx. Did you ever hear of such a thing? I can't be bothered to read it now. I'll read the rest after breakfast."

So she had crumpled up the letter and thrust it away in her bag and finished her breakfast, though she didn't eat much more. It was quite clear there had been something in the letter to upset her.

" Tell me," Mrs. Silver had again insisted. " If there's any bad news you mustn't hide it from me. You can't treat your mother like a little schoolgirl, you know! "

" No, darling, no," May had said, and got up and kissed her. " I'll read it to you, if you like. But it's all so boring. Really Susan was always such a bore." With that she'd gone upstairs, and there'd been nothing more said or done about it since then.

And then she had lately heard one of Sam's business friends saying that arrangements were being made for a regular postal service between England and Russia. As soon as that was done, she would write herself to Terkass. Perhaps, too, her daughter, Susan, might write to her then, from wherever in Russia she had got to. There was a suspicion of a tear in her eye. That girl Susan had never been a very devoted daughter. She was about as tender as a meat-safe, she said to herself crossly. Or perhaps Susan only *acted* like that ? And Susan, too, had a heart of gold hidden away somewhere behind that flat chest. Mrs. Silver was prone to believe that people really only *acted* like that ; they really had hearts of gold beating away quite busily somewhere.

And if ever she got some of them over from Russia, wouldn't it be a grand thing ! Naturally, if Alex and Leon should come, she'd wear the pearl necklace, their mother's pearl necklace, even if she didn't wear anything else. But if her step-sister Gallia should come, she would very carefully *not* wear it. It would be like crowing over her, and she wasn't one for crowing over people.

Her magnanimity made her feel a bit better. She turned to her dressing-table to spray a little chypre on her bosom.

Then her door opened. It was May. " Mother darling, you're late," she called out. " They'll be here in a minute or two, and you said you wanted to put some flowers out, and I wasn't to do anything about it. And it's too late, now. You wicked one ! "

" I'm sorry, May," she said. " I was looking out of the window, and I saw the fruit-trees, and I started thinking."

" Now, mother, now ! " May reproved her.

Mrs. Silver went up to the bed, and picked up a handbag which she had placed there. " Do you think this one is too much for a tea-party ? "

" Oh, my dear, I'm sure no one would think twice whatever you came down with. Of course, it *is* a little——" And perhaps it was, with its gold clasp inset with diamonds. " I wonder, perhaps, if it isn't the sort of thing one goes to the opera with ? " May mused.

" There you are," Mrs. Silver threw the bag on the bed again. " I'll never learn. How shall I learn ? Did I ever have any practice ? "

" You *shall* take it with you, so there. Even if a couple of princesses royal should be coming. And they're not. They're just women with title. Like the men father's got on his board of directors."

Mrs. Silver sighed. It was a sigh of contentment this time. "To think that my Sam should be sitting at the same table with lords and generals ! Would you have thought such a thing ? "

" Mamma darling, they're what you call guinea-pigs. I don't know much about it, but I know that's what you call them. And so are these women coming to-day—just guinea-pig committee-women. They don't do any work, but you've got to have them. The ordinary people think there's something wrong if you don't have them."

" I don't know what you call them. But these gentlemen that sit with Sam on his board—and they drink whiskies with soda together, and they give him big cigars—they're from the highest in the land, and you know it. They've got kings in their families."

" Of course, pet, I know. And why shouldn't they give father big cigars ? They can afford it. And it shows how wonderfully papa's made good, to have all these Knights of the Garter fighting to sit on his board. But I wish, poor dear, he didn't keep on working so hard. He works just as hard as he did in the old days—harder. We've got more money than we know what to do with. What on earth should he go on working so hard for ? "

" I know. It's like the sugar illness. The more you get, the more you want. And then you say you haven't got any." Then the line of her thoughts changed. " Is that one coming, the honourable one ? You know—how can you expect me to get his name ? "

" Oh, Wolfgang-Essex ? Yes, of course, he'll be here, too."

" You know, May," her mother said wistfully. " You know I don't want you to go from me ? "

" Yes, my sweet, I don't want to go away from either of you. But if we bring it off this afternoon, and, even if we don't, I'll have to go down south for a little time. If we get enough support this afternoon, the work starts sooner. If we don't, I'll have to hunt round for more, and the work starts later. That's all. But I have to go, darling."

" Yes, love. You think I want you to spend all your life here like my housekeeper ? I should ashame myself into an illness."

" Well, then, mother, so it's settled. My dear, look at the time. Isn't that a car coming ? We must go down, really we must."

" If they come, they can wait. I'm talking to you."

" Hoity-toity ! "

" Listen, May. You will spend all your life looking after this Country Home in—how do you call it ?—in that Sussex ? "

" No, dear. You know very well I said I wouldn't. I've got to get it on its feet. I've got certain ideas about it, and I can't trust anybody else to carry them out. It might take two years—three years, at most."

" And then ? "

" Then, mother, I'll come back to you."

" And be again my housekeeper ? "

" You're being a very troublesome woman."

" May, my daughter, why don't you ? "

" Don't I what ? "

" You know you're twenty-five. You're no baby. My mother married when she was fifteen. I married when I was——" She calculated a moment. Then her cheeks slowly reddened. She remembered her marriage was bound up one way and another with the pre-hymeneal imminence of her eldest daughter. " I'll tell you something, May. I know I should give them to the eldest by right. But I won't. Not if she will go down on her knees and beg me from to-day till next week."

" Give *what* ? "

Mrs. Silver opened her eyes wide. She was almost angry. " Give *what* ? What do you think ? My mother's pearls, of course ! I shouldn't give them to any of them, only to you, May, on the day you should get married."

" But, darling, I'm not getting married ! "

" This Wolfgang-Essex, do you think he has any interest at all in Country Homes for Jewish Boys and Girls ? "

" None at all, absolutely none. He invited himself to-day, as usual. He hitched himself on to his aunt, Lady Wolfgang."

" She's the German-*goy* side of the family, yes ? "

" Yes. Sir Ernest Wolfgang."

" But the other part of his name, Essex ; he's Jewish on that side, isn't he ? "

" Yes, Isaacs."

" May, May. I ask you. He looks at you like as if he were a dog. He's going to be a Lord. He's from one side a Jew. What more can you want ? "

" I don't love him, mother," she said, idling with the tassel of a curtain-cord.

" Love, love ! " her mother expostulated. " If you don't love him now, you'll love him soon ; a face like a picture. And it's not money he's after," she wagged her finger at her daughter. " With other young men it was money, you could see that with bandages round your eyes. But no, not with this one. He's not after money. He's rich."

" Yes, I know. He's a very pleasant young man."

" There you are, what did I tell you ? What was that college he went to ? Eton College. What more can you want than that ? Did you go to Eton College ? Did your father ? No, May, let me talk. You may be twenty-five, but you're young yet in knowledge from the world. Eton College ; and he's going to be a Lord ; and, from his father's side, a Jew ; and she makes difficulties. You wouldn't have to get married in no churches—like—like Elsie." The memory stuck in her throat. She tried to gulp it down, but it stuck there.

"Now, mother, darling, don't upset yourself. It wasn't really a church. Not like a place where you go and say Christian prayers. It was the private chapel in Bobby's country house. Not at all the same thing. His mother wanted them to get married in a real smart church, but Elsie thought that vulgar."

"Oh, yes, yes ; you've tried to explain it to me already. It was just Elsie having a joke. Yes, I understand. Well, I don't like jokes like that. If she has to marry a *goy*, let her marry a *goy*. Did I ever expect she should not marry a *goy* ? Anyhow, thank God a thousand times she settled down and married *somebody* ! And you can't get away from it, she's a Lady, too ! "

"Yes, indeed, mamma, she's a Lady ! And what's more, there are Ladies and Ladies ! "

"What do you mean ? " There was a note of suspicion in her voice.

"Well, I mean Bobby's the eighth baronet, something like that. So she's the eighth Lady, without counting dowagers. Or do baronets have dowagers ? "

"I don't know what you mean, May. All I know is, thank God it's a marriage ! "

"Yes, mother. And in a way you've got me to thank for it. I was the *shadchan*, the marriage-broker. You know I never got my commission ? "

"You mean—what do you mean ? "

"Didn't I get them introduced to each other, when I was working in the Hut, in Boulogne ? "

"I should say, thank you for it, eh ? "

"Oh, mother, really, you *are* hard to please ! All right, then, wash me out of it. As a matter of fact it was *quite* his own doing. Didn't he go round to the stage-door with flowers every night for six months ? Later on, when the War stopped, didn't he even follow her into the provinces ? Even Elsie couldn't stand up against that ! It made her feel like a corpse every night. And two afternoons a week, too. So she had to marry him."

" He said he'd kill himself if she wouldn't, didn't he ? " There was a note in her voice of satisfied maternal pride. " How often ? "

" Two or three times a week ! "

" Well, he's rich, anyway," Mrs. Silver added, not quite relevantly. " Oh, yes, he was a good catch. If only it didn't have to be in a *church* ! Why not a register office, to get it over quick, so nobody should talk ? "

" It's what they call a social convenience, darling."

" Well to me it's inconvenient, very inconvenient. Let me have *one* marriage in the family to give me *nachuss*, to give me joy, in my old years. One after another, it's been this way and that way. When Esther gets married, it's in a synagogue at least, but what sort of a wedding was it ? Like mice from churches. And then ? In a register office, Sarah gets married ; in a register office, Susan gets married ; and then, all of a sudden, Elsie becomes a high respectable lady, and she gets married in a church. Well ? Should I get fat from joy ?

" And now, you, May. You're the only one left. We're not so young as we used to be, your father and me." Hannah touched her eyes with a handkerchief. " And here's a chance for a wedding, he comes from Eton College, he'll be a Lord, he is rich, he is handsome like the sunshine, he's a long way a Jew . . ." She chanted his advantages with a sort of Friday-evening intonation. Then her voice resumed a prose measure again. " But do you need to get married in an old-fashioned synagogue like the poor people ? Why should you ? You could get married in the Reform Synagogue. Men and women sitting together ; a choir with an organ ; men without hats and women with hats ; you would think you was getting married in a church—and *yet* a synagogue ! "

" Mother ! "

" Yes ? "

" Did you love the man you married ? "

" Your father ? My Sam ? Well, what then ? "

" And you married him ? "

" Why, of course ! "

" I won't marry Mr. Wolfgang-Essex. I won't marry any man I don't love. It's extremely probable I'll never get married at all."

" But——"

" Please, mother. Not one word more. I don't want you ever to bring up the subject again. Father never does. He understands. I'm a little ashamed of you, mother."

" Oi, May, May——"

" Come now, mother. We've no right to keep our guests waiting. Now, now, don't cry. I know, darling, you're only thinking of my happiness. There, just powder your nose a little. No, darling, no. Of course I'm not cross with you. Ready ? "

" Yes, May dear, I'm ready."

" Come then ! "

" Oh, May, please ! "

" Yes ? "

" Do I make it any difference between the ladies with a title and the ladies without a title ? I mean when I shake hands with them ? "

" No, mother. Just treat them as if they were all equally human beings."

" But I'm so nervous from them, May. I'm so nervous."

" Never mind, darling, I'll look after you. And look here, mother. Before you go. One moment."

" Yes, dear ? "

" Those wrinkles on your forehead. Take them off this instant. I won't have them."

She went up to her mother's forehead, and sought, with cool fingers, to straighten it out.

" That's a little better, I think. I tell you, I won't have them. Come along now, darling."

11

It was very late when Sam Silver came in that night, well beyond midnight. He let himself in at the front door, turned out the light they had left on in the vestibule, and the light which was still burning in the hall. " Tut, tut ! " he said, a little annoyed at the extravagance. He was not a mean man, but he could not get himself to condone the burning of electric-light, hour beyond hour, when it could be switched on in a moment, as soon as it was needed.

He felt his way along the hall past the big drawing-room, and round into a narrow passage from which the " home-room " opened, as Mrs. Silver christened it with an un-conscious pathos. There had been no " home-room " in Ivanhoe Towers. That house did not lend itself to such treatment. But here, in Pennine Grange, the Silvers hardly used any other room, except to dine in, and when there was company. They had put up the old samovar there, on a shelf, though its chimney was battered ; and there the old brass trays were, and the candlesticks and the Sabbath evening beakers, on the mantel-piece. They had Oleander Street pictures on the walls, which, one way and another, had survived the two removals. There was Baron Hirsch, there was Disraeli, there was Queen Victoria, there was Dr. Herzl—the major Jewish figures of the Victorian era. There was a chart of the Forty-Year-Wanderings of the Jews from the Land of Bondage to the Land of Promise. There had been certain other images on the Oleander Street walls—Karl Marx, Tolstoi, Kropotkin. But these had been sloughed, whether out of sheer shame, or because there had been a definite swing to the right on the part of the Silvers during these last few years, keeping pace with the advance in their fortunes.

Very few of the bigger pieces of furniture were the same as they had been in Oleander Street ; but they were not egregiously different. And they still retained the parlour overmantel, at all events, and the small mirror, and the plush tablecloth ; and, of course, the metal stool by the fire. The family album stood in the middle of the table. Esther had been quite indignant about the retention of that penurious overmantel, though she calmed down when the undertaking was given that no visitors were to be allowed into that room. She would have preferred it if no servants had been allowed in, either ; but May would give no under-taking to that effect, for fear it got about among the servants that bodies were kept there. However, Esther anticipated that before long her mother would make that room her very especial care ; that nobody but herself would be allowed to labour there, with duster and crumb-scoop, at least. (Doubtless she would be forced to leave doughtier hands than her own to tackle the electric vacuum.) It turned out exactly so.

Sam Silver advanced up the narrow passage to the " home-room," where they always put out a glass of milk and buttered biscuits for him when he came in late. " Tut, tut ! " he said again. For the light streamed out under the door. They had left the light on there, too, as well as in the vestibule.

He entered.

" Darling ! " said his daughter.

" You ! " he said. " You bad girl ! Why aren't you in bed ? "

" Why aren't *you* ? "

" I've been busy, my dear, in the office ! "

" All day ? "

" Till now ! "

" If I'm not going to see you at night, when *am* I going to see you ? Off in the morning with the first bird. In at night with the first milkman. It won't do, father darling ! "

He lifted his hands to show these early goings and late comings were entirely outside his control.

" And look here ! You too ! They're getting worse ! " She went straight up to him and stared at his forehead.

" What's the matter with me? Have I some soot? " He looked round towards the Oleander Street mirror.

" No, those wrinkles ! I've been noticing them for some time now, and then forgetting about them. Mamma's got them, too ! I won't have them ! "

" Well, what do you expect, my baby? You know, May, you can grow to be a hundred and twenty, no evil eye, you'll still be my baby."

" Yes, it's dreadful, the way you both spoil me. The amount of money you let me have for my schemes——"

" If we shouldn't do that, what should we spend it on ? Can you put it all in the stomach ? We're so *rich*, May ; we're so rich ! "

" I know ! I know ! " Her head seemed to droop a little. " Well, papa, come, let's not be too miserable about it ! Sit down ! I think you'd best have a little brandy and soda to-night. It'll do you more good than milk. You look quite washed out."

" No, thank you, May. Milk, please ! Yes, it's been a long day. I sent for Sasha, you know, yesterday." (He meant his son-in-law, Alexander Smirnof.) " He came first thing to-day. That's one good thing. If he thinks I'm in trouble, and things are just getting a little mixed, he'll come from anywhere any time, let it be even Cape Town. I've just got to say the word."

" That man he put in his place when he went off to London, isn't he good ? "

" Oh, Huxtable's all right. Only I can't get his name proper, and he looks so frightening with his long blue chin and his high collar ; it's not so homely working with him as it was with Sasha. I must say he's got a fine head for figures, too. I don't know where I'd be without him. It's a big salary to pay him, but he's worth every penny of it."

" What did you send for Sasha for, darling? And why didn't he come in to see us to-day? How's the news with Sarah ? How's the new baby? She's not had another since last month ? "

" God bless her ! "

" He's at least got another hobby besides babies. He likes music. She's just got babies."

" Well, and why not ? Do you know from a better hobby ? I had girls for my hobby. I've had more pleasure out of it than from horses. There's only one wish I've got left in the world." He blew rather mournfully.

" And what's that ? " she asked suspiciously.

" That you, too, should start going in for a hobby for having babies."

" You didn't tell me "—she switched the subject off rapidly—" you didn't tell me what you sent for Sasha for."

" He's only just left me now. He's gone back to London by the midnight train. He'll only just catch his boat by going straight on to Paris and Marseilles."

" Yes, darling, I know. I know he's always charging about the Continent. How he manages to produce those babies so regularly is a puzzle. What did you have him up in Doomington for ? "

" Now listen, May, what do you understand from business ? It will only give you a headache, like it gives me."

" I want to share your headaches, father darling. I've done it before, and I hope to do it often again."

" What ? You want me to have headaches often again ? Well, there's a nice daughter ! "

" Tell me, father, there's a dear. I don't often ask you about business, do I ? I know it's all too mixed up for me— far too many figures. But, when you start looking worried like this, I do want to try and understand, and see if I can't help."

" Well, May, if you was a little smaller I'd put you on my knee, and I'd try and make you understand."

" Well, I'll sit here on the metal stool just beside you. Good old stool, isn't it ? Do you remember how I used to sit reading poetry-books here, hour after hour, and then when he was finished at the office——" She blushed. Almost as quickly the colour went out of her cheeks again. " Are you comfortable there ? Won't you have a cushion ? "

" And you won't let me go to bed ? Look how late it is ! "

" I tell you here and now. I'm not going to let you get up till ten in the morning. I'm going to lock you in your room. Now you must talk. I want to try and understand."

He uttered a sigh of resignation. " You're worse than Esther when you put your mind to something."

" Well ? "

" It's like this. This is the biggest thing from everything. You know Sasha ? "

" I do."

" Will you believe it ? "

" I will."

" Wait till you hear it. Wait till I tell you what I did to him."

" What you did to him ? You know perfectly well he'd never have gone a step without you. And he won't now. It's not *in* him."

" Wait a minute, wait a minute. Don't be impatient. I made him lose some money."

" Well, business is business. You made him gain a lot, too. "

" Did I say I made him lose some money ? "

" You did. "

" I don't mean some money."

" What *do* you mean ? "

" A lot of money. Thousands and thousands of pounds. And then more thousands."

" Nonsense, father."

" Do you know when we made a public company out of my firm ? "

" Yes ? "

" Sasha became a rich man, too. And then I made him lose—oh, I'd better not talk about it."

" It wasn't *your* fault ! "

" Well, in speculation it's nobody's fault. And yet it *was* my fault, too."

" In speculation? Did *you* speculate? What did *you* lose?"

" No, I didn't. All my money's good. What shall I want to speculate for? I don't believe in it. I want to go on making my raincoats and my waterproofs in my Longton factory, and my gumboots and my dummy teats and my hot-water-bottles in my Stretford factory. I'm happy like that, what should I want to speculate for?"

" Well, then, it's his fault. What do you want to worry your head for if he loses money speculating?"

" I was telling you. When we sold the company to the public, and we each of us got all that money, I wanted just to keep on being chairman, and he should be joint managing director with me, and to keep on manufacturing. Well, I was and he was. And we are now too. But he said manufacturing wasn't enough. What was the good of all that money for if you didn't speculate? You should have seen him in the office during those days when we had such a success selling the company, and he had all that money, and the shares he held went higher and higher, and he was getting richer every minute. He wasn't the same man at all."

" Yes, father, it's a little upsetting. You were rather excited, too."

" And shouldn't I be?"

" Of course you should. Please keep on."

" He's a clever man, is Sasha."

" Yes, of course."

" He already knew it, early on last year, things couldn't last so marvellous. He said he smelled it in the air, the way the prices of cotton and silver were going up and up, it couldn't last, and they'd have to come down."

" Yes?"

" That's why he said sell the company to the public."

" That's so."

" So, if there'd be a loss, the public would lose."

" That sounds just a little—— Doesn't it ? "

" No, darling, no. This is business. What do you understand from business ? " He looked at her just a little pityingly. " The public made fortunes, too. Hundreds of people
made fortunes with our shares. Do you know what the ten-
shilling shares were quoted at three weeks after, like we say,
the issue was floated ? "

" No, please, there's a sweet. No figures."

" You want I should talk to you about business, and you
say no figures."

" I mean, just as few as possible. I want the main outlines.
I see you're worrying, so I want to try and be in with you."

" Well," he said a little crossly, " don't talk like that about
selling our company to the public like we was selling baskets
of fruit with bad ones underneath. Have you seen who's
on our board of directors ? Two earls, with a brigadier-
general ! Do you think they would sell baskets of fruit with
bad ones underneath to the public ? "

She saw he was really upset and hurt. " Darling," she
begged him, " I confess. I really don't understand these
things. And if I seemed to say anything about the business
that I shouldn't have said, forgive me. I'm sorry, I'm sorry,
I'm sorry."

" All right, my daughter."

" Kiss me here, nicely, to show I'm forgiven. There.
Thank you. Won't you go on now, daddy ? I want to know
how you made poor Sasha lose all that money. Oh, sorry.
There I go again. That wasn't very tactful, either, was it ? "

" But that's true. There you are. That's why I feel so
bad about it. And he's been perfectly wonderful—an
angel."

" Well, of course, he's bound to get up on his feet again
with you to back him."

" Well, perhaps," he admitted. " I wouldn't say you was
wrong. I'll try and make you understand. It was with his
own money he was speculating, not the firm's or mine. You
understand that ? Clearly ? "

" Quite clearly."

" And it was in cotton. We've had a lot to do with Liverpool lately, quite outside our own factory. In fact we've got a cotton factory of our own, as well "

" Yes, of course you have."

" He said, in February last year, it simply wouldn't go any higher. That was before we sold out. Wonderful it was, the way he guessed it. And he was right. The market went slipping away like anything for five months. In July it had made a drop from nearly sixpence. You understand ? "

" Yes, I'm following."

" ' The market's touched bottom ! ' says Sasha. ' Not for long, but for just now ! ' I should live so, it was like those second-sight people in the theatre. They tell you what the number is on the back of your watch, and if your mother's name begins with S."

" Then there'll always be something for Sasha to turn his hand to. Can't you see his name in big letters on the bills ? —Alexander Smirnof, the Wizard Thought-Reader ! "

" Are you laughing at us, May ? Didn't I say——"

" No, darling, I'm not laughing at you. But the whole point of my getting hold of you to-night by the back of the neck—I mean, I want us not to be so frightfully frightfully serious. It *is* those wrinkles, I'm after. Out with them ! "

" All right ! " He was mollified. " Let me go on. In July he thinks the market's touched bottom. So he buys futures, and how much money he spends is nobody's business. Do you know what futures are ? " His own voice was, to a certain slight degree, uneasy.

" Yes, yes," she said rather hurriedly. She had an idea they were rather complicated things to explain at this time of the night, and that her father, too, might be not displeased to be spared the task of explanation.

" Next month he comes to me suddenly, all pale and excited, and says he wants to take a twopenny profit."

" And did he ? "

" I'm trying to tell you, aren't I ? I don't know what was

the matter with me that day. And perhaps I do. I'd just made a big deal with a firm of Swedish importers. Perhaps I'd had a drop of brandy, too. That's one reason why my stomach's turned against it. As you know, I always have a lot of respect for what Sasha wants to do. But that day I turned on him like an errand-boy, and it was funny, the more I treated him like an errand-boy, the more like an errand-boy he became. I said where were his nerves. He sees a twopenny rise in one month so he wants to take his profit. Let him wait two months more he'll have a three-penny rise, a fourpenny rise."

" It doesn't sound much," she muttered under her breath.

But he had heard. " Not much ? " he almost bellowed at her. " Not much ? What are you talking about what you don't know about for ? Each penny rise or fall is two hundred pounds on each future ! What do you think of that ? Not much, if you like ! It was like an earthquake on the cotton-exchange, not much she says ! "

She was very contrite. But he wasn't thinking of her blunder any longer. He was thinking of his own. He had more reason to be contrite than she.

" So he didn't take his profit," he continued wretchedly " In February of this year he had to face a loss of nineteen pence on each pound. That made—— No, no, it's no good making calculations. I've made calculations enough. It's a nice lump of money, God knows ! How often haven't I told him it's really all my fault, and that he should let me come in on his loss ! But no, as I say, like an angel. If a man speculates, on his own head, he says ; and if my advice had been good, would he have let me come in on the profits ? No, he says, as honest as the day is long. Fair's fair, he says. So what can I do more ? That's where it is ! "

" Oh, daddy, daddy ! " she murmured.

" Yes ? " he said heavily.

" Things were a lot simpler in the old days, in the old old days before you'd won the lottery. You remember, before you took on Horowitz's factory."

" Did I ask I should take it on, any of it ? " he asked listlessly. " It just happens. Life comes round you like this."

It seemed for the moment quite to have gone out of her head that her task that night was to make things as smooth as they might be for her father. Her tone took on the listlessness of his. " The fact seems to be that you weren't cut out to be a business-man ! " She stopped. There was silence for some seconds. She did not see the red point start in his cheeks, nor the angry flicker in his eyes.

" What ? " he cried. " How dare you say such a thing ? I should be no business-man ? You know what I call that ? Impertinence I call that, *chutzpah* ! "

She was so startled that she fell back and bruised her head against the wall. He did not notice it, nor did she, till some time later. She had never been able to make out just how good a business-man he was. Sometimes she was quite certain he had a streak of real, even of formidable, genius. There was no one readier to avow it than his colleague, Smirnof. At other times she was certain that Smirnof, no one but Smirnof, was the sole intelligence. There was no one readier to disavow it than Smirnof. He made her feel, from time to time, that he made almost too much a fetish of his modesty.

But she had never guessed that her father had this astonishing susceptibility to any imputation against his ability as a business-man. She knew that he, like most men, and all women, had his little vanity. She knew he liked to be considered a clever fellow, full of bright ideas. How could he not, when Smirnof, humorously always, but quite firmly, had been impressing on him for nearly ten years that he was exactly those things ? She had touched him on the raw. She hated herself for it. She had not suspected that she understood him so ill—him whom she loved more than anyone else in the world, saving one person only.

Infinitely dejected, she got up from the metal stool. There was nothing for her to do but get upstairs out of it. " I'm so sorry, father," she said, too miserable to look him in the face. " Good night. Forgive me."

" Where are you going ? " he asked. His voice had already changed its tone completely.

" To bed ! "

" Please sit down ! " She still hesitated, extremely uncomfortable. " Please do sit down ! " he appealed. His voice was mild and a little broken. His eyes were faintly misted over. He shook his head sadly from side to side. " That I should talk like that to my little May ! " he mourned.

" And that I should be so silly ! "

" Darling, you weren't silly. And darling, you weren't right, either."

" Of course I wasn't."

" You see, it was like a bit of pain for me hearing you say that, after I'd been telling you about that bad advice I'd given Sasha. That sort of a mistake all the biggest businessmen in business make sometimes in their life. And when you make it the other way, it isn't a mistake. It's—' Isn't he marvellous ? ' "

" I see."

" Are you sure you see ? "

" Yes, father."

" And now I've told you so much, I'll tell you why I telephoned for Sasha yesterday to come, and he came, even though he'll catch his boat only if he's very lucky."

" I'd like to know."

" Don't answer me like that, in a sad voice. Come to me, nearer. Did you forgive me yet for my talking to you like that ? "

She got up and rubbed her nose against his, and smiled into his eyes. " Go on, silly."

" A big girl like you, nose-rubbing. You ought to be ashamed from yourself."

" I am."

" Do you want me to talk to you more ? "

She sat down. " Please, let's get it talked out. You look

dead tired, but I do so want to be able to share things with you."

" Listen, May, business is bad in Lancashire."

" I rather thought things weren't so bright as they have been. But they'll get better again, father, surely? There's always ups and downs in business."

" They may or they may not get better. You talk to Huxtable about that. He'll give you a headful. How many hours a week they do in China ; how many they do in Japan ; how many they do here ; how many million yards India made for herself last year."

" It all sounds rather a long way off."

" I told you, a fat lot you'd understand. Well, I won't go into this or that. Business is bad in Lancashire. If I should start telling you what big stocks we've got, from the boom time yet—and no one's buying. Buying? I got a letter from Copenhagen last week cancelling a regular order from . . . I said I won't give you no figures."

" Poor old father, it's too bad."

" And how shall we pay the bank what we owe for naphtha, say. Let me give you just an example—naphtha. How shall we pay the bank for naphtha when they cancel orders in Copenhagen ? "

She made a gesture expressing her complete ignorance.

" I told you. It's bad. Huxtable and I, we've been going through the accounts. So I told Sasha to come. He's a bit out of touch with things up here in Doomington, what with our other companies in London, and he's going here and there, to Cairo, to Taranto, buying up these here dumps all the time."

" So he came and—— ? "

" I told him what I told you. He said it was worse than he thought. I said yes it was. I said he must make new connec-tions for us, when he travels about, to make up for the other ones that we've lost. I said if he wouldn't, there'll be a deficit this year, not a profit. We shouldn't be able to pay dividend even on the preference shares. You understand ? "

" Of course I do," she said dimly.

" Yes, he said, it was very necessary to make new connections. He had ideas. He would be in Paris, in Riga, quite soon, and he had big hopes. I said our public company in Doomington had lent the private trust company in London such a lot of money, some of the directors were getting frightened. He said not to worry. And when Sasha says you mustn't worry, you don't worry, you can't worry. And yet——"

" Please, father, one moment. I don't get it quite straight."

" Well, my baby, leave it. It isn't easy to understand. There's lots of men," he said with a certain pride, " who've been right through Oxford and Cambridge who don't understand, either. Anyhow, Sasha said yes, he agreed with me. He's going to work harder than ever with the trust company ; though I don't quite see how Sasha can work any harder. He eats and drinks work."

" What for ? "

" What for ? What a question ! "

" Hasn't he got money enough ? Haven't you, father ? "

" Ah, well, could you expect a girl to understand business ? It's not *money*. It's *business* ! Don't you see ? "

" Oh, my dear sweet parent, I do *not*. I do *not*. I leave it to you and Sasha. I shall never see. But I'm so glad you've talked it out with me, father. And I promise you I'll do what I can at my end, for what it's worth. I mean——"

" What do you mean ? "

" Well, for instance this committee-meeting to-day. It's pretty certain we've got all the social and moral support we want for the new Country Home I was telling you about You know—that big place I hope to get in Sussex—to be the Country Home for Poor Jewish Children. Like our Doomington one that we have in Cheshire, only much bigger."

" Well, and how will you help me ? "

" Like this, daddy." Her eyes were grey and serious. " I'd reckoned on getting quite a lot of money from you.

But there's no need to. With a little trouble, and one or two more countesses, we can work up any amount of public interest. Bazaars, and matinées, and so on."

" So you're trying to prevent me helping you with your new Home ? "

" I was only saying——"

" Have you ever heard from such a thing ? Shall I give up my best place in the synagogue because I'm so poor. Shall your mother sell up her necklaces, yes ? "

" No, father, no. I just thought that in my own little way——"

" A shame I call it, you should think of such a thing ! " He was quite flustered with indignation. Then a new thought struck him. " How soon do you expect to start it going, this new Home of yours ? "

" Oh, I don't know. There's all the organising and planning to be done. Dear old Emmanuel—you remember ? I expect him to be quite a lot of help, you know. I've seen the house I want already, as I told you. But there'll have to be lots of alterations. It will take months, perhaps a year."

" And then ? "

" Then as I said—I'll go and look after it for two or three years, get it running properly. I've got ideas about it."

" May—will you forgive me ? "

" Forgive what, darling ? "

" Am I a fellow who pushes his nose where it doesn't concern him ? "

" The last person in all the world ! "

" You've talked about my wrinkles, yes ? "

" Yes."

" Now, look here." He swivelled her face up a little. " Look at these lines here." He traced them gently with two finger-tips. " These lines between your nostrils and your mouth. They shouldn't be there."

" I'm getting on, you know."

" Yes." He sighed. " My baby, you love him very much, don't you ? "

She did no more than pass her fingers along the back of his hand to show how touched she was by his delicacy.

" I do."

" You wouldn't marry anyone else in the world than Harry Stonier ? "

" No, father."

" Do you ever see each other ? "

" Yes, just now and again. There's never been a quarrel, you know."

" As if anybody could quarrel with you."

Neither said a word for a little time.

" It wouldn't be any good at all," he started tremulously, " if I went to see him ? "

" Oh, father, don't you see ? "

" I can't understand it. Because you're a rich girl now, that's it, isn't it ? "

" Yes, partly that. He has a queer, queer sort of pride. And how magnificent, damn it ! "

" Damn it ! " he repeated. He was aware she rarely used even so mild an oath. " It's not like being a human man at all ! "

" Poets and saints are like that ! " she said.

" No," he mused. " How could I go and talk to him when I'm the bad one. I'm the one that made you a rich girl."

" Yes," she smiled. " You're the villain of the piece."

" But, surely, it isn't possible ! There must be some way out ! "

" Think of one ! '

He had a brilliant, a devastating, idea.

" I won't give you one penny. There. You can live in two rooms."

" We've thought of that. We've talked it over. Yes, yes, we've talked it all over. What would he feel like keeping me in two rooms, knowing that he's deprived me of—of all this, for what it's worth ? And me, too. Wouldn't there be bad moments when I'd hate him for it, for what he's deprived me of? Not clothes and theatres, I mean. The sort of things I like to do. Clinics, and babies, and things like that."

" Yes, I know. I know you've got to look after other people's babies, because, because—that's enough. I can cry like a baby myself."

" Yes, darling, it's because you're so tired. You were dead tired when you came in. Oh, it's a shame to have kept you down here all this time."

" You kept me, and I kept you."

" You'd share the blame, of course. Oh, just look at the time ! I dare you to guess the time ! "

" I'd rather not ! "

" To bed this instant ! "

" I'm going, darling."

" Good night, darling."

" Good night." He kissed her on both eyelids, like a lover almost.

" I'll put these things away," she said.

" No, no ; leave them ! "

" Yes, perhaps I will for to-night." He was going out now " Oh, father, just one moment, please," she said.

He stopped. " Yes ? "

" I know mother will still be awake, waiting for you."

" Do you think she will ? "

" I'm sure. Just go in and kiss her. She'll sleep better."

" Of course, I will, if she's awake. And if she's asleep, too."

" And I'll tell you what. Why not spend the night there, in her room ? There's room for you both."

He looked at her with shining eyes. " I love you," he whispered.

CHAPTER XIII

CAP FERRAT

I

THE HANDSOMEST man in all the world was 'outlined against the bluest sky and was about to dive into the bluest sea. He was balancing himself on the balls of his feet spreading his arms out like a bird's wings, letting the finger-tips quiver a little ; he was playing a little game with himself, the game of being about to dive.

The wife of the handsomest man piled up her cushions against her back and stretched out her oiled limbs more comfortably upon her oil-indifferent mattress. She was a lady once known as Elsie Silver in her profession, and outside it, during a career which had advanced from third-rate music-halls in the North Country to almost more than first-rate *théâtres intimes* in the West End of London. Her present name was Lady Malswetting. Her husband, Sir Robert, more frequently known as Bobby, was the eighth baronet.

Elsie looked at her husband. She knew that as he stood poised there, in that carefully manufactured attitude on that carefully manufactured rock, he was expecting her to. He would give her time to look at him before he dived. If he was within eyeshot of anyone else on Cap Ferrat, or anyone out at sea in a sailing-boat or a motor-boat, he would expect them to look at him, too. And, indeed, why should they not ? He was, as his American friends had said— and the greater part of his friends were American—an " eyeful."

Even the men were forced to take their hats off to his physique and his good looks. Elsie regarded them with satisfaction. He was tall ; he had magnificent shoulders,

and a chest deep and resonant as a bell. Then he sloped
down to hips which did not seem to be there at all. He had
firm flanks, just not slender enough to be out of proportion
to his chest. His legs supported the taut quivering structure,
like a stalk an iris. Yes, the image was somewhat appropriate.
He sloped inwards to his hips with lines similar to the lines
of an iris.

The bronze of his skin suggested rather a copper aloe.
It was quite Greek. He managed to preserve some flush of
it even in winter, with the help of unguents and his dexterously manipulated violet-rays.

No, he was not ready to dive yet. He turned round on the
carefully manufactured rock, which was connected by a carefully manufactured isthmus to the levelled and smoothed
rock-beach which had cost such a pretty penny. He smiled
at her, as if to say : " Well, darling, really, between you and
me, I *am* the handsomest man in all the world." And really,
between her and him, he was. Eyes could hardly be more
warm, brown, gazelle-like, than those eyes ; smile could not
be more winning—the eyes, the smile, which had first challenged her, appealed to her, across the haze of smoke and
the smell of strong tea in a hut in Boulogne during the late
Great War.

So this afternoon, on this perfect summer day, under the
lee of Cap Ferrat, with the scent of roses and mignonette
and heliotrope coming down in cascades from the walls and
gardens of their villa, and the honey murmur of the sea
within their ears, his eyes and smile again challenged her,
again appealed to her.

She had at once accepted the challenge ; she had for long
not submitted to the appeal. He was too beautiful ; he was
too rich ; his family was too socially impeccable ; his mother
was too formidable. But above all he was too beautiful. It
was not the sort of beauty you could get your teeth into. It
would bruise too easily. She did not want beauty. She wanted
ruthlessness ; she wanted blue eyes cold as glacier-water ;
she wanted pain and terror, humiliation and ecstasy.

Pah ! She put the tip of her little pink tongue between her lips and spat ! That old fatuous green-sickness which rose from her entrails from time to time and made her dither and twitter like a housemaid. She thought she had outgrown it long ago.

Bobby Malswetting came to her again and again and again. He had the most accurate taste in Milanese underwear, in scents, in orchids. He challenged and appealed to her again, and at length she submitted to his appeal, as she did now on the beach under the lee of Cap Ferrat.

" Yes, handsome man," her eyes smiled back at him, " whatever you like, as soon as you like, as often as you like."

His mind was never for two minutes together absent from love-making, in the clinical sense of the word—usually with her, often enough with other women. She did not resent that. She thought of a marriage as an arrangement by which a man and a woman declared it to be convenient to themselves to spend the greater part of their time together ; from which it followed they occupied the same house, and, whenever it was attractive, the same bed. She thought it as barbarous to expect a married man or woman never to sleep with another woman or man as to expect them never to have a meal excepting with each other.

But she thought you should eat when you are hungry, drink when you are thirsty. Or at least, if you are neither hungry nor thirsty, you should bring to your food and drink a certain vital curiosity, an intellectual, if not an emotional, passion. She deplored the woman—she could not remember whether she was myth or history—who ate hard apples while her husband beside her made strenuous love. She deplored Bobby's nonchalance in these matters, too. His friends called him, and he called himself, with a salacity which was somewhat repugnant to her, a stallion. But he was not. He was more like a cock in a hen-run. A flick of wings, a screech, and a moment later he was pecking away in the gravel for seeds, or whatever it might be. In his case it was chocolates.

He would point out to her a seemingly inaccessible window in a perpendicular façade of hotel-wall.

" Do you see that window, Mimsy ? " he would ask her. He called her Mimsy, because Lewis Carroll was the sole literature he read these days, with the exception of Surtees and Wallace. She saw that window. " That little American blonde hangs out there. You remember, the one from Akron, Ohio ? " She remembered. " I managed to get in that way last night. That's why I was so late. I hope I didn't disturb you ? " He had not disturbed her. " Good going, eh ? I only met her last week." She thought it good going. She thought it particularly good going to climb up a wall totally devoid of drain-pipes, so far as she could see. She remembered he had been an Oxford mountaineer.

The lady need not be a tourist merry-maker. A chamber-maid would do, even a governess. She found it inconvenient when one of their own maids caught his fancy. It made complications in the housekeeping. If she ventured an objection on these occasions, he would smile at her charmingly. " *Droit de seigneur*, darling ! " he would point out. She found it rather boring, and threw wine-glasses out of the window till she felt better. The fact was, he was slug-like in his indifference to the sort of leaf he made his meal of and his bed on. Or perhaps slugs have their fastidiousnesses too.

But if anybody on the Côte d'Azur made such odious comparisons regarding Bobby Malswetting as that he was a cock in a hen-run, a slug on a leaf, it was not his wife. He was not only handsome ; he was generous, he was brave. A cock or a slug is none of these things. Alike in the avocations of war and of peace, he was brave.

It had been too much, even for his mother, to convert Elsie into a hunting-woman. But she had followed the hunt in a car once or twice. And she had mother-wit enough, after a few meetings with them, to understand the language of the hunting-people, its special terms, its puzzling reticences, its more puzzling candours. She discovered he was the most dare-devil rider to hounds in the country. He had won his D.S.O. for a dare-devil feat which made people's breath stop short, alike when they witnessed it and when they talked about it later. The presence of an audience made him capable of any dazzling dare-devilry, but it was quite essential. In the absence of an audience, he was curiously timid. She could not induce him to go to a dentist, for instance. Those brilliant teeth he showed without reluctance were whited sepulchres. He suffered agonies of toothache. It was impertinent to hope he should not, seeing the quantities of chocolates he devoured. She could not induce him to give up chocolates either.

He stood there poised, a copper aloe against the burning blue sky. It was hot. There had been a slight breeze, but it was not blowing. She wished she had planted the big parasol into the hole in the rock prepared for it. It was hot. She had a sudden sense of the futility, the emptiness, of this, of him. The blue sky that encompassed them was like a huge blown egg, blue-painted. He was like a tiny egg, a chocolate Easter egg of the cheaper sort, which you crush between finger and thumb, and nothing is there.

She would be sick. She should have put on her smoked glasses when she lay down. She fumbled beside her for the handbag in which she kept them, but before her hand closed on it a dizziness descended upon her. The blueness was lifted out of the blue sky, like a tint that has been dropped before the beams of a proscenium spot-light, and has been withdrawn again. The sky was dead white, like an undischarged snow-cloud. A man stood on the rock outlined against the white sky. He was not her husband. He was a man whose face she had seen clearly for the first time a long time ago, in the Oleander Street kitchen. She saw it as clearly now as then. Now, as then, the face seemed only a few feet away, though the rock upon which he stood was actually a good many metres removed from her. The eyes of the man were blue and cold. There was a gold sheen in his hair, but the gold was not so bright as it had been in Doomington long ago. The mouth, of which the corners were so wryly twisted, was somewhat womanish. A long scar curved from the crest of the nostril round towards the mouth again. But it was broken by a network of small weals that had not been there before. The ash-white atmosphere dazzled with clanking globes of metal that some malignancy suddenly tore apart. The womanish mouth, the grim male eyes. . . .

Robert Malswetting, perched on his rock, made a sudden gesture. The sky's blueness flowed from his finger-tips back into the sky again. Her fingers closed on the handbag. She extracted her smoked glasses and put them on. A slight breeze started blowing again. Robert Malswetting, perched on his rock, had three dimensions again. He looked round for a last time, to make sure she was looking, though she was only his wife. He dived, like a seagull swooping.

Bobby moved his mattress alongside of his wife's. He arranged his pillows to his liking.

" Damn ! " he said. " I've forgotten ! "

" Forgotten what, Bobby ? "

" My vanity-bag ! "

He went and pulled a rope. A bell clanged musically in a little belfry up on top of the cliff. A few moments later a servant came pattering in rope sandals down the hewn stone staircase that connected the cliff-top, where the villa stood, with the bathing-platform below.

" Rosario ! " he said. " My vanity-bag ! " Rosario pattered up the stairs again.

" Did I look good, Mimsy ? "

" Extremely ! "

" Then kiss me ! "

" At this hour of the day ? "

" All hours of the day ! Ah ! Thank you ! "

He spoke with what is called an Oxford accent. The three brief disjointed phrases prolonged themselves like the slow unwinding of golden syrup from a spoon held above porridge.

" *Grazie !* " This to Rosario, who had come down again.
" Oh, and Rosario ! *Aspetti !* "

" *Signore ?* "

" Any chocs. down here, Mimsy ? "

" But no, darling ! We had the most colossal lunch ! "

" Rosario ! Some chocolates, please ! "

" How you manage to retain that figure . . ." marvelled
Elsie.

He looked at it with approval. " Yes," he admitted. " It
is one of God's secrets ! "

It was just as much of a godly secret how Elsie Malswetting, too, preserved that chaste silhouette. She had the
appetite of a plough-boy. But he did not often remember,
and she quite often forgot, that she, too, was a lovely
creature.

" You'll run all to belly in a night ! " she assured him.

" Monster ! Oh, please don't say that ! "

" I do ! The moment the least sag shows, I spread my
wings. I'm off ! "

He smiled at her indulgently. " Mimsy wouldn't leave
her little Bobby, would she ? She couldn't, could she ? "

" No, perhaps not her little Bobby. Not for a little time,
anyhow ! But she could manage to do without little Bobby's
little Americans. They give her a pain in the neck ! "

" Oh, Mimsy, how can you say such a thing ? They're
pets ! "

" I find them rather much ! You know just what I think
about them ! Another subject, please ! Shall we have the
parasol up ? I got quite a turn just now ! "

" By all means, darling, if you like ! " Rosario was down
again now, with the chocolates. " Rosario ! "

" *Signore ?* "

" Put the parasol up ! "

" *Si, signore !* "

" —Though this new stuff I've got, darling, is supposed to
be rubbed in in the strong sunlight. Must give it a chance,
you know ! I oughtn't really to have the parasol up ! "

" Then you can poke your head out of the shade, darling ! "

" Yes, come to think of it, I can ! " He opened up the bag Rosario had brought down. It was a sort of canvas hold-all, specially fitted up for him, with any number of jars, lotions, oils, creams. He arranged a few of the objects on the mattress beside him.

" Do you know, darling," she said, " you look positively sissy with all that stuff beside you ! "

He looked at her confidently with his gazelle's eyes. " Well, you know all there is to be known on that subject ! "

" Yes, O splendid male ! "

" Here it is ! " he exclaimed, taking out a bottle.

" What ? "

" This new stuff for the little . . ." He did not finish the sentence. He disliked exceedingly to put the little whatever-it-might-be into words. The whatever-it-might-be, the hush-hush, was a small bald patch in the centre of his beautiful brown silky hair. The brown silky hairs covered it, but only after a little manipulation. He had had the little bald patch for several years now, and had spent inconceivable sums of money trying to carpet it again with brown silky hair. He oscillated between fabulous expensive specialists and slum herbalists. He attempted irrational rituals which village women with barren wombs in the effort to conjure babies by voodoo would have spurned. But the little bald patch remained bald. The Achilles' heel persisted in the centre of his scalp.

" Perhaps," he asked, " you'd rub it in for me ? Other people's fingers are said to be more effective than your own. The electricity, you know."

" I *don't* know," she informed him. " There's one thing *you* don't know, either."

" Yes ? " he asked.

" That—that there——" She stopped. She herself did not like to specify the little bald patch, either. He had made her nearly as sensitive about it as he was himself. " I sometimes prefer that to all the rest of you put together ! "

" Darling ! " he cried, with great shocked eyes. " How can you say such a thing ! "

" It's true ! Come along then ! I'll rub the beastly stuff in for you ! "

" Beastly stuff ! " he grumbled. " It costs as much as if they made it up out of melted pearls ! "

" Pearls ! " she said. " If they'd have thought of using my mother's pearls—well, who knows ?—it might really have worked the trick ! "

" Has she got any specially jolly ones ? " he asked. He preferred not to discuss whether the new lotion would or would not work the trick.

" Hasn't she just ! "

" How much ? "

" Beyond price ! They're from Russia ! One of our ancestors stole them from Catherine the Great's jewel-box."

" I didn't know," he said, quite respectfully. But Catherine's jewel-box did not hold his interest long.

His little bald patch was as much as he could concentrate on at one time. " Rub a little harder, Mimsy ! That's right ! "

" How nice it is just now, with this little breeze blowing ! And it's so quiet ! Oh, what a rest it is, Bobby ! "

" What's the time, Mimsy ? "

She allowed the wide sleeve of her pyjamas to fall back and consulted her wristlet-watch. " Five ! "

" Oh, dear ! Oh, dear ! " he said. " They'll be here soon ! "

" Who ? "

" Oh, the bunch ! They're coming in for cocktails ! "

She made a *moue*. " I should have guessed as much ! "

" Mimsy dear, will you go and pull that cord again ? "

" I will not ! Go and pull it yourself ! " Her eyes had darkened and her chin acquired an unpleasant line or two.

" I do wish you'd get on better with them ! " he grumbled, as he rose.

" They'd be all right once a fortnight ! But every day, almost every meal ! Hell, no ! "

" I prefer them to that Boche woman you've picked up ! And her frightful brat ! "

" *Boche !* Really, Bobby, when will you grow out of that O.T.C. mind of yours ? You've licked 'em. Can't you leave it at that ? And I won't have you talk of Kathy in that way. She's the only creature I can talk to on the whole of this damn coast ! "

" But she's so glum, so dour ! "

" I admit she doesn't go screeching from cocktail-party to cocktail-party in beach pyjamas like your bright friends from Ohio. And perhaps you'll admit it isn't gay to lose your husband the first day of the war, a month after your honeymoon ! These Germans are the only people left in Europe with a little self-respect ! "

" Oh, for God's sake don't start ramming your Germans down my throat ! "

" Be reasonable, Bobby. Is it Kathy or is it your Americans who haunt this house all day and all night ? Is it or isn't it ? "

" I don't like Kathy von Schlettau, you know very well I don't ! She gives me the heeby-jeebies ! "

" All right, my pet. When I go to stay with Kathy all under the pepper-box towers near Breslau, I shan't ask you to come ! "

" Catch me ! "

" Though, poor dear, she tells me she gets poorer day by day. I mean, she doesn't *tell* me. I know. What with this German mark crumbling like a sand-castle——"

" Some old dodge of the Huns to get out of paying what they owe us."

" You're hopeless, my sweet. I only know when I go to stay with her we'll have to live on bread and dripping. She sort of warned me, the poor dear."

" Are you really thinking of going, Mimsy ? "

" Oh, I don't know, darling. One of these days. And only if your Americans make me."

" All right, pet. I'll go easy on my Americans. I won't have my Mimsy wandering off alone among the fierce Germans."

" You sweet. Roll over here. There. Was that a nice one ? "

He grunted his approval. " One more ! " he demanded She administered it.

" I'd best go and summon the dago ! " he said. He rose and pulled the bell-cord. The bell pealed in its belfry.

" Oh, Bobby, while you're up. There's a writing-pad against the cliff there ! "

" Here, darling ! Writing ? "

" No, I'm going to eat it ! "

" Now don't get snooty ! " He came and stretched himself near her on the mattress. " One more ! "

" No, darling ! I want to write now ! "

" One more ! " he pleaded. He always attached a great value to anything refused him.

" *No !* "

" Please ! " He looked at her, putting all he had of eye-craft into his gazelle's eyes.

She laughed. There was a note of uneasiness in her laughter. She was a little chagrined to find how completely the gazelle's eyes turned her into putty.

" Here you are ! Now go away ! Get into your own sty, pig ! "

He grunted comically as he rolled on to his own mattress. " Oh, Rosario ! "

" *Signore ?* "

" Cocktails ! A lot, and strong ! "

" *Si, signore !* "

" Who are you writing to, pet ? "

" It occurred to me I might drop a word to my little sister. I mean, talking about my mother and her pearls—it all sort of reminded me of the roses round the door."

" Mammy's darling, aren't you ? "

" And how ! "

"Which little sister are you writing to? There are hordes!"

"There are not hordes! Except Esther, the eldest. *She's* hordes!"

"I rather like the soft one, you know, with the curves!" He outlined them, a little prodigally.

"Oh, Sarah! Yes, she's a nice cow-sister. I quite like Sarah, too! It's May I'm writing to. You remember, the youngest?"

"Oh, yes, I remember quite clearly. The one with a passion for good works! Isn't she married yet?"

"Oh, shut up, Bobby! Let me get on with it!"

There was just time to get on with it before the bunch came.

"So, darling," the letter went, "do come. I can't tell you how lovely it is here. You'll have a bedroom all windows, with nothing but sun and sea to look at. And the cook Bobby managed to pick up—to steal, I should say, from one of his best friends in Antibes—oh, May, what a cook!

"And Bobby's marvellous. So good to look at, and he gets better every day. It's my duty to warn you. Anything new in the woman line knocks him silly for a fortnight. But between us we'll manage to keep his hands off you. Seriously, it would do you no harm at all to come out of your little shell a bit.

"And there's an awfully jolly German woman I've met here; rather tragic, but such a good sort. She's a Gräfin or a Baronin or something. I believe she and her husband both go back to Charlemagne. That's the way it's spelt, isn't it? I like the Germans here a lot, though there's only a handful of them, and they get fewer every day. I don't mean the big fat business-men with chins down the back of their necks, though they're amusing in their way. I mean the people I meet at Kathy's. That's her name, Kathy von Schlettau. I'd like you to meet her before she returns home. Apparently things are going rather badly in Germany. Their money is behaving oddly. She'll have to go and give things the once-over. But I intend to stay with her one of these days. She's awfully keen on it, and so am I. And why shouldn't you come too ? There's an idea. Then we could *talk*, and go out on horses. And when we'd come back you'd marry a Master of Hounds and I'd make Bobby's mother's eyes pop out of her head the way I'd take my fences.

" It's ages since we've seen each other. Any news from Susan, by the way ?

" Sorry this is so all over the place. But the speed-boats of the Americans are beginning to snoop in, and I hear the noise of their exhausts roaring up from Beaulieu. It *would* be nice of you to save me from said Americans for an hour or two. Apart from these same, everything here is lovely, lovely ! So what about it, O my may blossom ! I'll have to shut off now. Here come the Ziegfeld Follies !

" Love,

" Your respectable married sister,

" ELSIE."

II

Lady Malswetting's friend, the Gräfin Kathy von Schlettau, had been gone from Cap Ferrat two or three months by the time a letter arrived for Lady Malswetting from her sister, May Silver. The letter bore the post-mark Steyning, which is a village in Sussex, under the Sussex Downs.

" I can't tell you, darling Elsie," the letter insisted, " how sorry I am to have let all this time go by without answering your letter. I can only plead that I'm not usually so bad, am I ? You must try and forgive me.

" You remember earlier in the year I just dropped a hint about a big house my committee had its eye on ? You remember ? It's all in connection with my scheme for Jewish slum children. As a matter of fact, there's a whole literature on the subject already, pamphlets and appeals and so on.

I'd have sent a batch along to you ; but it's rather ridiculous—I hate the thought of roping you in, somehow. You seem, both of you, such a long way from Begley Hill and Whitechapel, if you see what I mean. And you haven't any children, either, worse luck. It would prevent me from doing anything about Susan and her husband, too, if they were accessible. (No, they haven't any children, either. Quite obviously they never will.)

" It's different with Sarah. Smirnof is probably richer than father now, since he's taken to company-promoting. And, God knows, they've got children enough. I honestly can't remember whether it's six and a seventh coming, or seven and an eighth. That's the scale it's on, anyhow.

" And then there's Esther. I've had a grand time with Esther. She's fair game. You'd be astonished at the way I've gunned her. She'll be astonished when she counts up what I've managed to screw out of her. I told her that suppose her own children needed the Chanctonbury Country Home one of these days, how would she feel about it if she'd been mean ? That made her purple with anger. But it terrified her, too. She reached for her cheque-book like a lamb.

" I'm not going to tell you what it's all about, darling, don't worry ; not in this letter, at least. But say the word, and I'll inundate you with appeals and illustrated pamphlets and bankers' forms till the floor's swimming with them. What I'm really trying to do is to explain why I've been so naughty and left your sweetest letter unanswered so long. I can't begin to give you an idea what there's been to do. First there was the house to decide on. I was keen on Chanctonbury House from the beginning. It's a lovely spacious early eighteenth-century place, not unlike your place in Oxfordshire, though there's no private chapel, so we'll have to fix our marriages up elsewhere. But, seeing that our guests are not to exceed twelve years in age, the question may not arise. I believe William Kent had something to do with Chanctonbury, too, as he did at your place, didn't he ? But you'll see it for yourself, my dear. (I'll come to that soon.) And, after a lot of wrangling, we fixed on Chanctonbury. Then there was a nice fat interval for documents. And then we had to adapt the place. Honestly, darling, adapt it, not spoil it. We're still on that now. We hope to open up soon after the New Year. And, odd as it may sound, it wasn't easy to get quite the right children. For the Doomington lot, old Emmanuel has been quite invaluable. Sarah gave a hand with the London lot. She's quite got her head screwed on the right way, our Sarah.

"Of course, the real work starts when the kids are in. We're not out merely to make their cheeks rosy, or to teach them what to do with peas and knives. It's something much more fundamental. But if I start trying to expound our ideals, I'll go on till morning. And I'm far too busy. Do you know, I've got to go over to mother's every few weeks, too? She's helpless with the servants. If I just left them to it, it would be Ivanhoe Towers all over again. So I've just got to mooch round now and again and put a spot of oil in the works. What was I saying? Oh, I'm busy ; and so are you, you lazybones, living the life strenuous out there, in your marvellous villa with your marvellous husband and the marvellous stolen cook.

"Anyhow, I do hope I've given you *some* idea, and that you've forgiven me. I should awfully like to meet your German friend, Kathy von Schlettau. Does she ever come to London? We're only a couple of hours from London, by way of Horsham. You can come round quicker by Brighton, though that would give quite the wrong idea of its place in the scheme of things. But you'll drive over, of course. If you haven't a car with you, acquire one of the Smirnof fleet.

"In other words, why not bring your German friend over? Or, if she can't come, why not come yourself? I don't want you to come now, darling. Not till we're going properly. Why not in the spring? We have lovely beech-woods here. Aren't you aching for a bank of English primroses, out there among your hot-house fungi? And daffodils? And cowslips? And I'll take you for strapping walks over the Downs, all the way along to Bury or Arundel. You must preserve that heavenly figure, my child.

" And I promise you, no Americans. How about it, Elsie ? And of course, I'd love Bobby to come. Though I don't quite know how he'd stand for an army of young ladies and gentlemen from Longton and Whitechapel, shrieking at the top of their voices. They will not be discouraged from shrieking if they feel like it, even if the Archbishop and the Chief Rabbi drop in for afternoon tea.

"Tell me how you feel about it. Tell me I'm forgiven. And give my best to Bobby, and kisses for yourself.

" With love,

" MAY.

" *P.S.*—You ask if there's any news from Susan. Yes. Letters are passing between the two countries now. I've asked her, when she writes to me, to write a special note which I can show mother, in which no reference of any sort is made to the Terkass business. Poor mother. She's written two or three times to Terkass, but the letters have all come back, marked : *Destinataire Inconnu*. There's no reason why she should ever get to know. Susan's working in Moscow now. Her husband has some responsible administrative position in connection with a new railway-line they're building in the Caucasus.

" We're a queer lot, aren't we ? Hasn't it ever occurred to you what a good turn we'd make on the halls—the Five Silver Daughters ? Won't you get Cochran or Charlot or somebody to consider the matter ?—M. S."

CHAPTER XIV

SMIRNOF AT HOME

I

LADY MALSWETTING had at last induced her husband
to go to the dentist. It had taken a long time, for it was now
the spring of 1922. It had become necessary not merely for
Sir Robert, but for his wife, too, that Sir Robert should go
to the dentist. He had lately developed the habit of coming
into her room and awakening her, whatever hour of the
night it might be, as soon as his teeth started off again. He
came in, got in beside her, and requested her to comfort
him. When she pointed out that a dentist could comfort him
a good deal more efficiently, he shivered and said she was
unsympathetic. She could never put her head on the pillow
with the certainty she would have a full night's rest.

By imposing upon her husband certain abstentions, and
curtailing his liberty in other directions, she had at last
blackmailed him into going to a dentist. He was a fashion-
able dentist in Nice. The car stood waiting outside the
dentist's door to carry them away after the dentist had concluded his odious labours. Bobby had entered the car at Cap
Ferrat with the reluctance a corpse might entertain on being
carried into his hearse, assuming a corpse knew what was
going on. He was sitting on a chair in the waiting-room
fingering a copy of *Vanity Fair*—for this was a very fashion-
able dentist, with an Anglo-American clientele. Lady
Malswetting sat opposite him, looking at his face.

His face was working towards a breakdown. His mouth
was trembling. His breath was coming shorter and shorter.
A mist was condensing upon his sad and beautiful eyes.

She had, in other words, a good twenty seconds in which

to consider the matter and to decide the course of action she should take.

Eighteen seconds, and twenty seconds passed. His face broke down. He was sobbing like a teething baby. She got up ; she had made her decision. She touched him lightly on the back of the neck.

" Yes ? " he blubbered, raising his gazelle's eyes aflood with tears.

" Excuse me a moment, Bobby," she said. " I'm just going out to powder my nose."

Those were the last words she said to him that day, or any day, ever at all.

" Don't be long, Mimsy darling," he implored her.

She closed the door behind her, went downstairs, and out into the street.

" Go straight back, please ! " she ordered the chauffeur. He looked up inquiringly. " Yes, straight back, please ! Drive quickly ! "

When Michaut drove slowly, he overtook everything on the road. Bobby liked him to be that sort of a driver. Now, driving quickly, he had passed Villefranche before he got there. They reached the villa at Cap Ferrat.

" Fill up with petrol ! " she told him. " We're leaving at once. We're going a long way."

" Shall I be away some time, madame ? " he asked. He was quite used to the sudden caprices of his employers.

" You'll need nothing," she told him.

She went to her room and called her maid. " I want you to pack a small bag," she said. " The sooner the better."

" Yes, madame," said the maid.

She got her jewels together. " Leave room for my jewel-box," she said. She sorted out her jewels. That took a little time. She did not take the jewels Bobby had given her ; it seemed to her indecent to leave him crying in a dentist's waiting-room and to run off with his love-tokens. But she had a fair amount of her own. She had had quite a jewel phase during that season at the Comedy Theatre.

" Madame will take a hat-box, will she not ? "

" Yes, quite right. That'll be all I need."

She was quite used to travelling long distances with a minimum of luggage—as much as was needed for her act, and little more. She needed no properties for this act.

She went downstairs, the maid going behind her with the suitcase and the hat-box. The chauffeur came forward and installed them into the car.

" Can I tell them when madame will be back ? " her maid asked.

" You cannot," said Elsie.

The maid hesitated. " Is there a message for the master ? " she inquired.

" There is not ! " said Elsie. " Are you ready, Michaut ? "

" Yes, madame ! "

" Let's go, then ! Oh, Jeanne ! " she called out.

" Madame ? "

She thrust her hand into her bag and brought out a few hundred-franc notes. " Just share these round ! " she said.

" Yes, madame ! " said the maid. Her chest was heaving. She broke down. She was howling at the top of her voice.

" Go on, Michaut ! "

" Where, madame ? "

" Up north. To Paris. Good-bye, Jeanne ! Don't take on so ! "

So Lady Malswetting went to Paris.

She lay back luxuriously in the car. She had not yet made up her mind whether she was going to visit Kathy von Schlettau in her Silesian castle or her sister May in her Sussex Country Home for Jewish Children. There would be time enough to decide that. For the present it was quite enough to sit back in the car, stretch out the limbs, and know there was no Bobby any more, there was never going to be any Bobby again. It seemed fantastic that such joy should have been hers for the asking for so long now, and she had never asked for it. She felt like a small bird carried forward high above mountain-tops between the wing-shoulders of a great sky-cleaving bird. She felt like someone soiled who has all day long been walking beside a clear stream and not thought to bathe in it, and suddenly the ridiculously simple thought has struck him, and he bathes, and he comes out clean.

They were halted at a level-crossing.

" Madame." Michaut turned round to her. " Could madame inform me where she would like to take dinner ? "

" I would like you to travel all night long, Michaut," she said. " You must get some sandwiches to eat at the wheel, and get me a few sandwiches, too. And a little fruit. And a bottle of wine for each of us. I don't want to go to Paris. Will you go straight to Calais ? If I'm asleep when we get there, don't wake me till it's time for me to get on the boat. Yes, the Dover boat. I want you to get me a ticket for London. You'll find the money in my bag here, if I'm asleep."

" Yes, madame. And then ? "

" And then, Michaut, you may return to Cap Ferrat."

The level-crossing bar rose slowly. The car started off again ; casually, without fuss, as if it was going in to the English Book Shop in Beaulieu for this week's consignment of the new novels.

II

Elsie liked the subdued tints of the carpet and curtains and furniture of her room at Claridge's. She liked the subdued tints of the London afternoon sun. After the white Mediterranean glare it seemed as if the sun shone through a grey gauze. She left the curtains undrawn and got into bed for an hour or two. She got back to herself very quickly after a night of little or no sleep. It was a gift acquired in, and retained from, her touring days.

She awoke in an hour or two, refreshed and hungry. By the time she had had a meal, it was clear she would be too

late to get to Chanctonbury House, whether by train or by
car—though the hotel people would get her a car in two
minutes. She remembered, too, that May wanted her to see
by daylight the country between Horsham and Steyning
and Chanctonbury. She thought the greenness of the Sussex
Weald would be very agreeable after all the shrill brightness
of the Riviera gardens. She decided to put off May till
to-morrow.

It then occurred to her she had another sister in this part
of the world—her sister Sarah Smirnof, in fact, who lived in
Kensington Palace Gardens. It would be pleasant to see old
Sarah again, and make the acquaintance of the latest batch
of Smirnofs. It seemed a far more satisfactory thing to do
than to go poking about on the telephone for one of her
ex-men to take her out somewhere. Yes, she would ring up
Sarah and ask if she might not go along after dinner.

The name was in the telephone book. " Who is that,
please ? " a courteous and capable voice asked.

" Please tell Mrs. Smirnof her sister, Lady Malswetting,
would like to speak to her."

" Yes, your ladyship."

" Elsie dear, is that you ? What a surprise ! "

" Yes, Sarah darling. I've just arrived. I'm at Claridge's ! "

" *What* a surprise ! You must come and see us at
once ! "

" I'm dying to ! "

" Is your husband with you—Bobby ? "

" No, darling. I've left him ! "

" You mean—you've left him ? "

" Yes, I mean I've left him ! "

" Oh, well," said Sarah, " why shouldn't you, if you want
to ? "

" He cried at the dentist's ! "

" Oh, Elsie, if I should leave my children when they
cry—— "

" I'll tell you all about it, darling. Can I come along
after dinner ? I'll have a bite here."

" No, have a bite with us. It will have to be a bite, too.
You see, we're giving a party to-night."

" A party ? "

" Yes, a musical party. Do you mind ? Will it bore
you ? "

Elsie was rather bored by musical parties. They were more
earnest, as a rule, than prayer-meetings. She knew Smirnof
took his music very seriously.

" What's going to happen ? " she asked, a little tepidly.

" I don't know that the people will amuse you very much,"
said Sarah. " Sasha's political and business friends, you
know ; rather on the old side, most of them. You might
be interested in the Russians—*you* know, generals and archdukes from the Tsar's time. Sasha has a lot of them about
always."

" We've got lashings of them on the Riviera, too," said
Elsie. " Who's going to play ? "

" Oh, Suggia at the 'cello ! "

" Not *Suggia* ! "

" Yes, Suggia ! "

" But I adore Suggia. I'd walk barefoot to Bradford to hear
Suggia. I mean, I don't much understand music, but I
worship Suggia. Of course I'm coming ! "

" And then we've got that Italian singing——"

" Which Italian ? "

" Gigli ! "

" Oh, my dear, how expensive it all sounds ! "

" Well," said Sarah, " what else shall we spend the money
on ? "

" Of course, dear ! What time ? "

" The party begins at ten. But you come before. Come
now. We'll have a bite of food."

" I wouldn't dream of it. I know what it means, feeding
relatives when your mind's full of party. Besides, I've only
got one suit-case. I'll have to work very hard to look respectable. I mustn't let you down before all those archdukes and
merchant princes."

" I'm afraid my frocks would be too big for you," said Sarah ruefully.

" Perhaps they would," said Elsie. " Look, I mustn't keep you. You must have lots to do. *Suggia !* What luck ! Good-bye till later, darling ! "

" Good-bye, dear ! "

It was certainly a stiff party. There was no getting away from that. But Elsie enjoyed it enormously. In the first place she enjoyed it because it was so exceedingly unlike all the parties she had been to this last couple of years in the smart hotels and the smart villas of the Riviera. She thought with delight of the expressions of terror that would over-spread the features of Bobby and his Americans should they suddenly find themselves set down in the centre of this party. It was a responsible sort of party. You had a sense of a casual word uttered by one merchant prince to another between a plover's egg and a mouthful of blue trout in jelly—and behold, a railway-line had been built here, an oil-field acquired there. One military-looking gentleman pointed out an item in the programme, or so he seemed to do, to another military-looking gentleman—and you knew that the scoun-drel who had brought off that *coup d'état*, his day was over, his doom was settled.

It was an agreeable feeling to be at a responsible party—for once, at least. Over in the South of France, you had a sense of crumbling, rotting, at their parties. Here you had a sense of wheels rolling, even of logs rolling, but they were logs of purpose and majesty.

Besides, Elsie scored a great personal success. She could not help enjoying that, too. It was so easy to score successes with the Riviera rabble ; but here, among these venerables, with their discreet decorations, it was really very gratifying. It was clear that in their circles anything so elegant, shocking, delicate, taut, dangerous, as Elsie was not a usual phenom-enon. The trimmed responsible beards got quite Left-wing at their edges. Certain of the faces about here were dimly familiar, as if she had seen them in childhood dreams, or in the illustrated supplements of newspapers. This, surely, was Mr. Winston Churchill in such affable close conversation with her brother-in-law? A vision pasted itself upon her mind of an enormous placard stuck on to a space of blank wall in Blenheim Road, round the corner from Oleander Street : " WHY ARE CHURCHILL'S PROMISES LIKE PIE-CRUST ? " It was election-time in Doomington. Mr. Winston Churchill was driving up to Unity Hall to address the Jews of Longton. The Jews on the pavement cheered as he passed. Mr. Churchill took his hat off, put it on again, took it off.

Who was this that had joined Churchill and Smirnof? Oh, he was clearly one of those generals from the Tsar's time. She had met one or two already. An archduke at the buffet was devouring roast pigeons hungrily, as if he had not had a square meal for a long time. Elsie had a particularly great success with the exiled Russian eminences. They implied it would be difficult not to make a morganatic Tsarina out of her when they overthrew the present iniquity.

No wonder the archduke was tucking away at the buffet. The food was royal, both in its bouquet and its quantity. So was the wine. Elsie had eaten quite heartily at Claridge's, but she found the food and drink such, and so many exquisite people insisting on serving her with it, that she ate and drank as if it were her first mouthful that day.

She enjoyed Gigli. She enjoyed Suggia. She enjoyed the spacious music-room, the dignified and magnificent house it was. She enjoyed its master, her brother-in-law, Alexander Smirnof ; she enjoyed the effortless good manners he displayed at the apex of his tree. He was evidently almost as much a statesman as he was a business-man. Or at least he was the sort of business-man whom statesmen confer with. He was admirably groomed. He was respected not for his money only. When he uttered a word about the latest conductor, the latest virtuoso, people strained to hear. He was charming to her, too ; genuinely delighted to see her, deliciously tactful with regard to the absence of Sir Robert.

She thought he looked a little tired, a little worried, almost. But how should he not, a man who, with his partner, Sam Silver of Doomington, controlled affairs of such gravity? And one of the children, Jackie, the eldest boy, had a temperature. He was a most devoted father.

But she enjoyed most of all the beauty and serenity of her sister Sarah. Sarah moved about, full and easy and warm in colour, like a madonna in a canvas of Palma Vecchio. She had advisers, it was true, in the preparations of so tasteful and ample a table, and the provision of such perfect drink to go with it. But it was evident she was the guiding genius of this hospitality, of the butlers and waiters who moved about so suavely to fill glasses, to hand cigarettes, to light them. She was the genius of the house, its men and maids that had it fresh as a rock scoured by the sea.

The party went on for several hours. And though no one noticed Sarah as she went, she was away a few minutes, at least, in each hour, up in the nurseries, seeing to the children, if they slept ; most of all, she went to the eldest boy, Jackie, who had a temperature. Once, not many minutes after she had come down again, a footman whispered a word to her, repeating a word a maid had whispered to him. A child was awake and crying. No one but his mother could send him to sleep again. Sarah went up, and Elsie went with her. It seemed to Elsie that Sarah was then most beautiful of all, leaning over a child's cot, murmuring into his ear, soothing his forehead with her lips.

The sight produced a sort of bliss, a sort of pride, in Elsie's heart. It also touched it with a minute cold point, of regret, of anger, of she knew not what. She was glad, therefore, when Sarah, her finger at her lips, beckoned her to come down again, and here they were once more among the merchant princes and the archdukes.

So Elsie left at length, one of the latest to go, though it was usually a vanity with her to be among the first.

"Darling! Darling!" she said. "How wonderful it's been!"

"It's been lovely to see you!" said Sarah. "Look, Elsie

dear. Why stay on in a hotel ? There's lots of room here ! We must talk about . . . about it all—you, and what you're going to do. I've not had a moment to-night."

" I should think you haven't, my dear. No, Sarah. I awfully want to go and see May to-morrow, and stay with her a day or two. I sort of promised, some time ago."

" Are you ? I'm glad, Elsie, I'm glad. I'm not at all happy in my mind about May. Go and see her, then, and come back here in a day or two. And then we'll see, yes ? "

" That's the idea, darling ! How lovely it's been ! Thanks so much ! Good night, Sarah ! "

" Good night, Elsie ! Give my love to May ! "

III

The Jewish children from Whitechapel and Doomington were up and around the grounds of the Chanctonbury Country Home. Some were playing croquet or battledore and shuttlecock or Red Indians on the lawns. Some were raptly attending their own little flower-beds, for each child had a flower-bed quite of his own to look after ; they sat staring at the soil as if they expected the seeds they had planted yesterday to break out of the earth and blossom before their eyes. Some were staggering under the weight of large stones, with which they were trying to build a rockery ; or rooting about for odd bricks to make borders with. Some lay sprawled over fairy-tales or little books of poetry. Some were chugging away manfully up the down to where Chanctonbury Ring spread its shade over the golden spilth of last year's beech-leaves.

The teaching staff were reading or resting ; the kitchen staff, having cleared away the mid-day meal, were getting on with their own. The Honorary Principal, May Silver, sat at her desk, biting vainly at her fountain-pen, in a room which opened through French windows directly upon the main lawn.

She heard a car approaching along the drive. She frowned.

She had a great deal to do. This was pioneer work in which a great variety of psychological and practical problems presented themselves from day to day. Obviously another of the county ladies was calling to let her know how frightfully interested she was, my dear, in your simply marvellous work, and anything I can do to help you, my dear, you won't hesitate to call on me, will you, I take that as a promise now.

The car drew up on the opposite side of the house. In a minute or two a maid presented a card.

" Show her in at once, Effie ! Good Lord, how lovely ! It can't be true ! "

A moment later, a young woman, hatless, her hair all over her face, her cheeks wind-flushed, her eyes shining, appeared. She held her hat in her hand.

" Elsie ! "

" May, darling ! "

" But how marvellous ! When did you get here ? Why on earth didn't you let me know ? "

" Let me look at you ! Yes, it's you right enough ! How glad I am to see you ! Can I have a cup of tea ? "

" Rather ! " Effie had been hovering discreetly in the doorway. " Effie, some tea at once ! China ? Indian ? "

" Indian for me, May ! Sorry ! I like guts ! "

" Indian for us both, Effie ! At once, please ! "

" Yes, mum ! "

" But, Elsie, what's it all about ? Is Bobby with you ? "

" No ! "

" Have you left him in town ? Why on earth didn't you bring him ? "

" I've left him ! "

" You mean—you've left him ? "

" I mean I've left him ! "

" Oh ! "

" Don't be depressed, darling ! I've not felt so happy for years ! It's *lovely*, having left Bobby ! "

" You mean—for always ? "

" Oh, yes ! " There was strong conviction in her voice.
" For longer than that."

" Well, I mean, do sit down Elsie, won't you ? Just let me
catch my breath a little ! "

" It's me that's out of breath. How glad I am you insisted
on my coming by car. What a gorgeous little village that is,
beyond Horsham. We were going like stink, but I made him
stop and turn back. Where there's a green, and a pond, and
ducks. I insisted on talking to the ducks."

" Partridge Green ! "

" I suppose that's it ! Green, yes—how *green* it all is, May,
how heavenly green ! "

" Yes, but——"

" Don't look so *worried*, my dear. I'll tell you all about
it ! "

" But, I mean, you'll understand my being a little—well,
a little taken back, won't you ? "

" I will. I do. And, come to think of it, I've never left a
husband before, have I ? But, darling, I simply must put
my hair where it belongs. Take me somewhere where I can
powder my nose." She was looking round for a mirror, then
she stopped suddenly, as if somebody had thrown a parcel of
books at her stomach. She roared with laughter, she roared
and roared. Her hair became quite dank with the sweat of
her laughter.

" Elsie, Elsie, what on earth *is* it ? Elsie, you're
mad ! "

" No—no—darling, I'm not ! " she gasped. " It's—it's
what I told Bobby ; those were my very words. ' I want to
powder my nose,' I said, just like that. And then I went
downstairs, got into the car, went home, and got a tooth-
brush—and here I am ! "

" This way, Elsie. I think you'd best have a little wash and
brush up. And then a cup of tea. And then perhaps——"

" Yes, May dear, forgive me ! " she said, clasping her
stomach. " I am a little hysterical, I suppose. It had to
come out. Thank God it didn't break out last night at

Sarah's party. That would have been frightful. Oh, Lord, my ribs ! "

" That's *not* where you keep your ribs ! " said May firmly. " This way ! You'll talk later ! "

Elsie had powdered her nose. She had got through two cups of tea, some slices of toast, some rock-buns, and a large chunk of currant cake. May apologised for the currant cake ; had she known Elsie was coming . . . Elsie assured her that one slice of English currant cake meant more to her than all the tottering iced follies of French pastry.

" More tea ! " Elsie said, holding out her cup. " Then perhaps you'll let me open my mouth ? "

" Yes," said May. " It might be safe now."

" Of course, it's very right and proper I should come straight from him to you. You remember, it's when I came to that hut of yours in Boulogne I set eyes on him for the first time ? So you're partly to blame."

" I remember. And I am partly to blame. And if you'd have asked my advice—— But you're not one for asking advice, are you ? "

" I suppose I'm not really, am I ? "

" But I had a feeling from the beginning something like this would happen. He was too beautiful."

" How right you are, darling. How exactly you've hit the nail on the head."

" He's not your sort. He's weak, too, isn't he ? "

She told her how weak he was.

" Elsie, you won't think I'm criticising ? "

" May dear, even if you were—— "

" I think I know what your feeling is about marriage. I don't think it can work out that way."

" You mean, both of you having an occasional adventure —outside ? "

" I mean that."

Elsie paused, and sighed. " I wonder if you're right. I'd hate to think you were. I must confess I couldn't help feeling just a little bit hurt when I saw him making eyes at every pretty woman we met, and sometimes they weren't very pretty, either. It was a bit thick to see him making arrangements, under my very nose, about when and where they might bring it off. Yes, it was rather painful sometimes. Yet it was absolutely part and parcel of the understanding between us."

" Oh, it's easy enough to come to an understanding about these things. That's the beginning, not the end."

" I, too, of course, once or twice——" Elsie said. She lowered her eyes and seemed to be scrutinising her finger-nails carefully.

" Yes, of course," said May, quite gently and quietly. " It was part and parcel of the understanding between you."

Elsie looked up. There was a flush on her cheeks. " I really mean it. Only once or twice."

" I can quite believe it. I suppose if a man's easy—loose, if you like—he can go on and on. It's just the same thing for a man, going on and on. But with a woman it's different. Each time it's a new thing, a fresh outrage."

" Perhaps you're right." Elsie's voice was heavy and wooden. Then she threw her head back. She spoke with some animation. " And yet, if it hadn't been for that once or twice, I'd have left him long ago. I'm absolutely sure of that. How do you explain that? Eh, May? Doesn't that stump you ? "

May gravely considered the matter. " I think not. It seems to me straightforward. Bobby was not your man. You were looking for him. You didn't find him. You're still looking for him."

Elsie looked up with startled eyes. " But, of course, that's true, that's dreadfully true. I'm still looking."

" I only hope, my dear," her sister said softly, " you'll recognise him when you see him."

Elsie leaned forward suddenly and seized hold of both May's wrists. " Listen, May ! Tell me, would you say I'm a spooky person ? Would you ? "

" I don't understand."

" I mean, a person with second sight, what they call
' psychic ' in Golder's Green—a nut-eater who has visions ? "

" I would say you're the least psychic person in all this
world."

" Quite true. I am. And yet—oh, how damned silly it
sounds ! "

" What ? "

" I've seen him ! "

" Who ? The man—the man——"

" Yes." Her voice was solemn. " I've seen him. I mean
I've seen him inside, with my mind's eye."

" What an odd creature you are, Elsie ! "

" I can sit here and describe him to you, May, quite
clearly, as if he were sitting a few feet away, there, on that
chair. He's tall, not handsome in the way most women think
men handsome. His eyes are grey or blue—blue, I think,
and very cold, and proud. The hair was gold once, but it
isn't now. It's grey over the temples, anyhow. He's not
young. He's got a queer mouth. Rather womanish. No, not
in the way Bobby's is womanish. We're not mannish or
womanish according to the people we go to bed with, and
the number of times we go to bed with them. There's something deeper in us than the body's sex. You, May, you—
you're the most delicate woman I know, and you're fifty
times more man than Bobby, than most of the men I know.
And I think I, too, could show them where they get off. . . ."

Then again her mind plunged forward on its task of evoca-
tion. She started forward in her chair. Her eyes, a little
dilated, stared hard upon the empty chair, as if, in truth,
a man occupied it. " He has a scar up against his mouth.
On this side." She lifted her fingers to her right cheek and
sketched a few movements with their tips in the regions beside the nostril and the mouth. " It's not a straightforward
scar. At least it was once, and it isn't now. It's all torn about
with little weals and ridges, as if something had happened
later . . . a shell exploding, perhaps. And what's this ? Did

I see it last time ? What's this patch of brown flesh up against the scar ? I hear the sound of broken glass and wood splintering ! I smell burning ! I tell you, I tell you . . ."

Her eyes blinked out of their fixity. She fell back loose and crumpled into her chair ; her hands and knees were trembling woefully.

" Elsie, Elsie darling ! Listen, it's me, May ! You're tired ; you're dreadfully tired. All that enormous journey to Calais, and the party last night. What time did you say you went to bed ? I insist you come straight along with me now and lie down. I insist, do you hear ? "

" Gosh, what a mug I am ! " said Elsie. " All right, big girl, show the way ! "

IV

" And now, my dear," said Elsie, " you bring out your crochet and I'll bring out my knitting. And what a joy we'll be for the prowling *Tatler* photographer. I'll be sick as hell if you've not arranged for one."

It was the middle of the following morning. Elsie had slept, as she informed May, like a hog. May had not slept so well. It is, after all, a little upsetting to have a sister, who has run away from her husband a few hours ago in the South of France, descend upon you suddenly in Sussex and start seeing visions.

" For you see," Elsie went on, " I'll probably want to get back on the stage again. And what chance have I got if nobody arranges the photographers for me ? "

" Sorry," smiled May ; " it shall be done."

" Not that I'm not going to have a damned good holiday first. You'd want a holiday if you'd been married to Bobby for—how many years is it ? Good God, it feels like fifty."

" She *shall* have a holiday. Indeed she shall. And then she can come and help her sister look after the little boys and girls from—yes, we've got a specimen from both Magnolia Street and Oleander Street. Dear old Emmanuel arranged that. Do you remember old Emmanuel? He's a great local patriot."

" Oh, dimly ! "

" We'll make a fine strapping woman out of our Elsie. And then, but only then, we'll start thinking of the stuffy old theatre again."

" You know, darling, it was just a toss-up whether it should be Kathy or you. Oh, no, it wasn't really. I had to come to you first."

" Kathy ? "

" That German Baronin woman I got so pally with down there, Kathy von Schlettau."

" Oh, of course, I remember. I asked you to bring her along, didn't I ? "

" Oh, my dear, she's dreadfully poor, she couldn't afford the fare now. Reading between the lines, I could see it was as much as she could do to pay for the postage-stamp. There she is, in her huge Silesian castle, scraping the dripping on the bread so that it'll go round. They're having a dreadful time in Germany. This inflation, you know."

" Yes, I've heard some heart-breaking tales. Well, why don't you go along and see her and be tactful one way and another ? "

" No." Elsie shook her head sadly. " There's something frightfully tragic about those Germans. And, my God, their pride ! Perhaps, if I rented a villa down in Amalfi or some-where, and asked her to come along with Toni—that's her youngster, you know. His father was killed the first week of the War."

" So was that one there. I mean his father, of course. That little red-haired chap, Barny Cohen, do you see ? "

" I see. Pretty bloody, wasn't it ? Doesn't seem to have led very far. Oh, what the hell ! This isn't the sort of day to sit about on deck-chairs croaking. What's that, darling ? That lovely fan-shaped fruit-tree, trained up against the wall there ? Surely it's an apricot-tree ! "

" Yes, an apricot-tree ! "

" Good God, an apricot-tree ! We've got a few beauties at
Cap Ferrat, too. How our family runs to apricot-trees ! You
remember that apricot-tree mother used to get so excited
about, way back in the ancestral estates ? "

" By Jove I do."

" And Susan, too. Do you remember ? Anything she could
dig up about jolly old Russia, you remember how she came
all over queer ? She was cut out to be a Bolshevik princess,
straight from the word go."

" Yes," May sighed. " I wonder if we'll ever see her again.
You know she's a very first-rate person, our Susan."

" They only let them out on dog-collars and leads, don't
they ? "

" I rather think that's the way of it. Ah, well, Germany,
Russia, it's a sad world one way or another. This is a good
country, after all ; the best of the lot. We've got a lot to be
thankful for."

" Yes, my sister. One hell of a lot."

" A lovely lovely country. The loveliest country in all the
world. The loveliest there's ever been."

" Perhaps you're right. No poetry now. I know that look
in your eye."

" I'll spare you the poetry. Not much point in saying it
when there it is all round you—the lawns, the downs, the
ring of trees up there, the flowers. Look, my dear, look at
that cypress-hedge ! Can you hear that willow-warbler out
in the orchard ? Look at that cedar ! The house ! No, you're
too near ! You can't get it ! Listen ! Do you hear that
blackbird ? "

" I thought it was Barny Cohen ! "

" Pig ! "

" Forgive me. But honestly, May, as one childless woman
to another—would it be just a little more perfect without
Hymie and Barny and Becky? Would it, or wouldn't
it ? "

" I don't think you've got the point, dear Elsie."

" No, as a matter of fact, I haven't. I've been hoping we'd

get to it sooner or later. What *is* the point, dear May ? What are you up to ? "

" You didn't read that stuff I sent out to you ? "

" Oh, May, I *am* a cad. I intended to, and then, what with one thing and another——"

" Perfectly, Elsie. I never expected you to."

" That helps, certainly."

" Well, I mean, to begin with—it's been rather odd. About ourselves, I mean."

" What ? "

" I mean starting off like that in Oleander Street. And all that's happened since."

" Yes, dear May, when you come to think of it, it's been too damned odd for words."

" Don't rag ! "

" I'm not ragging ! "

" Very well then. We know what it's like. At least, I do. I go on thinking and remembering. I remember long long days in that little kitchen in that stuffy little street—how my lungs were aching for fresh air, and my eyes simply couldn't see any more, because everything they had to look on was so grey and wretched. The only thing that helped me along was poetry. And then later, of course, Harry."

" Yes."

" And so, when all this happened to us, how could I possibly not do something about it—remembering it all as I do ? "

" Is that the only reason, because you remember it like that ? You wouldn't say that Harry Stonier has something to do with it ? "

May ignored the question. " Of course, it's all right, so far as it goes, letting the kids have a couple of weeks' holiday in the summer—in the way one or two institutions arrange it for them. But that's not enough. Oh, no, not at all enough. It's like letting a bird out of its cage, with a long thread attached to its leg, and letting it fly about for a few yards, and then whisking it back again."

" How long do you keep them here ? "

" A year, two years. Time enough to set them up in their little bodies ; and in their minds, too. That's sensible, isn't it ? "

" Yes, it seems to me a week or two might be almost worse than nothing. Upset the little blighters."

" Quite, Elsie. But there's more than that, of course, a lot more than that. There's the England side to it all."

" That's where I'm fogged. What are you after ? Do you intend to make little Anglo-Saxons out of your Jew kids ? "

" You've got it wrong, Elsie. Not little Anglo-Saxons. Little Englishmen. And little Englishwomen."

" I see," hesitated Elsie. " Or do I ? "

" I don't think you do. Listen, Elsie. I know it's an absolute chance that when father and mother decided to clear out of Russia, it was England they came to. It might have been Austria, Germany. They might have gone on to America. But they came to England. You might say I'd have felt about Germany or France exactly as I feel about England, if father and mother had gone to Germany or France. You may be right. But all I can say is, I don't think you are. Take Susan, for instance. Take yourself."

Elsie looked up. She was really interested.

" England meant nothing to Susan. It was Russia, Russia ; the whole time she thought of nothing but Russia. Whether it was the Russia of the past or the future, whether she wanted to pull it out root and branch, or anyhow keep that apricot-tree standing, her mind was set on Russia since she began to think at all. And you——"

" Me ? "

" I don't think England means to you what it means to me. Tell me, Elsie, do you think that's rude ? "

" Go on, May, don't be silly ! "

" I mean you were quite happy to be down there in the South of France all this time, weren't you ? I'd have hated it."

" It was rather more America than the South of France," Elsie grumbled.

" Oh, my dear, you *did* like it for quite a long time, didn't you ? "

" I did."

" And you'd be there now if——"

" Yes, if my little bit of England had come up to scratch."

" Quite." There was a note of triumph in her voice. " He helps me quite a lot. What on earth could be more Anglo-Saxon than Sir Robert Malswetting, umpteenth baronet ? "

" God knows, I don't ! "

" But he was just about as *English* as any other—forgive me, Elsie—any other Riviera lounge-lizard——"

" Go to it, baby ! "

" The son of an Italian vermouth king, or of a Detroit motor-car manufacturer, or Bobby Malswetting—they're not *English*, any of them. To be English is—how shall I put it ?—it isn't just lying on your back and kicking your legs in the air. It's something *positive*. You've got to *do* something about it."

" May, darling, this is all a little out of my depth. I'm not a runner in the Highbrow Stakes. You know, I've not thought about these things and they're not likely to upset my young dreams. None the less, what you just said—I rather think it's rot, that's all ! "

" What part of it ? "

" That to be English—you've got to *do* something about it. Isn't that what you call—what the hell do they call it ?— the Jewish inferiority complex ? Such an idea wouldn't have entered your old head if you'd been born straightforward English—a bucket-salesman's daughter, say, from Wolver-hampton."

" I'm not dogmatic about all this. You may be right. But I can only say I've thought a lot and hard about it—and you haven't. I've tried to say an Anglo-Saxon would have to work hard, too, to be English, like a Celt, or a Jew, or a Slav. Of course, he's got a start, a flying start. He's got the language, and he's born on the spot. And there are certain races, I think, who couldn't ever become English, excepting for certain special individuals. For instance—although they're almost as near to us as anybody in *space*, I think the Germans can't do it. Not that they want to ; I'm not saying that. Only supposing they *should* want to——"

" What I can't get, dear girl, is that stuff about your Anglo-Saxon having to do something in order to become English. Isn't that exactly what he is before he starts ? "

" I mean just this : I don't think a brainless ninny of a hunting peer or a beer-sodden navvy is English, not in the sense I'm driving at. You've got to know what England means, and has meant ; the tradition of England, the poetry of England, the flowers of England, the birds, the trees, the cottages, the churches. You've got to know the *soul* of England. And you can't do it over afternoon tea, either, prattling among the crumpets in the rectory drawing-room. It's a lifetime's job, and there's far more left to do by the time you're ready to die than there was when you started. For you never managed to catch up. And what's more, the English idea was growing, growing the whole time."

" I see," said Elsie, a little grimly. " Now we'll get on to our little boy-friends and girl-friends from Oleander Street. How do they come on in this act ? "

" We've naturally started on a small scale," she began.

Elsie looked round. She made a sweeping gesture with her hand. " Not so dusty, to start off with."

" Yes, people have been good to us," May agreed. "And of course father was a saint."

" I'm glad he's putting back some of the money where he got it from. Anyhow," Elsie said comfortably, " there's plenty more where that came from—if it ever became necessary to show the itching palm."

" He wouldn't let you down, Elsie, if you needed any-thing. He's too much the other way. But you know——"

" What ? "

" Things aren't swimming along so happily as they used to. The manufacturing end isn't quite what it was. But the

London end seems to make up for it. Oh, it's all beyond me. There's some sort of a slump on, I believe."

" There are always booms and slumps and things in business, aren't there ? " Elsie said lightly. " But look here ! Don't get me wrong. I don't want father's money. Strange, isn't it ? The thought of rich men's money makes me feel sick in the stomach at the moment. I've seen enough of Bobby's. The smell of it was all over the place, like open drains. Go on with your Jew kids."

" I get back to where I started from—England. I think to be English is the loveliest thing in the world. I think that Jews make a better job of being English than they make of being anything else in the world. I won't be dogmatic about that, either. There are Swedish Jews, I suppose, and I've no doubt they're good Swedes. I'm talking about England. I think that Jews become good English quicker than Gauls or Latins or Slavs do. They've had more training in adapting themselves, to begin with. And I think that what they bring with them fits in better with the English idea."

" Have I got a headache ? "

" Oh, have you, Elsie ? "

" No, darling. I was only asking."

" I've talked just about enough, you poor thing. What a bore I've become in my old age ! "

" Will you go on or won't you ? "

" All right. I want to make one thing clear, whether it interests you or not. Do I want these children to stop being Jews ? "

" Do you ? " May did not notice her frustrated yawn.

" No ! No ! The two things don't shut each other out. They enrich each other. You'll stay till Friday, of course ; and you'll see Miss Mosenthal presiding over the Sabbath evening candlesticks. It'll bring a lump to your throat. And on Saturday night you'll watch Miss Jenkins preside over the Morris dance. But we feel they'd get the Sabbath evening candlesticks in any case, in their own homes. The Morris dance wouldn't be so easy.

" The idea is to make it *easier* for them ; that's the word. They're put into our hands for a year or two, because they're not strong and the life they'll lead in the country will be good for them. And during that year or two we want to put into their way a number of adventures and discoveries that they'd normally take a lifetime over, perhaps a generation or two. The difference between hornbeam and whitebeam, and what dewponds are, and what a skylark's egg is like but you mustn't dream of touching it, and all about Sir Patrick Spens, and who said, ' Loveliest of trees the cherry now,' and what's the colour of pear-blossom . . ."

" You've got *me* licked, old girl ! "

" I think it would be rather late to make a nice little Englishwoman out of *you*. But I'd have liked to try."

" Me—doing a Morris dance ? *Me ?* Say, sister, you're missing on two cylinders."

" Do you know the time ? I say, what *is* the time ? Good Lord, it's nearly lunch-time. I simply *must* get some letters done ! Will you be all right here ? "

" Is there a book called *Foxe's Book of Martyrs* ? "

" There is. Why ? "

" You might let me have a copy. I want to put a chapter in, in handwriting."

v

One more conversation between May and Elsie Silver must be recorded here, for it had an important bearing on their history. It took place late the next night. Both girls were obviously tired, for May had put Elsie through her paces quite strenuously. Elsie had, of course, protested, but she had thrown herself heartily into the visits to class-rooms, play-rooms, sick-rooms, workshop, kitchen, flower-beds, chicken-runs, the whole varied work that May's creation under the Sussex Downs comprehended.

" Well, Elsie ? " May asked. " You look as if you've had about enough for one day. What about bed ? "

Elsie was silent for some seconds. She had seemed seriously preoccupied for a little time now, though she had yawned once or twice despite herself. Then she spoke. "No!" she said sharply. " I'm not going to bed yet. I want to talk to you."

" You've not had enough talk for one day? Darling! Won't it keep till to-morrow? "

" May, please sit down, will you? I want to ask you, May. Did you think it was only to weep on your bosom I came to see you? To weep about Bobby, I mean? "

" Well, partly that, I hope, though I didn't notice much weeping. And of course you came to see me just like that, too. As I'd come to see you if you were still at Cap Ferrat and I was within five hundred miles of you."

" Quite so. To see you. And I've seen. I'm going to shoot straight back to that night at Boulogne. You remember? "

" When you came to sing with the concert-party? "

" Yes, and I first set eyes on Bobby, too. But I don't want to talk about Bobby."

" Well? "

" The question came up about Harry Stonier. You remember perfectly well. I've never forgiven myself for the frightful way I let fly about him."

" *I* have, long ago."

" But then you are like that. You forgive people. I don't. I don't even forgive myself."

" You're not going to bring all that up against yourself *now*, are you? "

" I am. Because I'm going to go on with the same subject. I don't know what was wrong with me that night. I was tired, of course. I'm normally strong as a bull, but sometimes when I'm tired I go all ga-ga."

" You poor thing! "

" But it wasn't only because I was tired. I was really howling angry you still felt the same way about him. Please don't be cross with what I'm going to say now. I'm very, very quiet and self-possessed, and I'm saying it all because I—because you——"

" I think I understand," said May.

" Yes, I think you do. I still think what I thought then. I think he's sanctimonious. He's full of pride—the wrong sort of pride. He's a coward."

" You think what you think."

" You're not angry ? You promise me that ? "

" I'm not angry. Somehow I feel too tired to be angry."

" Yes. That's what I mean. Deep down, deep down, he's tired you out. I can see it in your eyes. I can hear it in your voice, too."

" Perhaps you're right."

Elsie suddenly switched the subject round. " What's your idea about this place ? How long do you intend to stick here ? "

" I don't know. Till it starts running properly. Then Miss Mosenthal takes over from me. A couple of years, perhaps."

" And then ? "

" I might start another. Or pay a little more attention to father and mother. They need it, you know. They're about as helpless as two children."

" It's not good enough ! " Elsie's eyes flashed. " You know perfectly well it's not good enough ! "

" Well, what are you going to do about it ? "

" That's just what I'm going to tell you. You said, didn't you, that I'm still looking for the man—the man I was cut out for, or who was cut out for me, anyhow ? I'm not absolutely certain they're always the same thing."

" I said that man wasn't Bobby. Yes, I said just that. You've still got to find him."

" And you ? But of course. You make no bones about it."

" No."

" I'm sorry it's Harry Stonier. You know I feel like that, and I can't get away from it. But this is your works, not mine. I know that Harry Stonier has made you ten years older than your age. I'm beginning to be bloody now. You must bear it. I know that he's pushed you into—all this ; Baby Clinics and Children's Homes. It's your substitute for

Harry Stonier. Yes, it is. I know it is. Oh, it's all very fine in
its way. But it can be managed by elderly widows, or by
elderly spinsters. Not by you. You're only twenty-six. You've
got your life to live. Don't kid yourself, you've not started
living it yet. It's all *right*, all this. It's fine. I think it's all a
little muddled somehow, but that's not what I'm after. It's
you I'm after ! "

" I don't see what you're driving at."

" You don't, eh ? Let me tell you. If you don't give me his
address, I can easily find it. I'm going to see him, wherever
he happens to live now. I'm going to knock sense into his
head. I know it's not—orthodox. But this isn't the time of
Richard Cœur de Lion. And, even if it was, I'm not going
to let him practise on my sister."

" I don't want you to go and see him," said May dully.
Even as she spoke, her own ear was astounded by the lack
of fervour in her tone. She would have thought that if anyone in the wide world had once more dared to make this
infamous suggestion, she would have shrieked her anger like
a fish-wife. " Father wanted to do that, too," she said.

" I should damn well think so. Which just shows. Father
loathes butting in on this sort of thing every bit as much as
I do, but to see you wasting like this, under our eyes—— Oh,
hell, no ! "

" Please ! " implored May. Her eyes were misty with tears.

" Oh, May, May ! " Elsie flung her arms round her
sister's shoulders. " I'm so wretched about it all ! We've got
to put it right ! We've got to, I tell you ! "

" I'm not asking you," May sobbed. " You're doing it
yourself ! "

" Come now, May, come to bed ! We can leave the rest
till to-morrow."

CHAPTER XV

DINNER IN CARDIFF

I

HARRY STONIER lived in Tasker Street, a street not more depressing than many other streets in Cardiff, and as little accustomed to the incidence of the most expensive sort of Hispano-Suiza. After finishing his work that day at the Cardiff Town Hall, he had taken his usual evening meal of milk and buttered toast at a Lyons café and gone on to the reference library, where he was studying the works and lives of certain contemporary Spanish mystics. Although the car, purposeful as a battleship and glittering like a chandelier, was drawn up outside number thirty-one, where he lived, it did not occur to him that it had any possible connection with him. Indeed, it was not of the order of phenomena which interested him. He was hardly aware of it.

But he could not help registering a phenomenon almost as unusual—the fact that the light was burning in the hall. It glimmered and sagged through the glass panels of the front door, as if this were a day on which a Lord Mayor or a Member of Parliament might be on a visit to Mrs. Morgan. And, seeing that neither under any circumstances ever visited Mrs. Morgan, the burning of the light in the hall was a mysterious matter.

Stonier let himself in with his key, and hung his hat and coat up in the hall. For Mrs. Morgan gave bed and breakfast only to the most reliable gentlemen, and to hang hat and coat in the hall involved no danger. Moreover, Mrs. Morgan had the hall well under survey. Even when she was upstairs at the top of the house, cleaning out the top back, she was aware if any unauthorised foot threatened to cross the strip of polished brass on the threshold, beyond which none but her gentlemen might venture. She would descend with surprising agility, despite her sixty years, and administer to the unauthorised foot such vigorous reproof that it would never again hover so impertinently over areas dedicated to feet more gentlemanly.

A moment after Stonier had hung up his hat and coat, she had traversed the distance between the kitchen at the far end of the lobby, and the hall-stand, which was its most imposing decoration.

" Well, there you are, Mr. Stonier ! " she said, her head shaking, and her voice hoarse with excitement.

" Good evening, Mrs. Morgan. Is anything the matter ? "

" Anything the matter, indeed ! Well, I wouldn't say that, no ! "

Her eyes glittered, but there was no menace in her tone. Stonier felt relieved about that. It was clear that he had not once again forgotten to turn the gas off in the bathroom geyser.

" Well that's all right then ! " he said, and made a movement as if to go up to his room. It was possible she had recruited an even more socially eminent gentleman than usual into the upper front, which had been vacant for some time : but it was too late now to listen to a recital of the newcomer's personal and ancestral merits.

" I should just think there was nothing the matter ! " she said. She leered into his face. She was positively coquetting with him.

" What do you mean ? Have you got anything to talk to me about ? "

" I have got something to talk to you about," she said. " I should think I have ! And it's a lady ! "

" A lady ! " He was genuinely surprised. And so in fact was she. It was understood at Mrs. Morgan's that ladies did not visit Mrs. Morgan's gentlemen. It was true that on more than one occasion, and very late at night, certain gentlemen of whom you would never have dreamed such a thing, never in all your born days, had attempted to shush ladies upstairs under cover of raincoats and loud coughing. But Mrs. Morgan wasn't born yesterday. That wasn't the sort of house Mrs. Morgan kept. She could smell the coming of ladies from the dark depths of that kitchen of hers where no living human being had ever been known to penetrate, except Mrs. Evans, the daily help, of whom you could say that she was not only Mrs. Morgan's daily help, but her heart's companion. She could smell which room they had sneaked into, though all the doors were closed and blank. And those ladies did not remain long in Mrs. Morgan's house to bring dishonour on Mrs. Morgan and the other gentlemen asleep in the chaste celibacy of their beds.

"A lady!" Mrs. Morgan repeated, and lifted her finger to her nose.

"What are you talking about, Mrs. Morgan? What lady?"

She chuckled. She knew that his surprise was genuine. Ever since Mr. Stonier had come to take her front bed-sitting-room, and a large room it was, dirt cheap, too, when you thought what you got for it—getting on for three-and-a-half years now, and Mr. Stonier the sort of gentleman who might easily stay on till kingdom come; saves so much trouble and worry these long lets—ever since Mr. Stonier had come to take her front bed-sitting-room, of ladies there had been neither hint nor trace. In fact, Mrs. Morgan, who permitted herself in conversation with Mrs. Evans a certain candour of conversation and speculation which she would very grimly have disapproved of, should any of the gentlemen have attempted them with her—Mrs. Morgan had made certain speculations regarding Mr. Stonier's physical constitution, which were quite definitely outside her province as landlady. "Well, his books is his young ladies," she summed up the situation, "so he will feel no lack." Mrs. Evans agreed. Mrs. Evans was a good chapel woman, as indeed Mrs. Morgan was, and both married, widowed, and the buriers of three and four children respectively, so that on the whole they should not be too hastily judged for analysing a curiosity which, in spinsters, would have been prurient.

" And even if he is," said Mrs. Evans, " why not ? "

" And why not, indeed ? " Mrs. Morgan echoed. And the two ladies shook their heads, and got on with the egg and bacon plates, which were that greasy—and why do even the most reliable gentlemen always put ashes on their egg and bacon plates, as if an ash-tray were not provided in each single room ?

But this lady that had come in the car was not merely a lady. Or, to be exact, she was very literally a Lady. Certain ladies might pretend they are Ladies for purposes of their own, but there was no pretence about this one. That motor-car was no soap-box on wheels. It wasn't even just a motor-car. It was foreign, and it had a solidity and a grandeur which were to be a legend in Tasker Street for many a long day. It had a chauffeur in uniform, of an immobility, of a magnificence, which could not be believed unless seen.

And as for the Lady herself . . . Mrs. Morgan dived with her hand and half her arm into a pocket in her skirt, and brought out a purse. With trembling fingers she opened the purse, and extracted a visiting-card from its central pocket. The name of Lady Malswetting was engraved on the card, which had been cleaner when the chauffeur had first handed it over to Mrs. Morgan. It had been cleaner, because it had already been produced a number of times since then. It had been shown, not only to a number of tradesmen, but to all the other gentlemen in the house, to let them know, if only belatedly, what sort of a house this was, in which the gentlemen were liable to be visited by titled ladies, just off-hand, when it occurred to them to go visiting their friends.

" Lady Malswetting ! " said Harry Stonier, turning the card over in his hands. " I don't know the name ! When did she come ? "

" Twice she's been here, Mr. Stonier. It was six o'clock on the dot, and the door give a ring. I opened the door, and there for you iss a chauffeur, looking for the life of him like a general of the Army. And he give me this card, and, ' Iss Mr. Stonier in ? ' he says. ' Lady Malswetting would like to see him ! ' ' No,' I says to him, ' he issn't in. I haven't seen him whatever.' So up I go to your room, and there you are, not in. And when I get down again, there she iss standing at the door, her own Ladyship."

" Is she here now ? "

" Wait, Mr. Stonier, I have not finish my storri. She paid ten pound for that costume, if she pay a penny, gospell truth, Mr. Stonier. And, duweth, Mr. Stonier, she look grand enough for an actress off the pictures ; she does really, and that sweet smile on her face, too ! So, Mr. Stonier issn't in, iss he, she says. When are you expecting him ? If he issn't in now, and yes, he's at the book-library for you, I tell her ; and half past nine iss his time for coming home, I says. And you're after half past nine, Mr. Stonier, issn't it ? She's been waiting more than half an hour for you. She's upstairs in your room, Mr. Stonier. I put one of my own shillin's in your slot, Mr. Stonier, because the evenin's iss turnin' quite chilly. So when you see it in your bill, Mr. Stonier, you'll know that it will be me in the right."

" In my room, you say ? Why didn't you ask her into the room down here ? "

" What's the matter with you, Mr. Stonier ? She won't give you a bite, she's a proper lady. And then I ask her if she want to wait here in the dinin'-room, and I pass the remark to her, would her Ladyship like a cup of tea ? No, she says, I would rather wait in his own room. Him and me iss old friends."

" Old friends ? "

" She says she iss a sister of a dear friend of yours ! " Mrs. Morgan's voice was full of roguery. So Mr. Stonier had dear friends, after all. Mrs. Evans and she would have to re-consider their decision about the first-floor-front's potencies. It was a pity Mrs. Evans had not been in when she went over with all the news. It would be a long time to wait till eight o'clock next morning before Mrs. Evans came in, and they could thrash out the matter in all its bearings.

" Very well then, thank you," said Mr. Stonier. " I'll go up now."

" Shall I make you a nice cup of tea for you and your Ladyship ? " called Mrs. Morgan after him, blinking up the banisters.

" I don't know. I'll tell you," said Mr. Stonier, in quite a brusque voice, and him so gentle as a rule that you wouldn't think he would kill a mouse.

He opened the door and went in. The scent struck his nostrils even sooner than his eyes registered her, sitting comfortably back in the wicker armchair to the right of the gas-stove. The scent was something more complicated and dangerous than the smell of the perfume which went up out of her hair and clothes. It was a scent which brought him back at once to the Silver kitchen in Oleander Street, where it subtly dominated the air, though so many other odours challenged its congestion. It was the scent of Woman, which had not once before arisen in that room, since Harry Stonier had taken possession of it.

He saw the silk-clad legs of the woman before he saw the face. It was almost as if he was intended to see them first, they projected so deliberately forward from the woman's lumped body. As he came in, the body made a movement downward from its hips, so that the skirt covered the legs down to the point that was seemly at that time.

" I beg your pardon," came the woman's voice. " I hope you don't mind my making myself comfortable."

" Not at all," said Stonier stiffly. " You are, of course——"

" Yes, I'm Elsie. I'm May's sister. You remember me ? "

" I do. I'm afraid—it's a long time since we met. Please tell me—is anything wrong with—your sister ? "

" Yes, a good deal. Everything."

" Do you mean—what do you mean ? " His eyes, which

would have seemed too large for his head if the forehead had not been so broad and high, dilated with alarm.

" She's all right, generally speaking. Any doctor would certify her A1, I suppose."

" I see. What can I do ? It's very kind of you—but what have you come for ? "

" What can you do ? What have I come for ? That's exactly what we are going to talk about. Do you mind, is this usually your chair ? There were some books in it, I put them down carefully, just here."

" No, I don't sit there."

" I'm taking it for granted you've forgiven me for breaking in on you like this. After all, we're old friends. Well—not perhaps *friends*, quite. We hardly met, really, did we, in Oleander Street. But you have known May for a long time, haven't you ? How long is it about ? "

" Ten years about, Lady—Lady Malswetting ! "

" Oh, we might as well cut that out. That's over. I'm going back to the stage. Elsie Silver's my name."

" As you choose, Miss Silver."

" Would you mind—it's rather cheek asking you to sit down in your own place like this ; but would you ? I'd prefer it if you would."

" Thank you." All the chairs in the room, but one, were piled up with books. Only one was free, the chair in front of the table which served as his desk. It was a stiff wooden chair, and he sat down upon it woodenly, on the other side of the gas-stove, as far away as he could get from her.

She looked at him—making no effort at all to disguise the fact that she was looking at him—head to heel. She was completely puzzled now, as she had been, ten years ago, by what it was in him that so enchanted May. She was more puzzled now than then, for then they had both been young, and girls have fallen for plainer men than Harry Stonier seemed to Elsie Silver. But the years had gone by since then. And she knew that May's love for this man had grown with the years to such a point that she must organise the most complex and grandiose structure to take the place in her heart that he refused to fill. He was no longer a young man. He looked nearer forty than thirty, though he was not thirty yet. His spell in Dartmoor as a conscientious objector, she concluded, was responsible for that.

He had a large forehead, with bumps at the temples like the knobs on the back of a toad. His nose was not so bad, but the cheeks were sunken. The mouth was thin, ascetic. He had not shaved well, or his chin was of the sort that cannot look well shaven for more than an hour or two. There was so little colour in his eyes that they seemed to merge imperceptibly into the irises. His hair was brown, almost sandy, a common sort of hair both in colour and texture. His hands, too, were common. They lay splayed out upon his thighs, the finger-tips squared off, like spades. He bit his finger-nails. His face was the face of a clerk. The hands, though they were almost revoltingly pale and flabby, were a workman's hands, the hands of a man whose father was a brass-moulder.

She looked at him steadily, then she dropped her eyes. She wanted to keep out of them the hostility she feared might be apparent in them. She feared that if he had eyes to see, he could not fail to notice the small spots which tingled coldly upon her face and all over her body. Her blood seemed to run hither and thither in her veins, as if it felt the pulsing of a blood inimical to hers several yards away. But no, she assured herself contemptuously, those were not the eyes which were sensitive to the tremulous adjustments of a woman's skin. The hands lay splayed out upon the thighs as if they were dead flesh.

She raised her eyes, and looked at him coldly through the fringe of her lashes. She realised in that moment how much she had always hated him. She recalled the night in France when she had extracted from May the information that May was still sick for love of him, and how odiously she had behaved as a result of that information. She remembered how, still earlier, long ago in the Silver kitchen, his presence had always made her go hot and cold with resentment, as it did to-night, in the bed-sitting-room in Cardiff. No, she did not merely resent him, she hated him. She wondered if he had always hated her as much, or merely despised her. His purity was to her a piece of preposterous impertinence, a challenge, a slap in the face. She violently wanted to slap his face, quite literally, to-night, this moment. She had to dig her nails into her palms to overcome the temptation.

Then he spoke. " I would have been obliged to you if you had given me some notice of your coming. We might have met in some more convenient place."

" I'm dreadfully sorry," she said. " There was no time. You see," she lied, without a moment's hesitation, " I was going off to Berlin to-morrow. It'll probably have to be the day after to-morrow now. I arrived a few days ago from the south of France. I've just left my husband. You don't mind my being frank with you, do you ? I just had time to run over and see May in Sussex. I've often been anxious about her, and now, after seeing her—I want you to understand one thing—all this is no more of a pleasure to me than it is to you. But I made up my mind, the moment I set eyes on May, that I wouldn't leave for the Continent without talking the whole thing out with you."

" Am I to understand she sent you ? "

" I said no such thing," she said sharply.

" I beg your pardon," he said. " Much more, I beg hers. I didn't know what I was saying. Your appearance here——"

" Yes, I can assure you. It cost a lot of money, and a lot of trouble."

" I'm sorry," he said.

" There's no need for you to be sorry. It's not for your sake I came. It's for hers."

" I can understand that. Might I suggest . . . would it be possible for us to discuss the matter outside ? It's a fine night, and perhaps . . . it occurs to me you might prefer it."

" I don't think you need worry," she assured him. " I'm an actress. I'm quite used to talking to men in their bedrooms."

" Very well, Miss Silver."

She had kept her eyes averted from him, after her preliminary intense scrutiny. She raised them again. She imagined, from a certain quality that his voice had during the utterance of these last words, that his face had grown scarlet. She found it was so. She saw the blush retreat immediately from his cheeks, leaving them more sallow than before. She looked upon his hands which he had not yet removed from his thighs. She became aware that they were not dead flesh, there was an infinitely minute trembling in them, like leaves on a day of hardly more than no wind. She became aware that the flesh of the thighs beneath the hands trembled too.

She became aware that Harry Stonier was afraid.

In that moment she realised that the course of action she had proposed to herself, if but vaguely, on her journey to Cardiff, must, as a consequence, be here slightly, there profoundly, modified. She had not reckoned that he would offer himself as her most potent ally.

" I know, Mr. Stonier," she said. " I know what landladies are." She was already adjusting the nature and angle of her attack. There was almost a note of banter in her voice. " Please don't let me frighten you. As a matter of fact, I don't mean to keep you up long to-night. Both my chauffeur and I have had a long day of it."

" Can't you say what you want to get said to-night ? "

" That's not very gallant of you, is it ? After all the trouble I've taken to come to see you. Yes, I'm pretty sure I could postpone my visit to Berlin for one day more. To-morrow we must really meet and talk. To-night—well, to-night I've hunted you down, haven't I ? That's almost enough for one night. And besides, as you say, there's the landlady."

He had not said anything at all about the landlady. With

a cry of impatience he got up from his chair, went over to his table, and started fingering some books.

" Mr. Stonier," she reproached him. " You will at least let me smoke a cigarette ? Do you mind if I have one of my own ? Would you like one ? "

" I don't smoke much, thank you ! My landlady said she'd make you some tea. Would you like some ? " he asked surlily.

" No, I think not, thanks very much."

" All right."

" Please sit down."

He sat down. " What do you want ? " he asked. The muscle on the side of his jaw twitched and hardened.

" You know perfectly well what I want. I want to talk about May."

" So you said."

" I think I ought to get one or two things said to-night. It'll give you time to think over them by the time we meet to-morrow."

" I'm engaged to-morrow."

" Oh, indeed you're not ! " she said angrily. " Don't you believe it. If you think you can treat *me* like a dog, you're mistaken ! "

" Like a *dog* ? What are you talking about ? Are you suggesting I've behaved badly to your sister ? "

" *Badly ?* " She looked her derision. " Badly ? If a man had treated me as you've treated May, I'd have poisoned him long ago." She looked quite capable at that moment (and quite frequently, indeed) of poisoning a man of whom she thought he had treated her badly. It was an element in her formidable charm.

" Isn't this," he asked evenly, " an affair between your sister and me ? "

" It *has* been, my friend, for ten years. It's an affair between my sister and you and me now."

He made a gesture of impotence with his hands. It was an unlovely gesture.

" You know, of course," she said, " how madly in love with you my sister is ? "

He did not answer. He bit his lip with pain.

" I'm going to give you the benefit of the doubt," she went on. " I'm going to conclude you're just as much in love with her."

He looked at her for several seconds, his eyes dilating again with their odd, terrible dilation. " I think it's unspeakably impertinent of you," he said, " to come here and talk to me like this."

" I think I'd agree with you," she said slowly, " if you weren't breaking my sister's heart."

He paused. He considered what he was going to say next, very carefully, for a full minute. " I'm not used to meeting women like you," he said. " I don't understand the words you use. You talk as if you were talking in a play."

" Do you dare," she cried out at him, " do you dare to tell me I'm play-acting ? The next thing you'll say is I'm hysterical ! You're even more of a cad than I thought ! "

" No, I didn't say that. You mean what you say as you mean it when you act in plays. But your words and mine are not the same."

" Are you accusing me of lying when I said that May was— that she was heart-broken ? "

" You see, you can't induce yourself to use the word a second time without embarrassment. I didn't say you were lying. I only said you were theatrical."

She was interested. She considered the matter. She seemed to be still considering the matter when she spoke. " I've not got the advantage over you. You say you're not used to meeting women like me. I can say the same thing about you. I'm not used to meeting men like you, men who can sit back on their behinds and start arguing about words like boys in a school debating society, all the time that some human being somewhere is slowly being turned round on a spit and dried and roasted. I'm thinking of a pub up in St. Pol behind Nice where they do trussed chickens like that. But that's over in an hour or two. You keep on at it, year in, year out."

" What d'you want me to do ? "

" In a way it's hopeless to expect you to do anything. If you were the sort of person capable of doing anything, you'd have done it long ago. But you're not. You're like something in a fair. You're a freak."

" Because I haven't asked your sister to come here and share a bed-sitting-room with me in Cardiff ? Have you any sense of human dignity and decency ? Do you think the only thing men and women want to do is to get into bed with each other like—like two pigs in a sty ? "

" Exactly. That shows the sort of man you are, the sort of mind you've got. Is that the only thing you can think of when a man and a woman are in love with each other and make love, as your father and mother did, and my father and mother did, and all lovers have always done, and will always do—is that all you can think of, two pigs in a sty ? You make me sick ! "

" I can't hope to make you understand. You can only abuse me and all I feel and think."

" What have you to say for yourself ? "

" If you think I'm going to justify myself before you, please understand—I am not. I could only try, without much hope, to make you see it from my point of view. And I do that, not because you're her sister, but because I see you love her—almost as much as I do."

" This thing is beyond the reach of a sister's love, excepting for one who'll dare to do what I'm trying to do to-night. And it's not easy. It's dreadful. It's hateful."

" I see that. You mustn't think it a further crime on my part when I say I think it admirable of you."

" We'll cut that short, anyhow. You were going to try to make me see it from your point of view. Try."

" You've given me the benefit of the doubt. I use your words. You are ready to assume I love her."

" Yes."

" I do. Far more than anything else I know in the world—
my books, my eyes, sunrise, springtime. She is the sum to me
of all those things."

" Keep going."

" I believe she loves me, too, even now, even after all these
years."

" Yes, God help us ! "

" I'm prouder of that than of anything else in the world.
It is, in fact, the only thing in the world I have to be proud
of."

" You've said it."

" You're good enough to agree on both points. But this is
the point at which we disagree. You think there can be no
love between a man and a woman unless they—unless
they——"

" Oh, don't be such a mammy's darling ! Unless they get
into bed and have a good time ! "

" I think, and I believe May thinks—I know May thinks—
love is possible without that."

" Is it because you think it's so filthy ? Tell me that, will
you ? "

" It's because I think, and she thinks, that it's the quint-
essence, the fine flower, to which and from which everything
leads, the golden gate that must not be forced. You think—I
know what you think ! I can see it in your face. You think
I'm talking romantic rubbish. But remember, it's not I that
forced this. It's you. I can only use the words which are
familiar to me to express the thoughts which are with me,
with us both, day and night."

" You're a liar ! "

" I expect you to treat me like this."

" You're a liar, and if what you say is right about her,
she's a liar too. When you get to bed at night, both of you,
it's not about golden gates and fine flowers you dream, like
hell you do ! You dream of lips and breasts and thighs. You
dream of chucking your arms—— You can't bear it, can
you ? What are you shutting your eyes like that for ? What

are you clenching your fists for? My God, man, you're sweating! Anybody'd think you're having all your back teeth yanked out!"

His eyes were closed and his chin thrown back; she noticed the ugly pulled tendons of his throat. He spoke with difficulty. "Miss Silver, if you are going to attack me with obscene words and images, I can only say I'll get up and go. You can stay there. You can stay there to-morrow and the next day. But I'll not set foot in this place till you've gone."

"How frightened you are of a bit of the truth, aren't you, Mr. Stonier? You get me wrong. I'm not trying to attack you. I've already told you I'm not interested in you. It's May I'm interested in. What would you do if somebody you knew was thirsty? You'd give 'em a drink. If somebody you knew was hungry, you'd give 'em a good rumpsteak. A hell of a fat rumpsteak you'd make for any woman. But that's May's funeral, not mine. Well, it's not food and drink you're both crying out for. Good God, you're shrivelled, both of you. Your eyes are popping out of your head. It doesn't take brains to see what's wrong with you. It takes just half an ounce of ordinary common gumption."

His voice was almost inaudible as he spoke to her now. His eyes were still closed. He was like the saints one sees in early paintings, undergoing a pain too great to bear. "Is it that you are suggesting—that your sister and I—that we should—that I should take her like a harlot out of the streets——"

"Don't be a damn fool! I don't ask you to get down to it before you get married, though that wouldn't do either of you any harm. You attach too much importance to it, big boy, with your golden gates and all that high-flown twaddle. It's just a natural decent job of work which every grown-up man and woman has got to get on with along with their other jobs. That's all. At the same time—it's queer; you don't attach enough importance to it, either. You think you can sneak round it. You can't. It'll just burn you up to a cinder. That's what you look like, both of you; burned up. You kid yourself with all your books, and she kids herself with her grand home for snotty-nosed babies. Don't you see, you damn fool, she wants a baby of her own ? And a man to get it from before, and a man to get another one from after ! Don't you see ? "

" You haven't answered my question," the faint words came.

" I will in my own good time. I was saying—what was I saying ? Oh, yes, come to think of it, I think if you *did* have a bit of a flutter it would simplify the whole damn thing. Then you'd realise what a fuss you've been making about nothing. But I'm not out to solve your problems for you. To get back to May. What was that you said ? ' Take her like a harlot out of the streets ? ' No, I don't think so. That's not May's strong suit. But, gosh ! you accuse *me* of talking like a play. ' Take her like a harlot out of the streets ! ' God Almighty, if ever a bum actor in a fifth-rate fit-up company shot off worse punk than that . . . No, you're not expected to do anything so noble. You've not got to make an honest woman out of nobody. Just write and say : ' Come along, kid, let's get along to old whiskers and fix it up ! ' " ·

" You mean, of course, I should ask her to marry me ? You mean also that it would make the whole thing easier if I presented myself besmirched with a night's whoring ? "

" Cut out the strong stuff, big boy ! Yes, I mean you should ask her to marry you. How did you guess ? Get to the top of the class ! "

" You think I should ask her to come and share this—this squalor with me ? "

" She's all right for funds. You could have the downstairs room as well."

Then he opened his eyes. There was a blaze of fierce anger in them.   His chin was grim. He shot his head forward.

" Do you think I'd let her keep me on her money, like one of your dirty little Riviera gigolos ? Have luxury and sensuality made you so blindly stupid ? And can I forget what sort of money it is ? Money squeezed out of the marrow of broken bones, sticky with the blood of slaughtered youths ? "

She shrugged her shoulders. " Well, there'd have been a lot more pneumonia, anyway, if not for father's trenchcoats."

He disregarded her. " That's why it's been impossible for me to—to do as you ask." Then his tone changed completely. " If I could have married her, I would have been the happiest man in the whole world."

" So what do you propose to do about it ? Just keep on like this—you here, she there ? "

" I can only say this. Some day I hope to get out of the office I'm in. You see there—those papers ? I'm writing. I haven't much faith in it, but I'm doing what I can. I work all through the night sometimes without going to bed. I go straight on from that table to my office. Some day I might have luck. It's come before now to people as unlikely as me."

" Well, well," yawned Elsie. " That's gratifying, anyhow. It makes me feel good that you're doing *something* about it, that there's some hope *somewhere*. Look here, Mr. Stonier, I'm beginning to sag a little. I'll have to be getting on to my hotel. I don't think we've done badly for one night, do you ? What about that meeting to-morrow ? "

" I don't wish to be discourteous, but it's very hard for me to spare the time. Is another meeting necessary ? "

" Now listen. I'm never going to barge in on you after to-morrow, even if you and May *do* get married. May and I will find some way of meeting without you and me making goo-goo eyes at one another. But I've got to see you to-morrow. In some ways I feel what you and I have got to say to each other has only just begun. We won't argue about it ; we're meeting to-morrow. Look here, I have an idea. You're engaged all day. Why not dine with me in the grill-room at the Queen's ? They gave me quite a decent meal to-night."

" I'm not in the habit of letting women take me out to meals ! " he said.

" Hoity-toity ! "

" If you feel you want to see me again, then please dine with *me* at the same place."

She smiled at him charmingly. She realised at once the

importance of yielding to him, even though the extravagance of taking a woman out to dine in the best hotel in the town should make him short in the pocket for weeks and weeks to come. " I couldn't very well *ask* you to take me out, so I put it the other way. Thanks immensely. You know, I shouldn't be surprised if you haven't the makings of a lady's man in you after all."

" What time ? "

" Well, what about seven ? Does that sound awfully early ? Then I might possibly start out for town that same night."

" Seven will do."

She rose ; her coat was over the back of her chair. She started to put it on, then looked at him, twinkling. " You might as well give a lady a hand."

" Sorry," he said, blushing again.

" I like you when you blush like that," she said. " My gloves and bag. Oh, there they are ! Thank you ! " And, while he handed them over to her, she suddenly raised herself on her toes and kissed him delicately on the forehead. Her laughter tinkled out merrily. " Now, now," she adjured him. " Don't be cross and nasty. After all, I did come all this way to try and make a brother-in-law out of you."

He was pale now, dead pale. He was less good with his manners now. He let her open the door for herself.

" Good night ! " she called out merrily.

He turned away from the door. " Good night ! " he said. His whole body trembled like an aspen-leaf.

II

Harry Stonier might be only a Town Hall clerk. He might have clumsy hands, with finger-tips square as spades, the hands of a man whose father was a brass-moulder. But he knew how to take a lady out to dinner. He did the job so well there was an almost suspicious perfection about it, as if, instead of attending to his Town Hall ledgers, he had been studying some manual all day long on *How to Take a Lady out to Dinner*. He did not falter in the correct spacing and sequencing of liquors, within the limits imposed on him by the Cardiff hotel; and, seeing that that mondaine manipulation was clearly outside the scope of his usual preoccupations, it seemed just to conclude he had studied the matter for the occasion.

In the zeal which, despite his evident fatigue, he brought to a ritual so foreign to him, it was possible he felt, in doing this particular thing as well as he might in honour of May's sister, he did honour to May herself, in a way he had never contemplated. Clearly, if the meal, expensive enough for a Town Hall clerk, had been ten times more expensive, he would have felt he was performing the rite so much the more piously.

Yet there seemed in the ceremony something more than a mere rendering of honour to one image. There was an element in it of propitiation to another. It was as if he said while the waiter brought round the vegetables or filled the wine-glasses : " You see, whatever I can do, I do, though so ridiculously little. Will you let me go now ? Will you return to your own territories ? "

" A cocktail, Miss Silver ? " he asked her scrupulously.

" I'd love one," she said. " A White Lady, please ! "

" Waiter, one White Lady, please ! "

" Oh, Mr. Stonier ! " she protested like a schoolgirl. "I simply couldn't ! I couldn't drink *alone* in a public restaurant ! "

" Waiter ! " he called out again, " two White Ladies ! " He hesitated a moment, as if trying to recall some injunction which had for a moment escaped him. " Oh ! " he remembered. " Will you have some olives ? Or some potato crisps ? "

" I'd *love* some olives ! "

The cocktails were set down. The olives were ordered.

" You're not touching it ! " she protested, lifting her glass to her lips and smiling at him across its rim. " You can't order a cocktail and send it back without touching it ! "

He sipped at it. He was clearly unaware how potent it was. He sipped at it again. He ordered the dinner, referring to her within certain limits, and referring (or so he seemed) at the same time to some mental pattern. She was glad there seemed to be no caviare on the menu. She felt it would have choked her. " Yes, I'd adore some smoked salmon. Thank you *so* much ! " She noticed he had finished off his cocktail without seeming to be aware he drank it. It was as if the choosing of the next course so completely commanded his power of concentration, he lifted the glass and drained it automatically. It might have contained nothing more than water which he needed to moisten his throat.

There followed a *Sole Suprême au Vin Blanc*. He ordered a Pouilly.

" I'm so glad," she said, " you haven't got any theories against wine."

" Certainly not," he gravely assured her. " Poets do not despise wine."

" We'll drink a toast," she said. " Neither of us can object to this toast."

He looked up quickly. " Oh, of course, May ! " he said.

" To May ! " said Elsie Silver.

" To May ! " said Harry Stonier.

The book, if book there had been, was a right-thinking book. There followed some roast pheasant and a thoroughly pertinent Burgundy. She noticed he drank, not of course like a connoisseur. He did not throw his head back and shut his eyes and roll the flavour of it in the cup of his tongue. He drank because he needed liquid. She drank more than he did, partly because she felt it might harass him a little if she did not drink, partly because she could have drunk three times the quantity without turning a hair.

He talked gravely, almost portentously. There was nothing contentious in what either of them said. He asked about flowers and birds in the Mediterranean. She knew little, but was surprised to find she could go quite a long way with it. She asked him about the literary work he was engaged on.

At first he showed a certain reluctance in speaking of it. But as the waiter filled his glass again, and still again, he became almost verbose on the subject, though his language became the more ornate the more loosely it flowed. He was writing a novel in which the characters lived simultaneously on two time-planes, so that certain helots of to-day were lords of a thousand years ago, lords whose names still reverberated through history, and conversely certain lords of to-day were reduced to their real proportions by their retropresentation as the helots of a thousand years ago.

" Crikey ! " said Elsie Silver. But she said it to herself. " How fascinating ! " she said aloud. " Where on earth these ideas *come* from," she marvelled, " that's what always gets me ! "

He was a little flushed now, and it was a flush which did not go. His hair, his almost sandy hair, was somewhat disordered, too, for he passed his right hand through it with some frequency.

They drank coffee. They drank brandy. She insisted now that he should smoke one of her cigarettes. He smoked it. With all a gentleman's nonchalance he paid his bill, with more than a gentleman's indifference neglecting to cast an eye over the items.

" Don't you think," she deferred to him, " we'd better go now ? " It did indeed seem the right thing to do at this moment, but she wanted to leave the initiative in his hands.

" We'd better go now," he said.

" My car's waiting. One of the men will find it."

They left. They stood about a moment or two in St. Mary Street before the car arrived.

" It's been perfectly lovely," she said. " I knew you wouldn't think me such a frightful old bully if we really met and had a talk ! "

" Indeed not ! " he said.

" And you were awfully decent, too ! " she said candidly.

" Thank you ! "

" And now ? "

The car was coming. He pointed to it.

She wanted the initiative all the time to seem to come from him. " Shall I be getting along to London now ? I suppose so."

" Your bag's in the car ? "

" Yes, I've got practically nothing with me."

He seemed to straighten himself out, like someone who slips a burden from his shoulders. His voice had a resonance in it, as of one given his freedom. " I'm glad," he said, " we've been able to understand each other to some extent, at least. May I ask you to give May my love ? Is it too impertinent for me to make you my messenger ? "

She stood there, ruminating. The man from the hotel held the door of the car open for her. She turned round to her late host impulsively. " But, of course, I wouldn't dream of letting you find your own way home. Number thirty-one Tasker Street ! " she ordered the chauffeur. " Where we were last night ! " She got in. " Do come in ! " she requested Harry Stonier. As if remembering a final injunction at the tail-end of his manual, he fumbled about in his pocket for a coin, and handed it to the man from the hotel.

" Thank you, sir ! " said the man.

He stepped into the car, his shoulders a little bowed, his chest fallen in upon itself. The car moved off. " It's very kind of you ! " he said. His voice sounded a little dull and blurred.

" I couldn't dream of not giving you a lift ! " she said again, " after that perfectly lovely dinner ! And it's no distance either, is it ? "

" No," he said. " He can get out of the town this way, if he likes. It won't add more than half a mile." He spoke with a curious hopelessness.

" That's all right," she said, settling herself back comfortably. " We'll be there in no time. But I wish," she said, " I hadn't drunk that brandy."

" Why ? " he asked.

" Brandy always gives me a headache. But my headaches

are nothing ; easy come, easy go. An aspirin drives them out in twenty minutes."

The car had arrived at number thirty-one Tasker Street.

" Here we are ! " he said. " Perhaps the rush of air will do you good. Shall I open the window a little more ? "

" Look here ! " she said. " Do you mind frightfully ? Do you think you have an aspirin upstairs ? Or your landlady might have one, perhaps ? If I could only sit in that arm-chair of yours for twenty minutes, my headache would go off."

" All right," he said, " I'll see."

He opened the door. They passed along the lobby and up the stairs. There was no Mrs. Morgan in evidence. Mrs. Morgan was not the one to go spying on her gentlemen when titled ladies went upstairs into their bed-sitting-rooms with them.

He opened the door of his room and lit the incandescent gas. Something had happened to the mantle. It was chuckling to itself busily. He tried to adjust it into silence, but it refused. It went on chuckling.

" Shall I light the gas stove ? " he said. His face looked grey and tired. The flush had gone quite out of his cheeks. She noticed there were pouches under his eyes and beside his mouth which she had not noticed before.

" Yes, please ! " she said. " It *is* just a little chilly ! Thank you ! If I might, I'll just take my coat off ! Otherwise I'll feel it when I go out."

There was a water-bottle with a glass inverted over it on his washstand. He half filled the glass and took an aspirin from a small phial that stood among the toilet things.

" There ! " he said.

" Oh, thank you ! You are a pet ! " She put the aspirin into her mouth, took a mouthful of water, closed her eyes, then threw her head back as she swallowed. She showed the line of her lovely neck, a curve like the bow of a master violinist. The perfect round of her breasts was thrust against the thin material of her frock. The slim length of her exquisite legs was visible. A scent arose from her like the stupefying scents which were shaken out of the incense-burners in the halls of the temple of Aphrodite.

She opened her eyes. She smiled at him with those dark lustrous velvet sensual eyes. In her eyes, her smile, the curling of her fingers, she packed all she had been endowed with by nature, and had acquired by training, of the technique of seduction.

" I only want you to kiss me ! " she said. " Just so that you should see ! "

He sat on his stiff wooden chair, his hands upon his thighs. His body was thrust towards her from the waist. His eyes stared at her like an animal's. The pupils seemed to have expanded till they almost filled the eye-sockets. A word or two rolled in his throat like a beast's growl. " As you choose, then ! "

The petal-frail kiss she had breathed last night upon his forehead might have been that one drop of acid dissolvent which will corrupt a large lump of chaste matter. The drink she had induced him to take this night may have consummated the process of disintegration. He was like a bone-dry heap of wood. In one moment he was one crackling conflagration of desire, the purity and sanctity a handful of ash.

He sprang at her like something released from a catapult. His mouth was on her mouth, his teeth biting her lips, her tongue. His hands were exploring her breasts, her thighs, all those secrets he had so long forsworn, or commuted into fleshly poetry. In that same moment the accomplished beast in her sprang out to the primitive roaring of the beast in him. She forgot the cunning plan she had laid for him, which was to make him howl like a small child in his humiliation, and to leave her smiling, malicious, triumphant—her hair a little perturbed, nothing more. She forgot the one love she had, the one loyalty. She forgot the other love which somewhere, some time, beyond some horizon, would present itself, and she would claim it. Her teeth fastened upon his mouth, her tongue thrust deep down into its cavern, explored his ears, the hollows under his throat. Her hands met his upon their infamous exploration. Their hands closed upon each other like two quite separate animals. They were carried to the bed as one object on the wind of their lust. Each tore at his own clothes and the clothes of the other, till they came ripping away like newspaper. She had not known in a copious experience an experience to compare with this tropical tempestuousness, that had come up with black thunder and devil's lightning into a sky so innocent.

They released each other at length. They lay upon their backs in a torpor of fatigue. A half-hour later, or more, thought and sensation began to course through the passages of her numbed brain again. She saw what there was to see as she lay there—the ceiling that needed whitewashing, the drab pattern in the upper reaches of the wallpaper. She smelled the drabness of the room, the coarse sheet she lay on, the second-hand books that had been rained on, the sour smells of gas-stove and washstand. She heard—she heard two sounds that interplayed : the mournful chuckling in the throat of the man who lay beside her, the crying, crying, crying of a small boy who knows he has been wicked beyond all forgiveness, and would die, there, at that moment, if death would only come to him.

She rose and stood beside the bed. She looked down upon him where he lay, turned round upon his face. She observed the coarse blotchiness of his skin, those great common hands that shut and opened like a cheap toy. She observed that that brown hair, which was almost sandy, had failed, like her husband's hair, in the centre of his scalp.

She was humiliated. She was soiled. Her stomach retched.

And then the thought came to her of her sister across the night, lying in her room that looked out towards the pale Downs. The thought was less a thought than a faint glimmer as of a moonflower, a faint note as of an instrument, almost too faint to maintain any burden of reproach—the thought of her sister, May, whom she had soiled so much more inexpugnably than she had soiled herself, whom she had robbed, of whom she might almost say she had taken her life from her.

She dressed herself with fingers that felt incompetent and swollen. The chuckling of the gas mantle and the crying in the bed retained their time and pitch. She staggered out of the room and down the stairs, aware that the landlady hovered above her on a higher landing somewhere. She opened the street-door and shuffled along to the car.

" Anything wrong, madame ? " the chauffeur asked, as he opened the door.

" No ! " she cried. " No ! No ! Get in ! Get to London ! Drive like hell ! "

CHAPTER XVI

BERLIN SATURNALIA

I

ELSIE SILVER had had some idea of staying in London long enough to do something in the matter of her husband, Bobby Malswetting. She knew there was not the faintest possibility of her returning to him. That business was over, dead. But he had been very fond of her, very kind to her, and even, in his own way, faithful to her. She bore him no malice. It was up to her to try and make him understand, as soon as he could get it into his head, that the partnership was over, and there was nothing more to be done about it excepting this fatuous business of a divorce. That would have to be managed somehow.

She had also intended to go up and see her father and mother at Pennine Grange. They were not bad old sticks. It would be fun to see him being a merchant prince, quite one of the big noises of the North Country ; and she must be rather a sweet sad spectacle among the rich women and the touts. They weren't altogether happy, she gathered. They'd really prefer to be back in the old Oleander Street kitchen, May had said, smiling, with the kettle perpetually singing on the hearth, and somebody having to go out twice a day to Mrs. Poyser's shop for more lemons.

Elsie didn't suppose it would add much to their stock of joy if she *did* go tootling up North to Pennine Grange. But one way or another, she admitted, parents are parents, with the corollary that daughters are daughters. " And how ! " added Elsie, reviewing in her mind's eye the little Silver beauty-chorus. " Les Cinq Silver Girls Cinq ! " she said to herself, seeing the name about two-thirds of the way down the bill for next week's show at the Pavillon Music Hall on the Grand Boulevard.

But when she returned from Cardiff to London, she did nothing about Bobby, and nothing about her parents up in their new house in Altrincham. She did not write to her sister May, either. Instead, she got the people at the hotel to make preparations for her departure for Berlin that same night. She had decided in the car that it was Berlin she would go to, no other city. In Paris she knew people ; she had no stomach for Rome, for she'd had enough of beauty and Latins for the time being. Vienna might be all right. She knew they were going through a bad time there, too, yet somehow the sound of it was wrong—Vienna, waltzes, Danube—— No ! No ! Berlin was the place. So far as she was aware, she didn't know a soul there. The few Germans she had met in the South of France she liked. What twaddle people always talked about Germans being sentimental ! They were austere, harsh, with a sort of tragic dignity. She liked the thought of them. The women were on the plain side, on the whole. But it never displeased her to find herself among plain women ; they were usually quite attentive to her, for, unlike many good-looking women, she was always polite to them. The men, too, were plain, with the heads that ran down straight into their necks, and their glass-bottle-coloured eyes. That was all right, too. She had had enough of pretty men for the time being.

Then there was Kathy von Schlettau over in that Silesian castle of hers. You would have to go through Berlin to get there. She proposed to go and see Kathy in a month or two. Kathy was one of the few people in the world she could bear the thought of seeing just now. But that would have to wait. She would have to get a bit more right with herself before she went visiting anybody.

She had thought of staying on in London an extra day or two to get some clothes. But it occurred to her she didn't want any clothes ; or, at all events, any fine ladies' clothes. She'd had quite enough of being a fine lady for the time being. They were a queer lot, these Silvers, she thought. The old man and woman had all along had a hankering after their slum kitchen, she gathered, however high up in the world they got. She herself, their daughter, Lady Malswetting, out of the expensive sun-and-sea-girt luxury of her villa on Cap Ferrat, often thought with nostaglia of the room she used to have as an umpteenth-rate variety artiste off Oxford Road, in Doomington. Her sister May, who could have anybody in the kingdom for the asking——

Her mind stopped suddenly at the thought of May. It was as it might be if a piece of glass had somehow got lodged inside you, and, if your body makes a certain movement, you come up against the point of the piece of glass. It was like that when her mind made a movement in the direction of May. It would be a long time before the point of the piece of glass became less sharp. She supposed some day May would forgive her. But she would have to forgive herself first.

She could buy clothes in Berlin. As a matter of fact, it would be advantageous from two points of view. She didn't want to have Paris or London written on her clothes ; for she didn't want to stand out in Berlin. She wanted to belong, to go about unnoticeable, so long as she was there.

In addition to that, she had gathered that the inflation of the mark had made things astonishingly cheap. She had met people on the Riviera—" valuta-vampires," she had heard them called—who spent all their time flapping about from country to country where the national currency was going down in value. They stuck their snouts in the shops and hotels and restaurants, and came up again with any amount of expensive dainties sticking out on both sides of their jaws.

" This fur coat, darling, do you know what it cost me ? Fourteen and twopence, every bit of it ! "

" No, darling, really ? Well, look at this silk cami ! I bought twelve like it ! They cost me eight shillings and sixpence the dozen ! But I had to be nippy, you know, or they'd have cost me eight and tenpence ! "

She had met that sort of person on the Riviera, though they belonged to a rather different social world than Bobby and she existed in. In her world, the hot sun, the indolent sea, were essential, however expensive they were ; and in their absence that world would have shrivelled to the dimensions of a dried pea. These " valuta-vampires " were rather of a lower sphere, at least financially. They were usually quite mild little people, excepting the retired colonels amongst them, until they heard there had been a new drop in some currency or other. Then they shot off to the fresh field of operations with the speed and strength of tigers. They were churchy spinsters, raddled actresses with young husbands, expatriate intellectuals from Boston who adored bull-fighting—all people in the several hundred a year field ; just money enough to keep them, but not to keep them in luxury ; excepting when the internal agony or the financial manœuvring of one country or another compelled the devaluation of its money. Then, for months, sometimes for years, they had their chance. With a hop and a screech they were away ; until such time as there was more to be made out of the exchange of their gold notes into liras or francs, or whatever it might be. Then with a hop and a screech they were away again.

Germany and marks were all the vogue now, if it was not Austria and kronen. But the " valuta-vampires " need not trouble her. She had had little to do with the breed and she was not likely to run up against them. She had a feeling that if they met her, they were hardly likely to see in her, solitary, the elegant wicked Lady Malswetting whom they had heard such a lot about in their stuffy little *pensions* all the way between Mentone and Toulon.

It was not because marks were cheap in Berlin she was going there. But it would be convenient. She had stuffed a fair amount of money in thousand-franc notes into her bag when she left Cap Ferrat. They were about, because Bobby liked her to spend large sums of money in sudden idiotic caprices, as he did himself. And they played bridge, and, much more, roulette, for high stakes, up and down the place in their own and other people's villas ; so it was always necessary to have a fair amount hanging about loose. It so happened she had been doing quite well with the wheel for a week or two.

But she had already spent a lot of that. Claridge's and the Hispano-Suiza had cost a pound or two. She had a current account in a bank at Nice, but on the whole she proposed not to draw cheques on it unless some strong reason impelled her—not till the whole Bobby matter was straightened out. Before the visit to Cardiff, she had intended to get her father to see her through till—till later ; till she knew where she was. She knew there would be no difficulty of any sort there. But now, after the visit to Cardiff, she felt it impossible to do anything about money up in Doomington.

So, on the whole, it was convenient things were cheap in Berlin. And, besides, she had her jewels. They were very much her own jewels, the jewels of the pre-Bobby era. They were nothing like so dazzling as the Bobby jewels, but they would be useful. It was not with much more luggage than her jewels that Elsie Silver arrived in Berlin, on the second night after the night in Cardiff. It seemed to her an extremely tedious journey.

II

It did not occur to Elsie Silver to invite herself to Kathy von Schlettau's castle in Silesia, for quite a long time ; not until a day of sleety drizzle at the beginning of the following year. The weather that day was as arctically cold and as penetratingly damp as it can be only in Berlin ; and it occurred to Elsie that it really was about time she did something about her friend. It was not at all in a fit of depression she wrote ; but rather in the mood of one who felt she had something to get over and done with, and to get it over and done with when the weather was so foul seemed plain sense. She had only written once to Kathy, some time in the summer, and she had had quite a cordial note back. That was all that happened. Then, when she wrote in January— this was the January of 1923—it took two or three months before she got a reply. The Baronin had managed to scrape up a few liras and had taken her son off to a cheap *pension* in Positano. The Silesian castle still remained hers—up in Silesia. She suggested that Elsie should come along to Positano, too ; it would be *entzückend*, enchanting, to see her.

But by that time Elsie had found something in Berlin so much more *entzückend* than anything she had known in all her life before that she would have sacrificed for its sake a Shah's treasury, if she had had it, and it had been asked for. And, seeing that she had not, she would have sacrificed for it an eye, a hand, ten years of her life. No demand would have been extravagant.

So she did not leave Berlin to go and stay in a *pension* with the Baronin and her small boy down in Positano.

Nor was it because she was depressed that she wrote to Kathy von Schlettau that day in January. She was not the sort of person who becomes depressed ; for, if she had been, she would quite certainly have committed suicide or homi- cide or both, time after time, during the Bobby period on Cap Ferrat. She could become bored, of course. And, when that happened, she would do something about it. She would hurl wine-glasses through the window out on to the rocks, if rocks were available. If not, the street would do. She got through quite a lot in the way of wine-glasses at Cap Ferrat. And that particular amusement used to make Bobby so helpless with laughter that it was an attack on her boredom from two angles. Soon she was laughing just as helplessly as he was, and everything in the garden was lovely again. If the wine-glass game was no good, she would eat. She liked good food and a lot of it, though the over-dainty food that

Bobby was keen on wasn't good for her. Sometimes, when she was bored, she ordered the next meal should be so vast that it gorged her as full as a small serpent with a large rabbit inside it. Then she would go to bed and sleep off her boredom.

Sometimes the eating game didn't solve the problem, either. She got up from the table and was still bored. Then she went out and looked round, for a week or two, may be. She looked round for a man, and found him, and had a good time with him. Then she wouldn't be bored for quite some time. She liked the looking round to take as long as possible. Often that process was more anti-boring than the fairly simple matter of coupling between the sheets.

She was not depressed when she wrote to Kathy. She was not bored. From the moment she got up in the Adlon Hotel, the morning after she arrived in Berlin, she was as little bored as she had ever been in her life. To put it more positively, she was more keyed up, more excited, and yet, oddly, more appeased, than she had ever known she might be, excepting in her girlhood, when she first learned how good a thing it was to have a room of your own, and no pimply anarchists for miles around, blathering, and swilling tea-with-lemon.

Elsie was aware that the febrility, the perversity, of the Berlin she had happened into was not a comic, but a tragic, spectacle. She was intellectually aware, that is to say, it was a tragedy, for she was not unintelligent. As she moved about, keeping her ears open, she gathered a fairly accurate idea of the various factors that made Berlin the thing it was in the inflation-time. She gathered that the Treaty of Versailles was not quite so intelligent a document as it might have been. She gathered that there were people in the Wilhelmstrasse who felt that it would be unwise, even if it were possible, to put a spoke in the wheels of the printing-presses that turned out these locust-swarms of mark notes ;

for the wheels solved quite a number of major problems, even if they created a number of minor problems of great poignancy for unimportant individuals like town and State officials, clerks, small *rentiers*, and, to a lesser extent, working-men. She did not study these matters, but it was impossible that she should not acquire the hang of them, for she met no other people than Germans all the time ; and these matters occupied a good deal of their thoughts during their saner hours—if they had any saner hours—when they managed to abstract themselves from that mad whirl of mark-spending, that whirled quicker and quicker and quicker, lest the mark, when spent, should buy less and less and less.

She was to some extent intellectually aware of the febrility and perversity of Berlin, but not emotionally. She was not shocked or distressed. She was, on the contrary, exhilarated. She was not the sort of person whom a hard-up story could impel to reach her hand forward for her pen and cheque-book. A really pitiable beggar, who was diseased or ugly, could under no circumstances wheedle a penny out of her. If he or she, and more particularly he, had youth and some suggestion of good looks, he might be driven hysterical by the sudden appearance in his cap or tin mug of a pound note. The misery which the inflational saturnalia involved left her quite cold. The dance itself intoxicated her.

An incident which occurred in a large well-groomed ladies' establishment on the Leipzigerstrasse the morning after her arrival gave her the sort of acute pleasure she was to renew again and again. She had brought with her a pale-blue woollen scarf which had some sentimental association for her ; a quite special man-friend had given it her. The scarf had caught on a point and was unravelling. She wanted to match up some wool with it and put it right. She deter-mined not to let a chambermaid or a page-boy get it, or whoever the hotel might send out ; partly because she knew she would not get the right shade, partly because she liked doing small things of that sort for herself, as she used to do in the old touring days. She had had enough of being cosseted for the time being. So she went into the shop on the Leipzigerstrasse and sorted out the wool she wanted; then she asked the price, and was told—in marks, of course. She informed them that she had not yet changed her money, so would they be kind enough to send the wool with the bill to the hotel, where it would be paid for.

The request seemed to paralyse the whole establishment. The girl who served her went to a shopwalker; the shopwalker addressed the matter to a higher authority. The decision ricocheted slowly back. It was regretted infinitely, but by the time the bill was made out and the wool was delivered at the hotel the wool would cost more in marks. Would the *gnädige Frau* be good enough to call again when she had the money?

She liked that enormously, the precariousness of it; the crust of suave organisation over such lavas of instability. Her own hotel gave her a thrill a few days later, when her chambermaid, a stolid blonde-plaited girl from Dresden, with a face like an ox, suddenly broke down in the bathroom where she was mixing a shampoo in the basin. Elsie liked to mix her own shampoos and do her own hair, but she felt lazy that morning; she was still in bed.

" What are you blubbering about ? " asked Elsie. She did not yet know much German, but she soon got the story. The girl had had an inconvenient baby in Dresden, as girls had a habit of doing these days; and that was why she had had to get a job in Berlin. Now her younger sister was going to have the same sort of baby, too. It would be dreadful if her parents got to know that their second daughter, too, was a sinner. She wanted to get her sister up to Berlin and arrange it all here. But she had no money either for the fare or the arrangements.

She possibly felt that Elsie had a sympathetic face; if she did, it was a misreading of Elsie's face. Or she was moved by the thought that Elsie was one of that golden race of *Ausländer*—foreigners—who had money that stayed firm as a rock, from month to month, instead of crumbling away like

sand between your fingers. Elsie inquired how much she
needed to adjust the matter. The girl made a calculation.
She would need a sum equivalent to fourpence for the fare
from Dresden. As for the other arrangements—she hesitated
a little longer ; then, faintly and fearfully, she specified a
sum equivalent to five shillings. Elsie was almost dizzy
with pleasure as she handed over a sum in marks equivalent
to three times what the girl had asked for. The girl for a full
minute remained speechless ; then she kissed Elsie's hand
till her coarse mouth nearly brought the skin off. Then a
sudden hideous realisation got hold of her. A sort of terror
entered her eyes which Elsie was to become more and more
familiar with as the months went on.

" But when the little one comes," said the maid, her
mouth twitching, " these notes, all this money, it will be
Mist—it will be muck ! "

The whole thing was several times more fun than it had
promised to be. Elsie's eyes shone with an excited gaiety.
" Come to me then, Rosa," she said. " I will pay for it all
in *valuta* ! "

Elsie did not stay on long in the Adlon Hotel. That was
not because it was expensive, though the international hotels
and the smart shops kept pace with the precipitate fall of the
mark with some approach to a reciprocity between value
given and money demanded. But it was beyond the skill of
the most inspired sliding-rule manipulators to prevent the
owners of foreign currency living in a fantastic millionaire
world, in which they felt that they had only to ask for a
thing in order to have it ; or, at most, to wait a few days
longer for it, till the mark dropped a few more thousands,
or a few more millions, to the pound.

Elsie had never had any sense of the delight of owning
things, beyond the delight of owning her own soul ; or,
seeing that she would herself have thought that phrase very
silly, the only thing she had ever liked to stick tight to was

the chance of keeping herself to herself when she wanted to.
As a girl, she had shared a bedroom with her sister May,
the person she had always cared for most in the world. But
she had been delighted to go and have her own room off
Oxford Road, despite that. It was a room she never cluttered
with an accumulation of toilet articles, dresses not good
enough to wear now but they might come in some day,
souvenirs of towns she visited, of friends and admirers. With
a minimum of toilet stuff she could produce an effect, whenever she wanted to, which would drive to despair many
women who had spent half a day with a maid or two violently
labouring among glittering shelves full of creams, sprays,
powders, greases, lipsticks, rouges, eyebrow pencils, and
electrical devices of one sort and another. Or she could
dispense with any aid at all, and produce an effect different
in kind, but equally potent in its results.

She had had many admirers in her days as a princess of
intimate revue in the year or so immediately after the War.
And whilst there were occasions on which her dressing-room
was alive with gay talk and the clink of glasses, and young
men and young women darlinging each other with indiscriminate enthusiasm, there were occasions on which her
door was grimly closed against everybody, even should he
be a prince of a royal house, as now and again he was. It
was said mournfully of her that " Elsie had the jim-jams,"
the inference being she had been having a good time with a
bottle of brandy ; it was even speculated that she was doing
things to her thighs with a needle. But neither was true.
She just felt she wanted to be on her own for an hour or two,
even though the hour or two coincided with the hour of the
show. She didn't feel she was any less on her own when she
went out on to the stage and did what she had to do. Indeed,
it was then she felt more thrillingly alone than she felt anywhere else at all. That may have had much to do with the
queer quality of her art—a something secret, a something
even ferocious, when she sang a song of the utmost banality.

She had insisted on a sitting-room, as well as a bedroom,

of her own in the villa at Cap Ferrat, too, being in this much, at all events, of the same mind as her eldest sister, Esther Tishler. If the situation be looked at for a moment from Bobby Malswetting's point of view, there was something to be said for the poor fellow having to go off now and again to find some other woman who might be sorry for him, when, having tried like any decent husband to get access to his wife's bedroom, she just lay there beyond a locked door and glowered and never said a word. The worst of it was that it was just at those times she was most infernally attractive.

So Elsie, on the same general grounds as these, left the Adlon Hotel and got herself an apartment on the Schöneberger Ufer, not far from the Potsdammer Platz. She liked to look down from her window through the tops of the chestnut-trees on to the black waters of the Landwehr Kanal flowing sullenly between their stone embankments. It was a water more in accord with her mood than the perpetual blue twinkling and prattling of the Mediterranean, which she had gazed at so long through her windows on Cap Ferrat that the prospect sickened her like an eternal diet of éclairs and meringues. It was noisy, for the two banks of the Schöneberger Ufer constitute one of the most important arteries connecting the older Friedrichstrasse centre of Berlin with the newer Kurfürstendamm centre. But Elsie was not of the sort whose slumbers were sensitive to noise. A good deal of frenzied building was going on all round (for the effect of the inflation was not to slow down but to quicken the tempo of every activity into a hysterical tattoo-time). And Elsie threw wide her windows at the top of the house to the slightly sulphurous winds of Berlin and its quite insensate noises, and she slept like a nun in a convent cell.

She liked her apartment because the rooms were large and light and clean, and she had a tiny kitchen all to herself if she wanted to be so utterly solitary that not even Frau Krantz, her landlady, need come in with morning coffee. There was no one else in the flat, for, though Frau Krantz had another room to let, Elsie settled that by paying for it herself. There was just a little difficulty about the sitting-room furniture, which was about as heavy and graceful as a fleet of tanks. Elsie did not like it, and said it must go. Frau Krantz showed herself unexpectedly firm. She said it belonged to her *Glanzzeit*, her golden age, when she and her husband, who had been killed in Mesopotamia, and her son, who had been killed in Belgium, had lived together a happy and prosperous life, in which they had the whole apartment to themselves, with no need to let rooms to any-body. There had apparently been a daughter, too, but she had disappeared lately, into a limbo where Elsie thought it discreet to pursue her with no inquiries. Elsie finally conceded a wardrobe, a vase that looked like a factory boiler, and an enormous painting of Monte Solaro, in the island of Capri, where Herr and Frau Krantz had spent their honeymoon, and acquired that painting. Capri, appar-ently, was an island which the Italian State Railways had built near Naples for German couples to go and spend their honeymoons in. She conceded the painting, too.

The room seemed twice as big without its colossi. Elsie did nothing about lessening its cubic capacity of air, though at certain moments in the catastrophic landslide of the mark she could have bought half Berlin, from stone palace to delicate intaglio. But she did not. She went on drinking, eating, watching with her dark and lustrous eyes, watching, waiting, waiting for something she knew in the secret places of her blood would not be long withheld.

Elsie ate vast meals, washed down with vast quantities of beer. It was not because she was bored, as she had been in the Cap Ferrat days when she ordered the cook to bring in food enough for a large family. It was because she liked German food and German beer. She liked the grossness and heaviness of it; she had had too much of those delicate French flavourings and sauces. It was of the earth, as she was. There was no nonsense about it. And she immensely liked the great variety of sausages you could get at any street-corner, if you had been up late, and dinner was a long time ago and breakfast a long time ahead ; or because you felt you hadn't eaten all you wanted to at your last meal ; or just like that, because you felt like a Wiener or a Nürnberger or a Frankfurter or a Thüringer *Bratwurst*, grilled over a fire, and thrust sizzling, far too hot to hold, into a cut roll.

The very sound of the names of the food was as gross and blunt as the food itself, and as exciting. She delighted in *Löffelerbsen mit Ohr und Schnauze*, which is pea-soup so thick that a spoon can stand in it, and is further thickened by the ear and snout of pig chopped small. The sound of *Schweine-bauch*, swine's belly, was as unctuous and tasty as the dish itself. With these came *Kalberzähne*, calves' teeth, a large peeled grain, or *Saubohnen*, it might be, pig beans. There was a dish called *Schlesiches Himmelreich*, Silesian kingdom-of-heaven, which put religion, she thought, in its proper place. This was a dish of stewed dried apples, pears and prunes, served with yeast dumplings and a fruit sauce. A cadaverous note was struck in *Dresdner Leichenfinger*, Dresden corpse-fingers, a crude cheese prepared with Kümmel. When she had ordered a second *Molle* of beer, and a third—like some peasant woman from the Spreewald come in to Berlin for the day and having a good time on her own—she began to be almost theological about this identification of heaven and hell with belly. " They've got it right, these Germans," she murmured to herself a little hazily. " Heaven's a damn good meal ; and hell's a stomach-ache. But there's only one damn place to get either in, and this is this little old world. Little old world, keep turning ! " she requested it. " It's a damn good world, and there's only one town worth living in, and that's Berlin ! " Then, " *Herr Ober !* " she called out. " *Nach eine Molle !* " For she never got more drunk than that, to become just a little speculative in a dithery sort of way. And she never got stomach-ache, either. She had a cast-iron constitution. Sir Robert and Lady Malswetting had this extraordinary faculty in common, that they could eat and drink like pigs and retain the extreme purity of their outlines.

Heaven's a damn good meal, and hell's a stomach-ache. She was convinced that her friend, Fritz, would be of the same opinion, too. He was not her friend, exactly, for she uttered not more than a single word to him in her life ; and she only set eyes on him twice, once in a restaurant and once again, some weeks later, in a dance hall. She wasn't sure that his name was Fritz, either. If it wasn't Fritz, it was Otto.

She met him one night in an eating-place called the Hamburger Klause. It was called Hamburger because the people of Hamburg have a reputation for eating well and heartily, and that was how they wanted you to eat in that place. There were a number of cosy little alcoves in the Hamburger Klause, where you could order a meal which was at once cosy and enormous. Enormous business-men and manufacturers from Chemnitz and Essen came here and ordered meals as enormous as themselves. They were having a good time in Germany these days.

It was also a favourite hang-out for a new race of German business-men, an entirely inflational product, which seemed to disappear suddenly, to be swallowed up into the mysterious twilight out of which it had emerged on the very day that Dr. Schacht announced the stabilisation of the mark. This new race of German business-men were almost no more than boys. They were lean, small, dark, adder-like in their movements. Their intelligences were quicker than the lumbering intelligences of the older, stouter men, with shaven polls and sheer skulls. They were not going to leave all the pickings to these aliens, these *Schieber*, who came in from Poland, France, Italy, England, with a certain amount of gold *valuta* with which they manipulated the market in industrial securities. These lean ones, these adder-like ones, had no gold *valuta*—to start off with, at least—but they had a newly engendered, highly pertinent inflational mentality. They dispensed with money in its intermediate forms as gold paper or mere Reichsbank paper. They traded a train-load of glass salt-cellars in a railway siding near Leipzig for a dump of contraband cigars in a Lübeck tug.

These were arduous labours, requiring several sorts of vigilance, and these young men needed feeding. They, like the more orthodox business-men, had a great fondness for the Hamburger Klause ; so had the *Schieber*, the foreign speculators, for there was always a hint or two to be picked up about how things were going on in this place and that place, between the *Löffelerbsen* and the *Eisbein*, the pig's-knuckle, which were the specialities of the Klause. Elsie Silver liked the place, too, for the atmosphere was so uniquely inflational-Berlin. It almost twanged with a sense of strain which threatened any moment to snap into hysteria; as it did on several occasions while Elsie was eating there, when the Klause's special runner came in and announced a sudden wild rise of temperature in the fever of the mark. Spoons were left standing upright in thick pea-soup, pig's knuckles were left shivering and shimmering in their heaped-up pinkness. Out lumbered the heavy elder business men ; forth darted, snake-like, the new slimmer schoolboy business-men. Only the foreigners took things a little calmly. They had the pounds, the dollars. They had the trump card.

There was always this sense of strain in the atmosphere of the Hamburger Klause. It was like a faint smell, a faint plucking in the air, above and around and below the thick solidity of the chairs and tables, the beer-mugs, and the food. The food had an aspect of immortality, so many coarse and simple generations contributed to the conception of it, so much care was exercised in its choice and preparation, so enormous were the helpings, too ; so enormous that one felt not merely human appetite alone, but the slow passage of time, too, must be impressed into their demolition.

One night, when Elsie entered the Hamburger Klause, the place was more than usually full. The waiter managed to find room for her in one of the more intimate alcoves, where one client was already seated on his little form, and there was room for one more client opposite him. The client was a very large gentleman in a very tight grey suit, of which all the buttons seemed ready to fly off like the corks of champagne-bottles if he made his bulk any vaster by distending it with one more mouthful of food. But, by some miracle, though he took a great many more mouthfuls during the next hour, his girth was not increased, and the buttons remained where they were. His head was quite clean-shaven, yet the roots of the hair made the scalp look a little dirty, like snow after it has stood near a factory for a day or two. He had a small nose, made small enough by nature, and still smaller by art, for a cartilage seemed to have been removed from it at some time. That nose and the small grey eyes and the recession of the lower lip and the jaw made him look a little pig-like, so that to see him eating pig had the distressing appearance of an act of cannibalism.

On the plate before him towered a monumental *Eisbein*, a pig's-knuckle, worthy of the proudest traditions of the Hamburger Klause. It was flanked by a mound of *Erbsenpurée*, mashed peas, and a huge bank of *Sauerkraut*. It was a vast pig's-knuckle, yet it had a sort of fragility ; it shook a little like a consummate raspberry soufflé. At the same time there was an oleaginous solidity about it, as if it were a lump of that primal slime from which our parent, the amœba, was engendered.

Elsie did not feel any discomfort at being a witness of this mystic wedding between the business-man and the pig's-knuckle. He was not good to look at, but she did not dislike him. She would not have chosen him to have an intrigue with, but she would not in her present mood have chosen the Apollo Belvedere, if he had been available. She actually liked Fritz. He was so completely *his* sort of German, and she liked all sorts of Germans. She would not have been displeased if he had shown some awareness that someone had sat down at his table, a thing Germans always do. " *Mahlzeit !* " they say punctiliously. But he did not. He went on eating his pig's-knuckle. He went on being unaware of her, which was, for her, a somewhat novel experience, and one which fortified her in her regard for him.

Fritz demolished his pig's-knuckle, the mound of mashed peas, the bank of *Sauerkraut*. He ordered neither cheese nor dessert, nor did he call for his bill. He ordered another pig's-knuckle, with the vegetables that accompany it. It was when he ordered a third that the terrible and beautiful thought struck her that perhaps the first pig's-knuckle she had seen him eat was perhaps not the first he had eaten that evening. Her eyes shone with incredulous delight. The morsel of *Schnitzel* which her fork was lifting to her mouth remained half way on its journey. Her mouth dropped. She stared at her vis-à-vis in a manner which could not be described as other than ill-bred. There was a faint dew of sweat upon his pig's-knuckle. There was a faint dew of sweat upon his forehead. Rhythmically his knife and fork impaled, cut, rose, impaled, cut, rose.

She did not know whether she uttered the word with her lips or only with her soul. But one or the other said : " *Oh, you pet !* " And in that moment, and for the first time, Fritz became conscious of her. He lifted his eyes from his pig's-knuckle, saw her eyes fixed in wonder upon him, and blushed. Immediately all the style went out of him. He finished his pig's-knuckle in the most perfunctory manner, like any amateur who only eats one at a time, and in a hurry. He called for his bill, paid it, put on his head a greenish felt hat a size too small for it, and went out.

Elsie had not much to do that evening. She had already opened up negotiations with the *Kabarett* which was shortly to recruit her on its strength, but the matter had not gone through yet. She dawdled over her sweet, her *Mokka*, her liqueur, her cigarette. Then she paid her bill and rose. She passed two or three alcoves on her way out, and then it chanced she dropped her bag. She did not even hint the gesture of stooping to pick it up, so used she was to having small groups of men squabbling like seagulls to pick up anything she might drop, by design or accident. But the fallen bag was invisible from the alcove in front or behind. It was only visible from the alcove at her left hand. She looked idly to see who the sluggish man might be who did not leap to pick her bag up. It was Fritz, Fritz with an enormous pig's-knuckle trembling before him, with a reef of *Sauerkraut* flanking it on one side and a hillock of *Erbsenpurée* on the other.

" *Mein Schatz!* My sweetheart! " she said to him, quite definitely with her lips, and with a real warmth of conviction. But he did not hear her. He went on with his pig's-knuckle.

And then, some weeks later, she saw Fritz again, in a *Tanzpalast*. Perhaps she might have seen him at that same *Tanzpalast* that same night, after he had got through his pig's-knuckle orgy ; but that night she did not chance to go there. She spent quite a lot of time among these dance-palaces, with which Berlin was prolific at that time. They were prolific, for money earned—at least marks earned—had to be spent, and one of the most rational ways of spending it was on women. There was a great demand for women, and those very conditions of despair and hysteria which had produced the demand created the supply. The trouble was that the supply soon exceeded the demand, vigorous as it was. Spending marks on women was at least as good a guarantee of getting your money's worth as spending it on tinned foods or underclothes. The women were never very well up in the latest quotations of the exchange market, and it was easy to fool many of them. They did not insist on payment in dollars, which was the increasing tendency on the part of the shop-people, though their gratitude was pathetic when some foreign client, or some native speculator, out of his noble heart paid them in gold currency. They did not set up in the dance-palaces, or in the cabinets of their private operations, the dial-indicators with which the shop-people at the end of the inflation-time protected themselves, whereon the hour-hand showed the sum due in dollars, the minute in marks. No, women were as good value as most things during that period of Berlin history, and a night of pleasure a fortnight ago was hardly more wasted then than a wad of marks not spent.

There were various varieties of dance-palaces. There was the dance-palace loosely Bavarian or Tirolese in character. These were got up to resemble Alpine chalets, with a great quantity of cardboard ice-capped mountains up and down the walls. The band wore green velours hats stuck with chamois-beard, shirts embraced by embroidered cross-pieced braces, and leather shorts. A rudimentary hand-knitted stocking went down from the calf to the ankle. The band did almost as much yodelling as playing on its instruments. Yodelling, on the part of the band, the waiters and waitresses, the dancing-girls and the clients, was persistent. The dancing-girls wore one variant or another of the costumes common to the *Dierndl*, the maiden, of the Germanic Alps. Their accents often as not were Alexanderplatz in Berlin or Reeperbahn in Hamburg. It was rather gay in these places, and all a little brutal.

Then there were the *gemütlich* dance-palaces, with a suggestion of how amiable everybody is in the Rheinland, and how romantic it all is, the castles and the vineyards, the moonlight and the ivy, the students, their scars, their caps, their beer-mugs.

There were the rather furtive dance-palaces, conceived on the system of the American speak-easy. It took a certain amount of trouble to get into these places ; there was knocking on doors, and sliding of grilles, and going up or down in lifts. The furtive note was maintained in the little curtained alcoves. The dance-girls were of the fatal type and rather French to look at. You might sometimes see a black man, or even a black woman, here. But they were, on the whole, rather naïve and very expensive. You could dance with your girl, and pay for an expensive bottle of the romantic imitation champagne called *Sekt*, and that was about all. You might even have to pay for it in dollars. Much more accessible dancing-places had departments where you could press more intimate attentions upon your partner.

The really strange and sinister *Lokale* of the Berlin of that period proclaimed themselves with blazing lights and equivocal images. They sent out platoons of boys and girls to stick bills into the hands of passers-by, to indicate exactly where they were ; and, when the bills were exhausted, they would stand outside the theatres and concert-halls, informing those members of the audience who were in search of further pleasure that they had *Nachtlokale aller Art*, night-places of every variety, at their disposal. But it was a formula by which a specialised variety was indicated.

It was in none of these that Elsie met her friend Fritz again. It was in a very elegant and rococo and gold and crystal dance-palace. It called itself, in fact, the Rokoko Tanzpalast. Prodigal as Berlin was at that time, there could not have been more than two or three dance-palaces so palatial. Indeed, when Elsie first wandered into it, her breath was so taken by the splendour of it that she thought she had stumbled into the Hofkirche, the Court Church, a place she had visited on one of her infrequent tourist jaunts. There was much similarity in the architecture and the fittings. But a moment's further examination made it quite clear to her that she was mistaken. She was certain the Hofkirche conducted no services at this time, and certainly no worshippers assumed costumes like these for worship.

The clients of the Rokoko Tanzpalast were for the most part business-men. There was that slightly macabre air about them which always hovers around business-men taking their pleasure. There were representatives of both varieties of the inflation business-man—the large fat shaven variety of which Fritz was an admirable specimen, and the lithe dark schoolboy variety, a type which on the whole, she considered, gave her a pain in the neck. Their warped minds were subtle enough, but they were as straightforward as the large fat men in the sort of sexual pabulum they asked for. They wanted women like these, here in this gold and crystal dance-palace, women themselves all gold and crystal. They were big women, with vast bosoms and hips, blonde women, mothers (if Fate had been kinder to them) of blonde babies. They were all so like each other that Elsie wondered how a man remembered which one his partner was, if he was called away a moment to wash his hands.

She set eyes on Fritz the moment she entered the Rokoko for the first time, and determined at once that Fritz would not distinguish more acutely between one woman and another than he would between one pig's-knuckle and another. They would all do equally well, so long as they were equally pink and succulent. Fritz was having a grand time. She noticed that the same little dew of sweat misted his forehead here, as he bent towards his woman, as there, when he hung over his pig's-knuckle. The woman looked stupid, but there was kindness in her face. She wished them both joy.

There were foreigners in the dance-palace, as well as native business-men. She sat down at a table, and immediately a foreigner—a Levantine probably—sat down too, and asked her would she like a drink. She did not want a drink, and she did not like that Levantine. She did not like any man, at the moment, in the relationship the Levantine assumed he was going to establish with her. She had not wanted to be any man's woman since the night she had been a man's woman in Cardiff. Her sexuality, in the sense of its immediate and local impulse, seemed to have been cauterised within her. It still remained the dominant influence and preoccupation of her life, but it had become abstracted from her own body's participation ; it had become, in a sense, mental, even impersonal.

She did not feel that in the Levantine gentleman she had found a mate whose sexuality would partner hers on so

austere a plane. She thought him a squirt, in fact, a word
which to her meant the utmost in contempt. She turned her
eyes upon him in a manner which gave just such a shock as
the hand receives in an aquarium when it gropes in a cold
tank for the electric ray. He started back, shivered a little,
then swaggered off with an assumed jauntiness.

" I really ought to do something about keeping that sort of
squirt off," she thought. " If I'd only been wearing trousers,"
she added, with a *naïveté* which it took her two or three more
Berlin months to plumb. " I suppose I'd look like one of
these sixth-form business-men if I wore the old coat and
trousers, same as I used to in the good old Ardwick Empire
days. Then, of course, the gold-haired Brünhildes would all
tramp up and try to make me. But they'd be easy to keep
off. And they'd laugh like hell when they found out. Yes,"
she decided, " I'll sally forth in the old coat and trousers
one of these nights."

She had already acquired coat and trousers for the
auditions she gave to the *Kabarett der Tsigeuner*, the Gipsy
Cabaret.

III

It was for a variety of reasons that Elsie determined to
start work again in Berlin. In the first place, there was the
money question. It began to be rather important for her to do
something about that. She had got through the money she
had brought with her, and had begun to sell her jewels. She
had not been extravagant, and a few French francs could go
a long way in Berlin, but she yielded to sudden extravagant
caprices from time to time, and didn't like to think there was
anything to stop her. She was not a good business-woman,
and the first time she sold her jewels she sold them for marks,
and didn't do anything about the marks for some time ;
with the consequence that they were not of much use when
she thought about them again. Then she sold some jewels
for dollars, through the agency of one of the little sixth-form

business-men, whom she thought a little less odious than his brothers. He took a large commission for his pains, so she might almost as well have sold them for marks. But she addressed herself to him again, none the less—it saved trouble—whenever she found she was running short again.

And then one day she saw a couple of detectives stop a harmless native, search him, and, finding he was carrying dollars in his pocket, hale him off to a police-station, to explain where he had got them from. She saw the same thing happen to a woman a few days later. She began to get uncomfortable. It occurred to her she might be doing something against the laws one way and another, and she didn't want to do that. She didn't want to get expelled from Germany. She found she was much too much attached to the place. And she was not a law-breaker, either. She thought most of the customs in the sex department quite idiotic, but laws as laws she had a healthy respect for.

That was one reason why she wanted to earn some money. Then she felt she wanted to establish some sort of place for herself in the society which she had wandered into, and which she found so sympathetic. She couldn't go mooching along indefinitely from restaurant to dance-palace and back again to beer-hall.

Then she was an artiste. She had ached quite violently from time to time in the Bobby days to pull herself out of that slime of indolence and get busy on the stage again. She liked the applause she got. She liked quite as much the hostility she felt herself evoking from time to time, the puzzled angry eyes her audience turned on her, which with a gurgle and a slap of the thigh she could convert at will into cow-like admiration.

She liked the intelligence and sophistication of the *Kabarett der Tsigeuner*, who had their small theatre near the Zoo station on the Kurfürstendamm. She thought it tremendously jolly to have your audience at little tables drinking beer and devouring sausages. How right that was, she thought ! When would the West End managers of London

take a leaf out of that book ? If the audience like you, they
would like you still more if they were free to take a swig of
beer. If they didn't like you, what impertinence it was to
prevent them turning their backs and forgetting all about
you in the bottom of a tankard !

She liked the personnel of the *Kabarett* still more when she
started working with them. For they saw that Elsie was
straight up their street, as it is phrased. They were only
" Gipsies " as part of their joke. They meant they didn't
give a damn where they wandered to, from Clemenceau's
night-cap to the ex-Emperor of Germany's commode. It
also meant what fun it was to watch the faces of the folk who
came in expecting a lot of zither and raggle-taggle and
finding a gang of rather corpulent and very cynical German
Jews, with a pleasant troupe of acrobats thrown in and one
or two jugglers. They saw that Elsie had style, intimacy, and
the faculty of irritation which was the *sine qua non* among
their qualities. She had little difficulty with her German,
though her strong suit was to sing in English and French.
They had the sort of audience who didn't worry what
language was sung at them. The Silver girls were good
linguists, when the occasion rose. And then her Oleander
Street Yiddish helped her a lot with the vocabulary. It even
helped her with her accent ; her German had quite a
Yiddish accent. But the *Tsigeuner* didn't mind that, being
Jews themselves for the most part.

There was a good deal of intelligence both among the
players and the audience. She found that most of them were
Jews. She found that most of the people she established
contact with through the *Tsigeuner* were Jews, the intellectuals of the various fields of activity—journalism, the stage,
the cinema, music, painting, the learned professions. The
West End intelligentsia of Berlin was definitely Jewish ; yet
she had never met Jews so unaggressive in their Jewishness.
Their Jewishness was not a thing in itself ; it was a heighten-
ing of all their qualities as honest-to-God Germans.

" What punk that is of May's," she said to herself (for she

had begun to remember May with no less shame, but with a little less anguish). " What punk that is of May's about Jews being by nature better Englishmen than they can be anything else ! These lads are the most German of the Germans."

They were, at least, their interpreters and their champions. There was often quite a virulent political note in their sketches and songs. And they spared their own compatriots as little as they spared those Allied statesmen who seemed determined to kick their prostrate country till finally they should kick it on to its feet again, shaking its fist and grinding its teeth. Now and again German business-men of one type or another wandered into the *Kabarett* thinking they were going to have still another leg-and-breast show served up to them. Then the *Tsigeuner* let fly their fleers and quips like a cloud of hornets about their ears—for there was quite a strong element of impromptu about the show. Time after time Elsie saw the business-men get up from their tables trembling all over with rage. " The poor fat darlings," she said to herself, " it will do them no harm."

Her colleagues, of course, did not fail to make love to her. But she made it quite clear to them that nothing was doing. If they persisted, she did her electric-shock trick again. Even the downiest intellectual recoiled from it. There was quite open speculation regarding the cause of this notable chastity. Some said with a romanticism unworthy of their brains, or perhaps with a romanticism which is never far to seek from acute brains—some said she bore bravely about with her a broken heart. Others said she was a Lesbian, though no little girl-friend could be adduced to support the contention. She smiled sweetly at the speculators, and went her way.

She had already decided it would be convenient to keep on her male clothes after the show was over, when she went wandering about the town on her own accord. She proceeded to do this more and more frequently, and to go about in them all day long. She began to be aware that she was not the only woman in man's clothes to be met on the streets of Berlin, and that there were men enough in women's clothes in that topsy-turvy world. She was turning, dressed as a male, from the Nollendorfplatz round into the Motzstrasse late one night, when a bevy of stalwart girls—she had thought them straightforward harlots—suddenly cleared their chests and started coughing out of heavy male lungs. It did not frighten her nor shock her ; nor was she frightened or shocked when one or two men pursued her. She realised that if they had known what she was they would have been more frightened and shocked than she.

It began to dawn on her that beyond the more or less familiar country of normal love-making there was a mysterious and equivocal territory in this wild dark city, wild despite all the rectangularity of its streets, dark despite all the blaze of its lights, where men and men and women and women loved each other. Again she knew nothing of fright or shock. It was true that she was woman of the world enough to be no stranger to that condition. But she began to be aware that this territory extended far and deep into the life of this tragic city. She had an intellectual realisation of the pain, the humiliation, the grotesque comedy of it all, even before she saw at close quarters the participants in this *danse funèbre*. But in her nerves she exulted at the strangeness of it, as she had exulted in the misery of Rosa, her chambermaid, when Rosa had pointed out that the paper marks Elsie had given her would be muck by the time they were needed.

She was exhilarated by it all. And when a runner, seeing her one night in the clothes of an elegant young man about town, whispered into her ear, " *Nachtlokale aller Art ?* " " Night-places of every kind ? " she demanded with amusement : " *Immer los ! Was Schwüles !* Let's go ! Something queer ! "

" *Los !* " the haggard boy requested her, and winked.

This was how she found her way into the *Regenbogen Diele*, where her life's supreme moment came to her.

IV

The intellectuals of the *Kabarett der Tsigeuner* had their theories regarding the phenomena of which the *Regenbogen Diele* was a notable specimen, and in the unparalleled frankness of that time they did not hesitate to propound them, duly converted into song or skit, from their stage. They were most of them violent pacifists now, though they had gone into the War with the high-mindedness of most normal young people in the various fighting countries, and their disillusions have been even more shattering. In the excess of their reaction against the treatment of their defeated country by the late enemy, they tended to throw in their lot with polemists, very much more stupid than themselves, who shrieked high and low that the Germans were as little responsible for the breaking out of the War as a meadow of shorn lambs. These intellectuals knew better ; and they had not refrained from saying what they knew, while the War was still on, and such candour required a great deal of courage.

Their errors were the errors of over-emphasis. And their insistence, despite their knowledge of recent political and economical history, that the Germans were completely innocent of the War, was so successful that the very Germans they had convinced worked out a philosophy according to which these same intellectuals were declared not only to have manœuvred Germany into the War, but to have demoralised her into accepting the shameful Peace. It was they themselves, in fact, who helped to induce a situation which was to involve them in desperate consequences of which neither they nor anyone else at that time had the faintest conception.

At all events, now, during the inflation-time, the *Kabarett* intellectuals were passionate pacifists. They were aware of the infinity of woe which the War had involved on both sides during its actual prosecution, in the way of death and wounds and separation and waste, and the suspension of all comely activities. They were aware that that woe had run by no means all its course on the day the War ended. But they were of the opinion that their country was involved in certain special pains and tragedies which might have been avoided if the victors had shown a little more generosity and sense ; which *should* have been avoided, for, however little or much their country had been to blame for what had happened, they had paid heavily, and would pay heavily for years to come.

Their diagnosis may not have been wholly accurate. But others, too, have blamed the terms of the Peace for the calamitous farce of the inflation ; and the *Tsigeuner* scourged with whips the profiteers, both native and foreign, who stuck their darts into the country's fevered skin and gorged themselves with its blood. To them the fine flower of the inflation was the *Regenbogen Diele*, which had its counterpart, not merely in every great city and in many minor ones, but in every quarter of Berlin—tough *Dieles* in the working-class regions for poor folk that had gone hurtling off their balance, smart *Dieles* for the elegants with monocles, male and female.

They defined normal sexuality as extrajection, in which a man or woman is impelled by his natural impulses out of himself to seek his spiritual and physical satisfactions in the opposite sex. Abnormal sexuality was introjection, in which the natural impulses were violently short-circuited, the man or woman was thrown in upon his own sex. Here too their diagnosis may not have been wholly accurate ; for it did not seem to take account of those cases in which no violent short-circuiting can be traced. It sought to place, perhaps, too large an onus on the War, for everything pitiable or evil in the pageant of that time.

They blamed the War as the fountain and origin of the *Regenbogen Diele*. They said that in the unnatural segregation of men in barracks and trenches, and under the conditions of monotony or intolerable nervous strain that those involved, many men must be forced into this introjection who would normally have been ignorant or incredulous of it. Something of the same sort applied to women, they said, who would be likewise thrown out of their just psychological order by the strain of separation and suspense. That would explain why after every war an increase of the phenomenon on both sides is invariably recorded. But the phenomenon in Germany was aggravated beyond all comparison with what happened elsewhere, because the War, or the terms of the Peace, had inflicted on Germany a calamity which no other country had had to bear, excepting in a minor degree—the calamity of the inflation.

The forces of dissolution which were loosed by the inflation were not the same in kind, but were equal in violence, as those which the War had loosened. In the War it was the unnaturalness of the restraint which had engendered the evil ; here it was the unnaturalness of the liberty. There was no sense or hope of stability anywhere. The air was full of a feverish passion for experimentation. There being nothing (excepting for the speculators) to do with money but to spend it, they spent it on wilder researches into experiences which lie far beyond the ken of normal people in normal times. These were the vicious ones.

But there were those who were not vicious. There are always cases, they maintained, who stand upon a sexual border-line, and these usually remain upon the right side of it because the whole pull of society is unconsciously exerted upon keeping them there. But in this time of the disintegration of the moral atom, these people of the border-line were twitched violently off their feet and thrown hurtling across it, across it and down a steep slope, into the tragic pit of the *Regenbogen Diele*.

v

That was the way the intellectuals of the *Kabarett der Tsigeuner* felt about it or, rather, theorised about it. Elsie Silver did no theorising. Her guide, the whisperer, led her into the place, stretched out a hand for some money, then left her to it.

She gave ear to her colleagues on the subject once or twice, but she carried away a conviction she brought with her, namely, that the more you talk about a thing, the less you understand it, *through the very act of talking about it.* She felt you either felt the truth straight off or there wasn't anything to do about it. May was like these Germans in her England excitement. It was all absolutely genuine. May loved England, and Elsie agreed that England was not a bad sort of place, really. But when May started the talky-talky on the subject, Lord, how cock-eyed she became !

These boys in the *Kabarett* were all much more intellectual people than May, of course. They had had a university education, many of them, and the languages they didn't know weren't worth knowing ; and when once they got going on Matisse and Massine and Modigliani, and all the other highbrows of Paris—Paris was the only place that made them feel small—there was no stopping them.

No doubt there was quite a lot in what they said in the why-and-wherefore of the *Regenbogen Diele*. But you just had to go in and sit about the place to see that a lot of it was pretty average punk, too. You went in, pushing aside a padded leather portière. There was a cloakroom where it was rather a tragedy if you didn't park your hat and coat, the poor painted youth who kept it was so ugly and looked so hungry. On his counter there was a weekly paper you could buy, called *Freundschaft*, and a monthly paper called *Die Insel*. These were for men. There were papers for women, too. They were all full of very sad bad little poems, and the advertisements of middle-aged ladies and gentlemen who wanted to establish relations with *solide*, respectable juniors of their own sex. There were also addresses of *pensions* where they could withdraw with people less *solide*.

On entering the *Diele* you found yourself on the edge of a dancing-floor, with little tables along both sides of it. Flanking the tables on both sides was a dais that extended for a dozen feet or so, where there were more little tables. Then, a stage higher, there were the invariable alcoves. You drank beer lower down, and waited for someone to pay for it, as a rule. On the dais, you drank wine. In the alcoves, it was expected you should drink champagne, which was brought round in ice-buckets, swathed in none-too-clean napkins. There were rather sickly pictures on the walls of gold-haired youths bathing in Reckitts-blue seas. There was a large engraving of an elder semi-nude Greek teaching a younger semi-nude Greek how to pull a bow. This was after an original by Lord Leighton, President of the Royal Academy.

There were men and men dancing together, and women and women. There were also demonstrably normal couples dancing among the rest, without turning a hair. Elsie remembered a dance-place of this sort she had been taken to once, somewhere in Montmartre. It was at once so vicious and so shabby—the screeching youths with bracelets, the coal-heavers in female *décolleté*—that it had turned her stomach. There was a little shabbiness about this place in Berlin, but it was too serious to be altogether vicious, even too sentimental. The men and men danced with each other, the women and women ; then they returned to their tables. Stolidly the normal couples turned round and round amongst the rest. It was, when she first saw it, so fantastic, so incredible, that she wanted to scream. And later, when the *Tsigeuner* expounded their theories, it was that stolidity of the normal couples that sometimes made her feel they were right. It was a world standing on its head, waving its feet in the air, as if that were quite the most unexceptionable place for feet to be in.

Elsie was a connoisseur in varieties of sexual experience, but her experience, both in practice and contemplation, had hitherto been confined within the boundaries of normality. As far as her practice went, Berlin made no difference to her. But it enormously extended the field of her contemplation. It should be stated there were two occasions on which she was shocked. A particularly large and prosperous business-man brought his mistress in with him one evening. She was dressed not so much in the height of fashion as with an extravagance in the way of jewels which many a leading lady would have envied. He had apparently not trusted himself to take her into a more conventional *Diele*. The lady was not fourteen years old. The proprietor came up, and was very courteous and very firm. The business-man withdrew, glaring evilly and profusely sweating. The same occurred when an elderly ephebos brought in a boy of about the same age. On both occasions Elsie's stomach heaved, as it had heaved up in Montmartre. But she suffered stomachic derangement on no other occasion.

She looked on, night after night, fascinated, with that quiver of excitement through all her limbs which Berlin produced in her from time to time, in the various manifestations of its agony. The very matter-of-factness of the people who defiled before her, sipping drinks from each other's glasses, dancing solemnly between the tables, humming the melody they were dancing to, accentuated that excitement till her eyes shone and the blood pulsed against her ears. One night she saw, for instance, a woman, in a tie and collar, a tailor-made coat and skirt, go up to a delicate gold-haired youth in female clothing and ask him to dance. He accepted. They danced, the woman leading. Then she took him back to the place where he had been sitting, bowed and thanked him. He, in his turn, graciously acknowledged her bow. Then he sat down. She stood about for a moment, then she turned to him again. Might she buy him a drink, she asked. He fluttered a little with embarrassment and thanked her. So they drank together.

Another night she saw two women in the most exquisite evening clothes, exquisite both in cut and material. She was first attracted by the clothes, for clothes of such quality were rare even in quite elegant straightforward dance-places. They both had beautiful blonde hair, admirably waved. They were very much in love with each other, for neither moved her eyes from the eyes of the other the whole night. Each was asked to dance both by men and women, and each refused. It was only when they got up to dance with each other that Elsie realised they were men. Their shoes were high-heeled and beautiful in design, but the feet they encased were just not small enough, the movements they made were just a shade too lengthy. The hands put the matter beyond any shadow of doubt.

Elsie was talking at the time with a rather pleasant and intelligent Austrian woman whom she met in the *Diele* now and again. The woman had had hopes which Elsie showed her very promptly would not be fulfilled ; but she reconciled herself quite easily to a blameless comradeship, during the times they should happen to meet in the *Diele*. It was convenient for both of them to be able to drink a glass together and exchange a word or two. Outside, each completely disappeared into her own world. It was to her Austrian friend she was talking when the two exquisitely dressed women got up, showed their hands, and indicated they were men.

Elsie suddenly threw her arms on the table, and buried her face in them. Her shoulders heaved with suppressed laughter. She laughed and laughed, her head hidden in her arms.

" What is it ? What is it ? " the Austrian woman insisted, plucking at her shoulder. " What is it ? "

At last Elsie lifted her face. Her eyes were streaming with tears. " Those two," she pointed out, " those two, do you see, with the marvellous *toilette* ? "

" Yes ? " said the other woman. There was a certain frigidity in her tone.

" No, never, never ! " said Elsie, breaking down again. " I'll never get the hang of it ! It beats me ! Ha ! Ha ! Ha ! "

The woman got up from the table, her eyes bitter with pain and animosity. " There is neither cause for weeping nor laughter," she said. " But, if you must do one thing or the other, you should weep." Then she left the table, and walked out of the *Diele*. When next she met Elsie there, she looked through her, as if they had never met.

Elsie smiled, and inclined her head. The defection did not trouble her unduly. There was always quite a lot to look at in the *Diele*, even when the clients themselves were a dull lot. The spectators, whose numbers increased from month to month, were sometimes a good deal more amusing. There were the scientists, the sexologists, as they were beginning to be called, who had little notebooks with them and took furtive notes, in order, later, to write articles in obscure reviews and give lectures in enlightened suburbs. There were the missionaries, who looked rather helpless, as if they perceived it was all rather more tangled than they had bargained for. There were the tourist young couples who came in expecting it was going to be rather a lark, and the young woman became more and more embarrassed and the young man more and more furious. There were the quite accidental visitors, who had strolled in because they had heard a burst of music as someone pushed aside the padded leather portière on going out. These Elsie found the most amusing. Sometimes they went on for a whole hour, perhaps even a whole evening, without the faintest suspicion that the place was the place it was, though so palpably the men and men, the women and women, danced together. It was obviously, even to them, a little unusual ; but it was so friendly and jolly, they even, in their innocence, danced themselves with members of their own sex. On others, swiftly or slowly, the dreadful awareness dawned. The blood left their cheeks. Their eyes became large and round with horror. They staggered over to the doorway, as if they would be sick any moment.

Elsie threw back her head. The laughter bubbled in her throat like a linnet.

VI

It was one night in the late autumn of that year, which was 1922, that Elsie Silver saw her vision become flesh.

She had had a little too much of her colleagues at the

Kabarett lately ; they talked a lot, and were very bitter, and got nowhere. And the *conférencier*, Adelbaum, had started making love to her again. She had had to put him in his place, and she was feeling rather cross and tired. It occurred to her that the *Regenbogen Diele* was just the place for a night like this. She went down, of course, in the male clothes she wore in the show. She very rarely wore anything else nowadays. Frau Krantz, her landlady, was rather horrified at first, and hoped she had an *Erlaubnis*, a permit, from the police. Elsie assured her it wasn't necessary, she was an artist. But she found out and made sure.

It was about one o'clock when she entered the *Diele*. She gave her black trilby-hat and her coat to the youth at the cloakroom, then she entered and looked round. She had got to know two or three people, and thought it might be pleasant to sit and have a drink with one of them.

She saw him almost immediately. He was sitting alone at a table on the dais diagonally opposite her across the dance-floor. His head was bowed a little, his hand was on the table, the fingers twirling the thin stem of one of those shallow glasses in which the Germans serve liqueurs. He looked a little sullen, and lost and lonely. The moment she set eyes on him, he lifted his head, and looked straight down the dance-floor, towards the entrance, as if he had heard his name called.

She for her part saw the scar before she distinguished any other of the features she knew so well—the scar which was the confirmation and the signature. It was less a scar than scars, on the right side of his face, from the nostrils going down to the chin. The scars were more tangled than she had envisioned them, in the Oleander Street kitchen once, and later on a stone ledge under Cap Ferrat, and most recently in a room in a large house under the Sussex Downs. There was a complexity of scars or cuts ; besides that, in the same region, the skin was brown, as if it had been burned. It could not be said of him with those scars that he was a handsome man. But the eyes were fine and blue and cold. The hair had been gold once, but the sheen was gone.

The mouth was slightly twisted, perhaps by the pull of the scars, perhaps by the wryness of his thoughts. But the lips were proud and beautiful, beautiful to a point that made them almost womanish.

Her eyes fell upon his eyes, his mouth, his scars. She knew in that moment this was the man whom all her years and thoughts and loves had portended. There was nothing hysterical in this moment of seeing in the flesh, as there had been before in those moments of seeing in vision. She knew with sobriety and absolute certainty this was he.

His head jerked again, as if he had heard his name called a second time. He saw the eyes of a youth upon him, the damson Arab eyes of Elsie Silver, the eyes of a slim youth, of good bearing. He smiled, shaking his head ever so faintly. He removed his hand from the stem of the wine-glass, and lifted the index finger in a slight gesture of reproof.

Elsie Silver strode straight across the dance-floor, ascended the dais, and stood at his table. She had no idea what must be the words she should first address to him. The words uttered themselves.

" *Ich habe Ihnen etwas Wichtiges zu sagen.* I have something important to say to you."

He remained seated at the table, as a man of the best breeding is thoroughly entitled to do when a youth he does not know comes up and addresses him in a public place.

" *Tut mir Leid, Bubi, ich bin nicht so einer !* I'm sorry, boy, I'm not one of these ! " he said, shaking his head with mock sadness, and indicating, with a comprehensive sweep of the hand, the fraternity he repudiated.

Then all the woman in her surged down in a fierce tide to her hands. They thrust forward to his wrists, and held them tight. They lifted the hands of the lover so long waited for, and pressed them like cups upon her breasts.

" *Ich auch nicht, ich auch nicht !* No more am I, no more am I ! " she sang exultantly. Her eyes were like a tree in bud that bursts suddenly into flower.

" *Na, wass soll das heissen* ? Then what's all this about ? "

he asked. He did not remove his hands from her breasts. They remained as if they were happy there. His mouth dropped a little comically. A gust of mirth swept across the blue waters of his eyes.

" I'll tell you, I'll tell you ! " she said. " May I sit down ? "

" Oh, pardon, a thousand times ! " He had not risen to his feet yet, but there had been something to explain his remissness. He got up, and bowed with infinite courtliness, made a gesture with one hand towards the chair opposite him, and with the other helped her to sit down in it.

She spread her arms out along the table, resting her hands palm downwards.

" You think I'm *verrückt*, dotty, don't you ? " she said. Her cheeks were blushing like a vase of peonies.

" Oh, no," he objected. " I think you're a very charming and beautiful young woman. Just a little—unusual, perhaps."

" Oh, this ! " she said. She pointed down with her chin to her male clothes. " I'm an artist," she explained. " I sing at the *Kabarett der Tsigeuner*."

" Oh," he said—a shadow passed across his face. " I don't like that *Gesindl*, that mob ! "

" Well, if there's any mob you like better," she said tranquilly, " just tell me about it ! "

" Excuse me," he asked. " From your accent—I take it you are English ? "

" Yes, I am English."

There was something more he wanted to ask, but it seemed to occur to him it would be better manners if he did not ask it. He looked, instead, at the beautiful bow of her mouth, and her glowing eyes, and the smooth fine pallor of her forehead.

" I think something's biting you ! " she said. " Yes, I'm Jewish ! "

" Please ! " He made a deprecating gesture. " How could you say such a thing ! "

" Well, I'm not so Jewish you'd know it a mile off," she

told him. " But don't *you* think for one damn moment," she
flared up, " I'm ashamed of it ! " She clenched her fists
where they lay upon the table. She was in such a state of
exaltation that it would have been as easy to dig her nails
into his cheeks as to throw her arms around his neck and
smother him in kisses. Either was easier than to sit there,
among all these nancies and horse-faced women, and talk
rationally, and explain the inexplicable thing, the inconceivable miracle which made thought-reading or making the
blind see as dull and simple as a cup of stale tea.

He looked at her with amusement. He observed there was
no expression her face could assume which did not make it
more enchanting.

" Shan't we leave that now? ' he hazarded. " There may
be time—later on."

Later on. . . . Later on. . . . Her heart leapt exultantly.
" He understands ! " her heart said. " He's got an inkling !
He realises it's not a pick-up, I'm not trying to make him !
There *will* be time, my God, there *will* be time later ! Yes,
my God, there will ! " Her lips almost fashioned the words.
He could see certain wild thoughts were racing through her
head. Then he ventured a word again. For, after all, he
considered a certain amount of explanation was due to him.

" What were you going to say ? " he reminded her.

" Yes. You're quite right. It's up to me to prove I'm not
mad. The fact is, I've known you for a very long time."

" Yet I'm sure I've never set eyes on you before. Believe
me, if I had——"

" I haven't either."

" Oh ! " he said.

They were both silent for a second or two. She corroborated the marvel which had taken place, in each of its details.
Yes, those eyes, that shade of cold blue ; no other eyes in the
world at all. That straight nose, that once-golden hair, that
still had pale lights in it, and was so fine and soft. Those
wounds on his poor face. She had also noticed that little
patch of brownness on the cheek. It looked like a burn.

Poor boy, it must have hurt him frightfully. He looked at her, this sudden apparition out of the gloom, the shame, the hopelessness—that dark flow of her hair, the heavenly curve of her eyebrows, the firm lips; above all, the eyes, like sloes, like damson-plums, like some sort of purple fruit. He had given up all hope of anything at all anywhere happening. Now this had happened. It was like picking up a book you had bought long ago on a bookstall, you could not remember where, and you were penniless, and you found a wad of good gold banknotes between the pages. It was like going back to a blighted garden in a ruined homestead and finding the garden blazing with a glory of flowers.

He blinked and shook his head. It surely wasn't one cherry-brandy that had done this ? No, no ; it was having a cherry-brandy on an empty stomach, which had been empty a couple of days.

He suddenly realised that he sat there so ill-manneredly, with a drink before him, and none ordered for her. A faint flush widened on his cheeks. He had a few mark notes on him, it was true, once good enough to buy a factory. They would not buy a crust of bread now.

He summoned the waiter.

" Try and forgive me," he begged her. " What will you drink ? " He spoke in flawless English, except for the slight gutturalising of the r's.

" What are you drinking ? "

" Cherry-brandy ! "

" That'll do perfectly ! " She clapped her hands. It was a minor portent that he should be drinking the one drink which should be exactly the drink for this superb moment.

" Waiter, another cherry-brandy ! "

The waiter brought it and put it down before the lady. He hung about, flicking at the table with his napkin.

" What are you waiting for ? " he turned round suddenly and rapped at the waiter. It seemed quite another voice.

The waiter stammered. " You see, Herr, the proprietor has ordered . . "

His eyes were hard as pebbles. " Go away ! " he said in a voice quiet and extremely formidable. It was the tone of one accustomed to command, who could not without danger be disobeyed. " *Canaille !* " he said under his breath.

A vein of delight beat in her throat like a tiny hammer. *This* was the man. *This* was he. In that way, in no other way at all, the man must speak when he demanded a thing should be done, whether he demanded it from her or from any creature else. She had made a further discovery. The thought of it went charging in waves through her head. She realised he had not paid when the waiter had asked him *because he could not pay*. It was not at all unlikely that the proprietor had warned the waiters that the gentleman must pay on the nail. He probably owed quite a lot for cherry-brandy. She saw in an instant's exact appraisement that the suit he wore, though in good style and of good material, had a suggestion of the threadbare. The shirt and collar and cuffs were scrupulously clean, but there was a hint of overlaundering in the thinning of material and the tiny fraying of edges.

Glory ! Glory ! She would have something to give him, for what it was worth. Not for nothing had Silver and Smirnof made raincoats and raincoats, but for the well-being of her lover and the glory of God. He was God. He was Love. For crying out loud, she was tight, she was tight, before she'd even had a smell of the liquor ! She raised her glass. He raised his. She placed her glass against his lips ; he followed suit at once and placed his glass against hers.

" *Zum woll sein !* "

" *Zum woll sein !* "

They drank. " Waiter ! " she called out. " Two more ! And then two more ! " She turned to him. " Please ! Please ! " she implored him. " This is inflation-time ! I've been paid to-night ! If we don't do something about it now, what the hell will it be worth to-morrow ? "

He laughed. " What a perfect little *Berlinerin* it is ! It's very convenient, to be sure. I came out without a million marks to my name ! "

They tossed off their glasses again. The waiter shuffled round in the most contrite obsequiousness.

" That's better ! " she said.

" Much ! " he said. He took her right hand where it lay on the table. It was a gesture of courtesy and possession, executed in perfect style, like a Herr Baron, a Herr Graf.

" I take it you're a Herr Baron or something ! " she speculated. " It would be fatuous if you weren't ! "

He rose to his feet, clicked his heels together sharply, and announced : " Graf Oskar Straupitz-Kalmin ! " Then he sat down again. " And you, madame ? "

" Well," she said, " in the sight of God I'm Lady Malswetting, wife of Sir Robert Malswetting, eighth baronet, of Sevenings, in the county of Oxfordshire."

" *Enchanté*, Lady Malswetting ! " he said, putting a hand on his heart and bowing from the waist till his forehead nearly touched the table. Then he added, his eyes twinkling : " I take it this isn't a piece of *Theater* ? I know you'll forgive me."

" I forgive you. It sounded like one hell of a quick tit-for-tat, I know. But it isn't. I am."

He went through the process again, hand on the heart, bow from the waist. He straightened up again. " But——" he began. " Unless you think me impertinent ? "

" But I'm Elsie Silver. I left my husband in a dentist's waiting-room in Nice, because he was crying."

" Oh—oh ! " His voice prolonged itself in an appreciation for which he found no words adequate. Once more he rose on to his feet. He bent across the table and put a hand on each of her shoulders. Then he placed his mouth, a mouth curiously soft and cool for a face so severe, upon her forehead. But, while his lips still rested there, Elsie rose, thrust her forehead back from them, and set her lips in her forehead's place. She threw her arms round his shoulders. They stood there united in a kiss which they did not suspend until they were uncomfortable for lack of breath. The waiter put down two further glasses of cherry-brandy. The men and the men, the women and the women, went plodding round and round like blinkered animals in tread-mills.

Elsie and Oskar sat down. She took a handkerchief from her breast-pocket and dabbed his lips lightly, then her own. " Now we can talk ! " she said.

" Now we can talk ! " he repeated.

" Doesn't this prove what I said ? " she asked. Her mouth, slightly open, showed her perfect teeth. His eye registered them—" Perfect teeth ! "

" What exactly ? " he asked.

" That I've known you for a very long time ! "

" *Pour ainsi dire ?* " he suggested.

" No, not that way at all ! "

" Where then ? How then ? "

" Listen ! " she requested him. " I know I've behaved like a madwoman. And you've not been very sensible, either, come to think of it ! "

" No," he admitted gravely.

" Will you believe me when I say that I'm—in England we say : a very-level-headed-little-woman-damn-it ! That's how your sort of man would put it."

" It's hard—but I *will* believe you. I'm sure you are—what my sort of man in England would call you—what is it ?—a very-level-headed-little-woman-damn-it ! "

" Good. I'm going to tell you something quite idiotic. I've only told it to one other person in my life."

" Your husband ? "

" Gosh, no ! "

" Who then ? "

" I won't tell you now. Oh, yes, I might as well. My sister. I was a pretty average sort of swine to her."

He lifted his eyebrows inquiringly.

" No," she said. " We won't go into that now."

" Don't worry," he said. " I feel the same sort of way, too. My wife, it happened to be."

" Oh," she whistled. " You've got a little problem play, too, waiting about on the old hearth ? "

" No," he said. " She's dead."

" Oh ! "

" Please don't let that disturb you. I didn't love her very much. I was only sorry for her now and again."

" Like me and Bobby," she pointed out, a little grimly.

" Probably."

" Well, I'll get on with it. Not that it's easy. God, it isn't easy. You'll think me crazy."

" No, I won't ! " His voice was quite earnest.

" I've seen you three times in my life," she said. " Three principal times, that I remember vividly. And just odd little peeps and glimpses now and again."

He looked very puzzled.

" Don't get me wrong. I wasn't spying on you anywhere. I saw you in a sort of—it sounds too balmy—in a sort of vision."

" Let me assure you," he said, " it doesn't sound to me as strange as you think. I've been a soldier."

" Yes, of course."

" I've seen visions, too. One night in the No Man's Land, this side of Tarnopol. A bit of shell got me. It did this—part of it." He lightly touched the complex of scars with his finger. " I lay out all night. I saw visions, too. But our men got me in again, unfortunately."

" No, don't say that ! " she requested sharply.

He smiled at her. " How exceedingly discourteous ! Please wipe it out ! "

" Go on ! "

" We were captured in the same area a few months later —by the Russians ! " His chin became stony and his eyes hostile. He did not seem to like the Russians ; or, perhaps, the things that had happened to him in Russia. " They carted us off by slow stages to Siberia. I was there during their two Revolutions. They kept me stinking there till after the War. Then I escaped. At least the War in the West was over ; it wasn't yet over between us and Russia."

He stopped a moment. " Does this interest you ? " he asked, almost savagely.

" Please ! " she begged.

" Well, I was saying I managed to escape," he resumed. " That was another night I saw visions, the night I crawled on my belly in the waste land between the Russian outposts and our own. So you see "—his voice lightened and his eyes smiled again—" I know something about visions, too."

" By gosh, I bet you do. But mine were rather different. I mean, they happened, just like that. Just sitting down, not thinking about anything."

" Yes, that's rather different."

" And I saw you, three times, quite distinctly, just as I see you now."

" I admit," he said, " it's odd."

" You're believing me ? "

" I'm believing you."

" It happened the first time in the kitchen of my father's house in Doomington, in the North of England. He was—a sort of tailor."

" Oh ! " he said. There was no shadow of meaning detectable in the intonation.

" Yes," she added with scrupulous casualness. " He's now one of the richest men in England—in the North of England, anyhow."

" Oh ! " he repeated, in exactly the same tone, for it was clear that neither fact could have the least bearing upon him.

" It's funny. You know," she went on, " these ! " She touched his scars with infinite delicacy. " You just had one sharp scar there, a clean line that stood out and curved round."

" Was that a long time before the War ? " he asked.

" Way before the War."

" Yes," he said. " I got that in a duel when I joined the regiment in Potsdam."

" Was she fair ? " she asked.

" It was over a boy."

" Oh ! " The sound was just as non-committal now on her lips as it had been on his.

" I must request you once again not to worry." He did not move his eyes from her ; but once more he made a gesture which indicated and dismissed the men and men, the women and women dancing a few feet away, staring sadly into each other's eyes. " That's not why I'm here."

" It's my turn for cheek," she said. " Why *are* you here ? "

" Why are *you* here ? " he had back at her. " I think the reasons are more or less similar. You've come here to watch ; so have I. But I rather wanted to die with them, and you——"

" I was kicking round till you'd turn up."

" I see. Please go on with your visions."

" That scar, the one I saw first. You got that in a duel ? "

" As I told you, over a young *Kadet*. I outgrew that. The next duel was over a girl. I wasn't touched that time. Go on, please."

" And then I saw you a second time, a good deal later—I mean when I saw you quite so *clearly* as I saw you the first time. It was one afternoon in Cap Ferrat, when I was making up my mind to run away from my husband, though I didn't know it at the time."

" Not so long ago ? "

" Last spring to be exact, over a year ago. Your face was gashed about a bit. Just as it is now. Forgive my talking like this."

" *Bitte*. That was the shell-splinter—I told you, near Tarnopol."

" And then, this spring. Before something happened that —that made me leave England and clear off to Berlin." She stopped. He waited for her to go on. " It was in a big house which my young sister runs to give slum children a year or two of living in the country. It was deliberate this time. I asked for it. I made you come."

" And I came."

" You'd changed. I saw you as you are now. Your face was much more torn. You seemed to have been badly burned. You poor poor fellow ! How did it happen ? "

His eyes stared before him, quite cold and terrible. His fists, on the edge of the table before him, went white, he clenched them so tightly. There was a slight quiver in his lips, enough to prevent the words being delivered from them until a second or two after he began to form them.

" It happened in a train, not far from Moscow," he said, his eyes rigid, like pale blue disks. " I was escaping. No ! No ! " His voice suddenly declined out of its levelness. He passed his hand before his face as if he sought to wipe out the phantasmal appearance of some horror too hideous to evoke. " We won't talk about it ! "

" Of course we won't ! " she soothed him. " Of course we won't ! " She passed the tips of her fingers over his forehead, where they encountered a dew of sweat engendered by his nightmare. " Do you know," she exclaimed suddenly, " I'm hungry ! And I want to dance ! I want to eat first ! And then I want to dance like hell ! "

He looked round doubtfully.

" No ! Not here ! " she said. It all looked incredibly shoddy and silly. " Oh, let's get out of this ! " she cried. " It's too damn silly ! And I'm hungry ! "

" So am I ! " he said, and then recollected that he had no money to do anything about it. " At least, I was ! " he faltered. " I don't feel much like food now. But, of course, you——"

" Come ! " she bade, quite roughly, and rose. He wondered vaguely if there was any eating-place anywhere which would give him credit.

" Look here ! " she said. " It's my night ! I know there's coffee and butter and rolls in my apartment. And cheese and fruit. I sometimes get quite hungry in the middle of the night, and I hate to mooch round and find nothing. I've got a little kitchen and pantry all to myself. We might be able to pick up a little cold chicken *en route*, eh ? "

" That would be grand ! "

" And I've got a gramophone with some damn good records. Then we'll dance. Just us two, alone up there, on top of the house, looking down on the Schöneberger Ufer ! "

" I should think you dance like a—like a devil ! "

" Not so dusty ! " she admitted. " And now for supper ! "

" And then for breakfast ! "

She looked at him, as he towered above her, tall and distinguished, and courteous and desolate. " I'll take that look out of your eyes ! " she promised him. " *Before* breakfast ! " she specified.

Frau Krantz was requested to make breakfast next morning, for Elsie felt a little too tired and shattered to go making breakfasts herself. Oskar von Straupitz-Kalmin looked so completely the Herr Graf, even in bed, with his one-time-gold hair a little disordered, that it was entirely impossible for Frau Krantz to refrain from doing a little curtsey as she approached with the tray ; even though it was quite against her principles that any female tenant of hers should be found sharing her bed with a man when morning came round ; and not merely against her principles, either—against the stated conditions of the let, too. But what with one's own daughter disappearing to lead a life of which the least said the soonest mended, and what with things being so bad as they were, and what with Fräulein Silber being such a very *good* tenant, she didn't quite see what was to be done in the matter. And one ought to be grateful, perhaps, that it hadn't happened earlier, which had been a very mysterious thing in some ways. Though some of the things that had been said by other people in the building, Fräulein Silber always going about in man's clothing, it wasn't possible to believe such a thing, but she *had* asked if she'd got a licence from the police to let her go about like that, so she hadn't any responsibility in the matter at all.

Anyhow, *that* was all nonsense, what with the *Hoheit*—he

looked every inch a *Hoheit*, even in that ridiculous silk
nightgown of Fräulein Silber's which he'd split all up the
back—lying beside her in bed like that. To be sure the bed
was a little narrow. It went against the grain of her house-
pride to see her tenant and her friend so cramped for room
in a bed of hers. She herself still slept on a double-bed,
though for all the use that was——

Apparently ideas somewhat similar to hers had been
passing through Fräulein Silber's brain, too.

" There is one thing you might do, Frau Krantz," said
Fräulein Silber. " You could put a bigger bed in this room.
It may be a little more useful than this one."

VII

They had supped ; they had danced ; they had made
love ; they had got a good deal said ; they had made love
again. It was love-making the whole time, whether they
supped or danced or talked or kissed. He was a very polished
and a very ardent love-maker. It was an art in which Elsie
was no novice, but she had to call on all her resources to be
his worthy partner.

It was queer, dancing at dawn high above the thinning
trees and the black canal rolling against their cemented
roots. It was queer to be embraced in their private delirium,
as at the top of a tower that looked down on the wide
delirium of Berlin. It was queer to evoke images so far and
strange as those that came gliding in through the door into
the room where they lay, mouth to mouth, their transports
for the time being ended, and speech coming fitfully from
him and her. . . .

A little rainproof workman from Doomington who had
become one of the richest men in the English North Country ;
a Prussian landowner, the brother of this man in the high
room, sitting ruined and virulent among his mortgaged
estates ; a handsome English ne'er-do-well who ate chocolates by the hour and made love to housemaids ; a Russian

sergeant who, having overwhelmed Oskar von Straupitz-Kalmin and his men in a lone outpost, had lost patience with two German soldiers who could not disentangle their hooked flesh from the barbed wire, and had shot them dead there and then.

The word " Russian " occurred over and over again in Oskar von Straupitz-Kalmin's random account of his days, and always with no love. It was the villain of his piece, though by Russia he clearly did not mean the Russia of the Tsar and the autocracy. He meant the mud of Russia which had come to the top these late years. It had at an early stage occurred to Elsie that it would be amusing to let this Prussian aristocrat know he had his arms about the sister-in-law of a Bolshevik Commissar. But it had quickly impressed itself on her that that would be a most unwise thing to do.

She asked him what certain small shrivelled tracts of flesh were below the back of his calves, and, as she asked, she kissed them. He told her. He said that during their month-long journey between the point on the Tarnopol sector where they were captured and the small town of Vitomir beyond the Urals where they were imprisoned for two years, his batch of prisoners went before a doctor. The doctor was a little half-baked Pole—a chemist's bottle-boy. He was not a Russian doctor. Russian *gentlemen* were all right. This was at Samara on the Volga. He had by that time developed a horde of sores on the back of his legs. He had no bandages, so that his underclothes, which were quite foul by this time, and, of course, he had no others, stuck to the back of his wounds. The lice had eaten their way in, so that the wounds now were festering abscesses. The batch was passed perfunctorily before the doctor. He, Oskar, made a request for a supply of bandages. The doctor said he could not spare any bandages, but would amputate his legs if he liked. The abscesses had given him continuous misery for two years, which those bandages would have saved him.

She passed her lips from his mouth to his eyes, then down

to his mouth again. " Hush, don't take on now ! It's all
over long ago. If ever you cut your finger I'll tie it round
for you with bandages of the most lovely silk."

" They are such fools ! " he said. " Millions upon millions
of snub-nosed gaping fools ! Do you know the peasants used
to flock round us at the stations and feel our heads to see if
we really had horns ? They had been shown photographs,
by their village priests, of Wotan with his horned helmet ! "

" But they're changing all that now," she murmured.

" Pah ! The Bolsheviks ! A pack of Jews ! "

He had of course forgotten that this was a Jewess with
whom he was at that moment placed so intimately. And
she, for her part, snuggling up against his chest, knew that
if this had been any other man in the whole world she would
suddenly have turned into a heap of claws like a wild-cat
there in his arms. And having scratched him till the blood
flowed, she would have ordered him to get out of bed and
be dressed in five minutes, and clear out to hell. But she did
not. She snuggled up inside his arm, and kissed him from
his chin down into the hollows above his collar-bones.

Like all people of extreme reticence, when once he had
broken down his barriers he gave away most of what he had
to give away. He did not use the actual word, of course, but
she gathered he was now a complete pauper. Here again the
" New " Russia played its sinister part. The Straupitz-
Kalmins were an ancient land-owning family in Mecklenburg. Oskar's father had inherited the estate as a young man.
He gave up his commission and had farmed the estate
honourably for some time according to the immemorial
traditions of their class. Oskar himself was a younger son,
and had been trained for the Army at the Dresdner *Kadet-
tenanstalt*. His elder brother had duly inherited the estate in
the early years of this century, but found it mortgaged up to
the hilt. For during the last years of his life their father had
fallen under the influence of a cousin of his, a mining-
engineer, a man of complete integrity and much brilliance.
He had induced old Straupitz-Kalmin to realise as much

money as could be squeezed out of the estate by sales and mortgage, and invest it, as he had himself invested every penny he possessed, in Siberian gold-mines. The Bolsheviks, of course, had confiscated the gold-mines. The Straupitz-Kalmin estates were left high-and-dry, derelict. It was true that the inflation had reduced the mortgages to waste paper. But what was the value of a large estate, without money, without beasts, with agricultural implements that dated back a thousand years ?

As for himself, his father had become rather unquiet towards the end of his life that so much of the family money was tied up in gold-mines, which were, after all, a speculation ; it was necessary to do something in the interests of his younger son, Oskar, something in the way of a gilt-edged investment. He had therefore bought in his son's name as many Prussian State Bonds as he could lay hands on ; and in order to make quite certain that this money, too, should not be used for speculation in Siberia, it was established in his will that the State Bonds should not be convertible into any other securities. The inflation had made them worth just a little more than the paper they were printed on.

" Money ! " said Elsie. " Money ! Isn't it odd ? "

" What ? "

" It's always run after me. I've never run after it."

" It has its uses, *kleines Mädchen* ! "

" Such as—— ? "

" Oh, if I had money, my child ! There's my wretched brother over in Kalmin ! I'd buy stock for him, and tractors, and——" He wasn't quite certain what else there is to buy before you put a ruined estate on its feet again. " And I'd hunt again, as I used to, as we all used to, the chamois in the Bavarian hills and the wild pig in the Polish forests. They've been stolen from us now, the Polish forests."

" What else ? "

" I'd buy you a great pale-green motor-car, an English one, a Rolls-Royce."

She felt it would be indecent to shout at the top of her

voice : " You shall, Oskar, you shall ! Anything you like in
the world. I shall be lousy with money the moment I lift my
little finger. You shall be a country gentleman and a town
gentleman, and have a hunting-lodge, and hunters, and a
great pale-green motor-car, an English one ! "

She felt it would be indecent to say all that to a scion of
a proud and ancient family, whom the Bolsheviks and the
statesmen had ruined. Was this a Riviera lounge-lizard ?
She said instead : " I was thinking of buying a cheap little
coupé to run about town in. But I can't drive. Can you ? "

" But of course ! "

" It would be grand if you'd drive me out some time.
Would you ? "

" But of course ! "

" Then I'll kiss you."

" And I'll say thank you."

" Then say please *now*."

" Please ! "

" Oh, my love, my love, my love, my love ! "

" You little black rabbit, you little black puppy, don't
bite so ! "

When he came in from his bath that morning, he found
her still in her pyjamas and dressing-gown, writing a letter.

" Who are you writing to ? " he said, with mock sternness.

" Only to my father," she said casually. " My allowance
is overdue."

" Oh ! " he said, as if the matter had as much bearing on
his own situation as the Tropic of Capricorn.

" It might run to that coupé," she hazarded.

VIII

Elsie Silver was no fool with regard to men, and she did
not delude herself into believing that Oskar von Straupitz-
Kalmin was in love with her. She knew that he was attracted
by her, and if he had been only a little attracted she would

have deployed more and more effective arts of allurement in order to attract him more and more. She was a mistress of them all, the art of withholding when pleasure seemed to come too easy, the art of mingling sweet with bitter when pleasure seemed to grow tame. In the spring of this same year she had scored, in Cardiff, a triumph which could not have been achieved by any but a major genius in these arts. She was anything but proud of her triumph ; but she was sensible enough to realise that it could be described by no other word.

Oskar was by no means a formidable achievement. He was no saint ; he had known gross nights with kitchen wenches in garrison-town and base-camp. But there was a streak of femaleness in him which had to be countered by a swift readjustment of all the sexual elements within her, so that to his femaleness she opposed a certain slim masculine tautness.

There were other difficulties. He did not like Jews ; but he seemed disposed to believe that to lie in the arms of a Jewess was not at all the same thing as liking Jews. She attempted once or twice to whip herself up into some such frenzy as had sometimes transported her when someone, totally ignorant that she was a Jewess, had uttered some slighting remark concerning Jews. But she could not. She bit her lip with vexation at the thought, but she felt that his feeling regarding Jews, which he was far too well-mannered to put into words, gave her a perverse pleasure and an increased respect for her own achievement. " What, my blue-eyed Prussian aristocrat, you don't like Jews ? You don't ? But you like *me* ! You've damn well got to like *me* ! You like my body, don't you ? You like my money, don't you ? Well, ride the high horse, sonny ! My horse rides higher than yours ! "

There was the further difficulty about money. It wasn't quite accurate to call it a difficulty, seeing that it was money, after all, which clinched the matter. Without money it might well have been an affair for a month or two or three. A woman like Elsie Silver had gifts to offer which need not cloy in three or four or five. But without money she would have had a great downward suck to combat—the suck down to the despair and darkness of the *Regenbogen Diele*. With money it was now, and would always be, a different matter ; an affair of years rather than of months—five years, say ; that would do to be going on with.

But the money part of it had to be handled carefully. He was not too proud to accept it, as the veriest paid sailor in Nice is not too proud to accept money for his services from the racked spinster who summons him to her villa up on the hill. If he had any compunctions, they were allayed by the knowledge that this money was earned in a War which had been won by the wrong side. If the right side had won it, the money would not have remained in the coffers of Jew profiteers, but would have fertilised the dried acres of his own country in the form of indemnities.

Yet it could not be denied that, as things stood, it was the Jew, Sam Silver, who now sat possessed of the money ; it was the Jew-girl, his daughter, who received a generous regular allowance out of it ; it was on himself, Oskar von Straupitz-Kalmin, that most of the allowance was spent. So it all had to be done with extreme tact, with a chemically perfect avoidance of the suggestion that he was a kept lover. In a manner of speaking, he accepted the money merely as a temporary convenience.

This much can certainly be said in the Count's favour. He believed implicitly, as Alexander Smirnof, the brother-in-law of his mistress, believed, that the Bolshevik régime could not survive more than a few years ; perhaps its collapse was far more imminent than the most sanguine optimists expected. When the Bolsheviks crashed, there would be a great many accounts to settle, among them the accounts of the Siberian gold-mines in general, and the Straupitz-Kalmin mines in particular. They would be settled, it had long been decided by the various creditors involved, at a handsome rate of compound interest.

There was the matter, moreover, of Oskar's private fortune which had been invested in Prussian State Bonds, and had dwindled to nothing in the inflation. It was firmly believed in certain quarters that the Government could not possibly condone for ever the injuries to its own citizens, of which the matter of the Prussian State Bonds was only a specimen. When Germany was rehabilitated, whether as the result of another war or the result of some more pacific reversal of the outrages to which she had been forced to submit, the whole question of the revaluation of all those dead securities would have to be taken up.

In moments of great gloom, these prospects of his rehabilitation seemed remote enough to Oskar. But they were not remote enough to prevent him being temporarily convenienced by a woman against whom all that could be said was that she was Jewish and, in her blood, common as dirt. But she was not the first Jewess he had had an affair with. Consciously blonde and Nordic as he was, he had not disdained to spend a night with a negress, and he had been quite sober. And Elsie was not merely the most attractive Jewess, she was the most attractive woman, he had ever met. He thought of his thin wraith of a high-born Austrian wife, who had been puffed out like a candle by the effort of bringing a child into the world, and had gone off taking the child with her. These Jewish women, these creatures risen from the dregs of society, had guts, anyhow. Yes, Elsie was attractive, full of guts, intelligent. And there was no denying it was pleasant to have money—far more money than you had ever had, in the family's palmiest days.

No, Elsie did not delude herself into believing that Oskar was in love with her. She had had quite as much as is good for any woman of men who were in love with her. Bobby in his own person was a whole regiment of men in love. She was in love with Oskar, as she had been for a long time before she met him ; that was good enough for *her*.

" I wonder," she speculated, " if it is more important for a woman to love than to be loved ? " Then she made a thoroughly American gesture of dismissal with her left hand. " Aw, punk ! " she decided. " There isn't any such thing as rules for men or women. You've only got to go to Berlin to wonder if there's any such thing as men or women at all. Some of us are made this way, and some of us are made that way. But that's only the beginning of it, not the end of it. Sometimes with Oskar I feel like a great husky guardsman, sometimes I feel like a teeny-weeny chorus girl, all chocolate-box and fluff. It's enough to drive a girl crazy ! "

But she liked being driven crazy. She had never been within a thousand miles of being so happy in all her life before. Her step was as light and airy as a bird on a twig. Her skin glowed like a wild rose on a day when there is wind and sun and rain. Her eyes were like spring-water. " Gee, I feel good ! " she said.

Then there was this idiotic element of the irrational, the super-rational, which was never out of her consciousness in her relations with him. She had seen him those three times, plain as a pikestaff, and not quite so plain a few odd times in between. She inquired a little plaintively if he was quite quite certain he had never seen her in that same way. He didn't want to be quite quite emphatic for fear it was bad manners, but he hadn't—he admitted it with decorous regret—he hadn't seen her in any vision. " And that's as it's bound to be," she said to herself. " For, after all, it's me that's in love with him, it's me that's been looking for him all this time. If I hadn't turned up, he'd just have gone all to seed, I suppose, in the *Regenbogen Diele*."

She had a sudden horrifying vision of what might have become of him, going all to seed in the *Diele*, more and more abandoned to the elements in him which she was cunningly anæsthetising, and killing off. She threw herself at him, launching herself upon his knees. She threw her arms around his shoulder. " Kiss me ! " she moaned with all that she could assume of weak and defenceless and chorus girl. She saw the big grand man in him rise like a trout to her manœuvre. " You funny little thing ! " he said. " What odd moods you have ! "

He never hinted for a single moment that he disbelieved her clairvoyance of him. On the contrary, he betook himself to explaining it as a thoroughly attested phenomenon, only a little supernormal. He made a small speech about wireless, too, the speech which is always made when minds slightly sceptical by nature discuss phenomena outside our usual faculties. He bought books by Flammarion and Schrenck-Notzing and others, and talked them over with her gravely. But she did not like it that way at all. It was her little bit of religion, her little mystical ewe-lamb. " Put those books away ! " she said. " Nasty old men ! I know what *they're* up to ! "

Previous to the discovery of Oskar, Elsie had had it in her mind more than once to do something for Bobby in the matter of a divorce. She knew he was too much of a perfect gentleman to take the initiative, unless he fell more desperately in love with another woman than he had ever been with her. That was unlikely, she knew. And besides, he probably wasn't quite so irresistible now as he used to be, though you never could tell what a woman would do for money. Yes, she thought once or twice of doing something about a divorce. Poor Bobby ; apart from anything else, a man like that needs somebody more than a housekeeper to run a house for him.

But the appearance of Oskar made the matter of a divorce from Bobby more hazy, not less hazy. There was no point, as far as Oskar was concerned, in being a " free " woman again. Their relationship was one to which the whole idea of marriage was irrelevant ; you might even call it silly. So it stood like that.

But Frau Krantz's double-bed was not quite good enough. Nor was the apartment on the Schöneberger Ufer. They moved to a much more sumptuous apartment not far away on the Tiergartenstrasse, which had all the spaciousness of the old Berlin houses, and plumbing as modern as anything in Grünewald.

They liked the Tiergarten, too. When they came in late at night they often went out walking among the sparse trees and by the borders of the thin channels that thread those sandy levels. They heard whispers, and moanings, and hushings. They saw the shadows of couples most strangely assorted : and they themselves were queerly perturbed and thrilled by it all, and squeezed each other's hands, and pressed their mouths together, as if they, too, were lovers who had nowhere else to go but the Tiergarten to conduct their love-making, or were afraid that any eye at all might witness it.

They duly acquired the large pale-green motor-car, a Rolls-Royce. And before the summer of 1923 they had rented a villa on the Schwanneneck, a wooded peninsula just beyond Wannsee, where the mob came and bathed on the warm sands. Here again they savoured the pleasure of being able to immerse themselves at a moment's notice among the mob, who exerted on them both a potent and recurring fascination ; and yet, a moment later, they could just as easily detach themselves and repair to their own grand villa, their own flower-girt terraces, their private beach, their sail-boat, their canoe ; they could go out on the slightly steaming water brushed by hanging willows, to sing, to talk, to be silent, in the expensive crystal isolation of their world, a world in which flesh was not only flesh but all the two lovers exercised of mind and spirit.

Oskar duly went to see his brother up in Kalmin near Stralsund, on the Mecklenburg estate of their family. He insisted with admirable courtesy that Elsie should come

with him too, all the more as he went up to arrange to spend
a good deal of Elsie's money on reconditioning the house and
bringing the farms up to date. But with tact equally admirable Elsie thought it would be better if, for the time being,
he arranged these matters himself with his brother. Later, it
was agreed, when things settled down, later . . .

He did not do as much hunting, either, as he had hoped.
He was invited to hunt the elk on one occasion, from an
estate in the north of East Prussia. He went, but he did not
like some of the people he met. He suspected that American
or Jewish money was involved somewhere, and thought that
deplorable. A friend also invited him to hunt the stag in
Bavaria, and there he had a much better time. He insisted
that Elsie must accompany him when next he was invited ;
his friend had travelled a great deal, he was a person of
understanding. Elsie smiled. She thought a stag would be
rather a handful. Her husband's mother had tried to famil-
iarise her with the fox, and that was more than she could
rise to. She did actually accompany him when he went
shooting wild duck in the Prussian marshes. They had a
jolly time in an old inn, bristling with antlers, ghostly with
stuffed birds with wings spread to fly. But it was even jollier
when they came back to the Tiergartenstrasse.

It was as if he were propitiating some ancestral godling,
when he went off with guns or rods or whatever it might
be, to go and be a country gentleman as his father had been
before him. He returned with quite a naïve relief from these
excursions to his black marble bath, his pale-green car, his
adroit warm mistress. Something of the quality had gone
out of him which had maintained itself in grimness and
silence among his forbears for many generations. Several
factors were responsible, in degrees which it would not be
easy to apportion—the compositeness of his sexual nature,
the hardships he had endured as a soldier and a prisoner, the
corrosion of his character through the inflation and the
poverty it entailed for him ; and, not least, his mistress.

His mistress was a creature of the town, the very

distillation of urbanism. She had endured Cap Ferrat because the whole of that sea-board between Monte Carlo and Cannes is the most luxurious of towns, and the very sea there puts on the aspect of a *super-de-luxe* swimming-bath. And when the sea, as it has a habit of doing even on the *Côte d'Azur*, shook itself, and got angry, and there was a fire in its eyes and a hissing in its beard—then Elsie got rather cross with it, and pulled the blinds down, and asked there should be several times as much fillet-steak for dinner that night.

So that, in Berlin together, they were extremely happy. Each had exactly everything he wanted, or, if it lacked, it could be bought in a minute or two round the corner.

Besides, gentleman that he was, Oskar was not content to sit eating porridge all day long with a golden spoon. The whole air of Berlin was full of the ticking of tape-machines and the making of money. It was felt that surely the inflation could not go on quite for ever. Therefore the tape-machines ticked more and frenziedly, so that more money and more money might be made, as much money as might be squeezed out of this misery and terror, until the good game was at last put an end to.

Everybody was at the game of money-making, from who knew what grave reverend senior in the seat of government to the very tramps on the benches of the Tiergarten, the *Bauernfänger*—the peasant-capturers, who played écarté for each other's benefit, and the three-card-trick for the benefit of the country noodle. Everybody was making money, why not Oskar von Straupitz-Kalmin?

So Elsie smilingly let Oskar have his little flutters, too. She displayed great excitement when he made something, saying that now she would be able to afford that lovely little parasol; and, when he went down, she said, " Better luck next time," even more cheerfully.

She liked the days when he came back from being one of the world's workers. He played a charming game of being a tired business-man ; and, indeed, it took very little in the way of even a suggestion of straightforward work to reduce him to limpness. On an aristocrat of his lineage, Elsie wickedly thought, the addressing of an envelope was a quite unjustifiable strain. She would kneel at his feet while he leaned back in a comfortable armchair, with his eyes half-closed, and take off his shoes and socks and freshen his insteps with a kiss, then fit on for him his lambs'-wool slippers. Then she would take off all his clothes for him, for she developed an extraordinary technique in removing them without making him budge more than half an inch. And she would encase him in one of his exquisite dressing-gowns, and get into one of her own, and sit at his feet, and look up into his eyes, adoring, adoring, with an adoration that retained always a bitter-almond flavour of comic irony which preserved it from cloying upon either of them.

They then became Hero and Leander, or Tristan and Isolde, or whatever rather patent pair of lovers their not extensive researches into world literature provided for their imaginations. But their favourite tableau was Othello and Desdemona ; she got an especial thrill out of converting her blue-eyed, till-recently gold-haired Prussian blond into a thick-lipped blackamoor. And, with a bottle of cherry-brandy on the small table at their side, he would proceed, in these moods, to tell tales of his soldiering, hardly less strange than Othello's disastrous chances, his moving accidents by flood and field. Their experiences were so far parallel that he, too, had something to say of his being taken by the insolent foe. He told her of the moment when he heard the Russians' fierce hurrahs. They had broken through on his left flank. The brown barbarians were sixty yards away. He swung the surviving gun upon them. There was still half a drum of ammunition left. The Russians were twenty yards away. The drum jammed.

> *But still the house affairs would draw her hence ;*
> *Which ever as she could with haste despatch,*
> *She'd come again, and with a greedy ear*
> *Devour up my discourse.*

He had, in fact, asked for some salted almonds, or a cigar ; and she went over to the sideboard, and brought them to him, and sat down at his feet again.

A minute or two later the enemy had them. A vast Russian was roaring at him as he drove him forward, poking his back with his bayonet. He wondered what might be the purport of the roaring, for he was already disarmed. He suddenly realised that his torch hung from a clip in his belt. The Russian thought it was a hand-grenade. He smiled, and the fellow had knocked him senseless with his rifle-butt.

He told her tales of the fighting in France, which had been deadlier, though he had come through it scatheless. His mind leapt forward to Siberia and half-way across a continent again to his efforts to rejoin the German front lines in the region beyond Minsk, after he had escaped from his prison-camp. He told her how he crawled, through mists, over frozen marches, expecting each moment to hear the ice crack beneath him, and feel the wire-like weeds wind themselves about his throat.

But she was always aware that there was a certain experience among the infinite diversity of his war-time experiences from which his mind shied away like an animal from a smell which forebodes catastrophe. She divined that this had taken place some time during his escape from Siberia ; she had a sense that it was somehow related to the brown patch of shrivelled flesh on the right side of his mouth. But she had questioned him on that matter once. She did not do so again.

Yes, he had been a good soldier, and had had adventures pitiful, wondrous pitiful. He had been a better soldier than he was now a business-man, or even a country gentleman for that matter. She filled his glass again, and got him another cigar, for the first had gone out. She pressed her cheek up against his calf, for he was the vision made manifest, the fine gold hair that was not now so golden, the blue eyes, the mouth, the scar, the scars. She worshipped the place he lay down in, and the ground he walked on. " My lovely

blond beast ! " she murmured, and got up from her stool
and bit his lip until it bled.

She had quite early given up singing at the *Kabarett der
Tsigeuner*, for she saw how much he disliked those acidulated
gipsies. They made him unhappy and bitter, to a degree
which might have produced a suspicion that they induced in
him a doubtfulness of himself, that they reproached him,
and he had no reply to their reproaches. He thought them
inferior, Jews, intellectuals. They seemed to unsteady his
standards, as if, for a hideous second, they convinced him
that he, Oskar von Straupitz-Kalmin, was inferior to those
Cohens and Levys, those sweepings from the gutters of the
Grenadierstrasse Jew-slum. Yes, it was clear he disliked them.
She gave them up. She wasn't going to entertain any longer.
She was going to be entertained.

The *Tsigeuner* smiled knowingly at each other, for naturally they learned quickly enough all there was to learn about
the *Graf* and the *Judin*. They tapped the sides of their slightly
aquiline noses. " The Jewish money smells good enough,
anyhow ! " they said. It provided them with the material
for a couple of songs, and quite a number of impromptus,
rehearsed and genuine.

" *I* should worry ! " said Elsie Silver, when she heard
about it.

" *Sau-Juden !* " scowled Oskar von Straupitz-Kalmin, with
a face as black as thunder.

They went about a good deal to the theatres and cinemas,
which were very brilliant at that time in Berlin, though
Oskar would have been much happier if there had been
less Jew about it all. They saw Liedke, Bassermann,
Massari, Eckersberg play ; they heard Schwarz sing ; he
writhed over the plays of Kaiser and Hasenclever, she
wriggled with pleasure at the female box-fights. They ate

and drank a great deal. Elsie was delighted to find that Oskar was as enthusiastic about eating and drinking as she herself was, and, like her, believed in quantity at least as much as quality. They danced. They danced so perfectly together that it was as much a pleasure for other people as for themselves. They danced in almost every place in Berlin where it was possible to dance, from the most elegant night-club, to the toughest little *Kneipe* on the Alexanderplatz, where you jigged about to an automatic piano. He had an urge towards places of a low kind, an urge to which she was herself no stranger, and she did not think it wise to curb it. She was not familiar with the phrase ; he doubtless was, and would strongly have repudiated its application to himself ; but there was in them both a marked *nostalgie de la boue*.

It was on an occasion when this nostalgia had led them to a fierce little drinking- and dancing-place near the Hallesches Tor that he displayed a characteristic which gave her, for once, a little displeasure. A quarrel arose among a group of three men, two large and one much smaller. The small man had said something which the larger men did not like. They liked it so little that they started hitting him. The small man tried to hit back, but found it useless, so he tried to get away. He was not allowed to. A fourth man joined the group and cut off the small man's retreat. Then the fourth man added his blows to the blows of the two first large men. In a minute or two, six or seven men were beating the small man so violently that at length he slid senseless and bleeding to the floor.

The host did nothing. The other men in the place did nothing. Oskar von Straupitz-Kalmin did nothing. The women jeered or screamed. Elsie Silver pulled at her lover's arm. " For God's sake, Oskar, why doesn't somebody do something about it ? "

" Don't be silly, my child ! " he said.

She looked on, miserably, for a moment or two. Then again she plucked at his arm.

" Oskar, I say ! Can't *you* go in and separate them ? "

" Really, Elsie ! He's only getting what he deserves ! "

" Oh, I'm sure, I'm sure ! But it's not fair ! So many against one, and him half their size ! "

" It'll teach him not to attack somebody stronger than himself ! "

" He didn't ! *They* started ! "

" Perhaps they did. Our people are like that. If something gets up against us, we've got to get it out of the way ! "

" But it's not playing the *game* ! Oh, do let's get out of it, then ! "

But he was quite enjoying the spectacle. He did not move. " Playing the game ! " he laughed. " I'm surprised at you ! English sentimentality ! "

" Bobby would have done something about it ages ago," she grumbled, " even if they'd have kicked his face in ! "

" I'm not interested in the way your husband would have behaved. If he'd have interfered, he'd have deserved all he got ! "

" Do you think you've had enough now ? " she asked wretchedly. By now the man lay bleeding under the table.

" All right, Elsie ! Come along ! But do understand one thing, please ! I am as I am. If you want me, you've got to take me as you find me. I won't try and alter myself into being and behaving like somebody else ! " He spoke with a bluntness quite unusual with him. She realised, even at that moment, while her cheeks were hot with indignation, how pleasant it was to be talked to by him in that way. She felt she would have liked more vicious handling.

" All right, Oskar," she said humbly. " I didn't mean to say anything to upset you, you know ! "

He changed the subject. " Shall we go on to the *Regenbogen Diele* to-night ? " They both contemplated the idea for a moment. " No, not to-night ! It wouldn't be quite right, somehow. No ! What about the Rokoko Tanzpalast ? Then we needn't go and change ! "

The Rokoko had it. It was not till a month or six weeks later they paid a visit to the *Regenbogen Diele*. It was Oskar again who proposed it. He quite liked returning there, every three months or so, not more frequently. She herself could have done without it fairly well. But she was far too sensible to make the place really irresistible to him by suggesting they should keep away from it.

So they went along duly to the *Regenbogen Diele*, one night in September. It was well after midnight when they got there. And the first person Elsie set eyes on when they entered was a person she had last seen in very different company, among politicians and Russian notables and merchant-princes, to whom he had been host in his princely house in London. There was only one other person in all the world whose appearance there, in the *Regenbogen Diele*, would have surprised her as much. That was Boris Polednik, the husband of another of her sisters. But there was a sense in which wherever Smirnof or Polednik went, Polednik or Smirnof was not far away.

CHAPTER XVII

SMIRNOF IN BERLIN

I

" What are you standing there for ? " asked Oskar, as Elsie stood just on the inner side of the padded leather portière of the *Regenbogen Diele* with her eyes starting out of her head. " Who are you looking at ? "

" It can't be ! " said Elsie. She blinked, and shook her head sharply.

" Who ? What ? "

" My brother-in-law, Smirnof ! " she said.

" You're mad ! "

" Of course I am ! But it's fantastic ! It's the very image of him ! "

" Who do you mean ? " He had been trying to determine who it was that could possibly be causing the excitement, but had failed so far.

" There ! At that table ! Do you see ? He's sitting alone there with his head between his hands ! But it *is* Smirnof ! "

Then he saw whom she meant. He had almost literally been looking through him, towards a table where a young couple were sitting whose clothes and colouring were so vivid that they might have made many a person more definite in outline and colour look shadowy. She was talking of a man in a sober dark suit, his shoulders round, his head round, with a faint blur of reddish hair above the ears and the temples. He had the air of one who preferred to draw no attention to himself, and even had the capacity not to draw attention to himself if he chose to exercise it.

" If it is," he said, " then go and speak to him."

" But it can't be, of course ! It's ridiculous ! In *this* place !

Anyhow, shall we go and sit down at the next table? It's empty!" They went and sat down, he with his back to the stranger, she looking towards him. She looked flushed and embarrassed. "I've never seen anything like it in the world. They're the spit of each other!"

"Every man has his double!" he said sententiously. "And every woman! Except you!" he added, with a touch of gallantry she made no effort to acknowledge.

The waiter came. Oskar ordered their *Regenbogen* refreshment *par excellence*—two glasses of cherry-brandy. The man at the next table did not lift his head from between his hands. He stared down on the table below him, where a glass of wine, untasted, stood beside an ice-basket from which the slim neck of a Moselle bottle extended.

"This place is queer," she murmured. "A place where you see people in the flesh you've seen in visions, and visions of people——" The words faltered on her lips. She had not removed her eyes from the man opposite to her since she sat down. As she spoke, the man gradually lifted his head from the cup of his hands. His eyes fell upon hers. Gradually recognition dawned in his, as certainty established itself in hers.

He removed his hands from his chin and spread them out. "Elsie!" he said. He rose and came over to the table. He bowed first scrupulously to the man who was her escort. The man got up, clicked his heels together, and bowed back. It was a meeting of two kindred spirits, moulded from a similar plasm, though one on his journey had remained a nobleman and become a gigolo, and the other had successively become a tailor's clerk and a merchant prince.

"What on *earth*——" cried Elsie.

"I'm delighted! How charming! There's no one in the world who could have given me greater pleasure!"

"Let me introduce—this is my brother-in-law, Mr. Smirnof. I've told you about him, often. This is my friend, Oskar von Straupitz-Kalmin."

The two men bowed to each other ceremoniously. Then,

with real warmth, they shook hands. They liked each other instinctively ; the sort of manners each had, the way in which each had risen to what was, in one way or another, a slightly embarrassing situation—the way of a gentleman, in fact.

" Come and sit down, Sasha, won't you ! " The waiter had come up by this time. He looked from table to table inquiringly. Yes, he was to bring over the honoured guest's wine.

" Thanks very much, indeed ! It's awfully kind of you, Elsie. If you're quite sure I don't——"

Oskar smiled at him. His eyes looked their bluest and frankest. Smirnof smiled back, and inclined his head in acknowledgment of Oskar's courtesy.

" If I'd have had any idea where you lived in Berlin——" said Smirnof. " Can you doubt it ?—I'd have asked could I come to see you." There was the faintest air of a remark made for a remark's sake in his tone and the words he uttered. For, after all, this wasn't a meeting in the sense that it would have been a meeting if they had come up against each other in the Adlon or the Esplanade Bar.

" That's completely my fault," said Elsie. " As a matter of fact, I made it quite clear to father that whoever asked for my address—— Of course, had I had any idea in the world you might be coming along——"

" And I might have insisted, too. All I knew was, you were in Berlin. And that you'd been heard—on the concert-platform."

Oskar thought it exquisite of him to put it like that. Singing in that *verfluchte Kabarett*, among that gang of Jews !

" Oh, I gave that up some time ago. He didn't like it." She indicated Oskar smilingly. It was about time she involved Oskar a little more explicitly in the situation.

" She has a most delightful voice," explained Oskar. " I didn't like her to throw it away like that."

" I quite see," said Smirnof.

There was an infinitesimal pause. The pauses would be

longer and quite frequent unless they got down to this odd matter of their meeting in this odd place. It was abundantly clear that it could be no matter of embarrassment to him, the husband of Sarah, the father of—how many children would it be now? And the *Regenbogen Diele* had become more and more of a show place the last few months—on the regular tourist round, like the Kaiserfriedrich Museum.

She plunged boldly at it. That was the only way to tackle it. "To see *you* here, Sasha! I've never heard of such a thing! How many children is it, God bless their little hearts? And you might let me know how my sister Sarah is!"

"Mother and children all doing fine!" he said, smiling. "Seven, to be exact. I think you all have a tendency to exaggerate."

"Come," she objected, "that's not bad, after all, for how many years is it—ten? Anyhow, don't shirk the other little matter! What are you doing in a place like this?"

"Please don't distress yourself. I don't intend to throw Sarah over and run away with a chorus-boy."

"There's never any telling," she said severely, "when men get to your age."

"I heard about the place. And I was feeling bored. So I thought I'd look in. It made me much more bored than I had been, and very depressed, too."

"So we noticed, Sasha."

"Yes, I can quite believe it."

"But you were such a nib on music! Sarah told me in London that all you do when you get a stomach-ache or a headache from counting up your money—you say hey, presto! and in marches Cortot or Ysaye or Pachmann with his Ten Thousand Pound Organ. And there you are! Pop go the wrinkles!"

"Well, if not Cortot in person, then a Cortot record. I went to hear Cortot this very evening. It's the first time I've been out since I came to Berlin, the first time I got back from the office before ten-thirty. I simply felt I must throw everything up and go and hear Cortot. Odd you should mention his name, isn't it? He was playing Brahms this evening at the Philharmonie. Cortot and Brahms—it's a combination I've never been able to resist till to-night—this very night. The Concerto in D minor—I'd make a special journey from Biarritz to Madrid to hear him play it. I think I did once, actually. And the Intermezzo in E flat minor. You remember it?"

"Well, as a matter of fact, Oskar and I aren't exactly high-brow in music," she explained politely.

"Oh, of course, of course not!" he said at once. "Forgive me. I didn't want to bore you."

"Please go on with what you were saying."

"Well, the Intermezzo. The serenity of it, the intimacy of it. And to-night I walked out. In the middle of it. *Me!* I'm afraid I can't quite explain to you how odd that is."

"And were you eating chocolate in crinkled paper all the way through? And did you tread on everybody's legs as you went out in the middle of it? But what on earth was wrong? Were you sick?" she asked, with quick common sense.

"Well, not exactly!" he said.

"Look here, aren't you well?"

"I'm perfectly well, Elsie. Don't start sending any scare letters to Sarah. I just wanted to explain how I happened to be here."

"But please——" protested Oskar, to suggest there was really no reason in the world why he should.

Smirnof smiled. "It is the last place in all Berlin where I should have expected to find you and Elsie." Oskar appreciated the effortless delicacy with which he coupled their names, his urbane acceptance of the *status quo*.

"We like it," said Elsie vigorously. "At least, we sometimes do. And, anyhow, he and I met here."

"*Voilà!*" said Smirnof, as if to indicate that the place could not possibly need any other justification. "I've heard about it several times, but, frankly, my curiosity was never roused. Then to-day my under-manager, Brauner, had a quarrel with an office-boy. I confess I'd never looked at the

young man ; one merely knows one's office-boy is there.
They had forgotten to close the door in their room, and the
door into my room happened to be open. So I heard what
happened. ' *Puppenjunge !* ' shrieked Brauner. ' Get back to
the *Regenbogen Diele* ! You think I don't know where you
got that gold cigarette-case from ? ' I'd best not repeat what
the boy answered back. I really couldn't have that in my
office. Schmidt, my manager, is very good at figures, but
useless in a situation like this. I got on the scene before Heigus
—that's the office-boy—had finished his speech. He really
looked like a very pretty little actress in a temper, with his
clustering gold curls and his eyes streaming with anger. The
next moment he landed his fist out like a champion boxer
straight on the point of Brauner's jaw, and Brauner just
slipped to the ground. Knock-out. The picture stuck in my
mind all day—the little choir-boy with a fist like the kick of
a horse. ' So that's the sort of person they turn out in the
Regenbogen Diele, that's the sort of thing that goes on ! '
I said to myself, as I gave my orders and signed my
letters."

" It isn't ! " said Elsie firmly. " You've come to the wrong
shop. There's a place Oskar could take you to near the
Hallesches Tor——"

" Please don't misunderstand. I'm not after that sort of
thing. You can get something like it in London, if you want
to. But it's so strange, it's so upsetting, this Berlin atmosphere. Everything is standing on its head."

" Yes," agreed Oskar, with something of grief in his voice,
and a sense of strain almost too great to bear.

" I got tired while Cortot was playing the Intermezzo in
E flat minor. Not tired ; *bored*. I've said already, I can't
hope to explain to you how odd that is."

" That's all right," Elsie assured him. " I saw you that
night at your house when Suggia was playing. I noticed you
weren't doing noughts-and-crosses with yourself on the
programme."

" When *was* that ? " he inquired, as if the specific date

were of some importance. " It was the spring of last year, wasn't it ? A lot has happened since then."

" That's quite true," she said, smiling into Oskar's eyes and lifting her glass to him. He repeated both compliments.

Smirnof seemed anxious to have it quite clear about Cortot and Brahms. " Now and again lately my mind's been unable to grip what was being said—in a piece of music, I mean. That's being tired. That can happen to anybody. But to-night I was *bored*, impatient. I had to get out. I wandered about the streets for hours, and then I remembered the little incident in my office to-day. I felt if I saw something strange and violent—it might make me feel a little better ; send me off to sleep, perhaps. So I came here."

" Strange, but *not* violent ! " Elsie pointed out.

" Quite right," said Smirnof. " I ordered a bottle of wine hopefully, and one or two odd people came and offered to drink it with me. I called the waiter and tipped him, and said my table was to be left empty. And then—and then——"
He looked up suddenly at Oskar and his face broke into an uneasy smile. " I really must apologise to you, Herr—Herr Graf. Am I right ? " He turned for help to Elsie.

" You know I wouldn't be satisfied with anything short of a Herr Graf," she said, smiling. " The last man I was matey with was the same way inclined, too."

Both men smiled. Smirnof continued : " I'm not in the habit of opening out like this. Forgive me. You'll be saying to yourself : ' How these ex-Russians *do* talk ! ' "

" Ex-Russians ? " asked Oskar quickly. " Of course, you left quite a long time before the War. I stayed on after it ! "

" What ? You were a prisoner ? "

" Yes, I was in the hands of the Bolsheviks till early in 1919."

" You did not like them ? "

" I did not like them."

The words were few and simple, but they immediately established between the two men a further bond, a bond more strict by far than the easy sense each had of the other that he was a man of race. They were bound together by a hatred more violent in each of them than the love of anything they loved.

" They are vermin ! " said Smirnof.

" I suppose it s much worse for you," said Oskar. " You lost—I suppose you lost a good deal ? "

" It was not money I lost. I owe to England, and even more to Elsie's father, whatever money has come my way."

" I'll tell father you're so nice about him," said Elsie, with an effort at lightness. The conversation was getting rather tense. It was always like that when that wretched Russia hove up over the horizon. It put Oskar off his food for days.

" It was more than money I lost in Russia," Smirnof went on.

" Oh—oh ! " said Elsie wickedly, but with a glum feeling it was getting her nowhere. " It'll be Sarah for the next letter—all full of revelations."

Neither of the men seemed to be aware of her ; or, if they were, only in the sense that a person of breeding is aware of the *gaucherie* of a person of none.

" I'm sorry," said Oskar quietly. He had no idea at all what Smirnof might mean, but he knew it was a profound grief, and one he spoke of but rarely, if ever at all. He waited. Smirnof did not continue. He knew it would be right at this juncture to deflect the conversation towards his own resentments, based on less desperate experience though it might be.

" I was in a filthy camp in Siberia for over two years. The Red soldiers found out about my family. They made me pay dearly for it."

" You escaped, you say ? "

" Yes."

" When ? "

" Early in 1919."

" I was in Russia at that time. A long way from you, of course. Did you come down by way of the Black Sea or across to Vladivostok ? "

" No, I went straight across Russia by way of Moscow to Minsk. I wanted to rejoin the German front."

" Of course, how stupid of me. It's a slight satisfaction, I know, in view of what's happened since, but early in 1919 I was in the South of Russia trying to do what I could. For us all, of course. We are together against them, aren't we, however we were placed in the recent War—English, German, French, Americans—and, of course, those of the true Russians who have survived ? "

" Yes. They're the enemy of us all. Where were you exactly ? It would be about the time I was making for Ekaterinburg and Moscow."

" I was at Taganrog, on the Sea of Azov. I was helping Denikin with his ordnance and commissariat."

" A pity it all fell through. If we Germans had been brought in, perhaps——"

" I think that's where we went wrong. We should have pooled our resources. Even so, we just didn't go far enough. You know the English proverb—spoiling the ship for a ha'porth of tar ? Churchill agrees with me. Lloyd George went so far as to announce at the Guildhall—rather indiscreetly, I think—that Great Britain had spent one hundred million pounds on the suppression of the Bolshevik horror. That was in November 1919. If we'd have spent another ten millions, fifteen at most——"

" Oh, crikey ! " Elsie burst in. She felt this was becoming the wrong sort of party altogether. The two men looked very bitter and very serious. It was not her idea of a night out. " The moment anybody brings up the name Lloyd George, I say it's time to put up the shutters. Do you hear, both of you ? "

Both men bowed, a little stiffly. They resented her breaking into a conversation which obviously was of such profound interest to both of them. But she was, after all, their hostess as it were. It wasn't easy to go on after so decided an expression of opinion. There was no doubt they would be able to continue the conversation under more favourable auspices.

" I'm sorry," they both said.

" That's a nice pair of little boys ! " she approved. " Can't you guess how excited I am to learn you've got an office here, Sasha ? You have, haven't you ? "

" I have."

" You might have let me know," she reproached him.

" My dear," he objected. " All we all knew was that you came to see us out of the blue that night ; and then you went to May for a few days—and after that, phew ! you'd gone. We tried to get your address from May, but she knew as little as we did. And your father and mother were dreadfully disappointed not to see you."

" Well, as a matter of fact," she said blandly, " my spies told me that Bobby was up and after me. And I simply wasn't going to have any scenes with Bobby. It took me a long time to make up my mind to leave him—three minutes, to be exact, in that dentist's waiting-room—and I simply wasn't going to have him making cow's eyes all over me again. I'm only a weak little woman. So I quit."

" We gathered it must have been something like that. But you can't reproach me for not letting you know I've opened up an office in Berlin."

" Where ? When ? "

" Not so very long ago—about the middle of last month, in fact. You see, I'm a financier." Then he turned to Oskar. " I hope you won't mind what I'm going to say now."

" Please."

" It's the business of a financier to make money where it is to be made. I'd already gathered early in the year what great returns might be expected in the stock market here for a slight outlay of capital. And on a much bigger scale, too, than during the earlier period of the inflation."

His apology for coming along to Berlin to profit out of the inflation won Oskar's heart. He was perhaps the only speculator among them all who had had the delicacy to utter a word of that nature. " I am a speculator myself, in a small way," Oskar pointed out, to put Smirnof quite at his ease.

" You'll have to take him on instead of the other little office-boy ! " Elsie laughingly suggested. Oskar was annoyed. He was afraid there might be a core of seriousness in Elsie's idea ; that she might want to push him for an hour or two a day into Smirnof's organisation because Smirnof was her brother-in-law. The thought embarrassed him. He knew it would embarrass Smirnof. He also disliked the thought of working anywhere regularly, for an hour or two a day.

" Now, Elsie, please don't be silly ! I'd be as much use in a regular office as an ape."

" Let's say a Borzoi. You'd look very decorative."

" As a matter of fact," said Smirnof, " it might be quite useful for us both . . . Oh, no ; oh, no ! I refuse to discuss a matter of business on our first meeting like this. I apologise ! "

" There you are, Elsie, it's all your fault ! " Oskar exclaimed.

" Go on, Sasha, go on ! " she ordered eagerly.

" Shall I ? " Smirnof enquired of Oskar.

" She commands," Oskar said.

" If you will permit me now and again to put you on to a good thing——"

" That would be lovely ! " cried Elsie.

" And sometimes, when it would be useful to have the backing of an old and distinguished name——"

" There you are ! " Elsie reproached Oskar. " Didn't I tell you how invaluable you'd be ? "

" I'd be enchanted ! " said Oskar.

" Just a word or two now and again would be all I want, or a small note of introduction. I'd like to work alongside somebody," he explained frankly, " particularly in a new area. It was like that with Elsie's father. It still is, in fact. It's almost a constitutional matter. I'm afraid this all sounds monstrous. But I do know that if it would interest you to make a fairly decent sum of money now and again——"

" Our estates in Kalmin are in a bad way. If I could make some money, it would be for Kalmin's sake."

" I think, frankly, it's very easy. I, for instance, have to make some two hundred thousand pounds by the end of October."

Elsie whistled. Oskar remained quite impassive, but there was a glint in his eyes. This was *money*, on any basis of calculation.

" It sounds a lot," said Smirnof, " but it isn't more than a thousand pounds, in a sense. It happens to be that figure and not this. It hasn't any relation at all with money as a commodity one spends."

" I get you," said Elsie doubtfully.

" What I mean," said Smirnof, " is this : there are a certain number of dealings in one's personal life one has to make in terms of thousands, or more. One buys one's house, one buys a car, one lays down a tennis-lawn, one pays one's income-tax, one buys a yacht. But one doesn't go on again and again buying a house or laying down tennis-lawns, however rich one is. Money, as you know it yourself, as you spend it yourself, that sort of money operates on a very unambitious plane. I mean, when you are spending for the things you touch, eat, see, sit on—palpable expenditure."

" I suppose you're right," said Elsie.

Oskar said nothing. He had bought with money of his own no houses lately, laid down no tennis-lawns.

" I need not say," said Smirnof, " how completely confidential what I've been saying is." The remark was addressed to Elsie.

" I think you can trust me," she said quietly.

" I know. I know. I just wanted to let the Herr Graf realise that, with an instinct for these things, money is to be made on a small scale or a big scale. It will surprise you both with how few thousand pounds I started my business here. I say that to let you know, Herr Graf, if you should care to speculate, how little money is needed in the beginning. It must be *valuta*, of course."

" We've had our little flutters in sterling already," Elsie

pointed out. Smirnof would have to draw certain conclusions, sooner or later, regarding the present financial basis of Oskar's existence.

"My dear girl, just a few hundreds would do, or less than that. If we convert it into a good many thousands, as we shall, I know that what little I shall have done in the matter will be paid for in my association with your friend."

"That's a good speech," said Elsie.

"You're quite hopeless," Oskar smiled.

"It's a good game—money," said Smirnof, closing his eyes. "A good game," he repeated. There was a note of affectionate crooning in his voice. "It is the most beautiful thing that civilisation has created, the most subtle and intellectual ; more beautiful than music, more beautiful than women even." He opened his eyes. "Whatever happens in Russia, they'll have to fall back on money. A country can no more do without money than a man without food or drink."

Then suddenly he lashed out at her with a question—a question which, apparently, it had been as far from his intention to ask her as it had been for him to overthrow the table they were sitting at.

"I don't suppose you've come up against your other brother-in-law here in Berlin ? "

"Which one ? " She looked quite startled. The mere thought of this other person that had come into Smirnof's head had made his eye malignant and his face dead-pale.

"I hear there's quite a lot of going to and fro between Moscow and Berlin," he replied savagely. "Polednik, I mean ! Susan's husband ! "

"No ! " she said, "no ! " Then her eyes were held by an expression which had come into Smirnof's eyes. He had turned his gaze from Elsie to Oskar. What he saw dispelled any other expression from his eyes than one of extreme astonishment. His mouth sagged, and a faint dribble of saliva formed at the corners of it, so astonished he was by what he beheld in Oskar's face. She turned round to Oskar, her heart beating an alarm.

Oskar's hands were gripping the table so tight that he seemed as if he must break off its edge. His eyes were full of a hatred more vicious than she had ever seen in the eyes of any human being before. The brown patch that was spread over his tangled scars was red with the blood that had surged up to it from all parts of his body.

"Polednik!" he said, his lower jaw hardly moving, so that the effect was queerly ventriloquial. "You mean a small man, with a long thin nose, and pince-nez, and rat-coloured hair?" His questions were directed, not towards Elsie, but towards Smirnof.

"Yes!" Smirnof replied.

"He is a Commissar, isn't he—some sort of official—in Russia, among the Bolsheviks?"

"Yes!"

"He's your brother-in-law, too?"

"Yes. He is the creature I loathe most on all this round globe."

"And I!" said Straupitz-Kalmin.

"You met him?"

"I met him!" He lifted his fingers to the brown patch of flesh which blazed so red now, and stroked it with the tips as if the blood that had surged there made it ache intolerably. "This is his mark!" he said. "The mark of the Beast!"

Elsie looked on, small, and terrified, and shrivelled-looking. Her shoulders were humped together like an old woman's.

Very softly came the words out of Smirnof's mouth: "Will you say how it happened then?"

"Yes. I'll tell you." Oskar's lips were white and his mouth a thin line. "It was so monstrous I made up my mind I'd never speak about it to a living soul. I wanted it to be as if it hadn't happened. I've succeeded more or less; except sometimes at night. Nobody's master of himself at night, of his dreams.

" It happened on that journey I mentioned to you, when I escaped from the internment camp in Siberia, after two years of humiliation and filth and sickness and hunger. It was much worse after the Revolution. I saw a gang of drunken private soldiers go up to a couple of officers in the court-yard and tear off their shoulder-badges and slap their faces. The officers and the men both knew we German officers were looking on. That gave us some sort of idea of what was ahead of us ; but it was much worse than we feared.

" I made my plans to escape early in 1919. If it interests you, I'll tell you about the journey some other day. It's this I want to get to, this——" Again he touched the inflamed patch against his mouth with his finger-tips. " I've often tried to reckon up how many days and nights it was I travelled in the corridor of the train coming from Ekaterin-burg, till—till the thing happened I'm going to tell you about. What happened after that I've never been clear about at all. I can't make it more than six or seven days and nights. Perhaps it was only six. But it seemed like weeks and weeks. I had to squat on the floor most of the time. Can you imagine how my bones ached ?

" It got better at Vologda ; that's the Petrograd junction. I got a plate of hot soup, too. It cost three and a half roubles, I remember that quite clearly. That was quite a lot of money still, and I hadn't got much on me. They stole nearly every penny that my people sent out to me. But I'd have paid every penny I had for that hot soup. I've never eaten any-thing that tasted so good in my life. A woman got into the carriage, half way to Javoslavl. A stinking peasant got out just at the same time, so I made a quick move and saw she got the vacant place. It wasn't only because she was a woman. One had the instinct she was—she was somebody lost ; she belonged to the other order.

" I was right. Of course it took a long time before we really got talking. I knew how necessary it was to be careful, and so did she, poor wretch. She was about as tired as I was. She'd been out on the station platform waiting for our train for about twenty hours. There was a waiting-room, but it was crawling with vermin.

" At a certain station a big fellow came in to the compartment and mooched about. He had great hanging arms like an ape. Then he lay down in the narrow passage between the seats and went to sleep. It's only later I worked it all out. I didn't pay any especial attention to him then. My mind wasn't very active after that enormous journey, or I might have asked myself, even then, why he should choose that point in the compartment rather than any other to throw his ugly carcass in, and why the guard didn't shift him. He was very much in the way.

" He started yawning and retching when we drew in to the next station. Then we stopped, and he lurched off. I suppose it was then he joined his superior officer, somewhere else in the train. That was our friend, Mr. Smirnof. He must have described us ; probably he even pointed out which we were. When the train started again, a small man with a pointed nose and pince-nez was lounging about. He had got into the carriage by the lower door. The other fellow had disappeared through the door behind us. He could easily have come in again without our noticing him. In a little time the small one had squatted on the floor, just as the other had done. He seemed to go fast asleep in a minute or two.

" It sounds ridiculous to have been taken in like that. But probably a less skilful performance would have taken me in too. He's probably had a good deal of practice in that sort of thing. I haven't. He looked quite completely asleep. Then the woman and I went on talking again. I suppose we were both knocked silly by meeting somebody of our own kind. We talked Russian first, then I slipped into German, and was thrilled, ten minutes later, to realise we'd been speaking German for ten minutes. We talked French, too. I'm sure we didn't say anything compromising ; but you can see enough had happened to excite the gentleman's suspicions. I offered her some *Zwieback* I had over. I think, then, she brought out a little bottle of scent. She was charming. It must have been worth more than rubies to the poor woman, that scent, that pathetic hang-over from her old life. She sprinkled a few drops on a handkerchief and dabbed my forehead with it, very prettily.

"Then the gentleman got up. He pointed a revolver at me. I knew, of course, the game was up. I tried to bluff it for a little time, but quite without conviction. I had the passport of a released Galician prisoner, with a beautiful row of stamps. He seemed to know by its smell it was wrong. I'd been primed with the name of the village I'd come from, but he knew all there was to know about it—unless he was bluffing too. I handed over my passport and told him who I was. Then—then——"

He was quite unable to continue for some seconds ; his whole face darkened and twitched with anger.

" ' Liar ! ' he said to me." Again he paused, his mouth working. The others remained silent as images.

"He called me ' Liar ! ' " he repeated. His fingers twitched, as if now at this moment they burned to fasten themselves round the throat from which this ineffable insolence had issued. Thump-thump ! went the musician on the piano. The listless feet clapped up and down and round upon the dancing-floor. " *Aber bist ja verrückt !* " a squeaky male voice protested. " *Du alte Tante, Du !* "

" *Dreck !* " pronounced Oskar von Straupitz-Kalmin at length. It was as if he had come back from the contemplation of himself thrusting his hands forward to strangle that other man, and the decision that he would not defile them by contact with such ordure. His nostrils quivered with disgust as he smelt the foul body of Commissar Polednik.

"What followed was worse ! " he confirmed. "I at least was a man twice his size. He betook himself to the woman then. A couple of peasants were sitting opposite us. He turned them out and shoved his own filthy carcass there.

Several soldiers had come up round us by this time. Then
he got going on her. It was monstrous ! I have never seen
anything more infamous ! It was—— Pah ! what else could
one expect ?

" We drew up at a station a few minutes later. His ape-
man got up, and was ordered to take me off to the first carriage, so that he could get down in comfort to the job of
hounding the woman. The next thing that happened . . ."
He paused again. It was clear that, even now, in the flow
of his narrative, it was no easy matter to transfer into words
the intolerable memory. " The carriage I was in—the front
carriage, I think it was—quite suddenly burst into flames.
I don't know how it happened. The woodwork was as rotten
as an old beam, and a spark from the engine could have set
it alight quite easily. The whole carriage was blazing so
quickly that you might have thought it must have been
deliberately set alight ; though I can't see how anyone could
guarantee it should blaze like that, or what chance he'd
have of getting away. . . . The train stopped. I can't tell
you much more. People came running up from other parts
of the train. The ape-man and I stood together in that hell,
our clothes blazing. We both saw the small man at the same
moment. I saw his rat-like face very clearly in the glare of the
flames. Then suddenly my warder cried, ' *Tovarish* Polednik ! ' at the top of his voice. Each syllable came out loud
and distinct, and very terrible. So distinct, I've not forgotten
the name, and never will. He said something more—I
realised a moment later what. Polednik lifted his revolver
and shot him through the head.

" As for myself—the agony was so acute that I did not
know whether I was already dead. I was convinced, whether
I was dead or alive, that the man must shoot me too. It did
not occur to me he possibly could not. He looked at me for a
moment quite calmly ; then he turned away.

" The action of his turning away awakened something in
me which had not been burnt up. It was anger. It was an
anger more violent than the flames around me. I insisted

that I was still alive, and would not die. I thought I saw a
gap in the wall of the compartment. I hurled myself at it
with a strength which I should think to be normally beyond
the strength of ten men. I was free. I was free. As I rolled
down the embankment I was conscious of something burning—a piece of wood, perhaps, or a lump of metal, that
seemed to have became part of my cheek. It was eating
through to the teeth. I tore it away. I rolled down into a
deep drift of snow. Then, at last, I was dead, quite dead,
for some hours. You can't suffer such agony, I say, and not
be dead. I managed to crawl away before dawn. I was not
going to be taken by that man again. It was like an animal
that had been trapped crawling away, leaving behind it a
limb that it had gnawed through.

"What happened then . . . what happened then. . . ."
His voice was getting louder and louder, his eyes wilder.
He beat his forehead with his clenched fist.

"Oh, enough, enough!" wailed Elsie. "For God's sake
leave the rest over for another time! Have some brandy,
Oskar! *Herr Ober*, some brandy at once, a large glass!
At once, do you hear?" Oskar's head sagged sideways, then
he pulled it straight again sharply. The sweat coursed
steadily down his forehead. He smiled wanly. "The rest
hardly matters, I think! I'm afraid it's rather a long story,
Mr. Smirnof! Forgive me for getting so excited!"

"My poor dear fellow," said Smirnof, "how they have
made you suffer!" He leaned forward and patted the back
of Oskar's head with great gentleness. But, as he patted it,
his eyes became faint and remote again. "They'll suffer for
it in their turn!" he said.

"You've not touched your wine, Sasha!" Elsie pointed
out feebly. She felt that a diversion at this stage would be
advantageous. Smirnof pressed two finger-tips against the
glass. The pads, seen through the green-tinted glass, looked
like small toadstools. "It's warm!" he said, with distaste.

" I should think so," said Elsie querulously. She leaned over to the ice-bucket and swished the bottle through the water it contained. " Naturally. It's all melted. What would you expect ? Waiter ! " she called out. " Take this glass away and put some ice in this bucket ! "

Smirnof did not seem aware of the trouble she was taking on his account. His eyes were still fixed on Oskar's. " He tried to strangle me," he said, " the first time I set eyes on him ! "

" Where ? The little rat ! Where ? "

" It was in Silver's kitchen, the night I first met my wife. Were you there, Elsie ? "

" I damn well think I was ! I just don't see why you should have to bring all that up ! "

He replied to Elsie, but his eyes did not move from Oskar's face ! " I feel it as a sort of duty to the Herr Graf. We are both so completely of one mind."

" I think I am going to feel the better for it, Mr. Smirnof, for getting this off my chest to-night," said Oskar slowly. " I feel that you, too, you carry memories about with you. If you could bring yourself to speak of them, it might be wise for you, too."

" I should have asked your permission to do so, Herr Graf, if you hadn't yourself been so kind as to suggest it. I've spoken of these matters to quite literally no other human being. Not to my wife ; to no one."

Oskar inclined his head in acknowledgment.

" Oh, hell ! " said Elsie, a tear starting in her eye. She was unused to breathing an air so rarefied as this. She could not remember when she had been so wretched. " Look here, Sasha ! " she commanded, striving hard to recapture something of her devil-may-care authority. " If *you're* going to open up now, we're going to clear out of this first ! " She felt that the two men had transported her to a world where her warrant was invalid. She had been far indeed from being bored by Oskar's recital. But it had produced in her a sense of helplessness as unfamiliar as it was abhorrent. What comfort could she proffer, with mouth or money, to counteract the sting of memories like those?

Sasha looked inquiringly up at Oskar. Oskar again slightly inclined his head, this time in affirmation. " And I think you'll find," he said, as if continuing his so-far un-spoken reply, " that we have a Bernkasteler Doktor that is quite drinkable. If you don't mind, I would like to refresh myself, too, with a glass or two."

They rose. Nearly all the honoured guests had gone by now. The personnel had been clustered anxiously round the bar for some time, wondering when those distinguished ones would take it into their heads to go too. " *Gott sei dank!* " the waiters murmured piously when at length they left.

II

" My father was a Roman Catholic priest in a small town in White Russia," said Alexander Smirnof. " The name I bear is not the one I was born with, if you could say I was born with any name. His name was one of the oldest and most honoured on all the Polish marches. There were many soldiers and diplomats in our family. I have been able to indicate this satisfactorily in my dealings with Denikin and Kolchak and the other counter-revolutionary generals, and that has been helpful ; although, of course, they would not have rejected the assistance of one so pledged to their cause as I am, even if my father's blood had been quite humble.

" My father, like my uncles, was destined for the Army or diplomacy. But he was one of those men who feel in their boyhood they must turn their backs on personal ambition. He became, I say, a parish priest in a small town in White Russia, not far from Vitebsk. The people there were as wretched and backward as anywhere in Russia, and the need for men of God was nowhere greater. He was a man of high intellectual attainments, handsome, and warm-hearted. He was well thought of by the authorities, even though his social views were considered rather advanced. His theology, too, was probably a little unorthodox, but his superiors in his province were not quite so alert as elsewhere in Russia.

" In the house of the local doctor, which was a sort of *salon* for the intellectuals, he met a young woman. They were immediately attracted by each other, and, of course, they considered it a purely intellectual attraction. I will attempt to give no account of their love-story. There were other elements of tragedy in it beyond the fact that he was a Roman priest. She was a Jewess, as intelligent as he was, and with burning ideas for the improvement of humanity— genuine ideas, however mistaken and perverse. She was the daughter of the richest Jew in that countryside ; he had the licence for the cutting down of all the forests for many miles.

" She was, in fact, already bound hand and soul to a secret subversive society, as dangerous as it was ruthless. I am no authority on these theories, and I have not studied the history of these organisations, though my later work brought me into contact with them from another angle. But I think it safe to deduce that the present abomination in Russia has a great deal to be thankful for to that society and its affilia- tions ; however much, and however differently, it has since codified its ideas.

" My mother—for, of course, you will have gathered I am speaking of my mother—had already developed something of the terror which used to sweep over her quite uncon- trollably later (and for reasons you will appreciate) at the thought of this wicked society to which she was so deeply committed. It is possible she confided the whole matter to my father. Her fears must have been very poignant to him. He was, as I have said, somewhat unorthodox as a church- man. Her people were fairly emancipated, as Jews go in those intensely superstitious regions. But you can imagine the horror with which the news of their disappearance was received in every corner, the excommunications and the curses. I was born of a father and a mother on both of whom anathema so deadly was pronounced that I have sometimes thought it is impious for the offspring of such a mating to beget children of his own.

" They disappeared as completely as if an earthquake had swallowed them up, or a river drowned them. In fact it was popularly believed, by both the Jews and the Christians, that heaven, or hell, had wiped them out in direct response to the maledictions that had been pronounced against them.

" But that was not good enough for the revolutionaries my mother had abandoned. They may have been afraid that she would hand over to the authorities knowledge which would be dangerous to them. But, when nothing happened to them after a year or two, they must have been assured that nothing of that nature, at all events, was to be feared. It is likely they felt that this was a sort of test case. It must not be felt among their adherents, or among wavering novices, that vows could be taken and secrets shared, and that thereafter desertion could be undertaken with impunity.

" I was born in a small cottage between Ekaterinodar and the shore of the Sea of Azov. I was a lonely child, strangely compounded. I was given no opportunity to learn self-reliance, for I was not allowed to mix with the country children, and we had no dealings with the Kuban Kossack families. My father and mother divided my education between them, but it was a sketchy affair, for periods of great happiness and activity alternated with periods of indolence and misery. In languages and figures, however, I developed great proficiency at a very early age, and both have been invaluable in my later career.

" I was about thirteen or fourteen years old when the revolutionaries from the Vitebsk area at last hounded my mother down. The story I am telling you now I have pieced together from things remembered or overheard when I was a boy, and facts subsequently ascertained during my career as a police agent—a miserable one, as all my careers have been, till good fortune came to me far away, in Doomington ; though how long that will last, who can say ?

" I remember the atmosphere of terror that settled closer and closer round the house. I remember how my mother used to bar the doors and close the double windows, even in the stifling heat of summer, to keep the terror out. I remember my father's alternate rages and fits of utter black impotence. I believe they finally succeeded in carrying her off, with the threat that, if she did not return to them, they would kill both her husband and her son. I got up one night, to hear my father sobbing and shouting, to see him shaking his fists and tearing his hair. She had gone. She had gone back to them.

" For a time he was paralysed with misery. But in a month or two a plan began to form in his head. He carried me off to a grain-merchant he had had dealings with, in the small port of Mariupol—Krolenko was his name. I was put to work in Krolenko's office, for I had already shown some aptitude for figures, as I have said. In figures I found something un-mixed, absolute, where I could find shelter from the doubts and indecisions of my blood, from the indeterminateness of a world in which I was neither aristocrat nor peasant, neither boy nor man, a lonely little nobody in a world of suspense and dismay.

" My father's friend had a wife and two daughters, who were extremely kind to me. They were very sensitive mu-sicians, such as you would sometimes find in those remote small towns at the dead ends of Russia. Music, like mathe-matics, was a liberation from my torments. I acquired from the Krolenkos a good deal of my feeling for music, though my mother, too, played a spinet very tenderly. When the Krolenko women played, I could almost bear the months and months of waiting that passed by till my father and mother should come back again—as I firmly believed they would. My father had gone in pursuit of her, as you will have gathered, and had arranged that he was to carry her across the German frontier. Krolenko was to have me sent to join them, when the word came through.

" The word did not come through. A year or two were

to pass before I learned what had happened. I think I can say I was useful in Krolenko's office during that time. He anticipated I would make a good man of commerce some day. I did it well because I had somebody to protect me, as it were, upon whom I could throw a moral responsibility, the moment my tragic timidity got the better of me. It was from the Okhrana, the secret police, I got my information regarding the fate of my parents. They very accurately calculated that it was the sort of information which would make me a likely recruit. And they were looking for recruits at that time, because the revolutionaries were beginning to inject their poison all along the Black Sea and Azov coasts, from Odessa to the mouth of the Don. Moreover the revolutionaries had taught them the usefulness of employing boys in their organisation. They could often do so much more than men.

" I learned from them that my father had got on to my mother's tracks. They had taken her off to Vilna, where she was helping to produce an illegal paper. He established contact with her, and though she tried to disown him, for she had a just premonition of what would happen to him, he overcame her objections. He attempted to carry her away, but they shot him dead in a street in Kovno. She hanged herself three days later.

" I think you will understand why I do not love the Revolution, which slew my father and mother and blasted my young years ; all my life, in fact, till I met a kind and simple woman who restored to me something of what I had lost so soon, and gave me something else I had never known. You will also realise how right the Okhrana was in putting me in possession of these facts, from the point of view of attaching to themselves a devoted agent.

" I worked for them for some time at Mariupol, but I found it difficult to stay in one place. I found the necessity then, which has been with me all my life, of moving from place to place ; for, when I do not move, the old doubts and miseries come over me more and more unbearably.

Despite my wife and children, I must still be moving, even now, sometimes rarely, sometimes more often. It was not by mere chance that I chose a form of business these late years, since the War stopped and it was possible to move freely, which enabled me, compelled me, to move about as I have always moved. It is because I flee from them, and at the same time pursue them, those fiends who shot my father and hanged my mother . . . who now lord it in the Kremlin . . . who will not be lording it long, I think . . .

" I went on from Mariupol, up and down the country. For a number of years I did useful work in various places —in the capital and on the Volga and up in the North. I brought off a useful coup in a pine-wood near Kiev once, and in one or two other places.

" And then—it is rather difficult to be clear about what happened then. It is probable that the revolutionaries had their secret agents amongst us, as we certainly had amongst them. I began to be aware of a certain atmosphere of doubt regarding me. If I had an invisible enemy, it could not have been too difficult to show that, after all, my mother had been a revolutionary from the beginning, and she had gone back to her activities after a lapse of years. What was to prevent me, her son, becoming a renegade ? I became aware of a certain tension and suspicion ; and I am the sort of person upon whom such an awareness works disastrously, who, in his nervousness, will act exactly in such a way as will confirm those suspicions.

" I was never actually dismissed. The suggestion was never put into words. But I realised they would prefer me to direct my activities along other channels. And when I myself asked permission could I go back to the Sea of Azov again, to try and start in business on my own, they most affably suggested that whenever I should get wind of something that might be of interest to them, I was, without fail, to let them know.

" I had some money, and my father's friend at Mariupol helped, too. I had some feeling for commerce, as I think I have proved more successfully in my later life. I tried to start in business as a grain-exporter at Taganrog, and failed. I tried oil at Baku and Batum, and I made other experiments elsewhere. I failed. People would not trust me, because I would not trust myself. But all the time I was convinced that I'd have made good if I'd stayed on in Mariupol with Krolenko, with somebody to lean on, that is to say. He was himself more of a dilettante than a business-man, and, though I was no more than a child when I worked in his office, he was quite ready to let me shoulder a lot of the initiative, while he went and played and talked and drank tea with his wife and daughters.

"And the fact is, I didn't mind taking the initiative in the least, as long as I had the sense of his support. Without him, without anyone to cover me, I failed—at Taganrog, at Batum, everywhere. I needed a Krolenko, and Krolenko proved he needed me, for he went bankrupt, I learned, a year or so after I left Mariupol, and he would not have done so if I'd been there.

"I felt I'd meet that man some day, the man I could lean up against. Not Krolenko himself, of course—for he died soon after his failure—but the man who needed me, and whom I needed. I met that man, as you will have gathered from all this, in Sam Silver, Elsie's father, in Doomington.

"How did I stumble upon him? How? I had almost forgotten. In all my experiments and wanderings it remained a matter of second nature with me to follow up any hint that might present itself, from any quarter, with regard to the activities of the revolutionary enemies of Russia. When at last I reached Doomington in my travels, I heard of a fearsome band of anarchists who held meetings in a waterproof-workman's house in Longton, in a street called Oleander Street. I hovered about for a day or two, and caught a glimpse of a woman more beautiful to me than I have ever known, save one. I managed to make my way, without attracting any attention, into the meeting of the anarchists, an art I have had much practice in. I found they were a pitiable crew, for the most part, though I must say at once, and Elsie will know I am not saying it because she is here, I immediately felt something of the attraction her father has always exercised over me.

" It must sound strange to you, Herr Graf, and Elsie will forgive this frankness. Her father was an illiterate little workman, but I divined in him a series of qualities I had not met before, and have not met since. A certain integrity, a certain gentleness—oh, and a good deal more beside—which have been the secret of his success, and, of course, of mine.

" That same night, the night I first entered the Silver kitchen, I was attacked by the gentleman we have been discussing this evening, quite suddenly, without any sort of provocation so far as I am aware ; though, when I review the past, I am compelled to speculate whether my activities in the Okhrana did not, at one time, in some way or another, involve him. If they did, I was not able to find out, doubtless because he was well protected by his pseudonyms, partly because my contact with the secret police was no longer a close one by that time.

" Sarah saved my life that night, or at all events, I should have suffered a great deal more if not for her. But the next day I moved on from that city. I did not see what should retain me. I felt it was not unlikely, some time, somewhere, I should meet Sarah again. It was in a very different *milieu*, and not in Doomington, I heard a humorous story of a little anarchist who had become a little capitalist, and how miserable he was, and how badly his anarchists were treating him, and how comic it all was. They remembered the name, because the very name, in this connection, was a little comic too. So I came back to Doomington.

" I have travelled a good deal since, as you know, Herr Graf, on journeys fortunate and unfortunate—fortunate for the most part. I count none of them so fortunate as this journey to Berlin, which has given me the honour of making your acquaintance and the pleasure of tracking little Elsie down to her hiding-place.

" Are you asleep, Elsie ? You are ? Then who am I to remind you of your duties ? But if your throat was as dry as mine you'd need no reminding."

" *Prosit*, Mr. Smirnof ! " exclaimed Oskar von Straupitz-Kalmin.

" *Prosit*, Herr Graf ! " responded Alexander Smirnof.

" And now," said Elsie Silver grimly, " I'm going to tell *my* life-story ! "

" How magnificent ! " both men remarked chivalrously.

" Like hell I am ! " she further specified.

III

The association, in a business sense, that was established that night between the Anglo-Russian business-man and the Prussian aristocrat was of no great importance to either man ; for Oskar was not of the stuff of which great business-men are made, though his successes, which were entirely due to the advice of Smirnof, went to his head, and convinced him he had quite a future in finance if he would only take it a little more seriously. There seemed, however, no particular reason to take it seriously, with a steady flow of pounds sterling (which had never been so valuable as now) coming in from Elsie's father in Doomington, and a highly dexterous Smirnof at the other end of the telephone making them breed and bear young on the most prodigal scale. Or, if Smirnof were absent, his manager, Schmidt, would do quite as well. Oskar did no more high finance than that, and succeeded in convincing himself he was a financier ; nor did the various occasions on which he acted without the advice of Smirnof, and lost every penny he invested, suggest to him that he was not.

As Smirnof had anticipated, he was able to make a little use of Oskar's name and a note or two of introduction from him, but he could have dispensed with them quite easily. He had made a point of Oskar's collaboration when Elsie, without much seriousness, had suggested it ; but his sense of good manners rather than his anticipation of profit had prompted his cordial suggestion. He meant what he said, none the less, when he declared that he liked to work alongside somebody, particularly in a new area. It had been like that, and still was, he had explained, with Elsie's father. It was a constitutional matter. The inference that the protection of Oskar's name would be a matter of real significance was a courtesy. Their business association, then, was not important to either of the two men. But their friendship, which had established itself promptly, meant much to both of them. There were great differences in their careers and characters, though there was some similarity in the blood that flowed in their veins. Yet there were profound resemblances, or, at least, sympathies, between them. They were both men of extreme reticence, who had managed, without difficulty, to keep the most desperate chapters of their lives secret from the women who, at this time, at least, were the most important persons in their lives. But they had not met more than an hour or two before they had disclosed matters to each other that were of such poignancy that they had always imagined they would take them down with them to their graves.

They did not regret their disclosures to each other, and the facts of those disclosures, as well as the nature of the things disclosed, were the foundation upon which a cordial intimacy established itself. It became cordial and intimate, even though they did not meet very frequently between the times of their first meeting in September and the day in November when a wire of the utmost urgency from Silver recalled Smirnof to England.

Smirnof, as a matter of fact, worked so hard during those two months—it was a matter of so much importance to him to make the large sum of money he had come to Berlin to make—that he tumbled into bed nearly every night, dead tired, at about eleven o'clock, having been at work in his office till about ten. He was off again to his office

next morning well before eight o'clock, for a day of complicated calculations and quick decisions in which the tension
hardly slackened for five minutes. He was too tired to see
Oskar and Elsie often, though they were the only indulgence
of any sort he allowed himself. The night of the *Regenbogen
Diele* had been a sort of catharsis. He would not a second
time have been bored to hear Cortot, though he would
have been too tired to make the journey. There were, in
fact, one or two concerts during those two months he very
much wished to go to ; but he either had no time for them,
when they came round, or he was too worn out ; too worn
out even to read music—an occupation in which he often
took great pleasure.

He was working against time in two ways. It was imperative upon him, for a reason to be explained shortly,
to make his two hundred thousand pounds clear by a certain
date in November. He had a strong and accurate sentiment
that the chimærical behaviour of the mark could not continue for more than another three or four months at most.
Either Germany would be precipitated into some catastrophe
of a nature not the most imaginative economist, politician,
or sociologist could foretell, or sanity must be restored to
the currency. The fever was of such a violence that the
patient must quite quickly die, or quite quickly, however
violent the remedy, be cured.

Alexander Smirnof worked hard, and he worked successfully ; it was not his fault that his success turned to dust on
his tongue.

It was in the March of this year that Smirnof's activities
first put out a feeler in the direction of the Berlin stock-
market. That was the month in which the mark, having
remained stable for three months at approximately one
hundred thousand to the pound, started sliding down the
steep slope towards that abyss from which a certain Dr.
Schacht finally rescued it on the twentieth of November of

that same year. This Dr. Schacht found the mark a purely imaginary concept, magically multiplied it by itself a million million times, and made it tangible. Then he called it a rentenmark, and convinced the world that four and one-fifth of such rentenmarks were positively worth one gold American dollar.

Towards the end of March, a certain Strauss, a German business friend of Smirnof, telephoned him from Berlin to inform him that the *Spass*, the joke, of the mark was really only now beginning. Strauss was a man whom Smirnof had helped once or twice to stuff a pretty wallet, so that when he suggested that Smirnof should pay into his account a thousand pounds to play about with on the *Börse*, the Exchange, Smirnof did not hesitate more than an hour or two.

He hesitated as long as that, though a thousand pounds was a negligible sum of money in the scale of his operations, because he happened to be disturbed in his mind at that moment about an affair of real magnitude. He had paid one million two hundred thousand pounds for a dump of military material sold him by the British Government. This he had in turn sold to the Government of a Balkan country, best called Cratonia, for one and a half million pounds. This sum was payable in six bills due in successive three-monthly instalments of one quarter of a million pounds each. He had deposited these bills with the bank, and had in addition given them a personal guarantee for the money, signed by Silver and himself, the two directors of the trading company which had carried through the transaction.

On that double security, the bank had lent him the necessary sum, which he had paid over to the British Government. He had then taken possession of the goods and handed them over to the Cratonian Government. Cratonia had honoured the first two bills, but there had been some delay in honouring the third. The settlement was two or three weeks overdue. Smirnof was nervous. The bank was nervous. But, during the hour that followed Strauss's telephone message from Berlin, he decided that a refusal to hand over to Strauss the paltry thousand he had asked for was a violence to his instincts as a financier. He was convinced that Strauss would make good use of it, for he was intelligent, and, as financiers go, honest. There was no question at all of Strauss making a penny for himself out of it. But it was more important for the sake of his own morale. A refusal would prove to him that, for the first time in his career, panic was threatening him.

His secretary, therefore, rang up Berlin and informed Strauss the thousand pounds had already been paid in to his account. He could not help smiling with pleasure at the rightness of his own instincts when the Paris agent of the Cratonian Government rang him up an hour or two later to inform him that, though the settlement must still be held up for a good week, it would certainly be made. It was a corroboration of his conviction that Cratonia would not, could not, let him down. The bank tolerated the week's postponement. For, indeed, it was not likely to make any real trouble, excepting if really serious postponements were involved, for a client of the distinguished integrity of Alexander Smirnof.

The story of Smirnof's dealings with the Cratonian Government must not be anticipated, though it is imminent. But there was again trouble, and more serious trouble, over the bill payable in May. It was hardly any mitigation, in any material sense, of the situation, that just at this time he received another telephone message from Strauss in Berlin, to inform him that the thousand pounds Smirnof had confided to him in March he had now converted, without working overtime, into two thousand five hundred pounds. Strauss suggested he should, as it were, double his Berlin stake. Smirnof was faced with the same set of considerations as faced him in March, though the two thousand five hundred pounds necessitated just a little more straining of the

muscles than it would have done then. But he acted precisely in the same way. The consequence was his doubled
stakes, namely five thousand pounds, invested in Berlin in
May, were worth not less than twenty thousand pounds in
July.

It was in July that certain political events took place in
Cratonia which looked as though they might prove very
embarrassing to Smirnof's whole career as a financier, as
indeed they did, though he did not then perceive how
decisive they were going to prove. But he did perceive their
enormous immediate gravity.

So much so, that suddenly the twenty thousand pounds in
Berlin assumed a new and startling significance ; not because
they were twenty thousand pounds, as because they had
been five thousand in May, and it was now July, and the
increment could be considered more than satisfactory—it
was sensational. Moreover, it had been made for him by a
friend, and not a close one, in the manner of one who
must do something with his spare time, and if he is not going
to collect moths, why not turn over a spot of money for a
friend ? If Strauss had been able to do so well for him
without breaking any bones, what could he do for himself,
with his own organisation, devoting himself to the Berlin
stock-market exclusively for the next few months ? The
money had to be made in the next two or three months,
before the next bill fell due for settlement. It was true that
it would then be one quarter overdue, and he knew he
would have to exercise everything he possessed of tact,
besides scraping up a sequence of interim small payments
from every conceivable source open to him, in order to
keep the bank inactive all that time. The sources now open
to him could not, alas, be induced to advance him more
than small sums. Things were not as they had been even
a year ago.

He also had the feeling from the beginning that the fantasy
in Berlin could not last more than three or four months at
most ; and it would be a matter there of doing what was to

be done, not to-morrow, but to-day, not an hour from now, but this very moment.

He opened up an office in Berlin, therefore ; his friend Strauss helping him to find his personnel—a by no means easy task. He had a manager named Schmidt, an under-manager named Brauner, and a dozen or more clerks and book-keepers. He had to keep on adding to their number, as the figures he dealt in became more and more compli-cated. Indeed, it was no exaggeration to say that one clerk was employed exclusively to write out the noughts in his transactions, which marched across reams and reams of paper. It was far more difficult to find subordinates who were not completely bewildered by these figures than to acquire the money they represented. There was also a sequence of office-boys ; but he was made aware of the existence of only one, and that but briefly. He also brought a man secretary of his own with him—Steadley by name.

He already had a capital in Berlin of twenty thousand pounds. He borrowed another thirty thousand pounds from Silver—a thing he had never done before, for he was ex-tremely hostile to the thought that Silver should be aware he was compelled to borrow a farthing from anybody. But there was no alternative open. It was quite imperative, at this moment, to realise, from whatever other sources were open to him, a sum of fifty thousand pounds, in order to be quite certain that the bank would be a little less restive during his next few months in Berlin than it had been lately.

He described to Silver the *Spass*, the joke, that the Berlin stock-market had now become, exactly in the same terms that Strauss had used earlier in the year. And indeed it was a *Spass*, and every financier who operated in it was an Alice in Wonderland. And yet the basic method of operations was rational enough. You bought securities in German industries—nothing but the best would do, even for specu-lators who did not mind a touch of the bizarre in their undertakings ; you bought a mixed bag of Farbenindustrie,

Siemens & Halske, A.E.G., Norddeutscher Lloyd. You bought them with the marks bought with your initial gold capital, or a little of it. And then you proceeded, on the security of your shares, to borrow another nightmare load of marks, with which you repeated the initial operation.

It was true that you paid fantastic rates of interest on the marks you borrowed. In October the rate rose to eighteen per cent per day. But sometimes your securities doubled and trebled their value within the course of twenty-four hours.

The basis of it all was simple enough, but it required infinite promptness and wariness, not so much to lose your money, for it was almost impossible to do that, as to make the best possible thing out of it—to realise, for instance, as Smirnof intended to realise, a return of two hundred thousand pounds within a few months on an outlay of fifty thousand.

There were persistent rumours from day to day, and from hour to hour, during the passage of these hysterical months, that the mark was at length going to be stabilised. There were, in fact, several attempts made at stabilising the mark before Dr. Schacht stabilised the rentenmark at four point two to the dollar on the twentieth of November, and with that one jab of his pen punctured the monstrous balloon of the inflation.

With what backing, asked certain of the speculators comfortably, are they trying to stabilise the mark ? Something is bound to happen in six or nine months, but we can sit pretty till then, whatever the bankers try to do. Then there'll be a civil war and riots and burning of the stock exchanges, and we'll all be put up against a wall and shot. But in the meantime—on with the dance !

A less comfortable variety of speculator was convinced that the Government would abrogate the kingdom of heaven any week, any day—as, in fact, it did. They conducted their operations with the air of those condemned voluptuaries who are determined to cram in the maximum of experience from moment to moment, till that moment when the heart bursts or the blood-clot breaks.

Smirnof was more collected, and had a surer instinct for the realities of the situation than most of his fellows. He sometimes managed to annul completely from his mind the galling behaviour of Cratonia, though not often. It remained almost perpetually a humming menacing bourdon under the shrill plucking of the wires. But when he did manage to forget, he was happy in a way he had almost never been. It was like certain cerebrations of Bach ; it was like a superb game of chess. One existed in an empyrean ; it was like juggling at the top of the sky's vault with an infinity of units ; up there they were stars, here they were marks, and they were equally prodigal. He had manipulated in actual value far bigger sums than he was concerned with now, but never had he, or anybody, dealt in figures so astronomical, so utterly beyond the scope of rational significance that they became pure poetry.

He was happy, or at least he was intellectually happy. Despite his anxiety with regard to the bank, he would have been as happy as he had ever been if he had had his wife beside him. He did not want her to discuss the day's affairs with him. But she would have been gracious and warm and comforting when he got back at night. He liked to lie in bed beside her, the feel of her finger-tips upon his forehead, of her soft hands smoothing his shoulder-blades. In the combustion of his passion, the day's detritus of littered figures was consumed. He sank into her fragrance and warm oblivion. Next morning, his body and mind set out fresh as a boy's again.

There was no chance, alas, of having Sarah beside him in Berlin. But, apart from her absence, he was happy. He was playing a game such as he had played in dreams, but had never hoped to play in sober fact, with the aid of sliding-rules and ledgers and typewriters. He played certain minor games, minor so far as the sums involved were concerned, but all bathed in the same wild poetry. He realised, for instance, that the copper pfennig pieces up and down the country—the value of which at this moment was not a value, but a puff of thought—would be quite a number of million times themselves when the stabilisation was carried through. He deputed an underling to organise the collection of them.

In addition to that, he was among the first to realise the possibilities of the situation that, in the two Germanies, the occupied and the unoccupied, there were two quotations for the mark. This happened in the last weeks of the inflation. The official Berlin quotation was four-point-two billion marks to the dollar. There was an unofficial Cologne quotation of seven, and even eight, billion marks to the dollar. It became the custom for small speculators, and agents of the large speculators, to sell marks for *valuta* late in the day in Berlin, to take the night train to Cologne, and wait till the banks opened there next morning in order to buy, with the same sum of money, nearly twice as many marks. The night train to Cologne, was, in fact, called the *Schieberzug*, and it was said of it it needed no fuel to propel it, because the *Schieber*, the pushers, did all the propelling necessary. The Cologne manœuvre was illegal, of course, but the alien authorities in Cologne did not exercise themselves greatly in the matter.

Soon after the middle of October, the feeling began to flood through Smirnof's brain, and his body too, that the fun was nearly over. It was the feeling called a " hunch " among gamblers both on the epic and the penny-a-line scale. With Smirnof it was something physical, to the point that he almost felt a rash come out on his forehead—as he laughingly explained to his wife, Sarah, one day, who took him too literally, and at once drenched him with a dose of Eno's Fruit Salts.

It was true that certain events took place after the middle of October which might have indicated to an extremely sensitive nostril which way the wind was blowing. But the nostrils of the financiers had become obtuse with the greasy smells of the burnt offerings heaped up upon their altars. Only Smirnof's nose twitched a little curiously when, on the fifteenth, a decree was promulgated for the establishment of the German Rentenbank. He cocked his ears when Dr. Luther, the Chancellor of the Exchequer, appointed Dr. Schacht as Currency Dictator on the twelfth of the month following. When, three days later, Dr. Schacht decreed the first issue of the rentenmark, the " hunch " that had unsteadied Smirnof for some time functioned somewhat in the nature of a series of minor electric shocks. He happened to be in Cologne on that day, and a major shock, to be described shortly, confirmed the impetus of the minor series. But the other financiers shrugged their shoulders, and wisely tapped the side of their noses. When, finally, on the twentieth of that month, the mark was stabilised, the consequences to their schemes were such that the fingers of the financiers were too numb to tap their noses, and their noses so frozen with horror that, tapped, they might have dropped off.

Smirnof had had the sort of " hunch " here spoken of on more than one important occasion ; as when, more than two years earlier, he so accurately divined the moment at which to sell the Silver firm to the public ; and, later, the moments at which to buy and sell the cotton futures on which he had gambled so vast a sum of money. It was true, he had not been allowed to take his profit, and no other person in the world than Silver himself had not allowed him to take it. Silver had so vehemently insisted that his associate was being premature that he had completely dislocated the finely balanced mechanism of Smirnof's " hunch." It had cost Smirnof a pretty penny, too. It had distressed old Silver beyond measure. But Silver could not be induced to see that it was not the formidable sum of money Smirnof had lost that really troubled him, so much as that he had played false to his own game—his game which was so subtle an interplay of calculations and intuitions. It would not have righted the matter at all if he had accepted Silver's ridiculously generous offer of sharing the losses in a certain proportion. Smirnof had pointed out, with complete sincerity, that it would not have occurred to him to hand over a portion of his gains to Silver if his advice had been fortunate. In an affair of this sort, you accept or reject advice on your own responsibility. You pay no indemnity, or, conversely, pay no commission.

No, Smirnof had hardly hoped Silver would understand. It was like a virtuoso. A triumphant success at a public performance of a piece which seemed difficult but was well within his scope would not atone to him for a private failure in his own drawing-room to play a piece which made a real demand on his virtuosity. The analogy was by no means exact, but it stressed the element of virtuosity which was entirely beyond Silver's mental compass to appreciate.

But in Berlin there was no Silver. There was, it was true, a Straupitz-Kalmin, who, now and again, gave Smirnof a certain ludicrous sense of having some sort of authority to defer to ; but he knew that that was the operation in him of a psychological flaw, it had no bearing on any practical issue. There, in Berlin, he was awaiting the exact, the triumphant, moment in which it would be supremely advantageous to realise all his securities, pay off his debts in marks, and convert the residue into the good gold, the two hundred thousand rock-like pounds sterling, towards which all his starry efforts had been directed. There was no Silver in Berlin who might advise him to hold on for another day, or another day, when he was at last convinced the moment had come—if it was conceivable that Silver could anywhere, under any circumstances, ever again presume to offer him any sort of financial advice.

On the night of Thursday, the fourteenth of November, Smirnof took the train for Cologne, where he arrived about

eight or nine next morning. It was his plan to consult with
Herren Lempert and Hildesheim that afternoon, regarding
certain important industrial possibilities, and to return to
Berlin that same night. He had a sleepless night on the
train, for his oddly physiological " hunch " kept worrying
him, like a phantom toothache which can find no tooth to
give it hospitality.

When he opened a paper in the morning, he was given a
further odd jolt when he read that a decree had been issued
for the establishment of the German Rentenbank. The
idea which had been forming in his mind during the night
at once crystallised itself. The moment had come. He would
be in Berlin next day—on Saturday. The Stock Exchange
would not be open till Monday. On Monday he would
realise all his holdings.

For the time being he would say not a word to anybody,
neither to Schmidt in Berlin, nor to his associates here in
Cologne—Lempert and Hildesheim. He was in Cologne.
He would make the best of this particular job, while he was
about it.

He was in Cologne. It was in Cologne, therefore, rather
than in Berlin, or Vienna, or Alexandria, that it was appointed that Boris Polednik should once more hurl himself
upon Alexander Smirnof, and squeeze his throat between
his fingers, and seek to throttle him with a success more
formidable than he had achieved one night, in Sam Silver's
kitchen, in Doomington, thirteen infinite years ago.

IV

Smirnof had left instructions with his English secretary,
Steadley, over in the Berlin office, that he could be reached
at Lempert & Hildesheim's office in Cologne at three o'clock.
But he was only to ring him up after consultation with
Schmidt, and if the matter was of absolute urgency. He
returned from a hurried lunch with Herren Lempert and
Hildesheim at half past two, and got down to the matters

in hand. They were extremely complicated, and he strongly hoped the telephone would not ring for him at three. But it did. He was informed that his secretary in Berlin required him urgently. Herren Lempert and Hildesheim tactfully withdrew to leave him the privacy of the telephone.

" Yes, Steadley, what is it ? "

" I have a telegram for you, sir."

Smirnof got many telegrams during the course of every day. Berlin business at that time involved a great many telegrams.

" Did you talk it over with Schmidt, as I asked you to ? "

" I thought it best not to talk it over with anybody. Besides, Mr. Schmidt is away from the office this afternoon."

" What's wrong with him ? "

" He came to the office and had to leave. He had an acute attack of diarrhoea."

" Oh, I see. What's it about then ? "

" I'll read it to you, sir."

" Yes, go on."

" It's signed Silver, and it's stamped Doomington."

" Oh ? "

" The text reads : ' Must request your immediate return to Doomington stop greatly puzzled and distressed stop long detailed letter received from Polednik Moscow this morning concerning Cratonian operations stop wire immediately.' "

The voice ceased on the wire. There was silence at receiver and transmitter. A tram clanged along its lines beside the offices of Lempert & Hildesheim. In some other room a telephone-bell rang sharply, ordering a handful of shares, perhaps. Or some harassed wife wanted Hans to remember to bring the coffee in from the stores on his way home. Or it was Fritz's girl, telling him she wouldn't be able to meet him, after all, to-night. Cologne was an occupied city. Fritz's girl was often ringing up to say she wouldn't be able to meet him, after all.

But of course he was the victim of some hallucination. He couldn't have heard properly. Steadley had got it wrong. An intelligent fellow, Steadley, to have realised it wasn't a wire to talk over with anybody—Schmidt, or Brauner, or anybody.

How much did Steadley know?

" Steadley ! "

" Yes, sir ? "

" Are you sure—you've got that right ? "

" Yes, sir."

" Read it again."

" Yes, sir. It's signed Silver, and it's stamped Doomington. The text reads : ' Must request your immediate return to Doomington stop greatly puzzled and distressed stop long detailed letter received from Polednik Moscow this morning concerning Cratonian operations stop wire immediately.' "

It was not only Steadley's voice, coming accurate and impassive on the wire from Berlin, he heard. All the way from Moscow the line came, where Boris Polednik sat at a table, his mouth at the mouthpiece, his eyes pink as a ferret behind his pince-nez. From over in Doomington two voices came, twisted round each other, like threads, into the single voice of Steadley the secretary.

" Greatly puzzled and distressed," came the voice of Sam Silver, a little peevishly, sitting in his office at the big factory on the Longton Croft.

" I told you so," said Esther Pliskin. " Didn't I tell you so ? Didn't I say you shouldn't start off like that on your own ? It wouldn't take you nowhere, I said ! Didn't you tell me, when once you start off on your own, it won't go ? "

The voice of Steadley came through again. " Are you still there, sir ? "

" Yes."

" Shall I hang on ? "

" Yes. Wait a minute."

The first thing to do was—what is the first thing to do when you stand on an island, and the stuff of the island crumbles beneath your feet and the sea is already crawling in, scratching with its thousand paws?

The first thing to do is to keep panic at arm's length. The first thing to do is to say something rational and matter-of-fact to the secretary at the other end of the telephone. There are other people to act for, beside yourself. You have a wife and children. In the last letter from Sarah she said that Jackie had another of his colds. He had a nasty hacking cough with it, this time.

" Steadley ? "

" Yes, sir."

" I want you to ring me up again in half an hour ! "

" Shall I hang on ? "

" Do as I say, Steadley. No. I'll get through to you. No. Hang on ! Do you hear ? "

" Yes, sir."

He walked away from the telephone as if Steadley might see his face or hear his thoughts.

What did Steadley make of this ? How much did Steadley know ?

The devil ! What was he worrying about Steadley for ? The wire had not been composed by Sam Silver himself. He felt a sense of grievance against Silver for letting someone else compose the wire. Why let someone else in on it ? He could have explained it all quite easily if it had remained a matter between Silver and himself—and his accomplice, Huxtable, of course. But it was not Huxtable. Huxtable had not ratted. There was no chance of that. Huxtable knew nothing about the Cratonian operations.

Polednik! The poisonous little toad ! Where the hell ? How the hell ?

He walked up and down the room trying to work it out. How had Polednik, up in Moscow, or wherever the hell he might be, how had Polednik got hold of it ? He walked up

and down, up and down, his hands behind his back. That
wasn't the sort of message you should transmit by telegraph.
There are the people who take down the message, the
people who receive it at the other end. There are people
who listen in on telephones.

If it had only remained a matter between himself and
Silver, he could have explained it easily, as he had always
explained everything else before.

But there had never been any suspicion before, not the
slightest shadow of a suspicion. For the first time in all these
years Silver suspected. The basis of the whole erection had
been that Silver had never had, must never have, one
infinitesimal iota of suspicion. Once he started suspecting,
it was like a rip in the fabric of a balloon ; it was impossible
that the pressure of the gases should not lengthen the tear ;
it was impossible that the balloon should not come down to
the ground, a blazing ruin.

He took his handkerchief from his pocket, and wiped his
forehead.

But Silver did not merely suspect. He *knew*.

What did he know ? How could Polednik—*Polednik*, of all
people—know what had happened in Trebinth ?

These things come out ; sooner or later they come out.
When you have entered into the arena of big-scale political
swindling, they will find out, sooner or later, in Copenhagen
what took place in Pernambuco.

Are you going to sit down sweet and simple, as if you were
a shop-assistant who has been helping himself to the till,
and has at length been found with a marked coin in his
pocket ? Are you going to sit down and stretch your arms
forward and let them slip the bracelets round your wrist ?
Why, that window there ; it was four floors above the ground !
You might as well throw yourself through the window at
once !

What ? Because Polednik had pushed you ? You were
going to sit down and let Polednik spring up at you and
press on your jugular vein again ?

Sarah wasn't here now to dig all her fingers into Polednik's hair, and pull his head sharply back, till his hands relaxed out of your neck. Sarah wasn't here now. She was away in London with all the children. They were a great many children to look after.

If you let Polednik strangle you or push you through the window—there would be no more Sarah again, no more children. That would be too much of a victory for Polednik, surely. Jackie ought to go to Derbyshire, or Clacton, with that chest of his. It would be a pity if there were no more Sarah ; Sarah at night, so soft, so warm, so silent.

A pity she hadn't been able to come to Berlin. She'd not been able to leave the children—she never would be able to leave the children—they were always having measles, or mumps, or tonsils, or something or other. They were a nice pack of youngsters, just the same.

How the hell had it got round to Polednik ?

The door had opened a full minute ago. Herren Lempert and Hildesheim were in the room. It was obvious the honoured visitor had had bad news. He seemed no more aware of them than if they were at the other end of the building. They did not know whether it would be less tactful to stay or go out again. The telephone was still off the receiver.

He caught sight of them. " Oh, excuse me, excuse me, I didn't see you were there ! "

" It looks a bit like—like bad news," ventured Herr Lempert. " Forgive me, if I make too bold. Perhaps—in that cupboard there, we always keep some good brandy."

" Brandy ! Thank you, Herr Lempert. Thank you ! Yes, there has been bad news. My wife sent a wire to Berlin. My eldest boy is very ill. He has been unwell for some time. I fear I shall have to leave by the night train for Flushing."

Of course. That was clear. He suddenly realised he must get back at once. He must get to Silver at the first possible moment, and explain it all. It was quite easy to explain.

The fellow, Polednik, had always wanted to do him an injury. He had tried to murder him the first time in his life he had set eyes on him. He was the victim of some delusion, some *idée fixe*. It was probable the fellow had somehow got wind of his association with Denikin, in 1919, during the Civil War. That must have aggravated the mania. Now he had got hold of some cock-and-bull story from some filthy international loafer, and was using it to try and gratify his homicidal lust from another direction.

It would be easy to explode the purulent nonsense. Nothing in the world would be easier. He must get back to Doomington the first possible moment. In half an hour he would have twisted old Silver round his little finger.

That is to say, in half an hour he would have blown the wicked libel sky-high. He must get back to Doomington, get hold of Silver at once.

But wait a minute. He had definitely made up his mind to sell out all his securities on Monday. That was only three days ahead. He knew in his marrow it would be dangerous to temporise. A delay of a few days might mean all the difference between triumph and disaster. This fellow, Schacht, meant business. If he worked the miracle, if he managed to stabilise the mark, the value of all securities would tumble catastrophically. He might stabilise the mark overnight ; he might stabilise it when you were out of the room, washing your hands.

Rubbish ! He was going silly ! You can't carry out an operation of that sort by dipping your pen in an ink-pot ! How often had they tried already, and failed !

It was not rubbish ! It was dangerous to delay ! He must sell out on Monday, not a day later.

But he was going to Doomington to-night, this very night ! It was even more important to get back to Silver than to sell out. Silver's belief in him was the keystone of the whole arch. If Silver's belief was withdrawn, everything went smash.

Couldn't he be back again on Monday ? Why not ? Let's

work it out now ! It's Friday now. We'll get to London to-morrow night—Saturday night. We could take a midnight train to Doomington on Saturday, or an early train on Sunday morning.

Why not telephone from Kensington Palace Gardens ? Why not telephone from here ?

No, that isn't good enough. We've got to get hold of Silver by the neck, and shake him and shake him till we shake the nonsense out of his head and the truth into it.

That brings us to Sunday mid-day. We could leave England again on Sunday evening.

No, we can't get back again to Berlin in time to do anything on Monday. The Stock Exchange is only open three days a week. That brings us to Wednesday. That might be too late.

Hell, what have we got a manager for ? Schmidt must sell out for us first thing on Monday. Look ! The telephone there !

We're still hooked up with Berlin. Steadley is waiting for orders at the other end of the wire.

"Excuse, me ; excuse ! " begged Herr Lempert. " Here is the brandy ! "

" Thank you, Herr Lempert ! Ah, that's good ! "

" We are so, so sorry, Herr Smirnof. If there is anything at all we can do ? " (Yes, there is, for God's sake, get out of the way !) " Shall we send a man round to get a ticket ? What *Pech*, what bad luck ! "

" We are sure when you get there . . ." Herr Hildesheim consoled him. " You know what mothers are ! But it's a terrible thing, most upsetting, getting telegrams like this, suddenly, out of nowhere ! "

" Out of Moscow ! " a voice behind Mr. Smirnof's teeth objected. " Out of Moscow ! " It was not a voice Herren Lempert and Hildesheim heard.

" If you would permit me," said Smirnof, " I promised my secretary to speak to him when I had made up my mind what I was going to do. Keeping the connection all this time with Berlin—will you excuse me ? "

" Please. please ! We will leave you. Perhaps, if you would ring twice on this bell whenever you are free for us again——"

" I thank you. It is kind of you. I am most grateful."

Herren Lempert and Hildesheim tiptoed out of the room, leaving the anguished father to make his further arrangements. He strode up and down the room for another minute or two, thinking things out, making swift decisions. Then he went up to the telephone.

" Steadley ! " he called. " Are you there ? "

" Is that you, sir ? Yes, sir ? "

" Can you hear me clearly ? "

" Yes, sir."

" I am leaving for London to-night."

" Yes, sir."

" I expect to be back on Monday, if possible ; if not, Tuesday. Let the others know at the office ! "

" Yes, sir."

" Keep my room on at the hotel. As for the telegram you read out to me——"

" Yes, sir ? "

" It was from my wife, to tell me my eldest boy was very ill ! You understand ? "

" Of course, sir."

" That's why I'm leaving like this, in such a hurry ! "

" Yes, sir."

" You'd best leave Berlin at once, too. Ring up for instructions at Kensington Palace Gardens."

It seemed better to Smirnof to have Steadley close to him during the next few days, while he was getting things explained, than to have him floating about loose in Berlin with the knowledge of the contents of that frightful telegram.

" Now get me Brauner at once, please ! "

" Yes, sir."

There was a short delay.

" Herr Smirnof ? "

" Brauner, is that you ? "

" *Ja, mein Herr !*

" I am leaving for London to-night. Steadley will tell you more about it. I want you to understand. You must give these instructions to Schmidt when he comes into the office to-morrow morning. They are instructions for Monday. If he does not, you must carry them out yourself. The orders are absolutely secret, of course ! "

" *Ja, mein Herr !* "

" I want Schmidt or you to sell out all my holdings on Monday morning, without exception, everything. Do you understand ? Everything ! You may tell Schmidt I am convinced the stabilisation of the mark can only be delayed a few days at most. You must convert all my holdings into cash, and pay off every penny I owe. Do you understand ? There must be no mistake ! "

" No, Herr Smirnof, there shall be no mistake ! "

" And—let me think, Brauner. No, that is all ! You have it quite clear ? "

" Absolutely clear ! "

" *Auf wiedersehen*, Brauner ! "

" *Glückliche Reise*, Herr Smirnof ; a happy journey ! "

There was a click in Berlin and Cologne of replaced instruments.

v

Smirnof was intensely relieved when at last he could get away from Herren Lempert and Hildesheim. Their eyes were large and almost tearful with sympathy. Their foreheads sweated sympathy, as if they had been eating and drinking too much. They threatened to take him over to their wives, who, they were convinced, would tackle the situation with even more loving delicacy than themselves.

He at last managed to get free. He went and bought one or two things he would need for the night—some aspirin, if he could not sleep ; some brandy, if the aspirin would not do its work. He bought a number of books. Perhaps he would be able to read. Perhaps he would not. He had the things sent to the hotel.

He had only a small bag, and he tried to pack it. But things kept dropping out of his hands, which seemed all thumbs. He rang for a valet, and requested him to pack for him. He also ordered that a man should take the bag to the station for him. He gave the number of his berth. He paid his bill, tipping lavishly, as his custom was, and went out into the town, for he still had an hour or two to kill.

He stared aimlessly at shop-windows for some minutes ; he sat down in a café, and tried to read a newspaper. The words ran together across the page in black streaks. He got up again. It was the wrong sort of café for his present mood. The officers and the smart whores made him feel uneasy. He got up and wandered down a side-street, descended a few steps into a low pub—a *Kneipe*—and ordered some brandy. They had no brandy ; they had only the inferior sweetish *Brantwein*, a native product. He sent that away, and asked for *Korn*, a powerful colourless liqueur distilled from wheat. He drank two glasses, three glasses. They did not go to his head, they merely made him morose. He drank another glass. Then he looked at his watch. It was quite time he left. He went off to the station.

He arrived with seventeen minutes to spare. The man from the hotel was waiting, having deposited his bag in the sleeper. He tipped him, and suddenly felt his face was familiar. He peered at him, and saw that it was familiar because it looked like the face of Brauner, his under-manager.

It was not a clever face. A rather narrow forehead sloped up from the eyebrows. The skull was graced by a pair of ears too big for it.

In that same moment he was almost knocked over by the realisation that Brauner was a fool. Brauner couldn't be trusted to give that messsge—that tremendously important message—accurately to Schmidt. He'd make a mess of it. He must get on to Schmidt at once. Schmidt had diarrhoea.

He was bound to be at home. There would just be time to get through to him and give him the order direct. He would have a *Blitzgespräch*, a lightning telephone-call. All the wires to Berlin would be cleared to let him through. It would cost him fifteen pounds.

" Listen ! " he cried to the man from the hotel. " Come ! You must help me ! I want to put a *Blitzgespräch* through to Berlin ! Where can I do it ? Can I do it on the station here ? Run at once to the station-master—no, the superintendent of the telegraph office ! Tell them they must put me through at once. What ? What do you say ? "

" Begging your pardon, Herr, it would be impossible at the station here, *sehr compliziert* ! If I might suggest the Dom Hotel just across the way . . ."

" All right, then ! Here ! Here is the number ! " He had an astonishing memory for telephone and all other numbers. He could hardly have used Schmidt's private telephone number more than once or twice. " There ! Run ! *Run*, I tell you ! I'm coming after ! "

He met the man hastening back towards him some twenty yards from the entrance to the hotel. " Begging your pardon, Herr, there are several people wanting to put a *Blitzgespräch* through. I think only if you give a big tip to the girl—it must be in English money——"

" For Christ's sake stop gibbering ! Here ! Take this ! " He thrust a handful of pound notes into the man's fist.

He seemed hardly to have passed through the swinging doors before he was standing in a telephone-booth, his breath panting and crackling along the wire all the long leagues to Berlin.

" *Herr Schmidt, bitte ?* " he rapped out.

" Yes, this is the apartment of Herr Schmidt ! "

" Bring him to the telephone immediately ! This is Herr Smirnof, his employer ! "

" It causes me much pain, Herr, but Herr Schmidt is out ! "

" What do you mean, he's out ? He can't be out ! He's got diarrhoea ! "

" Frau Schmidt gave him a medicine, and he felt much better. He thought some air would do him good."

" Bring Frau Schmidt ! Immediately, I tell you ! "

" She is out with him ! "

" *Scheiss !* " shouted Mr Smirnof, accurately but grossly, and banged the receiver down.

Brauner ! Brauner ! There would just be time to get through to Brauner. He would make quite certain of Brauner. He ran round, like one demented, to the girl at the telephone-counter. The man from the hotel ran with him. He, too, had been very handsomely tipped. He felt the gentleman needed somebody to look after him. The train would be leaving in four or five minutes.

" Get me through, at once, to this number ! " He thrust a wad of notes into the telephone-girl's hand, as if he would never have any use for money again. She said nothing. Her demeanour was that of a goddess who allows herself briefly to be deflected from her Olympian duty by an extra-special heaping of white heifers on her altar. She pointed to the telephone-booth. The *Schieber* whom she had intended to put through next shook his fist in fury.

" Excuse me, Herr," said the man from the hotel anxiously. " The train will be leaving in four or five minutes ! "

" To hell ! I must get through ! "

It took two full minutes to get through. It took a minute to get Brauner to the telephone. The man from the hotel was wringing his hands. " You will miss it ! You can't possibly catch it ! There is only one minute ! "

" Is that you, Brauner ? "

" Herr Smirnof ? "

" For God's sake, Brauner, what I said to-day, you won't forget ! What ? You can't hear ? I tell you, what I said to-day, carry out my orders—I won't, I tell you, I won't ! " The last words were addressed to the man from the hotel, who was shouting and sobbing and pulling at his coat-tails.

" Yes, yes, Herr Smirnof, I understand ! " came the voice of Brauner. There was a note of bewilderment in it which

Smirnof was in no fit state to register. He just managed to swing himself on to the train before it got moving too quickly.

VI

Oskar von Straupitz-Kalmin turned up at Alexander Smirnof's office about eleven o'clock the following morning. He was passing by, and he had a number of pound notes on him. He had had no idea in his mind that morning of playing about with them ; but the sight of the windows of Smirnof's office automatically put into his head the idea of a little flutter.

Moreover, he had not seen Smirnof for some time. It was true he was coming to lunch with them in a day or two, but he knew that, however busy he might be at the present moment, Smirnof would welcome him with open arms—if he were in, of course. If he were not in, the man Schmidt, the manager, could be given the commission.

He was shown in. Herr Smirnof, as a matter of fact, was not in the office. Would the Herr Graf like to meet Herr Schmidt ? asked the office-boy. Herr Schmidt would do, conceded the Herr Graf.

"How goes it, Herr Schmidt ? And you, too ? What is your name ? Brauner ? "

"Yes, Herr Graf ! "

"Not too well, Herr Graf ! " said Schmidt, in a slightly melancholy voice. "I have only just got to the office. I had to go away yesterday. And then it started again this morning."

"I am indeed sorry, Herr Schmidt. And what might it be ? "

"Diarrhoea, Herr Graf ! "

"Most disturbing, most disturbing ! And Herr Smirnof, he is not in the office ? "

"No, Herr Graf. He hasn't let you know ? He rang us up from Cologne. He had to go straight on to London last night ! "

Oskar found it unpleasant that Smirnof's employees should be aware of his personal plans, whilst Elsie and himself were ignorant of them. He might, at least, have sent them a wire. Besides they were lunching together in a day or two, weren't they?

"Yes—he rang me up, too," he lied quickly. "But he didn't say he was going on the same night. He hadn't made up his mind yet."

"And here is Brauner, saying—oh, we are in great trouble, Herr Graf!" wailed Schmidt. "I am very glad you called in."

There seemed to be something wrong with Schmidt, quite outside his intestinal disorders. And with Brauner, too. They both looked extremely worried.

"Now, now, just let me hear what you have to say!" said Oskar quietly. The tone was intended to suggest that he knew all they might have to say, and a great deal more.

"Well, Herr Graf, as I was saying. I had to leave the office yesterday, because of my—my——"

"Quite so."

"And then Herr Smirnof rings up from Cologne, and I am not here. So he gives orders to Brauner. And you know what those orders are? That on Monday, on *Monday*, we are to sell out all his holdings on the stock-market, everything. We are to convert all his securities into cash, and pay off everything we owe. He says that the stabilisation of the mark can only be delayed a few days at most. And everybody else says that that is *Quatsch*, it is nonsense; but if it is not nonsense, and the mark is stabilised, then the securities will fall, and there will be less money to pay the interest as well. You know what the interest we are paying is, Herr Graf? Eighteen per cent *per day*, Herr Graf? In five days you owe nearly twice as much. But Monday is a bad day to sell, and did he say sell, or did he not, after all? Did he?"

"Well?" Oskar asked non-committally, in the tone of one who will solve all outstanding problems when he deems the moment has come.

" Last night," Schmidt continued, his eyes rolling help-lessly, " while I am out for half an hour with my wife, he rings up from Cologne, a *Blitzgespräch*. The maid takes the message. He is very angry that I am not in. He utters one bad word, and bangs the apparatus down. Then he rings up Brauner. He seems in a great hurry for his train. Brauner is absolutely unable to say whether he rang up to confirm his orders, or to cancel them. I do not know what to do. It is terrible. He will not arrive in London till this evening. And then if his child is dying——"

" What ? "

" Yes, his elder son is dying. That is why he has been called home."

" Oh, he did not say it was as bad as that. He didn't want his sister-in-law, Fräulein Silver, to be upset."

" Of course, he is a man who thinks of everything. Well, here we are. What are we to do, Herr Graf ? Shall we send him a telegram ? Or ring him up ? Can we trouble him when his child is dying ? And yet it is an important matter ; a very important matter ! "

It *was* an important matter. It was important to Elsie and himself, too, if this were the right moment to realise your securities. They also held quite a number. It was certainly possible Smirnof had inside information about the mark. If there was any prospect that the mark might soon be stabilised, the quicker you got rid of your securities the better, that was evident. But if Smirnof *had* got wind of something, why hadn't he dropped the hint to them ? Oskar felt extremely piqued about it.

It was odd, that business of the double *Blitzgespräch* from Cologne. It looked extremely probable that he had somehow got later news which had made it desirable that his orders to Brauner should be cancelled.

" We didn't have much time on the telephone. We were both in a great hurry," said Oskar. " Did he say when he was coming back ? "

" I had a note from his secretary. Steadley also left last

night. He said Herr Smirnof might get back on Monday night. He gave orders that his room at the hotel should be kept on."

That settles it! determined Oskar. His brow contracted with the violence of the unaccustomed intellectual exercise that was going on behind it. It's plain as a pikestaff that the second telephone-call countermanded the first. Brauner's a born idiot. If he's coming back himself on Monday, why on earth will he want Schmidt to sell out for him when he can sell out for himself a day or two later? I wonder what game he's up to in London? Perhaps he's collecting funds for a last big flutter in Berlin here. That story of his boy being ill—it's all *Wurst*. Anyone can see that with half an eye. But, of course, it wouldn't do to let this pair of prize idiots suspect what *I* suspect. He wouldn't thank me for that. . . .

Come to think of it, it's rather nice of me to straighten out his mess for him. It would have done no one any harm if he'd have shown the same consideration for us.

Damn it! He *couldn't* have asked these people to sell out for him, without tipping us the wink, too! It's ridiculous. They've got it all balled up!

He looked up under his eyelashes, and smiled. He tapped the tips of his fingers together, like any greasy Jew financier. He looked almost top-heavy with the burden of weighty financial secrets he carried in his cranium.

" Well, Herr Graf, and what do you think? " asked Herr Schmidt miserably.

He quizzed the bewildered manager sympathetically. " You've had no wire this morning? "

" No, Herr Graf! "

Of course not! His reasoning had been sound as a bell from the word go. If Smirnof had wanted to confirm his order to sell by that second call, and not cancel it, he would obviously have taken some opportunity, at some stage of the journey, of sending a wire.

" Of course not! " he said aloud. " As a matter of fact,"

he lied suddenly and blithely, " I can set your minds at rest. He told me in his telephone-call that he *had* given Brauner orders to sell, but he'd thought better of it, in view of certain later information that had come to him."

He had by this time completely convinced himself about that second call. These dolts were still havering. How grateful Smirnof would be to him for preventing his lieutenants making fools of themselves, and him, and all of them !

" Really, Herr Graf, is that really true ? " Tears glistened in Schmidt's eyes.

" What do you mean, is that true ? "

" Oh, how can I thank you enough for coming in this morning ? If not for you, we would certainly have sold out on Monday, unless Herr Smirnof had sent fresh orders to the contrary."

" We might telephone to-night, Herr Schmidt ! " Brauner timidly hazarded.

" Tscha ! " Schmidt turned fiercely on his assistant. " With his boy, perhaps, dying ? Because you are such a fool you cannot take down a telephone-message properly ? Pooh ! " He spat.

" I don't think I should worry so much if I were you," the Herr Graf soothed him. " You're bound to hear from him quite soon, if he isn't back himself on Monday." He looked at his watch. " I say. I'm afraid I'll have to be going now."

" Again thank you, Herr Graf, and still again ! *Guten Tag*, Herr Graf ! "

Oskar von Straupitz-Kalmin shook hands with Brauner, and gave a quite immoderate tip to the office-boy. The wad of pound notes in his breast-pocket felt warm and friendly. There was no point in doing anything with them till Smirnof returned. He was feeling very pleased with himself, one way and another. He had done Alexander Smirnof a real good turn. And, after all, Alexander Smirnof and he were, in a sense, brothers-in-law.

CHAPTER XVIII

NORTH SEA

I

IT IS A GREY November day on the North Sea, with a wind blowing sudden flurries of drizzle into the face of the one passenger who is foolhardy enough to brave the elements. From hour to hour he paces the top deck, excepting for certain brief interruptions, when he descends the companion-way to his cabin and pours himself out a half-tumblerful of brandy. He sneezes once or twice ; he feels the muscles under the shoulder-blades shivering and aching.

" To hell with it ! I'm getting a cold, too ! " he mutters. " I'd best try and stick it down here ! "

But after a minute or two he feels there is not space nor air enough here. Here the enemy, confined within such close dimensions, is almost compressed into corporeal shape. You feel, you almost see, his fingers sliding slowly forward, all the way out of Moscow, to fasten themselves round your throat.

Upstairs the enemy is not more than a ghost padding after you, with a light now and again falling upon his pince-nez ; most of the time he is not even that, the wind blows so free upon your forehead. You are soaked to the skin, of course and have been for an hour or two. But your wife will see to that ; there will be a hot bath, and whisky and sugar and lemon and aspirin ; and your wife's hand on your forehead to send you off to sleep. You will be as right as rain to-morrow morning, clever enough to confound a hundred little Silvers, waiting puzzled and distressed to hear what you have to say on the subject of the Cratonian operations.

How the hell did Polednik get to know ? How did he manage to poke his long snout all the way from Moscow to Trebinth ? How the hell did Polednik get to know ?

He sat down for a moment trying desperately to worry out some sort of line which might connect the two points. In a cabin on the lower deck, just below the companion-way, a bored passenger put a record on his portable gramophone. It was some cheap sort of fake-Spanish orchestra-stuff, but it had a refrain which haunted him with its approach to something he knew. Perhaps the composer had deliberately gone to Handel for an idea or two, calculating that the people he composed for were no experts on Handel ; it may have been an unconscious reminiscence. Most probably it was no more than a coincidence, as it is sometimes only a coincidence that you will find in a bad poem by a bad poet some magnificent phrase almost identical with a phrase in a great and austere master of whom he is totally ignorant. " *Lascia ch'io pianga*," the air went, the sublime saraband from *Rinaldo*. The palm-trees of Rio de Janeiro swayed and curtseyed derisively against the curtain of grey North sleet. Smirnof rose from his seat again and shuffled round the deck, round the deck. His feet felt as heavy as lead.

Alexander Smirnof is not destined to be informed how Boris Polednik got to know about those Cratonian operations. But as he goes pacing along the deck, and down the deck again, so unwisely exposing himself to the wind and drizzle, the opportunity is allowed us of reviewing briefly Alexander Smirnof's career as a man of business, which was so seriously compromised by the menfolk of two of his wife's sisters— Boris Polednik in Moscow and Oskar von Straupitz-Kalmin in Berlin.

II

This narrative in its early stages elaborated the transformation of the little sweating-den by the river, which old Mr. Horowitz had foisted upon Sam Silver, into an organisation of first-rate importance in the industry of Lancashire and the North Country. The effort was made to make it clear that this gigantic success could not have been achieved excepting in the combination of the special and unique attributes of the two partners, the qualities of character in Silver supplementing the deficiencies of character in Smirnof, the qualities of ability in Smirnof supplementing the deficiencies of ability in Silver.

This process attained its climax in the conversion of the firm into a public company in June, nineteen twenty. In the legal actions which we will be called upon to speak of before long, the prosecution was not able to adduce even the suspicion of a single act of wrongdoing on the part of the firm during the whole period of the association of the partners in that initial enterprise ; a period which began in July nineteen twelve, with the appointment of Smirnof as Silver's book-keeper, and ended with the sale of their limited-liability company to the public in June nineteen twenty. Their association continued, of course, after that time, not only in other undertakings, but in the administration of the public company, for Silver became its chairman, and Smirnof its joint managing director.

The prosecution was able to adduce no single act of wrongdoing against either Silver or Smirnof during those initial eight years of their association, and it was to be remembered that those years covered the period of the War, when the record of a great number of companies, smaller and greater than theirs, was not without blemish. On the contrary, counsel for the defence was able to prove triumphantly that the company had fulfilled its contracts with an almost dazzling probity, and that it was precisely because of that probity that it had won the confidence both of the Government and many private organisations to an extent which enabled them so signally to outstrip all their competitors.

The inference was made on the part of the prosecution that those eight years of distinguished and laborious honesty were but intended to create a state of confidence in which those complicated dishonesties which were the subject of their examination might be more easily initiated. The inference called for a heated protest on the part of the defence, and was privately commented on by the public with great bitterness ; the judge himself was forced to utter a word of rebuke, for the possible inferences of that inference, he pointed out, were calamitous. No firm of the most unimpeachable standing could conduct its affairs with the utmost rightness for ten, twenty, thirty years, without laying itself open to the insinuation that it was acting with such propriety only to act the more efficiently with impropriety whenever it considered the moment had arrived.

In June nineteen twenty a company with a capital of two million pounds was formed to acquire the business for one million and a half pounds, the public scrambling most gratifyingly to buy up the six per cent preference shares. The question whether that operation was in any sense dubious was not a matter with which the law could occupy itself, once it had been established that the statements in the prospectus were, in point of fact, scrupulously accurate, despite the vehement efforts of the prosecution to prove the contrary. The discussion whether such operations are dubious belongs rather to the higher theology, the metaphysics, of commerce. At that time a number of firms, of which some went back several generations, sold themselves to the public, thus ensuring their owners great personal fortunes, and leaving the investing public to pay, if anybody should ever be called upon to pay, for a decline in absolute value which may, or may not, have been foreseen by the vendors.

Certainly Sam Silver & Company had assets tangible and intangible to show the public, which made a participation in the purchase of their interests a highly attractive proposition. There were tangible assets in the way of factories, machinery, and stock, valued at half a million pounds. They were able to show balance-sheets in which the profits of the firm gathered momentum from year to year like a rock bounding down a mountain-side. Five years' purchase of profits were adjudged worth one million pounds. If the public did not pay sufficient respect to the law of gravitation, and did not, as a whole, remember that the most exhilarating movement of that sort must come sooner or later to a standstill, there were certain members of it who anticipated the standstill and bought and sold shares to their great advantage, while the rock was still bounding merrily down the mountain-side.

Of the million ordinary shares valued at ten shillings issued, half a million were subscribed by Silver and Smirnof in the ratio of fifty-one to forty-nine, thus assuring to Silver the at least nominal superiority. Silver was firm on the point, with a firmness which Smirnof had, with his usual skill, himself suggested that Silver should not waver in. He realised that, so long as he desired it, the superiority was purely apparent, a matter of quite unpotent numbers. The purchase was indication enough of the confidence entertained by the former sole partners in the new public company to be formed. In actual money the public paid over the sum of one and three quarter million pounds.

Silver was delighted, he was almost appalled, by the social distinction of his board of directors, his two earls and his brigadier-general. He was not quite clear in his mind that it was not a spontaneous tribute on their part to the magnificent company he had developed out of such contemptible beginnings. He under-estimated the part played by the issuing-house in London, which took in hand the conversion of the private into the public company, in securing the collaboration of those distinguished gentlemen.

He was intensely proud of the company, of his directors, of the quality of the goods he turned out. His office in the factory on the Longton brick-croft remained the centre of his universe. He knew that Smirnof, on the other hand, had been contemplating speculation in cotton for a long time, as soon as he commanded sums of money large enough to make his weight felt on the market. It was true they themselves had large interests in cotton, but they were subordinate to their waterproof undertakings in their various ramifications. Smirnof did not neglect to let Silver know he intended to speculate in cotton immediately on a large scale, for he did not choose—at that moment, at least, or in that matter, at least—to hide so important a development in his own activities from his associate. It was suggested without vigour that Silver might speculate, too, if he chose. But Silver did not choose.

" What shall I want to speculate for ? " he inquired of himself, and Smirnof, in words identical with those he used in a conversation, elsewhere recorded, between himself and his daughter May. " I don't believe in it. I want to go on making my raincoats and my waterproofs in my Longton factory and my gum-boots and my dummy teats and my balloons and my hot-water-bottles in my Stretford factory. I'm happy like that ; what should I want to speculate for ? "

Smirnof, as that same conversation with May Silver indicated, did speculate, and to the tune of a considerable sum of money. It was the first time in his career that he had in his own possession a considerable sum of money to speculate with, and he had always intended to spread his wings the moment the golden heavens were open to him. It also happened to be a moment in which all the auguries were favourable, as his devoted studies of the situation indicated. The conversation of Silver and his daughter further demonstrated that Smirnof's speculation would have been as brilliantly successful as all his operations had been till that time, if it had not been for the unfortunate pressure exerted on him by Sam Silver himself, as a result of which he was the loser by sums so vast that Silver got an attack of colic every time he thought of them.

To what extent Smirnof found himself justified, by the loss Silver's advice occasioned him, in playing false to Silver in his later operations was not a matter which the lawyers could satisfactorily tackle, though counsel for Silver's defence thought the approach might be profitable, and made one or two efforts along those lines. That is a matter less for the lawyers than for the students of human character and motive. But there was no doubt that Silver was tremendously touched and influenced by Smirnof's magnanimity in the matter, for Smirnof did, in fact, behave with more than gentlemanliness ; he behaved with gentleness. And although it was inconceivable that Silver should under any circumstances have brought any action of Smirnof into question, Smirnof's behaviour after the cotton episode did certainly contribute to the thickening of that glamorous cocoon at the centre of which Silver sat enchanted, in a blindness for which he could hardly be censured, and in a vanity which was very blameworthy, and for which he was duly castigated. But the cocoon did not so completely isolate him but that Smirnof, even in matters completely outside Silver's competence in Doomington, did not succeed in insinuating a certain sense into Silver's mind of initiative and responsibility. It was a complicated situation, and one which exacted from the defence every power they possessed of elucidation and imaginative reconstruction.

By the time February nineteen twenty-one had come and gone, Smirnof had concluded that to speculate with other people's money is more likely to prove satisfactory, taking it by and large, than speculating with your own. It was for that reason, largely, that he determined to move his headquarters from Doomington to London. He was not allowed to do that without objection from one or two quarters.

" A fine idea ! " protested Silver. " And what should I do without you ? And when I want you should help me make up my mind about a new order, or a new process, or a new this or that, you shall have to come up to Doomington, or I should fly to London ? "

" There is always the telephone, Sam," Smirnof pointed

out gently. "Marriage has had a different effect on you than on me. It seems to be quite a journey for you to go to Liverpool, let alone London, though you, too, used to be quite a wanderer in the old days in Russia, weren't you? As for me, I promise you one thing : I'm just as ready any day to go to Rome or Vienna as to Rochdale. I'd rather travel than stay in one place, in fact, except that Sarah won't come. She doesn't like travel, and she won't move a foot without all the children. Apart from Sarah, London, Constantinople, Berlin—it's all the same to me. There's money to make, music to listen to, a game of chess now and again—what more can a man want? In any case, I have been away so often already, I assure you, you won't feel the difference."

" That's different. I always knew you was coming straight back here to Longton. But you said you was going to promise me one thing. What is it ? "

" So I am. Whenever you feel the telephone or a telegram isn't good enough, I'll come and do what I can . . . wherever I might be. Nowhere's too far. Does that make you feel any easier in your mind ? "

" Well, perhaps it does."

" And you'll find my man, Huxtable, the man who's been helping me all last year in buying up those dumps, you'll find him as useful as me. He's got a brain like an adding-machine."

" I know you wouldn't send me a man who wasn't absolutely A1, Sasha, I know that."

" But the most important thing is this, Sam—I feel we've only just started. We're going to make more money than we've ever dreamed of up here in Doomington, turning out raincoats."

" You don't say nothing rude about my raincoats."

" I wasn't, Sam. But there's so much more for us to do. You wait ! "

" Well, we'll make more money. And what will we do with it ? "

" What will we do with it ? Some day I'm going to buy up the whole harbour-front of Rio de Janeiro. I'll build the most magnificent opera-house in the world, and I'll collect the best symphony-orchestra there's ever been. And Sarah will give me *marrons glacés* all day long with a golden spoon."

" And me ? "

" You'll buy up Lord Street, Southport, and Blackpool Tower, and the Doomington Town Hall, and you'll give parties for the Aged and Needy Poor, the Incurables of Lancashire, and all the Poor Children from Longton and Ancoats. And you'll buy Hannah another pearl necklace."

" She has enough pearl necklaces. What ? You want to ruin me ? "

There was a conversation between Esther, the eldest Silver daughter, and Smirnof, which did not develop along such playful lines.

" So you're going to London, to start off on your own ? " Esther tackled him one day.

" I don't consider myself accountable to you for my actions," Smirnof countered sourly.

" You know quite well it'll do nobody any good your talking like that, neither you nor me nor anybody."

" I'm quite convinced my getting out of Doomington and spreading myself in London is going to do us all a lot of good."

" Oh, are you ? Well, I'm not ! "

" Very well then. The matter rests there."

" I know I can't stop you. I can only warn you."

" I'm much obliged to you."

" It's too important for you to answer me back like a schoolboy."

" I won't have you talking to me like a school-mistress."

" I'm not. I'm talking to you like a business-woman. Don't I know where Pliskin & Company would be now if it wasn't for Silver's ? Don't I know what would happen to it if anything happened to you ? You forget. There are quite a lot of other little businesses tied up with yours now."

" I don't forget. I'm merely going to add to them."

" What do you want to go to London for ? Why don't you stay in Doomington ? "

" Don't be ridiculous ! "

" No, I'm not being ridiculous ! You'll do a lot with father still ; you'll do nothing on your own ! "

He made an effort to suppress his anger, to keep his voice as level as possible.

" I think it about time I tried to do something for myself too. I think you'll all agree I've been fairly useful to your father."

" And to yourself."

" Of course."

" You remember what you said to me once ? "

" We've talked things over any number of times."

" You know very well when I mean."

" That's a long time ago now."

" Yes, but it's still true."

" What do you mean ? "

" You know it's no good. You can't start out on your own. You've tried before, and you've gone down."

" Pah ! I was a boy ! I've learned something since then ! "

" You're still the same like then. There are some things you can't ever learn."

" Don't be absurd ! It's like climbing mountains. At the beginning and a long way up it's steep and difficult. You need ropes and nailed boots and God knows what. But when you're near the top, all of a sudden it's easy. The slope is easy, the air is fresh and strong."

" Oh ! Don't talk nonsense like that with me ! " she said abruptly. " You think you can fool me ? "

" It's about time we both shut up ! I've had quite enough ! "

" You're only talking about mountains because you're not sure of yourself, just like I'm not sure of you. You want to

forget about it with words. What did you say that time?
You remember what you said? ' I can't do it, not by
myself ! ' you said."

" I'm sorry, I must leave now."

" You'll remember what I said. Some day you'll remember. You'll come to me and you'll say : ' Esther, you're
right ! ' "

" Good afternoon ! "

" Good afternoon ! Such a year on you ! "

The activities of Smirnof, directed from his London headquarters, were conducted along three channels—so far, that
is to say, as Silver was concerned. Smirnof remained joint
managing director of the public company in Doomington of
which Silver was chairman, and he managed to be of some
considerable use to Silver at the London end of the telephone,
when his nominee, Huxtable, did not seem able to carry all
the necessary weight. He formed a private trust company,
of which he persuaded Silver to become a director without
difficulty. He formed, in addition, a private trading company, to be financed by the trust company, of which also
Silver became a director. He formed certain subsidiary
companies, too, which facilitated the transference of funds
from one deposit to another whenever it became convenient.

But it was that triple chain of companies of which they
were both directors which drew up Polednik, as by a hook,
out of his musty office half a continent away in Moscow.
It caught Smirnof in its coils in Germany, where he laboured
so hard, and, it seemed, so successfully, to redress his
position. In this triple chain Silver in Doomington was involved to his undoing—though Silver himself would not
have considered the word quite accurate.

With respect to Smirnof's other company-promoting
activities in London, Silver was in no way involved. If
Polednik had not prevented Smirnof from disentangling

himself from his Cratonian complications, he might have attained the eminence of a Hooley or a Whittaker Wright in that territory. Considering the various elements in the case, it is not likely he would have avoided their ultimate destiny ; for the Smirnofs, the Kreugers, carry their fatal temperamental or intellectual flaw about with them, however microscopic it may be in its beginnings. Or if the impossible can be believed, and they leave the mould flawless in temperament and intellect, the world they are forced to operate in is not an absolute world. It is a relative and fallible world. A great deal of Smirnof's impulse in his financial career was æsthetic ; but he was deluded in his belief that he could lock himself up in an ivory tower and play marvellous music to himself on the keyboard of figures. The artist in sound and stone and word cannot wholly lock himself up in a vacuum, the financier much less. The figures he deals with, pounds, shillings, and pence, francs, dollars, are not mere ciphers. They are so many years of a clerk's work ; they are the difference to an artisan between no holiday and a fortnight's holiday by the sea ; they are dry bread and motorcars ; they are the doctor's bill for the dying child and a week-end of bought love.

Alexander Smirnof became a company-promoter. In that capacity he indulged his purer financial passions. It was an embarrassment to him to be forced to suspend those activities, or leave them in the hands of subordinates, during the Berlin period that extended from August to November nineteen twenty-three. But it had become a matter of absolute urgency to find that two hundred thousand pounds he went in search of. In the most dizzy company-promoting epochs in London or New York, at the height of their booms, you could not be certain of forcing the pace to the extent of making so vast a sum of money on so small an outlay in so short a time. To attempt so large a profit in London or New York, it was necessary to risk a loss as serious, and to be ready to devote much more time to the endeavour. In Berlin the task was not quite child's play, of course, but it

was a virtual certainty, if your stakes were just big enough
to begin with, and you kept your head.

Of course, there were certain outside eventualities you
had to bear in mind. You must not let them catch you
napping ; they must not stabilise their mark while you
stooped a moment to tie your shoe-lace.

And Schmidt, your manager, must not have diarrhoea ;
and Oskar von Straupitz-Kalmin must not pass your office
and take it into his head to poke his nose into your affairs.
Otherwise, it was a dead certainty.

How, then, did the triple chain operate which Smirnof
manipulated with results so spectacular ? It was in this way,
in the buying and selling of dumps of war-material. This
was an activity which appealed to another side of his
character. This also involved a great deal in the way of
handling and juggling with figures. But, in addition to that,
it involved travel over large areas, a difficult art of which he
was an effortless master. It involved intrigue, financial and
political, with minds sometimes as subtle as his own. There
was a good deal to do in that field in England itself, where
great dumps of war-material stood about ; where, in addition, great contracts for turning out this article and that had
been placed, or were still current, and could not be abro-
gated. All that kept Smirnof's and Silver's trading company
very busy. But it was comparatively straightforward work ;
it could be left more or less safely to subordinates.

But the work he himself took in hand was of a more international scope. The major Allied countries had dumps all
over the Mediterranean and Ægean shores, and were
anxious to dispose of them. The minor countries, some of
which had existed before the War, some of which owed their
renewed existence to the War, bought these dumps. It was
Alexander Smirnof who was the go-between for a great many
of these large operations.

We have seen Smirnof already occupied with business of

this sort in the early part of nineteen nineteen, when he was able to be of some use in South Russia to the army of General Denikin, who happened to be not only a soldier whose character and intentions were highly acceptable to the British Government of that time, but one who had had a certain direct association with the family of Alexander Smirnof. The sale to Denikin dirt-cheap of a great deal of material did not help Denikin's cause to ultimate triumph, and it was less profitable to Smirnof and Silver than their other operations of a kindred nature.

Smirnof was still acting at that time for the private manufacturing company in Doomington of which Silver and Smirnof were sole directors and shareholders. He extended these operations in nineteen twenty. In nineteen twenty-one he had several large contracts of the same nature running, some financed by the newly created public company, with the full connivance of the directors, some financed entirely by the private trust company. In the spring of nineteen twenty-two he was summoned by Silver to Doomington, to have the situation of the public company laid before him. Silver was in a state of great despondency. He feared that not even the preference shareholders would receive their dividend. He appealed to Smirnof to do all that was in his power during his travels to restore the fortunes of the public company by extending its connections. Thereupon Smirnof applied himself with special energy to this business of buying and selling war-dumps. Involved among these operations was a certain arrangement with the Republic of Cratonia, one of the largest of that sort he had undertaken ; it was the arrangement that twitched Polednik into activity, where he sat scratching away in his Moscow office, devoted and morose among the red shades ; it was the arrangement that toppled Alexander Smirnof over like a pack of cards.

The contract was concluded in the spring of nineteen twenty-two. It was the arrangement, previously described, by which Smirnof, acting on behalf of the private trading company, of which he and Silver were sole directors, bought from the British Government the residue of the war-material dumped by the Army some years previously in certain Ægean depôts. The material was sold and handed over to the Cratonian Government, who paid for it in six bills for one quarter of a million pounds, that fell due at intervals of three months. They were to pay, that is to say, one and a half million pounds in all. The sum borrowed from the bank on the security of these bills, and on the personal guarantee of Smirnof and Silver, was one million two hundred thousand pounds. After payment of the bank's interest, Smirnof would be left, when all the six bills had been honoured, with a neat profit somewhere short of three hundred thousand pounds. Of this sum rather more than one hundred thousand pounds was to go to the trading company as its share of the profits. A sum in the neighbourhood of one hundred and thirty thousand pounds was to be appropriated by Alexander Smirnof as his secret commission. M. Prokopedes, the Cratonian Foreign Minister, would receive as his share of the booty a sum in the neighbourhood of fifty thousand pounds, for his kindness in carrying through the deal on terms distinctly unfavourable to the public finances of his country.

From the nature of these arrangements it is evident that Alexander Smirnof had no desire that his associate, Sam Silver, should be in close touch with their developments. When the bank, therefore, requested the personal guarantee of Silver and Smirnof as an additional security for their loan, Smirnof—perhaps not for the first time—forged Silver's name, or had it forged. In so far as that forged guarantee was concerned, there was no intention on the part of Smirnof to defraud Silver. The money would be repaid to the bank with the utmost scrupulousness. It was purely a matter of convenience that Silver should not himself sign his name to that document. With respect to the Prokopedes arrangements, on the other hand, there was no question at all of the intention to defraud.

The first bills were duly honoured in August and November

nineteen twenty-two. The third bill, due in February nineteen twenty-three, was not promptly settled. There were disquieting rumours of political uncertainties in Cratonia, and Smirnof and the bank were both a little anxious. Some two or three tense weeks passed by, till at last the Paris agent of the Government rang him up to inform him that though the settlement of the bill must be held up for a good week, it would certainly be arranged. As indeed it was.

There was even more delay with respect to the honouring of the bill payable in May. The tone of the bank was extremely grave. It was quite impossible, now again, for Smirnof to raise so large a sum of money in ready cash without upsetting his financial arrangements in Doomington and elsewhere. The May bill, too, was at length honoured.

In July a *coup d'état* took place in Cratonia. The Government of which Prokopedes was Foreign Minister was overthrown, for he was not the only corrupt one, nor even the most corrupt one, amongst them. Smirnof spread his wings and flew swiftly and silently to Cratonia. He was shown that the sooner he spread his wings and returned the more they would like it. He pointed out there had been very serious delays in the honouring of the bills payable by their Government to his company. He hoped that these would not recur under a Government so much more efficient and conscientious.

He was informed with great regret that the further bills would not be honoured. The Government considered it had already paid over a sum of money far in excess of the value of the goods supplied them. Smirnof replied that the Government had entered into a solemn contract with his firm. It was inconceivable that Cratonia should behave with the abominable lack of principle of Soviet Russia. He was informed that the choice lay with him. They were quite willing to let the matter die a quiet death, for of course, though their justification in this affair was more than ample, they did not wish to acquire the sort of reputation that Soviet Russia had acquired in the field of international finance. But if he desired to carry the matter any further, the Government had the honour to announce that it possessed all the evidence relevant to the secret and criminal commissions agreed on between himself and the recently deposed Foreign Minister. They did not imagine he desired the matter to get to the ears of his partner in England, and his various associates up and down the Continent.

It did not seem discreet to Smirnof to be insistent. He returned to London swiftly and silently. Not many days later certain conversations took place between himself and his friend Strauss in Berlin, as a result of which he determined to devote himself exclusively for the next few months to the stock-market in Berlin. The matter of greatest urgency was to keep the bank quiet by the payment of as much as he could scrape together now and realise in a month or two, and by the exercise of all he knew of the arts of diplomacy.

He went to Berlin, as has been recorded ; he was summoned thence, as has also been recorded. But that was because of Boris Polednik. It had nothing to do with his success or failure on the Berlin Stock Exchange. He had, in point of fact, made the sum of money he had set out to make ; or had, at least, accumulated a holding of securities convertible into a sum at least as large, after the deduction of all interest.

The money was to be realised on Monday morning. It would be paid over to the bank with the minimum of delay. Then he could breathe again, and devote himself to London a little more steadily. He was a little tired, for the time being, of these international marketings. He would devote himself to London. He would have a good time. He had seen far too little of his wife and children lately. He had heard far too little music lately.

Yes, of course. There was the matter of Silver and Polednik to adjust first. That was all—Silver and Polednik. Silver and

Polednik ! Silver and Polednik ! the engines drummed as
they pushed and churned the grey cold waters.

III

The scene changes briefly to a rather shabby room in a
house in Moscow which at one time must have been rather
splendid, the house of some rich merchant. The windows
look down on the Kuznetski Most. The furniture in the room
was once splendid, too. The curtains are brocade ; the
furniture is of the Empire period, all bound and inlaid with
metal and decorated with sphinxes. But the general effect
is shabby. The brocade curtains are torn, and give out
clouds of sharp dust if you press against them. The surfaces
of the desk and tables are marked with the bottoms of tea-
glasses.

There is no time in Moscow, and certainly Boris Polednik
has no time, to attend to the beating of dusty curtains and
the polishing of the surfaces of furniture. Boris Polednik is
a high official in the Commissariat for Foreign Trade. He
has at this moment an important visitor, M. Mengalos by
name, the head of the deputation sent out by the Cratonian
Department of Foreign Trade to discuss the possibility of
certain commercial accommodations between the U.S.S.R.
and the Republic of Cratonia. M. Mengalos is very earnest
and very efficient. His Government has noted with great
interest the steps taken towards the resumption of trade
relations between the great country M. Polednik represents
and certain other countries. The Government of Cratonia
begs to make certain proposals to the Soviet Government.
M. Polednik listens carefully, his eyes glinting behind his
pince-nez in the half-light. What is proposed would be a
matter largely of adjustments in the interchange of certain
commodities, continues M. Mengalos, as from Soviet
Russia, timber, oil ; as from Cratonia, currants, olives,
fruit, carpets. The relations of the Cratonian with the
Rumanian Government being at this time not so cordial

as they might be, this might seem the moment in which a series of agreements in these senses might be of particular profit to both peoples, in the political as well as the commercial fields.

M. Polednik tapped his finger-tips together speculatively. He seemed as gentle as any mouse, sitting small and quiet behind his enormous Empire desk. Then suddenly his voice thrust out into the twilight like a fist.

" And what guarantees can you give us you will not treat your arrangements with us as you treated your contract some months ago with a certain English firm whose activities in the Eastern Mediterranean are well known ? "

M. Mengalos changed his position, his bearing, his tone of voice.

" That was straight from the shoulder, M. Polednik. I see you are well-informed."

" That is exactly the scope of my duties at this desk here, to be well-informed."

" Frankly, we imagined that the affair had gone no further. Neither we nor the opposite party had any desire that it should become common property."

" It has not become common property. But it is the duty of my department to satisfy itself as to the reliability both of Governments and private firms in this somewhat critical moment of our commercial history. Politically we have rather special reasons to dislike the firm we are both referring to. We have not forgotten its activities against us in South Russia some years ago. But we know nothing derogatory to its business *bona fides*.

" On the other hand, I am afraid that the behaviour of your Government in the affair does not reassure me. It hardly encourages me to represent to my Government the desirability of the arrangements you have been kind enough to propose."

" My dear M. Polednik, I fear that you have heard less than half the story."

" I have heard the significant part, from the point of

view of my Government. My Government would need satis-
fying that any agreements it entered into would not be
liable to suspension in the event of another *coup d'état*."

M. Mengalos felt like strangling the self-righteous little
rat there and then. The preposterous air of milk-white
innocence the Bolshevik brigand could assume when it
suited his purpose was exacerbating. He thought it best,
however, to subdue the impulse.

" You make it necessary for me to give you an account
of the facts, a thing which it had been more or less agreed
upon that my Government would refrain from doing in any
emergency."

" Proceed, please ! "

" The facts are quite simple. I do not wish to call into
question for one moment the *bona fides* of the firm involved.
The contract was arranged between M. Prokopedes, late
Minister for Foreign Affairs, and the firm's chief agent. All
that is involved is the personal honour of that chief agent."

" What ? "

The sound burst so explosively from Polednik's lips that
M. Mengalos looked up, quite startled.

" I beg your pardon ? "

Polednik's eyes were shut tight behind the pince-nez.
His clenched fists on the table were pale as chalk. " One
moment ! " he requested. There was no trace of emotion in
his tone.

M. Mengalos looked a little puzzled. " Did you wish to
ask anything ? "

No. Boris Polednik did not wish to ask anything—excepting perhaps for the loan of a hatchet. He wanted to go about
smashing the furniture in his sky-high exultation. He wanted
to tear the curtains from their rings and swathe himself and
M. Mengalos round with them, and go dancing, dancing,
among the shattered furniture, singing, singing, till what
was left of the ceiling-plaster came down in flakes.

" No," said Polednik. " I was trying to recall his name.
Oh, yes, I remember. Alexander Smirnof. Isn't that right ? "

" Yes, that's right. You are indeed well-informed, M. Polednik."

" Please continue."

" It was arranged between MM. Smirnof and Prokopedes that the contract should involve for both of them a secret commission on a scale which, even in the dealings of the last Government, must be considered excessive, positively outrageous."

" That is to say," Polednik deduced, " this man Smirnof made a large commission, all knowledge of which was withheld from his partner ? I believe his senior partner's name is—let me see now—Silver ? "

" Yes. May I say that I think the way in which you keep abreast here with what is happening in capitalist countries is most praiseworthy ? "

" Please listen, M. Mengalos ! "

" Yes ? "

" My department is aware of, and is much perturbed by, the behaviour of Cratonia in this particular matter. I must be in a position to convince them of the ample justification your Government had in refusing to honour your engagements."

" I should be delighted to furnish you with all the necessary proofs. In the strictest confidence, I need not say ? "

" Of course, in the strictest confidence ! "

" Well, then, assuming that has been done to your complete satisfaction, these are the arrangements I am instructed to propose."

Polednik switched the light on over his desk. " Let's get down to it ! " he said.

His voice was a little abrupt, but his manner was a model of official decorum. It would have surprised M. Mengalos to know how exceedingly close he had been to being embraced by a high official in the Soviet Commissariat for Foreign Trade and being kissed by him rabidly on both cheeks.

CHAPTER XIX

TRAIN JOURNEY

I

A CAR WAS waiting for Alexander Smirnof alongside the customs shed in Harwich. The chauffeur had found the journey from London to Harwich difficult, there had been so much fog the whole way. It was the chauffeur himself who suggested that, seeing a fast train for London was leaving immediately, it might be preferable for Mr. Smirnof to go home by rail. If he might say so, the sooner Mr. Smirnof got into London the better, he seemed to have so bad a cold coming on. He would immediately ring up Mrs. Smirnof in London, not to alarm her like, but to be sure that another car went to meet him at Liverpool Street, and she should be ready for him the moment he came in.

" All right ! " snapped Smirnof. " Go and get me a ticket then ! " He felt too cold and wretched to argue.

It was good to get back home again. It was good to have Sarah take him to her warm bosom, and cover his mouth and eyes with her large fragrant mouth. It was good to have her kneeling down to take his boots and socks off for him. It was good to lie in the hot bath and let her run in more and more hot water till it was almost too hot to bear. It was good to lie in bed with a stiff dose of whisky and lemon and sugar creeping gratefully along the chilled veins.

And how good it was to have the elder children brought down to kiss him on the forehead—just on the forehead, darling, for daddy's got a horrid nasty cold, and daddy wouldn't like Harold to have a nasty cold, too, would he, daddy? Daddy would not, Harold. And has Harold been a good boy? And has Hilda been a good girl? And Janey? And where on earth is Jackie, Sarah? Isn't Jackie all right yet? Just you go off to sleep, Sasha. Jackie's all right. He was asleep; I didn't want to wake him. He's still got that silly cough of his. He *won't* get rid of it. There now, children. Come along, Jackson, take them all away. No, Harold, you must go, too. Daddy must go to sleep now. He'll be better to-morrow. Daddy was a bad boy walking up and down in the rain high up on top of the ship. Yes, Harold, you shall go on a ship, too, some day. Daddy says we shall all go in a ship, to a place called Rio de Janeiro, some day. Won't that be lovely? Good night, children ; good night all of you ; God bless you!

"What's that you are saying, Sasha darling? You are going up to see father to-morrow first thing? Darling, don't be silly. You've got a really bad cold coming on. You mustn't think of going up to Doomington till you've got rid of that cold. He sent an urgent telegram for you? It's much more urgent for you to get well, darling. All right, darling, all right. The very moment you're fit. You've been working yourself to death over in that horrid Berlin. You must have a full week's rest, no telephone, no letters, no newspapers, nothing. Then I might let you go. And I'll come with you, of course."

II

Sunday and Monday passed, Tuesday and Wednesday passed. He fought furiously to oust the cold that had taken possession of him. He dosed himself with so much quinine and aspirin and brandy that Sarah was terrified he would do serious damage to his heart. The drugs induced in him a sort of sullen trance, but they had no power over that fierce obsession to get to Doomington, to get to Doomington, the very first moment possible to tumble into the train and get to Doomington, to see Silver, and explain away the abominable calumny. Now and again he mumbled a word about sending a wire to Berlin, or telephoning to Berlin, but the idea passed almost immediately out of his head, so dominant was the passion that had him to get to Doomington.

Thursday morning came. The concentration of his enormous will-power on strangling his cold had been more or less successful. He had no temperature, and the passages of his head were clear. But he was as weak as a kitten. He seemed to have lost pounds of flesh. His neck hung in flabby folds.

" Sarah," he said that morning, " I'm going to Doomington to-day."

" Darling," she moaned. " You can't. You're not fit. I won't let you."

" I'm taking the mid-day train from St. Pancras," he said. His eyes were lucid, with the hot lucidity of fire. She knew it was hopeless to oppose herself to those eyes. It was something to be thankful for that he had allowed her to dissuade him when, last night, he had suggested going up to Doomington by the midnight train.

" At least," she pleaded, " you might stay and have lunch here. It'll be a better lunch than you'll get on the train."

" Very well, then. Is Steadley about ? "

" Yes, darling."

" Tell him to arrange for the 4.40 from St. Pancras. By the way, I haven't seen the newspapers since—when was it ? "

" You came home on Saturday night, darling."

" My God ! Saturday night ! That's Sunday, Monday, Tuesday, Wednesday, gone ! Have them sent in, please ! "

" Yes, dear."

" Oh, one more thing. You said you wanted to come up to Doomington with me ! "

" Yes. The fact is . . . if you'd only wait a few days. You're driving me nearly silly between you."

" Who do you mean ? Is Jackie worse ? "

" No, he's not worse. He just doesn't get any better."

He rose from his chair and walked over to her. She noticed with dismay how weak his legs were. He patted her head. " You poor old thing," he said softly. The hot burning in his eyes was dimmed. " You do have a rough time. Don't worry too much about Jackie. Just you wait till I've fixed up this business with your father. It won't take long. I might even get back to-night."

" You can't ! You can't ! " she wailed, with real alarm in her voice.

" All right then, darling ! What a devoted little wife it is ! Then to-morrow, perhaps. After that—there's just Berlin. I've just got to wind things up in Berlin, then I'm free."

" Oh, how lovely ! So you'll be back in London again ! "

" I thought we might have a holiday, Sarah. We'll all go off to the South of France in a fleet of cars, eh ? "

" Oh, Sasha, Sasha ! Are you *ever* going to be able to tear yourself away ? You remember what you used to say about our going to South America, and having a house with palmtrees and fountains ? And you'd really have some rest at last, and give up wandering as if somebody was chasing after you——"

" Be quiet, Sarah, be quiet ! Nobody's chasing after me ! " His eyes were closed, and his hands trembled as he gripped the back of a chair. " I said we'll go to the South of France for a holiday. It'll do Jackie all the good in the world."

" Yes, darling," she murmured under her breath. " Though I'd have thought it would be more of a holiday for you to stay at home a bit."

" Please," he said abruptly. " Go and get me those newspapers ! "

" Yes, darling, I'll go and see about it at once."

The newspapers came a few minutes later. They stuck and came apart and slid to his knees, he held them so unsteadily.

The news from Berlin was sensational. The first issue of the rentenmark, on the Friday of the previous week, had been succeeded yesterday, Wednesday, by its stabilisation, at the rate of four point two to the dollar. There had been an immediate and resounding crash in the value of all industrial securities, which had only been supported at such rarefied heights by the perpetually soaring balloon of the inflated mark. The inflation was at an end. The balloon had exploded.

" My God ! " Smirnof said to himself, the sweat pouring from his forehead. " How right I was ! I knew it was coming, I *knew* ! Who'll dare to tell me now this business of a ' hunch ' is all nonsense ! I'm luckier than any man has a right to be ! "

His mind went off on a different tack. " How clever that man Schacht is ! What a wonderful piece of juggling ! The backing of the new currency isn't gold, is it ? It's the assets of the whole Reich, its land, its industries, its buildings, everything ! A little fantastic, Dr. Schacht, eh ? How am I to redeem a rentenmark if I'm impatient with it ? A rentenmark's worth of factory, please, Dr. Schacht ! Ha ! Ha ! Ha ! Ha ! Ha ! Ha ! " He laughed hysterically. His soft abdomen heaved and wrenched.

A ray of light from behind the curtains tapped on the polished surface of the telephone-receiver on the desk a few feet away. A face gloomed and glimmered in the ray of light. It was not a clever face. A rather narrow forehead sloped up from behind the eyebrows. The skull was graced by a pair of ears too big for it.

He had never realised Brauner's ears were as big. He had never realised so clearly before, Brauner had the face of a congenital idiot.

Why the hell hadn't he sent a wire to Schmidt to confirm that second telephone-call ? Why the hell ? He was damned lucky to have got away without a dose of pneumonia ! How could he have remembered to go sending wires, with a head stuffed full of burned rag ? But suppose Brauner had mashed it all up ! Suppose ! Suppose ! To hell ! The directions he had given had been clear and explicit as twice one are two. How could Brauner have mashed it all up ?

He ran unsteadily to the door. His knees shook so violently he almost fell before he got there.

" Steadley ! Steadley ! " he cried. " Come down at once ! " Steadley had a small room he used as an office upon the next landing.

Steadley appeared. " Yes, Mr. Smirnof ? " he asked. " What is it ? Are you all right, sir ? "

" Get Berlin for me at once, Steadley, do you hear ? Don't stand staring at me ! I'm all right, I tell you ! "

It took quite a long time to get through to Schmidt, the line to Berlin was very busy that morning.

" Here he is, sir ! " said Steadley at last.

" Schmidt ! Schmidt ! Is that you ? "

" Yes, Herr Smirnof ! *Gott sei dank*, Herr Smirnof, you've rung up at last ! "

" What's the position, Schmidt ? "

" The boy, is he better, please God ? "

" Yes, yes, he's all right ! "

" And you, too, Herr Smirnof ? We hope you're all right now, yes ? "

" What the hell do you mean ? "

" The *gnädige Frau* told us, when we rang up——"

" You rang up ? When did you ring up ? What did you ring up for ? " His heart seemed to be thumping violently not far from the base of his throat.

" On Monday, Herr Smirnof ! When we didn't hear from you, we thought it best——"

" You didn't *hear* from me ? You pack of idiots ! Didn't I ring up from Cologne twice ? But you sold out on Monday, of course ? Didn't you ? What ? Why don't you answer ? "

Schmidt seemed to be having some difficulty in finding his voice.

" No, Herr Smirnof ! "

" You *didn't* ? What are you talking about ? You *didn't* ?
Did you sell out yesterday ? "

" No, Herr Smirnof ! The fact is——"

" You imbecile ! You haven't sold out ? It's all still on
my hands, is it ? But you *have* sold out ! Brauner sold out !
I ordered him ! "

" You see, Herr Smirnof, Brauner couldn't quite make
out . . . he couldn't quite make out——"

" For God's sake, what ? "

" What you wanted him to do when you rang up that
second time. And then, next morning ; when the Herr
Graf came in——"

" Who ? What ? "

" The Herr Graf Straupitz-Kalmin. He came in specially
next morning. He told us you had spoken to him on the
telephone after speaking to Brauner. You did, of course,
Herr Smirnof, did you not ? "

" Go on ! "

" You told him you had changed your mind, he said. He
said that a wire or a telephone-message would certainly
come through in a day or two. And then Sunday passed,
and no word from you, though God knows, when one is
called back because a child is seriously ill . . . and on Monday,
in an hour or two the Stock Exchange would be shut and
still no word from you, so at last I made up my mind to
ring you up, and then it was the *gnädige Frau* came to the
telephone and said on no account must you be disturbed
with any business of any sort. You were ill, she said. Everything must wait. And then on Wednesday, that is yesterday,
of course. You heard what happened yesterday ? What ?
Are you there ? I can't hear, Herr Smirnof ! What ? What ?
Verflucht ! " cursed Herr Schmidt at the telephone-receiver
in Berlin. " *Verdammt nach ein Mal !* I have been cut off ! "

But Schmidt had not been cut off. The telephone-receiver had slipped from Smirnof's hand. His legs had slipped from under him. There was a chair behind him into which he collapsed like a sack.

" Mr. Smirnof! Mr. Smirnof! " cried Steadley. " Is anything wrong? "

Smirnof opened his eyes. He shook his head. There was a faint foam of saliva on the left side of his mouth. " Oh, no! " he whispered. " Oh, no! "

" Can I get you something? A drop of brandy? "

He nodded. " You might as well! " he breathed. It was as if all his sinews and tendons and nerves, all the strings that ran through a man's body and make it taut and sensitive, had lost all their resilience. His thighs, and the hands on his thighs, felt like dead flesh—as dead as butcher's meat.

How could he stand out against them all, he alone against so large and various an assembly? Behold what furies were gathered against him—the bank waiting with claw-like hands outstretched, the insolent Cratonian cheats, Polednik, Silver, Schmidt, Brauner, Straupitz-Kalmin. . . .

You, too, Oskar, you too?

And Sarah, too? And Sarah? Poor, poor, Sarah, little did you know what an ill turn you did me!

Steadley stood by. A quarter of an hour went by, half an hour. " Excuse me, sir, " he said at length.

" Yes? " asked Smirnof. His voice was very quiet, extraordinarily gentle.

" I hope you don't mind, sir. I think I've gathered—about all this—all this, in Berlin! "

" That's quite all right, Steadley! "

" If I may say so, sir, it may be possible to save something from the ruin! "

" Very very little, Steadley. You realise the interest has been mounting up at eighteen per cent day by day? "

" If you'll allow me to make out a wire, sir. Whatever happens, they must sell out now! You may come out on the right side, after all, sir! "

" You're a good fellow, Steadley ! I doubt it, I doubt it ! "

" Something like this, sir : How horrified we are at their disregard of our instructions. To sell all stocks immediately at best possible prices obtainable and pay off all loans. Then to wire report of position. Would that be right, sir ? "

" Anything you like, Steadley ! Yes, Steadley, yes. Forgive me. That would be right ! "

The door opened. Sarah came in.

" Come along now, darling. Lunch is ready. I've got such a nice little lunch for you. Boiled turbot, indeed ! "

" Yes, darling, I'm coming ! "

She supported him into the dining-room.

" You really are determined to go, Sasha ? "

" Please not again ! " he implored her.

It was, as she had said, a nice little lunch. But it did not tempt him. She played about wretchedly with her knife and fork. " Sasha ! " she protested at length. " You really must eat something, you know. How *can* I let you go off on a long journey with nothing in your stomach ? "

" Sarah darling, I'd rather you didn't worry me. It's all I want, thank you." His voice was so low she hardly heard what he said.

A sudden alarm fluttered in her breast.

" Look here," she said. " You ordered Steadley to get a ticket for himself, too ? "

" No, I did not."

" Then I insist you should take Steadley with you. Do you hear, Sasha ? Please, Sasha ! "

His eyelids fluttered very wearily. " I wish you wouldn't make trouble," he said. " I want to go up alone. I've just got to explain one or two things to your father. Then I'll come back. I'll be back again in a day or two."

She knew she could do no more with him.

III

The train was not crowded. Smirnof got a first-class carriage to himself without any difficulty. He was thankful for that, very thankful. He had thought once or twice he would go under in the car. What big eyes Sarah had made when he drove off. It'll be all right, Sarah ; I'll be as right as rain in a day or two.

He was tired, tired ; he could hardly move a finger. He was glad he had a carriage to himself. And yet—and yet, throughout the infinite hours that passed over his head, on the journey from Kettering to Leicester, Leicester to Derby, he had company enough.

Polednik got into the carriage as often as anybody. He sat down in the opposite corner for long minutes at a stretch, and ignored him completely. Then he would put his papers and pamphlets on the seat beside him, you could hear the rustling quite distinctly, and edge sideways slowly, nearer and nearer to Smirnof. Any moment you felt he would leap up from the seat and hurl himself at you, digging those hard ink-stained finger-tips against the pipes of your throat.

You pulled your chin down upon your breast, and blinked hard, and looked again, and he was not there, of course. But he came back again.

The bank director wasn't going to be easy to tackle. Oh, not at all easy, now everything had gone smash in Berlin. The bank director wore high stiff collars—six inches high, they must be, at least.

Yes, Esther, he was saying. It will be Rio, I think. Do you know, in the evening, in the cafés, the moon comes down through the palm-trees, and the little dagos in the orchestras—they don't shave from one month's end to another—they play great music, Beethoven, Handel, the hair almost stands on your head. Listen. I don't expect *you'd* know it, Esther. Can you hear ? That's the saraband from *Rinaldo*. It goes like this—*Lascia, ch'io pianga*. . . . Isn't it beautiful ?

It's a nuisance, isn't it, about Jackie ? He doesn't seem to get any better at all. I'm sure you've had the best people in, haven't you, Sarah ? No, don't worry about me. I'll be all right in a day or two, after I've seen your father. It was rather a mistake, darling, not letting Schmidt get through to me. Wasn't it now, darling? But how should you know, Sarah, how should you know ? No, darling ! Of course not ! Of course I'm not cross with you !

What ? This can't be you, Straupitz-Kalmin ? Of course it is ! How clear your scar shows up in this light ! I don't suppose that brown patch of burned flesh will ever heal up completely, do you ? You ought to try one of those flesh-grafting operations—I've told you before. We have an awfully good man here ; he lives in Wimpole Street, I think.

How *could* you, Oskar, how *could* you ? What harm had I done you ? What was the point of going into my office and telling them that lie ? It would make it a little easier to bear if I could understand what you could possibly hope to gain from it. We seemed to like each other, you and I. And in a manner of speaking we were brothers-in-law. What ? I can't hear ! Yes, you're quite right ! So was Polednik ! But what made you throw your hand in with *him*, Oskar ?

Get back, Polednik ! There's not room for both of us in here ! This is *my* carriage. It's not big enough to hold us both. Europe isn't big enough to hold us both. Get out !

Sorry, Sam, it's you, is it ? I thought it was that rat, Polednik. A fine brood of sons-in-law. No, it wasn't quite playing the game. But listen, Sam, I can explain it all ! Do you hear, Sam ? I tell you I can explain it all !

But suddenly it seemed that to explain it all would require so much effort, so much more effort than he had left in him, or could ever hope to collect again. It was silly how that cold had knocked the stuffing out of him. Lucky to escape pneumonia, after all. Of course it was silly to go walking up and down an exposed deck in the wind and rain.

The engine lifted its voice mournfully under a sky of moon and driven cloud. There had been fog all the way from London up to Leicester, but it was much clearer now. They were in Derbyshire, among the moors, with the low loose-stone walls running across them. The voice of the engine came mournfully back from the moors again. The train was approaching a viaduct, the train curved to the curve of the viaduct. He seized the handle of the door and turned it. The cold air thrust, sharp and kind, up against his falling forehead.

CHAPTER XX

THE ROCK TOMB

I

THE INVESTING public did not need to wait for the coroner's verdict before making up its mind that Alexander Smirnof had committed suicide. Its alarm was accentuated within a few hours of the news regarding Smirnof's death by the disappearance of John Huxtable, the general secretary of the Sam Silver Mackintoshery Company. It expected to learn, within the course of another few hours, that Sam Silver himself had either bolted like John Huxtable or committed suicide like Alexander Smirnof.

But Sam Silver did neither of these things. Secure in the consciousness of his rectitude, he faced the whispers of the crowd, and the formal requisitions of his legal examiners, with a chin firmer than it ever had had the knack of being. He gave no indication of the ordeals to which he was subjected for so many months, excepting that the grey hair began definitely to oust the black in his thick moustache, and the moustache itself drooped its towsled fringes a little lower over his upper lip. He did not remember to clip it so regularly as he used to.

Further and further he recedes from our eyes, wrapped round, like a mummy, in infinite swathings of legal complication, till you would think he is half dead ; and, if ever the swathings are to be unwound again, it will be a phantom of Sam Silver that will be turned away from us towards ignominy and darkness, or turn itself back towards the light again. But that is not so. Sam Silver will be less half dead than he has been for years when the swathings are unwound, and he is free to move his limbs again.

It had been a matter of careful arrangement between Alexander Smirnof and the issuing house that had undertaken the conversion of the private into a public company that the guinea-pig directors to be appointed to the board should be as guinea-pig as it was discreet to have them. Nevertheless, Lord Bamtree, one of the two noble lords on the board, had wit enough to be frightened almost silly by the report of Smirnof's death in the morning newspaper. His condition was not improved when, during the course of the day, it became evident that Huxtable had bolted. He had a certain tolerant affection for Silver, the little slum-Jew who had risen to such heights, who sometimes seemed so darned clever and sometimes seemed such a born fool. But he realised that with a little ill luck the directors were all on the verge of developments which might be extremely uncomfortable for people in their position, and he could not quite make up his mind whether it would be advantageous or not if Sam Silver, too, threw himself out of a train, as Alexander Smirnof had done. At all events, he motored post-haste to the Longton Croft factory, where he found Silver, with glazed eyes, in a sort of coma, and directed the secretary who had taken charge to telephone and wire the other directors, and convene a meeting for the next day.

Silver had to some extent recovered by that time from the coma into which the shock had thrown him, but it was at this meeting that Lord Bamtree definitely made up his mind as between darned clever and born fool. If he was either, he was the second. It was at this same meeting that General Tunstale, a colleague on the board, at last made up his mind on a subject which he had left open till now, namely that Sam Silver also was a crook, as he had for some time feared that Alexander Smirnof might be. He expressed this conviction to Lord Bamtree later, who ventured to disagree with him. But, born fool or crook, there was Sam Silver, and there were they, and they were all in the same boat, damn it, and they'd damn well have to pull together.

It was discovered at the board meeting that, with Smirnof

dead and Huxtable flown, and no one to prompt Silver either half an hour before the meeting or with a sequence of notes during the course of the meeting, no one knew very much how the company's affairs stood. General Tunstale was, of course, convinced that Silver was shamming ignorance. The wily little Jew wasn't going to show his hand. Lord Bamtree wondered how Silver could have imposed on them all, including Silver himself, with such an air of authority, when he now showed himself so completely at sea.

Whatever the directors felt about Silver, there was no doubt in any of their minds that Smirnof's suicide forboded grave discoveries and dire events. The meeting developed into a cross-examination of Silver, not only because of his early association and long connection with Smirnof, but because he was a director with Smirnof of two of those London companies whose situation had precipitated Smirnof into committing suicide. There could be no reasonable doubt of that ; for Silver had already laid the facts before them of the Polednik-Cratonian complications. He admitted that he had had no intention of laying those facts before them, until Smirnof had had the chance of explaining the situation. Further, the directors had been through to Steadley in London, who, under pressure, was induced to state that, in his opinion, his employer might have suffered extremely heavily in the recent crash of the Berlin stock-market.

It was decided by the board that an independent chartered accountant should be called in to investigate the affairs of the company. Silver was asked to permit the same accountant to investigate the affairs of the trust and trading companies in London, of which he was now the sole director. It was also realised how important it would be to endeavour to allay the fears of the public, stop rumours, and prevent a crash on the Stock Exchange here ; the decision was therefore taken that a reassuring statement should be issued to the Press. Finally it was decided that peremptory application should be made to the trading company in London for the money which the public company in Doomington had lent it, upon a mortgage over its assets.

The trading company, in the bewildered person of Silver, found it quite impossible to pay back to the Doomington company the money he and Smirnof had borrowed. It began to dawn on him that Smirnof had combined and played off against each other the trading company, of which he had invited his friend to be a director, and other companies of which he had not suspected the existence. He also learned for the first time the magnitude of the Cratonian operations in which he had been involved over his head. He further, and to his profound horror, was called on by the bank to repay the residue of the loan advanced by the bank to Smirnof and the company on a guarantee he had himself signed, as he now learned for the first time.

Payment from the trading company was not forthcoming. The directors of the Doomington company forthwith applied to the court to appoint a liquidator to wind up the trading company. The liquidator was appointed within a fortnight of the coroner's verdict.

The liquidator found himself faced with a task of considerable difficulty. It took him a couple of months, or more, owing to the magnitude of the deals the trading company had been involved in, the confusion in its books, and the necessity for corresponding with various foreign Governments and firms. The company was wound up. The Doomington company had nothing to hope for in that direction. It asked for a receiver to be appointed to Smirnof's estate. It was discovered that he had, of course, died insolvent, owing large sums to the bank and elsewhere.

At the same time the examination into the affairs of the Doomington company proceeded. It was realised that the losses caused through the failure of the trading company in London must be a severe blow to it. It would not have been a mortal blow if the company itself had been in a flourishing position ; but, precisely because the company had not, Smirnof had been asked, with almost criminal blindness, to attempt to redress the company's fortunes in those operations which were now so bitterly deplored. The Doomington company was not flourishing. Debtors abroad owed them large sums of money, which were required for payment of debts incurred in the purchase of dye-stuffs, cloth, machinery, and other materials. They had large stocks on hand they could not realise. There were heavy income-tax claims to meet.

Inexorably the weaknesses of the company's position were piled up. The expression in Sam Silver's eyes was like that in the eyes of a small girl who is informed by the vet. that her pet dog has this malady and that malady and another malady. She has known for some time the poor darling was sick. She has done all she can to cure him within the limits of her inaccurate knowledge. But something more drastic than washings and powders must be administered now.

Something more drastic, alas ! But it is not before her eyes that the vet. administers it. She is a brave girl, and goes up to the nursery and tries to occupy her mind with other thoughts.

There was no such solace for Sam Silver, who was, after all, a grown man, and should have needed none. It was determined that the Doomington company should be wound up.

And now the coils began to gather more and more closely around Sam Silver. The liquidator of the Doomington company now made a claim against him personally in respect of the moneys advanced to the companies in London of which he had been director, and which had lately been declared insolvent. At the same time the bank brought an action against him for repayment of the outstanding moneys due on the forged guarantee.

For, of course, the guarantee was forged. How could he have signed his name and not be aware of it ? How could he under any circumstances give a personal guarantee for so large a sum of money ? It was ridiculous. He was advised by his solicitors to do nothing to obstruct the proceedings. The case was heard a month or two after the Christmas vacation. There was much talking of expert witnesses, and signing by Silver of his name, and production of enlarged photographs, and squinting at signatures through microscopes. The bank was severely censured for not having been more minute in its examination of the signature, though it was pointed out at the very outset that it was exactly in virtue of the distinguished names and unquestioned probity of the signatories that the document was subjected to less examination than an ordinary five-pound cheque.

Silver won the case that the bank brought against him. He also won the case brought against him by the liquidator of the Doomington company. He remained a rich man, high and dry, marooned on the reef of his riches. Yet there was no period in his life when he was so unhappy as these months that followed now.

He had no real friends in the world of big manufacturers. Doubtless he had worked too hard in his factory either to have time to make friends or to look after his health. He looked an old and tired man now. But his factory had kept him busier and happier than a whole townful of friends. He had had few thoughts beyond the factory, excepting his love for his wife and daughters, and the working out of schemes to let them all have as much as they wanted from him, without seeming gross or stupid in his generosity. There were retired rich men, Jews and non-Jews, in the well-to-do residential suburb where he lived, who were ready enough to suggest ways and means of taking him out of himself and helping him spend a little of his fortune. He was not too old to take up golf—" Begad, you've still got a fine pair of shoulders on you, laddie." A country club had been started which wasn't too particular to have a lot of Jews on the books—" But you're different, old chap, you're a damn good fellah."

But those occupations did not seem to interest him, and

the slightly florid gentlemen who proposed them used to go off with a couple of whiskies and soda inside them, shaking their heads and puffing a little ruefully. " After all, old chap, you can't get away from it, he's just a little Jew-wallah. And that's how it is, old chap. Have another? I don't mind if I do."

And there were other more secret suggestions made to him, by people ill or well disposed towards him. He never attempted to puzzle out which it might be, for the suggestions made his eyes look hard and unpleasant, in a way you would not have believed possible. It was whispered to him that, after all, business is business ; and the whisper was often accompanied by a knowing tap of the forefinger against the side of the whisperer's nose. But was it really possible he could always get away with it, as he had got away with it already, and devilish lucky he was too ? Was it really conceivable that he and Smirnof had worked together all those years, and he'd never had an idea, never had the ghost of an idea, what Smirnof was up to ?

After all, he'd been the boss ; he'd said as much time and again. When people had praised Smirnof for his talents straight out, Silver had smiled darkly and indulgently, as if to let people know he didn't in the least mind Smirnof, too, coming in on the jam. There were rumours about that there were going to be criminal proceedings. It was all so complicated that probably the Director of Public Prosecutions would prefer to have action taken out of his hands. Why didn't Silver just sell up and go and live like a fighting-cock in Mentone or San Remo, or some place like that ?

But Silver behaved so oddly that these whisperers, too, went off feeling hurt and puzzled, wondering why they had been born into a world in which good advice and golden hearts were so little appreciated.

May, of course, as always, was his prop and comfort during those uneasy months. But it was impossible for her to be with him as often as she would have liked, and not merely because the work in her Country Home was so exigent. Her Miss Mosenthal, who was to be left in sole charge when May left the institution, rather surprisingly went and married a local nursery-gardener, though she had always seemed so inveterately spinster and so dogmatically anti-assimilationist. In addition to that, the care and comfort of Sarah and her children fell to May, in the way that always happens in a family when tragedies take place, and there is an unmarried son or daughter somewhere in the offing. Fortunately, Sarah was a strong and sensible woman. She had never been romantically in love with her husband ; he had been to her, so to speak, the first of her children. With that one out of the way, it was necessary to keep a stiff upper lip for the sake of the others ; and the preoccupation of the cough of a Jackie living was more constantly with her than a weak mooning over a Sasha dead.

As for Hannah Silver, she had at last found her level. Or if to say that she had found her level is to be a little indecorous towards the duchesses and countesses with whom she consorted, it would be accurate to say she had found her *métier*, at least. There had been no period in her life when she had not been abnormally conscious of the poor whom we have always with us. In her efforts to mitigate their lot she had only rarely used real common sense. To the beggars who came up and stood against the fence of her father's house in Terkass long ago, when she was a girl in Russia, she would creep out with an apron-load of dainties which would turn their unaccustomed stomachs. She made no effort to choose for them the simpler sorts of refreshment— bread and meat. When she subscribed to charities in Oleander Street, it seemed to her more important that she should be subscribing to charities than that she should know what charities they were, even if they were charities organised by Presbyterian elders in Dundee for the conversion of Chinese coolies in Hong-Kong.

During the indispensable period of ladies' committee-meetings which had preceded the foundation of May's Country Home, Hannah had come into contact with a certain Mrs. Proctor. Mrs. Proctor was a professional convener of committee-meetings, organiser of bazaars, balls, matinées, Olde English Fayres ; she did not despise boxing-matches, and might even have organised a bull-fight, excepting that the object for which she might have been asked to organise it would have been, more likely than not, the organisation of a Fund for the Eradication of Bull-fights. She made a good, though not a prodigal, living out of it ; and she probably could have made a good deal more as an ordinary business-woman, for she seemed to have inexhaustible energy and she had the gift of popularity.

She was getting on in years, her hair was grey and handsome, and her profile distinguished, but all her duchesses, countesses, and lesser titled ladies called her " Popsie." For that very reason, those of her clients who were not titled ladies, but merely the wives of rich men, were a little chary of calling her " Popsie," thinking it might be deemed a little forward. Clients, her duchesses and rich women exactly were. She made them feel it was a privilege to have their names, however lustrous in dynastic history or present commerce, blazoned on her *de luxe* programmes among the patronesses, or, even more, among the members of the working committee. She compelled them to work in her ragbag of causes for so long a working-day that any trade union would have gone hoarse with rage if its boiler-makers or coal-heavers had been worked half so hard.

She made an adequate living, but that was not her real reward. Her reward was that, as the duchesses called her " Popsie," she called them " Flossie," or " Susie," or whatever it might be. The wives of mere rich men called her Mrs. Proctor.

Moreover, she had a son. Perhaps the entrée his mother's activities gave him into high society gave her something of her reward, too. She was a widow, and John was the apple of her eye. Not much of a success with women younger than himself, he was a great favourite with women two or three decades their senior, and for two or three months at a time. It did not often last much longer, for ladies of that age like good conversation, in which he was lacking. He preferred to dance with ladies older than himself rather than with ladies younger, for younger ladies could never be induced to take him, or even his dancing, seriously. Though it would be unjust to think of him as in any sense a gigolo, it was clearly no disgrace to him if he, the son of a woman who worked for her living, allowed a countess to sign a cheque for his dinner when she took him out to the Berkeley. It would have been an entirely different thing, of course, if she had taken out a purse and paid cash.

Mrs. Proctor and Mrs. Silver had met over the organisation of May's Country Home. Mrs. Proctor was quick to realise that Mrs. Silver, or her husband's bank-book, was an acquisition after her own heart. Mrs. Proctor called Mrs. Silver " Hannah " on the third or fourth meeting, and when Mrs. Silver naïvely countered with " Popsie," Mrs. Proctor smiled indulgently. She did not think it courteous to point out that only Debrett had dealings with her on those terms.

Mrs. Proctor found Mrs. Silver as indefatigable in committee as she was generous with her money, and she realised how invaluable it was to have a plenipotentiary of such quality up in the North Country ; so indefatigable and generous, in fact, that, after a few months had passed by, the company of Popsie, and the tasks enjoined upon her by Popsie, became completely essential to Mrs. Silver's wellbeing. The more she had of them, the more insidiously she needed more of them.

Before long she took to spending long week-ends in London, to be nearer the hub of those grand philanthropic excitements. Then she spent weeks at a time in London with Popsie. Finally, towards the end of nineteen twenty-three, she took a suite in a smart yet comfortable hotel in South

Kensington, not three minutes' walk away from her darling Popsie's flat. So that, taking it by and large, she spent considerably more time with Popsie than with Sam during that period.

John Proctor complicated the situation very delightfully. It must be repeated that the relations of John Proctor with these charitable ladies in general, and Hannah in particular, were entirely unfleshly. Hannah would have been exceedingly surprised, or would flatly have refused to believe, that certain of her new countess friends did indeed have carnal relationships with men who were not their husbands. If it had been said by any cynic that they had such relationships with John Proctor, not merely would she have slapped the cynic's face. It would have been totally untrue. But she liked being made a fuss of by him. She liked being seen about with him. So grand he was—like he might be a general from the Austrian Army !

Her flirtation with John Proctor—for it was, after all, a rather sweet and sad and innocent little flirtation—cut not the minutest segment out of the large circle of her love for Sam Silver. He was still, and always, the sun of her being, all the more potently as she no more questioned his sovereignty than a flower or an animal questions the sun's. She did not reproach him for being able to spend so much less time with her, all the time he was a great big business-man, than he used to be able to spend with her in the Oleander Street days. She reproached the business for that. She did not reproach him for having a separate bedroom. She reproached Esther for that.

Besides, latterly he would often come in so late from the office, she wouldn't see him for days and days. So why shouldn't she spend a day or two now and again, or a week or two, doing good in London ? Why not ?

Sam Silver, for his part, never for a moment resented her frequent and long absences in London. He welcomed it, in a way ; she wouldn't see him pulling long faces and worrying the way things were going. He was extremely pleased that she was up to her ears in work she adored, over there in London. And he loved the thought of her going about with the nice young man, she in her great array of pearls, he in his fine tail-coat, showing all the duchesses in the land she was as fine a woman to look at as any of them.

She was, in fact, simply dizzy with happiness. The ladies of birth were kind to her, because of her transparent good nature and her delicious little *gaucheries*. John taught her to dance, insisted she should dance, and she did not know whether she danced on her head or her heels when he took her round and round, round and round, among the little tables on the smart dancing-floor.

And there was work to do. The smartness and the frivolity would have meant nothing to her, would have made her wretched, in fact, if Mrs. Proctor did not slave-drive her, as she slave-drove herself. She had all the opportunity for totally indiscriminate and irrelevant well-doing she had exercised in the Oleander Street kitchen at a penny per cause per week. She was happy and busy.

The two actions which were brought against her husband up in Doomington were only an impertinent interruption. She went up to be with him, of course, while they were on ; but she came back the moment they were settled. " Such a cheek ! " she said. " A black year on them ! "

It was much less Hannah than her friends, Popsie and John, who were frightened. They accurately gauged that if the verdicts went against Silver, there would be less serving on exalted committees for Mrs. Silver at so many hundred guineas for the privilege, and less dining with John Proctor at the Berkeley. But Silver won his cases. Hannah Silver threw herself more voluptuously than ever into her charity-organisings. There was such a fume of glory and virtue in her head that she was as dizzy as a drunkard. She did not realise that Sam Silver needed her companionship more than he had ever done before. She did not take it into account that he did not go to the office at all now. They could have retired to bed, in the same bedroom, at nine o'clock each evening, if they had wanted to. But she had to be up in Altrincham for that. And she was down in London, being charitable to other husbands than her own, or their wives, or their offspring.

So Sam Silver found his way back to Longton, to his friends in Oleander Street and Magnolia Street and the other streets of the flowering shrubs.

It is somewhat paradoxical to say he found his way back to Longton during the period of his suspense and loneliness, when the factory he had owned on the brick-croft was in the very heart of Longton, and he had made his way thither every morning in his life, excepting on Sundays ; and sometimes on Sundays, too. But it was as a stranger, in a sealed limousine, he had been carried to Longton each morning. He sometimes had the cadaverous fancy it was a hearse that was carrying him ; it was quiet as any hearse. Even the perverse spirits that rule over the mechanisms of motor-cars had yielded to him ; they could deny no longer that he was of that elect company to whom they owe the most disciplined allegiance. He went to Longton and returned from Longton in a limousine that behaved with the predictability of a planet.

There, all day, he would sit in his office, having his luncheon served to him in a small adjoining room, excepting on those days when his limousine carried him away for a luncheon in the Central Hotel with some big business-man. He was in the heart of Longton, but not of it. He would have been ashamed, embarrassed, to set foot in those old gay shabby oratorical streets, to which, even in the most staggering moments of his success, he still obscurely felt he had played the traitor. He knew that if any maxim is universal, it is this : that it is not criminal to grow rich. And yet it was not entirely universal. He knew just as certainly that though the majority of his associates in the Oleander Street kitchen would have given a limb or two to grow as rich, or half as rich, as he, there was a grim nucleus of one or two that would not. His son-in-law, Polednik, for instance, and that young man who would not become his son-in-law —Harry Stonier. He was not certain that Isaac Emmanuel, of Magnolia Street, would have allowed himself, without struggles quite violent, to get rich. Isaac Emmanuel would have despoiled himself in golden impossible benefactions as quickly as his wealth increased. He would have spent his life *spending* the money that had come to him, not making more money and more money and more.

Good heavens, had not *he*, Sam Silver, done what he could in the way of good deeds? How much money had not Susan, his daughter, had from him, precisely the one who was the wife of Polednik, the proud Bolshevik? They had not been too proud to ask him—or she had not, at least— to send over as much money as he could spare, to help the Swedish missions on the Volga during the great famine of nineteen twenty-one. Susan had been the organiser of the relief funds from the Russian end. And, though the Bolshevik Government let the world know how it despised capitalist money, it had taken no steps to hold up the large sums he had regularly sent Susan since nineteen twenty-one, to organise the distribution of food and clothes in various sorely smitten areas throughout Russia.

May, too—how far would her Country Home have gone but for him? And Hannah? She was simply pouring his money into the lap of that charity-woman, Mrs. Proctor. Had he not done what he could?

He was troubled. He did not believe that any answer he could give to that question would not be the false one. Somehow the question itself wasn't in the right time and place. He was not the sort of man who should have had to put that question and to answer it. He was a little wandering tailor, who had wandered up the country from Odessa and was on his way to Kiev, and thence to Vilna. But he had met a girl crying in the wood, and had come to Doomington instead.

So did that mean motor-cars ? Did that mean that colonels with red faces should come and patronise him because he was rich, and say come and join our golf-club, even though you are a Jew ?

There is but one life to be lived, he thought sadly, and you must live it so that it is true to itself. It must be lived in the truth of its quality.

What then about May, about Elsie, about all his daughters ? Weren't they living lives true to themselves ? Didn't May meet the long-established people of her southern county as if she and her father and her father's father had been long-established in this land, too ? Wasn't she quite effortlessly one of them ? Hadn't Sarah been an almost queenly hostess to the distinguished men and women who had frequented her drawing-room ?

That and that might be true. But he knew that in the last resort we are neither father nor mother, neither husband nor wife, nor child ; we are each a private and lonely universe, we must each live in the truth of our own law, our own quality.

It was while meditations such as these were passing through his own mind, where he sat forlorn in the " home-room " of his rich suburban house ; it was while he sat idly opening his letters, which had been lying about since morning, that he happened to take out of a halfpenny-stamped envelope a stylographed appeal from Mr. Emmanuel. It was an appeal for the latest of his causes, such as he had doubtless sent out to all the rich men of his acquaintance. He knew a great many, of course, in his capacity as Clerk to the Jewish Board of Guardians.

The latest Emmanuel idea was the setting up of a sports ground in the region which was now being opened up near Layton Park. Gentile boys and girls and Jewish boys and girls would play football and cricket and tennis with each other, in their season, on that sports ground. It would bring the Jews and the Gentiles together, in a way which the Great War had not quite finally succeeded in doing. The appeal slightly misquoted a celebrated dictum: "The Battle of Waterloo was won on the sports ground of Eton," and the inference was that the Duke of Wellington would have been very interested in the idea, had he been still alive, and would have given a liberal subscription, too. In which case, why not you, Mr. Higginbotham, and you, Mr. Silver?

Silver rose. He went out quietly to the little shut-off cloakroom near the front door and put his hat and coat on. He did not ask for the chauffeur of his limousine-hearse. He thought he would take the tram to Doomington, and get off at the Oleander Street corner, as he used to in the old days, opposite the clock-station, where the conductors clock in their times of arrival and departure. He knew he would have to change trams, and it would take a long time to get to Oleander Street, but he had time enough and to spare nowadays.

II

Silver walked a few feet down the Blenheim Road from the clock-station, crossed the road, and quite automatically turned into Oleander Street. He had walked a few yards before he remembered it was not a house in Oleander Street he purposed to visit, but a house in Magnolia Street. He had no place now in Oleander Street. He was a rich man; he lived in Pennine Grange, in Altrincham.

He knocked at the Emmanuels' door. It was Mrs. Emmanuel who came to open it.

" Is your husband in, please, Mrs. Emmanuel? "

" Who is that, please? "

" This is—Sam Silver," he said.

" What? " She peered into his face. " Well, I never! Is it really? Mr. Silver from Oleander Street? Oh, Mr. Silver, what did I say? From Oleander Street! You must forgive me! Excuse me, please! "

" Please ! " begged Silver. " Is he in ? "

She left him at the door, and ran excitedly down the lobby. " Isaac ! Isaac ! " she called. " Look who's come ! "

" Who ? " asked Mr. Emmanuel. " Why don't you call him in ? "

" Such a year on me ! " said Mrs. Emmanuel. Then she raced back to the door, waving her hands helplessly. " What is the matter with me ? Come right in, Mr. Silver ! "

Silver ascended the steps and followed her into the Emmanuel kitchen. Mr. Emmanuel was standing, long and lean, with his head shaking from side to side. He had taken his coat off, and was in red felt slippers. Evidently he was giving himself a holiday to-night. He was not going on the chase after rich men. Instead, a rich man had come to see him.

" Oh, it's you, Mr. Silver ? " he said. He held out his hand warmly. " Come in, sit down on this chair here by the fire ! Slatta, close the door ! " he bade his wife. " What is the matter with you, Slatta ? "

Mrs. Emmanuel came in and chirrupped about helplessly. Mr. Emmanuel took the situation in hand with *savoir faire* and natural good manners. " Have a cigarette, Mr. Silver ? I'm afraid they're just ordinary ones—Black Cat."

" What do you think I smoke, golden ones ? " objected Silver. " And since when you've started calling me ' Mr. Silver ' ? I've never heard from such a thing ! "

" Well, you're such a stranger, it doesn't come natural not to say ' Mr.,' " Mr. Emmanuel apologised. " Such a fog to-night, eh ? Where have you left the car ? "

" I didn't come by car. I came by tram."

" Oh ! " said Mr. Emmanuel.

" I just thought I'd like to come, just like that, to have a chat."

" Oh, that's fine, Silver, that's fine ! You don't mind I don't put my coat on ? "

" Tut-tut ! " Silver was almost annoyed. " I don't mind. Mrs. Emmanuel, no evil eye, you've made such a big fire to-night. It's lovely, but a little hot, yes ? Can I take my coat off ? "

" Here ! Here ! " she bustled up delightedly. " Here is a coat-hanger ! "

" That's fine ! " He stretched his legs out on the fender. " That's fine ! We might have a bit of talk about the sports ground, eh ? "

" Yes ! Yes ! " said Emmanuel eagerly, so eagerly that his always insecure pince-nez fell from his nose and hung dangling by its cord.

A charcoal drawing of a woman on the wall to his left hand attracted Silver's attention.

" By your son, eh ? " asked Silver.

" Yes," said Mrs. Emmanuel proudly. " My son Max ! "

" Who is it ? "

" Who do you think ? Me ! " she pointed out, her pride a little chastened.

" Of course it is ! The living image ! Isn't it funny ? My wife, she was on the committee for a big gala night from one of Mr. Cochran's shows. For the girls in Palestine, they should become farmers."

" Yes, I know," said Mr. Emmanuel. He was an authority on all charitable causes, and the means taken to provide funds for them. " She must come on the committee for my sports ground."

" I was talking of this gala night," Silver reproved him gently, " from one of Mr. Cochran's shows. And do you know, they had an auction as well, after the girls had stopped singing. And they sold a doll and they sold signed copies from books and then the people gave them back, they didn't want them. So they sold them again and once again. And then they put up a picture to be sold. It was by Max, your son Max. The first time, too, it made a big sum of money. But there wasn't a second time. The man who bought it knew he had a bargain, so he went out straight away. You should have heard how cross she was, Mrs. Proctor."

" I know Mrs. Proctor—she's a fine worker," said

Emmanuel, with the dispassionate approval of a colleague. " Talking about my sports ground——"

" I was just coming to the sports ground. Oh, if you knew how my throat was thirsty ! "

" Slatta, Slatta, what are we thinking of ? What will you have ? Some wine ? "

" Wine ? What for, wine ? Can I have some tea, yes ? "

" With lemon or milk ? "

" You should ask such a question ! Lemon, of course ! "

" Make it quick, Slatta ! I should like a glass, too ! Have you any nice cake or biscuits in the house ? "

" Please, please ! " Silver objected. " I haven't come to give you trouble like this ! "

" A trouble ! " laughed Emmanuel.

" Where are you going, Mrs. Emmanuel ? " asked Silver. She had slipped a shawl round her shoulders and was slipping out.

" I've just got to get one or two things at Mrs. Poyser's."

" Please, please, not to trouble ! Besides, it's too late ! "

" Oh, they'll only just be closing. If not, you think they won't serve me through the back door ? "

" The back door ! " repeated Silver. He turned to his host. A sudden memory had flashed into his mind. " Do you remember, Emmanuel ? You would always come in through *our* back door ! Your back door faces ours, no ? " He got up from his chair and looked through the window, where the blind had not been drawn, out towards the yard-wall beyond, as if he had hoped to see still further, in through the window of his own Oleander Street home. He shook his head, sighed a little, and sat down again. " You were ashamed to come in through the front door, do you remember ? We were such a lot of low lives and anarchists."

They both laughed merrily.

" What's happened to them all, I wonder," mused Silver " Wouldn't it be grand if we could all gather again in that kitchen there and tell what we've been through ? " He sighed again Emmanuel sighed too. They knew there were certain ones, killed in the War, or dead in the course of years, who would never come again. Silver resumed. " You are always hiring halls for charities. Perhaps you could hire that kitchen for a meeting of the old anarchists." Then he stopped. He slapped his thighs. " You'd have to pay *me* rent to hire it. I mean not me—my wife, Hannah. She is the landlord. It's her house."

" Of course it is," remembered Emmanuel.

" Yes, of course it is." Neither he, nor Hannah, nor any-one, had remembered it for years. The rent, such as it was, was paid in to the lawyer, doubtless. " Who lives there now ? " he asked a little sadly.

" Oh, Mrs. Silverstone. She is waiting to go to America with her family. Her husband will soon become an American citizen, so he can bring them over."

" So the house will be empty, yes ? "

" Yes."

" Then I'll tell you what," smiled Silver. " We'll come over and live here and we'll be neighbours again, and you can come in again through the back door."

" Well, I don't know," said Mr. Emmanuel seriously, after suitably acknowledging the joke. " If you said you wanted to come and live here, in my house, and I should go and live in your house—I don't know ! "

" Perhaps you're right," said Silver. " Who knows ? How much money do you need for the sports ground ? And tell me, do you really think it will do good ? "

" What ? " Mr. Emmanuel sprang from his chair. " What ? Do I really think it will do good ? Listen here now ! " He removed his pince-nez and shook them at Silver. Up and down the kitchen, up and down the kitchen, he went, haranguing Silver, as if he were a public meeting. His head swung about on his neck more and more un-steadily. His wife came in from Mrs. Poyser's with some cakes. She prepared the tea and set it down before them. She knew far better than to interrupt her husband. Mr Emmanuel at length exhausted himself. " Do I really think it will do good ! " he rumbled. " How much shall I put you down for ? " He sat down, noticed the glass of tea at his elbow, and lifted it to his mouth. " Slatta, Slatta, it's cold ! " he complained. " How's yours, Silver ? "

" That's all right," Silver assured him. " It's my third glass ! "

III

It was long after midnight when Silver let himself in with his latch-key at Pennine Grange. The trams had all stopped long ago, so Mr. Emmanuel walked with him from Longton to the Town Hall Square ; and there had been so much to talk about, he had walked half the way back to Longton with him, having intended to go just to the second corner ; and then Mr. Emmanuel had come back with him again ; and finally he had managed to pick up a taxi outside the Central Hotel.

He did not remember when he had had such a happy evening, not for years and years. Excepting, of course, for the rare occasions when May could manage to come up and see him. Not for years and years. He sighed and shook his head.

He felt like a prisoner, who has been let out on parole, passing between the gates of his prison again. He remembered once, a long time ago, it had been quite late, though not so late as this, there had been a light coming from under the door of the " home-room." May had been there ; she had been waiting up for him. There was no light in that room to-night, no May there. He went upstairs. There was no Hannah there, in the bedroom next to his own. He got into bed. He could not sleep for a long time, remembering how bright and cosy and warm it was in the Emmanuel kitchen. It was none of these things, here in Pennine Grange. Oh, yes, warm enough it might be. The steam slid silently and efficiently along the silvered pipes of the radiators.

A day or two later a most disquieting piece of news came to him. It was more than disquieting ; it was harrowing. He learned that an acquaintance of his, a man named Philips, had committed suicide. He had done fairly well in a small way as a waterproof manufacturer until a few years ago. They had had dealings with each other early in the War. After the War, he had given up waterproofing to open an estate-agent's office. He had invested more than he could afford in the Sam Silver Mackintoshery Company. The company's failure had hit him severely. Since then his affairs had gone from bad to worse. He had committed suicide two days ago.

He had committed suicide because the Sam Silver Mackin-toshery Company had gone into liquidation. Were there not other Philipses ? Might there not be more suicides ? Would the company have gone into liquidation if he had thrown in his own fortune to save it ?

Suddenly it dawned on Silver that the money he had in the bank was not his own money. It belonged to those other Philipses. It belonged to the widow and children of this Philips. The money Hannah was spending on charities in London, the money Susan was spending on starving *mouzhiks* in Russia, the money Elsie drew in a large regular allow-ance to live on in Berlin, the money with which May ran her Country Home in Sussex, was not their money. It was not his money. It belonged to the widow and children of Philips, of all the other Philipses who would not hang them-selves on the landing if the money that was rightly theirs were handed over to them.

It was true he had worked hard ; there had been a sort of outside happiness in his hard work. But he had sacrificed for his money the inward core of happiness. He had not worked hard enough for rewards so fantastic had he worked a thousand times as hard. He knew that brains must, in the nature of things, be recompensed on a scale quite incom-mensurate with the payment due to the work of hands. They are the chosen ones, those possessed of a certain type of brains. They may earn in a single day, in a single afternoon's operation, more than a working-man in all his years. But that was not the type of brains he had. He had been deluded into thinking so, but it was false. He had been vain, vain, strutting in his vanity like a turkey-cock. He had been honest in the sight of heaven and in the light of his own heart. But he had been wickedly vain. His vanity stank in his nostrils. He beat his forehead with his fist.

" They'll be on me soon ! They'll be on me soon ! Please God they come very quickly, and it'll be over then, and I'll be a free man ! "

IV

The Director of Public Prosecutions took three or four months to collect and consider the facts in the matter of Sam Silver of Doomington. Sam Silver received his summons to appear in the police court on a day early in May. At the police court Sam Silver reserved his defence and the magistrate decided there was a case for trial. The case came up in the Doomington assize courts some two months later.

The charge was that Sam Silver, with the assistance of Alexander Smirnof, deceased, had used his virtually dictatorial powers to have issued by the Silver Mackintoshery Company Limited balance-sheets and a prospectus which contained untrue statements. Standing for trial with him in the same court was one William Denton, the firm's auditor, in that he aided and abetted the deception. A warrant had earlier been issued for the arrest of John Huxtable, the general secretary of the company.

It is not the part of the chronicler to attempt the task of the legal historian, even if the crisis of the fate of one or more of his protagonists be involved in an outstanding episode of legal history. It would be as irrelevant as if he endeavoured to trace the course of an illness on the part of one of his characters, not merely in so much as the illness affected the behaviour of that character and of other characters who came in contact with him, as in all its pathological developments and the interaction it caused among the patient's affected organs.

It might be thought that the reverse holds ; that the lawyer trafficking in the stuff out of which legal history is to be made will concern himself rather with law than the infinite subtleties of the interplay of human associations. That is partly a matter of the legal tradition dominant in a country. In Italy it is possible to hear counsel defend a client accused of a purely technical breach of the law with the rhetorical passion of an evangelist and the arduous search into the springs of character of a psycho-analyst. In Sweden it is possible to hear counsel prosecuting a prisoner accused of brutal murder with the arid logicality and steady pur-posiveness of a problem to be worked out in trigonometry.

In the case of Sam Silver, a combination was inevitable of the logical and psychological methods. Infinite masses of figures were sifted and put before the court. But the final issue remained : was it humanly credible that a man of average intelligence could have been so completely under the thumb of his subordinate for so many years—and of an admittedly criminal subordinate ? An implicit alternative was that the accused was a man of less than average intel-ligence. To which the defence replied that against the machinations of a swindler so richly and disastrously en-dowed as the deceased Smirnof, a man of more than average intelligence could offer no defence ; as the case of Bottomley lately, and such cases as Whittaker Wright and Hooley earlier in the century, proved.

We must not be tempted into a resumption of the argu-ments on both sides, being already in possession of more relevant facts than Silver's counsel with the utmost industry could produce. But the speculation must be hazarded that if the exciting and highly relevant news of John Huxtable's arrest in Vienna had not been announced during the course of the trial, and the trial had proceeded to its conclusion without his evidence, it would have gone ill for Sam Silver. Counsel for the defence immediately requested an adjournment of the case till extradition formalities had been completed and Huxtable could be cross-examined. The stay was granted. The hideous suspense prolonged itself once again.

Faint and far, during the unwinding of these august and laborious proceedings, the voice of Sam Silver comes down to us with grief, and a little petulantly, as from a rock-tomb in the face of a vast hillside carved out into innumerable rock-tombs. They are walling him, standing upright, inside the tomb. The bricks are almost up to his shoulders now. He can only just lift out his hands to wave a gesture, bidding them be brave and believe in him, to his wife and daughters assembled far down at the foot of the hill. You can just make out his hurt voice coming thinly down on the wind :

" Have you ever heard from such a thing ? What do they say ? I make a false balance-sheet ? Such a black year ! I make rainproofs ; I make waterproofs ; what should I want to make balance-sheets for ? Now, Hannah, don't worry like that ! It'll be all right, I tell you ! Wipe your eyes, Hannah ! A shame, a grown-up woman like that should cry in public !

" That's you, May, is it, looking so thin and pale down there ? Well, May, whatever happens—and you never know, May ; it's a funny thing when they get you inside places like this, there's never any telling—I know I can trust you, May. You know I could quicker jump over the Town Hall tower than I could do a thing I thought it was dishonest ! Be a good girl, May ; just you look after your mother, yes ? "

The evidence of John Huxtable tilted the balance completely in Silver's favour. Huxtable confessed in full to all his complicities with Smirnof. He was sentenced to twelve months in the second division, the jury having added to their verdict the rider that Huxtable was greatly under the influence of the late Smirnof. Sam Silver and the firm's auditor, William Denton, were acquitted.

CHAPTER XXI

THE DECISION

I

FOR DAYS AND DAYS after the acquittal of Sam Silver there were merry-makings at Pennine Grange. Esther Pliskin was the grand organiser-in-chief, though she let May and Sarah and her mother take a hand in the actual carrying out of preparations. None of them knew that between them they had such regiments of friends, and the number of telegrams and letters of congratulation that were received was positively royal, as if some heir apparent or other had had a baby. Hannah summoned Popsie to the biggest of the dinner-parties, and Popsie cut a brace of duchesses to be present. Popsie, of course, brought John. Lord Bamtree honoured the party with his distinguished presence. Some of the local golfing enthusiasts were there, too. It was impossible to see in their hearty faces any trace of the horror with which they had learned, no long time ago, that the Jew-wallah they had invited to become one of them was a crooked financier. At least he wasn't, as the issue of the trial showed. But he might have been. And they had been horrified. Then Esther's great party came, and they were very generous. They washed out their horror in waters copious and lustrous, and their renewed pressure was so overwhelming that Silver found himself before the evening was out a candidate for election to the most exclusive golf-club in Cheshire.

Hannah Silver in her quite unbalanced excitement had asked if one or two of the people they used to know in the old days might come, too. She meant people from Magnolia Street and Oleander Street. Mr. Emmanuel, for instance, was often asked to really smart affairs. You might meet him in almost anybody's house. And the Bernsteins had moved from Longton to Withington, and they were quite big people in hardware. Mightn't the Bernsteins be invited, too ?

Esther Pliskin treated the suggestion with the scorn it deserved. And when the party came off, this extra-special particular party, and she looked around, and she saw who were at the table, lords and all the grandest people, she was very thankful, indeed, that no Emmanuels and no Bernsteins had been invited to let down the tone. She would have liked it to be a family reunion, too. Wouldn't it have been fine if they could have had poor Susan amongst them now ! Poor Susan, she thought with satisfaction ; she would probably have appreciated a good meal. But perhaps it was all for the best. Boris Polednik would not have fitted in with all these high aristocratic people, and he would have got angry seeing such grand expensive flowers about—so many of them you might think them paper ones. Well, perhaps those two were better in Russia where they were. But she wouldn't have minded at all if Elsie had been there, she was feeling so benign as that ! She and Elsie had never got on with each other ; but to-night, when they were celebrating nothing happening to father, she was sure it would have been all right. Excepting you could never tell with Elsie. She might suddenly let all the men see what she'd got till half way up her thigh. Or she'd let a shoulder-ribbon look as if it were slipping off her bare shoulder, till all the men got glass-eyed with hope and excitement.

Perhaps, on the whole, it was better that Elsie wasn't here, too. Anyhow, here was poor dear Sarah. All her children were upstairs at the top of the house. Sarah wouldn't move a step without the children anywhere. She was wearing a very nice quiet black frock ; for, after all, it wasn't so very long ago that her husband threw himself . . . Who'd have thought such things of him now ? A swindler, a forger ! And yet, sometimes, she had a sort of a feeling . . . Of course, she always understood, far better than all the rest of them, how *clever* he was, much cleverer than he ever let on, but he never even tried to deceive *her*. You could say they had been hand in glove with each other, in a manner of speaking, from the beginning. . . . But clever is clever, and —well, a swindler's a swindler and, if it hadn't been for that man Huxtable being found in Vienna, they wouldn't be holding any party to-night, with lords with eye-glasses sitting beside you, saying, "Would you like the salted almonds, Mrs. Pliskin?"

Sarah's frock was a simple one, Esther thoroughly approved of it. Yet she looked very beautiful, you could say the most beautiful woman there. You'd never have thought what a grand woman she'd make some day, when you saw her sitting about on the Oleander Street doorsteps with borrowed babies in her arms, making faces at them, and crooning. Of course there was never a woman who showed more clearly, almost from the moment she could walk, she wanted babies of her own. And she'd got them, no evil eye befall them, lots of them. No wonder she looked so beautiful !

Babies ! Poor May ! Esther sighed. If ever woman had old maid written all over her, it was May. Esther wondered why. She was certain May had knocked out of her head ages ago that old nonsense about the conscientious objector man —a clerk he was. Hadn't anybody else ever asked May to marry them ? She was a little thin, perhaps, not much in the way of bosom, but some men like them like that. And money, too ; she could have a dowry like a prince's daughter. No, Esther couldn't get to the bottom of it. She was puzzled.

May was sitting three chairs away from father. She had two quite nice young men sitting on both sides of her— Esther herself had seen to that. But no wonder she couldn't get off—she wasn't taking the least notice in the world of the two nice young men. She kept her eyes fixed on father the whole time—his least movement. You'd think she was his sweetheart, not his daughter, the way she looked at him the whole time. Of course, father was a bit pale and worried-looking. It was excitement. You can't go through what father had been going through without showing it a bit.

"Father!" Esther called out boisterously. "You're not eating anything! Cheer up! It's all made on the best butter!"

But even that pleasantry did not stir his appetite. His knife and fork moved very languidly, then slipped out of his fingers. His head jerked forward a little, as if he were going to fall asleep. In an instant May had risen from her chair, and was standing behind him, her hands on his shoulders. She whispered into his ear. He looked up into her face, and smiled. Then he got hold of his knife and fork again, and made a fair attack on his chicken. Mrs. Silver, at the head of the table, noted with pleasure that Sam was being a good boy and getting something down him. She lifted her hand, and played, tenderly, a moment with her pearls—her mother's pearls that he had stolen for her a long time ago in Terkass by the Dnieper.

Esther's husband, Joe, was somewhere down the table—a long way down. But, even though he sat so far removed from his wife, her shadow still seemed to hang over him, to reduce him to a little paper head and a little paper body. Esther remembered he was there. She looked to see how he was managing his knife and fork. He handled them scrupulously. Esther smiled, and inflated her large lungs. She heaved a happy sigh. It was a credit, her party, a credit to the whole family and to the Jewish people at large.

II

It was a couple of weeks after the junketings had been allowed to subside. May had gone back to Chanctonbury House again, though the new Miss Mosenthal was proving so satisfactory that May could have stayed away a week or two longer. Hannah Silver was still at home. Not even Popsie could with decency insist on Mrs. Silver leaving so soon the husband the kind gods had restored to her from the danger that had threatened him. Sarah had stayed on, too, till it was finally decided what was going to be done about her. She was, at all events, not going back to the boarding-house in Earl's Court, where she had been living since the house in Kensington Palace Gardens had been given up. There was ample room for the children in Pennine Grange. Their grandmother and mother were upstairs with the children that evening, a couple of weeks after the big party, when Esther Pliskin drove up in her handsome car. She asked to see her father. She found him sitting alone in the " home-room."

" Where are they all ? " asked Esther. Her father was sitting by the fire, on the low metal stool which each of the Silver daughters had monopolised in turn until, when she grew a little older, she had vacated it in favour of her next younger sister.

" Upstairs," he answered ; " with the children."

" That's good," she said breezily. " I wanted to see you alone."

He said nothing. He went on looking into the fire.

" Did you hear, father ? I said I wanted to see you alone."

" Yes."

"What's the matter, father? Aren't you feeling quite well?"

" It's all right, Esther. I feel quite well."

" Well, then, can I talk to you ? "

" Talk if you like."

" Father, you know it's a shame."

" What's a shame ? "

" All your money, you shouldn't be doing anything with it."

He made no comment.

" I've got an idea," she said.

Still he uttered no word.

" Why shouldn't you put some capital into our firm ? Why shouldn't you come in with me and Joe ? You know it's no good for you sitting about all day, doing nothing."

He still kept silence. An impatient word sprang to her lips, but she thrust it back again. If he wanted to take his time, let him take his time. Perhaps he was thinking over what she had said to him. Perhaps he wasn't. Maybe she'd made a mistake coming to him so soon after the other business. She judged it would be bad policy to force him into making some sort of comment now on her proposition. She decided that she'd best leave it for the present. He had heard her right enough. If he wanted to bring up the matter himself, well and good. If not, it would be as if she'd said nothing. Perhaps next week it would be a better time.

They both sat in silence for some minutes. She could be as obstinate as he was. She would wait till the others came down. She would wait five minutes, at least, then she'd go upstairs to them.

When he finally spoke, he spoke so low that it seemed he was not speaking to her at all. He did not turn his head to her

" You see," he said, " it's not my money."

" What ? What's that ? " she said.

" It's not my money."

" What are you talking about ? "

" I haven't got no right to it."

" Father, what are you saying ? Do you know what you're saying ? "

" I know what I'm saying. The money's not my money. I'm going to give it back to the people it belongs to. At once ! "

She felt her scalp freeze with horror. The blood was ice in all her veins.

" Father, are you ill ? I'm going up at once to fetch mother."

" Yes, I'm ill, Esther, but not like you mean. I want to get well again. I'm going to give my money back to the people it belongs to. I want to arrange it with my lawyers as soon as it can be done."

He had not turned his head. His voice had not risen out of its tired gentle monotone. She realised, as in one revealing flash of lightning, the danger that threatened her, her children, her mother, her sisters, all of them. She realised the necessity for action prompt as lightning. She must do something at once to hold up the malevolent operation of this poison.

" Father ! " she sprang at him. She caught at his shoulders. " Listen, father ! "

" I'm listening ! "

"Turn round! Do you hear? Turn round and look at me!"

He obeyed her and lifted his large and slightly pitiful eyes. " Well ? "

" You can do what you like with your own ! But it isn't your own ! You're not a single man. It's wickedness ! It's madness ! It can't be done ! "

" I shall do it, Esther ! "

" You don't mean it, father ! It's a joke you're making ! "

" It's no joke ! "

" No joke ! No joke ! God in Heaven ! " she called out. " Listen ! What will become of us all ? Me, it's not so bad for me ! But think of Sarah ! Think of her seven little children ! Think of mother ; of May ! You're not alone ! You're not a stone ! You can't behave like that ! You can't, I tell you ! God won't let you ! "

" God is making me ! "

" Father ! I beg you ! I pray you on my knees ! You mustn't do such a wicked, wicked thing ! All these years of hard work ! But it's not yourself, it's not me ! It's all the others ! You can't do it ! You mustn't do it ! "

" They must look after themselves ! If the money is not mine, it's not theirs ! It's bad money ! "

There was a solemnity in his voice she had never heard before. The tears streamed down her cheeks. She beat her clenched fists together. Then she got down on her knees to him. An idea had come to her she felt he could not gainsay.

" Listen, father ! If you're going to give it away, then give it ! But I say it's ours as well, and not only yours ! Give us a chance, all of us, to get together and talk it over ! All of us ! Yes, I mean Susan as well, and Elsie as well ! It matters to all our lives and our children after us ! I want you to promise one thing ! You can't not promise it, father ! "

" What is that, my daughter ? "

" You will do nothing in this matter, nothing, you will not take a single step, till we can meet, all of us, and talk it over ? "

" You mean till you collect them, yes, and between you you shall stop me ? "

" I mean—I mean—— Father, I beg you ! Will you give us this one month ? "

" All right, Esther, if you want this one month you shall have it ! "

III

There was a month to work in. A lot could be done in a month. A lot had to be done in a month. She did not delude herself into believing that the battle was going to be easy. It would need the utmost she possessed of energy, it would call for all her powers of organisation ; these would have to be backed up by the concerted attacks of the five other women—her mother, and her four sisters. The various children would be sharpshooters, pouring in their lighter fire from the flanks.

She was too clever to think of weakening the effect of her massed attack by engaging her forces in preliminary skirmishes. She did not want him to get hardened to the sense of being under fire. The barrage must be concentrated on him from all points simultaneously.

She was frightened. There was something in the mournful sobriety of his eye, in the profound gentleness of his voice, which convinced her, in moments of anguished self-distrust, of the certainty of failure. But these moments were succeeded by spasms of rage, by hectic affirmations of her own invincibility. He was just weak and old and dithering. The strain of the trial had unbalanced him a little. Well, she'd show if he was going to be allowed to sacrifice his wife and children and grandchildren for the sake of a nonsense, a madness ; *she'd* show him. She got to work at once.

The great gathering of the family was to take place on

November the nineteenth, exactly a month from the day on which Silver had avowed to her his iniquitous resolve. Her mother, Sarah, May, herself, were easy to collect. Susan and Elsie were the difficult ones. For, of course, Susan and Elsie would be as outraged as she was, as they would all be, the moment she told them about it. She determined to keep her mouth shut, for a day or two at least, until she had fixed up her plan of campaign.

Susan was a Bolshevik, of course. But that didn't seem to make any difference when it came to money, excepting that you took all the money away from the people who had it, and tried to spread it round among millions of people who didn't know what to do with it. Susan was as having as any of them. She had squeezed every penny she had been able to out of the old man, and gone about buying seed and cows and pigs, and giving it to starving Russians. Really, the amount of money the Silvers gave to strangers was chronic. First her father, then her mother, then Susan in Russia, then May in Sussex—chronic was really the only word for it. Charity begins at home, was her motto, and she didn't mind who knew it.

Susan was a long way away from Altrincham. She, herself, never had anything to do with Susan, of course ; she was a Bolshevik, and she didn't want to be mixed up with people like that. But she knew that Susan and May wrote to each other from time to time. She even knew that Susan's headquarters were in Moscow. Yes, that was a long way away from Altrincham. It was possible that just now Susan wasn't in Moscow at all, and Elsie mightn't be in Berlin, either. That was why it was necessary to book the big family meeting for a whole month ahead. Apart from that, there was a lot to be said for getting it over quickly, before the old man got any more screws loose.

She considered the idea of going to Moscow. She was ready to go anywhere, climb mountains, do anything. It was worth while. But going to Moscow seemed an undertaking outside all normal sublunar adventure. It was incalculable.

It would be different if they were straightforward savages over there in Russia, but they were not straightforward ones. If she went, she might never be able to get back. They might put her on a State farm, to be bred from. She had a husband and children of her own, thank you ; one husband and five children, and that was quite enough to be going on with. No, she decided she would not go to Moscow. She would write Susan such a letter that if Susan's heart hadn't just become a lump of stone inside her, she would pack up and come at once. Besides, Susan would have to come for her own sake, too, for those starving *mouzhiks* she was so fond of.

Berlin, luckily, was not so far as Moscow. She'd go to Berlin in person. She knew a lot more about Elsie than Elsie imagined she did. There were business friends of hers who'd gone to Berlin to pick up ideas and trade. They had seen Elsie up and down the place, with a ruined Prussian count. They were quite the talk of Berlin ; there had even been songs about them in a public *cabaret*. She knew Elsie was keeping the blue-eyed charmer on their father's money. She knew she was madly in love with him, though her wretched husband, Sir Malswetting, was drinking himself to death down in the South of France somewhere. What would you expect from Elsie ? She'd always been an " outthrow " from the beginning. Such a year should take her ! But she'd *have* to come to the family meeting. She'd *want* to come. She'd come flying in aeroplanes. What would happen to her beautiful Prussian count, if she hadn't got any more money to keep him ? He'd look out for some other woman, she supposed. Oh, yes, Elsie would come ! But she was taking no chances. She would go to Berlin to fetch her

Then there was May. It would be a serious blow to her Country Home if the big annual subscription from their father fell through. She had been talking lately of starting another one, somewhere in Yorkshire. Oh, yes, father's money was important to May. And yet, and yet . . she felt rather doubtful about May. She was the only one of them all she felt a little anxious about. They were rather like each other in some ways, those two, father and May. They were both liable to get the same silly sort of ideas into their heads. Besides, she knew that if there was one thing in the world May didn't like it was to see her father bullied. Bullied? They were just going to beg him on their bended knees not to spoil their lives for them, and their children's lives, that was all. Do you call that bullying?

And yet—May stuck like a fishbone in her throat. She remembered that awful occasion many years ago when old Horowitz had palmed his little workshop on to their father. A good thing it was, too. Thank God he had! But the fact was—how should May know what Horowitz's factory would grow into? She *didn't* know! She, herself, had begged her father not to throw away the fifty pounds he had won in the lottery; she had nearly burst a blood-vessel begging him. And she knew, she was absolutely convinced, that he would have given up his idea of buying the little workshop if May hadn't been in the room. May hadn't said a word, but, as sure as sure, she'd stopped him. That was because God had wanted her to stop him not buying the workshop.

It was very different now. The last thing God wanted now was that May should encourage their father to throw them all into the workhouse.

On the whole—it wouldn't be easy to arrange—but on the whole it would be better, one way or another, if May *didn't* come to the family meeting. The rest of them between them could manage the job of knocking the nonsense out of the old man's head. Of course she'd have to tell May all about it. She'd even have to make the journey to Chanctonbury House, too, to persuade her to come. If May got any idea that she, Esther, would really prefer her to stay at home, she would certainly come, to spite her. And that wouldn't do at all. It wasn't at all easy, but she'd fix it all right.

There remained her mother and Sarah. As for her mother, she would have a word with that woman called Popsie. That would settle *that*. As for Sarah—a widow with seven children;

what are you talking about ? That was all there need be said about Sarah.

She went home, sat down to her desk, and spent two hours writing the first drafts of her letters to Susan and Elsie. Then she wrote to May, asked when it would be convenient to go to Steyning to see her, and would she please send her Susan's address, in Moscow, by return of post.

IV

Susan Polednik was surprised at herself, shocked at herself. She sat waiting in their small two-roomed apartment that looked down over the Moskva River. She had come in late that evening from her office, but her husband had not come in yet. She could always rely on him to come home an hour or two after herself, however late she came in. Work took the place in Boris Polednik of food, drink, love. But even he could not dispense altogether with the first two. She should have got the Primus stove going, she remembered suddenly, and fixed up some food for him. That is, if there was any food in the cupboard to fix up.

She leaned forward on to the table and scrutinised the envelope, the letter, again. The envelope, as usual, had been steamed open. She felt, with a little resentment, they ought not to be so clumsy about it. Then she read Esther's letter still again, and put it down.

Of course she must throw her weight in with the rest to prevent the old man behaving in this imbecile fashion. Capitalism should not behave with such Christ-like quixotry ; any good Bolshevik who had it in his power to prevent a sentimental performance of the type her father threatened should do everything in the world he could to prevent it. It was the sort of thing that sometimes happened in the capitalist world, and put a namby-pamby nimbus behind the whole system. It made the workers go hot and cold with un-Marxian emotion. It was vicious.

She was confident Boris would endorse that point of view

He would also, like herself, strongly dislike the idea that the funds that were transmitted to her from a capitalist locker should be diverted from the starving peasantry whom she helped with it into a whole series of smaller capitalist lockers which would be by so much fortified in their anti-Socialistic activities. He probably would not put that point of view into so many words. The authorities had never expressed themselves in so many words on her activities. No one doubted what a great deal of good her money, or her father's money, had done, first in association with certain Swedish relief organisations, then, when these had suspended their work, in the organisation she had herself created. The work was unofficial, of course. The Kremlin had all along turned a blind eye ; but it had been a benevolent one.

It was not for revolving such thoughts as these that Susan was surprised and shocked at herself. It was because, in addition, she was wildly excited at the thought of going back to England. Despite herself, despite her abhorrence of its social system, she had begun to sentimentalise about England in the deepest recesses of her mind, as she used to sentimentalise over her mother's family's home on the Dnieper, the orchard and the apricot-tree. She wanted to see how the family was getting on, of course. But it was not that that so wildly excited her. She wanted a hot bath. That was what it amounted to—a great marble bath, with bath salts and flannels and loofahs and scented soaps and endless hot water and a plug in the bath to keep it all in. She was tired of hip-baths and enormous ex-Romanof full-length baths with a cork for plug and a quart of hot water boiled on a Primus to bath in.

It was fantastic. For she had never been a luxurious person. She had been clean, that was all she could say of herself, and that is all anybody need say of herself. And she had not grown up in a grand house with a private bathroom to each bedroom. She had been born in a slum, and spent most of her life in England in a slum. It was fantastic, but it was true—she had a fierce nostalgia for good plumbing—for a hot bath, and bath-towels as large as a room, and smooth lavender-smelling face-towels, and decent underclothes to get into—not prima-donna silk underclothes, just decent clean soft fresh underclothes ; and breakfast in bed—even that—breakfast in bed ; to be waited on by another human being every bit as good as herself—wearing a neat little cap and a neat little apron—who would draw the curtains and put the tray down on the small table beside the bed ; and there would be boiling milk and boiling coffee in silver jugs to be poured into a large breakfast-cup ; and a sweet boiled egg ; and a kipper—how marvellous to have a kipper wait-ing supinely for you under the silver dish-cover ; and marmalade, marmalade, marmalade !

No wonder Susan Polednik was shocked, as well as surprised, at herself.

It was not the last of these emotions she expounded to Boris Polednik when he came in. She said, frankly, she thought she ought to go to Pennine Grange, but she did not say it with any enthusiasm. All Bolsheviks were the same in this ; if you ever expressed any enthusiasm for any scheme or idea—outside the strict lines of Marxian orthodoxy—they at once wrinkled their noses and started sniffing round, for heaven knew what, counter-revolution, sabotage, espionage, heresy. She carefully kept all enthusiasm out of her face and voice ; yet, even so, she was surprised at her effortless victory over him.

" Of course," said Boris, " there's no doubt about it. You should go. He should be stopped. The change will do you good, too."

How splendid of him to think of it from that point of view as well ! She felt like throwing her arms round him and kiss-ing him. But she kept herself carefully under control.

" I don't know about that," she said. " It'll be rather sickening in some ways. The big family meeting is fixed for November the nineteenth. I'll get there a day or two before,

and stay on two or three days after. I'll try and get into
touch with the local Communist group and see how things
are progressing."

"Don't hurry back," he said blandly. "Make a holiday
of it. Stay on for a couple of weeks. Why shouldn't you?"

She looked up a little suspiciously. Such gentleness in Boris
was not a phenomenon she, or anyone who knew him,
welcomed. But his face, if it had looked amiable for a moment, looked so no longer. He was rooting about among the
papers on a table, his pince-nez harshly glinting and darting.

"It'll do no harm to anybody," Boris Polednik said to
himself, "if she stays away a fortnight—or a month, if she
likes. It might do her some real good, too, if she gets a
noseful of capitalist stench again." He was not altogether
pleased with her; nor were the Party authorities for that
matter. Nobody minded her rather sweet schemes for suc-
couring the victims of drought and flood. But somehow her
methods and motives were never quite right. She did not
make any proper discrimination between the people who,
when helped, might be of real use to the Union in the
establishment of Socialism, and the people who, to say the
least of it, might be only a dead weight.

How odd it was, he thought. She was in some ways as
addle-pated a philanthropist as her mother. He recalled the
grease-spattered flyblown charity collection cards which
covered half a wall in the Oleander Street scullery. Blood
will out. Only a few days ago they had been going to an
important co-operative meeting. They were walking down
a side street, when they came upon a man lying on a doorstep, his body in the shade and his head out in the sun. He
was some piece of indiscriminate riff-raff that had seeped
into Moscow from the countryside. He was an oldish man,
sixty or so, too old to be of any use. Perhaps he was all that
was left of some counter-revolutionary country lawyer or
doctor. The sooner he was out of the way the better.

And, in fact, he was dying. A glaze was coming down on his eyes. His forehead was damp with the last sweat. He would probably be dead in an hour.

Suddenly Susan had torn at his sleeve. " Boris ! Boris ! Can't we do something about it ? "

He pointed out it was too late to do anything. The old fellow would be dead soon.

" But that doesn't matter, Boris. Don't you see that doesn't matter ? We can't leave him to die out here like a dog ! "

" It *is* rather a nuisance ! Why the hell don't they keep to the country ? What are the ditches for ? "

But she hadn't heard what he said. She was kneeling down by the old tramp, with his head in her lap, and mopping his forehead, and sending for a droshky, and altogether making a sentimental idiot of herself in her best manner. It wasn't as if there were any chance of *saving* the old man. And what was the good of making him hang on by the eyelashes for another month or two ; what was the good to anybody ?

He had gone on alone, furious, to the co-operative meeting.

It would not be unpleasant to have her out of the way for a little time. They would both appreciate it.

v

Esther wrote Elsie a very full and touching letter explaining the whole situation. She made it quite clear that it was all so terribly urgent that, if Elsie wanted her to come to Berlin to explain in fuller detail, she would come without a moment's delay. But, as a matter of fact, she found it would not be necessary to go to Berlin after all.

Elsie's first reaction was : " Hell ! Am I going to have Esther and Oskar doing a grand masonic get-together ? Hell I am ! I'm no snob, but there *are* limits ! "

Her immediately subsequent reaction was : " God Almighty ! If the old lad's going to do this Sign of the Cross stuff—there won't be any more nice monthly cheques from the home burg ! And, if there aren't any more nice monthly cheques, Oskar won't be quite his happy little self, will he ? Oskar's not the boy for love in a cottage, and, Go and pump some water, there's a darling, and, Hell, the baker's boy's forgotten us again to-day ! No, the wandering daughter must go wandering back to papa and make big eyes at him, and tell him that when papas behave like moo-cows that's one way girls go naughty. The other way is to have a clergyman for a papa."

So she sat down at once and wrote to Esther, telling her she wouldn't dream of putting her to all that trouble ; and how frightened and horrified she was ; and poor old Sarah with all those children ; and she'd be at Pennine Grange the nineteenth of November, Esther could put her shirt on that. And thank her very much for bringing her into it, she had so often felt awfully miserable at being completely cut off from the family like this ; and how she was looking forward to seeing Esther herself, in particular, and Joe and their children, bless their little hearts, and she remained her affectionate sister with love and kisses.

Esther received the letter, read it, and snorted. " The tart ! " she said, with the bitterness of a woman who does not attract men towards the woman who knocks a man back with the tap of her little finger. " But she'll be there right enough ! " she said.

Then, after Elsie despatched her letter, she had a further reaction. She had learned in Esther's letter that the whole family would be assembled to knock sense into the old man. That meant May would be there, of course.

That would be a blow. She could not face up to May. She would never be able to face up to May. She again tried to argue herself out of it. She had all her life long maintained that everybody attached far too much importance to the sexual act. You went through with it and that was that. But, surely, to make such a fuss with herself about that twenty minutes in Cardiff with Harry Stonier was to go right over to the other side, to the girls with bonnets and the long-jawed lads with dog collars. Surely it was. She argued with herself like any-thing. But it was no go. She had been the complete mutt. She hated, like poison, the thought of facing up to May.

Then she thought of a world without Oskar, without the money to pay for Oskar. It would be like biting into an apple of which the inside is cotton-wool. It would be like drinking a glass of Perrier water after it had been left standing a week. She would have to go through with it. May and she were both perfect ladies. There would be no scene.

Poor dear sweet little May, what a goddam swine I was !

Elsie and Oskar sat in their Tiergartenstrasse sitting-room before the beautiful English hearth they had had expensively built in. The logs spat and crackled. A valet was mixing a cocktail for them.

" They're bats ! " she informed Oskar.

" Bats ? " he asked her politely, for there were quite a number of her neologisms he did not understand.

" Batty ! " she further explained. She pointed to her fore-head. " Bats in the belfry ! "

" Oh ! " He understood now, or he understood the phrase, at least. " And who is it that have bats in the belfry ! "

" Business men ! " she said comprehensively.

" And how so ? "

" First, poor old Smirnof chucking himself out of the old train ! "

" Yes, that was very sad ! "

" And now father ! " She shook Esther's letter before him.

" But surely, my dear, he hasn't .   "

" Oh, no, not that ! Hard-hearted as I am, I wouldn't be sitting about sipping cocktails, if *he'd* thrown himself out of a train, too. Put some more in, Hartkopf, will you ? "

" What is it then ? "

She explained the contents of the letter.

" You are going ? " he asked, with scrupulous casualness, as if he asked were she going to the hairdresser

" I've written and told her I'll be there."

" Good," he said calmly. " Hartkopf ! " He made a gesture towards his cocktail glass.

" Look here ! " said Elsie suddenly. " It's not absolutely fool-proof, you know ! "

" What do you mean ? "

" I mean, whatever *we* do, there's no guaranteeing what *he'll* do. He gets queer ideas sometimes. This is the queerest of the lot, God only knows."

He daintily removed an olive-stone from between his teeth. " Well ? " he said. He threw his olive-stone neatly at the flaming head of a log.

" Oskar ! "

" Yes ? "

" And suppose there's nothing doing, suppose there ain't no more goose laying any more golden eggs ? "

" My dear, why do you run forward like that ? Why do you need to utter such unpleasant thoughts ? "

" Oskar," she said sombrely. " I'm going to get drunk to-night ! "

VI

Esther felt that merely to write a letter to May, or even to write her several letters, would look like a suspicious lack of enthusiasm. She thought it best to make a personal visit to Chanctonbury House. She went away with very mixed feelings as to the result of her mission.

" I'll come," said May, " if you want me to. But if you think I'm going to try to persuade father against his will, you're mistaken."

" Then you think what he wants to do is right ? You know how Sarah's been left with all those children ? Is it fair to mother, after he's let her have her own way all this time, he should make her live like a beggar again ? And your work ? Don't you believe in it ? Were you just going in for it for a hobby, like a society lady ? "

" No," said May quietly. " It means a great deal to me. And I see a lot in what you say. But if father thinks what he wants to do is right, I think he ought to do it. I won't try and stop him."

" Listen, May ! " Esther begged her. " I've told you Susan's coming all the way from Moscow."

" Yes."

" And you'll want to see Susan, won't you ? You're the only one who's kept in touch with her all this time. She thinks she'll only be able to stop a day or two in England."

" Yes, I'd like very much to see Susan."

" And Elsie's coming."

" Yes."

" And you want to see Elsie again, don't you ? "

" Yes."

" Well, that's what I mean. We'll all be there. We *must* all be there—you, too, the whole family. Just so that he can see it's not only one of us or another of us, but all of us—he wants to ruin all of us."

" *You'll* be all right, Esther."

" Yes," she proclaimed with triumph. " I'm the best off of the lot. Yet I'm the one who's taking all the trouble. It just shows."

May wasn't quite certain what it just showed.

" So you'll be there, May, with the rest of us, just to back us up ? "

" I'll be there."

The nearer Esther got to Doomington, the more she was convinced that May would be rather a liability than an asset at the family gathering. She felt she had done her duty, anyhow. She had gone all the way down to Sussex to show how much she wanted May to come, and if she didn't come it was her own fault. By the time she got to Stockport, she had no doubt at all May would be a serious handicap at the gathering, sitting about like a little Virgin Mary. Perhaps it would be possible to arrange that May should not come.

May did not want to come. In the first place, she immensely did not wish to see Elsie. She had understood from the very beginning what had happened between Elsie and Harry at Cardiff. Elsie's precipitate flight had made it quite clear to her. Her knowledge had been confirmed by the fact that neither Harry nor Elsie had written to her from that day to this. They were both sick with shame

She did not want to see Elsie. On the other hand, she hated to think of her father being set upon by this mass attack of ardent females. She hated to think of him being forced to give up doing the thing he proposed to do, if he thought it was the right thing to do. As against that, it was repugnant to her to try and influence him to a course of action which would have such serious consequences for other people, many of them children. The least of her considerations was her Country Homes, the one already established, and the projected one. This one could stand on its own feet now ; or could be made to, with a little trouble. The Yorkshire Home would have to wait two or three years.

It was a difficult dilemma. She might, of course, make some excuse at the last moment for not coming. She shrewdly suspected that Esther would be extremely relieved if she did not come. But that was a rather mean thing to do. She realised that the factor which was most pressing upon her was her disinclination to see Elsie. That decided her. She must go, because she must not have her course of action decided for her by her own inclinations or disinclinations. Elsie and she both had a certain amount of good manners. They would be able to carry off the situation with decency. For the rest, she would remain as unemphatic and unobtrusive as she knew how. She would leave at the first possible moment.

That implied, of course, she would turn up at the latest possible moment. Esther had decreed six o'clock in the evening of the nineteenth as the hour when the bombardment should commence. There would be a jolly little high tea before, at which Esther hoped everybody would be present. May worked out a sequence of moves—car to London, train to Doomington, car to Altrincham—which would get her to Pennine Grange a little before six. She wrote to Esther, giving her the times. She was afraid, however, she would not be able to get there in time for tea.

On the morning of the nineteenth, about an hour before she had arranged for the car to take her to London, May was having breakfast at Chanctonbury House. It was a rather early breakfast, and her morning mail was delivered during the course of it. There was a telegram on top of the letters. She opened it. " Most urgent see you to-morrow Tuesday," went the message, " could you possibly come Cardiff forgive." The telegram was signed, " Stonier."

May carefully folded the telegram and put it back in its envelope. Then she took it out again and examined the office-mark. The telegram had been duly sent from Cardiff.

She finished her cup of coffee. She smiled. How very ingenious of Esther ! And to go to the trouble to send an accomplice all the way to Cardiff, too ! And how carefully thought out it all was. The accomplice had sent off the wire last night, so that it could not possibly arrive before the next morning !

How beautifully it resolved her dilemma for her ! Of course she would go to Cardiff ! Perhaps the poor boy really *was* in some sort of trouble, she told herself Jesuitically.

As for her father—she thrust her head back, and her eyes were proud. She knew, however heavy the odds arrayed against him were, he would act as his fine heart instructed him.

As for Harry, her love, in Cardiff—how could he resent it if she came post-haste to him when he sent out to her so urgent a message ? She knew that the flowers of his spirit were scorched and wilted within him ; it was time that the healing waters were poured over them.

CHAPTER XXII

THE FAMILY GATHERING

There was a rather funereal air about the family high tea. Esther had given careful orders that no one was to bring up the all-important matter before the conference proper took place. It would clearly be rather an anti-climax when it came up at the conference, if it had already been worried over in company with the currant cake and the trifle. They had all seen each other individually during the course of the last day or two, and there had been enough tongue-wagging for a meeting of the House of Commons. Particularly Susan. It was extraordinary how much talking she did, all the more when you remembered what a silent and preoccupied girl she had been in the old days. She had talked even in her bath, to herself or to anybody who would come and listen to her. She stayed in the bath for two whole hours, as if she had not had a bath since she went to Russia.

Both the foreigners were there at high tea, Susan the Muscovite and Elsie the Berlinerin. Elsie was doing much less talking than Susan. She looked very smart and bewitching. It was pathetic to see the way Susan took the stuff of Elsie's frock between finger and thumb and caressed it, and asked her what you called that material. It was pathetic. Berlin was clearly a more comfortable place to live in than Moscow. Mrs. Silver was at the head of the table. Esther was at the foot of the table. Sarah sat in between. There were troops of children up and down. There was the old man himself, of course.

He wasn't in a very good temper. Pleased as he was to see Susan and Elsie, he was very upset that May wasn't there. You would have thought that May lived in Vladivostok, and Susan and Elsie had come in from Blackpool

and Southport, the way he took it for granted that Susan
and Elsie should be there, and the fuss he made because
May was not.

It was a difficult tea-party, because when people are
specifically requested not to talk about a subject, it is the
one subject that they cannot keep their minds from. Tea
came to an end finally, and Esther proposed they should ad-
journ to the big drawing-room and wait till May came. It
was nearly six now ; May said she would arrive close on six.
Old Silver declared categorically against the big drawing-
room. He had his wife and all his daughters together for the
first time for many years, and he insisted they should repair
to the little room, the " home-room," with the candlesticks
and brass trays and Queen Victoria and Lord Beaconsfield.
It might be a little crowded in the " home-room," but they
had often been crowded enough in the old days, and the
sooner they got used to the thought of being crowded again
the better.

That sounded a little forbidding. Elsie protested they
couldn't possibly get all the children into the stuffy little
room. Her father said, God bless them, he didn't want the
children in that room. He had a bit of a headache, and he'd
be pleased if they'd all be packed off upstairs. That was
disagreeable, too. Esther found herself deprived of one of her
principal effects. She had intended to make much rhetorical
use of poor Sarah's orphans at appropriate moments. But
there was nothing to be done about it. Off they had to go
upstairs.

The father, the mother, the four daughters, repaired into
the " home-room." Elsie sat down on the low metal stool
near the fire, and made her eyes look large and pathetic ;
she was the complete poor-little-thing. Susan felt a bit of a
hypocrite ; Sarah felt a bit of an exhibit ; Mrs. Silver thought
dinner at the Berkeley with John Proctor was much more
amusing. Only Esther thrust her bosom stoutly forward,
like the prow of a battleship. Silver tapped with his fingers
on his thighs and grunted and fidgeted. His fidgets conveyed

themselves to the others, to all but Esther. She seemed carved out of oak.

Six-fifteen ! Six-thirty ! It was strange. May was always extremely scrupulous about being on time. Had anything happened to May ? Was Esther sure May knew the right day and time ? Esther was absolutely sure. She had a letter from May in her bag there, confirming the day and time. Six forty-five, and still no May ! Silver was extremely worried. Esther suggested that perhaps one of the children had got taken ill suddenly, and she had been prevented from leaving Chanctonbury House, after all. " Then for why she doesn't send a telegram ? " snapped her father.

Then Elsie suddenly threw out another suggestion.

" Perhaps she didn't want to see *me* ! " she said.

" For why on earth not ? " asked Esther.

" Oh, I don't know ! We had rather a nasty row just before I left ! "

" Oh, is that so ? She never said anything. Well, perhaps you're right ! "

" She should have sent a telegram ! " insisted her father.

" She should, she should ! " repeated Esther, a little huffily. " But she hasn't ! And it's seven o'clock ! We won't wait another minute for her ! "

" I shouldn't ! " corroborated Elsie. " Start talking ! "

There was a note of acerbity in Esther's voice as she addressed her father. The gathering hadn't turned out quite as she had intended it to. It was to be all twilight, and gentleness, and fluttering children holding out their hands, and a little muffled sobbing coming out of the darkness from time to time. God in heaven ! How she'd worked to fix up this thing ! God in heaven, how much depended on it ! She'd been forgetting that ; they'd all been forgetting that ! Just because his precious May hadn't turned up, and he was cross about it and had made them all nervy and fidgety.

" Well, father," she started off, " I've told them ! They know all about it ! "

" Of course they do," he said, " or they wouldn't be here ! "

"No !" She recoiled. This was not in the least the way she expected her father to talk. " And they're heartbroken ! "

" I'm sorry ! " he said. His voice was rather intransigent.

" Sorry ? " she flared up. " What do you mean you're sorry ? You want to ruin yourself and your wife and your children, and all you say is you're sorry ! "

" I don't worry to ruin anybody ! " he said, with extra-ordinary mildness. " If you haven't made a good thing out of it, you've been slow, all of you ! "

" My dear daddy," complained Elsie virtuously, " do be fair. Anybody would think we'd all been sitting around with our hands in your pockets for years."

" Quite so," Esther backed her up. " Whatever Joe and me's had from you has always been in the way of business. It's been a loan, at so much per cent, and you've had it back every penny."

" Is your business in a bad way now ? Do you want any more loans ? "

" No, thank God, we're in a very sound position, and we don't care who knows it."

" Well, then, you're all right. It won't make no difference to you."

" Now look here, father. If you think I've got the family here together to-day, from all the world over, just because I want to borrow money from you, you're mistaken. I'm not asking anything for myself at all. Some day, when you get this—this wicked idea out of your head, and we all settle down again nice and proper, and if the firm asks you to invest a little sum of money on the side, why shouldn't you ? It isn't as if you've got a business of your own now. Or as if you've got any more daughters to marry."

" What are you saying ? " cried Mrs. Silver, in an an-guished voice. " No evil eye, is there not our youngest one to marry ? She will yet marry a somebody, a big man ; she will surprise you all yet ! "

" She's quite right, Hannah," said Silver softly. " We shall never need money for May to get married. If she'd ever have needed it, she'd have had it, every penny I've got."

" Well, daddy," said Elsie, with a mouth like a pink chocolate cream, " you have got other children, you know."

" You didn't let me finish, my daughter," her father said. " I said if she'd have needed it once, she'd have had it. But to-day, if she'd need anything, it wouldn't be there. It *isn't* there ! "

Esther made impatient noises with her tongue. She turned to Susan. " Susan, why don't you say something ? "

" It's very difficult for me to say anything, because in some ways I think father's right. It *isn't* his money ! "

" What——"

" Please let me talk. It *isn't* his money ! You know I can't say things like this very easily, but I insist I'm very fond of father. I only found out in Russia how fond I am of him, reckoning it all up. But I can't hide from myself he's an exploiter. It's sweated money. And the money he hasn't sweated out of his workmen——"

" Now, Susan, now ! " her father objected hotly. " Everybody always said our firm was one of the best in the trade. The architects had special orders to make the biggest windows possible for the money, and our sanitary arrangements were a model. We were building a sports ground out at Stretford——"

" Yes, father, I know, I know. I shouldn't be surprised if you weren't quite the best of a bad lot. It's not *you* I'm attacking ; it's the system. I was saying what money you didn't get out of sweated labour you got out of investors, and that money came out of sweated labour, too. That's where *all* money comes from, from the workman and the peasant ; it's they who create the wealth, and what do they get out of it ? "

" I say, Susan, old girl," suggested Elsie, " cut the patter and let's have the tricks now ! "

" I wish you wouldn't interrupt," said Susan sourly. " I was going on to say that if I'd have heard that father was going to give back to the workmen the money he's made out of them, I'd have stayed on in Moscow, where I've got my work to look after. But that isn't the idea at all ! "

" No, not all ! " corroborated Esther.

" It's going to the investors, the creditors of the firm. I think that's in the highest degree foolish."

" It's going back where I got it from," said Silver quietly. " What they do with it, is their look-out, not mine. I didn't get no money out of my workers. I got work out of them and they got wages out of me, as good as any in the trade. If the business could have been run on a higher wage-scale, they would have got it."

" I don't think we need go any more into that," Susan said a little pityingly, conscious of the immense advantage she had over them all in economics. The schoolmarm expression had come into her face, an expression which always used to make Elsie want to throw things at her. Susan continued : " I'm not pretending to have any claim on you, father, as the others have, I'm sure. I've turned my back on your world and all it stands for, and they haven't. But I do want to put in a claim for common sense. You know all about what I've been doing with the money you sent me. It's unofficial work, but there's a lot of it to be done still, unfortunately. Whenever there's a famine, or a flood, or an epidemic shows up anywhere, my organisation is informed, and we see what we can do about it. It's got nothing to do with politics at all. Most of the people we've helped have still only the faintest idea who Lenin was, and as for getting into their heads what dialectical materialism really means—well, as I've been saying, that's not our job. Our job is purely humanitarian——"

" That's right," broke in Mrs. Silver, recognising the word. " That's what Popsie and me do in London, too."

" I'm sure," said Susan, " though I venture to believe that the wretched *mouzhiks* out on the tundras have fewer people to look after their interests than the people you work for, mother."

"What is she saying, what is she saying?" Hannah asked. She hadn't quite got the hang of it, but she felt that Susan was running down the lovely limpid work she did in Bethnal Green. At least she did it *for* Bethnal Green. She did most of the work itself in committee-rooms in Mayfair, or selling programmes in Shaftesbury Avenue.

"Now, now!" Sarah objected. "You two mustn't quarrel about your charities. I'm sure the work you both do is simply wonderful."

"Did you say, Susan, that the work you do in Russia is unofficial?" Silver asked.

"I did."

"Well, it will have to be official now."

"What do you mean?"

"I'm afraid you can't get no more money from me to help *mouzhiks* in tundras."

That had a certain air of finality about it. Susan wondered if it was worth coming all the way from Moscow for. It suddenly occurred to her she could have another bath to-night. There was no reason in the world to wait till to-morrow for the next one. She thrust forward her lank limbs. They felt clean and fresh and new. She had been putting things on to her hair. She caught hold of a hank of it, twisted it up against her nose, and sniffed.

That was a check, definitely. It was almost as if Esther had signalled to Elsie to weigh in, Elsie followed up so promptly after this reverse.

"You do remember, daddy, what I said to you before?" asked Elsie.

"No, Elsie, I don't. And I don't remember you ever calling me daddy before. Nobody ever does. I like being called daddy." His voice was rather withering.

"It's about time somebody started," she said; but he had brought a flush into her cheeks. It really wasn't going to be such a damn-fool easy game to get round the old man as she had thought. "Let's be sensible, daddy. You're a business man, and you know what's what. Is it fair? You will admit it isn't so very long ago I asked you to give me a hand. It's not as if I've been sponging on you for years."

"If you like, I'll look it up. I can tell you just when you wrote to me and how much you've had till now."

"Oh, there's no need to make out a balance-sheet," she said lightly. Then she realised that that was rather a gaffe, in virtue of the recent happenings at the assize courts. "I beg your pardon, father," she said. Which made it a little worse, perhaps.

But no. He was quite amused at her discomfiture. "I can stand it," he said. "That counsel for the prosecuting— he was worse."

"I made my own living for years and years." It sounded in her ears like a line in a sketch she had played in some time, somewhere. "I never asked you for a penny. Then I married a rich man. Again I never asked you for a penny. Then my husband and I—fell out." She simply could not resist a slightly tragic fall of the voice and droop of the head. "I had to leave him."

"You poor, poor girl!" sniffed Mrs. Silver.

"I went to Berlin. For a time I tried to earn my own living. I went back on the stage again, though it was hard, very hard, after living such a life of luxury, and being waited on hand and foot."

"Where was that?" her father interrupted. "In Olean-der Street you were waited on hand and foot?"

"On my word, father!" Esther protested. "Can't you see how upset she is?"

Elsie resumed. "I couldn't do it. I couldn't keep it up. I was just about to write to you, daddy, and ask for your help, when I got a letter from my husband. He'd heard somehow I was nearly starving. He offered to help me. It was either you or him, daddy, and I chose him. I thought I had more claim on him. He hadn't anybody else to think of, and you've got such a big family. It went on like that for some time. He made me a regular allowance, though I never saw him. I suppose he thought he'd buy me back that way. But I couldn't face it "—her voice broke—" I couldn't face going back to him."

Mrs. Silver mopped her eyes with her handkerchief.

Elsie resumed. " Then, at last, so far as I've been able to make out, another woman came into his life. The money stopped. So I had to ask you, daddy, for the first time in my life."

There was a silence. It really was a very moving tale. It was rather grand of Elsie to have been able to hold her end up so long and so bravely, though Fate had dealt so unkindly with her.

" Well," Silver proclaimed breezily, " how do you say it ? The going's been good, yes, while it lasted ? "

" Father ! " Esther protested. She found herself doing a lot of protesting.

" I hope you put a bit by for a rainy day," he said.

Elsie now took out her extremely dainty pocket handkerchief and dabbed her eye with it. " I wish I had. I would have done if I'd have known you'd treat me like this when I came to see you after so many years. Was it my fault my husband gave me such expensive ideas ? If I'd have known, I'd have put the money by regularly. I'd have just kept enough to pay for a small room and a crust of bread——"

" But you said you went on the stage again ? "

" Yes."

" Did it go down well ? You aren't no back number yet ? "

" Say, where did you get that idea from ? "

" Well, that's all right then, Elsie. You can go back on the stage again, yes ? "

" I suppose I can," agreed Elsie sullenly. Really she had underestimated the old man. He was as wily as an eel. But she wasn't quite through yet. " I'm not expecting you should keep on with that regular allowance," she said. " I suppose it was rather a lot of money."

" Yes ? What then ? "

" If, instead of that, you'd let me have a sum down——"
There was something to be said for one long last glorious
burst with Oskar. And then perhaps—well, it was impossible
to say how dependent on her he'd grown. After all, he'd
have to pay good money for most other women, and very
few as good value as she was.

" No ! " said Silver, quite pointedly. " Next, please ! "

Elsie flushed furiously. It was all she could do not to
hurtle out of the house there and then. Esther nearly
exploded with anger. She hadn't expected her turns to be
ticked off like items in a shopping-list. Nobody said a word.
Mrs. Silver was wondering who John Proctor would be
dining with that night, and would there be any chance at
all to get up to that All-Star Matinée at the Palladium next
Wednesday in aid of the Dockers' Settlement. Sarah was
thinking how much better Jackie was up here. His cough
had been troubling him a good deal less. The more bracing
northern air seemed to be good for him.

" Sarah ! " her father said.

" Yes, father ? "

" What do you think of it all ? "

" Well, father, I hope you won't do it ! "

Esther would have liked her to put a little more guts into
it. After all, it was she and her seven children who were
more deeply concerned than anybody else. If she hadn't
had so many children it wouldn't have been so much of a
problem. They might not have been there that evening,
any of them.

" Yes, Sarah, I can quite understand," her father said,
with a note of gentleness which had not yet been heard at
the conference. " I've got to ask your pardon, Sarah, for
what I'm doing. But it's not my fault I'm doing it."

" But who'll pay for it, eh ? " Esther wanted to know.
" Not three children, not four children, seven children ! "

" Well, thank God, I had five. And you all look nice and
well, bless you ! "

" Yes," Esther countered swiftly. " They had a father to bring them up ! "

" Yes, that's true ! You have got a bit of money you had on the side, Sarah, eh ? What does it come to ? "

" A few pounds a week ! "

" Not bad ! Not bad ! And, of course, they've got a rich auntie. If it's not enough, perhaps she'll help some time ! "

" Who do you mean ? You mean Esther ? No father, no ! We'll manage somehow."

" I like to hear you talk like that. I think you understand, better than the rest of them. You and May. I do wish May had been here this evening."

His voice seemed rather weary. Esther was on the alert at once. He had been holding out quite firmly till that moment. She watched him like a cat a mouse.

" Of course," said Esther, " I'll do what I can, though I've got children of my own to look after, too ! "

" No evil eye befall them ! " wished Mrs. Silver hurriedly.

" Though seven's a great number," Esther went on, " and some of them very delicate, very delicate. How's poor little Jackie's cough, Sarah ? "

" Oh, it's a bit better ! It seems to agree with him up here ! "

Esther bit her lip. Sarah really was a bit of a fool. She wasn't taking her cues at all well.

" Yes, up here ! In a nice house, with every comfort ! " She was trying to retrieve Sarah's error. "But what happens if father gives his money away ? He won't be able to keep on a house like this then ! " She turned triumphantly to her father. " You never thought of that ! You'd have to give up this place. It costs quite a lot of money to keep up this place ! "

" I have thought of that, of course I have ! " Silver corrected her. " Naturally I don't expect to stay on in a big house like this. What should I want to stay on for ? "

" What ? " wailed Mrs. Silver. " You are going to sell up my house, too ? What shall I do, what shall I do, what shall become of me ? " She swayed from side to side as she wailed, like poor women behind their partition in slum synagogues.

" That's more like it ! " said Esther to herself. " That's more like it ! "

" Now, now, Hannah ! " her husband protested. It pained him to hear her going on like that. " You know this house is much too big for us ! You know that when we're together we only use the two bedrooms and this room down here. Well, we can have one bedroom, like we used to have ! "

The tears ran heavily down Mrs. Silver's cheeks. " What will Popsie say ? " she sobbed.

" If I should worry what Popsie will say—— "

" And I have so many friends down in London, from the biggest people in society, countesses as well ; what will they say ? Oi, oi, what will they say if I become a beggar-woman again ? No, no, Sam, I've been a good wife to you, Sam ! What should you want at the end of our days to bring such misery on us all for ? What have we all done ? You can't do it, Sam ; I can't go and be a poor woman, like it used to be ! I'm too old to change, Sam ! "

He sighed heavily. His eyelids drooped with misery. " You have a lot of jewels, Hannah. They are all your own. I gave them to you. Perhaps, if you went to a smaller hotel, with those jewels you could manage for a long time. Did I say you should come and be a beggar-woman with me ? You can go, and perhaps you can stay in the same hotel with Mrs. Proctor—— "

" What ! " She suddenly suspended her wailing and swaying to and fro. A tear hesitated on her eyelashes and dropped heavily on to her bosom. " What ? You think I will let you go and live in two rooms somewhere, and I will leave you ? You think I will go to London and stay with that woman ? Is it my husband, my Sam, that says such things to me ? It can't be ! I didn't hear ! Oi ! Oi ! Oi ! " Her wailing was twice as loud as before.

" Yes, Hannah," he said quietly, " we've been together a long time, haven't we ? It would be a pity if we shouldn't

be together, now that we're an old couple, even if it was only
in a couple of rooms ! "

" But I could keep my mother's pearls, peace be upon her !
You wouldn't like me to sell my mother's pearls ? No, no,
Sam ! I have promised them to May, though she is only the
youngest. God will give her a bridegroom ; it's not too late
yet ! "

" Hannah, you can keep what you like to keep. I cannot
take back what I have given. Your pearls—a question ! Why,
didn't I steal them for you myself ? It was a good thing the
judge didn't know or he would have given it a different
verdict. And besides, there's another thing."

" Yes ? "

" You mustn't forget you're a property-owner, too ! "

" What ? "

" You know—the house in Oleander Street. It is yours.
It was bought for you. It stands in your name."

" Mine ? Yes, of course it is mine ! " Her eyes shone.
" Don't I get rent for it ? That should help us a little ! "

" Well, it's empty now. There were some people named
Silverstone living in it, a woman and three children. They've
gone to join the husband in America because he got his
papers he should be a citizen."

Esther's blood froze as his hideous idea began to dawn on
her. Her heart seemed to be beating at half its normal pace.

" But it shouldn't be hard to let it again ? " Hannah said.
" Those houses, they weren't ever empty for more than a
week ! "

" I was thinking," said Silver, " of paying you rent
myself. You think I will live in my wife's house and pay her
no rent ? I shall go to work again, and I shall be able to
afford it ! "

Sarah, Susan, Elsie, looked at him in a sort of horror. His
wife looked at him in a sort of ecstasy. Then at last Esther
sprang to her feet. Then at last, as once, many years ago,
when she had sought to batter him into repudiating the
arrangement he had entered into with old Horowitz, she

strode up and down the room, roaring and ravening. Now as then, but more tremendously, the air darkened as with a cloud of torn leaves. Once again twigs cracked like whips, whole branches went careering through the air. But there was a sense in it now, of the certainty of triumph. May, who had baulked the triumph then, was hundreds of miles away, lured away by her cunning, the master-stroke of her organisation. She saw him fall back, as if indeed an actual tempest assailed him. Mercilessly she roared and roared. She said no more than had already been said by the five women assembled there ; she resumed all their arguments, blunting their fine points, indeed, but it was not by the fineness of her points she would prevail.

" You will not, I say, you will not make paupers of your family ! You can't do it ! It's madness ! You should be locked up ! You will not ! You will not ! Do you hear ? Say you will not ! Answer ! Answer ! Say you will not ! "

She stopped. She waited. He looked like one who in one moment more would have all the life in him battered into senselessness.

" I will ! " he said.

Then she crumpled out of her towering height, and fell on her knees and tore at his right thigh. She had one more card to play. Her hair fell loose among the shower of her tears. Her corsage creaked and gaped. She made one last appeal to him, as the eldest of his children. She knew that if his heart told him to do a thing, he must do it. She knew that conscience must come before wife, children, grandchildren, everybody. Let it come first, but let not the rest come nowhere. Let him divide his fortune—half of it should go to the creditors, half of it should go to the family ; it should be kept on trust for the children. Her bosom heaved with her sobbing ; she spoke with extreme reasonableness. Again, as a long time ago on that other occasion in the Oleander Street kitchen, he suddenly felt very tired and weak. He wanted to go to bed. He wasn't as young as he once had been. All those children, seven orphans, no evil eye befall them ! He heard Sarah sobbing quietly, with no intention in the world that he should see or hear. Here was his daughter Susan, come all the way from Moscow. Here was his daughter Elsie, getting up from the metal stool like a little beaten animal, kneeling up against him on his left thigh. She rubbed her head miserably up along his trousers, as if to seek reassurance and comfort.

" You will do that, father ? Yes, father ! Please ! Say you will ! "

In the half-light the low metal stool which Elsie had vacated glowed and glimmered—the low metal stool where May used to sit reading her books of poetry. He became aware that May in the spirit was as much in that room, every fibre as much in that room, as May in the body would have been. He saw her mouth even more clearly than her eyes. " No ! " proclaimed the pursed-up lips, a little less rose-like than they had been on that occasion long ago, but still pure and exquisite as running water. " No ! " bade May. " It is either all or nothing, either all or nothing, either all or nothing ! "

" No ! " said Sam Silver, and got up from his chair. " No ! I'm tired ! I'm going to bed now ! "

CHAPTER XXIII

THE SILVER KITCHEN

I

MAY SILVER took up her station outside an office door in an echoing corridor of the Cardiff Town Hall a good half hour before the offices closed down. The clerks who passed up and down, with pens behind their ears and sheafs of papers in their hands, wondered who the bloke was in Room 143 who was going to get it in the neck from the bright-eyed jane. Harry Stonier appeared at length. He had a handful of books under his arm, and a battered hat on his head. The tendrils of his reddish hair escaped under his hat and clustered above his collar. He was looking very neglected. She saw a hank of thread on his overcoat below the lapel, where the top button should have been.

" Harry ! " She caught hold of his elbow. " Don't you recognise me ? "

He stopped and turned round. He blushed like a small schoolboy. " May ! What on earth are you doing here ? "

" I got a telegram from you ! "

" What are you talking about ? "

" You're going to deny it, are you ? "

" My dear May, what *are* you talking about ? "

" If you don't mind, I'd rather not talk about anything here ! I never knew town halls were so draughty ! Will you give me a cup of tea somewhere ? "

" Of course, May ! There's a Lyons round the corner. What on earth—— But it's lovely to see you ! Why on earth didn't you let me know you'd be round this way ? "

" What ? Let you know ? When you send me a telegram that frightens me out of my wits ! " She laughed merrily.

He looked at her pathetically. " Honestly, May——"

" All right, my dear. I'll let you in on the joke when we sit down ! "

They entered the café. He put his books down on the table, hung up his hat and coat, sat down, and turned to her.

" What'll you have, May ? "

Then suddenly the dreadful awareness flooded him that this was not the first time he had sat down at a table in a public eating-place in this town and asked one of Sam Silver's daughters exactly that question. A flame seemed to be licking his cheeks and devouring the lobes of his ears. He put his hands up to both his cheeks, as if to hide them from her.

" Harry," she said, her voice as gentle as a tiny runlet among grasses. " I think I can understand how it went."

He did not look into her face. " Did she ever tell you ? " he asked woodenly.

" No, she just disappeared. She went to Germany. I have never heard from her from that day to this. She must have suffered hell, too."

" I don't know how you can bear to sit near to me ! "

" I love you more than I've ever done before."

" I can't understand you. You're more beautiful, more incredible, the more I know you."

" There's not been much knowing lately."

" How could I ? How could I ? "

" My dear ! " She became aware of a waitress, in a little cap and apron, standing up against their table with a little pad and pencil. " Do order *something*, Harry ! "

Something was ordered and drunk and eaten, neither knew what.

" How could you ? " she repeated. She pondered the question. " No, I know you too well. You couldn't. And how could I ? We've been in an impasse, Harry. But I think this telegram is going to open up the road to us." She got it out of the bag and laid it before him. " Read that ! "

He opened his eyes in utter bewilderment. " But, my dear May, it's ridiculous ! I know nothing at all about it ! What on earth does it mean ? "

" Oh, my dear, I know you don't. My sister, Esther, sent it. At least she sent somebody all the way to Cardiff last night in order to send it—to get the stamp right, of course."

" But why ? What on earth for ? Surely I'm the last person in the world she wants to throw you up against ? You remember that awful, awful night ? "

" I remember ! When she called you names, and I nearly pulled out two handfuls of her hair ! "

" Yes, what a nightmare it was ! "

" Quite possibly, if I'd have been up in Altrincham to-day, I'd have done the same thing. Her telegram saved her that, at all events ! "

" Please explain, May, there's a good girl ! "

" I'll tell you, very simply. You know my father's firm went into liquidation ? "

" Yes, I read about it."

" He's not been the same man since that time. It goes back before that, as a matter of fact. Since Smirnof died—you remember, his partner, the one who married Sarah ? "

" Yes."

" I could gradually see the idea getting hold of him, that he had no moral right to the money he possessed."

" You mean, because it was chiefly the War——"

" No, Harry, frankly. I don't think that influenced him at all. It's rather complicated. Anyhow, that's what he felt. He felt his money belonged to the firm's creditors, not himself."

" What a grand chap he is ! "

" But while these law-suits were on, of course, he couldn't do anything about it. He had to clear himself first."

" I see that."

" Then came the big trial. You've read about it ? "

" Yes, you poor dear. It was then, more than ever, I wanted to write to you, or come and see you. But I felt—

you know how I felt. . . . If it had been anyone else but a sister of *yours*——"

"You mustn't torture yourself, Harry. Be a good chap. Put it out of your mind. Yes, it would have helped me through if you'd come. It was a bad time, but it's over now. He decided to give up everything he had about a month ago. Then Esther got to know about it."

"Yes?"

"Then she got busy. She got him to hold his hand for one month. You know what a demon she is for organisation? She had the greatest time in her life. She organised Susan out of Moscow, and Elsie out of Berlin——"

"She's in England?"

"Don't worry, darling. We're not likely to meet, any of us. I'm convinced she nearly died of relief that I didn't turn up."

"Turn up where?"

"It was for this evening"—she looked at her watch—"this very minute, the big family reunion was fixed up. They'll be hard at it now. The idea was, we were all to give our various points of view why father shouldn't hand over his money; all of us—mother, the five daughters, all the grandchildren. He wouldn't be able to stand up against such a combination, that was the idea. Sarah standing about like Niobe; Elsie doing the languishing touch; mother in floods of tears——"

"And you?"

"Oh, Esther realised I was the weak spot in the attack. She had to ask me to come, of course. She came all the way up to Chanctonbury House to do it. I wasn't to smell a rat; I mean I wasn't to realise she'd rather I wasn't there."

"You were not to be there because your influence would count the other way?"

"I think that's it. It was rather a rotten responsibility. I didn't like the thought of Sarah's big eyes following me about reproachfully for the rest of my days. Though I don't think she *is* like that, somehow. Still, seven children are rather a handful."

" May, there was never a girl with a lovelier heart than yours."

" Let me go on with the detective story. That was why Esther sent that wire."

" But you were bound to find out."

" She was clever enough to realise that a wire from you was the one thing certain to get me out of the way. As for my finding out, what did it matter ? It was worth it. The stakes were pretty big, so she could risk making a fool of me. Besides, she could always line up Sarah's orphans in a row, and say what did a fake wire matter compared with them."

" What's going to happen ? "

" Up there, you mean ? "

" Yes, at your father's house ? "

" Happen ? " She threw her head back proudly. " He will act as his heart orders him. You and I both know what he'll do ! "

" Yes," he pondered. " You're right. There's not the shadow of a doubt. Besides——"

" Yes ? "

" If he didn't—he'd not be your father ; you'd not be his daughter ! "

" Thank you, Harry ! You make me very proud and happy ! "

" And now ? "

" Well, now, Harry, we're back where we started from ! "

" You mean, long ago, in Doomington ? "

" Yes, that's what I mean. I shall be a poor girl, and have to work for my living. I might get a job in the Country Home in Yorkshire. They're thinking of starting a new one."

" May, I've a piece of news for you ! "

" Yes ? "

" I only heard last week. I wanted to write and tell you about it. But, of course——"

" Oh, Harry, Harry, what a lot of time we've wasted ! "

" Do you think, May, that time is wasted, when the soul

realises it has battles to fight, and fights them, even though peace mayn't come for years?"

"I think peace may be coming now."

"My love, my love!"

"It would be nice if this café were a little less—just a little less popular. What is your news, my sweet?"

"It won't sound much to you!"

"Tell me!"

"I had my first novel accepted last week!"

"Oh, my dear! How marvellous! I'm sorry! I must kiss you! Even though this café *is* so popular!"

"I got an advance, too. Fifty pounds. It's quite a lot for a first novel."

"It's gorgeous! You'll have to write a novel about us some day!"

"Who's us?"

"The five Silver daughters."

"Oh, my darling, I think one at a time is as much as I'd manage."

"I'll type it for you. I'm quite good at it."

"Yes," he said seriously. "The typing's an awfully big item. Do you think, May——" Again he paused. Again the deep schoolboy blush suffused his cheeks.

"Go on."

"Do you think we might—manage it?"

"I'm not so powerful a manager as Esther. But I've learned a thing or two at Chanctonbury House."

"Oh, May, we'll read poetry to each other again, hours and hours and hours of poetry—Traherne and Thompson and Marvell."

"But, my dear, you'll have to leave me *some* time for darning the socks."

"I've become rather a good hand at that myself," he said, a little shamefacedly. "You'll do the typing, and I'll darn the socks!"

"Agreed!" she said. "Is there anywhere we can go and see ships? Come, let's go and see ships!" she commanded.

II

Mrs. Silver and Sarah and Susan were sitting at breakfast in Pennine Grange a week or so after the great family conference. It was rather late, and Silver had already left for Doomington. He had a great deal to fix up with his lawyers these days.

There was a letter beside Susan's plate—a letter from Russia, from her husband, Boris Polednik.

Mrs. Silver was a little fretful. She had not quite got over Elsie's prompt departure the day after the gathering. " You would think," she complained, smashing her egg viciously, " a daughter who has not seen her mother all these years, she would stay on for a week, at least. She was never a daughter for her mother," she resumed bitterly.

" Well, mother," Sarah pointed out gently, " she *did* make it clear that she'd have to hunt after a job again, so the sooner she started at those managers the better ! "

Mrs. Silver snorted. " Managers ! I bet you she's got a man over there she's crazy about ! Fine managers ! " She turned to Susan. " Well, Susan ? And your husband, has he a greeting, perhaps, for his mother-in-law ? "

" Yes, mother," said Susan. She was reading her letter through a second time. " May I just finish ? "

" Don't let your kipper get cold ! "

This is an extract from the letter Susan Polednik read :

" I do not know how much pain this letter will cause you, or if it will cause you any at all. But I have been thinking the matter over very hard since you left. I consider it would be desirable if you did not come back to Russia again. I personally should miss you, but I think it would be better on general grounds. You are not a good revolutionary. You are a humanitarian and a sentimentalist. You have a great capacity for work, and you have done some very fine work, for which the Revolution is grateful to you. But, frankly, we can't wholly trust you. Your ideology is sound, but your origin and temperamental leanings get the better of you. I want you to understand this is in no sense an official order. You are perfectly at liberty to return if you choose. But it is right for me to say the authorities would prefer it if you did not. Will you please convey my greetings to the various members of your family."

" Does he mention me by name ? " asked Mrs. Silver.

" Yes," said Susan.

" There you are ! " said Mrs. Silver triumphantly. " I only wish Elsie was here, she should take a lesson ! It's a great pity, Susan ; it's a great pity ! " Her mind had veered suddenly in another direction.

" Yes, I'm sorry she's gone," said Susan.

" No, I don't mean Elsie. I mean the family in Terkass. You, Susan, you were always the one that made me tell big tales about the old times in Russia. We always keep the album in the ' home-room ' ; the old album I mean. We keep the new one in the drawing-room."

" Yes," said Susan. " I've seen them both."

" It's a pity you never took the trouble to go to Terkass and give them a greeting from me and your father."

" I told you, mother, it's a long way from the capital. And I've always been terribly busy."

" You shouldn't be so busy you can't go and see your own grandfather, no evil eye befall him, and your uncles and all your cousins. But it's a shame on them, too, they should never write all this long time."

" The post is very uncertain in Russia," said Susan.

" You got your letter quick enough," Mrs. Silver pointed out, " from your husband ! Like he sent it from Leeds ! "

" It's different. He's an official."

" Oh, I see. Perhaps it's so. You haven't finished your kipper. Where are you going ? "

" I'm just going to 'phone through about the boat services to Russia. They've called me back to Moscow. I've got to get there as quick as I can."

" Did you ever hear of such a thing ? " Mrs. Silver shrilly protested. " What is the good of having children ? They come from the North Pole and they go away in five minutes. Susan ! " she called out.

" Yes, mother ? "

" Talking about Terkass—perhaps some day, after you get back, you might go in and see how they're getting on, eh ? Perhaps your work might take you that way. You could give them a greeting from us. Don't tell Shevka and Gallia we're going to live again in Oleander Street, will you ? I shouldn't like them to know ! "

" No, mother, I won't tell them ! "

III

Early in the spring of 1925 the Silver régime was restored to number eleven Oleander Street, though, of the five Silver daughters who had lived there once, only one Silver daughter returned with her parents. The Silvers were, after all, a good deal better off than many of their neighbours in Oleander Street and Magnolia Street and Laburnum Street, for they had no rent to pay—they were their own landlords. Or, more accurately, Mrs. Silver was her own landlord. She had her house, her pearls, her daughter, her husband—she couldn't grumble.

Sam Silver got a job, quite easily, as a " maker " ; he had always been a good workman. He was getting on in years, but the trade wasn't so busy that it took too much out of him.

May hadn't got a job yet, but she could get one without too much trouble if it ever became necessary. For the time being she could get along without a job. She had a certain small sum of money of her own, which had almost accidentally survived the recent admirable exercises in abnegation.

She could have lived in a somewhat more imposing neighbourhood than Longton on her money, but there really was
no point in that. No one recognised with more good humour
than she what poetry it was—there was no other word for it
at all—that her family should have gone back again to the
shade of their oleanders.

And the house, within its limits, was really quite comfortable. Mrs. Silver called it her " palace "—a word she had
never used, excepting in misery or derision, concerning her
more imposing residences. It was true that May felt it
necessary to do something drastic and expensive with the
bathroom out of her own money. She had a really good bath
put in, though it had to be a trifle on the small side ; she
also had the bathroom walls tiled. Further, she had basins
with hot-and-cold water put into her own bedroom, and the
bedroom of her parents. Her father and mother shared the
same bedroom, of course, even though there was quite a lot
of space to spread themselves in nowadays, with one sole
daughter living on the premises, where there had once been
five. Mrs. Silver was just a little nervous about these sanitary
modifications. " And shall your father go to work in a
morning-coat and trousers with stripes on them ? " she
objected.

" But it's improving the property, mother, don't you see ?
It's improving the property ! " The formula was almost
magic in its potency. " I see now," she said keenly. She
would not have minded, on those terms, installing two or
three hot-and-cold water basins in each bedroom.

Sarah went to live in St. Anne's-on-Sea. One way and
another she managed. The North Country air was excellent
for the children. Jackie throve on it. Jackie became a positive
Kossack, shouting, " Ho ! Ho ! " up and down the golden
Lancashire sands.

Letters came, from time to time, from Susan in Russia
and Elsie in Germany. They kept well, it was gathered.

As for Esther—Esther appeared in Oleander Street in person. She appeared in fine silks and expensive furs, according

to the season. She drew up in a car of such magnificence that it would have made Hanover Square or the Avenue Friédland look a little shoddy. She had no intention of abating one jot of her splendour, however much it might embarrass either her parents or their neighbours. Her husband came with her too, often, but the one who opened the door of the car was her chauffeur.

It was, in fact, only during these appearances of Esther Pliskin that the return of the Silvers to Oleander Street involved any sense of strain or embarrassment for anybody. The situation was handled from the beginning with exquisite tact. It was as if they had been living for some time in some Oleander Street in Hulme or Miles Platting somewhere on the other side of the town, and they had found it pleasanter to come back to their own district, now that they had married off their daughters, all but one of them. Mrs. Silver took out an account again with Mrs. Poyser, who kept the grocery-shop at the corner of Magnolia Street. Mr. and Mrs. Emmanuel slipped, quite often, out of their own back-door, through the back-door which immediately faced it, into the Silver kitchen. Before many weeks had passed by, the Silver Saturday nights were in full swing again.

There was no conspiratorial rapping of once-twice, once-twice again, on the front door, as there had been in the old days. That was felt to be a little pre-War, a little childish, even. And, of course, there was a great change in personnel. Of the old anarchists, some were dead, some were rich, some were in Russia ; but quite a few stalwarts reappeared. The tone of the gatherings was certainly milder than it had been. People were allowed to believe in God, or Zionism, or even the Monarchical System, without losing caste. The rivers of tea-with-lemon flowed again, and here ancient custom reasserted itself. They sucked it, now as then, in the Russian fashion, through a cube of sugar wedged between the teeth. But the Gentiles did not need to drink tea, as had been expected from them once. Bottled beer had been added to the commissariat. Some of the Jews drank beer, too.

And, when there had been enough intellect for one night, Silver took out the cards, now as of old time, and they all played " Pishy-pashy." And he stretched out his feet, and his daughter, May, was beside him, unfastening his shoe-laces. And, when she had pulled his slippers on to his feet, she went back to her metal stool by the fire, which had survived Ivanhoe Towers and Pennine Grange, and took out a book, or sat staring into the red depths of the fire, dreaming. Mrs. Silver was too busy to dream. There were more lemons to cut up, and the sugar-basin was empty, and it was time to put fresh tea-leaves in the pot. The firelight gleamed on her Terkass pearls, which her mother had worn on her wedding-day, and they had been taken from her, and her husband had found them for her again.

May was her youngest daughter, but it was to May she had promised the pearl necklace, long ago, as soon as she found a husband for herself, in a lucky hour.

" No," said May, " no, mother. That's cocoa, isn't it ? I think *this* is the packet of tea ! "

" Who would dream from such a thing ? " laughed Hannah Silver. " It will be soap-flakes next time, yes ? "

IV

This narrative ends where it began, in the Silver kitchen in Oleander Street. It is a Saturday night, as it was then. But there is no crowd of anarchists sitting about, talking, talking, sucking numberless glasses of tea through cubes of sugar. The fire is almost out, and will be quite out soon if nobody makes it up. If there is any water in the kettle it must be cold now.

The neo-anarchists are all over in Mr. Emmanuel's kitchen. Mr. Emmanuel has not pulled down the blind, and the window is a square of orange light. A ray from that apocalyptic illumination has managed somehow to climb over the two walls that separate the two back-yards. There is a roaring, like the sea, in the Emmanuel kitchen. The Silver kitchen is hollow with the echo of it, like a sea-shell.

Mr. Emmanuel has some grandiose scheme afoot, which almost certainly bears on the elimination of the factor of hatred from interracial and international relationships. He has summoned the Silver anarchists to constitute themselves into an executive committee. Hannah Silver has been over in Mrs. Emmanuel's scullery for some time, giving Mrs. Emmanuel a hand. But Sam Silver himself is not there. Where is Sam Silver? One or two of the anarchists are getting restive. A Saturday night meeting, even in Magnolia Street, without Sam Silver isn't quite proper somehow.

"Sam—where's Sam?" asked an anarchist, a little peevishly.

"I've said already!" called out Hannah Silver from the scullery. "He's in our kitchen! He's coming soon!"

"It's time he was here!" said another anarchist firmly. He made a movement towards the yard-door as if to go and fetch him over.

"You should leave him!" said Hannah Silver quite sharply. "He said he'll come when he's ready! He'll be here in a minute or two!"

Sam Silver sat in his kitchen, on a chair drawn up near the fire. Between him and the fender sat his daughter, May, on the low metal stool, leaning back against him, between his knees. Slowly, delicately, with the tips of his fingers, he stroked her forehead from the centre to the temples. Many minutes had gone by, and neither had said a word.

Then at last he spoke. His voice was hardly louder than the ash sifting through the grate.

"He will be here soon?"

"Yes, father."

"I'm so happy for you, May my baby."

"You've always been . . . you've always been. . . ." Her voice broke.

"Hush now, May! What? On a night like this, you should start crying, no less?"

" Do you think I love you less, father, because he's coming
.. and because when he goes—"

" Yes, my child. You shall go, too."

" I shall go, too."

" Didn't your mother go, when I came for her? And it
was a longer journey, no? "

" If I go with him to the end of the world, I'll be with
you, too—always here "

" Yes, my daughter, yes." He took hold of her hand and
placed it against his cheek, and held it there for some
minutes. Then he passed his lips along it three or four times.

" I am glad," he said suddenly, " it should be to-night. It
wouldn't have been so nice, if they'd all been in, making a
noise like that. Listen to them! "

" You know, father," she whispered. " I told Mr.
Emmanuel he was coming. Nobody else, only you and
mother and him."

" I see," ruminated Sam Silver. " I see. It was clever of
him to arrange it. He's a nice man ; only perhaps if he didn't
talk so much—"

" He can talk as much as he likes to-night."

" Are you cold, my baby? I'll put some coal on, yes? "

" Don't move ! Oh, no, don't move ! There ! Your fingers !
That's right, daddy ! "

Ten minutes passed again, fifteen minutes, with no word
spoken. Slowly, delicately, he stroked her forehead. There
came, at last, a knock on the front door.

" Harry ! " she cried. Her breath stood arrested in her
throat. She did not move from the metal stool. It was as if
there had been no knock at all on the front door.

Sam Silver rose from his chair. " Come, my love ! " he
said. He lifted her to her feet. " Kiss me just once, my baby !
Ah ! That's fine ! Now open the door, May. I'll go over to
the Emmanuels. They'll be wondering what's happened to
me. Do you hear, May ? Open the door like a good girl ! "

She stood there, not moving, staring after him through
brimming tears. He had gone out of the kitchen now, down

the single step into the scullery. She heard the click of the latch on the scullery-door, as he let himself out.

There was a knocking at the door a second time, a little louder than before. She turned towards the knocking. " Oh, Harry, my love, do I keep you waiting ? " she called. She raced like a child along the dark passage.

THE END

BERLIN—LONDON—PARIS,
November 1932–May 1933.

GOD OF A HUNDRED NAMES
Prayers and meditations from many faiths
and cultures
Collected and arranged by Barbara Greene
and Victor Gollancz

Reaching across the barriers of time and place, the prayers in this moving and often surprising collection range in author from Elizabeth I to an Arab chieftain, from Socrates to Edith Sitwell. Together they express the deepest needs of the human spirit.

"A book to cling on to when the world seems falling to bits" – Sir John Betjeman

ISBN 0 575 03645 1

NICHOLAS AND ALEXANDRA
Robert K. Massie

The internationally bestselling biography of Russia's last Tsar and his family, whose violent deaths still provoke speculation and debate.

"An exquisite story of love and compassion" – *The Times*

ISBN 0 575 03589 7

GOLLANCZ PAPERBACKS

YOU'RE A BRICK, ANGELA!
The Girls' Story 1839-1985
Mary Cadogan and Patricia Craig

This witty, enlightening, thoroughly researched and hugely entertaining look at girls' stories ranges from Victorian moral tales, via the schoolgirl yarns of Angela Brazil to the novels of the eighties.
  "Such brilliance, energy and expertise. It's all super!" – Arthur Marshall

ISBN 0 575 03825 X